The Tower of Light

A
Children of the Links
Novel

Adam Dyer

Mecharical Publishing and Wizardry
Duluth, GA

Initial editing by Amy Miles

ISBN 978-0-9848660-1-4

For those who kept faith in me
though I had thought it lost in myself.

Contents

One:
To Wake a Lion

The platform was crowded with children moving inexorably toward the long trains. Crying toddlers led by boys and girls merely a handful of years older than them, brothers and sisters huddled together in corners, and chains of siblings linked tiny hand in tiny hand to prevent separation, being prodded and jostled onto the trains away from their homes. It was the end of the Child Rebellion and the remainder of the young soldiers' families were to be exiled by order of law. There was to be no second rebellion and this was the surest way, as the New Dominion saw it, to ensure that.

The station was the last in the land before the Cold Sea and the Straits into Romara. Outside the station, snow coated the ground and the air was crisp and cold with a steady wind from the sea not far to the west. If the wind gusted enough, Rebecca could catch a hint of the salt from the sea. The train docks were crowded with shipments of crates of various supplies and imports from the Wilderlands beyond Romara; exotic items within the crates would fetch handsome profits for those lucky merchants with decrees from the New Dominion to sell them. The Trader's Mark, it was called.

Gray light came though the frosted pane glass ceiling supported by black arched steel trusses above the train platform. The light from even cloud-covered skies would have added some warmth to the station, similar to a greenhouse, but the wind from outside would whip away any warmth due to the openings at either end of the station for the trains to come and go. The children moved about progressively

1

closer to the trains to take their places on the passenger cars, modified to fit ever more small bodies for transport away.

Rebecca was one of the lone children dotting the crowd here and there. Some like her moved with no purpose other than to avoid the men doing the herding. Wherever she looked the faces were all portraits of loss and despair. Here a boy or girl with face smeared with grime, the only clean areas to be found were the tear streaks down their cheeks. Most wore all that they had left to them in the world, clothes so worn and battered that they were about equal parts air and fabric. Some carried sacks made of cloth, tied over their little shoulders, or dragged behind when their strength failed them.

There was no hope that anyone's mother or father was coming or even elder brother or sister for that matter. There was no one left to these children, to Rebecca, but to whomever they were clinging or could find to help carry a bag or satchel. Wading along in the throng of displaced children, Rebecca longed for the home lost to her now for almost half a year. She and the other children had been marched and carted to this train depot to send them away from their homes. All she could think about was trying to find a new place to call home, somewhere that wasn't a makeshift camp or fenced pen. She had turned thirteen in one of those pens and the memory of the absence of her family at that time still made her heart hurt. She felt helpless and lost; a tingling at the back of her mind felt like nearing desperation; she had felt it there growing as time wore on. Rebecca plodded slowly toward the gaping mouths of the train cars that would carry her and the rest across the Straights of Romara into a foreign land to be housed in scattered universities, built decades before the wars to house and educate children in the great fields of study.

The New Dominion, having taken possession of this country like so many before, would educate and house these lost children now, for, as they would say, were they not without mercy for the innocents? Those children who were old enough would be taught the value of work for the society and would be required to learn the new, correct, histories of the time. They would be taught why their families were traitors to their homelands and why they, the children, had to be held to account for those that now lay in the soil of the battlefields on which they fell. Those children too young to work would be housed in orphanages to be raised as loyal New Dominion citizens. The children of the rebels were now wards of the very state against which their predecessors had fought – that would not be forgotten.

Rebecca moved, eyes on the ground, toward one of the cars. She edged away from one of the large guardsman with the long rifles at hand, eyeing the crowd for any disturbance in the flow. The guards were like menacing wool statues in their uniforms of dark gray, with the red fist of the New Dominion embroidered over the heart on their long overcoats. Some of these men were from her own country. They had been forced to pledge allegiance to the New Dominion after the disastrous battle that claimed her brother, even so, the men looked on the children with disregard at best and at worst...

With her eyes intently studying her boots, she did not see the patrolman moving amongst the children, looking for weapons or anything of value he could find; she had time only to see a second set of boots in her field of view before being shoved roughly backwards onto her backside. She landed with a thump on her satchel.

"Watch where you be heading girl; you just about ran into me," said the patrolman, "we wouldn't want to be accusing you of assaulting a patrolman of the Red Guard would we now?"

"No sir," said Rebecca, "no sir, I wasn't assaulting you by any means, I was just going to that train just there…"

"Stop yer ranting girl and gimme that there sack you be carrying," said the patrolman.

Rebecca gripped hold of her satchel; it was all she had left and its contents were precious to her. The patrolman wore the Red Guard's uniform but it hung on him; he was lean and had a vicious look to his face; his eyes were devoid of anything resembling pity. A sparse scattering of beard coated his cheeks and neck and he spoke with a definite accent, not one of her countrymen. She moved the satchel further from the patrolman, which was precisely the wrong decision. His face twisted in a mix of what appeared to be anger and joy, the last froze Rebecca's stomach.

Reaching down, the patrolman gripped her by the collar of her coat and hoisted her, one-handed, into the air, feet dangling, and brought her eye-to-eye with him. She could smell the stink of alcohol as he breathed into her face, and see the pockmarked skin he was attempting to hide beneath the scraggly beard.

"We're gonna be going through that there bag, you and me, little girl, and if you be very lucky that's all we're gonna be going through," he said in a hoarse low voice.

She turned her head away from him, unable to stop him as he began to rummage through her satchel pulling her belongings out in handfuls. A scarf her mother had knitted for her he dropped to the ground, her brother's triangular compass he pocketed along with her father's big pocket watch, he threw down her half finished leather bracelet and the gloves she had knitted herself. All her belongings scattered about and displayed for all to see, her spare clothes and bits

4

of food she managed to scrape together before she had to flee her home.

She felt as though this man was pulling out her heart bit by bit, stealing the pieces he found shiny and disposing of the odd ends for which he saw no use. This was like being told all over again her family was dead and she was now going to have to work off their debt to society. She could feel the desire to surrender creeping up on her from behind, edging closer, about to take hold.

He came to her grandfather's old journal pulling it up so he could flip roughly through the yellowing pages written decades before she was born. He eyed them briefly before flipping a page perhaps looking for pictures; he didn't look the sort to sit and read a book. She could remember sitting in her father's lap, her brother sitting cross-legged on the floor in front of them, as her father would relive the accounts of her grandfather's expeditions across the globe and his descriptions of the wonders he found there. She would marvel at the maps and drawings her grandfather had laid down while traveling to distant islands and countries.

"What's this girl some ratty old book?" Dropping it to the ground, the man smiled into her face. "Well, we got what we were looking for."

Releasing his grip, she dropped back on the ground among her dispersed possessions. This was too much to bear; the despair had its hands on her mind and was pulling her down.

"You be lucky girl, carrying contraband items like these," he said, patting his pocket where her belongings now rested. "I might have had to take you back for questioning for carrying these. You should be thanking me. Well, go on, thank me."

Tears welling in her eyes, she whispered, lowly, "Thank you, sir."

5

"You be very welcome my young lady, after all, you now be under the protection of the New Dominion's Red Guard," he said with a big yellowed smile, "and we wouldn't be letting nothing happen to our young new children, now would we." He chuckled as he turned and began walking away.

Rebecca could feel a hole in her middle that this man had opened and been rifling through. The hollow feeling wanted to be filled with something, anything. Slowly from afar, something began creeping in to fill that hole – rage. A red burning rage began to fill the hole in her. She could feel her face heating from the anger as well as the embarrassment of what had just happened to her. This man, this pig of a man, would not be walking away with all she had left of her life before.

Gathering the remainder of her belongings, careful with grandfather's journal, she stuffed them back into her satchel and gathered herself up off the ground. Keeping an eye on the patrolman, she moved back into the crowd, edging in and away from those children who had witnessed the encounter between herself and the patrolman. They took quick glances at her then stared at the ground so as to avoid the same happening to them. She moved parallel to the patrolman, keeping her head low so as not to be seen. She stalked closer to him as he walked along the train, pushing a child here and there. She had a purpose now, for the moment anyway. This man would not get away with her belongings.

He was one of those vicious people that took pleasure from any feel of power he could get, even the power to hassle children, none older than fourteen. This man, like those in the camps, felt it wasn't enough to have taken her family. He needed to steal all she had left.

She was going to enjoy removing some of the pleasure that this man thought he had won from her.

She shied closer to the patrolman. He was moving in on his next intended victim, a small boy, maybe ten, carrying a little rough sackcloth bag tied with twine over his shoulder. The patrolman stepped closer, about to make his move on the boy. Rebecca crouched low, getting nearer the patrolman. The boy stared at the patrolman with wide-eyed horror as he realized he was this man's next target.

Rebecca ran and plunged into the back of the patrolman's knees; the boy squealed with fright and ran; the patrolman yelled as he fell. Without time to break his fall with his arms, he smacked face first with a "thwack" into the paving stones of the train-loading platform. The man groaned as Rebecca recovered her footing; she moved in like a raven on a dead rabbit, picking at exactly the right spots. She quickly found her belongings in the patrolman's pocket and stuffed them back in her satchel; dipping once more into his pocket, she found a coin purse and some other trinkets stolen from unsuspecting children. *Pig*, she thought. Without looking she emptied all the patrolman's pockets into her satchel and began to dart away. She felt a grip on her wrist as she started off; turning, she saw the patrolman had her, staring knives into her.

"You? Girl, we'll just..." was all he had time for before she kicked him in the nose, and saw the blood begin to flow, his nose broken, obviously. His grip instantly released as he grasped his broken face. Running with her heart pounding in her throat, she disappeared back into the crowd of children, ducking low; she looked back with satisfaction as the patrolman stood, hunting for her, his hand stained red over his nose, and eyes watering. She felt warm now. It was not the burning rage as before but warmth that she had her family's

7

belongings back, warmth that she had not been helpless. She had escaped from the patrolman unharmed. She felt a smile come to her mouth as she moved in the crowd. Looking back for one final glimpse of her vanquished foe, she thumped into something solid and made of fabric. She froze and her heart stopped for a moment.

Turning with dread, she was face to chest with the patrolman; he had gotten in front of her somehow. He looked down with merciless, drunken eyes filmed in tears from his broken nose and a fan of blood covering his wicked grin. He gripped her collar again and pulled her close as he breathed down in her face.

"Well now girl, we're just gonna have to do some really rough questioning now aren't we," he said in a thick nasal tone, blood running down his chin and dripping onto his coat collar. He began to pull her away.

Suddenly, the patrolman was laying flat on his back, scampering back onto his elbows to see what had happened to him. A large guardsman stepped in front of Rebecca, his enormous back blocking her view. She stepped sideward and looked around at the patrolman lying on the ground.

"Looks like you must have tripped, Carson," said the enormous back in a deep throaty voice. "You should be more careful; these children shouldn't be arriving at their destination all bruised up because some wretch of a patrolman fell on them."
Rebecca looked up at the enormous back's face and saw a grin that made her shiver.

"Er, Captain Gaston, sir, we wasn't doing nothing hurtful now was we girl?" said the patrolman with pleading in his voice.

She eyed the patrolman with disgust. "We didn't get a chance to do anything hurtful now did we, Carson," she said with all the spite she could muster.

The patrolman's eyes widened as they shifted up toward Gaston. "Now, sir she's just being prankful is all. We weren't meaning her no harm we were just gonna give her a little frightening is all," he said, slithering further away.

"Get up and get out of here Carson," said Gaston, "and don't touch another one of these children."

The patrolman skittered to his feet and ran off into the crowd. Gaston stood staring after him for a moment then turned and knelt down to Rebecca. He was a huge man, his face filled almost her whole view. A kind face, the color of cinnamon, with deep lines from smiles, but the grin she had seen directed at the patrolman still gave her pause. Gaston spoke in a deep warm tone though and he made her feel comfortable for some reason.

"That man is an evil wretch I swear to you," Gaston said with a smile. "What's your name child?" he asked.

"Rebecca, sir," she said, looking down a hair. He waited for a moment and she reluctantly gave her family name. "Dulac, Rebecca Dulac, sir."

"Heart of a lion you have there, Rebecca," said Gaston with a harrumph of a laugh. "I saw the whole thing. Sorry I couldn't get close before he got your things but looks like you took care of that yourself."

The grin returned to her face still looking down; Gaston gently raised her chin to look at her. He studied her face a bit, looking deep into her with a hint of recognition.

"No need for you to be eyeing the ground young Rebecca," Gaston said. "What you did there was a fancy bit of fighting but I know you took more than was by rights yours to be taking. See to it that those trinkets get back to those you can get them back to; I know you would have anyway. That wretch had no right to be making you children suffer more than you already are and you did right by me by setting him straight, but you go now and keep your head low. Don't be attracting any more attention than needs be."

Gaston leaned in close to her, taking a close look in her eyes with a smile. Then he moved in to whisper in her ear.

"I did know a Sebastian Dulac once; you have his eyes," he said lowly. "Brave young man your brother. He's the reason any of us got out of that pass alive. You see, not all of us have a strict allegiance to this *New Dominion*," he said, plucking at the fist over his heart. "We're going to be in need of hearts of lions again one of these days; you make sure yours is amongst them my lady."

And with that he kissed her forehead, stood, turned and walked away. Rebecca was numb. What was that about lions? He knew her brother? Who was he? She made to follow him but Gaston was gone. With no answers, she was alone, just Rebecca, standing on the loading pier waiting for a train to send her away from her home.

Two:
A Train and a Timekeeper

Boarding the train, Rebecca felt her last ties to this land that was her home finally snapping. From this point on she was going to have to find her own way, alone. How she would find the strength to carry on she had no idea, but she would survive. What she had done to the patrolman back on the platform had awoken something in her; that something was more than she had felt since leaving her home.

Approaching the train, the belching fumes from the long dark engines stung her eyes; they smelt of oil, rancid oil and coal. The soot traced back over the first few cars obscuring the once bright painted surface. She made her way to one of the rearward cars to afford herself some comfort on this awful expedition.

Gripping the hand rails, she trudged up the few metal rungs into the dim interior of the pathway between coaches; she walked through the door leading toward the rear car. The cars were made from steel and lined with wood paneling. The halls were lit with gas lantern sconces along the outside aisle. In the cabins, Rebecca could see more lanterns to light those spaces as well. These cars, oddly enough, were once used by students of the universities traveling to and from the Homelands. They had once been quite luxurious. Now though, the cars had been converted to hold more children so as to reduce the trips necessary to move the vast numbers; this was the last trip. Compartments had the benches removed, as well as the doors, to provide more floor space for huddling children. At least the coaches had been constructed with the cold of the Straits of Romara in mind; the walls were insulated to prevent the cold from invading.

Rebecca moved to the rear of the car toward one of the less cramped compartments. Entering, she stepped over a huddling boy wrapped in what appeared to be three wool coats, probably all he owned. She sat in a corner against the wall below the window, noticing that they had been sealed shut to prevent escape. Sinking down into a tight ball, she pulled her satchel around and rummaged through its contents.

She removed the trinkets she had pilfered from the patrolman and examined them for signs of their owners. She had a small locket in the shape of a heart, perhaps belonging to a young girl. Flipping it open, she found a small portrait of a woman and a man in an embrace; *mom and dad,* she thought. Replacing the locket, she picked up the next object, a watch made to be worn on the wrist, flipping it over she found some initials, S.J.B. *That should help* she thought. Moving on, she found a small gold wire-wrapped hand mirror; taking it up, she examined herself.

Her face was a bit pink about the cheeks and nose from the cold and her dark red-brown hair was windswept around her head. She straightened it; satisfied, she examined her face closer. *What was it that Captain Gaston had seen?* she thought. True, she had her brother's features, in feminine form, they came from their mother she had been told. Her eyes were similar as well, a green so light they bordered on yellow; they were definitely father's gift. Some had found her eyes a bit difficult to stare into, saying it was like looking into the eyes of a hungry lion. She was proud she had been given the eyes of her father though, for, she could always look to a reflection and see her father looking back.

"Hey that's mine," said a small voice from across the compartment, "you stole that from that patrolman didn't you?"

Rebecca looked at the small girl. She had tear streaks running down her face and was bundled in a similar fashion to the boy she had stepped over to get in, with a head of ruffled blonde hair and large blue eyes.

"No, I didn't steal anything from that pig I simply returned the favor he offered to these people," she said, showing the girl the other trinkets, a grin spreading across Rebecca's face. She reached the mirror across to the girl who took it smiling and started bouncing slightly with excitement.

"Michael," said the little girl, nudging the bundled boy near the door. "Michael, wake up, look."

The boy shook out of his sleep and turned to the girl.

"Wha' I was sleepin'," said the boy in a muffled voice, looking at what the girl was holding out to him. "Mom's mirror," he said, coming out of his stupor. "Where'd you get it? I thought that man had stolen it from you."

"She got it back for us," said the little girl, pointing at Rebecca.

The boy looked at her in shock; they had seen one another before, on the platform. The patrolman was going to attack this boy for more goodies before she had stopped him.

"You," he said, gaping at Rebecca, "You really hit that guy good but I didn't stick around to see what happened, sorry," he said looking down. "But I got scared and ran, I thought you were going to get killed for sure, but, hey, it looks like you got away right and you got this back for us, thanks," he said in a rush.

Rebecca felt warm again; she had returned these two some joy that had been stolen from them. Maybe she could give some more back to the other owners of the possessions she had. She smiled at the two.

"Don't be sorry," she said to the boy, "but you can help me with something. I am going to see that these get back to their owners," she said, holding out the objects. "I could use some help finding who lost any of these. Do you think you could help?"

Michael looked at the possessions Rebecca held out to him, looking crestfallen.

"I don't know. I mean what if that patrolman finds us with these," said Michael. "We're not as big as you or smart neither. We two would get beaten for sure," he said, looking down. "I promised mom I wouldn't get Sam hurt, and I swore I wouldn't. Didn't I Sam, didn't I swear?"

"He did swear," said Sam, looking despondent, then she shot a look at Rebecca. "But maybe, we could just ask around, maybe ask anybody who looks really sad if they got something stole from them," she said with a gleam in her eye.

Rebecca looked at the two. "I'm afraid if we did that, Sam, we would be asking everyone on this train. Everybody here seems to have had something stolen from them, if not by that patrolman." The girl looked down again. "But look," Rebecca said, getting to her knees and holding out the watch, "this has someone's initials engraved on the back. We could ask around, introducing ourselves, and find someone with these initials."

The children's faces lit up. They were bouncing at the thought of being able to help. *I've found,* Rebecca heard her brother's words in her mind, *when what is before you has you beaten down, find something else to do that lifts you back up.* "Alright, I'll hang on to these," she said, putting everything back into her satchel, "and we can move out of here once

14

we're moving. I'm Rebecca by the way," she said, holding out a hand to each in turn.

When the platform was empty of children, the guards walked the length of the trains, locking the outside doors of the coaches. Then, after a time, a low whistle sounded ahead, the train shuddered and slowly rolled out of the station. The cars rocked, rebelling against the sudden movement of the engines. The undercarriages creaked and groaned as the ice that formed on the wheels from staying stationary for so long, broke away. Slowly, the cars crept from the station housing into the grey landscape on the tip of the Arnoran shore, leading out to the Straits of Romara.

This far north the dark soil was patched with snow a majority of the year and the ground was always hard and cold, but grey-green grasses clung to the icy ground. The tracks swept along the coast moving toward the shortest gap between Arnora and Romara. The shore was a cliff of bright white chalk that reached down to the blue-green waves hundreds of feet below.

Mashing her face against the window, Rebecca could see the Straits moving closer and then, like a steel web strung over the thickening glaciers covering the sea, the Great Span. A series of bridges, constructed decades before to cross the Straits, marched out across the blue-white ice. The dark line of trestles and suspension bridges reached between huge steaming pylons; they sunk deep through the bedrock below, harnessing the heat to melt the progressing glacier. The Great Span could be seen for miles before disappearing in the distance like an ever thinning line suspended on a cloud.

Quickly, she switched her view. Pressing her face hard against the window, she looked back the way they had come. She could see the station getting smaller and there, behind the station, Landfall, the last town in Arnora. Somewhere back that way further south laid Arinelle, her hometown. She felt a pang of loss as the last of the lands she called home moved away from her and there was nothing she could do to stop it.

Rebecca sat back and wiped a tear that had appeared in her eye before the younger children could see it. No need to upset them; they were talking heatedly among themselves about how they would find the owner of the watch. They actually had smiles on their faces. Now they were debating about what his name was.

"How do you know he's a *he*?" said Sam with a serious expression painted across her face, "My name starts with an *S* too."

"That's stupid. Look, it's a wrist watch. What girls do you know that wear those, huh?" shot Michael. "Besides look at it, it looks boyish don't it?" he continued.

"Well, I think the name is Sarah Jennifer Brown, that's what I say," said Sam, pouting and huddling back against the wall of the compartment. A guard moved down the outside aisle toward the rear of the train.

"You brats keep it down," he shouted, "I can hear you halfway down the damned car," he said, motioning the way he had come and moved off toward the rear access door to the next car.

"Come close you two," Rebecca said, motioning them toward her. "These guards aren't going to want us doing anything that looks like we are working together for any reason. They are going to look suspiciously on any whispering and darting looks. If we are going to find the people who belong to these," she patted her satchel, "then we

16

are going to have to go about it in a way that looks perfectly innocent."

"Well, what do we do then? We can't just go down the aisles screaming 'Got a watch here. Hey, any SJB got a watch stole off him by some mean guard back there at the station?'" said Michael.

"You're so thick," said Sam with a look of disgust. "All we have to do is go about and walk up to the compartments along the train and say, 'Hello all, I'm Sam and what are your names?'" she said with a satisfied grin. "Then when Sarah Jennifer Brown says her name, we just give her the watch and say, 'Here I think you dropped this back there somewhere.'"

Rebecca had to stifle a chuckle. Michael eyed Sam sideways with a look of disbelief. Rebecca put her hand on Sam's shoulder with a very serious look and, holding back a smile, said, "That's a very good idea but I think that Sarah Jennifer Brown may not be the only *SJB* on this train and that way might take a little long." Sam looked down a bit and screwed up her mouth, thinking. "Here, look at the watch," Rebecca said, pulling it out once more. "What do you think this can tell us about the owner?"

The two looked at it intently as Rebecca held it out and rotated it for them both to get a good look.

"Well," said Sam, "I guess it could be a boy's watch."

"Finally." said Michael, throwing his hands up.

"Good, what else?" prodded Rebecca.

"He's bigger," said Michael.

"Whaddaya mean bigger? Bigger than what?" asked Sam, pushing Michael lightly.

"Stop," said Michael, half pushing her back. "I mean he's bigger than you or me or even Rebecca. Look at the strap, the smallest you can make it would be dangling around her wrist," he said, pointing at the strap.

"Good, Michael," said Rebecca, brushing down his stand-up hair. He smiled and blushed pink around the ears.

"Hey," said Sam, "look at the strap." They all moved closer. "It's kinda dusty see," she said, pointing, "looks like it's been on for a while. I bet we will know for sure the watch goes to whoever we find if he has a clean band where the watch would sit."

Both Rebecca and Michael looked at her with a look of astonishment. Even Rebecca hadn't noticed that. Rebecca reached out and pulled Sam close in a short hug. Sam smiled and stuck out her tongue to Michael.

"Alright, now you two listen to me," said Rebecca as they all got to their feet; she put a hand on each of their shoulders. "We are going to stick together. We are just some kids from the same town looking for our friends. We are going to move from one compartment to the next; if we see a bigger boy then I'll do the talking. If anything goes wrong, I want you two to run and hide back here, alright? Michael, remember what you swore your mom." Michael nodded his head in agreement, looking down a hair. "Now follow me and stay close. If we see a guard, just keep your eyes down and look like you did back on that platform. Any smiles or laughing is going to draw them on." They all agreed. Slugging on all their bags and sacks, they moved out of the compartment toward the front of the train. Fortunately, they had chosen the last for children; any potential recipients of the items were forward of their compartment.

Rebecca led the way followed by Sam then Michael; they moved out, heading up the train toward the engine. Rebecca looked out of the window as they left; the train was now moving out over the glacier, leaving the land and traveling along the bridges over the straits. The view was breathtaking, if a bit unnerving; she could tell they were now about sixty yards above the coast and glacier, seeming to fly out into the open air above the frozen sea below. Dusk approached quickly at this latitude. The sky began to melt into shades of pinks and violets, darkening slowly to midnight hues the further up she looked, and stars began to appear, flecks in the darkness.

Walking slowly up the aisle, all took on looks of sorrow and loss as they moved forward. The door at the front of the car opened and an armed guard moved down the aisle toward them; Rebecca could feel Sam tense as she saw him. Rebecca squeezed Sam's hand and led them past the guard, all with eyes pinned to the floor, to the next compartment. Rebecca entered the first cabin to appear; pulling both children after her; she could see the relief in their eyes.

Turning, Rebecca took note of the others in the room; crammed against the wall nearest the door were two small boys hunched together for warmth or for comfort; she was not sure which. Along the wall with the window was a large boy who stared at them as they entered. His face was contorted in anger or fear or both. Rebecca certainly hoped that this was not the one they were looking for. She walked into the middle of the cabin and knelt down with the rest of the occupants.

"I...I was wondering if any of you had noticed that patrolman back on the station platform?" Rebecca said in a low voice. She looked down so as not to leave any impression on these children, best not to be remembered if the worst were to happen. "My friends here lost some of their belongings to him. I was hoping..."

"What...what were you hoping?" said the large boy near the window. "We didn't take anything, the guy back there did. Now get

19

outta here before you get us in trouble." All of the children in the compartment nodded their agreements.

Rebecca stood with Sam and Michael and apologized as they made their way back into the aisle.

"That didn't go like I planned," said Rebecca. The others shook their heads slowly as they agreed. "Well, let's keep moving," she said, taking the lead as before.

Rebecca led the siblings down the next two coaches with similar results from each compartment they tried; Rebecca and her friends seemed to have little effect on the downtrodden children, but the third coach proved more fruitful.

Entering the first cabin they came to in this car, the mood became apparent immediately. A girl perhaps a year younger than Rebecca was sobbing on an older boy's shoulder. He was attempting to console her as the other children in the cabin looked on.

"I'll never forgive that man," she said through shaking breaths, "How...how could he just take it from me like that."

"It's alright, I know he's just a bastard like the rest of them around here," said the boy, his shoulder becoming increasingly sodden.

Rebecca knew that this girl had been plundered just as she had been – she had had the same thoughts this girl was expressing in choking gasps. She took Sam and Michael by their hands, leading them into the crowd as they had in each cabin they had tried.

"Excuse me," Rebecca said to the girl, "but would you be talking about that patrolman back at the station with the yellow teeth and scraggly beard?"

The girl looked at Rebecca in a pause, cutting off one of her sobs midway. She nodded her head, confirming Rebecca's thought.

"I was just wondering what it was he had taken from you, because he attacked my friends here," Rebecca indicated Sam and Michael who nodded to the girl, "and he did the same to me." She stopped Michael from spilling all he knew with a squeeze to his shoulder as he opened his mouth and took a breath; he closed it again and let out the breath.

The girl wiped her eyes and said in a little muffled voice, "My locket with my mom and daddy in it." Tears began to flow freely from her eyes again but before she could resume her lament Rebecca hurried into her satchel and found the silver locket with the pictures; she pulled it out slowly and held it for the girl to see. The girl's face brightened and fresh tears streamed down her cheeks. The other children stared at Rebecca and her friends with looks of awe.

"How did you get it?" asked the girl, streaming tears and laughing simultaneously. "I never thought I would see it again."

Rebecca made to answer but was bowled over as Michael jumped forward and recounted the events as he believed them to have occurred.

"Well, that pig was gonna hit me next," he said. "Rebecca saw and wasn't going to have any of that. So, she ran up and knocked him down, then, she grabbed all the stuff that jerk stole from us and came and found my sister and me and handed back the mirror the jerk pig stole from us. And then…"

The kid's eyes in the cabin were locked on Rebecca with a look of wonder.

"Well, that's not exactly what happened," said Rebecca, pulling Michael back by the shoulders. "All that matters though is that I'm

21

giving this back to you," she said, reaching over to the girl and lowering the locket into her outstretched hand. "What I was hoping was if you could point me to anyone else that was robbed back there."

The girl began to straighten herself from all her crying; she wiped her cheeks and began pulling her clothes to rights.

"Yeah, I saw a boy back at the station get smacked in the face when he tried to get something from that patrolman," she said. "He was a tall boy, maybe a head shorter than the patrolman but he got hit pretty hard and went sprawling. That was before the patrolman came over to take this from me," she said, indicating the locket she was sliding into an inside pocket of her jacket.

"Big you would say," asked Rebecca, "what did he look like?"

"I didn't get a real good look at him before he hit the ground but he had blond hair and was wearing a black coat, I think," said the girl.

"Thanks, we are just going to move up the train," Rebecca said, motioning with her head then looking around the cabin at the children. "We're going to be in the farthest compartment back later, after we find the boy you described. Anyone who wants can come and join us; it's empty back there." She smiled at the girl and the rest of the kids and again moved out into the corridor of the car.

The light outside had faded to a deep blue-black and the stars were awash across the sky. Rebecca stopped and gazed with open mouth astonishment at the sight of streaming bands of green and violet waving across the night sky. The glacier below was a ghostly mirror, reflecting the celestial inhabitants above. She pointed for Sam and Michael to see. After a few moments, they moved on, peering from one window to the next as they went along.

Finally, they came to the walkway vestibule between cars and moved through the rocking passage into the adjoining car. This car

22

was identical to the one from which they had just come; the small gas lanterns spaced along the aisle spilled pools of flickering light down the hallway. The car rocked as they came to the first compartment and walked in to again begin their inquiries.

Immediately, Rebecca knew this was not the place to be. This compartment was filled with several large lumps of boys; angry scowls and cruel grins marked their faces as they caught sight of the trio. Sam and Michael shrank up behind Rebecca so as to use her as a shield against any potential violence. When she made to back out of the cabin one of the brutish boys stepped up behind the three, blocking their exit.

"Wha' 'ave we 'ere?" said a large slab of a boy with pitted cheeks. "Looks like we got us some more compn'y, I'd be sayin'. An' look 'ere this one brought us a gift," he continued, pointing at Rebecca's satchel. "Why don' you jus 'and it over little girl?" he finished with a smirking grin. The other toughs in the cabin made amused guffaws and edged toward the three.

"I'd not be doing that if I were you," said a voice from the door. The attention immediately refocused on the speaker. "I hear this girl took down one of those Red Guard patrolmen back at the station." Again the young toughs attention switched to the three small figures standing in their midst, disbelief plain on their faces. Rebecca looked around to see who was speaking; she saw only a mop a disheveled hair silhouetted in the doorway.

"So, like I was saying, you gents might as well let this catch go before you all get unintentionally bitten," the speaker continued. The tough blocking Rebecca and the others' path slowly sidled away from the opening; turning in place Rebecca put her hands on Sam's and

Michael's shoulders and herded them toward the speaker at the doorway, not looking anywhere but toward escape.

Once they crossed the frame they walked quickly toward the front of the train; their savior behind them took up the shepherding from Rebecca and including her in the flock, moving them away from the wolves behind them.

"In here," said the speaker behind them. "Quickly now, there you go, inside, inside."

Once inside the cabin, the three slouched to the ground, breathing in relief. Sam huddled next to Michael who had thrown an arm over her shoulder and hugged her to himself. Rebecca looked at them regretfully; she had almost gotten these two hurt while they attempted to give her help. She couldn't ask these kids to risk themselves to help her. How could she ask anyone to risk themselves for her?

"You three almost got yourselves really wrecked up back there," said the speaker from the door. Rebecca turned to look at him and realization hit her. "You were lucky I was coming down that way or you might have been another bruised up bunch...well, that would be one thing we have in common," he said, turning to the three. He had a cracked lip and a darkening cheek that looked like it ached. His golden brown hair was a mop on top of his head and his black coat was buttoned to keep out the cold that was now trying to creep through the glass of the windows. He had a kind face and looked at them, smiling with warm brown eyes.

"James Bligh," said the boy, holding out his hand to each in turn; when he reached Sam he bent down and kissed her tiny hand. Sam's eye shot to the floor with a giant grin smearing her face. Michael tugged on Rebecca's coat sleeve, trying to get her attention. When she looked at him, he gestured to James's left arm with his head and eyes.

The thick wrist of his left arm had a telltale light band where a watch easily could have once rested.

Rebecca nodded to Michael to show she understood and then looked to James who was turning to his bag in the corner by the door. "Um, thanks for helping us out back there," she said. "We were looking for anyone who wanted to join us in our cabin in the back. It was getting kind of cold with just us three and..."

"Well, you might want to work on your lies a bit more my friend," said James.

"What...I wasn't," Rebecca tried to say but he talked over her.

"A guard found me in the crowd back at the station a while after that thug ran me down. He said to be on the lookout for a girl, trying to return some valuables that that skink was stealing from us. He was a dark fellow, guess a southlander, built like an ox he was so I told him I'd keep my eyes pried," he smiled at Rebecca. "Sorry, but I was expecting a big cow of a girl to have taken that one out like I heard you did. You know you broke his nose; I saw him run past."

Rebecca grinned and looked down. "Yeah, I know, he tried to grab my arm, I didn't even think, my foot just jumped out," she said. "He looked like he was going to pay me back double for it though when he found me again, but Gaston, the big guard you were talking about, stepped up and sent him sprawling – he saved me."

"Well, it's still better than I did," said James, brushing a hand through his hair and looking a touch ashamed.

Changing the subject, Rebecca reached in and grasped the watch in her satchel, she pulled it out but did not show it to James; he could still not be the one they were looking for, but she hoped he was.

"Look," she said, "a girl back that way gave us a description of a boy who got something snatched and I was wondering if you had."

25

She caught his eye as he turned, looking puzzled. "You know something valuable that the patrolman might have taken from you."

"Rebecca," said Sam with urgency in her voice, "his name is James that doesn't start with an *S* at all…"

"Shut up," Michael hissed, catching on to Rebecca's plan.

"You mean you have it," said James, "my dad's watch, you have it?" He stepped up to Rebecca, his eyes gleaming with hope.

"I just want to make sure. Is there anything you might be able to tell me to convince me that what I have belongs to you?" said Rebecca, edging back from him slightly in case he made to grab for her.

A big smile split his face and his lip; it cracked as he grinned and he winced at the pain.

"You're keener than I thought; yeah, there are initials on the back for my dad, Simon James Bligh. Dad gave his first name to my older brother; I got his second," said James.

"We found him," Sam squealed.

"Yeah, but you could have blown the whole thing if it wasn't him," said Michael, scowling at her but she was bouncing up and down and didn't notice.

"Here," said Rebecca, opening her hand and pushing the watch forward. "I was telling the truth though, about asking people to our cabin, if you want to get out of here that is."

James took the watch, rubbing his eye in a way that told Rebecca there had been a tear. He put the watch on, looking at her and her small companions.

"Yeah, I think I would like it back where you are staying."

Three:
From a Worn Satchel

The group moved back past the toughs, through the lantern-lit aisles of the adjacent cars, past all the no-luck compartments, finally coming to the start of their little hunt. When they walked through the door the four stopped at the sight before them. Children had gathered in the cabin and were all looking at the doorway with gleams and smiles on their faces.

"I guess word got 'round that this was a friendly cabin," said James, nudging Rebecca from behind, breaking her away from her shock. When they had left this cabin it had been just the three taking up the space. Now there was barely room for the four to squeeze back against the windowed wall of the compartment.

"Sorry," said a girl from behind them when they moved in. Rebecca recognized the girl she had given the locket immediately. "I kind of started spreading what you did for me. These others just wanted to come see the one who stood up to that brute. My name is Helen by the way and this is Paul." She went around, introducing the rest of the half dozen other new guests. A pair of brothers had a roguish look to them; they were about Michael's age, named Gene and Lester. There was a boy, about eight years old, named Mac, watched by his older cousin, older by about two years, named Marissa. There was a sulky girl named Elizabeth, hiding behind her dark curtains of hair, and a pudgy boy named Arthur who kept darting looks at Rebecca and then everywhere else.

"They were all wondering," said Paul, sitting beside Helen after she had finished. "Well, they were hoping that you had maybe gotten some more from that guy back at the station 'cause each of them got something took," he finished, pulling Helen close protectively.

"There were a couple of other things," said Rebecca, squishing in between James and Sam against the wall and pulling her satchel around to her lap. "I didn't really look at all of it I just kind of emptied his pockets." She smiled, "I think I probably ended up taking his things too."

The gathering laughed nervously and edged in as she opened her satchel. She began rummaging through the contents.

"Let's see," Rebecca said, looking at Elizabeth. "What did you lose?" she asked, holding open the top flap of her bag.

"I...I lost my gramma's brush. It... it was made of ebony with a bird carved into the back," Elizabeth said in a low soft voice.

Rebecca saw it; she ducked back into the satchel and pulled it out, revealing it slowly, with a grin. She handed it to Helen who handed it down the line to Elizabeth; once in her hands she pulled it close to her chest and thanked Rebecca in an equally low tone.

"Arthur was it?" said James from beside Rebecca. "Let's have it son; what did you get nicked from you?"

"Um... well, sir I... uh, um lost my, my uh," he stammered.

"No need to be scared Arthur," said Rebecca, eyeing James with an accusing glance.

"My ma's silver sewing kit, it was a little box with some etchings in the metal all... all the way round," he finished in a whisper.

Digging through the leather pocket inside her bag, she found the square box inside. It had intricate swirling patterns etched in dark lines all over it. Rebecca pulled it out, the contents clinking lightly, and reached it out delicately to Arthur.

"It's very pretty," she said to him.

"Thank you," he said, reddening.

"Boys did you lose anything?" she asked the young brothers.

"That brine-sucking slug took our unc's knife," said Lester.

"Said it was dangerous paraphernalia and we could be taken out and beaten for having it, the dung-wallowing maggot," put in Gene.

"Well, we are in agreement on our feelings for our friend the patrolman, aren't we?" said Rebecca.

The children gave a more full heartened laugh.

Reaching in again, she looked through the contents; the children seemed to be taking these little revelations with much enjoyment, as much as it gave Rebecca to be doing it. She found the folding knife that she had thought was a carving of a fox but now she noticed the little release hidden between the foxes laid back ears. She pulled it out and tossed it over to the brothers, who caught it and looked up again, grinning from ear to ear.

"Marissa did you lose anything?" asked Sam in a consoling voice.

"No, but that jerk took my little cuz's magnifying lens; it was his favorite thing in the world." At this Mac's eyes welled with tears and he clutched his cousin's arm and wept into the wool jacket.

Rebecca put up her finger and made a spectacle of reaching into her bag, slowly rolling out the lens in its leather case. One of Mac's red-rimmed eyes poked out from behind Marissa's sleeve and clamped onto the familiar shape. Rebecca handed it over to James; Mac's eye followed its travel. James slowly reached out the lens to Mac.

"Here you go big man," he said to Mac in a low voice.

29

Mac didn't say anything but took the lens from James and latched his eye back to Rebecca's; she smiled at him then turned to the rest of the gathering.

"I think that's all," she said as she looked back into the bag for the last time. "All I've got left are my things and one Red Guard coin purse." She smiled to the kids as they giggled.

The children began to talk quietly amongst themselves, passing away the hours. As the talk dwindled and they began to lay down for sleep, Rebecca got to her knees and turned to look out the window at the night lights, flickering overhead; the stars winked through the sheets of color as they melded into one another, blending and brightening as they touched. James shifted his gaze up to watch her looking out.

"The aurora, they're bright this time of year. Really beautiful aren't they?" he asked.

"I just wish I could have seen them with family." She folded her arms on the window sill and rested her chin on her hands. "My brother would have liked to see this," she said, "He loved looking at the stars and with my mom when we were younger. She would point out a cluster and he would name the constellation; he knew them all," she said, shifting her head to look at James, "I couldn't remember more than a handful but he always knew." She quickly turned back to the sky before he could see the tears form. "I guess there's no use hoping for what can never be, right?" she said in a soft voice.

"There's never harm in hoping. You just can't rely on it to carry you through," he said, turning to look out to the sky with her. "First time I saw these," he said, putting a finger against the window and drawing a line across it. He turned to look at Rebecca with a smirking smile, "I cried because I thought the sky was on fire and we were going to be burned alive. My dad took me up and put me on his shoulders. He said 'Don't you cry now, this is the First Father's paintbrush at work; just sit back and enjoy the show.' When I looked again, I swear I could see the bristles hitting the sky as the First Father painted the night."

They knelt there together for a time while the train trundled down the rails; the glaciers groaned and cracked at the load passing above. Night lingered as the children slumbered.

Finally, resuming a more comfortable position next to James, Rebecca opened her Satchel and pulled out the journal her grandfather had created.

"Here," she said, "I want to show you this." She opened the old book to one of the maps, looking for the Straits of Romara. "Here is where we are, about," she said, finding the map she was hunting for and circling a finger around the line indicating The Great Span. "And here is where we're going, I'm guessing." She dragged across the page to Romara's lower boundary, a horn sticking out into the Cold Sea, with little stars marking towns and villages around a larger mark, noting the universities. "I heard my brother talk about going to these," she said, "He wanted to be a master smith, you know making really intricate scroll work for buildings and the like."

"I thought about going there too, but I was headed down a different path," said James. "My mom wanted a Cleric in the family; so, I got history and archeological studies instead." Looking over the map he said, "This is a really well made map, where did you get this?"

"My grandfather, it's his travel journal, he made this along the way while exploring all over the world."

"This text looks odd though, I don't recognize the script," he said, pointing at the notes below the map. The script sketched across the page in little glyphs, each made of slanting lines and little sweeps.

"I don't know," said Rebecca, squinting at the characters. "I never noticed these before." She turned to the next map in the journal, one of the university's plans, and saw this map too was footnoted with foreign script all along the bottom. She could have sworn she had never seen it there before. As many times as she had sat looking at the sketches and maps in the book, she would have noticed these characters.

"Well, I don't suppose you can read it then?" asked James, looking at the new page.

"No, I can't," she responded in a distracted whisper.

They sat together, looking through the journal and the strange script covering the pages, until James became very quite. Rebecca looked over at him; he had fallen asleep, leaning against her shoulder. She set the journal back in her bag careful not to jostle James awake. She leaned back against the wall and James. She sat for quite a while, thinking about the journal's new addition. How could she have missed such an obvious detail in the book? Had it been in there all along and she had never noticed, or had it somehow formed there of its own volition? More importantly, what did the incomprehensible lines of text say?

Four:
A Book by Its Cover

Light poured through the window above, creating incandescent shafts of dust and haze in the center of the compartment. The train still thumped away and the cars gently swayed as the wheels coasted down the steel rail.

Stretching, Rebecca found her back quite stiff from the odd position she had slept. James was still there but he sat awake, looking down in a way that made Rebecca assume he was deep in thought. He noticed her shifting and looked down at her leaning against him.

"Morning," he said.

"Morning," she returned, sitting more upright and cracking her back as she did so.

The rest of the younger kids still laid breathing softly or snoring like a ripsaw, so they kept their talk to a low whisper.

"I was just thinking, what do you suppose they are going to have us doing wherever they are taking us?" he asked her.

"Not sure, but I think we can get through whatever lays ahead," she said, looking at the sleeping forms about the floor. "James, whatever happens, we should stay together."

"What?" he asked, looking a bit bewildered.

"We have lost our families, but kids need a family, and we can be one for each other to keep from breaking," she said. "You had to have seen some of the children in the holding camps before they took us to the train. . . they had a look on their faces, as though they were looking off ten thousand miles. I don't want to see that look again; I don't want that look. It's the look of the broken," she finished, looking him in the eyes.

He nodded slowly.

"I see, well, we will have to stay together then, whatever they have waiting for us," he said resolutely.

The silence was shattered with a clanging from the aisle of the train. A bell rang followed by the cry of a guard.

"Everyone up, up I say, get up an' follow me. This way, this way, come get your chow now you wretches, this way to the grub."

The guard walked past the cabin and shook the bell in the doorway.

"Get up you lumps, get up," and then he went on to the next doorway.

As all the children began to wake, Rebecca, James, Helen, and Paul, the oldest amongst the group, got the children in order and followed after the guard. Other groups of children spilled out in ones and twos. Down the aisles they marched, passing through six cars before reaching a dining car.

This car had been converted like all the rest; it had all its finer appointments removed in favor of a long horseshoe table where large kettles were lined up. Cooks stood behind it, ladling out soup into bowls which were thrust on the first child to step toward them. Down the table, a plate of bread was stacked; another cook dropped each bowl holder a hunk of the hard crusty loaves. Around a loop at the front of the car and back down the other side of the horseshoe, a series of pitchers and mugs sat; one last cook poured water into each mug then handed it off to the next in line. Finally, the line looped out the way they had come.

Rebecca was at the front of their procession and led the smaller children through the workings of the mass feeding; she had seen the like back in the camps, during the start of this wicked expedition, and knew how a child could get flustered with such rapid handling. Taking the bowl that was shot out at her she made sure Sam got hers, before proceeding to the next station. Forward and forward they all passed; James tailed the group to prevent stragglers from getting displaced. Putting her bread in her bowl, she grabbed the mug and made sure Sam followed her lead but by this time Sam was making sure Michael was following procedure. Smiling, Rebecca led their little flock toward their cabin.

"Does anyone else feel a bit like a pig going to the feeding pens when they do that to you?" asked Lester as they walked into their cabin and found their spots.

"Yeah, I was thinking something near enough myself," said James, last through the door.

They all ate and talked about what meals were like when they were home. They all laughed when Gene heckled Lester about how he would eat so much he would have to sit a whole thirty minutes before he could stand and walk away from the table.

As they finished eating, the children got up and began to stretch their legs a bit; James warned them not to stray too far from the cabin.

"You sound like my da'," retorted Lester.

"Well make sure you heed me like your da'," said James with a smile.

"Oh, no I don't think you'd be wanting that at all," said Gene. "His backside can attest to how well he listened to our da'."

"It's like leather it is," said Lester.

"Go on," said James, shooing them.

Rebecca giggled as the children moved out of the cabin and James came back to sit near her as she paged through the journal.

"Well, what do we have then?" he said, settling to look down on the open pages.

"I was hoping to find some kind of key, some way to begin to solve what the symbols are but I can't seem to find one," she replied, turning the page. "I know now though that this was not here before we left Arnora," she said, pointing to several lines of the text under a drawing of an enormous tree, judging by the tiny figure of a man drawn next to it for scale. "I remember this page distinctly. This was one of my favorites in the whole book. I couldn't imagine a tree being this large."

"But writing couldn't just appear on the pages like that," James said, moving to look closer at the page.

"Maybe… I mean, what if… never mind, it's just fool-headed childishness," she said, shaking her head.

"What?"

"Nothing it's just… not possible," she said, sitting back from the book.

"I'd like to know what you were thinking was not possible because I haven't an idea what you are going on about."

"Well, this is ridiculous I know, but what if the book… knew it had left Arnora, somehow, and this," she drew a finger down the text, "was unlocked when the book passed the border, maybe to give the holder more information on where she was."

"You're right; that is impossible," said James, moving his face back away from the book as if it might burst into flames.

"I told you," she said, closing the journal with a *thwump*.

"That sort of thing hasn't been possible for years now," he said like he was saying the sky was blue.

"What?" now it was Rebecca's turn to be confused.

"That sort of thing hasn't been possible since," he looked to the door to make sure no one was listening, "the *Scouring*," he finished in a whisper.

Rebecca looked at him with a confused twist to her face.

"Surely, you've had to have heard of *that*."

Rebecca gave a little shake of her head. James looked again toward the door; seeing it was still clear, he moved in closer to her, beckoning her to lean in.

"The Scouring happened before Arnora fell to the Red Fist Army, before the slaughter at the Last Stand, around the time of the Return of the Exiled.

"In the past, people with a certain…touch and the knowledge to do so were able to create objects that worked with the *Kilaray*, the nexus between this world and the invisible world that the First Father set in motion. Clocks, compasses, carvings," – he looked down at the book and put his finger tips on the closed cover – "books, anything Linked to the Kilaray could be made to do… things, depending on the ways they were Linked; like, well, like what you just described," he finished.

"How can that be? My grandfather was an explorer; this journal was a record of his travels. My father never said anything about the book containing links to anything beyond that."

"Maybe he didn't know; maybe he was trying to protect you."

"Protect me from what?"

"Adarianites, the followers of Mandagore Adarian and the Red Path, they saw any who touched the Kilaray as blasphemers, heretics to their Path. They destroyed all that they found relating to the Kilaray Links."

"You said this Linking hasn't been possible for years; how can that be? Surely whoever created these objects must be able to recreate them."

"No, they can't. The Adarianites swept through the Homelands before they were exiled into the Broken Lands. The Old Religion libraries, all the devices, objects they held, the volumes of history on the creation of Links and manipulation of the Kilaray, all were put to the torch. The Clerics who refused to convert to the Red Path were butchered. The few objects that remained intact disappeared between the time of the Exile of the Adarianites and the Return. I never heard the Clerics speak of having seen a Linked object firsthand."

"But what about the people able to touch the Kilaray? They must still know how to make these Linked objects."

"That would be, if any survived. The First Order of the Touched, those most capable of touching the Kilaray Links, the Philistari, were killed before the last battle to exile the Adarianites. Those who remained, the Mecharicals, held only a portion of the gift required to manipulate the Kilaray directly; they were dependent on the devices that the Philistari taught them to create that Linked to the Kilaray; even they were not safe from the reach of the Adarianites though.

"Murders, assassinations really, followed the Exiles' Return. All the victims were renowned Mecharicals and their descendants. The last remaining group who had any knowledge of the Kilaray Links, the Palantean, were killed at Ronan's Folly in the Anderwill Mountains, trying to give the Homelands time to muster a defense against the Red Fist Army. Mandagore Adarian literally had the lands Scoured to purge the knowledge, written and living, of the Kilaray Links.

"This can be very dangerous to you, and me, and anyone else who knows about it," James said, pointing to the book. "If the Red Guard knew what this was, or what it could be, our lives would be forfeit."

"Do you think they would kill me for having this?" she asked, wrapping her arms around the book, hugging it to her chest.

"Maybe. You said your grandfather created it. Those with the gift to touch the Kilaray often passed down the trait to their children."

"My grandfather was an explorer; my father was a carpenter. They were not Mecharicals; I don't have any gift, James."

"Perhaps, but that doesn't explain how you have in your possession maybe the last remaining Linked object from the Homelands. And you did say it was your grandfather's. You must keep this secret, you must keep it safe. Rebecca this could be very important for anyone who can figure out how this book is Linked," he said.

"Hey, what are you two playing at?" asked Lester, standing in the doorway. "Why are you leaning so close all of a sudden?"

They looked at him with shock painting their faces. Noticing how close they had been leaning to one another, they sat up quickly, and then, realizing how that must look to the boy, they unnecessarily straightened their clothes.

"We were...talking," said Rebecca first.

"Exactly," said James, noting the unfolded fox-carved knife in Lester's fist. "We were betting on whether you or your brother was going to get that nice little blade snatched by some passing guard."

Lester whipped his head around, looking for guards as if they would appear by mere mention. Then folded the knife and slipped it back in his coat pocket.

"We were just noticing a town not far ahead. I guess we made it to Romara and didn't notice," he said, looking at them with a guilty expression. "Were you really betting on us Rebecca?" he asked in a little voice.

She shook her head and smiled. "Show me this town now," she said, getting up and taking his hand. He led her to where the other kids were pinned to the windows along the aisle. She walked up and stood on tiptoe to see over the children's heads.

A town lay in the distance. The very ground here seemed alien to what she was used to. Dark brown, nearly black, rock covered the majority of surface, that which was not covered in snow. Steam rose in the distance from some unknown source but there seemed to be buildings encircling that source. The buildings themselves seemed strange to her. They were painted in bright colors, perhaps to contrast with their bleak surroundings, and they seemed to be made of some material like concrete with wood being used sparingly as visible supports for steep-peaked roofs, and door and window openings. The sight filled her with wonder and, at the same time, made her feel even more adrift than she had back at Landfall Station in Arnora.

Remembering the map of Romara from the journal, Rebecca realized that they were nearly to their final destination now. Butterflies flapped in the pit of her stomach; what was to become of the little family she had helped to gather? Would they all be forced to separate? Would she ever again see any of these friends? What of James —funny that. Why had he stood out among the others?

Just then, James stepped close behind her.

"I'd say we were near there now," he said, bending his neck to whisper in her ear.

She grimaced and nodded. "Almost there," she said softly.

Five:
What's in a Name

Rebecca could tell the train was beginning to slow; she rocked forward with the deceleration. They had passed three more outcropped villages along the way; each marked by a jetting plume of steam at their centers. From what she gathered some construction had been built over the source of the plumes and pipes ran from the housings out to the buildings all around the jets. *Maybe*, she thought, *they were using the heat from the ground in a way similar to the pylons of the Great Span.*

The brakes began to scream as the train neared the final destination. The station itself looked as though it had been constructed of the same material as the buildings in the villages, but where there had been simple box shapes, the station grew from the surrounding dark rock. The supports for the arching roof looked like the ribs of some long dead leviathan, jutting from the ground. The train came to a stop at the platform finally, jerking to a complete halt.

A squad of Red Guard stood waiting on the pier as porters unlocked the outward doors of the coaches. Then the clanging came again as the guards walked from the rear, signaling the children to get off the train.

Rebecca led the group from the train and onto the platform where guards had begun to organize the children.

"Two lines here," shouted a large man with a shaved head and a thick, dark beard. "I want two lines, no pushing, no talking."

"Stay close and link hands with the person behind you," said Rebecca to Sam standing behind her.

The chain of children did as she said and they walked to the lines, coming a little way back from the front line, nearest to the train. Red Guards, carrying steel batons, walked the lines making sure none of the children stepped out or disappeared. Wind howled through the openings for the train; Rebecca wondered why they did not build doors on train station platforms. The station had been made to welcome the students entering the university here and it was made to impress. The arching supports flew high overhead, supporting colored glass tiles between their ribs. The light cast in a rainbow of hues on the people below gave a cheery look to the crowd. Tiled floors on the platform of the station made intricate patterns that swirled in on themselves in shades of blues and yellows. At either end of the station, where the trains came and left, there were amazing stained glass images in the semicircular portions at the top of the openings.

Eventually, all the children were organized into two orderly columns. The guard who had been doing the bell ringing walked to a man wearing a long dark fur coat that looked very warm.

"Train is clear, sir," he said curtly to the man.

"Good, then get that engine turned and the cars loaded with as much as they can take," said the man.

"Aye, Sir," said the bell ringer, turning on his heel after a fisted salute over his heart. The bell ringer issued orders to men who began loading the train with crates and furniture.

The man turned to look at the children; he walked slowly to the end of the columns, no one spoke. He was a tall man, imposing. His face was lean and clean shaven. What remained of his hair was bright white and cut close to his skull. He stared at them with a gaze that looked as though he was seeing what price he could get for them at market. When he reached the end of the columns he turned and walked back to the head of the lines; he began to speak.

"I am Colonel Dormon and you are now under my command. You will be marching to your new home, Valgerhold, in a few short minutes," he said in a voice used to shouting orders. "Consider yourselves fortunate, this university is by far the most prestigious in Romara. We will produce the finest quality goods for our great New Dominion's desires. Valgerhold will house you, Valgerhold will feed you, and you will thank Valgerhold by working your very hardest. Eventually, when you have all learnt what we have to teach you and sufficiently repaid your families' debts to the New Dominion, you will be returned to the Homelands." He stopped at the front of the columns and turned to face the children. "Any who do not follow my command will have the mercy the New Dominion has bestowed upon you revoked and will be dealt with as traitors."

He turned to the bearded man. "Commander Postam you are in charge," he said in a gruff quick voice, then turned and quickly moved off, exiting the station.

Commander Postam turned to the children with a menacing cast to his face.

"You will be marching some distance; any who cannot march will be left where they drop. Now move," and with those words Postam walked toward the station exit.

The children followed after him; the other Red Guard on the platform followed the columns with batons at the ready for stragglers. Postam led them out into the open Romaran air; the cold quickly began to burn Rebecca's nose. The wind whipped across the open rock surface of the land surrounding the station and numbed any

43

exposed flesh. Rebecca pulled her scarf from her satchel and wrapped it around her head and face to cut the wind. She turned and saw many others devising similar coverings from anything they had to hand. Surprisingly, Postam looked completely at ease in the torturous biting gusts, with his bald head exposed to the full force of their attacks.

"Nothing like a brisk walk to clear the mind, ay," shouted Postam through the roar of the wind in a mocking voice.

The columns of children struggled through the elements and staggered along the path cut into the dark rock plane that led from the station. Rebecca could hear whimpers whenever the rushing sound of wind died momentarily. She turned to make sure her friends were still behind her; they all walked heads into the wind, and bent over to diminish the blasts to their faces.

The marching seemed to go on for hours but when she turned back she could still see the station; they had only come about three miles by her judgment. *How much further did they have to go before they could rest?* Finally, looking ahead, she could see a village looming, perhaps another two miles on.

The road from the station led down to the village, this one much larger than those they had seen from the train. Rebecca looked for the plume she knew would be here and found the telltale fan of steam pouring from the top vent of a large housing. Pipes protruded from the walls and traveled up to cement towers, holding the piping aloft. The pipes seemed to be dressed in wool blankets. *Perhaps keeping out this blasted wind,* she thought. The piping followed all the main streets, branching off to smaller tubes to feed buildings down narrower streets.

The buildings here too had been painted in garishly bright colors with dark wood supports, doors, and shuttered windows. The roofs were tiled in slate that seemed to echo the rocky environment in which they were constructed.

As they entered the streets of the village, the structures cut the wind. But when they would pass a street with a clear view to the rock planes they had crossed, a torrent of air would rip the relative warmth away and tear at their clothes.

Rebecca could see the inhabitants of this town every once in a while running between buildings or hurriedly strolling down the streets bundled in thick, dark coats. Men drove wooly oxen quickly through the town; even the animals with dense fur seemed to hurry. Thick-coated dogs huddled together or curled with their noses in their tails to stay warm. *These must be the Romarans that taught at the universities before the New Dominion had taken over*, thought Rebecca.

Continuing past several buildings that looked to house various industries, the columns came at last to a structure like none Rebecca had ever laid eyes upon. The main building and immense walls seemed to have been constructed of the same dark stone that made up the planes. There was a vast doorway in the outer wall perhaps fifty feet tall with an arched opening; the massive doors, bound in intricate scroll-worked iron, were opened outward. Above the huge walled opening, Rebecca could see other structures behind the dark arched crenellations atop the walls, reaching skyward. The main feature was a minaret supported with stone buttresses; they arched up to meet the spire which was topped with a green clay tiled dome hundreds of feet up. The whole of the spire had been adorned with the masterful carvings of the craftsman that had studied here. Other structures could be seen to either side of the main tower, all vast and topped with the same green clay tiles as the dome. Valgerhold, she assumed, resembled a grand fortified castle complex more than any place of learning.

45

As the columns of children walked – faces pointing skyward and ogling the immense structures looming overhead – through the doorway, they entered into a huge courtyard space. The wind, thankfully, could not breach the walls and they were finally given some respite from its relentless onslaught. The courtyard was paved in a light-colored stone that was laid in patterns with great skill. Around the space were raised sitting places with planting areas within their circumferences. Hardy looking trees had been planted to give shade to any who would dare sit in this cold.

Around the perimeter of the courtyard, carved stone columns supported a second story walkway with openings that led to darkened hallways. Rebecca could see flights of tiered stairs leading to the second story through a massive dark wood door. At the far end was an arched opening that led to a grass-covered space that looked remarkably vibrant in relation to the cold weather.

The children marched to the center of the courtyard where Postam shouted for all to halt. Panting breaths puffed from the lines of children; they all seemed exhausted after the march. The Red Guard escort took up positions around the courtyard and locked into place. Colonel Dormon came down one of the spiraled stairways, he, apparently, having traveled by some other means. He walked into the courtyard and took up a position flanking the columns.

"All face the Colonel now," shouted Postam and the children hurried to comply.

Rebecca found herself in the row nearest the Colonel; she could have hit herself for choosing this line to march in. The Colonel had at his side a spindly man, holding a ledger with pen and ink at hand. Postam walked to what had been the rear of the line and turned to face the boy he found at the front row.

"State clearly your name, family name first, given last," commanded Postam.

The boy glanced about quickly then licked his lips, "Taylor, Anthony," he said in a rush.

Postam looked at the boy for a moment then gave him a full-armed backhand across the face which sent him sprawling. The children near him flinched away from the scene.

"You are to follow all answers with 'Sir' when speaking to any that have your charge," said Colonel Dormon as if the incident had never occurred.

The boy got to his feet and stood with tears in his eyes.

"Name," said Postam.

"Taylor, Anthony, sir," said the boy. The spindly fellow scratched down the name and Postam moved on to the next in line.

"Tines, George, sir," said the following boy.

On and on, name after name was given and recorded. The daylight dwindled and the sky became pink above the courtyard. The cold seeped through Rebecca and she began to shiver uncontrolled.

"Name," Postam said off to her right.

"Bligh, James, sir," came from down the line. She turned to look; Postam had arrived at her group. The clerk scratched the name on his ledger and Postam moved down.

"Fletcher, Mac, sir," said a little voice next to James.

"Albret, Marissa, sir," the girl's voice ringing in the courtyard.

Postam moved ever onward down the line.

"Flannery, Eugene, sir," said Gene in a clear voice, defying anyone to laugh at his name.

"Flannery, Lester, sir," Gene's brother spoke.

"Uh, Galbright, Arthur, sir," said a jittery staggered voice.

47

"Roberts, Elizabeth, sir," said a voice that would be just enough to carry to the clerk.

"Caldwell, Paul, sir," said the next in the group.

"Foster, Helen, sir," a voice much stronger than the first time Rebecca had heard it.

"Talbert, Michael, sir," Rebecca could see Postam two down from her.

"Talbert, Samantha, sir," said Sam in her bright voice.

She saw Postam loom before her; he eyed her up and down, squinting as he looked into her eyes as if remembering something he didn't like.

"Name," he said when she didn't answer immediately.

Rebecca's heart began to pound at the base of her throat. She hadn't planned for this. If the Red Guard learned her last name it was bound to cause trouble. Postam made a move as of rearing back to swing at her.

"Dulac," she blurted, her voice bouncing back to her off the walls of the courtyard.

Postam froze and she could feel all eyes in the courtyard pin to her; James leaned forward and looked down the line at her with a gaping expression. Colonel Dormon, who had until she had spoken seemed to be calmly listening to the line of names as though committing each to memory, became very rigid and stared at her with a sharp look in his eyes. Rebecca regained her wits and continued.

"Dulac, Rebecca, sir."

Postam leered at her with a snarl barely concealed, twitching his lip. He turned to look at Colonel Dormon. Dormon continued to stare a hole between her eyes then, breaking his stare, he waved

Postam on. Postam took a deep breath as he returned his gaze to her and released it, moving on to the next member in the line.

"Baxter, Angela, sir," she barely heard as the fear that had gripped her when Postam had stepped before her released. Warmth seemed to be draining from her stomach out of the bottoms of her boots as the adrenaline that had coursed through her faded. She had feared this would happen, been dreading it. She knew her brother had made an impression on the Red Guard but she did not realize how big that impression had been until this moment. The only word that could have described the looks on Postam's and Dormon's faces was hate, pure hate, but there was more than that; what had it been? Fear – yes, that was what she had seen there too; fear hid behind the walls of hatred. She realized she was in danger now, more so than before these men knew who she was. She was the sister of Sebastian Dulac, The Boy General; he had held Palder's Pass for months against the Red Fist Army in its attempt to break the Arnoran borders. Oh yes, she would be in danger here without a doubt.

The listing and recording continued for perhaps another hour and then silence seemed to reverberate through the courtyard with the lack of the constant calling of names. Dormon walked forward finally and looked side to side, viewing his new charges. His eyes lingered on Rebecca. He spoke, slowly returning his gaze to the whole crowd.

"You are now in the courtyard of Valgerhold. You will soon be escorted to your dormitory accommodations. But first, let it be known any action any member of my command determines to be... rebellious...will be punished swiftly, severely, and without question. It has been an eventful day; as I am sure you would agree, you will rise tomorrow and be fed, then your service will begin."

49

Dormon turned and walked out of the courtyard the way he had come, up the spiral staircase. Postam gathered two guards and spoke some instructions to them then walked to follow Dormon.

"Girls follow me," said one of the guards Postam had spoken to.

"Boys this way," said the other.

The two guards walked to the tiered staircase Rebecca had seen through the large door along the opposite wall from the one through which Dormon and Postam had exited. The columns of children broke apart and scattered after the two guards. Rebecca's friends caught up with her as she turned to follow after. James walked along side her; the others gathered round to hear what was said.

"Why didn't you tell me?" he asked. There was no need to ask of what he was speaking.

"You didn't ask," she said, not looking at him and continuing after the guards.

She noticed glances from other children directed at her. She looked down to avoid their stares.

"That's ridiculous," James said in a heated whisper. "Postam looked like he was going to personally tear your heart out. Rebecca you need to be careful these Red Guard are bound to hold a grudge for what your brother did. Bast! Half these guards were probably in the Red Fist Army at Palder's Pass."

"I know," she rounded on him. "This is why I didn't tell anyone; I am not my brother," she turned and resumed walking.

They had arrived at the tiered stairs; the group climbed after the guards in silence. Windows in the stone walls above the landings lit the stairwell's tiers; gas lanterns mounted on the walls around the stairwell would cast pools of light at night. Up the switchback stairway past the second floor they climbed. Rebecca could see that the landings on this

50

level led out to the walkway that wrapped the courtyard; there were also two closed doors to either side of the landing. Rebecca's legs began to burn as they climbed two more flights of stairs to the fourth floor landing. Two massive wooden doors on either side stood open; Rebecca could see the two guards at the end of either of the hallways to which the doors led. Before the group separated, Rebecca turned to James.

"Take care of them," she said, indicating the boys of her group who had gathered around him to make their way down the halls.

"I will; you do the same," he said, looking at the young girls behind her. "And Rebecca," he paused, "take care of yourself too."

"James," she said as he began to turn, "remember what we talked about on the train, about staying together, talk to them about it, alright. And James, I should have told you, I'm sorry."

"I understand, goodnight," he said and turned toward the boys' stairwell.

The guard had stopped, waiting for all the girls to finish their climb of the steps. The hallway was made of lighter stone than the rest of the castle complex and anchored along the walls were large thick material banners to keep out the cold as best they could. Tall windows, looking out into the courtyard, streamed the fading light of the day across the hallway onto the walls. More gas sconces lined the halls here. Along the peak of the arched ceiling ran a wide vent that disappeared into the walls at either end of the hall. It appeared to be the pipes of the steam jets from the town.

Once the guard saw that the last had arrived he began to speak, looking up as if to pull something from memory.

"You are now on the fourth floor of Valgerhold," he said in a monotonous voice. "This is the girls' dormitory. The stairwell will be locked to prevent your leaving. The lavatories and washrooms are down this hall to the right," he pointed with his arm. "Behind is the sleeping chamber; inside you will find, uh, inside you will find that there, um. Well you get the idea," he said, losing the thread of the speech. "Jus' go in an' sort yourselves out," he said, dropping into his native dialect.

The guard walked out of the hall, slamming the door and latching the lock on his way. Rebecca heard his steps fade as they went down one, two, three flights and then she heard the squeak and thud of a large door closing, the door to the courtyard.

She gathered up her friends and belongings and walked to the large arched doorway that led into the sleeping area. The doors were already open and girls could be heard arguing over the sleeping arrangements. The sleeping chamber was a round stone-tiled room with a wide spiraling staircase at its center, leading to three other levels. Arched alcoves along the perimeter walls held four to six beds in each. The beds she had expected to be meager things at best, but was surprised when she saw, in the alcoves, well made four-posted beds with thick hangings attached to keep out drafts. Everything inside this university had been crafted here, from the beds to the buildings themselves. This had been the last of the universities to be constructed and as such, had benefited from the experience the students who had studied here gathered from the other facilities.

She led her small group to the spiraling staircase at the center of the room and began stepping up to the higher levels. As they wound round the center column, Rebecca admired the enormous stained glass window that stretched to the ceiling. It depicted an image of a lion, grasping a green shield with the coat of arms of Arnora clearly visible - a young girl protected by two Arnoran soldiers, swords bared, with hands signaling halt - the workmanship was excellent. The beds up here had remained empty even though the group had been near the last to enter; it seemed no one wanted to climb any more stairs after the long march. Rebecca had noticed the vent from the hallway connected to the center column of the staircase; she was relieved to find her thinking had proven correct when they found the alcoves at the top warm from the air vented from the column.

The alcoves formed a semicircle, all facing the large window; the beds mirrored the semicircle along the round alcoves. Mosaics of flowers were inlaid in the floor in tiny tiles of various colors. The one they chose had an orchid; the arched ceiling had been painted with stars and the moon. Rebecca chose the bed nearest the opening of the alcove, Helen took the one across from her, and Sam picked the one nearest Rebecca on the inside of the alcove. Marissa and Elizabeth took the two beds next to Helen, leaving one bed empty, which they utilized as a storage area for all their belongings, next to Sam.

The girls all sat in their beds, looking at one another once they were settled; no one spoke for quite some time. Then Sam turned to Rebecca and asked, "Why was James upset with you?"

"Because she held out very important information from us," said Marissa before Rebecca could answer.

Rebecca looked at her with fire in her eyes that made Marissa lean back.

"I didn't hold back anything," she said. "No one gave their last names on the train except James and he wouldn't have done that if I hadn't been trying to return that watch to him."

"You should have told us anyway," Marissa shot back.

"Why, so you could start making assumptions about me that I can't live up to?"

53

Sam looked very concerned for having started this line of conversation.

"She had no reason to tell us any more than she wanted," said a quiet voice next to Marissa. Elizabeth held her carved ebony brush. "We have no reason to expect anything from each other, that's what the New Dominion is doing. We aren't responsible for the actions of anyone else. Just because our relatives may have stood against them doesn't mean we will follow the same path."

They all looked at her considering her words.

"I'm, I'm sorry," said Marissa after a moment. "I was just… shocked."

"It's alright," said Rebecca. "I knew the reaction I would get from the Red Guard; I just didn't guess at the reactions of my friends." She looked at Marissa.

Relief washed Sam's face, and she asked more carefully, "Rebecca what is it about your name that has everyone worried?"

"Her brother, Sebastian, was the one who held off the Red Fist Army's invasion into Arnora," said Helen in an almost reverent tone, "He and the First Born of Arnora held against a force of thousands at Palder's Pass. Our brothers and sisters - little older than Rebecca or James – held to try and give their compatriots time to evacuate us, coincidently, here to the universities. They were going to get us all across the Straits of Romara and then destroy the Great Span so the Red Fist Army couldn't get to us."

"But they were betrayed," Elizabeth whispered.

Helen went on. "One of their own showed the Red Fist through the gates of another part of the border wall Arnora constructed before the war to keep out the Return. The First Born were overrun and were forced to surrender," she stopped, speaking and looked at Rebecca.

"Sebastian worked out the terms of surrender with the Red Fist's general. Sebastian and his command would give themselves over for execution in return for the lives of the rest of his army and their remaining families, us. He had ensured that his command consisted of only children who had lost their parents in the Last Stand and had no brothers or sisters to think about. In other words, they were children with nothing to lose, that was, except him."

Rebecca had tears running down her cheeks when Helen finished.

"He promised me he would come back; he promised," said Rebecca, looking at her hands. She felt tiny arms wrap around her shoulders and looked over to find Sam, tears staining her cheeks as well, hugging her.

"Her brother sacrificed himself for the rest of his army and our lives. He is the only reason that anyone walked out of Palder's Pass; he's the only reason we're still drawing breath," said Marissa quietly.

After a time the others began to ready themselves for sleep. They pulled the curtains on the beds and wrapped themselves tightly in the covers and began to fall asleep. Rebecca lay, looking out of the alcove, with her blanket pulled to her chin. Tears continued to leak from her eyes, pooling on her pillow as she imagined her brother, hoisted into the air, feet kicking, face turning violet black, then slowly, slowly becoming still, swinging from the gallows on some far off battlefield.

"You promised," she whispered.

Six:
Crime and Punishment

Rebecca was awake before anyone else had stirred in the room. So, she heard the footfalls approach the large door leading into the dormitory. The doors swung open and a large guard walked into the middle of the sleeping quarters.

"Everyone up, now," he shouted.

Rebecca could hear the gasps and half suppressed screams as girls jumped up from their slumbers.

"You have one quarter of an hour to get dressed and down to the main courtyard," he continued in a carrying voice. "These quarters and the rest of the floor will be searched at that time; anyone found will be publicly punished," and with that, he turned and exited the room. Silence filled his wake as girls realized the full meaning of his words. *Publicly punished?*

Rebecca heard a wave of rustling sheets and thrown curtains sweep around the chamber as girls jumped from their beds and ran in every direction. Some ran for the lavatories; some attacked their bags and sacks to throw on some warm clothing; others just seemed to be running round and round the staircase in the sleeping chamber.

"Do these gutter rats enjoy tormenting us at every turn?" asked Marissa, as she rolled from her bed. She began to put back on the clothing in which she had arrived.

"Yes, they do," said Rebecca, as she stomped her feet into her boots. "They despise us."

"Well, I still think they could start to treat us a bit less like hardened criminals; we're kids for Father's sake."

"You can forget about kind treatment from the likes of these...people. They are sadists, it's in their blood and bones. We are the children of the men and women who exiled them. They will extract as much pleasure from us as they can," Rebecca said to the girls, as she finished tightening her coat and scarf.

"We are going to have to watch out for ourselves, aren't we?" asked Elizabeth.

"I think we are," said Helen.

"We need to watch out for each other," said Rebecca. "None of us is going to be able to get through this without help."

They all looked at Rebecca. "We have to act as each other's family now. James and I talked on the train, he agreed; we need to be strong to stand against whatever they throw at us. That means we need others to turn to, family."

Rebecca looked around at the others in the alcove; they each slowly nodded in agreement.

"Come on then, before they decide fifteen minutes is shorter on this side of the Cold Sea," said Marissa.

The group walked from the dormitory stairwell after finishing their morning preparations; their shoulders held a bit straighter, heads a bit higher. The sun in the courtyard was blazing down; the sky a blue so bright that when Rebecca looked down, she had tears in her eyes. Guards were posted as before but there were more now, lined along two long rows of wooden tables stacked with dark brown and gray clothing piled all along them. Postam waited in front of the tables, glaring toward the children as they approached.

Rebecca and the girls spotted James and the boys and they moved toward one another. When they were together, they walked toward the other children lined up in front of Postam; a guard was directing the children into more manageable rows than the two long snakes from the previous day. They approached and were ushered into a row four back and to the far left of Postam.

When they were in their positions, Rebecca leaned over to James. "Did you talk to the boys about sticking together?" she whispered.

"Yeah," he said curtly; he was holding his ribs in a peculiar way.

"Well?" she asked.

"They agreed," he said in just as short a tone. "It was a good idea," he said, seeming to release a held breath and wincing. "The younger ones latched on as soon as I brought it up. Paul needed a little more... convincing."

Rebecca noticed James looked a bit more battered from the last time she had seen him in the courtyard the previous day. Leaning forward she saw Paul had a similar roughed-up look about him.

"What happened?" she asked.

"Paul thought that if the guards found we were keeping an eye out for one another they might try making an example out of us."

"So? That doesn't explain your faces," she hissed at him.

"Let's just say he felt this might be the start of things to come with you; he didn't want to be led into anything that was going to leave him and Helen..." James paused and looked at her with a sympathetic eye.

Rebecca looked down. "Hanging from a rope," she finished his sentence.

James gave a small nod. "He eventually came around though and he seemed to be sorry for it, so don't hold it against him."

"I won't, but you shouldn't have hit him," she whispered.

Postam walked toward the children once they had all been settled into position.

"Today begins your repayment to our New Dominion for the rebellion of your predecessors," he said, with a cruel smile on his beard-covered face. "These," he said, gesturing toward the long tables, "are your new uniforms, they will be kept clean and pressed. Depending on the tasks that we set before you, you will receive various other accoutrements. After you are inspected, you will be issued your uniforms and your tasks will be assigned. First meal will be served after you have begun your exciting tasks," he finished with a mocking guffaw.

One of the other guards stepped forward from the table and shouted, "First Row." The children walked to the long tables. The skinny clerk from the previous day, as well as another clerkish looking fellow, each held a ledger. A guard separated the boys from the girls as they approached. Another guard stepped up and made a few quick measurements which were recorded in the ledgers and uniforms were issued. The children moved along the tables, where stacks of clothing were foisted upon them; by the time they got to the end of the tables the smaller ones could barely see over the tops of the piles.

"Return to your row when you have finished with uniform issuing," shouted the guard. Postam stood with his arms crossed over his massive chest with a satisfied grin. Rebecca noticed a pair of guards walking from the stairwell that led to the dormitories. Between them, a boy of about ten was struggling against the guard's grips on his arms to no avail. They dragged the boy to Postam who turned to them as they approached.

"Sir, this child was hiding in the washroom on the boy's dormitory level," said one of the guards holding the boy.

"Well, well, our first hero emerges, and I thought it might be some other candidate," said Postam, looking toward Rebecca. "Attention children," shouted Postam, "we have a special treat for you this morning. This young man has decided to gift you with an example of the type of punishments you can expect for your transgressions against the command here at Valgerhold," he turned and spoke to the guards. The boy's eyes grew very large and wet as Postam finished. Postam patted the boy on the head and sent the guards off toward a construction in the courtyard Rebecca hadn't seen here before. It appeared to be a platform with a short wooden mast projecting from the base, with a cross beam at the top.

The guards dragged the boy up the step of the platform removed his shirt and tied his wrists to the crossbeam of the mast; Rebecca felt sick as she realized for what the construction had been built. The guards then turned to Postam for instruction.

"Ten I would say would impress upon this young man the importance of following orders."

The guards nodded and one of them walked over to the post and removed a long leather whip. He stepped from the platform, turned toward the boy, and reared back, releasing the tail of the whip.

Rebecca refused to close her eyes as the boy's screams filled the courtyard; the guards' faces brightened with each crack. The boy's back opened in long red stripes with each caress of the tail of the whip. The bright red drops sliding from the gashes made an arc behind the little figure tied to the mast. Blood sprayed across the guard's grinning face as he reared back for each lash. Again and again the boy's screams ripped across the courtyard until finally the silence shook Rebecca from her open eyed trance.

The guards untied the boy; he dropped like a wet cloth to the base of the mast.

This is the New Dominion, she thought. The guards picked him up by the arms and dragged his sagging body to Postam; he lifted the boy's chin to look in his face.

"Did we get through to you the importance of our orders young man?" he asked with feigned concern; the boy wobbled his head in agreement, tears streaming from his eyes. "Then guards take this child to the infirmary, for we are nothing if not merciful to those who acknowledge their mistakes," said Postam, turning to the rest of the children with a smile across his face.

The children in the courtyard looked on Postam's smiling face with cringing fear, their faces red from crying or pale from shock, all except Rebecca. She had a look of utter serenity, complete calm; her yellow-green eyes met Postam's ruddy-brown and his smile slowly melted into a cruel grimace; it fit his face more appropriately.

"Continue with the uniforms," he shouted to the guards and spun, walking quickly toward the stairs that he had taken to follow Dormon the previous day.

Rebecca stared at his back for his entire retreat, holding the look on her face.

"What is the matter with you?" asked James with a look sheer horror. "You didn't even flinch. That kid's blood is fanned across this courtyard and you watched the whole time like nothing was happening in front of your face."

Rebecca turned to look at James. Her thoughts turned in her head, finally all fell into position.

"We have to tear them down," she said in cool unemotional calmness.

James head spun around, looking over his shoulder for guards. "Don't say that out here."

"We have to end these people, James."

"Rebecca, keep quiet, please, we'll talk later I swear just keep quiet until we get out of earshot of these guards."

Rebecca swallowed and nodded her head as their line began to move toward the tables for uniforms; she hadn't heard them call for their row she was so focused on her thoughts.

The children waited to be measured and issued their clothes, weeping for what they had just seen. The whole time Rebecca's brain spun, devising ways she could hurt her captors. *What would it take to bring the New Dominion down?* More than she could conceive. *Who am I to think such things, a little girl, what could I do?* More than they would expect. *They have a flaw Rebecca;* she heard in her head. *They see us as children. They won't expect anything from us and because of that; they won't be ready for the attack. We're going to hurt them Rebecca; we're going to hurt them bad.* Sebastian's words echoed through her racing thoughts. Anything that she could do to fight back against the New Dominion control would be more than they were expecting.

"What?" asked Rebecca, rousing from her thoughts.

"I said you look strange, are you alright?" asked Helen.

Rebecca hadn't noticed she stood behind Helen while she had been thinking. Rebecca noticed the redness around Helen's eyes; she had obviously cried for the whipped boy.

"I'm alright, I was just… thinking," she said still half in her own mind.

"I can't believe they did that to the poor boy, for hiding. I just can't believe it."

"I believe it," said Rebecca, fully coming to her senses. "Helen, this is what we can expect from them; they'll have no mercy for us and they'll enjoy the cruelty they inflict. Did you see those guards' faces; they smiled the whole time. We need to start to think of them," she looked around, making sure none of the guards was close enough to hear, then lowered her voice just to be sure, "we need to think of them as...as our enemies."

Helen's face had grown very pale while Rebecca spoke and her eyes were wide with fear. She shook her head slightly.

"Paul was right. You *are* going to get us killed," she said quietly. "Rebecca, we can't fight these people; we aren't strong enough and they have all the power in the world to do whatever they like. If we resist we will die. What would your brother's sacrifice have gained us then, nothing?"

Rebecca didn't know why Helen and James were reacting this way. Why was she the only one not frightened by the New Dominion's Red Guard, but outraged? Why did no one else have the same thoughts running through their heads? Why were the children cowering when they should be rising to fight? What would it take to get the others to stop fearing these men and stand against them?

Rebecca had nothing to say; she knew what Helen was saying was right. But, she also knew that the New Dominion needed to pay for all they had done. Not just the pain they caused the boy they had just whipped, but all the pain, not just her brother's death, but all the deaths they had caused; they needed to pay for it all. She looked at Helen though, saw the look of sheer terror on her face, and knew she needed to gain the support of the others first. She couldn't hurt these

Red Guard by herself, she needed the other children. *We all know what's at stake Rebecca; we stand together. Remember what dad used to say; together the weak can bring down the mighty.* Her brother's words came to her again, but if she couldn't convince her friends, how was she going to get the support of all the rest? She needed to gain their loyalty. More than loyalty, she needed to gain their trust; it was going to take more than returning some lost valuables to her friends. She was going to need to find something that would garner her support. Not just support of friends but those who would see her as Paul did, someone that could get them killed. What she needed most was to break the fear that held these children; she needed their fury. She needed to show them what was at stake if they didn't stand strong. She needed to become like her brother; she needed to find these children's courage, where they had hidden it. She needed to set it free; she needed to set it afire. Even though she didn't think she had it in her, she needed to become a leader.

Rebecca followed after Helen to the clerk with his ledger, followed by Marissa, Elizabeth, and Sam. His face never moved from the scratching he made on the ledger as he noted the answers each child gave to his questions. Rebecca stepped up when Helen went to gather her uniform from the guards down the tables.

"Name?" asked the clerk.

"Dulac, Rebecca, sir," she said, making sure to keep her voice as low as possible.

The clerk paused in his scribbling for a moment and looked up from under one grey bushy eyebrow to peer at her, then returned to his task. He flipped through the pages and asked her questions.

"Age?" he asked in a businesslike tone, as if recording a shipment of beans.

"Thirteen, sir," she said.

"Height?"

"Five feet, sir" she responded.

"Weight?"

She answered all his questions as to her measurements, her health history, if she had any mental deficiencies that would hinder her performance at any physical task. Then she felt a pang of loss with his next question.

"Your mother and father's previous fields of occupation?" he asked.

"My father was a carpenter, my mother was a teacher of astronomy, sir," she recounted.

"Do you have any proficiency in your father's field of occupation?" he asked.

Rebecca could remember helping her father in his shop behind their house, outside of Arinelle. The smell of woods from around the world mixed in her nose with her father's cologne; he would hold her hands steady while she carved into some soft piece, learning. He taught her the right way to work the grains of the woods. He had told her she was born to the craft when she showed him the small bird she had carved from the scrap he had given her to practice. She would sit at her father's bench, practicing, while he built the fine furniture and intricately carved objects that brought their family their income.

Feeling a burning in her eyes, she answered. "I was born to it, sir."

He made a small check at that and ushered her on to the tables. The first guard there handed her a set of dark grey undergarments; the next tossed her a folded dark brown pair of pants and gray shirt. A knit woolen cap came next and a pair of gloves, then a dark brown wool overcoat, and a set of thick leather boots. She balanced her pile as she moved back into the line next to James who had a similar pile in his arms. When all the rows had finished one of the guards stepped from the table.

"One quarter of an hour, be dressed in your uniforms and back in this courtyard," he announced.

The neat columns and rows exploded as children, balancing their piles, rushed for the large wooden doors that led to the dormitories. Rebecca and her friends remained calm and walked to the doors.

"Rebecca, what are you thinking? You haven't said anything for a while now," asked James quietly, keeping from piquing the others interest.

"I'm thinking that we need to find someplace to talk where we don't need to worry about anyone overhearing what might be said," she said.

As they came to the stairs and started up the flights, Rebecca examined the stairs and corridors more carefully. She looked for any way they could get out and meet one another where the guards wouldn't hear.

"Rebecca, I don't know if the others are going to be willing to even risk what happened to that kid back there happening to them, and I don't blame them. If these people think we're scheming at something they'll kill us, especially if it's you," he said as they neared the dormitory floor.

"James," she said, spinning to face him. The others began breaking off to go their separate ways. "We need something to keep us from giving up hope. Something small, like talking when we want, might be enough for now."

He looked her in the eye for a moment, then his eyes caught on something over her head; Rebecca turned to see what had his eye. There, above the doors to the separate dorms, was a transom on hinges, probably used to take advantage of air flow in the summer. It was high but if they could get up to it and through they would be able to access the stairwell to the courtyard and other levels. Maybe they could find someplace to meet where they wouldn't be missed when the guards locked them in at night.

James stepped closer so only she could hear. "Alright, tonight after they lock us in wait for everyone else to fall asleep then see if you can get out and I'll do the same," he whispered, looking down into her face.

Rebecca, her face beaming, smiled up at James. "Thank you."

They turned and hurried into the dorms. Rebecca could hear girls changing in the lavatories so she continued to the sleeping chamber, up to her bed to change into her uniform. She took note of anything she might use to climb to the window to escape. As she topped the spiral staircase to her floor, she saw small dressers placed around the short wall that wrapped the opening for the staircase. She might be able to take one of those to get a boost; she could jump to the sill and pull herself up the rest of the way. Her plan set, she changed hurriedly into the uniform, stashing her clothes in one of the dressers. She went to the alcove where her bed was and found her friends, finishing dressing.

"Well, at least we'll be warm," said Helen, as she pulled the wool cap over her brown curls.

"We look like a bunch of dock workers though," said Marissa with a wry grin on her face.

Elisabeth was making sure her curtains of dark hair properly hid her face from beneath the cap.

"I've always liked the idea of wearing pants," said Sam as she tightened the suspenders on her britches. "I hate the wind blowing around my legs. Whaddaya think Rebecca?"

"I think it fits you Sam, well, at least the pants do," she said to Sam, standing in boots two sizes too big.

"They said little kids grow too fast; so they give us bigger boots to grow into," she said when she saw Rebecca looking.

"They wouldn't want to waste leather on the likes of us, now would they?" Rebecca said under her breath. "Come on, I can give you an extra pair of socks to fit them better."

She led Sam to her dresser and pulled the extra pair out and handed them to her. "That should help a bit."

"Thanks Rebecca," Sam said, pulling off her big boots and pulling the extra socks over the pair she had on.

When they were all ready, they made their way back down to the courtyard for the next phase of their initiation into Valgerhold. As they left, Rebecca took note of the window above the door. It was set back into the thick wall but didn't appear to be sealed with anything more than a latch; *the Red Guard must have just overlooked it*, she thought.

Returning to the courtyard, the guards lined the children back into the rows as before. There was a guard at the front of the rows standing with several sheets of paper; Rebecca could see as the guard flipped through the sheets that they contained the clerk's scribbles. Also, along the wall, behind the guard, was a group of men and women dressed like the people Rebecca had seen scurrying about in the town outside Valgerhold.

When the children were in place the guard spoke.

"When your name is called, you will come and gather to my right. When all the names have been called for each work group, you will be led to the facility where you will be working until such time as you are released."

He began calling names in no particular order. When he had finished with the section, a man walked from the group, Romarans Rebecca assumed, along the wall to the gathered children and escorted them through the arched passageway, leading into the grassy space at the end of the courtyard. Rebecca could hear the man giving the children behind him instructions as to what they would be doing.

The guard continued with the list; Elizabeth was called and hesitated before she walked to the group. This time a woman walked to the children; she led them out the same way as before. James was called in the third group. Rebecca's stomach felt queasy; she was nervous for her friends. The large Romaran that stepped forward carried several leather aprons which he handed out to the group gathered there. He then led them through a different passage, going down a hallway between the columns around the courtyard. The guard called both Rebecca and Paul for the next group. As Rebecca walked from the lines to the gathering group, she caught sight of the rest of her friends. They all had worried looks painted across their faces. Rebecca caught up with Paul.

He had a scowl etched into his face. "Where do you think she'll go?" he asked in a whisper. Rebecca didn't need to ask who he was talking about; Paul had kept a close watch over Helen since before Rebecca had met them. He obviously was not keen on being separated from her.

"She'll be alright Paul," Rebecca whispered to calm him.

"What do you know?" he hissed back. "We don't know what they'll do when we walk out of here."

"No," Rebecca whispered back, "we don't know what they have planned for any of us, do we?" She eyed him with a serious expression. He returned a scowl but understanding of their situation seemed to come to him now. He nodded slightly to her.

A Romaran stepped forward to lead the group away. He was a tall man with a thick steel-grey mustache and close-trimmed hair. He looked the group over before taking the lead, walking out through the columned exit to the hall James's group had taken. She saw James up ahead, moving toward a doorway at the end of the long hallway. The large man heading his group gestured with his hands in a way, like hammering, and she could hear deep rumbles, echoing down the hall, emanating from the man's barrel chest.

"Charles Broheim," said Rebecca's group leader. "It's Broheim though, none of that sir nonsense with me, got it?" he said, turning back to the group. "Bast! The morons act as though you're a bunch of fresh recruits; you're kids for the Father's sake," he said half to himself. "And you got any questions, you ask 'em. Because you start doing something and you haven't a thought to it; you'll be losing fingers left and right."

He led them through a large door into another hallway, running off from the one down which James's group had gone.

"Woodwork is what you'll be doing, got it?" continued Broheim. "We used to make all the furniture you see laying about the place," he said, waving his hand around the conspicuously empty hall. "Now we make stocks for the Red Guard's rifles. It's all we make now; so, once you learn what you're doing it should be easy enough for you."

The hall came to another large door which Broheim stepped to and pulled out a ring of keys, Rebecca eyed them with intent, unlocking the doors. He stepped through, throwing the doors wide. Rebecca was amazed at the room she entered. Large windows along the walls let in bright light to fill the space casting warm yellow shafts across the large room. The floors were of smooth finished concrete. The walls were covered in light wood panels that continued up to the ceiling. From the vaulted stone ceiling hung large gas lanterns with mirror-finished reflectors for late night work. It was similar to her father's shop but much, much larger; smaller workshops were placed

71

throughout the space. There were large wooden tool chests in each small shop and lathes for turning wood; table saws and presses for making holes stood in the center of the room for access to all. Along the back wall were pallets full of wood of various species. She could see walnut and cherry, ash and maple, and some she couldn't identify from the distance. This had been a facility to train master woodworkers and it was equipped with the best that could be found to do that.

Broheim stepped into the space and turned to the group of children.

"Now, I don't expect many of you to know what you're doing right off. So, let's get one thing clear, ask questions," he said, waving a finger at them to emphasize. Rebecca liked him; he seemed to be the first adult she had run into that talked to them like humans.

"We're going to start off a bit on the slow side so let's get names first," he said. "You, you there boy, what's your name?" he said, indicating a red headed boy to the back of the group.

He stepped forward. "Geller, David, sir," recited the boy.

"I told you boy no 'sirs' here. Alright, you're gonna be 'Red' 'cause I'm horrendous with names," Broheim said.

A chuckle went through the group. Next a large round boy was called on.

"You, you're Tiny, got it!" said Broheim.

The group continued naming themselves while Broheim reassigned each a name of his choosing. Paul was given the name Sunshine for the scowl still plastering his face; this, of course, caused the scowl to deepen. When at last he came to Rebecca, the nervousness she had felt ever since the first time she had been asked her name returned.

"Rebecca," she gave, leaving off her family name in hopes Broheim wouldn't hassle her for it.

"Rebecca? Rebecca what? Out with it girl, last name," he said.

"She's Dulac's kid sister," came a boy's voice from the back.

She spun to see who it was, her face reddening with anger.

"Is that so, Fats?" responded Broheim. "And your given name would be what?"

"Gregor Mathiason," said the slab standing in the back.

"Thank you for your help Fats, but I think I can handle this on my own," said Broheim, returning his attention to Rebecca. "Now, is that your name my dear, Rebecca Dulac?"

She nodded, looking him in the eye. He squinted his eye closed and stroked his mustache with his thumb and forefinger.

"Skinny," he said, pointing at her at last. "You're gonna be Skinny, to go with Fats back there," he said, waving to the back as he turned around to walk back to the center of the room. "Alright, now we got that straightened out, next we're going to be covering some shop rules. Second, after ask questions, is you walk out of here every day with all your fingers. So, keep an eye on them at all times. Next, keep this place clean; sawdust can get slick when it piles up…"

Broheim continued to show them the shop and how everything worked. The steam vents apparently were used for more than just heating here; they powered the tools and everything else that required turning force. The steam was sent into heavy spinning flywheels. Shafts running below the floors engaged the wheels when power was needed. Leather bands running into the floor connected the tools to the shafts for power. It worked similar to the waterwheel-powered shop her father had built at home.

They were each assigned a small shop that would be their workspace; Paul was next to her, the boy Broheim had named Red was on her other side. She liked this space, it felt familiar – it felt like home.

A bell on the wall sounded after a time and Broheim said it was time to break for first meal. He led them back down the hallway and down another that opened out into a smaller courtyard, with a large cylindrical well at its center. A stone stairway wrapped two walls; it led up to a balcony above. As they walked through the courtyard, Rebecca noticed Colonel Dormon standing at the balcony, looking down at the group walking to the dining hall across the courtyard. Behind him, in the shadows, she could see Postam, peering over the edge of the balcony's railing. She eyed him as she walked. He stepped up behind Dormon who watched her move through the courtyard; Postam leaned in and began to speak into Dormon's ear. He put up his hand, cutting Postam off. Postam turned in place and walked out of sight.

"You're vying for trouble Skinny," Broheim whispered down to her. "Postam doesn't like you and Dormon is still measuring I'd say by that look on his face. You be careful and keep your head down."

"Everyone seems to think that's the best course to take," she said, not looking at Broheim. "But I think keeping my head down is going to lead me into just as much trouble as not." She looked up into Broheim's lined face. "They know who I am Broheim."

He nodded thoughtfully. "Mighty big boots to fill you got there, Skinny," he said, leading them into the dining hall. "You just be careful when you put your head up, as there might be an axe waiting for it." He moved off to a long table where the other Romaran teachers sat. Rebecca caught up with Paul, moving toward Helen and their friends.

Rebecca looked around the group; the smaller children were missing. Rebecca quickly looked around, hunting for them.

"Relax," said James. "They're here in the dining hall; they already ate, they're on cooking crews." He was massaging his shoulders as he ate. "At least they don't have to do anything really hard. My shoulders are already killing me."

"What are you doing?" Rebecca asked.

"Blacksmithing, you know I never realized how tough my dad's job was. He would let me watch while he and my brother worked. They made it look easy," he said, smirking.

Helen was stretching her back and Paul was ensuring she wasn't hurt. Rebecca felt bad for the others. She actually looked forward to working in the wood shop; she liked it there and she liked Broheim.

"What do they have the rest of you doing?" she asked, taking a seat next to James.

"Alchemy," Helen said with a worried look on her face.

"Alchemy?" Rebecca asked confused.

"They have us grinding different minerals and rocks. Rebecca, they're making gunpowder, lots of it. My daddy taught me some of his chemicals, enough to know what to stay away from anyway. I know what these make when they mix right. They're going to blow us up," she said, wiping a dark smudge from her cheek.

Paul looked at Rebecca, a worried look on his face.

"They have us grinding by hand because they think the powered equipment might cause a spark," Marissa put in; she too was rubbing sore muscles.

Elizabeth sat next to Marissa, her head resting on her arms folded on the table before her. Her cheeks displayed prominent gray mud smears.

"Elizabeth, what are you doing?" she asked.

"Ceramics," she said not lifting her head.

"Hey," said a cheery voice next to Rebecca. It was Sam with Michael at her side. "We brought you food, look," she said, setting down the tray she and her brother carried, bowls of porridge waited there.

"They have us cook all the meals," said Michael, looking sad. "I can help in the forges James, I can."

"I don't think you'd want to once the work started, Michael," James said to him.

"Well, where are the others?" Rebecca asked.

"Mac is helping us; he's bringing apples around in a little while," said Michael. "But I haven't seen the others yet."

Just then one last group came through the door from the courtyard outside. Arthur, Lester, and Gene came in and plopped down next to Rebecca. They smelled clean, really clean, and their hands were pink and wrinkled.

"Laundry, they have us doing laundry," said Lester.

"Our ma' never even made us do laundry; said we'd just mess it up anyway," said Gene.

"It's, it's not that bad," said Arthur with a small smile.

"Speak for yourself, you get to iron, we have to wash everything," said Lester, looking at Arthur.

"That's because you bur...burned the sheets they gave you to iron," Arthur said.

"Yeah, yeah," said Gene, taking one of the bowls from Sam and Michael.

Eventually, Mac and some other small children filtered out from the kitchen going amongst the long trestle tables in the dining hall, carrying baskets full of red apples for the children. They snatched them and quickly gnawed them to their cores; then finding their hunger unsatisfied most ate the cores as well.

When Mac made it to the group his basket was nearly empty, he offered the remainder to his cousin first; Marissa took several and began handing them around, finding she was two short for the whole group.

"Mac, go back and get more for the rest," Marissa instructed him.

"Can't," he said to her, "that's all of them."

Marissa looked at the group with a grimace.

"He says there aren't any more to go around," she said slowly.

Rebecca had begun to rub the wax off the fruit and looked forward to eating it but she noticed that Paul, and Marissa were the last without the fruit. Knowing that what Marissa was doing was far more strenuous then her own work, Rebecca tossed the apple to her.

"You need that more than I do," she said as Marissa caught the spinning red fruit in flight.

"Thanks, Rebecca," she said, looking away as she bit into the ripe flesh, juice spilled down her chin.

Paul watched as Marissa gulped down the last of the fruit, wiping her chin with the back of her sleeve, leaving a dark smear from the powder on her uniform.

The children spent the remainder of their time talking about the tasks the Red Guard had them doing; most complained about their assignments and commiserated with one another. After a time, a bell sounded and the Romaran group leaders stood, gathered their children, and headed back to the separate facilities.

Walking back through the courtyard, Rebecca looked to see if Dormon or Postam were watching, neither were. She continued and walked past the large well at the center of the courtyard. She leaned to look over and saw that this was not like the wells she had seen before; there was a grated opening in the wall of the well at the water line and there appeared to be a tunnel behind the grate. Rebecca wondered what fed the well.

"Skinny, catch up," shouted Broheim. "I'll have no stragglers working for me."

When she caught up, she walked next to Broheim; she felt at ease with him. She could tell that he actually cared about the children that he was training. He acted gruff but the comments he let slip about the Red Guard gave him away.

"Broheim?" she asked.

"Yeah, Skinny?" he said.

"What feeds that well back there, it's not groundwater?" she asked.

"Why do you ask?" he said back as they continued down the hall to the woodworking building.

"You said to ask questions didn't you," she said, with a mocking expression.

"You're gonna look pretty ugly when that smirk gets stuck," he shot back.

"You know, don't you?" she asked again.

"There's a lake fed by a river from the north; a pipe connects the lake to the well. There are a couple of filters along the way to keep out fish and frogs. That answer your question?"

"Yes, thank you," she said, smiling.

"You're sharp, Skinny, how'd you know that well is not groundwater fed?"

"It's not very deep for one, and the ripples coming from the tunnel gave it away too."

"Come on kid," said Broheim, clapping a big rough hand on her shoulder. "Let's get back to it." They walked together through the door to the shop.

"Alright kids," Broheim announced, "now that you know where everything is and how it works we're going to go over the process for making these stocks. I'll walk you through the first couple and then I'll leave you to it."

He walked to one of the smaller workspaces and had all the children gather round so they could watch. He showed them how to cut the blanks and mount the pieces on the lathe. He moved with quick smooth movements, handling the gouges and tools. Her father had the same sureness to his movements when he worked; he said it came from practice. When he had roughed out the shape and turned the parts that needed turning, he took the piece over to a press and showed them the templates to use to cut the holes to the right size. He then chiseled out pockets in the wood for parts to attach. All was complete in a relatively short time.

"When you have gotten to this step just set it aside for now," he said, showing them the completed stock. "I'll show you how to finish them when you get a handle on these steps. Alright, everyone to your spaces and get working. Remember the first rule, just shout for me if you get stuck or need help, got it? Well, what are you all standing around for, get!"

The children scattered to their spaces and gathered their tools and materials as Broheim had shown. He walked around from space to space, commenting on the work as the children began. He showed why one blank was better to use then another, the correct woods to use, how to hold the tools properly, helped mount the blanks in the lathes, how to engage the belts to give power to the machines.

When he eventually came around to Rebecca he found her working on honing down the stock, already mounted correctly. She was working as she had done under her father's supervision. She was lost in the actions. The turnings peeled from the wood; her gouge moved along the brace, feeling for knots or if she was working too quickly. She smelled for the telltale burning that would tell her to back off a bit. She checked the guides to gauge her progress; she worked as if in a trance.

"Skinny," Broheim said, shaking her a bit by the shoulder. "Hey, wake up."

She turned to look at him, feeling the haze she had been working in lift. She blinked at him, coming back to herself. He smiled, his arms crossed, looking at her work.

"You've done this before haven't you?" he asked.

She nodded and watched as he took her gauges and checked thicknesses and measurements.

"Looks good," he said at last. "Do you think you can move on to cutting the fittings without my help?"

"I think so," she said, smiling at his approving glance.

"Then I'll leave you to it, but remember…"

"First Rule," she said.

He smiled and moved on to the next space.

"Red, what in the name of the First Father are you doing?" she could hear him shout as he walked on. She giggled as she took her work from the lathe and moved on to the presses. She was the only one this far along in the process; she could see others, concentrating on moving the tools properly and checking work too often, making sure they hadn't gone too far. *I was born to this*, she thought as she mounted her piece in the press and returned to work.

Rebecca and the others continued to work in the shop. The light, streaming through the large windows, faded. The night approached fast in winter here, far to the north, and soon the gas lamps began to spark on as light diminished. They were escorted to mid meal at the tolling of the bell and had another meager meal. The children doing laundry had moved on to making uniforms, with the laundry done for the day. James, Helen, and Marissa all returned to the dining hall, seemingly more exhausted then at first meal. Sweat stains marked all three and they were coated in dark soot and char from the work the Red Guard had them doing.

After a time the bell to return to work sounded; a guard approached Broheim as he gathered the group to return to the shop. The guard talked to him and he listened with a look of concern on his face. He nodded in a resigned way and walked to Rebecca.

"Skinny," he began, "this guard is going to escort you to see the Colonel." He didn't meet her eyes. The guard stepped over to her and roughly took her by the arm, marching her toward the courtyard and the stairway leading up to the balcony where she had seen Dormon and Postam earlier.

"I want that girl back in my shop after the Colonel is finished, you hear me?" Broheim shouted after the guard. The guard didn't respond.

Rebecca looked back over her shoulder, meeting Broheim's eyes; his thick mustache hid his lower lip in the grimace on his face. Their eyes met and locked until the guard dragged her around the corner of the staircase, up to the balcony.

The guard dragged her across the balcony to a set of double doors that let into a hall lined with tapestries and paintings. This section seemed to have retained the fine furniture the university had produced. The floor here was stone tile, like everywhere Rebecca had seen, but covering the tile were long carpets woven with intricate patterns; she assumed they were from Beltarus, judging by the bright colors and pattern. The carpets muffled their footsteps as the guard brought her before a dark wooden door covered in finely made iron scroll work. The guard knocked and waited.

The door opened and Postam greeted them at the door. His bald head was bright red and his face was contorted in anger. He stopped and glared at Rebecca; she met his stare defiantly, not allowing him to cast fear in her. His mouth began to work and he made a step toward her.

"Edwin!" Dormon said forcefully, from within the room.

Postam spun and looked at Dormon for a moment. He turned and walked from the room, down the carpeted hall, not looking again at Rebecca.

"Bring the child and leave us," Dormon said to the guard. He quickly complied.

Rebecca was dragged before a massive desk behind which sat Dormon. The room here was warm and lit from above by glass windows in the ceiling; the light from the fading sun cast the room in an orange glow. A lantern was placed before Dormon on the desktop. In front of him was a disassembled gun which he appeared to be in the process of inspecting. He sat in a high-backed leather chair as rigid as a steel bar, picking up one part of the gun at a time, rotating and examining the pieces. His eyes locked on each part like a hawk with a mouse in its grasp. His face showed no hint to his thinking but all Rebecca felt was that she was looking at a predator.

The door thudded shut as the guard left and Dormon looked up at her as she stood before him. She felt unnerved being caught in that stare this close.

"A fine mechanism, this," he said, indicating the gun spread across the cloth on the desk. "We do not make such, from where I come. We do not waste time, adding useless decorations to our tools, nor do we skirt so near blasphemy in our designs as they did here in Romara, before we took control."

Rebecca stood, staring at the parts, seeing how each fit into the other, where each screw fit to hold parts in place, and how the springs would cause the parts to rotate in certain ways with each pull of the trigger. She stepped closer to the desk; she felt a pull from the parts and the fine detailed etchings made in the metal.

"It wasn't made here," she said, not realizing she was speaking. "It's an Arnoran revolving pistol." She stepped to within arms' reach of the parts and slowly extended her hands to the array; Dormon did not stop her. She picked up the cylinder and inserted the axel on which it rotated, sliding in the springs, and turning the parts to lock them in place. She slipped the assembly into the frame and placed the screws and pins in their holes, working, as she always had, when she saw how puzzles fit together. It was a gift her brother had had as well, knowing just how to move a part, how to manipulate pieces of some puzzle, to make them work together.

Dormon watched with his measuring eye as she laid the completed pistol back on the cloth before him.

"My Commander Postam seems to think you are likely to cause trouble in my ranks," he said, ignoring the feat he had just witnessed. "He thinks we should break you before you can instigate any action that would cause chaos in my university."

Rebecca stood, staring at him with her yellow-green eyes fixed on his ice blue; neither flinched.

"I met your brother one time before," he said after a moment. "It was at his end, before the gallows."

Rebecca felt a stab of pain from the unexpected statement, her stare faltered.

"You have a similar look about you as he. A brave young man he was. He gained you and your countrymen the mercy of the New Dominion in his surrender. You would be wise not to waste that gift," Dormon said as he took the revolver from the cloth and slid it into a holster at his side. "You may leave me."

Rebecca walked to the door with her mind in a daze. Dormon, she could tell, was dangerous, more so than Postam. While Postam was more prone to violence, Dormon had sought out her weaknesses. Broheim was right; Dormon was measuring her and if she did not fit into his designs she would either be cut to fit or discarded.

She met the guard on the other side of the door as she exited. He escorted her back down the hall, through the courtyard, and into the passage leading to the woodshop. When they reached the door Broheim took her from the guard with his hands on her shoulders.

"You tell Dormon that if he wants these kids to produce the quantities he's proposed, he'd be keen not to take my best workers," Broheim said gruffly.

"Keep your comments, Romaran," said the guard as he left.

"Come on Skinny, I'm going to show you how to finish your work," he said, walking her to her workspace.

When the last meal bell tolled and the group walked through the gas lamp lit courtyard, Rebecca spotted Dormon and Postam standing at the balcony; she kept her eyes down.

Eight:
Testing the Waters

For the final meal of the day they were served a thick stew. Rebecca noticed the lack of any meat to fill out the meal. When she commented on it to Michael and Sam, as they passed out the bowls, they told her they had cooked some but that it was reserved for the Red Guard and command. This was met with some angry words from the others in the group.

"We do all the work and they just stand around looking violent," Marissa grumbled, "and all we get is their leavings to eat."

At the sounding of the bell the Romaran group leaders gathered their groups and instructed them on what was expected of them the following day. Broheim told his group to get a good rest and be ready for more independent work in the morning. When all the instructions had been finished, guards came to escort the children from the dining hall back to the dormitories.

The group walked together up the flights of stairs, coming to the two opposite doors leading to the separate dorms. Rebecca, walking next to James, talked in a low voice, avoiding the ears of the rest of the group.

"If you are too tired you can wave off the plan for tonight," she said to him.

He looked at her with grime covering his forehead from where he had wiped a hand across. "And have you sulking all tomorrow, I don't think so."

She smiled and wished all the boys a good night and followed after the other girls to the sleeping quarters. The girls climbed the staircase to their alcove where they found more uniforms on their beds, with undergarments and socks, sleeping clothes, and towels. Sam explained that the children doing the laundry had distributed all the uniforms. Arthur had told her. They had been escorted, the guards and Romarans recording where each child had taken up residence, dispensing spare uniforms. *They know where we sleep*, Rebecca thought.

The girls in the dorm changed for sleep; most went to clean the grime from the day in the washrooms, especially those who had not taken the time to do so that morning. Rebecca and the others prepared for sleep afterwards, talking quietly as they lay down. As the others began to drift off, Rebecca lay awake, staring out through the large stained glass window set in the wall opposite the alcoves. She could see the moon shining brightly down outside. Off to the west she saw a dense wood she had not taken the time to notice before. There was a field of open grass that led into the wood which appeared to be mainly pine. Rebecca wondered what lived in that forest in this cold place.

When Rebecca was sure all the others were asleep, she slipped from her bed and quietly crept to the small dressers along the wall of the top floor. She tested the weight of one of the empty dressers, it seemed manageable. Lifting it, she made her way down the spiral staircase, careful not to make any noise. Goosebumps appeared on her arms from the chill in the chamber and from her nervousness. When she reached the bottom of the chamber, she carried the dresser to the door and set it down. She hurried back up the stairs to grab her coat; she didn't know where she would end up and didn't want to be unprepared.

She slipped through the chamber door, carrying the dresser. Her bare feet padded on the stone floor as she made her way down the hall toward the entrance to the dorms. She set the dresser to one side of the door and climbed on top. She had to jump to catch the ledge of the sill to the hinged transom. Pulling herself up, she found the thick walls had enough room for her to sit in the opening into which the window was set. She unlatched the window and pushed out; it swung upward and she stuck her head out underneath to make sure the landing was clear. She turned and stuck her feet and legs through, sliding out on her belly, gripping the other side of the wall to keep from falling. She inched out farther and farther and then froze as a pair of hands gripped her thighs. She fell into the hands which lifted her down from the ledge. She turned and found James standing before her. Her heart dropped from her throat back to its normal home.

"You scared the wits out of me," she said to him with a relieved smile on her face.

"Well, it looked like you could use a hand," he said, grinning down at her. "Come on I've already checked; the stairs are clear."

They slowly padded down the steps to the lower floors. They came to a door on the floor below. Checking, they found it locked; they crossed the landing and checked the opposite door, the handle turned and clicked in James' hand. He opened it enough to look in through the opening; finding it was empty, they stepped through into a small hall with large windows that looked out to the forest Rebecca had seen through the window in her dorm. They moved down the hall and found a door that opened onto a balcony that swept around the base of the two dormitory towers in a semicircle. They walked out into the cold night air. The balcony was covered in grass with stone pavers sunk into the lawn in patterns. They walked around, examining the space they had found. There were domed glass windows protruding from the ground around the courtyard and stone benches carved into the bases of the dorm towers. Rebecca looked up to the towers, seeing the large windows with their inset images. The boy's tower had a snow-white owl clutching a lantern, the symbol of the Clerics of the Old Religion. They came eventually to a stairway that led down into the lawn. At the bottom of the stairs, they found a door; it was unlocked and, after checking, they moved inside.

They found themselves on a walkway that led around the top of a library located on the second floor. They could see there was a spiral staircase that led down to the floor below. Apparently, students were once able to take books from the library out to the courtyard above to read on fine days. They walked to the entrance of the library and checked the door; it too was unlocked. Opening this door, they found the stairwell leading up to the dorms. They closed the door and returned to the library. They walked past row after row of tall dark wood bookshelves, holding hundreds of thick leather bound books. Finding a secluded corner, they settled in to some overstuffed leather chairs to talk, away from the door in case there were any unexpected guests.

"Well, we should be able to meet here without much trouble when we want to talk," James said at last.

"I think we might be able to bring the others with us next time. We just need to be careful that we don't wake the whole dorms doing it," she said.

"Rebecca, I don't know if that's such a great idea," he said, leaning forward and resting his elbows on his knees. "I'm sure that some of the others wouldn't mind coming for a chat but Paul was even more adamant about not bringing the guards down on us after today. We all saw what these swine consider proper punishment and I don't want to be responsible for bringing that on any of the others. You said yourself we need to watch out for one another."

"James we can't just take what they're doing to us without a fight; there are more of us than them and I'm almost certain some of the Romarans would help if we stood against the Red Guard."

"Rebecca, come off it! They have guns; we're just kids," he shouted as loud as he dared.

"So were our brothers and sisters," she said, looking at her hands.

"Yes, and look where they got us," he said.

A tear slipped down her chin and landed on the back of her hand.

"I'm... I'm sorry. I shouldn't have said that," he said.

"You're right, I'm just being a fool," she said in a low voice. "We should get back to get some sleep; our Red Guard *masters* will have more for us to do in the morning I'm sure."

She stood and walked away toward the exit to the stairway. James stood and as she left; he drew his hand down his face over his mouth and chin, shaking his head. He hurried after her.

Back at the landing, James gave Rebecca a boost to the window and pushed her up and through. Before she disappeared through the opening, he called after her.

"Rebecca wait," he called.

She turned in the space behind the window, sticking her head back through to see what he wanted.

"Have you gotten any further in deciphering that journal?" he asked in friendly tone.

She shook her head. "I haven't even looked at it since the train."

"Well, if you figure anything out tell me and we can meet again. You know, go over whatever you find."

She nodded and began to turn away, closing the window.

"Rebecca," he called again she turned back to him. "I am sorry. I just don't want to see any of the others get hurt, or you. I'm scared Rebecca, I am."

"Me too," she said, "but we can be brave and scared at the same time."

He hesitated then nodded in agreement.

"Goodnight James."

"Goodnight," he returned.

She turned and slipped back down the wall, reaching out with her feet, feeling for the dresser. Her toes felt as she lowered herself and then touched the top of the dresser. She slipped back down to the floor. She picked up the dresser and made her way back to the third level. She replaced the dresser where it had sat, then climbed quietly back into bed. Remembering what James had said, she reached out of the canopy of her bed, feeling beneath for her satchel. She grabbed it and found her grandfathers journal. She opened the book and flipped slowly through the pages, looking for a key to the script that now seemed to coat even more of the pages than before.

Nine:
A Step too Far

Rebecca awoke with the shouting of the guard below; she had fallen asleep with her grandfather's journal opened across her chest. She lifted the book and peered, blurry eyed, at the pages she had before her. The page showed some part of the Wilderlands farther west from Romara; the mysterious script ran in lines under a sketch of a sheer cliff, with trees clinging to its face; their roots worked into the cracks between the rock. She remembered the symbols floating through her mind as she slept. They seemed to connect and make sense for a time, then they would drift and become incomprehensible again. Angry with herself that she had made no real progress in deciphering the text, she closed the journal. She replaced the book in her satchel and stashed it back under her bed. The others were groggily rubbing sleep from their eyes and massaging sore muscles from the labors of the previous day.

"I don't know if I can do all that again today," Helen said, twisting her palms against her eyes. "I'm exhausted."

"Same here," Marissa said, stretching her back. "I feel like I haven't slept in a week."

"What did that guard say," Rebecca asked, swinging her legs from her bed. "I only caught the tail end."

"Same as yesterday, one quarter of an hour or public punishment," Marissa said, mocking.

The girls dressed and made their way down to the courtyard where the others were gathered. Guards stood at their posts around the perimeter of the space. A Romaran man waited for the guards that had gone to check the dorms to return. When they came back from checking, they gave a sign for the Romaran to begin. Without much surprise, the guards had returned empty handed this time, the lesson from the previous day learned.

The Romaran man looked lean and fit; he stepped forward as the children got in their lines.

"I am Ben Frowler; I am in charge of seeing that you maintain healthy bodies here at Valgerhold. Every morning you will go through your exercises before we take you to first meal. Then you can go off to work for the rest of the day," he finished.

He then proceeded to lead them through stretching and exercises to get their hearts pumping. Some of the children were winded by the time Frowler said that they had done enough for the morning.

"Are we not doing enough work for these pigs already?" James asked, breathing heavily as they were led into the dining hall.

The younger children were led away to begin serving what they had prepared yesterday for first meal. The group began walking to find a place to sit when Rebecca heard a boy's voice from behind.

"Oy, Dulac, why don' you do us all a favor an' offer yourself up so the rest of us can get out of those exercises?"

Rebecca's friends stopped to find a gang of rough looking boys gathered behind them. Rebecca had seen them before; they were the group of toughs from the train.

"Watch your mouth, street scum," James growled at the pocked boy who had spoken.

"Looks like you got yourself a love Dulac," said another squat freckled boy in the gang.

James stepped forward, grabbing the boy by the front of his shirt, and pulling him into his face.

"I can see to it that you're in no condition to work for these dogs if you'd like," he said into the boy's face.

The rest of the boy's gang crowded in to help their comrade. Rebecca's friends moved to James's aid when Broheim broke up the coming brawl.

"Skinny, what is going on here?" he shouted, pulling James's hands from the boy and stepping between the two groups.

"I'll not be having my workers involved in fights, got it?" he said, eyeing Paul and Rebecca. "Fats, that goes for you too," he said, turning to face the boy from the woodworking group in the gang. "Now go eat," he finished, turning back to face Rebecca as the gang of boys moved off. "Girl, get over here," he said to her as James and the others began to take seats at one of the tables. "Those boys back there give you any more trouble you tell me, got it? I saw Postam talking to some of them; I think he may have given them the idea you were an open target. So, you be careful around them." He eyed her for a moment then went to sit with the other Romaran group leaders.

Rebecca found her place next to James. He was still angry from the confrontation.

"Thick bastards," he said. "Some people can't just let others do the tormenting, they have to join in."

"Don't worry James," Rebecca said to him, trying to calm him. "I couldn't care less what they say."

"I don't understand you Rebecca; you're keen to get on the bad side of the men with guns but the wretches licking their boots you're going to shake off," he said, leaning in so the others didn't hear.

"I'm trying not to set my standards too low; besides, the men with the guns are the root of the problem," she said back.

The first meal was served and the children wolfed the food down as fast as it was brought out. The meal proved just as piddling as the previous morning. The children didn't look eager to join their groups to begin work on such small fare.

When Broheim gathered his group and led them through the courtyard, the boy Broheim named Fats knocked her from behind as he passed. When she recovered she looked to the Balcony and saw Postam staring down, smiling at her. So, he *was* responsible for the boys. If he couldn't break her personally, he was going make her life here more miserable than it already was.

In the shop, Broheim gathered the children before him.

"Alright now, listen up, Dormon has given all the Romaran leads here quotas to meet," he said. "I've done the calculations and you each need to make about six of these stocks a day. You are going to have to make at least that many; I won't have any shirking for someone else to pick up the slack. Once you finish your six for the day, I'll see if I can't find you something a little less tedious to do. I'm going to be coming around if any of you need help; so remember…"

"First Rule," they said in unison. He nodded and they broke off to their separate spaces.

Rebecca began to work to produce her pieces. After a time she was roused from her work; Paul was tapping her on the shoulder. She turned to him to see what he wanted.

"I know you met up with James last night," he said. "I want to come along next time, alright."

His tone left no room for arguments and Rebecca didn't want to anyway. She had thought it would be good for others to come with them.

"Alright, I'll talk to James," she said to him.

Paul nodded and returned to his space.

When the bell for mid meal rang, Rebecca made sure to let Fats go before her to avoid any unwanted confrontations. The group met for the meal and took their places. The girls at work in the Alchemy facilities looked wrung out; they were visibly exhausted. Paul looked concerned for Helen; she tried to reassure him that she was alright but he could see for himself that she was tired. James looked like he was having a hard time of it as well.

Rebecca leaned over him as he was scraping the remains of his meal from every corner of his plate. "We need to talk," she whispered as the others were talking.

"What is it, something in the journal?" he brightened a bit.

"No, Paul," she said, looking over at him; he caught her eye as she did. James looked at him.

"What about him?" he said, looking at Paul with a suspicious glare.

"He wants to meet with us next time," she said, leaning back to James.

James stared at her with a hurt expression on his face.

"I didn't tell him; he saw you leaving and figured it out himself," she said quietly.

"Alright, when do we meet?" he asked.

"Tonight I suppose; I can tell Paul on the way back to the shops," she said.

James agreed and finished his meal.

On the walk back to the shops, Rebecca told Paul how their plan worked and he agreed to keep quiet to the others. As they were walking, Postam stepped onto the Balcony gloating. She could tell from his face, he was expecting something. Just then she heard heavy footfalls quickly approaching from behind.

She pushed Paul out of the way as Fats made to plow them both down. She stepped sideways in time to miss him, leaving her foot extended to catch the large boy unprepared. His legs caught in her outstretched boot and he went sprawling across the courtyard pavers.

"Fats, watch where you're going," Broheim shouted as he pulled the boy from the ground. "You could have hurt my best workers, and I'll have none of that."

Paul recovered from the shove Rebecca had given him and got to his feet on his own, smiling at the large boy laid out on the ground.

"Serves the oaf right," he said loudly.

Rebecca turned to see Postam at the balcony; his gloating expression had vanished and was replaced with a look like murder. She caught his eye and there, in the center of the courtyard, staring into Postam's enraged eyes, she slapped her fist over her heart in mock salute.

"You," the entire courtyard fell silent as Postam roared, "get up here now!"

Broheim stared at her with a look of horror.

"Commander Postam," Broheim said, turning to face the man whose bald head was red with fury. "This girl is my best pupil so far. I need her to…"

"Shut your mouth Romaran, before I cut out your tongue," Postam cut him off. "Dulac, move your ass."

97

Rebecca began to climb the stairs she had the previous day when Dormon had summoned her. She felt a whirl of excitement at having taken Postam's tormenting and turned it so easily. She also felt that she may have gone a little too far with the salute. She couldn't stop the smirk from climbing across her face though.

Postam was shaking as she approached, staring defiantly into his eyes.

"I am going to enjoy this, girl," he growled, grabbing her by the arm. He dragged her across the balcony to the hall that led to Dormon's office. He led her past Dormon's office, down the corridor, to another large wooden door with iron scroll work. He slammed the door open and threw her through the opening to land sprawling on the hard stone floor. She landed in a pool of light cast from the windows above; she was temporarily blinded while her eyes adjusted. Postam stood in the door with a cruel grin marking his face.

"I knew from the second I saw those eyes, girl; I knew. Those damned eyes, like some beast from the pit of Discordia. I'm going to get what I wasn't allowed to from your brother; he got off easy. Your bastard brother killed a lot of my friends in that pass but you don't care about that; do you?"

"You vermin have only yourselves to blame for your losses; you should never have come back to the Homelands," she screamed at him with tears coming to her eyes.

Postam stepped forward and grabbed her by the front of her shirt pulling her to her feet. He brought his hand back and punched her, full force, across the face. She fell back to the ground with the impact. Her lip split and blood streamed from the cut onto the stone floor, a bright red pool in the light. He stepped toward her; his shadow cast across her face. She looked up; his head was a silhouette against the light. He grunted and she felt his boot in her ribs; she doubled up, lying there on the floor of his office.

"Edwin," said a voice from the doorway.

Postam turned in surprise to find Dormon, standing in the doorway, Broheim at his back.

"Edwin, that is enough for now," he said calmly. Postam stood hulking and panting with anticipation of revenge.

"Anton, this girl is going to pay," he shouted at Dormon.

"That she is, Edwin; but not this way, not yet."

"Anton she mocks us openly in front of those whelps in the courtyard," he screamed.

"Colonel, to me, it looked like she was saluting the Commander," Broheim said respectfully from behind Dormon.

"You shut your mouth, old man," Postam screamed at Broheim. "We know what side you Romarans were on in the war and don't think we will forget!"

"Edwin, come with me please," Dormon continued in his calm voice.

Postam's shoulders slumped forward as he walked to Dormon's side; he followed like a beaten dog out of the door and down the hallway, toward Dormon's office.

"Mr. Broheim take your charge back to the facilities and get her working," Dormon called down the hall.

"Yes Sir," Broheim responded. He swept through the door, lifted Rebecca from the floor beneath her arms, avoiding her ribs.

"Rebecca, what were you thinking?" he said to her; the use of her actual name came as a surprise to her. "That man has killed more men than I care to know and you needle him just by breathing. What was going through your head girl? I told you to call on me if you had any more trouble not go jeer the Red Guard."

"Did you see his face, Broheim?" she said, smiling up at him. "He lost his mind." Broheim looked at her like some rabid creature he had picked up by mistake. "He sees my brother in me and he hates me for it; he wants to kill me, the whore's son. I'll make him do it, Broheim; I'll make him kill me personally." Tears streamed from her eyes. "He wants to do it; I'll make him work for it." She broke down crying and slumped back to the floor, sobbing in gasps. "They can kill me…they can kill me like they killed my brother."

Broheim knelt to her and wrapped his arms around her shoulders; she pressed her face against his chest, bawling into his shirt. She sent a stream of muffled curses into Broheim's chest in choking gasps. He held her in his arms, rocking her back and forth until she calmed.

"You are a brave girl, Rebecca, but you're trying too hard to join your family," he said in a comforting voice. "I know what it's like; I know. You have to keep trying though. Don't give up on life so soon; you have friends here that need you." He pulled her back by her shoulders and looked into her face. Her eyes were red and her lip had swollen. He smiled at her and wiped the tears from her eyes. "You are going to get out of here I know you are. You have great things set before you girl; you just need to make it to them, you got it?"

She nodded at him, wiped her lip on her sleeve, and accepted his help to stand.

"Broheim, why are you doing this for me?" she asked him. "You could get yourself into trouble with the Red Guard."

"Because Skinny, like I said, you're my best worker," he said as they walked from the room and made their way to the courtyard.

"Broheim, I want to know, why?"

"Let's just say even though Romara stayed neutral in the war, some of her younger, more idealistic, sons and daughters thought to aid our neighbors to the east." They walked down the stone staircase into the courtyard. "Some of those who went were caught up in the First Born's last battle." He rubbed his eyes with two fingers and wiped tears on his shirt. "My boy..." he began and cleared his throat, "my boy ended up in a prisoner of war camp rather than being slaughtered, because of what one brave young man did at the end of that battle."

She had her answer. He felt he owed her, another person looking to repay her for her brother's actions. At least he wasn't looking to pay her back with a boot to the ribs.

When they returned to the shop, Fats grinned at her as she came through the door with her swollen lip. She eyed him like a predator staring at her prey; he slunk back to his work. Broheim walked her back to a small office in the corner of the shop where there were medical supplies. He pulled a box down and removed a small brown glass jar filled with some liquid. He blotted some of the liquid on a square of white cloth and held her chin while he patted her lip with the cloth. She winced as the liquid seeped into the wound. He replaced the jar and pulled out a small vile of some clear cream he dabbed some on his little finger and rubbed a daub on her lip.

"Try not to lick that off for a while," he said to her. "It'll help it heal faster and take some of the pain with it."

"I'm sorry I'm causing you so much trouble Broheim," she said in a whisper. "I don't know why but I can't take what they're doing to us here."

"It's in your blood child," he said to her with a cocked smile. "You Arnorans always did have a strong spirit, and hot heads." She smiled at him. "You just let me take care of any of those thugs from now on and that will make up for it, got it?"

He led her back into the shop and sent her to work on her parts. She finished her quota before any of the others and Broheim gave her some wood she could carve while the others caught up. When the last meal bell rang, Broheim called Fats back and had some heated words for him. The large boy sunk back into his shoulders; he then went to clean the shop. Broheim locked the doors; he would come back later to check the thug's progress.

In the dining hall, the gang of toughs found another place to sit, away from Rebecca's group. James and the others looked at Rebecca with concern but she reassured them she was fine. The meal again disappointed and the children began to expect it to remain so.

Walking to the landing, James stopped her. His face was worried.

"Rebecca, Paul told me everything that happened in the courtyard," he said. "You can't take them on alone; you know that don't you?"

She realized that he was truly concerned about her; in fact, the whole group had seemed genuinely concerned about her run-in with Postam.

"I know, I won't do anything that stupid again, if I can help it," she said, smiling.

He still looked worried. "Tonight," he asked, "after they go to sleep, right?"

"After they're asleep," she agreed.

They went to their dorms and the guards followed after to lock the doors. They all washed and got dressed for sleep. Rebecca pulled her grandfather's journal out and began where she left off that morning, going over the script for any clues. She sat, examining the pictures and Arnoran text, looking for any parallels. She felt warm in her bed and her eyes began to feel heavy. Turning page after page, she felt her eyes begin to itch in a peculiar way. She rubbed at them with her fists and looked back at the page she had turned to in attempt to stay awake. Then her eye caught something in the lower part of one of the pages relating to the Wilderlands. The text was about something called the Barrier:

...and though we have yet to find any entrance permitting any to pass within alive, we remain confident that in time we will discover some access to the land beyond this Barrier. We have explored nearly the entire perimeter; even the gaps in the physical walls do not allow any to pass beyond. We have lost good men who wandered into such gaps, thinking they had found entrance; they traveled no farther than a few steps before dropping to the ground dead. We dared not even retrieve their bodies for fear any who tried would meet a similar fate. To the families of these brave men, I am truly sorry I did not see the Kilaray in time to stop them. I take full responsibility for their deaths and I beg your forgiveness.

Rebecca stopped reading, feeling a chill run up her spine. *I am truly sorry I did not see the Kilaray in time...* Her grandfather had been able to see the Kilaray. Why had her father never told her about this? She felt her head spinning. She was the granddaughter of one of those with the touch to see the Kilaray. James had said that the gift traveled in families; was it possible? Had her father been able to see the Kilaray as well? Had he been protecting her from it? She felt sick and got out of her bed to get some air. She walked out to the wall around the spiral staircase and stood, staring down at the floor below. She breathed in slowly to calm herself.

She slowly came to her senses; she heard the sounds of sleep all around her. She remembered the meeting and hurried to grab the dresser. She was not sure how long the others had been asleep but she was sure it was long enough. She placed the dresser by the dorm entrance and ran back to the alcove to grab her coat. She thought about taking the journal to show James but thought again. She didn't want him to know about her grandfather. She didn't know if *she* wanted to know about her grandfather. She raced back to the dorm door and leapt to the ledge, pulling herself up to climb through the window.

When she stuck her head through to check, Paul and James waited.

"We were starting to think you'd fallen asleep," James said.

He helped her down and they snuck to the library, to the corner her and James had met the night before.

"Now what did you want to talk about?" James asked Paul.

"I'm worried about Helen," he said.

"Well, that's certainly news to us," James said, throwing his hands up in exasperation. Paul looked down embarrassed.

"Go on, Paul," Rebecca said to him. He turned to her and relaxed a little.

James took one of the overstuffed leather chairs.

"I know we all feel tired from what they have us doing but, I don't know; she seems to be pretty bad off. Worse than the others, you know. Maybe they need to feed her more or something. I don't know if she can keep doing what they have her doing; she can't take it."

"Well, she did look really exhausted at last meal," James said, turning to Rebecca. "Do you think the Romarans in charge of the kitchens might be able to slip her a little more? Or maybe we could give her some of ours for the time, until she looks better."

Paul looked to Rebecca for an answer; she didn't know how to respond. She doubted that the Romarans were actually in charge of anything here so she didn't think they would be able to increase anyone's portions. She also didn't know what would happen to the others if they began shorting themselves of the little sustenance that the meals provided. Seeing no other option, she answered.

"I'll go first," she said. "We'll rotate between any who is willing to share their meals. We can't force anyone. If they feel like they need the food then that's that."

Paul's shoulders raised a little. "Thank you, Rebecca. She won't take long to recover; I can tell. She's really strong. You should have seen her when we were in the camps."

"I'm sure she will be alright, Paul," Rebecca reassured him. "We all just need to get used to the work they have us doing and we'll feel better."

"Should we get going?" asked Paul, looking toward the entrance of the library. "You didn't stay out long the last time."

"We can go if you don't have anything else you want to talk about." James said, looking to Rebecca. Rebecca knew he was asking about the journal, she was still shaken about her discovery and didn't want to tell him.

"I don't have anything right now," she lied.

"Well, let's get going then, I guess," James said. He stood from the leather chair.

The three made their way back to the dormitory landing and as before, James gave Rebecca a lift to the ledge. She wished them a goodnight and slipped back to the ground on the other side of the door. She turned; Sam stood before her with a sleepy expression, watching as Rebecca stepped from the dresser.

"Hi Rebecca," she said. "What were you doing?"

Rebecca was at a loss for words. She hadn't expected to get caught; especially on her second attempt.

"I...I was..." she began but Sam interrupted her.

"Was that James you were saying goodnight to," she smiled at Rebecca in a conspiratorial way.

Rebecca grinned at the little girl and nodded, taking the opportunity for a way out of explaining.

"Yes it was; now, what are you doing out of bed? It's cold out here," Rebecca said, taking the girl's hand and leading her back toward the sleeping quarters.

"I had to go to the bathroom; I came out when I heard you in the window."

They climbed the spiral stairs quietly to the third floor. Rebecca tucked Sam in when she crawled into her bed.

"Sam, can you keep what you saw a secret?" she asked. Sam's eyes were already drifting shut.

"Sure, Rebecca, like on the train when we needed to find James to give him his watch," she said in a haze.

Rebecca had a memory of Michael hushing the girl before she blurted out too much information and felt sick.

"That's right Sam; only this time you can't tell anyone, understand?"

The girl nodded once and was asleep. Maybe she could convince Sam it had been a dream if it came to it.

Rebecca climbed into her bed and her feet hit something hard, the journal. She had left it in her bed after she had read the passage that caused her so much confusion. She considered putting the journal back in the satchel. Perhaps she could convince *herself* she had been dreaming, but she knew better. She picked up the journal where she had left off. She was hunting now for more than the key to deciphering the script; she was looking for keys to deciphering her past.

In the morning, Rebecca awoke exhausted; she had spent hours reading the text, looking for more clues to exactly what her grandfather had been. She had finally collapsed against her effort to stay awake. She went to the lavatories to splash water in her face in attempt to wake herself. When she looked in the mirror, she saw that her lip was now a hideous red-violet around the cut but at least it was closed. She returned to the alcove and went to her dresser to pull on her uniform; she felt her stomach drop. She saw the empty space where the dresser she used to reach the ledge was supposed to be. She had forgotten it when she took Sam back to bed.

She put on her uniform and walked with the others down the hallway leading out of the dormitory. She could see the dresser, sitting in the corner by the door. She hoped no one took notice but her hopes were dashed when she felt a tug at her sleeve. She looked down to Sam who was nodding toward the dresser. There was little chance of convincing her she had been dreaming Rebecca decided.

"I see," she said to Sam under her breath. "Remember what I told you about secret."

Sam nodded her understanding.

Rebecca silently thanked Sam for keeping quiet.

Out in the courtyard, Ben Frowler led them through their exercises and then led them to the dining hall. Michael and Sam came around with the bowls of porridge for first meal; Rebecca took hers and a second one pouring half of one into the other then handed the larger to Helen. Rebecca handed out all the rest to the others at the table. Paul gave her a small smile when he saw Helen's bowl.

The day seemed to drag as Rebecca, already tired from a lack of sleep, continued to half her own meals for Helen. She could feel her stomach protesting as she worked the stocks in the shop. Broheim asked her if she was feeling well when she didn't finish ahead of the others in the shop as she had the previous day. She said she just hadn't slept well and Broheim left it at that.

At last meal, Rebecca was thoroughly spent. She wanted to crawl into bed and sleep. She was brought momentarily out of her stupor when James leaned over at the table and whispered in her ear.

"Sam says she'll take tomorrow; so you can eat."

She turned to him with a look of utter confusion. How did Sam know what she had been doing? She had made sure the girl hadn't seen her splitting the portions.

"She told me she caught you meeting me last night," he had a grin on his face. "Quick thinking, ay, she wants to come next time we meet; looks like you're going to have these meetings your way after all, if this keeps up."

"Well we're even now, we've each been caught once," she said back.

He grunted a chuckle.

The children finished their meals and were sent to the dorms. Rebecca was awash in relief as she trudged through the courtyard on her way to the dorms and her bed. Then she froze, standing at the balcony, Dormon and Postam stood watching her. Postam's chest rose as he took in a deep breath. Rebecca walked with her shoulders slumped and head down. She would give them the impression she had learned her lesson, for the time being.

At the landing, James' and Rebecca's usual goodnights were exchanged but this time Paul approached before they separated.

"Thank you," he said. He stared at her a moment then nodded once, turning to go down the boy's side of the dorms.

"Well, I think you're gaining a loyal follower," James said to her.

"I thought I already had one," she said, grinning at him.

"Hey, I'm not following; I'm at your side. You just seem to keep taking odd turns and I have to rush to catch up."

"Alright, that works for me," she said, conceding.

"I know you're tired but have you been looking through that journal?" he asked. "I would really like to know if you find anything."

"I'll tell you if I get anywhere," she said, looking down to hide the lie.

"Well, maybe you could bring it next time we meet and I can help you look," he said.

She hesitated, looking up into his eyes. "James, there is something I found." She was nervous. She didn't know if she really wanted to tell him yet what she had found out about her grandfather.

"What? I knew you had to have found something by now," he said, brightening.

"There was this passage about... about a barrier and..." she said.

"*The* Barrier, what was it?" he said his eyes wide with anticipation.

"Break it up you two," said a gruff voice, coming up the stairs. The guard who locked the dorms had arrived. "Move it along lovies," he said, deriding.

They split up and went to their dorms, the doors slamming behind them. Rebecca had never thought she would ever thank one of these guards for anything in her life but she did now. She climbed the spiral stairs, her legs felt like stone. She flopped on her bed and was asleep without even changing. She awoke in the night; something had made her remember the dresser. She got up and walked down the stairs. Groggily she retrieved the dresser and returned to the alcove and her bed. Sam was sitting up watching her.

"James said I could come next time," Sam whispered.

"I know," Rebecca whispered back. "I'll tell you when, alright."

She nodded happily and lay back, going to sleep. Rebecca changed out of her uniform and into her sleeping clothes. She climbed under her covers and was asleep in an instant.

Her mind didn't rest though; it turned all night long. She worked the puzzles as she had worked the pieces of the revolving pistol in Dormon's office. She saw the glyphs before her; she turned them this way and that, looking for their connections. The mysterious script wrote messages to her in her mind, trying to explain their meanings

110

but she couldn't understand them. She felt her mind flashing on the text of the Barrier passage. She saw the image of the stone wall with the trees growing from them.

Her eyes snapped open and she reached for her satchel. She grabbed the journal and flipped through the pages, searching for the key her mind had found in the turnings of her dreams. There, on the page, with the sketch of the rock wall. How could she have seen this page and not noticed the symbols inside the sketch? There, as clear as day, was the key her mother had made her and Sebastian remember from as far back as she could remember. The Gates, The Gates were the key.

Eleven:
Happenings in the Night

He sat awake this night with his dark thoughts. He would sleep at night, sometimes, as he had once; now the leisure of sleep was but a tie to what he had been. This night though, he sat awake and Reached.

He sat on the dark red mat he used for contemplation. The mat lay on the fine marble floor before the large glass windows, looking out on Pelos, capital city of Felsof. The lanterns on the distant streets were like ground-born stars in the darkness. The columned buildings in the capital city reflected the yellow light of the lanterns, giving ghostly hints at their grandeur, only fully appreciated in the daylight. Mandagore preferred this palace to the hovel in which he had lived for so many years in the Broken Lands; that was before he had set his plan into action.

If he closed his eyes, he could still smell the brimstone and burning air of that land to which he had been exiled. The heat and dryness of that place had made his lips crack in mere hours. The land itself repelled life, with its scorching rocks and biting ash-riddled winds. The pain and anger that came with the memory of his exile to that land broke his concentration. He stared at his clenched fists, sitting atop his knees. He opened one of his hands and stared at the palm. The skin was slick and shiny; if the light in this place were brighter, he knew the skin, from finger tips to midway up his forearms, was a red pink color, the color of burnt flesh. His feet crossed beneath him, he knew they too bore the scars from that land.

He had been forced to flee in the night unprepared for the harshness of his destination.

His followers too bore scars, some anyway. They looked on them as reminders of the injustice that had been dealt them. The Homeland traitors had received their retribution. His scars now sent fear through the hearts of the people here, scars that had given name to an army, his army. The Red Fist Army had fulfilled his greatest desire; they had handed him the Homelands.

He had gained that which he had sought since the day of his betrayal at the hands of his one time friend, vengeance. He had gained something more with his vengeance, that which every Felsofese child hungered for from the time they grasped the idea of political intrigue. He had gained power.

That power is what kept him awake this night though. He had felt it in his meditations, an itching at the back of his mind, a sign that something happened that touched on him. *What could it have been?* He dreaded the feeling; it was one of the few remaining Philistari teachings he had received before he had been cast from the ranks of the Palantean. He relied now on different teachings, stronger teachings. He dreaded for more than the feeling's reminder of his past but for what he knew would accompany such a feeling.

He stood from his mat and stretched muscles, tight from sitting in one position for so long. He walked to his wardrobe and pulled a robe from within. The robe, so dark a red it neared black, fit his mood. He had only just gained his power and repaid the Arnoran filth for their hand in his exile; now, something was happening that might threaten his vengeance. He knew he didn't have long before his visitor would arrive, not after the implications of the feeling he had.

He walked to the entrance of his chamber and pulled on one of the large gilded rings attached to the center of the carved door. He opened the door and stepped out into the light of the hall. The multicolored marble walls reflected the light of the stand lamps spaced down the corridor. Large canvases hung along the walls with scenes of Felsofese glory, the Senate's expulsion of the Philistari Council, his coronation as Emperor of the New Dominion in the Grand Square of Pelos, and, placed outside his door so he could see it every morning when he exited, the betrayal of Ronan Arcand, Captain of the Palantean, at the gap in the Anderwill Mountains.

That betrayal had been the turning point in his plan to retake the Homelands. With the gap cleared, his Red Fist Army had flooded back into the Homelands. They met hardly any resistance; the lands were ripe for the picking.

Mandagore turned and walked to the large, gilded, dark wood doors at the end of the hall leading into the greeting room of the palace.

They had swept the lands like a tide, tearing down the last vestiges of the Old Religion, destroying what its libraries contained. His anger at the injustice was aimed at more than the mortal realm. After what he had seen of the First Father's will, he had remade the Red Path to replace the old beliefs. He forced the Red Path upon the Old Religion Clerics and those who refused met their ends.

City after city, those that opposed him fell before his Red Fist until none stood against him. Felsof remained nearly unscathed for its role in the Return of the Exiles. The others though, they were made to suffer. Garmon to the north, Silvari to the west, each fell in time. Mandagore hoped they found themselves in Discordia for daring to refuse him. When the dust settled, the only land that remained opposed was Arnora.

Arnora, that blight on his mind. The country had been as its namesake, ever persistent. The Red Fist had been trained to be ruthless, merciless; what he hadn't been able to make them was fearless. When his forces had met nearly the entire citizenry of Arnora, armed and ready, at the borders, his commanders feared it was impossible to take such a land. He had shown that it was possible with his machines and fury to drive them.

Mandagore had returned to Pelos when Arnora's Last Stand, as it had been called, finally broke. But it wasn't her last stand. One name stood out above the rest in the days that followed that supposed Last Stand. It had taken a place next to that of Ronan Arcand in his mind of those he hated.

His commanders sent word that he must return to break Arnora, again. *How can this be*, he had thought, *those capable of fighting are dead?* When word reached him that it was a force of children, he had thought he must be losing his grip on the world.

Dulac was his name. Boy General, Little Lion, Arnora's Revenge, his name had taken on legendary standing. He had actually retaken battle lines that had been drawn months before, pushing into Silvari. Mandagore could not believe his eyes as he saw his New Dominion contracting instead of expanding. The boy fought like an enraged beast; his child soldiers seemed to be what he had been unable to make in his own forces, fearless. Finally, Mandagore was forced to retake the field, to whip his Red Fist Army on, driving them like stubborn mules all the way back to the Arnoran border wall.

If it had not been for that one weakness that, like a fleck on a beach, had caught his mind's attention, Mandagore would have never seen his revenge break that land most responsible for his exile. It was fitting, somehow, that the defeat of Arnora came in the form of a betrayal. He had turned the Dulac boy's attempt at a quick end to the war into Arnora's ultimate defeat.

When he finally came face to face with Dulac, he had not expected what he saw; the boy had the eyes. It explained everything that had happened. It should not have been possible; the Wanderer had promised him those like Dulac were lost. The boy had the eyes though; somehow his lineage had been hidden in the Scouring. Mandagore had ensured that the boy was killed. Dulac would not be his undoing.

The New Dominion had its final jewel. When Arnora was finally taken, Romara came willingly into the New Dominion. Everything was falling into his hands. The Wilderlands made agreements to continue to supply the New Dominion with its raw resources with Mandagore's decree to help them expand into the Tremen territories. The Beltari would soon find that their beloved wall could not hold out his Red Fist for long.

But now the itching at his mind, something lay in wait for him. The Philistari methods were so ineffective nowadays. Every other lesson the Wanderer had taught him had worked but this last was impossible for him for some reason. The future remained as a fog in front of him; a light approached in that fog, a spark of what was to come. He remained unable to determine the source of the light, what the pathways of his Reached Vision led to. Until the future came closer, he would be blind to it. His reliance upon this method had led to his exile. He would not allow that again.

He stepped through the doors leading into the greeting room. As he expected, the Wanderer waited for him in the center of the room.

116

The room was meant to inspire awe in its guests, to intimidate. The thick marble columns around the room supported a large domed ceiling. The center oculus had a chrysanthemum inlaid in the glass, the symbol of the Felsof nobility. The floors were dark thickly veined marble; large finely made carpets from the looms of Beltarus spread across them. The walls had vast windows all around, giving the impression that they stood in the open air of a temple. The entirety of the room's grandness was wasted on its current visitor. These meetings always left him drained and shaken. He wondered, sometimes, if his agreement with this…thing had been worth the cost, but his revenge was worth any cost to him, even his soul.

The figure stood before him as it always appeared. Its waxy white hands protruded from the thing's deep red robes clasped at its waist, a death-gray gnarled staff held in the crook of one arm. A smooth pale chin and gray pink lips peaked from the shadows of its drawn hood. Its form betrayed no hint as to its gender, whether it was old or young, human or something else, but one thing was clear, this thing was not meant for this world.

"I have seen what your mind has felt," it said in a voice that dimmed the light in the room. "You are in danger Mandagore, you must take precautions."

Mandagore shuddered.

"Show me," he said, stepping forward as the Wanderer reached to pull back its hood.

The fires in the lanterns of the room burned but their light traveled no further then the extents of their flames, points of light in the darkness. The air in the room became thick and stale. Mandagore could see nothing but the blackness before his eyes; the Wanderer had vanished with the lifting of its hood. He knew the Wanderer held him in its gaze; he was inside his own mind now. The fog that had laid over Mandagore's Visions had been lifted when the Wanderer took possession of his mind. The light he had seen in the fog of his Vision moved closer now. The mote of light had a green-yellow cast to it; in the darkness, it came toward him.

The light approached slowly, Mandagore had a feeling of recognition before it was upon him, around him. He saw the flashes of what was to come but something was wrong. He had seen this already, lived it. The Palantean took the field of battle, their Blades blazing in the night. Arnoran soldiers encased in that accursed Mechanical armor, Linked to the Kilaray, repelling all but the direst of assaults, bearing weapons that pulled their power from the Links. This was the past not the future, from before the Exile. Why was the Wanderer showing him this? But wait, there was something different; his forces then had been his loyal Adarianites and the dregs of Felsofese mercenaries and assassins guilds. They had been armed then with ancient weapons, swords and bows, pikes and war hammers. They had been overwhelmed by the superior weaponry of the Homeland forces. Now though his forces fired guns and artillery, and there, in the sky, his Dreadcaster airships floated like great manmade clouds, supporting ships that rained down fire. The Palantean entered the fray; the streaks of their Soul Blade illuminated paths like multicolored lightning slashed through the ranks of his forces, his Red Fist Army. This *was* the future. *How could this be? The ways of the Kilaray Links were lost;* he thought desperately.

His Red Fist Army was turning to retreat, but in the sky his Dreadcasters threw down flames and explosions ripped the battlefield. Perhaps his terrible inventions would turn the course of this battle. Then to his horror, streaks of flame shot from some unseen source toward his airships. The streaks stuck into the membranes of the great envelopes of gas; they remained there only a moment before...

The light from the explosions lit the battlefield below and the clouds in the sky above. Silhouetted against the fiery burning airships dropping from the sky, Mandagore saw men on the backs of winged beasts.

The Palantean's captain, identifiable by the dark blue bristled crest arched along the ridge of his helmet, was assessing the battle. He turned to his commanders to issue orders, touched thumb and forefinger knuckles to the bridge of his nose, collapsing his face shield, and removed his helmet. Mandagore moved, in his mind, closer to see who this man was. Shock ripped through him. Impossibilities were coming true; for, before Mandagore Adarian was a ghost from his past.

The Palantean commanders removed their helmets to take their captain's orders. Children, they were children; none could have seen his nineteenth year.

"We have them on the run, Captain," said one of the young Palantean.

"Good, keep on their backs; take no quarter," commanded their captain.

"What orders for the Icari, Captain," said another young Palantean with a winged brass badge attached to his cloak.

"Tell my granddaughter to send these dogs back to Discordia." Their captain turned and Mandagore was face to face with his old enemy, his old friend, and the man who had sent him east, into the Broken Lands, Ronan Arcand.

Mandagore felt himself shaking in his body; if the Wanderer didn't release him soon he knew his heart would fail and he would die.

His mind's view shifted suddenly; he was high above the carnage of the battlefield, soaring toward a dark winged shape. The rider on the beast pulled down the scarf covering his mouth and nose from the wind. He lifted the odd eye coverings and looked down at the ground to see the battle. When the rider turned back, Mandagore was looking into his, no her face, the eyes, the eyes, those damnable eyes.

The green-yellow light flashed around him and he was pulled back into the marble greeting room of the palace. The Wanderer was settling its hood back over its head. Mandagore lay shaking on the marble floor. Sweat slicked his body and tears ran freely down his cheeks.

"Those eyes," he repeated in whispered pants.

"You must take precautions. The Barrier must not be breached; the Tower must not be taken. I will not allow you to fail me," the light came back to its normal luminance with the last word from the Wanderer's lips. It slipped away between the blink of Mandagore's tear-filmed eyes, back to where it dwelt.

This night Mandagore sat awake, shaking. He watched from the huge windows in his marble lined bed chamber. From his Pelos palace, frightened horses drew a dark coach, carrying dark creatures toward the port into the Gulf of Beltarus. The passengers, while shaped like men, bore little in common with those weak beings. They had their instructions; how they did enjoy carrying out orders of this kind. With a description of their target, they were given a single command. Kill.

Twelve:
A Need Met

It had been nearly three weeks since Rebecca and the others began to share their meals with Helen. She had shown signs, at first, of recovering her strength but now, as the days continued, she seemed to be losing the ground she had gained. Paul was on the edge of panic. Rebecca saw that the four splitting their meals were beginning to suffer the lack of food. Something would have to be done or they would all end up without the strength to continue.

"Rebecca, we need to do something; she is slipping. I won't let her down now," Paul said as they sat together in the library on the second floor of Valgerhold.

Sam sat in James's lap, curled up asleep; they kept their voices down to keep from waking her. James's face was set in tired concern. Rebecca sat in one of the leather chairs next to James, watching as Paul paced back and forth.

"I can't watch her waste away like this. These bastards here have to do something for her; we are doing their work for them. How can they just let one of us just wither away? Don't they want us producing these goods?" he said. Angry tears peeked from his eyes.

"Paul, they don't really care if we die or not; you must realize that by now," Rebecca said to him softly. "What we need to do is get out of here; we should be trying to…"

"Not now, Rebecca, please, we can't stand up to the Red Guard if we can barely stand to begin with," Paul said louder than he should have.

Sam stirred in James' lap and looked on the scene before her.

"Why are you shouting Paul?" she asked.

He looked at her with a mix of anger and sadness.

"He is worried about Helen," said James to her.

"So are we all," said Rebecca. "I think that what we need—"

"Rebecca," James warned.

"Listen, what we need, all of us, is more to eat," she said, turning to face James. "We can't keep up strength with the food they're feeding us. Sam, is there any way you could sneak some meat into our food, somehow, without it being missed from the kitchens?"

She sat up in James' lap and looked down, scrunching up her face in thought. At last she looked up with a pained expression.

"They watch us real close when it comes to the meat we cook. They would see if we were skimming some for ourselves. I saw a boy get beat last week when he tried to cut himself a nibble of a venison steak."

"Do you know where they get the meat? Maybe we could just steal it from the source," said Rebecca.

"No, I'm not sure. The Romarans bring it in but I'm not sure where it comes from," she finished.

"Look it's getting light outside," said James, looking up through one of the domed ceiling windows into the courtyard above. They had been staying out longer and longer with these clandestine meetings. Rebecca had tried to increase the group's size but James and Paul felt it would be too risky.

"Let's get back before the guards come," said Paul. "I'm going to ask the Red Guard watching the kitchens if they could help with Helen."

122

"I wouldn't do that Paul," said James. "You may not agree with Rebecca on these dogs but I wouldn't bring any undo notice on her state."

"What else can we do?" he asked in a pleading tone.

James shook his head. "I just don't think it's a good idea."

They snuck from the library to the fourth floor landing, leading to the dorms. Paul and James helped Rebecca up to the window and Rebecca, once in the alcove above the door, turned to pull Sam up through the opening. They had gotten better at the escapes.

"Goodnight," said Sam to the boys. Rebecca switched positions in the opening to help her down to the dresser on the other side. Once Sam was on the ground, Rebecca turned and stuck her head back through the window.

"Goodnight," she said to Paul and James. "Paul, try to be patient. I know you're worried but be patient."

Paul nodded his head reluctantly and took James' boost to the window ledge. He slipped through onto the other side of the door. James returned to her as she leaned through the window.

"Remember next time, bring that journal," he said to her. "I want to see this code you've been deciphering."

She grinned at him and nodded. "James, I can't believe how obvious it was; it was right in front of my face. I can almost read the script like normal Arnoran now."

"Good, maybe we can find something about the Kilaray in there; Rebecca, I wasn't lying when I said that book could be very important."

She looked at him thoughtfully. "James, I already found something about it in the text."

"Why didn't you tell me?" he asked, looking hurt.

123

"I was nervous. I swear, next time we meet, I'll show you and you can help me make sense of what I found," she said.

Just then they heard keys inserted in a lock below them. The door to the courtyard was thrown open with a bang and footsteps echoed up the stairwell.

"James, hurry," she hissed at him as he bolted for the opposite door.

He jumped and caught the ledge, pulling himself through in one fluid motion, practice had paid. She heard his feet slap the stone on the other side of the door. She turned and slid back to her side of the door. She slipped through, caught the dresser with her feet and pounced down. She whipped up the dresser and urged Sam on when she made for the sleeping chamber.

The guards were unlocking the dorm doors as Sam and Rebecca snaked around the spiral staircase to their beds. Rebecca replaced the dresser in its normal place and leapt for her bed. Her heart pounded in her chest as she yanked the covers up over her. Sam was snuggling into her own bed when they heard the guard step into the bed chamber.

"Everyone awake," shouted the guard. "One quarter of an hour be dressed and in the courtyard for morning exercises."

Sam popped up and made a show of stretching as the other girls sluggishly woke and sat up.

"What a night," said Sam as the canopies were drawn on the girl's beds. "I had the strangest dream," she said with a secretive smile directed at Rebecca. Rebecca knew if she let Sam continue with these blatant displays, eventually the rest of the girls would catch on to their late night activities. That is why she let them continue.

"Sam, I don't know what you do to be so awake in the mornings," asked Helen as she rose to her feet. "I feel like I just went to sleep five minutes ago."

Sam looked at her with worry. Helen had dark circles under her hazel eyes. Her skin was paling as time continued. She looked exhausted. Marissa, doing the same task, by comparison looked tired but no more so than any of the rest of the children.

Rebecca wondered if Paul was right. Maybe if the guards saw how she was faring, they would act, at least to keep up production.

In the courtyard, Ben Frowler ran the children through their daily workout. Rebecca had become used to the activities and was able to complete each exercise without much difficulty; it was all in the breathing she found. Her body, already slim, had had any extra fat melted from it. Her muscles had grown tight with the weeks of exercise and she felt good after the daily routine, more awake. The rest of her friends had similar results; that was all except Helen.

"Foster, you're done," called Ben Frowler to Helen.

They were in the middle of pushups and Helen strained to get fully off the ground. This had become a regular event; Helen had collapsed once in the middle of one of the exercises when Ben Frowler had urged her to continue. Now, he saw as Rebecca's friends did; Helen was not well.

Rebecca had believed that at least some of the Romarans actually worried about them. She had seen Frowler arguing heatedly with the guards, directing his stares and gestures toward Helen as she trudged from the courtyard toward the dining hall. Unfortunately nothing had come of these arguments in the way of aid.

Rebecca knew that if anything was going to be done to help Helen, it was going to fall to her and her friends.

When Ben Frowler released them to go to the dining hall, Paul helped Helen down the passageway. When they entered the dining hall, they took their seats. They waited for Sam and Michael to bring them their usual breakfast; Helen wobbled in place at the table. Paul looked to Rebecca with fear plain on his face. Rebecca shook her head at him, trying to dissuade him from what she could tell he was about to do.

He grimaced, furrowed his brow, and stood from the table. Rebecca and James watched as he approached one of the guards near the door to the kitchens. Paul began in a meek way; they watched as his mouth worked, pleading with the guard. His gestures became more and more overt as he continued, the guard showing no concern. Eventually, Paul started flinging his arms wildly about.

"You dogs have to do something; you're responsible for us for the Father's sake," Paul shouted at the guard.

The guard punched Paul in the face, landing him on his back on the ground. James and Rebecca leapt to chase after Paul, struggling to get to his feet. The rest of Rebecca's friends were on her and James' heels. Broheim stepped between Paul and the guard, catching Paul as he leapt for the guard. The whole of the dining hall was in shock, staring at the scene unfolding in front of them.

"Come on Sunshine, settle down," Broheim said through gritted teeth, trying to hold Paul back.

"Romaran, let that boy come and get what he wants," taunted the guard with a grin across his face.

"You shut your face," Broheim said, spinning to the guard with Paul caught in a head lock. "The boy's looking out for your charges, which is more than I can say for you."

"The boy was blaspheming, and threatening the Red Guard. I should take him out and lash him myself," said the guard.

Broheim turned to Rebecca. "Take your friend back to your table Skinny." He handed Paul over to Rebecca and James; James grabbed his arms and held them pinned behind his back; Rebecca stood, pushing on Paul's chest, holding him against James.

Broheim stepped up into the guard's face, talking in a low malevolent whisper. The guard shied away from him.

"Well, that's the last time, you hear? This is a warning," said the guard, shrinking back.

"Fine then," said Broheim. "Get going Skinny," Broheim said, turning to her. "I'm going to have words with you boy when we get to the shops," he said, pointing at Paul.

"I don't care," Paul shouted at him. "I just want that..." The rest was muffled as Rebecca clamped her hand over his mouth, still spewing vile curses at the guard. Paul's nose began to bleed over Rebecca's fingers as she held back his words.

"He'll listen to you when we get to the shops," Rebecca said, pushing Paul back toward their table; James pulled as much as she pushed and they eventually got Paul to the table.

Helen had tears running down her cheeks. She hugged Paul when James got him seated. James sat next to Paul, whispering in his ear. Whatever he said worked; Paul's head sank and tears dripped from his downturned face. He nodded as James finished speaking.

When the bell to go to work sounded, Rebecca caught James by the arm.

"What did you tell him?" she asked.

"Well, I think I may have just put off an explosion for later," he said, looking into her eyes.

"What do you mean?" she asked, puzzled.

"It's on you now," he said. "I told him you were working on something that would help Helen and if he started fighting with guards it was going to ruin it."

"James," she gasped. "I don't have any plan. Why did you tell him that?"

"It worked didn't it? Besides, you'll come up with something, I have faith in you."

She stood there as James broke to go with his work group to the forges. Her mind spun. What was that boy trying to do to her? Paul was going to kill her. How was she going to get out of this? She watched as a group of small children walked from the kitchen, exiting at the other end of the dining hall from the entrance the children used. She could almost see the children's mouths watering, looking at what they carried. Between them on a silver serving tray, roasted to perfection, was half a dozen rabbits. She almost heard the pieces fall into place in her head.

She hurried after Broheim when he called after her. She walked next to him for a while, getting out of ear shot of the guards in the courtyard leading to the shops.

"Skinny," he said to her before she could speak. "Whatever it is you have, it's spreading."

"What?" she asked.

"That disease you have that makes your heart drive you instead of your brain; your friends are catching it," he said.

"I didn't know it was contagious until just now," she said.

He chuckled. "I thought maybe that big blonde boy of yours, not Sunshine. I didn't see it coming from that one."

"Well, he's been worried a lot lately," she said. "One of our friends is sick and he wanted the Red Guard to do something for her."

"That girl isn't doing too well – anemia they call it. Ben told me," he said.

"I was wondering Broheim," she said. "Is there anything you or the others could do to help her?"

"I want to Skinny, I truly do, but the Red Guard watch us nearly as close as they watch you."

"Well, maybe you could just answer a question for me then?"

"Perhaps," he said, eyeing her with a raised steel-gray eyebrow and twitching his mustache to the side.

"The rabbits I just saw, would they come from the woods to the west of Valgerhold?"

He looked at her for a moment, thinking, and then he nodded. "They're rather fat this far north; might be, one could snare a few in the night, if they had means of getting into the forest that is."

He walked her through the doors of the shop

"Sunshine, follow me," he announced. "Skinny, you too." He continued to the small office in the back of the shop. Rebecca walked beside Paul following Broheim.

"Is it true?" Paul asked when they were together. "Are you planning something?"

"Maybe," she said. "I'm working on something."

He nodded and brushed a sleeve across his nose; it had begun to bleed again.

When they were in Broheim's office, he closed the door and took a seat at the small desk.

"Sunshine, I thought you would have learned from Skinny here," he started.

"Don't call me that," Paul growled.

"What should I call you then, Thickhead, Dimwit, or Dead Boy? Because that's what'll happen if you try something that stupid again," Broheim yelled, standing from his chair with his hands spread on the desk. "You damned Arnorans and your hardheads," he said under his breath. "I don't know why I should expect you to be any different than your parents," he said, returning to his seat. He smiled at the two of them.

"Do you two know what kind of trouble I'm going to be in if you get caught?" he asked. "Of course you don't but that would also make you no different than your parents. Arnorans inspire rebellion whatever their age." He pulled the ring of keys Rebecca had seen the first time she met Broheim. He unhooked one and placed it on the top of his desk. "This key unlocks the grating of the vents that heat the place," he said as he leaned back, placing his crossed feet on the desktop, looking at the ceiling. "I've heard some of my colleagues talking about how they have been finding books out of place in the library and furniture rearranged in a particular corner. We have had an infestation of large rats recently; if these rats were to somehow get a hold of this key, they would be able, from the courtyard atop the library, to gain entry into the vents which, if they study well enough, will lead them to the grassy field, leading into the woods." He stood from the desk and looked at the two children before him. He smiled. "Funny thing, I think I must have misplaced my copy of that vent key some months ago." He walked to the door and stepped back into the shop.

Rebecca looked over at Paul with a broad smile on her face. "My plan is coming off so far." She jumped for key on Broheim's desk and stuck it into her pocket. "Come on Sunshine," she said, grabbing Paul by the hand and leading him, looking very confused, back into the shops.

At mid meal Rebecca leaned over to James and whispered something that made his eyes widen.

"All of them?" he asked, looking at her very concerned. "Rebecca, I'm telling you it's going to get us found out."

"We are going to need them James," she said. "Tell them tonight; we have to get this together quickly."

Paul smiled at James and Rebecca; it was the first time they had seen that in weeks.

"Alright, all of them," James conceded.

That night Rebecca and Sam woke the girls in their alcove quietly. They led them down the spiral staircase, Rebecca carrying a very useful dresser. Sam led the procession to the dormitory door. Rebecca set the dresser in the corner and climbed up, cupping her hands to helping Sam into the opening. The girls followed her lead.

The group waited for Rebecca to slip down from the ledge with James' help.

James led the group down into the library, into their corner. When they were all settled, Rebecca stood in front of the group. She pulled a key from her pocket.

"This is what is going to help Helen," Rebecca said.

"What do you mean help me?" asked Helen.

"We've been trying to build your strength," said Paul next to her. "We've been splitting our meals with you but it hasn't worked so far."

"Paul," Helen gasped, looking at him. "I thought they were just giving us more to eat. If I had known…"

"You wouldn't have accepted it," said Rebecca.

Helen looked at Rebecca with a hurt look.

"You need something that you aren't getting and by my guess that something is meat," Rebecca continued. "This key leads to the vents; it can get us out to the forest to the west. If we can get out there, we can trap something to eat. That's where the rest of you come in." She looked to the two brothers. "Gene, Lester, do you two know anything about snares?"

"Bet your britches we do," said Lester.

"Our unc' used to take us with him when he went hunting," Gene put in. "Showed us everything he knew, he did."

"Good," Rebecca said. "We're after rabbits. Arthur," she said, looking to him; he tried to hide, suddenly the focus of attention. "Gene and Lester will tell you what they need. It's up to you to find it in the sewing rooms." He nodded. "I'm going to need the rest of you to keep guard and prepare whatever we can find; so, we're going to need something to cook with. Sam, Michael, what can you do for me?"

"Rebecca, I already told you they watch us close," said Sam, looking distraught.

"Not me," said a little boy's voice. Mac stared at Rebecca, clutching his magnifying lens. "They send me to take the pans and pots that wore out to the forges. They don't send no one with me. I could maybe get lost on the way with one of 'em."

Rebecca smiled at him. "Mac, do you think you could get one here without much trouble?"

Marissa looked at her little cousin, worried. Mac looked down, thinking, then looked up and nodded. Marissa clapped her arm around him.

"We can get the wood in the forest but we need something to start the fire," Rebecca said, looking to Marissa and Helen.

"It shouldn't be too hard to get some of the powder out of the alchemy lab; we're coated in it when we come to meals," said Helen.

"James, we need steel," she said, looking to him; he had a wry grin on his face.

"Aye, Captain," he said, putting the knuckles of his thumb and forefinger to the bridge of his nose, an old Arnoran salute.

"Elizabeth, do you have any flint in your ceramics shop?" Rebecca asked, unable to hold back the grin James had put on her face.

Elizabeth bit her lip and nodded. "They use it to grind the glazes in the mills there," she said in her soft voice.

"When we have everything in place, we'll move," said Rebecca. "Helen you hold on for this; we can't let one of our own down."

Helen grimaced and nodded her head in agreement, wiping a tear from her eye.

When the children got up to leave, they had a purpose and their spirits were high. They were on a mission to save a friend.

With all the children back on the other side of the doors James and Rebecca were alone on the landing. She raised her arms for him to give her boost to the ledge, it didn't come. She turned to see James, smiling at her, his arms crossed over his chest.

"What is it?" she asked.

"How long did it take you?" he asked.

"What do you mean?"

"How long did it take you to come up with that plan after I pushed it on you?"

"I don't know, not too long, I guess."

"You didn't bring the journal with you."

"No, I forgot. What is this about James because…"

"Bring the journal with you next time Rebecca," he said, stepping closer, looking into her peculiar eyes. "I think I know what you found in there because I've been thinking it since I met you."

And with that he picked her up and helped her to the ledge.

"Goodnight, Rebecca," he said to her.

It took the children only a few days to gather all the supplies that they needed to carry out the plan Rebecca had devised. They gathered the supplies in the library, hiding them in their corner out of sight of anybody who would happen by on chance. When they had nearly all the materials, Rebecca decided it was time to explore the vents.

"We are going to be looking for an access to the outside. We need to be careful, from what Broheim has told me, there are several hatches at different levels within the vents. So, we might accidentally step out twenty feet up." Rebecca stood in front of her friends in the library corner. "I'll go first; I brought my dad's pocket watch. It has a material on the face that casts a faint light; so, we won't be entirely blind in there. I need another volunteer to go with me."

All the children's hands shot up immediately, a wave of giggles through them.

"Paul," Rebecca said. "How are you with tight spaces?"

"I'll be alright," he said.

"Alright, you're coming with me. If we can find our way out to the field, we might as well gather the wood we'll need. So Arthur, give Paul that sling you made."

Arthur had managed not only to gather the cords needed for Gene and Lester's snares but an odd assortment of scrap fabrics and wool that he thought might come in handy. He had put together a sling to carry whatever they found in the woods. He was working on sewing together some woolen over shoes to cover the group's boots to muffle their footfalls in the forest.

When Paul had the sling, the group followed Rebecca up to the courtyard above the library. They stepped out into the chilly night air. Winter was breaking, finally, and the days had become warmer as spring approached, but the nights here were still frigid. The children were bundled in their work coats and hats. They followed Rebecca to the hatch covering the vent between the two dormitory towers. Rebecca removed the key Broheim had given her and unlocked the covering of the vents.

When the hatch was opened, steam billowed from the opening as the warm moist air met the cold night. Rebecca removed her coat and tied the sleeves around her waist and lifted herself into the opening. She felt around with her feet, eventually finding steel rungs mounted inside the vent. She climbed down into the pipe and called for Paul to follow.

Once they were both inside the venting and the hatch closed behind them, they crawled along using Rebecca's father's watch as a makeshift lantern. The dim green glow cast little light for them to see by but, as their eyes became accustomed to the darkness, it was manageable.

The heat inside the vent soon had the two sweating. They passed several intersections in the main run; having walked this section out in the library, they continued forward. Eventually they came to a down shaft in the vents; Rebecca signaled for Paul to stop.

"This looks like it could take us down to ground level," she said to him. She pulled a length of cord from her pocket and tied it around the watch; she handed the cord to Paul. "Lower this down so I can climb without worrying about dropping it."

He did as she told him; Rebecca slipped her legs over the edge of the dark opening leading downward. Her hands were slick from sweat as well as fear and her stomach was doing flips as she felt with her feet for the rungs. Lower, lower, she was beginning to think they had not built rungs into this section. Her hands lost their grip on the vent floor and she slid backwards down the shaft. She let out a little scream, the echoes bouncing around the inside of the vent. Her feet caught the rung as her hands came to the edge of the opening. Paul hurried to look over the edge.

"Are you alright?" he asked.

"Yeah, I'm alright. They make these rungs for people a little taller than me though."

"Well be careful; we don't need you waking the guards screaming," he said.

"Thanks for the concern," she said, looking up into his face in the green glow of the watch.

"Sorry, you know what I mean," he said, apologetic.

Rebecca moved down the rungs of the vent. She passed several hatches as Paul lowered the watch from above; it twirled slow circles casting its green light on the walls of the vent; its soft ticks in the vent beat a rhythm for her descent. Rebecca's arms ached from the climb. Slowly, the ticking became quieter and the green glow moved away as she climbed farther.

"Paul, lower the watch," she called up in a whisper.

"Can't, we're out of cord," he called back.

"Alright then I'm going to try the hatch nearest me."

She pulled out the key and twisted around for the hatch mounted behind her. She unlocked the cover and pushed out on the door. She climbed up a few rungs and stuck her head out the opening. Through the clouds of steam pouring from the vent, she could just make out the ground ten feet below. She pulled the hatch closed and locked it.

"We're almost there," she said. "I'm going to come up and take the watch; you climb down and meet me."

"Alright, tell me when you have it," he called down to her.

Rebecca moved up a few more rungs and took the watch, dangling in mid air above her. "Alright, I've got it, come down."

She heard his feet above her grip the rung and he climbed down. From the darkness above slowly materialized, out of the black, a set of ghostly green boots. When Paul was just above her, she looped the cord around her wrist and climbed down the rungs again. They passed the hatch Rebecca had opened and a second about five feet further down, coming at last to a hatch that Rebecca figured had to be at ground level.

She twisted around again and unlocked it. White clouds of steam washed over the grass just below the open hatch. Rebecca stepped from the rungs and out into the open grass field. Instantly, shivers hit her. The sweat from the climb had soaked though her undershirt and her bare arms prickled with goose bumps. She untied the coat from her waist and hurried into it as Paul passed through the opening. He too had a similar reaction.

"Bast! It's freezing out here," he said.

"Put your coat on quick before you catch something."

"Yes Mom," he said smirking.

She shook her head and turned to look around. They were in the grass field below the dormitories. She moved out further into the field and looked up to the courtyard above. The others leaned over the side looking down to them. She signaled to them and they waved back. She turned and looked at the field. It was placed between two of the various shops that the children worked during the day. The field was a bit faded from the winter but the grass was still held its color. The wood she had first seen from the dorm window loomed some five hundred feet away. A feel of freedom washed over her.

"Rebecca, what's to keep us from just getting the rest of them and leaving this place," asked Paul as he looked up to the others above them. "We could get away from here and never look back."

Rebecca hadn't thought of that; she was too concerned about helping Helen to have run the possibility through her head. She wondered if they could do it; get all the children down the vents out into the woods and just keep running. Then she thought about all the others, those not in amongst her friends, she knew they would be stranded. Who would help them? They would no doubt be punished for the escape; the Red Guard would not believe they had no knowledge of the plan. What about Broheim? He defiantly would be punished for their escape. No, she couldn't risk it; not for the other children's sake and not for Broheim's.

She turned to Paul and shook her head. "We can't leave the others here; they'd suffer for our escape and I won't have that. They are still our countrymen; we have to stay loyal to them."

"But we could be miles away from here in the morning," he pleaded.

"The others would be here to take the beatings for our good fortune."

"Fine then," he said, his shoulders slumping. "Let's get the wood and get back up there." He looked up to the others.

The two crept into the woods, watchful for any patrols that might be out at night. They didn't see any; the Red Guard had locked them in the dorms and they were still there for all they knew. Her brothers words came to her again...*they see us as children. They won't expect anything from us.* She smiled to herself and slipped into the woods with Paul on her heels.

In the woods, they hunted for firewood and kindling. The pine needles covering the forest floor muffled their steps without Arthur's wool overshoes. She wouldn't tell him they wouldn't need them. She gathered some of the straw and picked up dry wood. When Paul and she had gathered enough to fill the sling, they began to make their way back to Valgerhold.

They walked back the way they had come, moving quietly. As they walked, Rebecca heard a noise off to her right and stopped dead; Paul froze in place. They waited for the sound again, a rustle off a little to their right. Rebecca knelt down in case it was a guard; Paul followed her lead. Hiding behind a dense thicket, the two peered between the branches.

There in the center of a small clearing in the woods, a doe stood picking at some berries on a bush. Rebecca's heart leapt; these woods were alive and they were going to help their friend live as well.

Backing slowly away from the thicket, the two moved out into the grassy field.

"What I wouldn't give to have been able to bring that back tonight," said Paul. "Forget rabbits, we should be going for deer."

"Just how are we supposed to bring down a deer," she asked, looking at Paul.

"I don't know," he said, as they came to the hatch leading back to the vent. "Why don't you figure it out?"

Rebecca paused as Paul climbed into the vent. She turned and looked back to the forest, thinking. She could almost hear clicking as the pieces worked against one another, attempting to fit together. She turned back to the vent, closed the door, and climbed.

Fourteen:
Answers Questioned

Back in the library, they found a place to stash the wood with the other supplies. They set the time for the following evening for their hunt. The excitement was palpable as the children readied to go back to the dorms. James pulled Paul aside as Rebecca was telling the others about the deer they had seen in the woods. He whispered something into Paul's ear which made him smirk. Paul nodded and Rebecca looked on the exchange with suspicion.

"Alright let's get back to the dorms," said Paul to the others.

The group began to make their way to the exit to the stairwell; James caught Rebecca by the arm and pulled her back from the rest.

"Paul can get them through tonight," he whispered in her ear.

Rebecca turned to look at her friend. He watched her in a way that made her nervous.

"I noticed while you were gone that you brought the journal," he looked down at the satchel at Rebecca's hip.

"I did," she said, feeling her heartbeat quicken.

"I was looking through it while we waited for you to return," he said, smiling now.

Rebecca turned to look as the rest of her friends left; she thought some of the others were giggling about something Paul was telling them.

"Do you know what I found?" he asked, putting his arm around her shoulder and leading her back into the corner.

"What was that?" she asked; her hands and feet went cold.

"Why don't you hand me the journal and I'll show you instead." he said as he sat her down in one of the overstuffed leather chairs; he knelt in front of her.

She hesitated then lifted the flap of her satchel; pulling the journal from inside, she handed it over to him with a grimace.

He took the book delicately and opened it, flipping through the pages and examining them as he did.

"Just like before," he said in a whisper.

"What is just like before?" she said, leaning forward to look over the top of the book.

Slowly, he turned the open book to face her; what she saw shocked her. He turned the page, then the next, and the next.

"Notice anything?" he asked, a knowing smile on his face.

"It's gone, all of it," she whispered, furrowing her brow as she looked at the pages. "All the script is gone."

"Exactly," he said. "Rebecca this book was not linked to Arnora; it's linked to you."

He stood and nudged her to squeeze in next to her in the chair. She squished to the side as he slid down next to her.

"I want to see it happen," he said, holding the open book out to her.

She slowly reached for the journal. Its worn leather exterior was so familiar to her for her whole life; now it was like something entirely new. As her finger tips touched the cover, the sweeps and lines bled into the pages, filling the margins and adding lines of text under the pictures. James watched wide eyed as the words finally fully appeared on the page.

"Amazing," he whispered.

"How, how?" she began, looking at him confused. "I don't understand, how did…"

"I don't know but Rebecca if I'm right on this, I'll bet I'm right on the other," he said, looking into her peculiar eyes.

"What James?" she asked. The nervousness she had felt was replaced by a desire to know anything that would answer her questions.

"I think one or both of your parents had the Father's Touch, Rebecca," he said, looking into her eyes now glistening with tears. "I remembered when I looked at the window in the girl's dorm tower. Your eyes, Rebecca, you have the eyes of the Philistari."

"What are you talking about?" she said, looking away suddenly conscious of his admiration. "I have my father's eyes."

"Then it was probably him that was Touched. Rebecca, the young girl on the coat of arms on the shield the lion is clutching, that is supposed to be Arnora. She was the first, the first Philistari. They said her eyes were like something from the animal world, not entirely human. They were said to be a particular shade of green. It was a trait that stayed with the Philistari until their end. Although not all had them, those with the eyes always had the Touch to see the Kilaray."

"James, it can't be. Why wouldn't my father ever have told me?" Tears streamed down her cheeks. James put his arm around her shoulder. "Sebastian, he had my father's eyes too. He never said anything about having a touch. If I have it why didn't he?"

"He probably did," said James, holding her to him. She shook with what he was telling her. "It would explain why he was so skilled at leading the First Born. Rebecca he held off an ocean of the Red Fist and actually gained ground for a time. How old was he seventeen, eighteen? It was like he knew what they were planning."

Her head spun; the words in her grandfather's journal flashed before her eyes… *I am truly sorry I did not see the Kilaray in time…* She knew it was true, what James was saying, but she didn't want to accept it. If she and Sebastian had this Touch why then did their father never tell them of it? How could her mother have not told her about her father? Why had these secrets been kept from her? Why had her parents gone off to fight and die as her brother had, leaving her alone with no answers? Anger flared in her. Her family had lied to her, her whole life, and now they were gone, taking the answers with them.

"Why didn't they tell me?" she shouted, standing from the leather chair, her grandfather's journal toppling from her lap onto the floor. The script vanished as the book lay open in front of the chair.

"Rebecca, keep your voice down," James said.

"I don't want to keep my voice down," she shouted. "I want to wake the dead. I want some answers for the Father's sake."

"Calm down," said James, standing from the chair and stepping toward her. She stepped away from him.

"No, I won't calm down; this is insanity. I'm not special; I don't have the Father's Touch. I'm just a girl; I won't believe it." She slumped to her knees suddenly light headed. James caught her as she fell.

"Whoa, there, I got you, come on," he said, helping her back into the chair. She sat looking out, seeing nothing.

Her mind settled slowly; reason returned. James was brushing the hair from her face gently. She calmed; her thoughts still spun but she could see what they pointed to. James knelt, looking into her face. She thought back to her childhood. Had her father and mother truly never told her?

You two are going to be great one day, their mother had told them as she and Sebastian sat before the telescope. Their mother had been teaching them the constellations. *You two will burn as bright as these stars one day. You are going to help this world more than it can know now.* Their mother had looked into their eyes as James was looking in her eyes now, with wonder. *You two have a special gift, you'll see it in time. Yes especially you, Rebecca.*

...I am truly sorry I did not see the Kilaray in time... She wanted to see; before it was too late. James had his hand at the nape of her neck his thumb on her cheek below her ear. She looked into his warm brown eyes.

"Are you alright?" he asked, looking worried.

She sniffed and wiped her eyes with the backs of her hands. "I'm alright, sorry about that," she said, feeling embarrassed. "I'm just a little scared just now."

"I understand," he said, leaning back from her. "You scared me there for a minute. I thought you were going to faint."

"I thought I was too," she said.

"Well, what are you thinking now?" he asked carefully.

"I'm thinking I should show you this," she said, taking the book from where it had fallen. She moved to sit next to him on the ground. She flipped the pages to the passage about the Barrier that had started her confusion. She showed him the words her grandfather had written; he read them twice over.

"Well, that proves it then," he said, looking at her. "Rebecca, you are going to need to be even more careful. If the Red Guard finds this, you are going to be in very serious danger."

"What do you think I should do?" she asked. "I don't see any Kilaray; I don't even know what to look for."

146

"What's with the change of heart all of a sudden?" he asked.

"I can't change the past and I can't find answers where there aren't any. I might as well accept what comes and move forward before it's too late to do anything about the present," she said, looking at him seriously. "Now, how do I go about finding these Kilaray?"

He nodded his head. "It's not that simple; from the histories I've read, the Clerics sought out the children most likely to have the Touch, but it was left to them to discover how to see them."

Rebecca watched as James went through her grandfather's journal. He wasn't scared of her. She had been worried that if he knew, their friendship would be at an end. Now, he knew and he was doing as he had from the first time she had met him on the train, he was trying to help her. She got to her knees, leaned over, and kissed him on the cheek.

"What was that for?" he said, smiling at her. "Not that I mind."

"It's to thank you, for being my friend," she said.

"My pleasure, my Captain," he said, saluting her.

She punched him in the arm and he laughed.

"Not very friendly of you," he said, rubbing his arm.

She leaned against him and they sat looking at the Journal together; James put his arm around her shoulders.

"I nearly forgot," she said after a time. "I have been looking at all this script and I never showed you what it means." She flipped through the pages, looking for the image of the cliff with the trees growing from them. When she found it she pointed to a series of points above the trees in the sky.

The points were nearly a mirror of one another, arching in two slightly curved lines into the sky. Next to the points was a line of the script. "My mother would have killed me if I ever forgot this one," she said, looking at the points on the sketch. "This is called the Gates," she tapped the points. "It's a constellation in the western sky; she said you can see them better in the south."

James was not looking at where her finger pointed; he was instead staring wide eyed at the image of the cliff.

"Hey, you aren't paying attention," she said, nudging him.

"The Gates of Yuriah, bast! He found them," he whispered to himself.

"How did you know what their called?" she asked, looking confused.

"This," he said, pointing to the cliffs. He pointed to the stones hidden partly behind the trees; they were a stone copy of the stars in the sky, arching slightly as they reached skyward. "This was supposed to be the entryway to the Barrier. In rumored histories those able to open the Gates would pass between the stones to the land beyond. Somewhere in that land was supposed to be a great hope. Your grandfather found the Gates, Rebecca."

Fifteen: Naming Feast

The next morning, Rebecca awoke with a sense of purpose. Tonight they would help Helen and she would continue the search through the journal for more clues about the Kilaray. She was determined to learn to see them. She had shown James how her grandfather's code worked. She explained that once she saw the constellation in the sketch with the name written in her grandfather's script, she had known she found the key.

Each letter of the standard Arnoran alphabet had been replaced with a different glyph. When she found the Gates of Yuriah written in the code next to the constellation diagram, it was only a matter of time before she worked out the rest of the symbols.

They had sat for nearly an hour while Rebecca read the script to James. He would stop her every once in a while to ask her to go back over a section again. In the end though, they had not found any further information on either the Gates or the Kilaray. They had to rush back to the dorms when they saw light streaming through the glass domes above.

Now, Rebecca sat in anticipation of the coming night's events. The other girls awoke and dressed for work.

"You didn't come back until late this morning," said Sam to Rebecca with a grin. "What were you and James doing?"

Rebecca blushed; so, that is what Paul had told the others. *Well, no need to let them in on her discovery just now,* she thought. "We talked," she said. She smiled and went to retrieve her uniform.

"Awful long talk," said Marissa, smirking.

The others grinned like cats with canaries.

"Yes it was," said Rebecca, tucking in her shirt. "And that's all you're going know about it," she said. She grinned back at them.

They met in the courtyard for the morning workout. Helen finished all the exercises; she wasn't going to risk being punished when she was so close to help. They all went through their regular day's routines, working and breaking for mid meal.

Rebecca had become accustomed to seeing Postam at the balcony, watching for when his cronies actually managed to catch her off guard. Fats had become increasingly desperate and his attempts to knock her down had landed him on his face twice and had him cleaning the woodshop every other time. When he made his run today, Paul heard it before she did.

"Fats is coming," he whispered to her.

"I hear him," she whispered back.

When the large clumsy boy neared them, Rebecca spun to face him.

"Gregor Mathiason, we were just talking about you," she said loud enough for Postam to hear. "That was a pretty good joke you told about the Commander in the shop; how'd it go again, 'What's the difference between Commander Postam and an ox?' You told it better, you finish it."

Fats had a look like he had just been struck dumb, which wasn't much of a change. He looked up to Postam at the balcony, mouth agape, and shook his head in denial. Postam reddened and, shaking his head, he turned to walk from sight.

"Skinny, move it along now," called Broheim. "You too Fats."

Rebecca smiled at the hulk of a boy in front of her; she turned to catch up with Paul and Broheim.

"Pretty quick girl, but you could have left Postam out of it," said Broheim as they walked to the doors of the shop.

"I don't know what you're talking about Broheim. It was Fats's joke," she said.

"I'm sure it was; now go get your work finished."

She gave him the Arnoran salute and went to her workspace.

She finished her parts ahead of everyone else as usual; when Broheim came to her, she had planned what she was going to ask.

"Finished again Skinny? Alright, this time I'm going to give you something more challenging to work on for the rest of the time," he said, looking over the row of stocks drying on the rack.

"Broheim, I was wondering if I might be able to use some of the other woods to make something," she put forward cautiously.

He eyed her with suspicion. "What might that be Skinny?"

"My father showed me how to bend wood in a certain way and glue it together with other types to give it strength. Can we bend wood here?"

"Yes, the steamer is in the corner, haven't had much use for it lately," he said. "What precisely would we be bending this wood into?"

She signaled him to come in closer. "A bow," she whispered.

He stood up straight, shaking his head. "Last I checked it didn't take much to stop what you are after. I think that might be a little overkill; don't you?"

"We've already got what we're after planned for," she whispered. "But I saw something bigger that would be better pay for the risk we're taking. Only, I can't take it with twine and twigs. I need something with more power."

"Let me think about it Skinny," he said, ruffling her hair. "For now, you're going to be making a chess board. We can play when you've finished it. You might learn something from the game. Perhaps you might even learn some caution."

"Alright," she said to him, feeling slightly defeated.

When last meal broke and the children were escorted to the dorms, Rebecca felt her stomach fluttering. She was excited about what they would be doing that night. If everything went to plan, by the morning, Helen would be on her way to recovery. The others would have seen that they can work together to accomplish great things. Rebecca hoped that would begin to break the fear that held them from standing against the Red Guard.

The girls sat in their beds in the alcove, trying to rest while the others in the dorm drifted to sleep. Rebecca sat with her journal and read through the script, watching as her friends tossed and turned, waiting. After about an hour and a half, snores echoed around the sleeping chamber. Rebecca tucked the journal into her satchel and got the others ready. She only needed to touch a shoulder and the girls sat up wide awake.

They grabbed their coats and hats and made their way to the dorm door. They slipped through the window to the hands of the boys on the other side of the door. They snuck to the library, into their corner, and retrieved their supplies. Up on the courtyard above the library, the children put together the wood to make a fire.

"You'll wanna wait until one of us throws you a signal before you set the fire," Lester told the others. "No use wasting wood if we don't have anything to cook over it."

They had decided to send three into the woods – Lester, Rebecca and Paul would go first. They gathered the snares and wool overshoes Arthur had made them. Rebecca told him they were excellently made. They made their way into the vents. Rebecca went first; Lester and Paul followed her into the vent. They used Rebecca's watch to find the down shaft. Rebecca had to help Lester to the first rung, he was shorter than her. Once on the grassy field, Rebecca's heart leapt.

The three sprinted into the forest. Lester set the first snare, showing them where to look for trails and the proper placement. After, they divided the snares and split up to set their traps. After about an hour, the three met at the head of the forest. They sat waiting and praying that at least one of the snares would catch something. Lester told stories about hunting with his uncle, how he had nearly wretched the first time he had to clean an animal for cooking. They laughed at his stories and it helped to relieve some of the tension. After a few more hours, Lester decided it would have to be time enough if they wanted time to cook whatever they found.

The three returned to their snares, looking for a catch. Rebecca's heart sank when she found her first snare empty, and the second. On her third she found a fat hare's lifeless body caught head first in her snare. She paused as tears blurred her vision.

"Thank you," she whispered to the rabbit. "You have helped my friend and I thank you for that."

She gathered the rabbit and moved on. She found another of her traps empty; she continued checking her traps. When the three met at the head of the forest, Paul held three brown rabbits up for all to see. Rebecca had gathered two; Lester had only managed to catch one.

"It's first timer's fortune it is," he said, looking at the two. "You watch, next time I'll come out ahead."

They put their catch in the sling and hurried back across, signaling the whole way across the field for their friends to get the fire going. The three climbed the vents as fast as they could to the courtyard. When they stepped from the hatch at the top, the scent of burning wood met Rebecca's nose immediately. She put her coat on and walked to the fire, blazing near the edge of the courtyard. Paul sat the full sling on the ground with a smile; he opened it for the others to see. Lester stepped up behind Paul with his hands on his hips.

"It was first timer's fortune, I swear it was," he said to the group.

"Well brother, as unc' used to say, 'Hunters get to rest while the other's do the cleaning'," said Gene, opening the fox carved folding knife.

Rebecca had the other girls take Sam away while Gene began the gruesome act of cleaning the animals for cooking. Rebecca watched the whole procedure, feeling queasy at first. Once she saw the first couple done she felt better and helped the others cooking the meat in the pan Mac had managed to get out of the kitchens.

The smell of cooking meat brought the girls from across the courtyard from where they had taken Sam. They gathered round the fire, watching as the meat cooked. When it was ready, Gene pulled a large leg from one of the rabbits and handed it to Helen.

"It's gonna be hot so be careful," he said to her.

She took the leg and looked around at the group watching her. "Thank you, all of you," she said and took a bite from the leg. The juice ran down her chin and she wiped it with the back of her hand, laughing. "It's good," she said. "Well, I can't eat it all." She gestured to the pile of sizzling meat.

The group pulled the meal apart and, in a short period, the only thing remaining was a greasy pan and a stack of bones. The group sat back and looked at the fire as it was dying down.

"We need a name," said Marissa. "We need something to call our hunting party."

"I agree," said Helen, pulling the last bits from a bone.

"Rebecca's Rabbit Raiders," said Sam with a grin.

"No, no, no, I'm not taking credit for this," said Rebecca, shaking her head.

"Come on, this was your plan," said Elizabeth, across the fire.

"Maybe, but we all worked together," said Rebecca.

"What about Arnora's Rev, Revenge?" asked Arthur. "That wouldn't be, be, be so obvious if the guards hear us talking."

Rebecca looked into the fire, the light burning into her eyes, making purple white shapes when she looked up.

"That still draws attention to Rebecca," said James. "They know who that refers to."

"Second Born of Arnora," said Michael, "that won't draw attention to anyone in particular."

"Here, here," said Lester.

"I second that," said Marissa.

Rebecca smiled; she saw the first cracks in the fear that had held her friends. "Sounds good to me," she said.

Sixteen:
Lessons from the Past

The next morning, Rebecca's friends awoke with a revitalized look on their faces. They had gone to sleep with full bellies, a first since leaving Arnora. The color in Helen's face seemed to have returned. In short, the children felt better than they had in a long time. When they went for morning exercises, none of Rebecca's friends had the slightest difficulty finishing.

"Foster," Ben Frowler called to Helen when he had finished the routines. "You look better. What have you gotten up to?"

"I guess I just had to get used to the cold," she said to Frowler.

Rebecca's friends sat at first meal and ate the meager porridge without any longing; their hunger had been met for the time. Rebecca felt sorry for the other children sitting at other tables though. She could tell, by comparison to her friends, that the poor quality of food the Red Guard fed them was having poor effect on them. Rebecca feared that, in time, more of these children would end up as Helen had, struggling to keep working.

She wondered if it would be possible to bring the other children in on the hunts without alerting the guards. Then she thought better. Hundreds of children running through the forest at night couldn't be missed, even if every last one of the guards were blind. Perhaps they could keep the Second Born small yet still manage to feed the others. She would have to figure something out because she had plans to turn the children against their captors. The best she could manage for now was to supply them with a proper meal.

In the wood shop, she worked on her daily quota of stocks, working with a purpose. If she finished the stocks faster, that would be more time to work on Broheim's side projects, more time to convince him to let her work on her own. She managed to finish four stocks before the mid meal bell sounded. She would quickly complete her share of the work when she returned from the meal. She walked with Broheim to the dining hall.

"I'll finish my work soon after we get back from mid meal," she said to him.

"Uh huh," he grunted.

"We were able to get what we were after last night."

"Glad to hear it," he said, looking straight ahead down the hall. Broheim acted odd; it was not like him to be so short with her.

"Is something wrong?" she asked.

"Some of the large rats I told you about didn't clean up their mess completely when they were finished," he said, looking down at her. "Some of my colleagues found char marks in the courtyard atop the library. They wonder if it's such a good idea for us to help these intruders."

Rebecca felt sick. She had finally achieved some real goal and now her friend was having second thoughts.

"I'm sure the rats will be more careful next time," she said.

"I certainly hope so," said Broheim, looking at her with a frown. "Because a larger catch is going to cause a larger mess," he smiled.

"You mean?" she asked him with hope.

"I think we can forgo the chess board for now," he said. "While some of my colleagues don't believe we should aid the vermin, the ones that count were impressed with the rats' resourcefulness. They think the leader must have a good head on her shoulders."

Rebecca's smile stretched from ear to ear as she sat at the table with her friends. She ate her meal in near silence. Her mind raced to work out the problems of bringing down larger game. It would take longer to cook for one and there was no way her friends could eat all that came from the animal. They would have extra and that she would not see wasted, not with all the children slowly deteriorating from malnutrition. They would have to figure out a way to preserve the meat so they could give it to the other children to keep.

She looked to her friends, talking happily to one another. She would need their help to plan such a task. It wasn't enough to merely fell an animal; the preparation of the meat would take more than she knew.

"Gene, Lester," she whispered to them.

"Aye Captain," Lester responded with a cocked grin. The others had taken to James' title for her.

"What do you know about preserving meat?" she asked.

"Well, you can dry it," Gene said. "Smoking takes a while, but it'll last a while too."

"Do you think you could do it in the forest if we had the materials?"

Gene and Lester looked at one another and whispered for a time, finally they turned to Rebecca.

"It would take some setting up but we could manage," said Lester.

"What are you thinking now Rebecca?" asked James.

"Look around, James," she said, turning to scan the children at the other tables in the dining hall. "These others need what we had last night. We can help them," she looked to her friends. "We should help them."

Her friends looked to one another.

"What do you need from us?" asked Helen.

Gene and Lester went over what they would need to cure the meat they caught. James was sure he could make some knives and smuggle them out of the forges. Elizabeth had become friends with the Romaran ceramics leader, a woman by the name of Gelda Hume; she thought she might be able to get out some pots to cook the meat. The others volunteered themselves for anything else that needed doing.

"Remember," Rebecca said, "keep as quiet as you can. We may be trying to help the others but we have to look at them as potential leaks until we can trust them."

"How are we going to bring down something bigger, Rebecca?" asked Paul.

"That's where we come in. You have to pick up the pace on your work, Paul," she said to him.

Back in the wood shop, Rebecca finished faster than she had in the past. When she had set her last stock on the racks to dry, she went to the small office in the back. She could smell the sweet smell of tobacco, wafting from the open door. She stepped through and found Broheim at his desk, feet propped up, and a pipe held to his lips. He seemed to be thinking; so, she knocked gently on the door frame.

He turned to her, setting the pipe in a dish on the desktop. He put his feet down and gestured her to take a seat in front of his desk.

"Come, sit Skinny, I was just running some things through my head," he said in a voice that wouldn't travel into the shop. "I was trying to remember the last time I had a student with as much talent as I see in you. It's been a long time I'll tell you that much."

"Thank you," she said, "I just finished my last stock for the day."

"I'm not surprised," he said, putting his feet back on the desk and resuming puffing on his pipe.

"I was wondering if I could start work on the piece I want to make," she asked, getting a strange feeling from the way Broheim was acting.

"Postam is watching us," he said to her, making her spin to look at the door. "Not now, girl. He sees us talking together. He says he has his suspicions about the relationship between teachers and students he sees developing at the university. Seems to think we Romarans are forgetting that we are associating with traitors to the New Dominion."

Rebecca didn't know what to say so she sat and let Broheim continue.

"You and your friends need to be careful who they trust amongst us, Skinny." He looked at her with a serious expression. "Do you know about the battle called Ronan's Folly?" he asked her.

"I've heard of it," she said. She could remember her mother crying when she heard the news of the battle; Rebecca's father had tried for hours to console her mother.

"Do you know why that battle turned out the way that it did?" Broheim placed his feet on the ground and leaned on his desktop, looking at her with a hard expression.

"The Homelands were betrayed by the Felsofese soldiers that went to hold out the Red Fist, in a gap in the Anderwill Mountains," Rebecca said, feeling a little uneasy.

"That was the result of a decision that should have been foreseen," said Broheim, leaning back in his chair. "Trusting the wrong people was the cause of that disaster. Ronan Arcand needed those Felsofese soldiers; his need outweighed his caution. Everyone knows you can't trust the Felsofese; they're treacherous, devious, and underhanded. Ronan disregarded his knowledge because his need for assistance was that great. He was betrayed because he trusted the wrong people." Broheim looked her in the eyes with a frown. "Do you see what I'm trying to tell you?"

She nodded. "Even if my need for help is great, don't let down my guard when help presents itself."

Broheim smiled. "It would appear we are going to have those chess matches after all, even if we don't get to touch a board." He stood from his chair snuffed out his pipe and walked around the desk. "Let me show you how the steamers work."

They walked to the rear of the shop where the steamers were kept. A gas line ran into the machine. Broheim checked the water level on the steamer, struck a match, adjusted a knob, and held the match to a little hole in part of the gas line. Rebecca heard a "whoosh" and the machine began to warm. While the steamer heated, Broheim went to a large wooden cabinet on the other side of the shop. He opened the door and began sorting through some large sheets of paper. He came back to her with a tube of paper held with a piece of twine. He untied it and laid it out on a workbench near the steamer.

"I figure we need to make it just strong enough that you can use it. No use making something so powerful it requires a full grown man to draw it," he said to her.

The paper showed diagrams of different pieces of wood of varying shape that needed to be bent and glued in certain places. The shape of the final construction was an elegant looking curve; the two ends swept away from the main curve which ran through a grip constructed of another block of wood.

"We'll use some of the scraps from the stocks to strengthen it, and make the grip," said Broheim.

"I just thought of something Broheim, how long will this take do you think?" she asked.

"Couple of days at most, if you can finish about the same time," he said, looking at her.

"And if we had help do you think we might be able to make a second?" she asked.

"I'm already stretching my neck out here, Skinny," he said, glaring at her.

Just then, Paul walked over to where she and Broheim stood at the rear of the shop.

"I'm finished with my stocks," he said to Broheim.

Broheim spun with a worried look on his face. Seeing who it was, he slouched a little, using the table to support himself.

"You kids are going to end me; I swear you are," he said, gripping his chest. "I suppose this is your help Skinny," Broheim said, turning to Rebecca.

She nodded, smiling at Broheim.

That day, the three managed to cut all the pieces they would need for the two bows. Broheim said he would hide the parts while they were being made; it would look less suspicious if the parts remained in the shop.

That night, the Second Born of Arnora met in their library corner and went over plans to help their fellow countrymen. Rebecca sat, feeling warm; she was doing what she hadn't believed she would be able to do. She was turning her friends into soldiers.

Seventeen:
Motives Revealed

It took Rebecca and the others longer to complete the tasks than it had for the rabbit hunt. That didn't surprise her; what did surprise her was the complexity of the plan they had devised. There were several key processes that needed to go into just preparing the meat, let alone hunting and bringing down the deer. They were able to slowly build up enough of the chemicals from the gun powder production Gene and Lester said they could use to preserve the meat. Elizabeth had managed to talk Gelda Hume into letting her take some of the defective pots from the ceramics shop. Rebecca had checked with Broheim to make sure the Romaran ceramics teacher could be trusted first.

It seemed Arthur's woolen overshoes would come in handy after all. The children had checked to make sure the deer were regular visitors to the forest near the school. Each time they had come upon the animals, the soft footfalls on the pine needles was enough to scare the deer into bolting.

In the wood shop, Rebecca, Paul, and Broheim soon finished the two bows. Rebecca realized she had overlooked a vital piece of the plan, arrows. Broheim assured her it wouldn't be a problem; he kept a small shop at his home in the town outside the university. He had his wife preparing the arrows for them; she, apparently, was quite taken with Broheim's description of the Arnoran rebels held within Valgerhold.

All told, it took nearly a week to prepare everything for their hunt. In the meantime, Rebecca had taught James to read the script in her grandfather's journal. They took to staying in the library after the other children broke to go to sleep.

They had started from the beginning of the journal and read through the whole book, looking for anymore description of the Kilaray or the Gates of Yuriah. Her grandfather, she was realizing, had remained vague about both the location of the Gates as well as any way of entering them. He also apparently took his ability to see the Kilaray for granted; when referring to any of the Kilaray Links he encountered, he simple wrote a brief account of his attempts to adjust them or to attune to them. None of these accounts shed any light on how precisely one was to go about learning to see the Kilaray, or just what it was he was adjusting and attuning.

Rebecca lay on the floor, her hand resting on the edge of the book, while James read through the script.

"Put your hand back," said James as she began to drift off to sleep. "The script is fading again."

She shook awake and moved her hand back onto the pages. This had become their routine. Rebecca would read while James rested; then, she would rest while touching the book for James to continue where she had left off.

"James, I don't know if we're ever going to find anything this way," she said to him. She rolled over on her side to watch him read.

"We haven't even gotten halfway through the book and already you're ready to give up," he said, looking at her.

"I didn't say I was giving up," she said. "But what is the likelihood that my grandfather would have put a Kilaray primer in the middle of his travel log?"

"Not that great I'll admit," said James. "But we might be able to figure out how to get through the Gates if we keep going."

"What good would that do us, James? We're stuck here; we aren't going anywhere." She got up on her elbow to look at him straight. "We need to get out of here James. If I'm ever going to learn to see the Kilaray, it's not going to be here."

"Well, when the Red Guard releases us we can go to the Wilderlands and search for the Gates," he said.

She didn't know why, but his words angered her. "They aren't going to release us, James."

"What are you talking about; of course they'll release us. Why wouldn't they? We are only a burden for them to support. Eventually they'll have to let us go."

"No they won't. If they don't starve us with their food, they'll just work us until we die. We're free labor James. Why should they give that up? We can't stop them, you said so. Who else is going to make them let us go?" she asked, sitting up. The script faded from the pages as James watched. He sat and contemplated.

"They made an agreement with your brother that they would release us back to the Homelands," he said with a pained expression.

"They also told us they would release us when we learned we were traitors. I don't see any lessons being taught here other than don't do anything the Red Guard doesn't like."

"Well what should we do then?" he asked anger filling his words. "Storm Dormon's office and demand we be released, we'd be killed in an instant."

"We need to get the other children to come to the idea that there is going to be no end to this work. We need them to come to our side of this fight. We need allies."

166

"That's what this hunt is about isn't it?" he asked, looking hurt. "This isn't about helping the other kids. It's about building an army. We're just soldiers aren't we *Captain*?"

"James…"

"Aye, Captain. What can I do for you Captain?" he said, saluting her.

"James, stop it."

"Aye, Captain."

"You are more than soldiers to me. You, all of you, are my friends."

"You could have fooled me. You've been planning this since that first day," he said, standing. "You met us and you thought 'I can use these people'. You just had to work us to get us to fit into your plans."

"James it's not like that at all. I …"

"You…you are going to get your revenge against them aren't you? We are just a weapon you think you can use. However many of us it takes, you'll avenge your brother. Well, I won't do it. I do care for the others; really care, like I do for you."

Tears ran down her cheeks. She didn't know how to stop him. What's worse some of what he said was true. She had seen the children as weapons she could use against the Red Guard. She looked into his warm brown eyes and saw his anger flaring. How could she have been so one minded? He was right; these weren't soldiers, they were children and she had no right to use them. But the Red Guard had even less right to own them. She was sure of it now; if she couldn't get the children to fight for her, maybe she could get them to fight for themselves.

"You're right," she said at last. "You're right, James, I wanted revenge. I was wrong James; I was wrong. Please, listen to me." He had turned his back to her, his arms folded over his chest.

"I do that and you'll just twist my brain back to your thinking," he said.

"James, look at us," she pleaded. "We're huddled in this library, hiding from these people; they won't let us go. You know I'm right about this. We aren't going to be freed. I don't want you to fight for me but I do want you to fight. We are Arnoran; they can't change that. We weren't meant for captivity."

James turned his head a notch, listening.

"If you won't fight for me, that's fine. Fight for yourself. You aren't a slave, James. None of us are slaves. There are worse things than death, James," she finished.

He stood quiet for a time. "I don't know if I'm angrier at you," he turned to face her, "or myself. I know you're going to get me killed, but I know you're speaking true. Father have mercy," he said, looking up, "this girl is going to get us all killed."

Rebecca felt a little hope. Looking into his face, the anger in his eyes faded.

"This is our arrangement," he said. "No more manipulations, no twisting me to fit your plans. You want me to do something, ask. It'll be up to me whether I think it's a good idea."

She nodded. "Alright, no more, I promise," she said.

He stood, staring at her for a while, then shook his head. "You knew you were going to turn me didn't you?" he asked.

"You knew what I said was the truth; you turned yourself," she said, smiling.

"Well, what now?" he asked.

"I think it was still your turn in the journal," she said. She sat next to the book and, while watching his face, she extended one finger to the page. The script bled into the parchment.

"I never get tired of seeing that," he said.

James sat next to Rebecca and read where he had left off. They talked while he went through the text. Rebecca was careful not to upset him again. She had feared that she had lost him as a friend when he had realized what she had been doing. She didn't think she would stand much of a chance without James. She had come to rely on him; he was her closest friend here. She had thoughts about him when their nights were over. He lingered on her mind when she tried to concentrate on some aspect of planning.

She moved closer to him to feel his warmth. He paused in his reading for a moment as their knees touched, took a deep breath, and continued. It was brief but Rebecca had noticed. She looked down into her lap and smiled to herself.

"Wait, that doesn't make any sense," he said.

"What doesn't make sense?" She hadn't really been paying attention.

"This section, it makes no sense." He pointed to the bottom of one page, the paragraph continued over to the next.

There seem to be certain artifacts that need to be either found or created to pass through the Barrier. We were able to gather this… and with that the Tremen bade us farewell, our questions still unanswered.

It seemed that the two sections were not meant to run into one another.

"It's like something is missing between," said James.

Rebecca looked into the valley between the two pages, searching for a cut page. There was nothing to find.

"Well, there doesn't appear to be any missing pages," she said.

A shaft of light moved onto the pages the two were examining. James whipped his head toward the domed windows above. Day was breaking. Rebecca slammed the book shut and the two raced to the exit of the library.

When they opened the door they heard the guards, climbing the stairs below. James grabbed Rebecca's hand and pulled her back into the library.

"Up, we need to go up," he whispered.

They ran to the spiral stairs to the courtyard atop the library, bursting out into the brightening day above the grassy courtyard. They ran through the doors that led to the stairwell connecting the dorms and the main courtyard. The echo of footsteps approaching met them as they climbed to the fourth floor landing.

James grabbed Rebecca by the waist and hoisted her to the window ledge. As soon as she gripped it, he darted for the opposite door. Leaping, he caught the ledge and slipped through the opening. Rebecca lowered herself through onto the other side of the door. The dresser was gone. The others must have taken it when she didn't come back with it in the early hours of the day. She dropped the last couple of feet to the ground, rolling backwards to break her fall. She ran.

The door began to open from the landing. Seeing the door to the lavatory, she turned sideways and rushed through. The sound of boots approached. Closer, closer, her heart pounded as she leaned on the door to the hall. Closer, and then, they moved farther down the hall. She was safe.

"One quarter of an hour be dressed and down in the courtyard for morning exercises," she heard echo from the sleeping chamber. When the guard walked back past the lavatory, she waited until she was sure he was in the stairwell. She opened the door and slipped back into the hall.

Climbing the spiral stairs, she walked to her bed and sat on the edge. The other girls watched her with fear in their eyes.

"That was close," she said to them at last.

Eighteen: Warning a Friend

The coach pulled to a halt at the front of the large dark stone university, Valgerhold it was called. Ramon Garler looked out of the glass windows of the coach at the massive structure before him. He momentarily forgot his reason for traveling to this university. Turning his mind back to the task at hand, Ramon prepared his thoughts. Ramon felt he owed his old friend a warning of what was coming his way. Anton Dormon and he had survived more together than the battles to take Arnora. Anton had saved him on several occasions. That is why he made this visit in person; it was only right.

Pulling his dark fur collared coat closed, Ramon opened the door to the coach and stepped from its opening. The memory of those creatures visit to his university had left him with nightmares. He wasn't a religious man. He had his doubt about those who did believe in the First Father, but when those things had left him, he had prayed that he should never have cause to see them again. A sudden shudder went up his spine; it had nothing to do with the weather, which finally began to show signs of spring.

"Wait here, this won't take long," Ramon said to the Romaran driving his coach. The horses stamped with pent up energy from their journey across the cold stone planes that dominated this land. Ramon turned and walked to the entrance of the school.

These universities were truly marvelous structures. Ramon had always enjoyed architecture. In his childhood he had marveled at the buildings in his home of Pelos, in Felsof. He had wanted to help design those structures but he was Felsofese, and not of proper heritage to be educated in such a field. Instead he joined a mercenary guild before the Exile; that's where he had first met Anton. They had watched each other's backs while they moved up in the ranks of the guild. His trust in his friend grew as they gained more prestige as hired killers. It was rare to find someone in Felsof one could trust, but Anton was a rare person indeed.

He walked into the vast courtyard where the Arnoran children were running through morning exercises. Anton's idea most definitely, the man knew how to keep people occupied so they couldn't think of anything that might cause trouble. Ramon walked across the courtyard and talked to one of the Red Guard standing watch over the children.

"I'm Colonel Garler, here to see Colonel Dormon," he said.

"Aye, sir, I'll show you to his office," said the guard.

The guard led the way through the twisting stone hallways up to the second floor. Ramon tried not to show his awe while examining the craftsmanship of the carvings and tapestries, the paintings and the decorations. Who would have expected a low cast, Felsofese child would ever come to oversee such marvels of design and craft?

The guard stopped before a thick dark wood door with iron wrought scrollwork adorning it. The guard knocked and waited. The door opened and a large burly man Ramon seemed to remember met them at the door.

"Colonel Garler, to see Colonel Dormon, sir," said the guard to the man who had appeared at the door.

"Ramon?" came from within the room.

The large man swung the door wide for Ramon to enter. His friend sat behind a large wooden desk. What appeared to be a gun lay on a cloth on his desktop, the parts removed, and placed as for cleaning. Anton stood and moved around to greet Ramon as he walked into the room.

"Ramon, it is good to see you," Anton said, gripping his forearm. His eyes had grown harder since the last Ramon had seen his old friend, not that they had ever been soft.

"What brings you to my doorstep?" said Anton, offering Ramon a seat. He waved it off.

"I'm afraid I don't come under the best of tidings, Anton," said Ramon. No point to beating around the bushes with Anton, he liked things direct. Ramon signaled to the large man still in the room. "Is he trusted?"

"You do not remember Edwin Postam, Ramon?" Anton said, gesturing to Postam.

Now he saw it; the last time Ramon had seen this man he had been all of about fifteen. He had put on about ninety pounds of muscle and his beard seemed to have finally grown in.

"Great Father, look at you man," said Ramon, extending his arm to Postam.

"It's good to see you again, Sir," said Postam, taking Ramon's forearm. He didn't seem pleased at all. That had been the result he had seen in too many of those who survived Palder's Pass. Their spirits had been hardened; it was like they were the walking dead.

"Now, what would bring you from across this cursed rocky waste?" asked Anton.

Ramon's stomach suddenly leapt, remembering for what he had come.

"Adarian has loosed the Blind Men," Ramon said to his old friend. The hint of a smile that was on Anton's face drained to a grimace.

"The Blind Men, why?" Anton asked in a whisper, looking at Ramon.

"They are searching the universities for something," Ramon said. "Anton they wouldn't speak of what it was but they are on the move. It'll take them a couple of weeks to reach this far. You know how they work; methodical doesn't begin to describe it."

"No word on what they hunt?" asked Anton, falling into one of the chairs in front of his desk.

"I suspect it's one of the Arnoran children, I'm sorry to say," he said, looking down. "Poor wretches don't know what they have coming for them."

"Sorry, Sir, but if you are referring to these Arnoran spawn, you shouldn't feel sorry for them," said Postam behind Ramon.

He turned to the large bearded man. "Have you ever seen how the Blind Men cull their prey?" he asked the man, stepping closer.

"No sir, but with all due respect, you were not in that Pass. They deserve whatever it is these men do to them."

"Edwin, you know not of what you speak," said Anton. He looked pale as he sunk into the chair.

Ramon stepped closer to Postam. "They look like men but I can assure you they are not. They are not natural. When they find their prey, it starts gently so there won't be a struggle until the victim has no chance for escape. It almost looks like a lover's kiss. At last the Blind Man reveals itself but by then it's too late. When it's over," Ramon shook his head, "there is nothing left. Bodies yes, but something is missing, the soul, or some essence; whatever it is animals can see it. Vultures, wild dogs, bast even the maggots, won't go near the body. Whatever the Blind Men do they utterly destroy the person they take."

Postam had become quite pale.

"Father, protect us," said Anton from the chair. "Strynges, here."

* * *

Ramon made his apologies for the news he brought; Anton assured him there was no need and thanked him for the warning. The guard was summoned and led Ramon back to his coach. Climbing inside Ramon felt a weight lift from his chest. His duty to his friend was done. He could return to his university to the east and try to leave this business behind him. He signaled the Romaran to take the coach out.

Ramon thought. What he knew of Strynges made their visit to the universities peculiar. Strynges usually had no troubles taking humans. They enjoyed it from what Ramon knew, but they had seemed cautious, if one could assign such an aspect to the creatures. They had not simply stalked through his university culling children as they willed. They had been standoffish from the children until they had eliminated them as their target, and then they moved on to the next. The last time he had heard of the Blind Men behaving in such a way, they hunted Philistari. That made no sense now though; for they were all dead.

* * *

"It's her Anton I know it is," said Postam. He smiled.

"You may be correct Edwin but don't let your joy show so," said Dormon, staring blindly at the disassembled revolving pistol on his desk. "It's unseemly."

"Unseemly it might be, but that girl is going to finally get what she has coming," said Postam, taking one of the chairs in front of Dormon's desk.

"Edwin, keep watch on her. No more of your bootlicking turncoats, we need someone close to her. We need an infiltrator," said Dormon.

"I don't know Anton; she seems to stick to her cadre of friends," said Postam.

"Do your best, make promises, give rewards, whatever it takes. Search her belongings also, leave no sign. See if she has anything of interest," Dormon said, slowly reassembling the pistol.

"Aye, Sir," said Postam, standing from his chair. "I'll report what I find."

Postam left Dormon's office. The light from the windows above poured in on his desk. It took him almost five minutes to reassemble the pistol. When he had the gun together, he looked at it lying on the cloth on his desk. It took him at least double the time it had taken Rebecca to piece it together.

"How did she do it?" he whispered to himself.

* * *

"Who do you think he was?" asked Paul.

"I don't know," said Rebecca. "He was dressed like Dormon though."

"Maybe he was another Colonel then," said James.

"Maybe," said Rebecca, "I just have a bad feeling is all."

She had felt a shiver go up her spine when she saw the man enter, while they were at morning exercises. She felt dread course through her. They sat at their table in the dining hall.

"Well, everything will be ready for tonight unless you think we should wait," said Helen.

"No, it's nothing. We go tonight if everything is ready," said Rebecca, giving her friends a reassuring smile.

Rebecca sat and ate while the others talked over their parts in the plan. Her stomach felt queasy. The feeling she had was peculiar, it felt distant, as if from someone else. It was not like anything she felt before. She figured it was just her nerves. The bell to go to work sounded and shook her from her thoughts.

Nineteen:
Rules of the Game

In the wood shop, Rebecca and Paul finished their work ahead of the others as had become custom. They went back to Broheim's office where they found him smoking his pipe with his feet propped on his desk. A chess board sat on the desk next to the tray to hold his pipe.

"Come you two, I figured you deserve a break from all the work you've been doing," said Broheim. He put his feet down and motioned them to sit.

"Broheim," said Rebecca, "we are going need our project tonight." She walked in and sat in one of the chairs in front of his desk.

"I see," said Broheim, stroking his mustache. "Well, there will be something waiting for you when you go for your walk tonight then. Now sit, Sunshine. What do you two know of the game of chess?"

"My mother used to play with my brother and me," said Rebecca.

"Good, good, then I don't need to explain the rules to you. This game has been used for hundreds of years to show the importance of planning ahead. You must not look at each move as independent; everything is tied together. You have to plan for every move your opponent might take to stop you. Plans within a plan, this is what is necessary to be a great chess player."

"What is the point to this?" asked Paul.

"The point, Sunshine, is that unless you plan for the worst, the worst will find a way to plan for you," said Broheim. "Look at us here;

we are in the position we are in because those with the power to affect our situation failed to plan for the worst. Now, let's play shall we. Skinny, you first, we'll let Sunshine catch up on the rules as we go," Broheim finished and set up the board.

Rebecca moved her chair closer to the desk. She took the white side of the board, Broheim the black.

"Now, the key is to realize, Sunshine, that every piece on the field has its role," he moved his pawn forward. "The least important piece on the board can still take the highest if one plans correctly."

Rebecca moved her pawn forward. She listened to Broheim's words but she was following the pieces. Her mind turned, shifting pieces this way and that.

"You see, Sunshine, Skinny has got the look. She is no longer with us she is on the board. She is planning ahead, seeing where I will move next." He moved his knight out from behind the pawns. "This move eliminates some of her plans, but the key is to have others in place for this."

Rebecca heard his words; they washed over her. The moves in her head fell away and were replaced with others. She continued to listen but Broheim was right; she wasn't really in the room anymore. She was on the board.

Pieces left the board as Rebecca and Broheim made move after move. Broheim continued explaining the happenings on the board to Paul. Finally, only a few pieces remained.

"Now is the time when the players must be careful," said Broheim. "A handful of moves remain to either. Make the correct ones, and you'll win, but fail to see the game to the end and you've planned defeat."

Rebecca could see the last moves remaining for Broheim; she knew where he was going. She could see the end of the game. She made her move. She took his queen and put his king in check.

Broheim smiled. "You see, Sunshine, you plan for the worst and you will come out ahead, but you must also know the rules of the game you play."

Broheim moved his pawn one last place to the far side of the board and replaced it with both queens; they surrounded her king.

"Checkmate," he said.

Rebecca looked up from the board at Broheim; his smile was gone.

"You can't do that," she said.

"It's a little known rule," he said, leaning back from the board. "A Felsofese variant, it's called turn-of-the-tables. You should always know where you stand before you begin."

"You cheated," she said, becoming angry. "You were going to cheat all along."

"Knowing your opponents intentions also helps," he said.

"Broheim, you can't do that I've never heard of Felsofese rules," she said, standing from the chair.

"Sit Skinny," he said to her gently.

"I won, that's all there is to it," she said.

"Sit down Skinny," he said firmly. She sat, scowling at Broheim. She slowly sank back into her chair.

"You can never rely on your opponent playing by the rules. This game is set to follow certain laws. You can't trust that to happen in the real world. You're right Skinny, I cheated, but so will others you run into. Not everyone plays by the rules; it seems fewer all the time these days do," Broheim leaned forward, placing his hands on either side of the chess board. "Always look for signs your opponent is going to cheat, that is the worst and if you've prepared, you can catch your enemies off guard. Planning betrayal often depends on more than playing by the rules; one overlooked item and the foundation crumbles, leaving no room to move."

Rebecca's anger subsided; she knew he was helping her. He was trying to teach her to watch out for herself.

"Broheim, if we have to always watch behind us how can we ever look forward and plan our strategies?" she asked him.

"At some point you simply have to have trust in your allies. There is no helping it; one person can't take on an army. The key is to know your allies, and know your enemies better," he said.

"How do you know your enemies better than your allies?" asked Paul.

"Ah, Sunshine, you figure that out and no one will ever be able to stop you," said Broheim.

Broheim and Rebecca played another game; he promised he would use Arnoran rules this time. Rebecca kept her eye out though just in case he lied. Broheim had taken it easy on her their first game, apparently just to teach her a lesson. She struggled to follow his strategies. They were wild and reckless offering up key pieces for sacrifice while lower value players moved in for check. He knew the game well; he had no need to cheat. Rebecca lost as many games as she won and Broheim actually seemed to enjoy when he was pinned and had to declare defeat.

Paul began to play; Broheim gave him hints as to where to move. Rebecca scaled back her attacks to encourage him.

"Don't you hold back Skinny, I see it and I don't approve. I'm working as Sunshine's commander; he's my captain. I give him advice he chooses whether to heed it. You take it easy on him and he'll never see the reasons behind my advice. He won't grow as a captain."

Rebecca played harder. She improvised moves, trying to catch Paul and Broheim off guard. Her mind whirled to invent ploys to draw them in to traps. She led them to believe she was attacking one target while the whole time advancing forces on another. She could see how this game was like planning for a battle. She was about to catch Paul and Broheim in checkmate when the bell for last meal sounded.

"Well, that was close; it seems the hand of the First Father rescued us for today Sunshine," said Broheim. "Would you two like to continue this tomorrow? You might be more prepared after a good night's sleep."

Rebecca had forgotten what was to happen tonight while she had played. Her stomach made a leap of anticipation. She smiled at Broheim.

"No Felsofese rules tonight, right?" she asked him.

"I promise," he said.

Twenty: Giving Thanks

Rebecca and Paul went to sit at their table in the dining hall. Her friends had looks of worry on their faces. The scale of what they were to do that night finally made its impression on them. Rebecca was nervous but she felt she should encourage her friends.

"Everything is set," she said smiling. "The Second Born of Arnora earn their name tonight."

The others turned to her, brightening at the thought of success.

"Aye, Captain," said James.

"Aye, Captain," said Paul.

The rest joined their agreements.

The last bell of the day sounded and Rebecca's hands went cold. She went with her friends up to the dorms. Her mind ran through all the possibilities she could think of. She tried to figure out what to do if one of them got hurt, if someone got caught, if they couldn't get everything done in time. What if something didn't work like she planned? She decided she would have to just trust in the plan in the end.

The girls sat in their beds, looking at one another with nervous smiles.

"Do you think it will work?" asked Sam.

"Of course it will work. Rebecca has the luck of Arnora behind her," said Marissa.

"Don't go hexing us from the start," laughed Elizabeth.

"Everything will go to plan," said Helen, looking to Rebecca. "Right Captain?"

Rebecca nodded. "Everything will go to plan," she said to her friends, praying to the First Father.

They all laid down to rest while the other girls in the sleeping chamber slipped off to sleep. Slowly the sounds they had grown to recognize as the sounds of sleep drifted up to their alcove.

"It's time," whispered Rebecca.

They stood in the library corner, watching Rebecca, nervous. She could feel their eyes on her. James smiled encouragingly at her and nodded for her to begin.

"We are the Second Born of Arnora," she began, "our brothers and sisters were the First. They achieved great things against great odds. We are going to prove we can do the same. We need to trust one another out there; we need to know we can rely on the person next to us. This may not be easy, it probably will be harder than we think, but that's no reason not to try. If we carry this off, every one of those children sleeping above us will benefit. That's what soldiers of Arnora hope for, the benefit of others," she looked at her friends before her. She felt pride for what they had done.

"Let's move," said James.

They climbed the spiral stairs to the courtyard above. They climbed from the recessed doorway to the grassy courtyard around the dorm towers. Rebecca led the group to the hatch into the vents. She unlocked the door and removed her father's pocket watch to use for light. They climbed into the vents after tying their coats around their waists.

Climbing through the vents, Rebecca led the group past intersections to the down shaft leading to the outside. She handed the watch back to Helen behind her to hold while she climbed down. They had taken this course several times in the planning of this night; they had memorized the number of rungs to reach the hatch they needed. As Rebecca approached the last few rungs, her foot hit something; it clattered lightly. She reached down and felt for the object. She knew it at once. She had helped build it; it was her bow. She climbed down and unlocked the hatch, steam billowed out and dim light reached the inside of the vent. She saw, tied to the rungs, the two bows and two quivers full of arrows.

"Thank you, Madam Broheim," Rebecca whispered.

She climbed out of the vents and removed the two bows and quivers. The others stepped from the hatch into the grass field leading into the woods; the moon shown down on them. The night was cool but not frigid as it had been. The woods showed signs of the beginnings of blooms.

When the rest of her friends had stepped from the vents, Rebecca closed the hatch and locked it. She showed the group the two bows and quivers. They had agreed that Rebecca would take one and James the other. The rest of the children were going to be used to flush the deer toward the two archers. Arthur produced eleven sets of woolen overshoes which they tied over their boots. When they were prepared, they marched into the woods.

They walked softly when they reached the forest. The overshoes worked to muffle their steps but they remained cautious. Rebecca and James readied arrows and tested the draw of the bows. The group moved through the woods, coming to their smoking preparations, several clay pots set up with dry wood inside them. The salt peter from the powder in the alchemy shop along with salt from the kitchens was in other smaller pots with wax seals to keep them dry. They had produced quite an impressive operation in this forest, under the Red Guard's nose. When they were in their camp, James stopped them and pulled a heavy cloth from inside his coat pocket.

"I thought I would wait until now to give you these," he said to the group. He unrolled the cloth and handed them each a rough steel knife. The blades were about as long as Rebecca's hand with cloth wrapped hilts. "They aren't as good as could be but they should make a neat cut in whatever we manage to find."

They thanked him for his gifts. He seemed a bit embarrassed by the praise he received. He turned to Rebecca, pulling another cloth from within his pocket.

"I thought our Captain should have something a little finer," he said to her.

She opened the cloth he handed her; it was nearly the same as the others but there was a small round pommel on the end with an engraved lion's head. She smiled at him.

"Thank you," she said.

He knuckled his forehead in salute.

The group readied themselves for the hunt and started off deeper into the woods. The others split off into groups to look for signs of deer. They stalked through the forest nearly silent. It felt strange, moving through the forest at night with only the sounds of night birds and the soft rustle of the branches in the wind. The night enveloped the children; the browns and grays of their uniforms blended into the forest colors. Rebecca thought it was good of the Red Guard to provide them with hunting clothes.

Suddenly, a twig snapped somewhere up ahead; the gray brown shapes of the children froze in place. Rebecca saw Gene point in the direction from which it had come. The children sunk low to the ground and moved to flank the sound. Rebecca's heart pounded in her throat. She and James took up positions for the maximum field of view to find the approaching animal. She watched as her friends disappeared into the forest.

Silence followed for a long time. Rebecca could barely hear over the thud of the blood through her ears. She looked to James, standing apart from her. He squinted into the night, looking for movement. Cracks and snaps from ahead made her jerk. She looked forward.

"Whoop, whoop," came from the trees. Thuds from ahead made her whip her head in the direction from which they came. More branches snapped in the woods.

"Whoop, Whoop," closer now. Running sounds approached from the left.

Thudding hooves met the two archers' ears. She drew her bow back. Small trees and branches moved in a wave toward James and her. The thudding was much closer. Rebecca took a deep breath and released it. The night glowed to her eyes, she could see more clearly now. The sounds intensified, she pinpointed the direction. Everything seemed to slow. Suddenly, a brown shape burst from between the bushes, running straight at her. She saw the antlers of the buck and the wide dark eyes. She saw her friends, chasing after, drop to the ground as they came to where the archers were. She pulled back on the bow. The twang of the string whipped past her ear. She reached for another arrow and heard a second twang from her left. The buck still ran for her; she readied the arrow and drew again. Twang and she jumped to the right as the buck crashed toward her.

Getting to her feet, she turned and saw the buck lying on the ground, motionless. Three arrows protruded from the animal. Her friends rushed up after her.

Their faces glowed with joy, fear, and excitement. Rebecca felt the blood drain from her head. Everything became less defined. She began to breathe again, not even realizing she had been holding her breath. Crashes and snaps came from the trees as the rest of the flushers approached.

"We did it." Sam jumped in circles.

James walked to the group. "I thought it was going to run you down," he said to Rebecca.

"I wasn't thinking anything," said Rebecca.

"Well, we've got one but that's only the first part," said Lester.

"Right," said Rebecca, "let's get him back to the camp. Sam you go with Lester and get the fire going."

"Aye, Captain," she said. She grabbed Lester's hand and pulled him toward the camp.

"We'll need the rest of you to help pull him," Rebecca said to the gathered children.

"Maybe we should say something," said Helen, looking at the buck with tears in her eyes.

"It's a deer Helen it's not like a person," said Gene.

"She's right," said James, "we should say something. This animal is going to help all of us." The children gathered round the deer and they all bowed their heads. James began to speak. "Thank you First Father for this animal; you have given us what we need to help your children."

When he had finished Rebecca spoke.

"Thank you deer for your sacrifice," said Rebecca. "I'm sorry we had to do this to you, but you have helped us with your life."

With that the children each gripped hold of the buck and began to pull it back to the camp. It was a large animal and by the time the children had gotten the buck to the camp, they were exhausted. The glow of the fire waited for the rest of their plan though, and Rebecca and the others willed themselves to butcher the animal.

They removed their coats and put on the aprons Arthur had made from scrap material he smuggled from the sewing rooms. Gene and Lester led the children through the process of butchering the deer. Several of the children had to stop and walk away from the sight of the blood. Rebecca had to hold her own stomach for a moment. It took them nearly two hours to finish removing the skin and cutting the meat. Those who had been unable to do the butchering were recruited to season the meat with the mixture of chemicals and set it on cloth to rest. The pots were prepared for the smoking and the children gathered water from the lake near the forest to dampen the wood.

While the meat cooked, the children took turns sleeping by the fire to keep warm. Those who had done the butchering went to the lake to wash up. The water was freezing cold and Rebecca shivered by the time she had finished getting off all the blood and gore. James held her coat for her when she was done and she climbed into it. They walked back to the camp together.

"Fine plan I would say," said James, smiling.

"I can't help but feel some pride at how it's going," she conceded.

"Well we're not done yet," he said. "We still have to get this back into the dorms."

"Yes and we have to distribute it to the other children once we get there," she said. "Can you imagine the looks on their faces when we give them this?"

"I don't know; I think it'll be good to see some smiles. Do you think we should just give it to them, *all* of them?" he asked.

"What do you mean?" she said.

"Well, what about those guttersnipes that Postam has hassling you? Do you really think we should reward them for acting like the dogs of the Red Guard?"

Rebecca thought about it for a moment. She couldn't help but feel like James; those boys had tried their hardest to get a pat on the head from the Red Guard. While it would be just rewards for their behavior, she knew better than to give them cause to try harder than they already were.

"They need to be given this more so than the others," she said. "Those are the type of people we need to convince that the Red Guard are not people to turn to for help. We need to convince them that we are all Arnoran, together, and we stand together."

"You are more forgiving than I. The Clerics would have loved to get their hands on you," he laughed.

The two walked into the camp. The last of the meat was put in the smokers as they readied for the return to the dorms. Night still held but it wouldn't be long before the gray light of dawn crept up to the east. The children wrapped the meat in cloth and stacked it in the slings Arthur had made. Rebecca sent the children back to the library as their slings filled. When the last of the meat was ready, she bundled it up, while Gene put out the fires with the water from the lake.

"My unc' would have been proud of us tonight," Gene said to her.

"You should be proud," she said to him. "We did well tonight and it's thanks to all of you."

"Aye, Captain, but we have you to thank for getting us moving. We'd be lost without you. Your brother would be proud of you," he said, looking up into her eyes.

"Thank you, Gene," she said, feeling a burning in her eyes. "Now, let's get going."

She helped the boy get his sling on and they marched out of the forest as the first line of gray snaked along the horizon. They ran to the vent and climbed inside. Rebecca pulled the hatch shut and locked it. She made sure the bows and quivers were securely fastened to the rungs and then she followed up after Gene.

Rebecca marveled at the piles of dried meat when she and Gene returned to the corner of the library. They had each hauled back slings filled with dried venison, eleven piles sat on the floor of the library.

"You really must have Arnora's luck," said Michael when he saw Rebecca.

"Rebecca, how are we going to get this to the others?" asked Elizabeth.

"We'll split one of the slings into the other ten and take half the meat to either tower. We have to hurry now; dawn is coming," she said. She moved into the corner and put her sling with the others.

They divided up one of the piles into the others and quickly bundled everything together. They made their way up to the landing and started through the windows above the doors. Rebecca handed up the sacks to Helen in the window and she in turn handed them to Marissa on the other side. James did likewise at the boy's window, handing the slings to Paul. When all the children and meat were on the

192

other sides of the doors, Rebecca and James stood alone on the landing.

"Well, we actually did it," he said, smiling at her.

"We did," she said.

"It truly is a wonder watching your plans unfold," he said. "I have never seen anything like it."

He stepped to her and hugged her; it felt good to be held. She returned the embrace.

When he released her she looked into his eyes.

"What was that for?" she asked and smiled. "Not that I mind."

"I was wrong before, you really do care for these kids, don't you?" he said.

She nodded. "I feel I have to help them James, the guards are trying to break us down, to keep us from following what our brothers and sisters did. If we show the others that at least some of us are willing to do what is necessary to help them, they will begin to turn. We can turn them and they will stand for themselves; they're Arnoran after all."

"You sound like a general rallying the men," James laughed. "Come, I'll lift you up," he began to move away, Rebecca stopped him. She wrapped her arms around him and pulled him to her, resting her head against his chest. He put his arms around her hesitantly.

"Thank you James," she said, the words coming out muffled through his shirt. "I couldn't have done this without you."

"You're the one that couldn't be done without; you are a very rare person Rebecca. If I can thank the Red Guard for anything, it's sending me here with you."

She stood for a while, feeling his breathing against her face, and the warmth from his chest. He ran his hand through her hair and rested it on her back. She looked up into his eyes and he down into hers. She looked from one to the other, seeing the kindness they held. He bent his head to her and she craned her neck to him.

The doors below opened with a thud as the guards came to wake the children for the morning. The two looked at one another with regret, as much for the timing as for the fear of getting caught. James took a deep breath and moved with Rebecca to the window; he lifted her to the ledge. Once in the opening above the ledge, she turned and looked at James. She smiled a roguish grin and watched as he turned reluctantly and bolted for the boy's window, slipping up and through the window in one smooth motion. She climbed back to the other side where the girls waited for her.

"We must hurry," she said to them and grabbed up the dresser by the door.

The girls rushed down the hall, the five bags of dried meat in tow; Rebecca lugged the dresser. Up the spiral stairs they climbed to their alcove, waiting for the sounds of the guard to enter the sleeping chamber.

"One quarter of an hour be dressed and in the courtyard for morning exercises," grunted the guard from below. The routine seemed to be wearing on the guards as well as the children.

Rebecca and the girls sat and waited for the guard to leave the chamber. Then they rose with the sacks. Rebecca let Sam lead the way, one bag over her shoulder. Rebecca's friends made a fine procession, conquering heroines bringing the spoils of war to their countrymen.

"The Second Born of Arnora come bearing gifts," announced Sam as she walked round and round, descending the staircase. She held a strip of dried venison as though it were a scepter. The other girls preparing for their morning turned to see who spoke. They watched Rebecca and her friends march down the stairs. Their eyes latched on the dried meat Sam carried, hunger visible on their faces. Slowly they gathered around the base of the spiral stairs. Rebecca's friends followed the script they had decided upon while preparing the meat.

"Know this," Marissa spoke, "the Second Born of Arnora stand for Arnora and with her people."

"We are the Second Born of Arnora," said Rebecca, looking from face to face, "all of us. We stand together to support those who stagger. Take this offering from we that stood so that you too may stand."

Rebecca and her friends had all eyes on them now. They stood shoulder to shoulder around the column of the spiral staircase. Rebecca knew James and the boys repeated these words in the opposite dorm. She hoped that they were having a similar reaction.

"Accept this offering and join us," said Helen, presenting the dried meat.

The girls' faces were wide, gaping; the meat held their attention as much as the speakers. The first girl approached Sam tentatively, as a stray dog would approach a stranger.

"Stand with us," said Sam as the older girl took the piece offered her.

The girl nodded when she had the meat grasped in her fist, as though fearful Sam would snatch it back. She bit into the strip and relaxed. Finally she spoke. "I will stand with you."

Slowly, the girls moved following the lead of the first. They took the offering and said the words as though entranced. The fear she saw in the girl's faces, fear of their own countrymen, angered Rebecca. The guards had worked long on these children and the results were plain. Rebecca had worried about the children's spirits breaking; from what she saw they hung by a thread. Living day to day with no support, no hope, had taken its toll on all here. Rebecca's rage at the Red Guard flared.

The line of girls dwindled as did their supply of venison. The last girl in line took her offering and walked to the gathered girls gnawing what they had accepted. A few girls had remained on the outskirts of the line. They stood facing Rebecca and her friends, nearly empty sacks hung limp from her friends' shoulders.

"There is more for you, if you'll have it," said Sam, a strip held out to one of the girls who had not joined the line.

"What would you have of us if we take your offering?" a tall lanky girl with dark blond hair said. The question was directed to Rebecca.

"This is a gift. It comes with no bindings to who accept it," Rebecca said.

"That's a lie; no one gives anything in this place freely. Everything comes at a price here," the tall girl said. The girls at her back looked ashamed and eyed the floor. Rebecca examined this group. Every other girl in the room was lean to the verge of emaciation all but these. They were of an age with Rebecca or older, signs of womanhood clearly forming. All wore lost expressions on their faces, frightened and humiliated at once. A thought slithered through Rebecca's head like a filth covered snake. She could see why these girls were leery of their gift. She had known girls in the camps that had met with this sort of treatment. She could imagine the guards tempting them, kind words and promises, luring them away from watchful eyes. Then, there had come the pawing and the groping; the thought made Rebecca sick. She welled with pity for what these girls must have experienced at the hands of the guards.

Rebecca stepped closer to the group of girls. She spoke with compassion in her voice. "The guards here may have offered you rewards and gifts, better treatment, more food, less work. But the price you paid is too high. You will not be shamed amongst us; we are sisters of Arnora. We give this gift with no price and no expectations. Please take it." Rebecca held out a strip of the venison to the tall girl who had spoken first.

"I will not die for you," she said, snatching the meat from Rebecca's hand. The others holding the meat looked at it as though they held poisonous creatures in their hands.

"We aren't asking your life for this or your dignity," said Rebecca. The others behind the tall girl stared half at Rebecca and half at the ground unable to look her full in the eye. "The Second Born of Arnora support our brothers and sisters here; for, we are far from our home. We're offering aid to those who would have it. If they find the strength to stand with us, we would gain by it. If they cannot, we still provide for our countrymen."

The girls stepped from behind their leader and took the strips Rebecca's friends offered to them. They avoided the glares their leader directed at them as they did so. Rebecca stepped closer to the girl so as not to be overheard.

"What is your name?" she asked the girl.

"What does it matter Dulac? I know yours and I know what you're doing," the tall girl spat.

"I am giving you an alternative to what the guards would have of you," Rebecca said calmly.

"You're trying to be your brother. Well, you do that and you follow him to the gallows; I won't do it. Better to face what the guards have then to end up dangling by your neck," said the girl.

"What did they offer you, other than food?" asked Rebecca.

"It doesn't matter what they offered me. I took the offer and I'm going to get it; I've already paid for it," she looked down for a moment, her cheeks reddening, and then glared back at Rebecca. "So you can keep your gift; I won't have it if it comes at the price I know you'll ask." The girl shoved the dried meat into Rebecca's chest and walked away to her alcove, hurriedly grabbing her uniform for work.

Rebecca turned back to the others who had taken the meat. They chewed away happily, talking to Rebecca's friends. They had agreed to keep secret the details of how they had acquired the venison. Until they knew they could trust the others, Rebecca would heed Broheim's lessons. Rebecca approached one of the girls that had stood with the tall girl and pulled her aside.

"Who is she?" she asked, directing a glance at the retreating back of the tall girl.

"Elisa Ruteg," said the girl.

"Do you know what the guards offered her?" Rebecca asked quietly.

"They offered us all kinds of things," tears welled in her eyes, "food mainly. "Some had trinkets; others said they could lighten our burdens."

Rebecca put a hand on the girl's shoulder. "You aren't to blame for what you did, know that. Know also, we don't judge you for taking what they offered. We have had the support of each other to keep our spirits; too many here have lost their dignity. What is your name my friend?"

"Theodora Fergus, I only took what they said because I was scared. They had us alone and we were all so hungry, even Elisa. They didn't even give us most of what they had promised. They kept coming back though, saying they were pulling strings with the Commander or they were waiting for a shipment from the Homelands. We believed them because we had no other choice. They liked Elisa most; they would get her alone and whisper things to her when they had finished with us. I don't know what they said they could give her but she was convinced that they were going to come through with it."

Rebecca's stomach boiled; these poor girls had become the Red Guard's doxies, for the promise of food. She felt ashamed at the thought of feasting on rabbits while these girls had been treated to the sick desires of the guards.

"You don't have to turn to them anymore, Theodora," Rebecca said, smiling at her. "None of you, Elisa included. Whatever their offer, it's not worth your pride."

"Thank you," said Theodora, tears streaming from her eyes. "I didn't want to keep going with them but they said if we refused, they'd cut our rations until we died. I was sure they would make true on that promise."

"You just come to one of us if your need anything from now on, anything," said Rebecca, hugging the girl to her. "You are a Second Born of Arnora now as are the rest of these girls. We watch out for one another."

Theodora thanked Rebecca again for the gift and returned to her friends to tell them the words Rebecca had spoken. The girls, realizing how much time they had to prepare, rushed to dress; most ignored washing. When all the girls were dressed, they walked to the courtyard.

The atmosphere there was palpable. The children's collective spirits were lifted higher than they had been since arriving at Valgerhold. The children met Rebecca's eyes with smiles or nods, silent thanks. Rebecca's friends took their places for morning exercises. Rebecca stood near James.

"Morning Captain," said James as he saw her approach, others around them could hear the title clearly.

"Morning, James," she returned.

"Looks like you had luck on your side of the dorms," said James, a cheery smile on his face.

"You too, any hold outs?" asked Rebecca smiling just as broadly.

"A few, no surprises as to who they would be," he said as the children began to stretch.

"The toughs from the train," she said.

"Some of them broke though when they saw the others gnawing on the gifts," he said. "Most came around by the time we had to come down."

"Gregor Mathiason?" she asked.

"Fats, he held out till the end along with that squatty leader of theirs with the freckles. We had words with him at first meal a while back. I think they get rewards for their attempts at harrying you."

"Some of the girls were getting...special attention also, for other reasons," she said, not going into too much detail. James seemed to understand though.

"Bast! These people have no limits to the depths they'll sink," he said under his breath. "Surely the girls must have come around when you told them we could help them from now forward."

"All but one, she was promised something and she is convinced it's coming to her," she said.

"Poor girl," he said, shaking his head. "They must have said they could give her something big to have her not jump at a chance to avoid...well, avoid that kind of treatment."

"Whatever it was James, we can't trust those who refused," she said as Ben Frowler began to lead them through exercises.

"What do you mean?" he asked.

"If we are going to continue with our late night activities we need to keep them out of it until we are sure they aren't going to betray us."

"Do you really think they would turn us in?" he asked.

"We have to plan for the worst," she said.

201

Twenty-two: If You Need It Done

"And this was all you found in her possessions?" said Dormon.

"Anything else she must keep on her person," said Postam.

"This journal, it was an old travel log you say. Was there anything incriminating in the contents, anything blasphemous or unnatural?" said Dormon, turning from the windows behind his desk to look at Postam.

"Truth be told, I thought it was a book of fancy at first. The drawings are a bit too incredible to believe they exist in this world. It's old though, I would guess from before the Exile," he said with hope in his voice, anything to give him a reason to grab the girl.

"There was no mention of the old ways?" Dormon asked, leaning on his desk, fists planted.

"No sir," Postam said. His hopes at retaining Dulac for the Blind Men dwindled.

"And, what news of infiltrators?" Dormon asked. He sat in his leather chair.

"There I have some promises," Postam said, smiling.

"Then, we have an informant." Dormon looked at Postam with a cocked eyebrow; a hawk looking at a mouse would have the same expression.

"Three possibilities, two boys and a girl, my ferreters worked the girls and winnowed them down to one. The boys I had giving Dulac special treatment were willing to take oaths to the New Dominion until a few days ago. Then suddenly, their cooperation seemed to have faded. I'm still trying to figure out what happened there," said Postam; Dormon gestured for him to sit.

"Yes, very strange that," said Dormon.

"Anton, I believe some of the Romarans are aiding the Arnorans in some fashion. I think they have some kind of underground resistance movement operating within Valgerhold. A few of the loyal Romarans have gotten short shrift from the others and the Arnorans seem to be at ease with some of their Romaran leaders. I suggest we replace the Romarans with our own men. If we can keep the Arnorans off kilter then…"

"Then we will never get the quantity of goods they are currently producing. Edwin, I need these children to produce. Adarian wants to make them suffer; he wants to benefit from that suffering. If they cannot produce, they are all but useless and we can have done with them. As it is now, they are extremely efficient and our New Dominion gains from their work.

Now what of these three; how close are they to our target? Are they trusted?" Dormon finished.

"Not as of yet, Anton," said Postam

"Make it clear that they will be given all that was promised if they can provide information on Dulac or what the others are doing."

"Aye sir," said Postam. He stood from his chair.

"Edwin, do not trust these children. Some may indeed be willing to sell out their countrymen but others may be playing you for the fool. Go now my friend," said Dormon.

"Aye sir," said Postam as he turned and walked from the room.

Dormon sat staring at his desk. The midday light streamed through the overhead windows onto the desktop. He looked at the manifest that Postam had brought of Dulac's belongings. Nothing indicated what he was growing to suspect, that the girl was indeed the Blind Men's quarry. The girl had all but shriveled from his notice since the first few days though. Not the usual quality of those with the Touch; they had a drive, a need to take command of people. That, above all else, is what the Red Path decried; a man was free to choose his Path without the shepherding of those with the Touch. Like what he saw developing with the girl.

True, her friends seemed to be overly dedicated to her, and the others seemed to be moving in the same direction over the last couple of days. Dormon suspected that the girl had done something to garner support from them. That must have been what dried up Edwin's leads.

If the girl was what the Blind Men hunted, then he had to look forward to them culling her within his university. Bast! But that would cause trouble. Not to mention the questions to answer as to why he had not noticed the girl earlier. He did not like explaining to bureaucrats the ways in which he worked, and they would never understand his desire to puzzle her out before retaining her. If she was indeed a re-emergent of the old ways she was worth studying before she was destroyed.

Dormon did not like being without a plan. Too much relied on others here; he preferred to rely on himself. He knew he could trust himself; in the unlikely event of things going awry, he knew he could depend on himself to land on his feet. Now though, he was forced to rely on Edwin. The man could be so vicious at times; his desire to cause the Arnorans pain drove his wits from him. Edwin would get the three to work for him though; he had his ways, no matter their *distastefulness*. Ferreters, only Edwin would name the vile scum in such fashion. Dormon wondered if the Red Path could be supported with its foundations rooted in such rotten soil. Surely the First Father would not reward the likes of Edwin at the end of his Path. For that matter Dormon was convinced he would be spending his life at his Path's end in Discordia, with so many of his comrades. No use dwelling on what could not be changed.

If the girl was the Blind Men's target then he would hand her over without hesitation; he was loyal to Mandagore Adarian in the end, and Adarian must be trusted to know the course of the Red Path. He had proved as much since the Exile and the retaking of the Homelands. The only righteous handling of the old ways was left to Adarian and those he chose to burden with the Touch. It was not Dormon's place to question his decisions. Dormon would use Edwin's infiltrators to get the information Dormon sought. If the information turned out as he thought, he would seize the girl and take her to the Strynges himself. It would be worse, though, to give the Strynges the wrong target than if he let them find her themselves. Once the girl proved true, no one would ask questions as to why he had not brought her to the attention of the New Dominion earlier.

A shiver ran through Dormon's spine. He did not like the idea of witnessing the Blind Men at work. Although he had abandoned most of the feeling long ago, he felt some remorse for the actions he set for himself; a prickling of pity for the Dulac girl itched at his mind. He pushed the feeling away. He had grown used to doing unseemly business. This would be just one more action in a long past that would see him placed firmly in the pit of Discordia.

Twenty-three: Sheepdogs

"We can't take them all, James. I know they want to help but it would be a complete disaster to expand the hunters anymore," Rebecca said as they sat at the table for mid meal. They had been planning another deer hunt for the past few days. They were inundated with requests from the others in Valgerhold to help with the next hunt. So, Rebecca and her friends were busy trying to find chores and ways in which a couple of hundred new friends could help them.

Rebecca was happy for the first time in a long while. The assaults from Postam's bootlickers had relented when most of the gang had joined the Second Born. Now they worked as bodyguards for Rebecca's friends.

Rebecca and her friends had become a bit like head commanders of the rabble of displaced children. Even the youngest, Mac, had a following of children, as young to slightly older, looking to him for information and instructions. It was almost eerie the way the others had taken to their new roles. It felt right though; they all agreed. Rebecca was trying to convince James that bringing more children out into the woods would only lead to them being spotted. It seemed strange to her that she was the one now arguing caution when it had been her who had wanted to expand the group at its beginning.

"We can have them sweep wider in the forest, Rebecca. We can flock more game together and then it will be easier to take more animals," he said, arguing heatedly.

"I understand that James. It's just that we have to remember the more we bring out, the more mouths there are to be overheard speaking where they shouldn't," she said, stirring the bowl of meatless stew they were served for mid meals.

"Come off it Rebecca," he laughed. "We have to trust them sometime. We even broke one of the hold outs, Jason Ganty by name. Now, it's only two who aren't with us, Fats and Elisa," he said, smiling. "Your plan worked; you just don't want to believe it's worked so well."

"James, what concerns me is *why* that boy joined us. We haven't done anything since that first day to make anyone think we can pull it off again." She furrowed her brow in worry.

"Broheim has been giving you more lessons, hasn't he?" asked James. "The man wouldn't trust his own mother until he had interrogated her to his satisfaction."

"Maybe, but then he would know he needn't worry about his mother stabbing him while his head was turned," she said.

"Alright, we keep the hunting parties small but we could cover more ground if we split up this time," he said.

"I agree, and if we do that, we will need some more flushers, but we keep it limited to those we can trust the most," she said.

"Right, then we'll start gathering parties together. What about the curing? We need more for that if we bring down more deer," he insisted.

"You're right. Mac, Michael, and Sam can find them from the kitchen crews; they should be used to handling meat by now. Besides, I trust the younger children more than the older for being loyal," she said.

"True, when do you want to set the date?" he said, excited.

"Three days should be enough time I would think," she said.

"Very well, oh one more thing," he said.

"What's that?" she asked.

"Don't forget we have our Commanders' meeting tonight," he smiled a wolfish grin.

Rebecca flushed bright red and nodded quickly, looking down.

The two sought a secluded spot during their night time gatherings with their friends, to read the journal. So far, they had managed to keep their escapes secret from the others, waiting until they slept, were wrapped in conversation, or kept watch for guard. Even so, curiosity was unavoidable, even in her friends. When Mac had voiced a question it had been Paul who gave them their excuse. "Captain's privilege," he had said, "It's a Commanders' meeting, to work things through." Now whenever they would make their way to a private area during one of the night's gatherings, someone would announce for all to hear, "Commanders' meeting," which was followed by waves of giggles and laughter. Rebecca had flushed the first time and had been unable to prevent it when she heard the words still. James seemed to enjoy needling her with it.

The bell sounded for everyone to return to work; Rebecca punched James in the shoulder. He rubbed it with feigned pain and rose to join his crew gathering to return to the forges.

Rebecca joined Paul and made her way to Broheim, waiting for them. Paul smiled when they met Broheim; he, on the other hand, looked concerned and Rebecca's heart beat faster.

"You look like you're finally taking to your name, Sunshine," Broheim said in a forced cheery voice, his face still held hints of concern.

"I wish you'd stop calling me that," Paul said as they walked toward the wood shop.

"You know I'm not good with names and I don't think I could recall your proper handle if I was at the point of a gun," Broheim said. He led the group across the courtyard between the dining hall and the corridors to the shops.

Rebecca ran her fingers over the stones of the well at its center as they passed. Looking over the edge, the water below moved in slow ripples away from the grated opening at the side of the well. Broheim had told her it was fed by the lake near the forest. She wondered how long the tunnels would take to traverse. She sometimes did this when she wanted to avoid a problem, come up with questions to keep her mind from nibbling at the edges of a larger issue. That issue was the chatter she knew Broheim was worried about. She could not help but hear the whispers in the dining hall, when the children thought no one would be listening. This was what she was trying to avoid in increasing the hunting parties. Human nature was to gossip. That was what Broheim had told her. Try as you might, word travels faster than fire when secrets are involved. She was glad they had not brought any of the others out to the forest yet, or even to the library. That particular bit of gossip could get more than her and her friends killed.

"Broheim, I'm trying to do as you say," she said, interrupting the banter that had continued between Paul and Broheim. The two looked at her, Paul with a puzzled look, Broheim a knowing one. He nodded.

"Come with me Skinny, we have a game to finish," he said, motioning her to follow.

They walked to his office, Paul trailing behind. Broheim closed the door and took his chair behind his desk. He took up his pipe and searched a drawer for a box of strikers. He snapped one alight and held it to the bowl of his pipe, drawing until thick aromatic smoke puffed from his mouth. His moustache hid his lower lip in a grimace when he pulled the pipe stem from his teeth.

"I know you're trying Skinny but word is spreading. The guards are beginning to question us Romarans away from one another to see if they can catch us off-footed. Those who know anything important are keener than these guards; so, we aren't going to betray anything that's going on under their noses. But Skinny, you children haven't lived long enough in this world to know how the workings spin. One of your new friends whispers something to a close friend, that close friend whispers to another, on and on, until the whisper reaches the ears of your enemy. Too many mouths are speaking in corners and that's about as obvious that something is happening as if you were to announce it to Dormon himself."

"What do you mean?" asked Paul. "I haven't noticed anyone saying anything. They wouldn't betray us. We are helping them,"

"They wouldn't do it on purpose Sunshine, that's the point. One day one of these guards is going to snatch you and bring you before Dormon. He'll have evidence on you that may have been whispered from your own lips. That's how it works."

"I don't believe it; what could they have heard?" Paul asked, looking confident.

"The Second Born of Arnora offer aid to those who would stand with them," Broheim announced, moving his hand flamboyantly as if he read a banner posted on the back wall of his office. Paul's eyes went wide. "Aid and succor to those who would stand with the Second Born." He waved his pipe about, streaming smoke. "Anything one has need of need only ask and the Second Born of Arnora shall provide." The last Paul had used himself trying to convince Gregor

Mathiason to join them the other day at mid meal. "If I heard then I'm sure Postam has heard and you can bet your eyes Dormon has."

"What do we do then Broheim?" Rebecca asked worried. "We need them with us or we won't stand a chance when the time comes to do more than hunt." Paul's mouth tightened. He was the main obstacle Rebecca had convincing the others that what was needed was to stand against the Red Guard here in Valgerhold.

"You be as careful as you can and remember most people are not as headstrong as you. Most people prefer to follow rather than lead. When it comes down to it, people are very much like sheep. All one needs is to get the first in the flock to start moving and the rest will follow along. It wouldn't hurt to have some good sheepdogs to keep the wolves at bay," he said, replacing his pipe in his teeth and puffing.

Rebecca looked at her hands thinking. Paul spoke up, "Well I'm no sheep,"

"Really Sunshine," Broheim said, looking surprised. "You seem to take to being led by your – *Captain* - fairly quick." Rebecca looked up in surprise. For him to have heard the title the others called her from whispers meant the chatter was getting closer to important information. The purpose in naming the group as they had had been to keep its members anonymous from the guards *if* they were to overhear. "Don't look at me that way Sunshine. Some of the greatest men in history have been as sheep to their captains. Just because you're following most of the time doesn't mean you don't try moving the flock one way or the other when you're at its head." Paul looked a little less insulted.

"Where do we find sheepdogs?" she asked. She still looked at her palms, trying to follow the labyrinth of spirals there with her eyes.

"They will be from the children here, just as likely to speak as any other."

Broheim smiled at her; he had pride in his eyes. "There you go Skinny," he said, leaning forward and resting his forearms on his desktop. "A good sheepdog is somewhat of a cross between the sheep and the wolves. He looks, from afar, like a member of the flock. Up close his features, his teeth, give him away for what he is in his heart. The sheep flock away when he is too near, they see only his wolfish parts. The wolves though, the wolves will see him as but a sheep, until they threaten his flock, then they'll see him for what he is, a wolf in sheep garb."

"The toughs," she said, looking into his eyes. "We need the toughs to be our sheepdogs." He nodded thoughtfully.

"They would be a good choice if you could train them; the best sheepdogs are often very much like just tame wolves," he said, leaning back into his chair.

"Gregor," she whispered.

"Are your brains addled?" Paul hissed. "Fats, you want us to get that lummox to help protect from the guards overhearing us."

"He's perfect Paul," said Rebecca. "The children are all scared of him because he's so big and Postam seems to have disposed of him as one of his bootlickers. He's adrift without a line to lead him. If we can bring him in, he can work for us."

"He may be intimidating Sunshine," said Broheim. "But that's because you're looking at him through sheep's eyes. He's scared I can see it. He's alone now and vulnerable. He may not be getting pats on the head from Postam anymore but he's still an opening that Postam could tap. He hasn't made a move to attack any of you since his gang seems to have joined you either."

"We'll bring him on the next hunt, we'll give him the glory of bringing down the deer. That should give him some sense of loyalty at least to start."

"Rebecca, you seem to be forgetting that he has yet to join us. In fact, he won't have anything to do with us. You saw how he reacted when I tried to get him to give over and join us. I thought he was going to rip my skull from my shoulders," Paul said as he paced back and forth across Broheim's office. "You go to him," Paul said, now tuning to Rebecca with an expression between worry and fear, "you tell him what we're doing, and you'll have killed us, as sure as if you had asked Postam to join us. You will have killed us."

Broheim sat nodding as Paul talked. He looked at Rebecca with a raised eyebrow. "He's got a point there Skinny. Any plans to avoid that?" Broheim sat, drawing on his pipe still staring at Rebecca.

She looked at her palm again and followed the flow of skin around and around until she reached the center of one of the spirals. She looked up, "We hold off until the night we go. We bring him in at the last minute. He won't have time to tell Postam anything if he doesn't know and when we get him out with us, we will have some leverage on him if he gets second thoughts. He'll be one of us then at least in the eyes of the Red Guard."

Broheim stabbed his pipe stem at her, smiling. "You see Sunshine this is what I've been trying to show you with these chess matches, plan for the worst."

At last meal Rebecca told James what she had planned, Paul voiced his disagreements but James sat thinking.

"I don't know, Rebecca. Bringing in someone raw like this, it could be dangerous. How do we get him to come along? How do we

213

keep him from going to the guards as soon as he knows how we get out? There are a lot of things that can go wrong."

Paul nodded as James spoke. "You see, you listen to James. He knows what he's talking about."

Rebecca ignored the comment. "He'll follow us James, I'm sure of it. He hasn't come to us because he's still scared of Postam. I know it seems strange but I think he just needs to see that what we offer gives him a place to hold onto. He is acting as if the gang of toughs is still with him. He hasn't seen anything to offer him a place yet. We give him a place to fit James and he'll be with us."

James sat staring at the table, he looked at Paul. Paul's eyes gleamed with hope.

"Alright, we'll try it your way," James said. Paul's shoulders slumped. "If he makes to turn on us though, we're going to have to put him down, somehow." Paul's eyes went from sullen to shock in an instant.

"How do we 'put him down' exactly?" Paul hissed.

"I don't know; but we can't have him knowing our secrets and running to Postam with them. It'll be us or him at that point, Rebecca, and you know it." James looked at her in concern.

Rebecca nodded regretfully. She had thought of that as well. Could she do it if she had to? Kill a man, a fellow Arnoran at that? She prayed it wouldn't come to it. She prayed harder than she had in a long time.

Twenty-four:
A Spy Among Them

"What do you mean she doesn't trust you?" Postam said, his a voice near a growl. He sat at his desk in his dim office, the gas lanterns on the walls turned down low. The flickering orange light made the shadows on his face dance. He looked on his last remaining hope of infiltrating the Dulac girl's inner circle. He found that dealing with children could be harder than grown men. At least men knew the depravities that another would sink to, to gain what he wanted. Children hadn't had the experiences to know those depths yet. They still trusted too much, but he was hoping to impart some of his knowledge on this child tonight.

"You are telling me you have not joined their group yet." He pulled his dagger from his belt and tested the edge with his thumb. He looked at the child, flanked on either side by one of his ferreters, and made his most concerted effort to cast terror in the child's heart. "If you can't get close to them, you are of no use to me. Do you understand? I can leave you with my two friends here to do with as they please. I can assure you they hold as much animosity toward Arnorans as I and I don't think they'll be as friendly." He gestured to the ferreters at the child's sides; they each grabbed a shoulder. The child wept and begged for mercy, pleading and struggling as the ferreters began to pull away.

"Wait!" He paused to give the child time to latch on to the opening he was going to give. "Wait, I think I might know a way for you to appeal to them. You are going to have to be vigilant. I want to

215

know everything that Dulac is doing, especially if anything seems strange to you. If she has any devices on her that behave oddly or if she does anything – peculiar, I want to know it."

The child nodded vigorously. It was hard to see with the lights so dim but Postam was sure he saw tears streaming down the child's face. He liked it when he caused fear. He liked it better when he caused pain and that was just what he intended. He stood and walked to the child.

"I'm going to give you something that will make them believe you are really one of them. You just remember what you have to lose. Freedom waits for those who aid the New Dominion's Red Guard."

* * *

The last day before the hunt saw the Second Born's plans nearly done. Michael, Sam, and Mac had recruited several of the kitchen crews to be their meat curers. Michael assured Rebecca that the children knew what they were doing; they were in charge of preparing the meat served to the guards in Valgerhold. Sam and Mac vouched for their loyalty. Some of the new recruits had seen the whipping post more than once for trying to sneak from the kitchens. Arthur, Lester, and Gene had found more children to help make Arthur's woolen overshoes for the flushers.

James had questioned Jason Ganty, the latest member of the Second Born, about his reasons for joining. James said that Ganty was offered many things to pass information to Postam, including freedom. He had said the only reason he hadn't taken the offer was because his parents had told him never to trust a Felsofese man on his word alone. Postam refused to show him anything that would lead him to believe he could make true on his promises; so, Ganty had joined the Second Born. He had decided at least he could get a meal out of the deal. The words hadn't inspired the most confidence in the new boy but at least the words sounded authentic.

Elizabeth offered some more intriguing news. Elisa had come to her, asking if she could join the Second Born. Elizabeth said the girl had come crying, her face swollen and bruised. She said that Elisa had been with the guards the night before. She had asked about the progress of the promises they had made her. When they put her off she had badgered them until one had lost his temper and begun slapping her. Elizabeth hadn't been able to tell the story without crying. She said Elisa had come to her because she was ashamed to approach Rebecca after the way she had talked to her. That left one man standing on the outside, Gregor Mathiason.

Rebecca had made sure that everyone did what they could to isolate Gregor. She wanted him weak and off guard when she made her move on him. The children had snubbed him at every turn. His former gang refused to speak with him. He was forced to sit away from everyone at meals. In the wood shop children made efforts to avoid eye contact. He was alone and without ground to stand on. Rebecca hoped that she could act before Postam made use of him. She decided to move at last meal, the night of their planned hunt.

The meal nearly finished, she stood and walked over to the hulking boy, sullenly eating his stew in silence. He was larger than some of the guards and he wasn't fully a man yet. He was an intimidating form most of the children. Rebecca approached him from behind and tapped him on the shoulder. He half turned his head and peered at her from over his shoulder, his thick brow hiding most of his eye.

"What?" he grunted.

"Can I join you?" she asked with confidence in her voice.

"No, now, you can leave," he said, turning back to his stew.

Rebecca stared at the back of his closely cropped skull; the brown stubble swirled around the back of his head. From this angle he looked like some enormous baby, the thick layer of fat and rounded shoulders fit at least. But those ham sized hands would have been out of place on any infant. She walked around the table and sat in front of him, watching as he shoveled the stew into his mouth. He paused mid-chew and looked up from those heavy brows.

"I told you to get out of here Dulac," he mumbled around the food in his mouth.

"You seem to be alone a lot lately," she said, leaning forward.

His chewing reminded her of the times she went into Arinelle with her family; the cows at market chewed their cud in the same way. She smiled.

"I don't need nobody following me around," he said, looking back to his bowl.

"I understand. You're a large fellow; I'm sure you can take care of yourself, but what if you couldn't? See these guards; they're watching us right now." She rearranged herself on the bench, getting to her knees and leaning in toward Gregor, over the table. "You see the guards, they don't particularly like me."

"Neither do I," he growled.

"Well, that may be but to these guards," she gestured toward the men, standing at the entrance and exit of the room, they seemed to all be looking her way, "we look like friends just now." She reached out and patted him on the shoulder.

"Why are you doing this?" he said, spooning the last bit of stew into his mouth. "I never hurt you, you were too quick. The Commander doesn't talk with me since you spoke to me in the courtyard, says I'm damaged goods. And don't start any of that Second Born nonsense; we aren't never getting out of here and we had better get used to it. That's what the Commander says at least." He seemed to realize he was talking a second after he finished the last sentence. His eyes went wide.

Rebecca was shocked. She had her thoughts that the Red Guard wouldn't let them leave but for Postam to come out and say it to one of them, she couldn't believe it. Her head spun as fast as it ever had. She made quick steps in her planning of this conversation.

"Gregor, did he say that to you? They aren't going to let us leave?" she asked, truly leaning in to whisper to him. He seemed to slowly understand that she had heard what he said.

"I won't tell no one else, no one will believe you heard it from me," he said, his large dark eyes going wider still. "You listen to me Dulac; if you try taking me down with you…"

"Gregor, listen to me," she cut him off, "the Second Born of…"

"No, I won't listen to that. Bast! You are as bad as they say. They said you'd be trying to do this, take control, and start leading everyone in a revolt. I won't be a part of it I'm watching my own skin now." He made a move to get up but Rebecca found herself pulling him down. She looked around and caught the looks from her friends across the room. Shock filled their faces and James had turned and looked on the verge of doing something brash.

"Gregor, sit down for the Father's sake," she hissed at him. "I'm not trying to do anything to you. We need you." He looked at her as if she were speaking some foreign tongue. He lowered himself back to the bench and looked at her with a steady hard gaze.

"We need a guardian, someone to help watch *our* skins. You are the man I chose. I need you." He began to relax and leaned an arm on the table.

"What do you need me to watch your skin for?" he had a look on his face like Rebecca had just asked him to dance.

"It's not like that, you lummox," she spoke before she thought. *Oh wonderful Rebecca, insult him before he's with you,* she thought. He chuckled to himself though, a deep rumble of a noise that shook his shoulders.

"Don't worry Dulac, anyone with half a wit knows you got that Bligh bloke hung on you," he said. Rebecca wondered if he was as plain dumb as he looked.

"I'm trusting you with this much Gregor, got it." He hesitated then nodded, she continued. "James and some others are going to wake you tonight; go with them and I'll explain what we're doing."

Rebecca's heart pounded as Gregor looked at the table, silently thinking. She had given him enough information for him to bring Postam down on her. He looked up at her at last. The last bell tolled and the light outside was growing pink as he stared at her.

"Aye," he grunted. He stood and walked from the table.

Rebecca slumped back, sitting on her feet on the bench at the table. She watched as Gregor walked through the throng of children; a wake surrounded him where no child would enter. *Just like a sheepdog cutting through the flock,* she thought.

Twenty-five: The Hunt

Rebecca couldn't relax as she lay in her bed, waiting for the guard to finish locking the door to the courtyard. There was no point to waiting for the others in the chamber to sleep now. They knew Rebecca and her friends had managed to find a way out of the locked dorms, out into the woods. Rebecca had insisted they keep the particulars of their escapes secret from everyone else. There was no way to hide it forever. This night would see more children in the library below than had been there since the New Dominion took control of Romara.

Rebecca rose from her bed and gathered what she would need for tonight. Her coat, her father's pocket watch, and for later her grandfather's journal, she put them all in her satchel and took a deep breath. She tried to calm her heart's pounding but the more she tried the higher in her throat it seemed to climb. As much blood as she felt pumping through her, she found it odd that her hands and feet felt like ice. If things went sideways tonight, she and her friends might not live long enough to see tomorrow night.

She turned to her friends; they had mixed looks on their faces. Fear, nervousness, excitement, all blended together with a kind of anticipation. They looked to her for a sign it was time to move. She nodded and they walked to the spiral staircase.

Walking around the stairs, the others in the chamber stared fixedly at the group descending. Some stood still; others seemed to be dancing from foot to foot. Theodora caught Rebecca's eye and she knuckled her forehead in the Arnoran salute; Rebecca smiled at her. At the foot of the stairs a gathering of girls waited. They all wore the grays and browns of their uniforms, coats and boots, hats and gloves. This was the group of new recruits Sam, Michael, and Mac had chosen. They were so small to Rebecca's eyes. They looked up to the group as they reached the floor, gleams of pride in their eyes. Rebecca knew these children's lives were in her hands and if she stepped wrong, they would pay for it.

A young girl stepped to Sam and saluted. "All's set Ma'am," the girl's voice was so small and the scene so ridiculous, Rebecca had to hide a grin. *Children playing war, was that all they were?* Rebecca wondered. She hoped they were more than that.

"Good work Lain," Sam said to the girl. Sam turned to Rebecca, "Captain, the new crew is ready."

Rebecca nodded and looked around the room. Eyes gleamed with tears, hands clasped together over mouths in silent prayer, and looks of envy. She saw that too, others wanted to come along tonight; she found that comforting for some reason. Rebecca caught Theodora's eye again and gestured the girl to come closer.

"Aye, Captain," the girl said when she approached.

"I need it kept calm in here tonight. What we are going to do took us almost the entire night last time. I don't want anyone coming to find us if you think it's taking too long. Whatever happens, you keep these girls quiet and in here, understand?" Rebecca finished.

Theodora nodded and wished her good hunting. Rebecca gathered her friends and the new girls that would be going and they made their way down to the end of the corridor to the door. Rebecca turned back as Marissa set the dresser at the door. The others were gathered around the entrance to the sleeping chamber, looking down the hall at those at the dorm entrance. *Well, here your secret is lost,* she thought as Helen followed by Marissa climbed to the window ledge. Helen pushed open the transom and slipped through. Rebecca could see the girls' astonishment as they stood at the opposite end of the hall. Elizabeth helped up the last few girls and followed after, leaving Rebecca last to go. She saluted to the girls down the hall and climbed up and out of the window.

On the other side of the door James waited for her. His face was a study in nervousness. Gregor's hulking mass was nowhere to be seen.

"Where is he?" Rebecca asked James quietly.

He nodded to the door. "Other side," he paused and looked at her, a disbelieving grin climbing across his face. "He's helping the others reach the ledge."

Rebecca turned and watched as boy after boy climbed through the opening above the door. Paul helped them down to the landing. When he saw Rebecca, his face was half way between laughing and astonishment. He shrugged and helped the last boy down. Suddenly a large form filled the opening and two thick legs came through the window. Gregor lowered himself to the landing. He turned and walked to Rebecca, James staring up at the boy with raised eyebrows.

"What now?" he asked; his voice seemed to fill the stairwell even in his whisper. The other children gathered round shifted their glances between Rebecca and Gregor and back again.

"Now, we move," she whispered. "James if you'd lead the way please." He nodded and waved for the others to follow him. Moving quickly but sure to keep the noise low, James led the forty children down to the library two floors below. He ushered them in when they arrived and Paul took the lead from there, guiding the procession to the hidden corner. James waited for Rebecca and Gregor to appear then followed them through and pulled the door closed after him.

The other children marveled at the library. Row upon row of dark wooden shelves held hundred if not thousands of books, most covered in dust from lack of use. The children gathered in the corner Rebecca and her friends had used to hold their meetings. They sat; their numbers crowded the space. Arthur and others handed out the woolen overshoes. Rebecca and James stood before the group. Gregor stood to one side, his massive arms crossed over his chest, eyeing the proceedings. The children looked at Rebecca and James for instruction; their eyes continued to dart to Gregor though, as if he was some half tame beast waiting to fall upon them.

"This is how it works," Rebecca began. She looked sidelong at Gregor as he shifted. "We leave here and exit up through that door." Rebecca pointed to the door to the courtyard above, the children followed her finger. "When we reach the courtyard above, we are going to slip into a vent. Now, it's dark and a bit tight so, if you don't think you can take it say now, there is no shame," Rebecca waited.

Michael stood. "Captain that was one of the things we looked for first, they all say they can handle the vents." He sat back and Rebecca nodded.

"Very well, you follow your leaders and stay together. There are crossways and down-shafts that we are all used to by now but you won't see them until you're already down them. We guide the way with this." Rebecca held up the pocket watch. "It takes a bit of getting used to but once your eyes adjust you should be able to catch hints of the vents. We exit through one of the down-shafts and out into the grass field you can see from the dorm windows." She gestured toward it. "If we're going to be seen, it's going to be crossing that field. Watch for your leaders to give the signal then move quickly." The children nodded.

A hand went up and a girl stood in the back, it was Elisa. James had talked Rebecca into including the other new members along with Gregor so as to keep an eye on them. "Rebecca, if I might, what is he doing here?" She pointed to Gregor who smiled at her maliciously.

"He is our second bow tonight." A murmur went through the children. Gregor looked at her with wide eyes. James spun his head to stare at her. She went on. "I'm going to act as a flusher tonight. It will be James and Gregor tonight on the bows."

The children quieted and Rebecca continued. "If we're all ready then we will move out."

As the children began to move, James leaned over to her. "I don't know if this is such a great idea Rebecca. I thought we were going to talk these things through before you acted."

"I didn't think about it until just now," she said back. "What could bind him more to us than to have him act as our second bow though?" James hesitated then nodded in agreement.

Gregor came up to the two. "I don't know about this Dulac," he said to her. Rebecca was surprised to see worry on his face. "What if I miss: I could kill one of these kids or at least not bring anything down." The fact that he had been concerned about the others first gave Rebecca hope.

"Don't worry, Gregor, you'll do just fine. Just remember to breathe and relax. It worked for me the first time." She moved to follow the line of children following Paul up to the catwalk and door above. James stepped up and slapped Gregor on the back.

"It's great isn't it?" he said, smiling.

"What's great?" Gregor grumbled back.

"Being led around by a girl half your size. Well, I guess she's only three quarters my size but the feeling's the same. Don't try to fight it though – you'll lose in the end." James followed after Rebecca.

"That girl's going to get us killed, you know," Gregor said, catching up to James.

"Yeah, I know that too," he smiled a mischievous grin back at the huge boy, climbing the stairs after him.

Out on the courtyard, Rebecca looked up to the stained glass windows above. Boys and girls lined the windows at either tower, looking down to the group exiting the door from the library below.

Rebecca unlocked the hatch and swung the door wide. James went first. Rebecca handed him the watch and he tied his coat around his waist. He slipped through the steaming entrance into the dark and disappeared. The next children followed his lead, tying their coats around their waists and climbing into the vent. The line of children dwindled and it was her and Gregor last. She motioned him into to vent, he reluctantly stepped in. His form barely fit inside the opening. Rebecca wondered if he would call off, but he slipped in and crawled after the others. Rebecca closed the hatch after her and counted her movements; she and the others had memorized the number of steps to the features of the vents in case they needed to negotiate them in complete darkness.

After a few minutes' crawling, Rebecca saw the green glow that said James was ahead with the watch. James had to press flat against the wall in order to let Gregor pass to the down shaft. Once he was moving down, Rebecca waited on the edge to give him time to gain some distance. Before she slipped over the edge, James stopped her. He stared into her face in the green glow and smiled. He leaned forward and she met him half way. The minutes seemed to stretch as

226

they kissed; his hand held the back of her head and she brushed his cheeks with her finger tips. They parted and she could feel her heart leap in her chest.

"Good hunting," he said with a grin.

"You too," she said, and slipped over the edge to the rungs below.

She climbed hand after hand down the rungs until the gray light from the night said she had reached the open hatch below. She stepped out of the steam, billowing from the vent, to join the others in the field below. Paul held both sets of bows and quivers, he stepped to Rebecca.

"Are you sure you want to give *him* one of *these*," Paul whispered, indicating Gregor who was looking around at the buildings and the field. She nodded and Paul walked over to Gregor. Slowly, Paul held out the bow and quiver to Gregor towering over him. Gregor took the bow and hung the quiver around his shoulder. He tested the draw on the string and nodded to Paul. James stepped from the opening and Rebecca closed it behind him. Paul handed James the other bow and quiver and the children waited for the signal to move.

James took the lead; a small group followed after him. Next, Paul led another group when the first had disappeared into the forest. Group after group slipped into the forest beyond until they were all hidden. Gregor and Rebecca crossed the field last and dashed into the forest after the others.

"How did you plan all this without the guards finding out?" he asked.

"Luck," she laughed, "pure luck."

Rebecca and Gregor joined the others at the camp they had prepared. Sam, Michael, and Mac took the lead guiding the group in charge of curing. They readied the clay pots and gathered wood. The flushers got their woolen overshoes and gathered near their assigned bowman, a wider space around Gregor than James. Rebecca joined the group around Gregor.

"Why don't we just run?" he asked when she approached him.

"Don't think about it. We wouldn't make it far with this many of us. The guards would be on us before midday," she said. "Besides, what about the others back in the dorms? Would we just leave them for the guards to take out their anger?"

He looked at her thoughtfully. "Is that why you are still here? You could have been gone long ago from as much preparation as I see here."

She nodded and his jaw tightened; after a moment, he nodded.

Rebecca explained to the other flushers how they were to move. They practiced a bit and then they moved deeper into the woods, James' group going off another way. Once Rebecca's group had found a small clearing to flush animals toward, she found a place for Gregor to wait. She led the flushers out into the woods away from Gregor.

They swept wide into the forest. The only thing she could see was the movement of the gray brown shapes in the distance; slowly, even they faded into the trees. The air was cool but warmer than that first time they had done this. The trees foliage was denser too. The moon was full and cast the forest in a cool blue-gray light. She listened for the sounds that the flushers had come on a deer. The muffled steps from her woolen overshoes barely registered in her ears. She stalked quietly into the forest, listening for snaps of twigs or stamps of hooves. Nothing. The woods were utterly silent. Her heart sank. Maybe the game had moved off into better grounds.

A wolf's cry broke the silence, a mournful sound that reached to her soul and sent shivers along her limbs. So, they weren't alone in these woods. The cry sounded far though. She hoped the others wouldn't spook and turn back. She continued deeper into the woods. She edged through a thicket and, as she was about to step completely through, she caught sight of a shape moving. Head down, the deer nibbled at a small bush of berries. From the corner of her eye, something shifted. She looked slowly over and saw another, larger form, moving in the dark. She quietly backed out through the thicket and stalked wide around the two. When she had some ground between her and the deer she began her run.

"Whoop," she cried out. The sound of running hooves came from beyond the thicket. She chased after them. Somewhere off in the woods she heard cracking limbs and leaves shifting.

"Whoop," came from the trees to her side, she smiled. Someone else tailed the deer. Chasing the sound of the crashing animals, she spotted Lester, a grin plastering his face.

"Whoo-oop," he cried out when he saw her.

She ran through the brush and heard more crashes around her; the other flushers were closing the trap. She could see the clearing up ahead. More cries and the deer were in full panic in front of them; nearly colliding with one another, they tried to escape. She saw flashes of white as the deer jumped over fallen logs. Suddenly, they burst into the clearing.

"Down," she cried out, as the others ran into the clearing. They dropped, sliding in the leaves and pine straw. Arrows thwacked to the sides of them. *Please Father, let him take one of them before he kills one of us,* she prayed. Suddenly, one of the shapes faltered and fell to the ground. She could see Gregor, working the bow as fast as he could, trying to take the other. She closed her eyes and concentrated on him. *Calm, breathe, relax,* she tried sending her thoughts to him. She pushed her own feelings out, reaching, *calm, breathe, relax, calm, breathe;* something inside her moved. She felt the ground beneath her but it felt like she was falling even as she lay on the leaves and pine straw. Startled, she opened her eyes and watched as one last arrow flew after the gray brown shape leaping away. It crumpled in mid-stride and fell in a rolling heap to the forest floor. He had done it; he had taken them both.

Everything froze in that instant after the deer toppled to the ground; the flushers who had urged the deer toward Gregor lay looking ahead at the scene before them. The forest was silent; Rebecca thought she would be deafened from the thud of blood through her head. Gregor's chest heaved as he let out a last held breath and his shoulders slumped, the tension in them released. He looked at Rebecca, his dark eyes wide with shock. A grin twitched his cheek, vanished, and then slowly spread back across his huge face. Nervous laughs – as though testing to see they could still breathe – from the flushers began in a wave as they stood, brushing the forest debris from their clothes.

Lester approached behind her as Rebecca rose from the ground, leaned over, and whispered from the side of his mouth. "I wouldn't have believed that much man could move so quickly if I hadn't spied it myself." He shook his head in disbelief as he moved on to where Gregor stood near the deer. "Nice shot, man," he shouted to Gregor.

"I cannot believe it," Gregor said in a breathy voice. "I was lost with that last. It kept coming on but I couldn't focus," he continued to stare at Rebecca, walking after Lester. He blinked and swallowed hard.

"Something happened, something strange. I can't explain it. It was like I was standing here, the deer escaping, and it... it moved,"

"Of course it moved, it was trying to keep from getting your shot through it," Lester said, slapping the large boy on the back. "Which, I might add, you seem to have put solidly through the poor creature's heart." He bent to examine the deer.

"It wasn't like that," Gregor said as they stood looking down on the collapsed animal. "Everything... everything," he looked around the forest and the ground too as though to make sure it was still there. "The ground, the trees, everything but that deer seemed to be moving and shifting; I felt calm, relaxed, I breathed and took the shot as the deer moved like it was falling through cold molasses." He looked down into Rebecca's eyes. "As soon as the shaft left the bow I knew it was going to hit its mark, I knew it, and then everything fell back. The forest stopped and the deer ran at full tilt and the arrow hit and... and I don't know; it was like I said, strange." He still gaped, wide eyes staring down at Rebecca.

She felt cold bumps climbing her arms and the back of her neck. *Everything fell back he had said, and my own thoughts, calm, relax, breathe, from his mouth. What had happened?* She didn't know but she felt her stomach flutter and her hands felt weak. She noticed the other flushers had formed a circle around them; the patted Gregor on the back and looked at the deer with disbelief plain on their faces. Whatever had happened, it didn't change the fact that they still stood in the forest with work to do.

"Good job," she said, pausing to take the fear out of her voice. "We need to get these animals back to the camp, but first, we give thanks." She went on with the words she and James had said over that first deer they had brought down; not forgetting to thank the animals for their sacrifice to help them. She felt that was almost as important as thanking the Father for providing the animals for them. They, after all, had to end their lives.

With the words said, the children gripped the animals to haul them back toward the camp. Gregor managed to carry most of the weight of the larger of the two animals himself. When they spotted the light from the fires of the camp, some of the energy that had been flagging as they wrestled with the weight seemed to return. Rebecca noticed the line of silhouettes of small children staring into the woods, watching for the hunters and flushers' return. They leapt and jumped in celebration as the first to spot them pointed and gave cry to the others.

"Rebecca's back," she heard from a voice she thought was the girl Sam had named as Lain. Rebecca smiled and pushed her thoughts back. The time to think over what had happened in that clearing was not now.

"Two!" Sam said in astonishment, looking on as the animals came into the firelight. "Bast! How did he get two?"

"Watch your language Sam," Rebecca admonished lightly. The girl was just excited. "You have your crew start work on this one while we start on the other." Sam nodded, her smile never faltered as she gathered her small friends from the kitchens. They began to skin and cut the deer for cooking. Rebecca was surprised the younger children had such hardy stomachs for the work. She thought she might wretch the first time she did this. "Sam, have you spotted James yet?"

She shook her head. "Not yet, but we heard his flushers not long ago from the other side of camp. So they may be coming soon."

As if the talk had summoned him, James and the other hunting party stepped into the firelight across the camp from where Rebecca stood. He carried a buck by the antlers with the other flushers reaching in to grab the animal where they could. He stopped and smiled as he found her eyes.

"You seem to have come out in front Captain," he yelled to her and resumed walking to where the others prepared the animals. "You've brought two to our one and our newest man on top of it, working the bow. I begin to wonder if you don't have Arnora's luck."

"Complements will skin you none of these animals James," she said, unable to keep the mirth from her voice. Her relief and joy had pushed her thoughts further back in her mind. "Gregor is a fine bowman, I must say," she said, looking at the large boy. He had stared off at the fires as though thinking. He looked at the two of them and his grin returned.

"I guess I am at that," he said in his deep voice.

The work took less time than the previous hunt had, with so many more hands to do the cutting and scraping. Before too long, the carcasses were reduced to bone and sinew and the meat was prepared and cooking in the clay pots. Rebecca and the others went to wash the gore from themselves in the nearby lake. The water still felt like ice even though the air was warmer, and the children shivered and breathed hard by the time they were clean. The time slipped away though and the meat from the hunt still needed to be moved back to the dorms. Arthur produced more slings to carry the meat that had finished cooking back to the library; as soon as the first batch was off the fire Rebecca's friends led groups carrying full loads back toward the vents.

When all the fires were doused and the cleanup of the campsite complete, Rebecca, Gregor, and James were the last outside of the library. They gave the camp a once over to make sure no embers continued to burn. That done, the three started back.

"What say you Gregor?" James asked as they walked through the forest. There was still no sign of dawn. "You seemed pleased with yourself, bringing down those deer."

The huge boy looked to James with a wry grin. "I never knew I could shoot one of these," he said, hefting the bow. "Did pretty well for a first go at it."

"You said something back there, Gregor, about the forest falling while you were shooting," Rebecca said. After the work had been completed, the thoughts crept back into her mind. Her stomach had not stopped its fluttering and her hands still felt weak like she had just woken from sleep and her strength hadn't come yet. "You said everything shifted and the deer stood still."

"What are you talking about?" James said with a nervous laugh.

"It was nothing. I think it was just the heat of the hunt that took me," Gregor said but the grin had faded from his face and he looked near worry.

"Rebecca, why do you ask?" James looked at her, his brow furrowed in concern.

"I felt something back there when I was lying on the ground. I was watching Gregor shoot at the last deer and he was missing. I just wanted make him remember to be calm, to breathe..."

"Relax," Gregor said. "Calm, breathe, relax. It ran through my head when I thought I was going to lose the last one. Then everything shifted like I said."

James looked on Rebecca his face concerned. Rebecca stared back with worry in her eyes.

"I felt something in me move. It felt like my whole body was falling for a moment then it was over. I reached out, trying to push calm to him, trying to get him to relax. James, my stomach feels like there is a swarm of bees flying around in it and my hands are weak. I think...I think I did something back there."

James looked down at the forest floor as he walked, thinking. "I don't know Rebecca. I never learned anything about what was possible with the Links. Maybe you did do something."

Gregor looked like he was listening to complete gibberish. "What are you talking about?" he asked. "What did she do to me? I'm telling you Dulac, if you did something to me, I want to know it. Bligh you answer if she can't; what did she do?"

James looked torn. He looked from Gregor to Rebecca. Rebecca stared at her hands as if just noticing them for the first time. Gregor goggled wide eyed in fear. James looked at Rebecca and spoke words that, if Gregor were to tell Postam, would see her hanging before daybreak. "Rebecca has been trying to learn to do something forbidden by the New Dominion and the Red Guard. She may have had an encounter with something they deem blasphemous."

Gregor relaxed, his shoulders slouched to their accustomed position, and his breathing smoothed out. He stared at Rebecca with mixed expression that neither James nor Rebecca could understand.

Gregor took them both in as he spoke. "You spoke of Links, the Kilaray." Now it was James and Rebecca who stood gaping. Gregor reached into the collar of his shirt and pulled from within a charm on a length of leather cord, a snow white owl grasping a lantern in its talons, a symbol of the Old Religion. "My grandmother was a devout believer in the First Father and the Links he created. She told me if I was ever Touched with the Kilaray I should consider myself blessed."

In the distance a wolf cried out, the mournful howl brought the three back to where they were standing.

"I will show you something but we need to get back," she said, shivering. The three made their way back to the hatch and into the library where the children were gathered. Stepping down the last few stairs to the lower level of the library, the three were greeted like heroes. The children encircled them as they made their way to the corner of the library. All the while, they were given slaps on the back and had their hands shaken. Rebecca knew that these children needed the hope that came from this hunt as much as the nourishment it would provide.

When the congratulations settled and the children fell silent, Rebecca gave direction as to how the meat should be divided. There would be more than enough to distribute to those in the dorms; so, they would have a supply of meat to last for a time. She sent the children back in groups, her friends acting as leaders, to take the meat to the others above. When they began to move, Rebecca and James broke off, asking Gregor to follow.

In another secluded corner of the library, Rebecca sat on the floor between two leather chairs. She set her satchel in her lap and waited for James and Gregor to take the two chairs. When they were seated, Rebecca took her grandfather's journal out of the bag and handed it to James.

"This is a travel log my grandfather left to my father. It was one of the few things I was able to collect from my home before we were forced to the camps." James handed Gregor the book to look through. He stared at the first few pages and then looked back to Rebecca as if sensing that there was more to be said. "When I was young, I would look through this journal, my brother at my side and we would daydream about visiting the places my grandfather had described and drawn. I was intimately aware of every aspect of that book. Later when I showed James the journal, something happened. It may have happened sometime earlier, I'm not certain but what I am sure of is that this book is very special." She got to her knees and moved closer to Gregor holding the book, watching intently what Rebecca was doing. Ever so slowly, she extended her hand and touched the cover of the worn leather journal. Gregor's eyes bulged from his skull as he watched the sweeps and lines of script leak into the pages. His gasp seemed to hold the space in silence.

"You see Gregor," whispered James, "this book has Links to her and her to it. We need to keep this secret, because if the Red Guard here were to learn of this and what it means, Rebecca and I, and now you, would be killed."

He nodded slowly and reached, with shaking hands, to turn the page and look at the next. "First Father, send me courage," he whispered under his breath.

* * *

The three sat in the corner talking. Rebecca explained what the text was; what she could tell from what was written. But a set of eyes watched from the shadows and their owner needed hear no more. Staring from behind one of the old bookshelves, a listener heard words that had given the spy hope. Rebecca had given the spy the information that Postam had asked. Silently, the eyes turned and the spy crept back toward the others leaving for the dorms above.

"Come on now, that's a Commander's meeting over there," said Paul, escorting the spy into one of the groups headed for the dorms.

Now to tell the Commander and gain my freedom, thought the spy.

* * *

On returning to the dorms, Rebecca had much on her mind. The puzzles were piling on one another and sorting the pieces had become frustrating. She was certain that she had done something in the woods to reach out to Gregor but she was at a loss for what that was. She had tried again in the library but without any effect.

Rebecca felt nervous; what if what she had done broke something in her? What if she had done something wrong and now she would never be able to see or touch the Kilaray? James tried to reassure her that that isn't what happened but they knew neither could be sure.

Gregor finally dismissed himself and went to make sure all went well in the dorms. He had taken to being a member of the Second Born almost as soon as Rebecca had talked to him in the dining hall. She had been right about him; all he needed was a place in the group to feel at ease.

The other two new recruits had worked well also. Jason Ganty and Elisa had acted as flushers for James. They had located the deer that he had brought down. Something still bothered her though. The stories the two had given were just convincing enough to make the group let their guard down. Ganty was smug and conceited and his story fit that he was working for the best deal. Elisa's face, still yellow and brown in places, lent her credence. Something nagged at the back of Rebecca's mind though like the first touch of a web that would entangle her if she made one more step.

Her time alone with James though pushed the thoughts away for a while. He had embraced her the moment Gregor exited, his arms held her close and his mouth found its place against hers. She felt abuzz all over and the fluttering in her stomach had diminished. She sat with him on the floor, resting her head against his chest, listening to the beat of his heart. He caressed her cheek softly and ran his fingers through her dark red-brown hair. She craned her head to look into his face; his cheeks were flushed and his warm brown eyes were nearly all pupil. She smiled at him; he bent and they kissed again.

She shook her head, coming back to where she was, but the smile remained on her lips. She walked down the corridor now after she had made her difficult separation from James on the landing. He had sighed deeply as he watched her climb through the window and she had chuckled at him. Now, she approached the entrance to the sleeping chamber. She walked through the doors into the round chamber, the gray light from dawn threw greens and blues and yellows on her from the stained glass. Her breath caught when her eye took in what waited for her.

All round the chamber, girls stood stiff the knuckles of their thumbs and forefingers pressed to their foreheads. Helen stepped to her, saluted, and spoke.

"The Second Born of Arnora welcomes back our Captain."

Rebecca felt her eyes burning, on the edge of tears; she held them back. All the girls stood in salute to her, waiting. She had felt that James acted a fool with all this saluting but now she realized that the others hadn't. They were proud to be a part of Rebecca's army and they waited for her. She saluted them all in return and started to speak.

"Thank you," she began and had to stop to clear her throat before she could continue. "You have done well and I am proud of you. You bring honor to your families and yourselves. Now, please eat and hide away that which you can for later."

The children around the room relaxed and came to greet her first hand. After they had all spoken what they wanted to say, Helen told them to return to their beds before the guards came to wake them, for it was nearly that time.

Returning to their alcove, Rebecca and her friends were awash in relief and pride. They sat in their beds smiling at each other and to themselves; waiting for the sound they knew would come.

The footsteps approached and then the guard walked into the chamber.

"One quarter of an hour be dressed and down in the courtyard for morning exercises." The guard turned and left. Rebecca heard the sounds as the others quickly jumped from their beds, beginning their day as true members of the Second Born of Arnora.

Twenty-six:
What Lay Ahead

In the courtyard, the exhaustion of a busy night couldn't compete with the excitement of what the children had accomplished. Ben Frowler commented on how lively they all seemed and eyed Rebecca with a worried smile. Did he know? Had Broheim talked to him? Rebecca meant to ask when she talked next to Broheim. She had been so concerned about the plans for the hunt and bringing everyone to her side that she hadn't thought about what was next. She didn't know where to go from here.

After first meal, Rebecca walked close to Broheim; his eyes were tight and his mouth set in a grimace as he led the group to the wood shop. Rebecca felt concern immediately. She walked near him around the big well in the center of the courtyard; her mind seemed drawn to that well; it tugged at her thoughts. Shaking her head, she brought her mind around to the problem at hand. She turned to Broheim and asked if everything was alright.

"What?" he said harshly as if looking for an enemy, then, realizing it was Rebecca, he began again in a milder tone. "Oh, Skinny it's you. I was just lost in my mind there for a moment."

"I asked if all was well," she said again.

"Yes, yes, it's nothing to concern you child." He looked to the balcony that led to Dormon's room. "Not yet at least," he said under his breath. Rebecca didn't think that he had meant to say that out loud. She knew something was wrong; it wasn't like Broheim to brush her off like this. She decided to wait until they were in the shop.

Once there, she followed him as he walked into the shop. He signaled her to follow to his office. He waited outside, ushered her in and looked to make sure no one else followed. He stopped Paul with a shake of his head. Paul looked confused but turned to his workspace. Broheim stepped in the office and closed the door. He rested his hands on either side of the doorframe, his head on the door itself. He looked frightened.

When he turned, she saw how haggard his face looked then, noticing her concern, he took a deep breath and walked around to sit in his chair. He picked up his pipe in shaking hands and pulled the box of strikers out to light it. His hands shook so much he snapped the thin stick of the striker before he could snap it into flame against his desk. He gave up and set the pipe on the tray to hold it. Rebecca noticed the pipe didn't even hold any tobacco for him to light; he seemed to have forgotten to stuff it.

"Broheim something *is* the matter," she said quietly, feeling her hands and feet go cold.

He stared at her and she could have sworn she saw a tear forming before he turned his head away, speaking in a think voice.

"Something is coming." Rebecca felt cold bumps climb her arms and neck.

"What is coming?" she asked, barely audible.

"I heard it from some fellow Romarans to the east. Word often travels faster than coaches." He dry-washed his hands; this was the most nervous she had ever seen him. "The dogs called them heretics but *they're* consorting with bloody *demons*." He didn't make sense. He seemed to talk to himself, forgetting she was in the room. "Eaters of Souls, Masked Ones, Faceless, demons of the between worlds…" he turned, eyes focusing on her, "Blind Men." Rebecca began to shake.

"The bloody fools are sending Strynges, girl. They're coming for you; we know it."

"Broheim, what are you talking about?" she said, barely able to hear her own words. She had heard stories of the Blind Men; she had believed them tales to frighten children. *Don't swear or the Blind Men will come for you. The Blind Men take children who misbehave. Don't run away from home or the Blind Men will find you.* She believed the children who told her these stories to be somewhat dim. Who would believe such nonsense?

"Adarian has sent his Strynges into Romara and they're searching the universities for something, someone. They'll hunt anyone for the pleasure of the culling, but they can't resist the pull the soul of one with the Touch for the Links, girl."

Rebecca shook her head in refusal. "No, no, I don't, I can't," but her words were lies in her own ears. She knew very well that she could, and she had.

"They came for the Philistari like vultures on carrion, we couldn't stop them then. We didn't know what they were at first. They pushed through us like we were gnats between them and their quarry. We did what we could but the Palantean were the ones to finally drive them off. We formed an alliance there, over the bodies of our beloved friends, the Brotherhood of the Three Knives. 'We won't let them have the next so easily,' we told ourselves but we failed again and again to stop them. It's the way they move, you see; they don't exist fully in this world. They slide between worlds, reaching through to pull the souls from the living."

"What...what are you talking about Broheim; I don't understand? How did you know about me? What is this brotherhood?"

243

"Your heritage was hidden from all, to keep you safe; but your name has been known to the Brotherhood since you were born. We were to keep you safe from those who would see those with the Touch wiped from this world. We are friends of the Touched Ones, Philistari, Mecharicals, and Palantean. We ourselves lack the Touch but we stand with those who have. And now we stand between the monsters of Adarian and you.

"The Blind Men some call them, but they don't need eyes to see you; you'll stand out to them like a beacon on a hill. Some of the others here know of their approach and are trying to figure a way to get you out. Frowler thinks we can sneak you out through the vents, like you do to do your hunting."

"Broheim, I don't want to leave the others. I want to make sure they are alright. I want to get them out of here too."

"You would, wouldn't you," he said, smiling at her. "Rebecca you are a special girl, you must know that. We can't afford to lose you. The clerks knew you would be coming, sooner or later, and they made sure to put you under the watch of one of us in the Brotherhood." Rebecca was shocked; she had hated those clerks, sorting the children that first day. Now, to realize that they worked to protect her felt strange to her. "Gelda Hume, Ben Frowler, Angus Freen, Pater Janns, they are all here in Valgerhold to make sure you are well. Well, well enough. We didn't dare draw any more attention to you then need be because that would only make Dormon suspicious. But with the Strynges coming, we can't afford to leave you out in the open."

Some of the names Broheim mentioned she knew, Ben Frowler of course, Gelda Hume was the leader of the ceramics group, and Angus Freen was the blacksmith who led the group in the forges, but who was Pater Janns? Rebecca focused on the dust in the corners

244

while the house burned down around her. She brought her thoughts slowly around to what Broheim was saying.

"Broheim, if you have some sort of brotherhood here watching after me, why then haven't you acted to fight the Red Guard?" She felt so helpless sitting in that office when, somewhere, a force Rebecca couldn't fathom bore down on her.

"We wouldn't stand a chance against the force they have just here at Valgerhold. We are agents of stealth, child; we sneak and listen at corners. We aren't the type to take up arms and storm the gates. But that's neither here nor there. Listen and follow close. We are going to get you out of here. Once out, we are going to take you west into the Wilderlands. Somewhere near the border, there is a man with which we will entrust you. He will see to your safekeeping until you are needed. He is very odd at times but he knows what he's about, so you mind him."

She cried now unable to stop the flood of emotions. Broheim looked at her. His face was full of sympathy, his moustache drawn down over his lower lip, the strain in his eyes released.

"Now child," he said, coming from around his desk. He knelt to look into her face. "You have your heart hung on these kids, that big blond boy especially, don't you? I am getting too old." He shook his head, admonishing himself. "You have given your friends hope; it's the best you could give them for now. But you listen to me; you have more to give, something only you can. Your friends will be safe enough here; the Brotherhood will see to them when you are away. It's you that the Strynges hunt. You will only put your friends in danger if you stay here."

She reached out her arms and Broheim pulled her close while she sobbed into his shoulder. "I don't want to leave him, or the others, or you. Broheim, I'm scared."

"I know child, I know, but you can be scared and brave at the same time. That's what that lion's heart in you can do for you. Come now, dry your eyes and try to put this out of your mind. The woman who passed me the rumor of the Blind Men said we had two, three days at most. We will get you out tonight, though, and pass you away from this place so you can be readied."

"Readied for what?"

"Readied for your part in what comes. I don't know the whole of it but I know you're going to be needed at some point." He looked away from her and his eyes became lost in thought. "*And there shall stand the child of the lost. The child shall be descended of the blood of the lost. The child will go beyond and that which has been lost shall be found anew. The rebirth of the Orders shall come at the hands of the child and the heart of one beyond this world.*" He looked at Rebecca after he finished as if coming out of a dream. "Those words the last of the Philistari spoke as he lay half dead. We don't know what the words meant exactly but the words were like those we had heard before. They were what we knew as a *Reached Vision*, a possible future. Those words became the foundation of the Brotherhood of the Three Knives; our purpose. We were to find, protect, and see that that child fulfilled the Vision. You, we believe, are that child Rebecca; you have to be. We know of no other."

Rebecca's head and heart fought for her attention. Her head spun the pieces about, puzzling. Her heart ached with each beat trying to force through her chest. She felt utterly drained. She longed to wake and find herself safe in her bed in her home, her mother wiping a fevered dream away with a wet cloth. She longed for her father to come into the room and sweep her up in his powerful arms, to carry her to safety. She longed for her brother to pull her close and ruffle her hair, making her feel like nothing would hurt her as long as he was at her side. But none of those things would ever happen again. She realized she had built a new family here. James, her friends, even Broheim had become her support. She had become attached, if not to this place, to her friends here. Now, she was going to lose the anchor that held her in the storm her life had become since her family had been killed. She was going to be alone again here in this land of unknown dangers, feeling her way blindly.

She looked into Broheim's eyes; his face was a study of compassion. How was she to just leave her friends behind? They would see her as having deserted them. She would leave them when she had started them on the path to resist the Red Guard here. Broheim would have to let her explain to her friends and she said as much to him.

"No, we can't risk word spreading. If Postam or Dormon catch hint of an escape, they'll lock this place tight as a prison. We'd never be able to sneak you out. As much as it hurts, child, you must keep quiet." He was still on his knee looking at her eye to eye.

"Broheim, maybe they could help, that way they could at least know I wasn't just running. They would help me escape, to reach whatever it is you say waits."

"I'm sorry, Rebecca."

His use of her name gave finality to the words. Anger flared in her at what he was making her do. He would make her look like a coward to her friends. While she was safe in the home of some caretaker, they would be here, brooding on their craven Captain. The girl who had made them believe there was hope and then run out on them. She would not have it; she would at least tell James. She would make him understand. When she was away, he would explain to the others why she had to go.

"If that's the way it must be; so be it," she said, hoping Broheim didn't see her lie.

"You look like you're trying to swallow a bitter fruit, Skinny."

"I will do as you say, Broheim."

And with that, they both stood. She dried her eyes and returned to work. He stood in the doorway, watching her go.

The bell for mid meal sounded after a time and Rebecca joined Paul to walk to the dining hall. She left without waiting for Broheim as she had every other time. When Paul commented on it, she turned to him as they walked.

"The man worries too much,"

"You two have a falling out?" Paul asked.

"A difference of opinions," she said, continuing on her way to the dining hall. She never looked back for Broheim. She never saw the two guards approach him from an adjoining corridor and take him aside. She never looked back to see them escort Broheim away from the corridor.

In the dining hall, she hurried to the table where her friends waited. She took her place next to James, thinking of the best way to word what she needed to tell him. She didn't notice, at first, the worried looks on the others' faces at the table. When she worked out what she meant to say, she turned to James and caught sight of the number of guards in the dining hall. Usually there were two guards at either entrance, dressed in their uniforms of dark gray with the Red Fist over the chest, marking them members of the Red Guard. At most they would carry a steel baton to intimidate the children. But now there were guards placed all along the walls, carrying rifles as well as the batons at their belts. She turned to ask what was happening.

"The guards started pouring in after we all arrived," said James, his forehead furrowed in concern. "Where is Broheim? I didn't see him come in with you."

Rebecca turned to the Romarans' table and noticed Broheim's absence. Her heart pounded in her chest and her fingers froze in an instant. Had the guards learned of the Brotherhood's plan to get her away tonight?

She looked around the dining hall, checking to see if anyone else was missing. All the members of the Brotherhood Broheim had listed, that Rebecca knew, were at their table. She looked to her friends; they were all there, including the new member at their table, Gregor. She quickly scanned the remaining children. *Was anyone missing?* She couldn't tell. She asked if the others knew of anyone who hadn't come to mid meal.

"Jason Ganty's gone," said Gregor, in a rumbling whisper. He had been leader of Gregor's former gang until his conversion. Rebecca had worried about the validity of Ganty's story.

"Elisa didn't come into the ceramics shop," Elisabeth whispered next to Helen. "She isn't in here either," she said, looking around. *What was going on*, Rebecca wondered.

It didn't take long to find out. When the bell to return to work sounded, the guards moved to block the entrances. The Romaran leaders stood and made moves toward the guards, talking over one another to know the meaning of this.

"You will all be escorted to the main courtyard where the Colonel will address you," a brutal looking guard with a close-cropped beard and hair said.

The guards arranged the children and Romarans to walk to the main courtyard. They gathered the children into lines; the Romarans took the lead, the guards flanking to ensure no one made to escape.

The procession wound its way through the corridors to the courtyard the children had their morning exercises that day. This was also the courtyard that had greeted them on their first entrance into Valgerhold. The day was overcast at its start and now, thick clouds gathered overhead. In the distance Rebecca heard thunder roll off the rocky landscape to the north. The wind gusted even over the tall walls of the courtyard and the first splotches of rain marked the stone tiles of the courtyard. The trees in the raised circular surrounds, with the benches cut into the stone, looked ready for a downpour. Their tiny leaves, the first of the coming spring, were light as they flipped in the wind.

Dormon was nowhere to be seen yet but Postam stood at a stone pillar, to the side of the opening of the spiral stairs that led to the upper walkway around the courtyard. The children were lined up as if they were to have another round of exercise, facing the stairwell entrance. The Romaran leaders were lined along the pillars to the side of Postam. Yet more guards led Romarans, the ones who did the hidden work of cleaning and maintaining Valgerhold, into the courtyard to join their countrymen. Rebecca noticed they all had looks of fear clear on their faces.

When everyone was arranged into place, Rebecca heard the sound of approaching footfalls, descending the spiral stairs. Her heart beat harder than it had in her life and she had an urge to run. James took her hand and squeezed, she returned the gesture.

From the dark, Broheim stepped into the gray light of the day. Rebecca's heart froze for an instant. Then Dormon pushed him forward and walked into the courtyard. Postam walked to stand behind Broheim to the left of Dormon. The satisfied look he wore made his bald-headed, bearded face look wicked. Dormon stepped forward and stopped, eyeing the children; a hawk would have more mercy in its eyes for a mouse than his held. He wore his heavy dark fur coat over his uniform with a belt strapped around his waist, holding the Arnoran revolving pistol she had seen in his office.

"You were warned when you came here," he began. "Any rebellious acts would be punished severely." He turned to look at the Romarans that stood against the wall. "You too, were warned about aiding the prisoners of the New Dominion in any actions that were against my command." He looked to one of the guards standing near the entrance to the stairs. "Bring the child." The guard turned and disappeared into the dark opening of the stairwell. Rebecca was at the edge of her nerves, near panic. The courtyard was lined with armed guards and there was nowhere to run.

The clouds thickened and roiled in the sky. Rain patted down, making snapping sounds as it hit the leaves of the trees and the courtyard stones. A light hiss rose as the rain increased. From the darkness of the stairwell, a form took shape. A girl with the yellowing of fading bruises still on her face. Elisa. The guard walked her to Dormon's right side and turned to return to his place by the opening.

"Some will know the punishment of which was warned. Others," he put his hand on Elisa's shoulder; she shuddered and was still, "will know that the New Dominion rewards loyalty." Elisa's head whipped to stare at Dormon, a relieved smile on her face. Rebecca wanted to get a hold of the girl. Traitor, she had been a traitor the whole time. She had told Dormon everything. Postam must have given her the bruised face to convince them of Elisa's story. Rebecca lurched forward but James held her back.

"Now, you will all witness what becomes of those who rebel against the New Dominion, the Red Guard, and my command here." Postam pushed Broheim forward. Rebecca felt sick. He had a stoic look on his face but he found her eyes in the rows.

"Do you have anything to say for yourself, Romaran," Postam said from behind Broheim, his satisfaction clear in his voice.

The courtyard grew silent; the patting of the rain was the only sound. The water rolled off Broheim's steel grey hair and his sharp eyes twinkled at Rebecca. His moustache twitched in a cocked grin and he nodded to her.

"Yeah, I reckon I have a word or two to say for myself," he looked relaxed, resigned, and Rebecca's heart went out to him, standing before all these eyes. Suddenly he stepped forward straight as a steel rod and snapped the knuckles of his right thumb and forefinger to the bridge of his nose, an Arnoran salute. "Fight long, fight hard, Second Born of Arnora!" he shouted. His voice mingled with a strange loud crack, echoing off the stone walls of the courtyard.

Rebecca didn't realize she was screaming until she felt James pulling her to look away. Dormon stood, his right hand outstretched; the revolving pistol's barrel still streamed smoke. Broheim staggered and fell to his knees, his eyes still locked on Rebecca's then he fell face first to the stone tiles. She had seen the dark hole in his forehead leaking blood before he fell.

Everything became chaos. Dormon shouted at the guards, something Rebecca couldn't hear for her screams, as she tried to run to Broheim. James pulled her back, yelling something to the others around them. The guards moved in with their batons in their hands.

The Romarans huddled together, crying and looking on, afraid to move. Gregor's huge form appeared before her, pushing her back. Screams and shouts filled the courtyard in a cacophony. Cries of pain added to the noise as the guards reached the rows of children. They were trying to get to someone. Tears filled Rebecca's eyes and her screams continued, unable to stop them. Her vision faded to gray around the edges; the only thing she could see was Broheim, lying on the stones, a pool of dark blood forming in the rain that poured down.

Elisa yelled at Dormon about an agreement. Dormon thoroughly ignored her. Postam waded into the fray, taking a baton from one of the guards. The guards used their batons and the butts of their rifles to push through the children. There was a wake of children, clutching foreheads and noses, crying behind the guards. They moved in closer. At last James and Gregor realized who the guards were after. James shouted to the children, the words were lost to Rebecca. She thought it vaguely sounded like, 'Rally Second Born, Rally to the captain', but that made no sense. The children thickened in a tight ring around Rebecca and James who held her back. She thought she could here battle cries of some sort, 'Rally Arnora, Rally the Second Born.'

James and Gregor fought two fronts, the Red Guard pushing in, and Rebecca pushing to get to Broheim. Gregor single handedly threw guards back as they came near. James pleaded for Rebecca to come back; she was not there to hear his words though. Suddenly, Gregor hit the stones of the courtyard and a guard loomed before Rebecca. From the outside, it looked like she fought to get to the guard and away from James. James pulled her back behind him and was knocked flat to the stones opposite Gregor. With the release of James' pressure against her, Rebecca shot forward into the guard. He seized her by the shoulders.

254

Paul leapt for the guard holding Rebecca. The guard, unprepared for the attack, fell to the ground as Paul careened into him. Snatching up the guard's dropped baton, Paul brought it down viciously into the guard's temple and he went slack. James began to recover his feet; Gregor was making his way, staggering, back to Rebecca. Rebecca was on her knees unable to move after the guard had released her. Paul went to Rebecca and faced her. He shouted something at her, his eyes wide with fear, and something else, excitement? Rebecca slowly began to hear fully again, she stopped screaming, and her vision began to clear. The words her friends shouted were beginning to make sense again.

"We have to get you out of here," Paul yelled over the shouts of fighting. "They are after you, Rebecca. They want to take you, Captain."

Rebecca nodded hesitantly and took Paul's hand to get to her feet. Paul was, all of a sudden, pushing her back to the stones of the courtyard. He seemed to be lying on her for some reason. She looked over his head and saw Postam standing behind Paul, looking at her with rage filled eyes. His hand held a pistol and smoke issued from the barrel. The sound of the shot echoed back into her ears as the sounds in the courtyard abruptly ceased.

Rebecca realized, with horror, why Paul lay on her. She rolled him over and laid his head in her lap, looking into his eyes. She noticed the dark wet patch growing on his chest. James stood to her right, eyes wide, and mouth agape; Gregor to her left, anger and fear playing for space on his face. Helen was suddenly there, clutching Paul's hand. She was crying. "No, no, no, Paul. Oh, it's not so bad you'll see, Paul. Oh Father no, no," the words tumbled out of her.

A ring of children faced the scene, mouths covered with hands, arms hugging themselves, tears rolling down cheeks, knuckles clenched white. Rebecca looked down into Paul's face.

"Paul, I'm sorry," she said, tears dripped on his hair. "I'm so sorry, Paul. Please, I should have listened to you. I should have listened to you from the start. Please Paul, forgive me." She grabbed his hand when he offered it, Helen squeezed the other, crying into his shoulder.

"Nothing," he began in a gasp, "nothing – to forgive – Captain. It's…" he paused to take a shuddering breath. "It's not your fault. You did good by me, Captain, you did good by me." He gasped again. Rebecca held his hand tight and shielded him from the rain as best she could. Thunder rolled out in long peals. Paul squeezed Rebecca's hand and pulled her in close. "Make sure Helen and the others make it out. You get them out Rebecca. Make sure you get them out Captain." His eyes were filming over. He took a deep hard breath. "Fight hard, fight long, Second Born of Arnora!" he yelled with his last breath, the last words fading with his strength. He died in her arms and Rebecca held him for as long as she could.

Postam was on her too soon. Other guards were close behind with rifles at the ready. One knelt to the guard Paul had attacked and gripped his wrist, feeling for a pulse.
"Dead," he said, turning to Postam. Postam pushed Helen aside and grabbed Rebecca's arm, pulling her from beneath Paul's body. She was careful to set his head down gently.

Once up, Postam pushed her ahead of him toward Dormon. She pushed back for a moment beside Broheim lying in the courtyard. Postam roughly moved her along to Dormon.

"I told you before child, not to waste the mercy of the New Dominion. Yet you listened to nothing," Dormon said to her, still clutching the revolving pistol. Elisa was behind him trying to hide from Rebecca's sight. Rebecca expected, very strongly, to join her lost family soon and didn't waste the time she had left on the traitor.

"When I see my brother next, I'll be sure to let him know you and your *great* New Dominion won't be joining us. You see, you're going to be burning in the Pit of Discordia, Dormon, where you belong." She spit in his face with the last word. Postam thanked her with a crack to the back of her head that made the world go black.

"I know child," said Dormon under his breath, wiping the spittle from his face. "I know you are correct." He turned to Postam. "Take her to the chamber to await our guests." Postam hefted Rebecca's limp form over his shoulder and trudged to the stairwell through the rain. Dormon looked after his catch as she left.

"Colonel Dormon, Sir, I demand to receive what I was promised," Elisa said, finding courage now that Rebecca was gone. "We had an agreement and I demand that it be fulfilled this instant. I want to be away from here as soon as possible."

Dormon turned to the Elisa, her yellowed face indignant and pouting. The rain laid her hair in strings across her face and her clothes were soaked through.

"Your demands will be met," said Dormon, his voice like rock. He raised the revolving pistol to the girl's forehead and pulled the trigger. Her face looked indignant till the end as she dropped in a boneless heap in the courtyard.

"You demands are met. Fair you well on your journey child," he said, turning to walk to the stairs. "Guards, get these children locked into their dorms, and lock those Father forsaken transoms." With that, he disappeared into the dark stairwell.

Twenty-eight:
The Messenger Boy

James watched Postam march Rebecca to Dormon. He could see their mouths moving. He saw as Rebecca spit in Dormon's face and Postam hit her in the back of the head with the spent pistol he carried. Gregor grabbed his shoulder to keep him from going to her. The other children gathered in, watching as Postam carried Rebecca away; most were crying. He watched as Elisa, she had already become *the traitor* to his mind, yelled at Dormon. Dormon raised his pistol calmly and shot her in the head. Gasps and screams filled the courtyard. The girl's limp body fell to the courtyard and Dormon turned to leave, issuing orders to the guards.

The guards pushed in with their rifles leveled. They yelled orders to return to the dorms and the children complied. Several guards followed the children to the dorm floors where they led them into the separate chambers. Two guards went to the entrance of the boy's dorm; one cupped his hands while the other climbed up to secure a lock on the window above the door. Their only way of escape had just been sealed.

James walked to the sleeping chamber in a fog. He didn't listen to the questions the boys asked. He moved as if watching his body from the outside. *What were they going to do to Rebecca? What was he going to do without her to lead them?* He remembered yelling at her once about how she saw him and the others only as a means to revenge. He realized now how wrong he had been. She had given them all purpose. He didn't think he could move the others the way she had. What's more, he didn't think he could move himself the way she had. Rebecca had said something about being brave and scared at the same time, but he only felt scared now.

Gregor shook his arm, trying to get his attention. The other boys stood close by intently watching, asking questions when they thought he was listening.

"Bligh, snap out of it," Gregor said. "We need to decide what to do next."

James felt his fear lash him into anger. "What we are to do next? What we're to do next is wait here until the Red Guard decide to put bullets in every one of us. What do you expect of me?" he shouted at Gregor and looked around at the rest of the boys in the sleeping chamber, their faces filled with shock and fear. "I'm not her; I don't make the plans."

"Well, if that's your attitude Bligh, I may just have to go see if the girls are more up to it than you," a voice said. It came from the back of the chamber, near the large stained glass window, showing a snowy owl carrying a lantern. Jason Ganty stood, a smug look upon his face, leaning against the stone wall next to the window.

James looked at the boy; he wore a condescending grin. "Where did you go?" James asked him slowly, walking to where he stood. "Why weren't you there in the courtyard with the rest of us?" James grabbed the boy's collar; the grin vanished in an instant. James pulled the boy's face into his. "Are you a traitor like the other one, because I saw what Dormon did as a fit end to traitors."

Gregor stood at James' back, arms folded, staring at the two. Ganty's eyes flickered around to the other faces looking on. None looked like they would lift a hand to help. James shook the boy for an answer.

"Alright, I'm no traitor," he said, going wide eyed at the look on James' face. "I was with a man named Janns; he's the head clerk. He has me working in his office, his personal assistant, allegedly. He's a member of some Brotherhood that's here in Valgerhold. They were supposed to be looking after someone, to make sure she was well. Guess that's Dulac."

"That doesn't answer my questions; why weren't you there, and where did you go?" James said, releasing Ganty a hair.

"I wasn't there in the courtyard because I take my meals with Janns. You see, he's trusted in Dormon's eyes. The guards all but ignore the clerks; makes them perfect spies for the Brotherhood. Janns caught me one day eluding some guards after exercise. Thought I'd find myself a place for a nap. He requisitioned me for his use and I've been running messages for him since. Broheim, poor man, he was in this Brotherhood too. They were going to try to get her out tonight but…well; you see where there is a problem." He finished looking hopeful.

"Yeah a bit of a snag in the plan," said James, letting the boy go. He turned and rubbed his chin thinking. "What does this Janns mean to do to get her out of Dormon's hands?"

"That's where these come in," said Ganty, pulling two bits of thin metal from behind his belt. "Living on the streets, you learn to keep your valuables well outta sight, as well as certain useful tricks. This," he said, tucking the bits back into his pants, "is a master key to the university. Those bloody fools think we're stuck in here with those locks on the windows when we can walk through the door like we own the place."

James tried to think of what Rebecca would do; her plans seemed to always come off without a hitch.

"Problem is, none of us can get up to where they're taking her," said Ganty, relaxing back into his normal mode. "If they see any of us up where she'll be, we're as good as dead. And we can't be known to have had anything to do with getting her sprung or Dormon will come down on us."

"Did this Janns say why this Brotherhood was trying to free her tonight?"

"No, but the man looked white as a sheet. Something has got to him, I never saw him scared before. It's not like these fellows to use kids to do their work. They must be desperate if they're turning to us now."

"What are you thinking Bligh?" asked Gregor.

"I think we are going to have to run a distraction for Rebecca. She is going to have to get herself out," James said. "I need to know if this Janns can get to her. I need to know if he can get her a package."

"Shouldn't be much of a problem; this gent is a sly a fox."

James hoped some of Rebecca's fortune had come his way because for this to work he was going to need all the luck he could afford.

* * *

Rebecca awoke some time later. It felt like her eyes were swelling in their sockets and the base of her skull was stiff. She opened her eyes and looked to see where she was. The room was dark. The walls were blank stone except for a narrow window at one wall and a thick wooden door in the opposite. She sat up and let her eyes adjust to the dim light from the window. A flash lit the room from outside and thunder rumbled the walls. The room looked to be a cleared out storage closet, long since abandoned. She had seen the prints of boots in the dust on the floor when the lightning flashed. She stood - her head spun for a moment then settled - and walked to test the door. The handle didn't budge. She was trapped.

She walked to the window to peer out; it was a just low enough for her to see out on tip toes. The courtyard was visible below, the main entrance sealed shut. She judged she was on the third floor of the main building by the height. She could see the green clay tiles covering the walkway around the courtyard. Rain sheeted against the glass in the window, making the night move in waves. Looking across the courtyard, she could see the two dorm towers. *What were they doing right now?* She thought. She put her back to the wall and slouched down to the floor, hugging her knees tight to her chest.

She had lost two friends today, or was it yesterday? What time was it? Strange thoughts to have when she should be grieving for them. But time mattered now. How long had Broheim told her when they last talked? Two, maybe three days, he had said, until the Blind Men arrived and sucked out her soul. Now, it had to be down to one or two days, judging by the dark outside. She had been so stupid, so trusting, to believe all the children would follow her. Had she learned nothing from what Broheim had tried teaching her? She thought on all those lessons, all his words to her about trusting people. Now, her hope in trusting one person too many had gotten Broheim and Paul killed. She rested her forehead against her arms on her knees and began to cry. *What was she going to do now? Probably die,* she thought.

Twenty-nine: Plans Forged

The next morning, the guards awoke the children in the dorms as usual, except for the several armed guards that followed them. The children went to the courtyard where the disasters of previous day had played out. The rain still poured down and it didn't look to be letting up any. Exercise was skipped and the children moved off toward first meal in the dining hall. Ganty slipped away unnoticed, carrying two messages, one for this Janns man, the other for Rebecca. He had no fear that Janns would read the second; for, as far as James knew, Rebecca and he were the only two who knew the script her grandfather had used in his journal.

The children ate their meals in silence. Guards lined the walls now, armed and on edge. He couldn't blame them; Paul had killed one of their comrades. *Good for him*, James thought viciously. The Romaran leaders cast quick glances from time to time at the men with the rifles along the walls. James guessed they would be of no assistance in what he was plotting.

Helen and Marissa had started his plan rolling. Ganty demonstrated his skills with the two thin strips of metal he carried. He had made quick work maneuvering the tumblers of the door locks. Before James and the others had known it, they were strolling into the girls' sleeping chamber to begin planning. Talk of distraction led to talk of what would draw the guard's attention fully. Fire. Fire in the alchemy lab, where the gunpowder was made and stored, would draw all eyes like flies to honey. James was surprised at Helen. She had not taken Paul's death as he had expected. She wanted revenge. Now, his plan, worked out with the help of the others, rested on a complete stranger and a boy James didn't trust over the distance he could throw him.

James had thought about why this Brotherhood, whatever it was, would be here, secreted away, to guard Rebecca. What he came to stretched his trust in this man Janns a bit farther. If they knew what Rebecca was, perhaps they had been trying to get her to safety? If they were trying to keep her safe then perhaps James could trust them, at least for the time. He had learned from Broheim's words, spoken through Rebecca.

When the bell tolled to go to the shops, James gathered with his group. Angus Freen led the other boys to the forges. James noted that all the groups had tails of armed Red Guard. The four that followed the forge group took up their places outside the large wooden doors that let into the hot smoky room James had come to enjoy. The furnaces blazed yellow-white around the edges of the doors, keeping in the heat. The furnace's heat paled to his anger at the Red Guard for what they had done to Rebecca, and Paul, and Broheim. He didn't know the man personally but Rebecca had become fond of him, and so, James had too. He spoke wisdom, through Rebecca, close enough to the words of some of the clerics James had known before he had to leave his studies and home to come here.

Paul had been a friend, as close to a brother as he had found here. They had often fought over James' belief in Rebecca but they were not heated battles. The few times they had actually come to blows James had found himself laughing with the younger boy afterwards. Now, he was left to fend for himself and the others. It had been Rebecca who led, James who backed her, and Paul a questioning conscience for the two. *How do you back someone who's not there?* he thought.

James began hammering a piece of thick steel stock. He pounded the metal, envisioning Postam's face in the white hot metal. By the time the bell sounded for mid meal, he was exhausted. He walked with the others into the dining hall in sullen silence, the guards trailed behind. He joined the others and methodically ate his stew. Looking into his bowl, he noticed chucks of some tough meat. He laughed to himself. If that Father forsaken Dormon had done this at the start none this would have happened. The minor rebellion the children had been involved in had been started over a lack of proper food. *Now they give in*, he thought.

It took James a moment to realize Michael tugging at his sleeve. He looked over to the golden haired boy. James saw a face that spoke of worry and that he hid something. If the guards had noticed they hadn't given sign.

Michael carried a basket full of crusty loaves for the stew. He had been nervously stepping from foot to foot, waiting for James to notice him. Now, that he had, James noted the piece of parchment sticking from under one of the loaves.

"I think the top one is the one you want, James," he said, his voice cracking with his nerves.

"Thank you Michael," James said, reaching in and taking the note and the loaf in one hand. "I've been looking forward to this all day," he said to Michael with a wry grin.

Michael moved off, his shoulders relaxing with his message delivered. What was Ganty thinking using Michael to ferry messages? James laid the parchment near his bowl and began eating the loaf as he read.

266

Blacksmith, I admire your handy work, a fine design indeed. Be assured that your intended recipient will receive the parcel on schedule. I would like very much to see more of your work, perhaps when times are fairer.

It was signed "Janns". Not Ganty then. This Janns had received his message and was going to help. Rebecca would get the package he had Ganty deliver to Janns. Now, all he needed was to wait until dark and hope Rebecca was up to the final part in his plan.

* * *

Rebecca woke from troubled sleep to find the rain still pouring against the glass. It was light outside, but a gray light. She took better stock of the room she was in by daylight. The walls were undressed stone, no need wasting time to finish something that wasn't to be seen. The window was little more that a square hole to aid the staff in storing whatever had been here before. The ceiling was high with no vents. The door in the opposite wall was unadorned dark wood, solid though, and iron bound. She put her ear to the wood and heard nothing from outside.

Her clothes were stiff and wrinkled from drying on her. Her neck and back were stiff from sleeping huddled against the wall. Her head no longer hurt but when she felt through her hair, she found a large bump on the back of her skull. She needed to use the washroom but she was afraid to call out. She took off her coat and shirt and laid them on the floor. She started exercises, in her under shirt and work pants, to take her mind off the situation. She always thought more clearly after her blood got flowing.

Once she had worked herself into a sweat, she had enough courage to see if anyone was on guard at the door. She called out and heard a shuffling from down the hall approach the door. The clank and click of keys inserted into a lock and the door swung open. A guard with a rutted complexion and uneven hair stood in the open doorway. His eyes looking on her made Rebecca feel filthy and the sneer he gave her made her put back on her work shirt. She had known some of these guards had taken advantage of the girls here, like Theodora and Elisa. That was the only compassion she had for the girl; she could not forgive her treachery. It suited, the way things were falling, that she would have one of those despicable sorts on watch on her door. She would have to sleep light until the Blind Men came to take her.

"I have to use the washroom," she said to the guard, trying to keep her face smooth.

"Step along then," he said, pulling a steel baton from his belt. "You flinch and I'll make you wish the Colonel had killed you with that old Romaran yesterday."

She struggled to keep her mouth closed as the guard walked her down the hall. He stood too close for Rebecca's comfort. As she walked to the washroom she took note of every feature of the hall. The walls here were plain stone and the floors bare. It must have been some kind of maintenance floor. She saw a stairwell that led down as she neared the washroom. She could see tapestries and paintings on the walls below, and brightly colored patterned rugs. They had a similar look to the ones on the hall floor of Dormon's, and Postam's rooms. She went into the washroom, she was glad the guard waited outside, and she hunted for an escape in the room. All the windows were sealed and the vents were too high to reach. Disheartened, she relieved herself and washed herself in the basin. Rough linens were piled to the side of the basin and she dried her hair and face. She looked into the mirror and steeled herself for whatever was to come next.

When she exited the washroom, the guard gave her another of his disgusting looks. *Definitely must sleep light*, she thought. The guard walked her to the storage room, pushed her in, and then slammed and locked the door after. She noticed a bowl of stew and a crusty loaf as well a roll of wool blankets and a pillow. Other guards must have brought them. She sat and ate the stew. Picking up the napkin to dab her face, a note slipped from inside. She picked up the folded sheet and her heart leapt. On the outside of the note in her grandfather's script was her name.

Hurriedly she unfolded the note and read the message. When she had finished reading the note, her appetite had left her. She forced herself to eat every scrap. If what James had planned was to work she would need every bit of strength she could muster.

Thirty: Fire and Water

It was a long day's wait for Rebecca. The day stretched with nothing to occupy her time but her thoughts. The rain continued unabated outside and she stood until her calves were sore, tiptoeing to look out the window. The courtyard remained empty for a long time. She longed to see one of her friends scamper across it. She heard the bells toll, telling her what time it was. It would be last meal, *not long now*. The light gray sky gave way to dark gray and night crept in. She checked the blanket again to make herself believe what she had found was real. It was and she calmed herself for what she would have to do.

Eventually, the last bell tolled and Rebecca's stomach went to ice. Her friends would be on their way back to the dorms across the courtyard. She peered over the window edge and smiled. The first clumps of children ran for the stairways to be out of the driving rain. She saw a tall boy pause a moment, his dark blond hair, darker for the rain, gave him away, James. He stared at the upper windows, glancing around; he raised a hand, she put hers to the window. A larger boy with cropped hair came along side him and put a hand on James' shoulder, Gregor, and led James back to the stairwell. She watched as all her friends crossed the courtyard until they vanished within.

James had said, in his note, she would know when the distraction had been put into effect. She had no doubt in him; her only doubt lay with herself. As night thickened, she heard low snores from down the hall. *Not long now*, she thought.

* * *

James and the others had everything prepared nearly as soon as the guards locked the dorm doors. Flint, knives, fuses – made from wool, left over gun powder, and beeswax; everything was set. Helen insisted on being a part of the distraction team; James couldn't refuse her. Ganty was needed to open doors but others wanted to come just to be a part of freeing their Captain. He had to have Gregor put the fear of the Father into them before he was sure none of them would tag after them. Rebecca had been right about Gregor; he was as loyal and as fierce as a sheepdog. Once James had determined the time to be correct, Ganty, Helen, and he lashed on the woolen overshoes Arthur had made; they would work as well on stone as leaves.

They made for the third floor door opposite the one that led out to the courtyard above the library. This door had been locked the first time Rebecca and he had made their escape from the dorms. From what Ganty had told them, the door led to service hallways. They could move along them to the main halls and work their way into the Alchemy shop. Once in, they would rely on Helen's knowledge of the chemicals to determine what to set the torch to.

They moved along the darkened halls in silence. The three kept eyes and ears open for signs of guards. They moved down the service halls without problem. Once to the main hall they faced a more daunting task; the guards patrolled these halls. They moved from shadow to shadow, James leading, Ganty bringing up the rear. They had to back track twice to avoid patrols. It took longer than James expected but eventually, they arrived at the large double doors of the Alchemy shop.

The shop was kept down a longer hall than any of the others. Fire was a distinct possibility in any Alchemy shop but this one especially, for the volume of powder being produced. The storm outside gave the plan a cover; lightning could very well spark a fire in this place.

Ganty moved to the lock and crouched down, pulling the bits of metal from his waist band. James drew the rough knife he had made for the hunting expeditions and stood guard. Helen did likewise; she had a fierce look in her eye that said she was more likely to use the weapon than he. Ganty cursed softly at the lock. The time seemed to stretch. Finally, the lock clicked and Ganty pushed the door open.

"Come on," he whispered.

The three moved into the shop. Helen chose out the jars of colored materials and vials of liquids from wooden racks to place near the powder. The fire, she hoped, would feed on the chemicals faster than if left unaided. They needed the full attention of the guards for Rebecca to work her way out of the university. With everything in place, James stuffed the end of the woolen fuse in a keg of powder and unwound the cord to the door of the shop. He pulled the flint from his pocket and knelt down to where the end lay.

"You two get moving. I'll be on your heels as soon as this takes," he said quietly.

They turned and moved back the way they had come. James gave a long count to thirty, giving them a lead. He said a silent prayer that everything worked as it should and struck the flint along the edge of his knife.

* * *

Rebecca lay on the unrolled blanket, the pillow rest over her hand in her lap, her back to the windowed wall. The second blanket covered her to her waist. She hoped whatever it was James and the others planned would happen soon. She was nearly giving herself fits at every bump and groan she heard. The storm continued outside her little window, the flashes of lightning made flickering blue-white squares against the far wall.

She heard a noise from the courtyard. She jumped from the blankets and stretched to see down. The tall dark doors to the courtyard were opening to the outside. She had only seen those doors opened twice since she had come here, once when they had arrived, the second to admit a visitor who had arrived by coach. She waited, looking into the dark downpour. The sound of axels turning and the clump of horses' hooves came from the open doors. Guards stepped from beneath the covered walkway below Rebecca. Dormon, in his dark fur coat, wore a cap to keep the rain off his head. He walked out to face the opening.

A dark carriage rolled into the courtyard; lightning flashed overhead showing it to be utterly black. The driver dressed in dark midnight hues didn't seem to mind the weather he rode through. Rebecca could see he wore strangely loose clothing when he hopped fluidly from the driver's bench. A swath of material covered his face from chin to eyes, his head covered in a kind of hood. He flowed back to the door of the carriage and opened it.

Rebecca's heart pounded in her chest; her spine felt like the lightning outside was playing up and down it. *Two or three days he had said,* she thought, *Broheim had said two or three.* She knew now that her luck had finally run its course; for, what stepped from inside the carriage, drove the hope from her heart.

One after another, numbering five in total, man-shaped things stepped down to the stones of the courtyard. They seemed to wear fine gentleman's clothes in dark wool with white collars laid against their chins. All wore thigh length coats with dark capes clasped over them, reaching to their knees. Each carried a thin straight dark cane that, when on the ground, came to their waists. But it was their - what could you call it but a face? Their faces looked to be a mockery of what a man's should be. She could tell from this distance the faces seemed to be masks drawn over something not quite the shape of human underneath. Their eyes were covered with smoked spectacles and each had a tall hat atop its head, dark spills of hair fell to their shoulders. Their *wrongness* could be felt from here. Rebecca wanted to scream. These, she knew in her heart, were the Blind Men.

They moved their legs as though walking but the distance they traveled was too great for a normal stride. They seemed to move as on ice, one step and the ground slid beneath their feet. They didn't bob up and down as a normal man would walk either, but instead remained at constant level. The first of them moved toward Dormon, the others falling in line behind. The horses whickered and whinnied, trying to pull free of their harnesses as the things passed by them. The first came to within two steps of Dormon and slid to the left, the next to the right, so that it looked as though the five were being poured against a glass wall. The final *man* slid into place before Dormon and waited.

The guards looked to one another and back at their guests; Rebecca could see they were uncertain. The Blind Man in the middle in front of Dormon opened its mouth; the guards shuttered, putting their hands over their ears, wincing. Dormon only shook slightly. Dormon must have spoken because the Blind Man tilted its head in a

274

way that said it was listening. Dormon turned, gesturing for the Blind Men to follow, when suddenly, a bright blazing yellow orange ball leapt up from the shops opposite the open doors to the courtyard. The Blind Men, as one, shielded their faces and turned from the light.

The room shook with the concussion of the blast. The clouds above the university moved as if a wave rippled through them; the blaze lit them from beneath. This must have been James' distraction. Gathering her wits she covered herself with the blanket and whipped the pillow over her hand and what it held. She took a deep breath and released it, *calm, relax, breathe,* she thought.

"Guard, guard, come please. What was that noise?" she called out.

She heard the shuffling from the hall, more hurried now. The keys in the lock, she gathered her courage. The door opened; light silhouetted the guard in the opening. She hoped it was the same fiend from that morning. She lay in her undershirt, squinting into the light from the hall, appearing completely helpless, she hoped. *Come on you pathetic wretch,* she thought, *you can have your way with me with none to know you had.* The man took a step and halted. Then another and another, into the room he walked, into her trap. The man stood over her now. He breathed heavily. She caught the hints of strong alcohol from him.

"Guard," she said in her weakest voice, "what was that? It frightened me."

In an instant, the guard dropped to his knees and forced her into the blankets, his hand wildly groping at her. She was suddenly not so sure of her plan. The man was stronger than he looked and she struggled to get her hand, pinned between them, from beneath the pillow. She pulled with all her strength; if the man had not been in such a state, he may have seen the gleam on the lion pommel dagger as it plunged into his back.

He reacted, wrenching away. Rebecca held tight, pulling the knife from his back. She was up as a flash of lightning lit the room in stark white. She darted for the man on his knees, reaching back at his wound. She plunged the knife into his neck, gritting her teeth in a snarl. Hot wet spray splashed against her face. Another bolt of lightning showed the man's eyes, wide with fear and a ruined throat, blood gushed out in spurts, coating Rebecca and the walls. He fell over backward and died.

Rebecca's blood beat in her head. She couldn't think straight. She took a deep breath, and released. *Calm, relax, breathe,* she reminded herself. The beating of her heart slowed and her mind returned. She needed to act, and quickly.

She pulled the man to the blankets and searched his body. She found a leather sheathed dagger and a cloth sack with some coin. She went through his pockets and found a flask. *That'll teach you to drink on duty,* she thought savagely. Grabbing up a blanket, she wiped the blood from her face and chest as best she could and pulled on her shirt and coat. She stuck her head into the hall to see if anyone else was there. It was clear. She hurried back to the window to see into the courtyard. The carriage was still there but the Blind Men, Dormon, and the guards were nowhere to be seen. *They'll come here first,* she thought, *they'll take me first then deal with the fire.* She covered the man with the wool blanket and tossed the pillow over his head. She grabbed up both knives and the coin pouch then, remembering James' note, she pulled that from beneath the bottom blanket and stuck it in her shirt pocket. She pulled the door closed behind her.

Out into the hall, she ran. The ring of her boots on the stone thundered in her ears. Leaning against a wall, she pulled off her boots and continued in her socked feet. She came to the stairs leading to the hall below. She could see shadows moving toward the stairs on the patterned carpets, one ahead, and five behind, gliding more than walking. She turned from the stairs and dashed into the washroom. She heard only one set of boots climb the stairs but she was sure the Blind Men were there.

"Where is the guard I posted here?" she heard Dormon say, agitated. "If the man has left his post to use the washroom, I'll gut him."

Rebecca's heart froze. They were going to come this way. They were going to come in here and find her trapped. They were going to find...abruptly, she found herself, unbidden, gripping her ears to stop the sound from entering. Slowly she heard what the noise had been.

"Perhaps, he waits with the prey in the room beyond?" A voice like the death rattle of some cursed unnatural thing. It sounded more air drawn in than out, like life pulled out of the world.

"Yes..." Dormon hesitated, "perhaps he does. I'll skin him if he's done anything to your prey."

Again Rebecca gripped her skull to stop the sound.

"It matters not to we. As long as the soul lives, we can feed."

She heard Dormon's steps move away toward the storeroom. A rattle of keys, the door squeaked open, and Rebecca threw open the washroom door and bolted for the stairs. She ran across the patterned carpets, down tapestry and framed-painting lined halls. She tried to get her bearings. She couldn't make for the main courtyard; that strange carriage driver had been standing wait for his passengers. She needed to get out of this place.

Turning a corner, she found herself in a familiar hall. At the end lay a double set of doors, leading out to a balcony. Down the hall lay several intricately worked iron bound doors. Dormon's room lay down this way and in the small courtyard beyond the balcony...

She ran down the hallway past Postam's door and nearly past Dormon's. She paused and looked into the open room. For, set on his desk laid an all too familiar shape. A worn leather satchel rested on the desk, its contents laid out on the top. She rushed into the room and grabbed the bag, tossing in all that she found on the desktop. Her brother's compass, father's watch, scarf, bracelet, and the all too important journal, all went into the satchel. She looked around the room for anything that she could use to keep the contents dry. Nothing seemed adequate for what she had in mind.

Back out in the hall, her eyes fell on the large canvas oil painting outside Dormon's office. It was perfect. She reached up and took the framed painting from the wall and pulled the lion headed knife from her waist band. She cut around the border of the large painting and set her satchel, boots, and coat inside. She undid her shirt and stripped off her work pants. She bounced around, pulling her socks off, and threw all into the center of the oiled canvas sheet. She cut a strip from one side and pulled the whole contents up in a rough sack. She twisted the top as tightly as she could and wound the strip around the top, making a loop for her to carry it.

She stood in the hall in her underclothes with a once-oil-painting-sack, containing her belongings, and a knife stuffed in her waistband. She took a deep breath, committing herself to the plan. She strode calmly out the double doors into the rain soaked night. She could hear shouts and yells, and the roar of a fire from the shops. As she walked down the stairs wrapped around the courtyard, she thanked James and the others for saving her life.

Thirty-one: Separate Courses

Dormon stood in utter disbelief. How could so many things go wrong at once? He stood in the ruined end of the hall leading to what remained of the Alchemy shop. The charred timbers of the ceiling stuck from cracked stone, still dripping from the storm in the night. The shop had been transformed into a black and gray burned out shell. Nothing remained of the stores of gun powder that he had produced. The Romaran in charge here said that perhaps some of the other chemicals had added to the blaze and subsequent explosion. Perhaps! Was the man blind? That sent a shiver up his spine.

He stepped across the blackened floor stones. They crunched beneath his boots; most had shattered from the heat and the rain dripping on them. Everything that wasn't burned was soaked. The smell of char and chemicals hung heavy in the air. The roof of the shop was gone completely; the doors were nothing more than melted bits of iron lying where the frame had been. The walls had mostly crumbled down; nothing stood but a stretch here and there. He had his suspicions that, unlike what the Romaran had said, this fire was intentionally set. The coincidence was too great for anything else.

The fire had been astounding. As the rain fell into the open hole of the roof, instead of diminishing, it had flared more brightly. The fumes that were carried aloft had his men choking and gasping as they tried to battle the blaze. If that Romaran Alchemist had not shown up when he had, more of Dormon's men would be laid in the infirmary with ruined lungs. He had to watch and wait for the fire to burn itself out. That had taken most of the night. By the time it was out, his main problem had already taken his full attention. The girl was missing.

The Blind Men and he had gone into the room where he had her held and found a shape lying under blankets. When the Blind Man whipped the wool away, the sound it produced had shattered the glass in the small window in the wall. Dormon could still feel the Blind Man caressing his soul, like a cat toying with a mouse it intended to eat. They had fled from the room and hunted the corridors, looking for their prey. If he had not gone to his room to take a drink of the strong brandy he kept in his desk, he would have had to pay for wasting the Blind Men's time. He had come upon an empty picture frame lying in the middle of the floor. When he went into his office, the other gift he had been meaning to present the Blind Men with was missing as well. The girl had come that way he was sure of it.

They had searched the whole of the university by the time the fire was down to smolders and turned up nothing. At last resort, he led the Blind Men to search the dorms. He would have to deal with the consequences of that later. Children could be so troublesome at times. When Postam had reported fish in the well in the small courtyard near his office, he knew where she had gone.

* * *

Walking down the last few steps, Rebecca paused to look at the well in the center of the courtyard. She found it odd, it had drawn her mind again and again for some reason and now it was going to be her way out. She hefted the painting canvas over her shoulder and walked through the sheeting rain. She began to shiver. It was not as cold as it

281

had been but she was wet and the wind was gusting. She hurried over to the big round well and peered over.

The rain, over the last days, had raised the water level to above the grate in the wall. She would have to hold her breath the whole time. She prayed her brain had worked out the distance clearly. She held the sack over the edge and dropped it down into the water below; it floated on top. At least the things inside would be dry if she got through, no not if, when.

She lifted her leg up and straddled the edge. She felt a fool, strolling about in her underclothes but one does what one must. She lifted the other leg and in one motion pushed off to land in the center of the pool below.

The water knocked all the air from her lungs and sent her in to uncontrollable shivers. The pain was intense and when she surfaced, she breathed in heavy fast gasps. She needed to move fast or she would freeze before she could drown. Grabbing hold of the sack, she breathed deep as she could, and dunked her head into the dark water. She felt along the walls for the grated opening and slid inside. The walls were slicked in slime and her hands slid along, unable to get a firm grip. She pulled and kicked her way along until she hit a wall.

Panic hit her and she had to calm herself. *Filters*, she thought. Broheim had said something about filters to keep out fish and frogs. She pulled the lion headed knife from behind her waistband and felt forward. She found the wall, it felt like some kind of mesh material. She pushed the knife into it and heard it ripping in the water. She slipped through the opening and moved on. Her lungs heaved in her chest. She was almost out of breath. She came to the next filter and cut through. *Almost there*, she thought. She continued onward.

Her vision started to fail her. Her arms and legs no longer pumped as hard as they had. Her lungs burned in her chest for air, pushing in and out while she clamped her mouth and nose tight. She wasn't going to make it; she couldn't turn back though. Desperately, she pulled along the slimy walls of the tunnel.

She saw a dull glow ahead of her. It must be the entrance to the tunnel. She pushed herself to go on. She pulled and...ran into a series of steel bars. The tunnel opening had bars over it.

She knew now that she was going to die.

* * *

James was amazed he still drew breath. He and the others had made it back into the dorms without being spotted, even after guards started pouring down the halls. He had managed to light the fuse on the first go and was so surprised, he almost forgot to run.

The fuse sparked alight and began burning its way into the room. James watched it go and then turned, using his long legs for as much as they were worth. He saw Helen and Ganty, waiting for him, at the opening leading back into the service halls. He frantically signaled them to keep moving, when a wave of hot air rushed down the hall after him. The sound didn't come until he laid face down three feet past where he had last seen Helen and Ganty standing. James' ears rang and it felt like a giant had punched him. A roar, like all the furnaces in the world, came from the Alchemy shop.

He rose to hands and knees and slowly to his feet and staggered back to the opening. He found Helen and Ganty on their backsides staring up at him with shocked faces. "Come on, that will have gotten someone's attention; it sure as the Blazes got mine," he said, limping up the stairs to the upper halls.

Now, they stood looking at the wide eyed faces of the others in the dorms, Gregor's among them.

"What in the blazing pits of Discordia did you three set off?" he asked. "We felt the whole building move like it meant to get up and dance."

"Helen showed these dirt sucking rats how dangerous it can be to leave chemicals where children can get to them," James said with a laugh.

They all went to bed that night feeling like they had accomplished something. Something that, if it didn't repay the Red Guard for all they had done, went some way to setting things right. When they awoke in the morning, they were certain that this day would not be like any other.

Dormon stood in the center of the sleeping chamber. His arms folded behind his back. James noted the guards at the chamber entrance.

"Awake!" Dormon said loud enough to summon the dead. Every head stared at him in the entrance to the sleeping chamber. "We have had an incident this past night," Dormon said when he was sure they all saw him. "One of your fellow compatriots has…died." James smiled. The man had 'lie' plain across his face. "Young miss Dulac is dead. She died while trying to escape during the fire. I have brought some men with me who will be examining you. So, if you will come this way." This was not the way of Dormon as James had seen him. He was uncertain, shaky, rattled. That more than anything made James nervous.

The children filed out of the sleeping chamber with a bounce to their step. They had seen the hesitation when Dormon said Rebecca was dead. They knew she had gotten out. Whatever high spirits that thought had raised vanished at the sight of the five men waiting to *examine* them.

Dark clad men-shaped things stood at the entrance to the dorm. They each held a cane and had tall topped hats on their heads. Smoked glass spectacles covered their eyes. They never spoke but the guards and Dormon halted each boy, as he made his way to leave, before the things. As James approached something itched at his memory. *No eyes to see you by, but by and by they'll find you Bligh,* a torment from his childhood. Some older boys had tried to scare him into running home at night; they spoke of the Blind Men. Strynges. *Oh, Father, protect me,* he thought. As he passed them, they turned their heads to look at him. The faces were a charade. Their mouths too wide, the cheeks to narrow, and the slack way the skin hung gave their appearance a *wrongness* that would set anyone's hackles up. They never moved more than their heads, not even a chest rose and fell to say they breathed; and their silence was somehow more terrifying. When James exited the dorms, his knees buckled as he attempted to descend the stairs. He found himself among others; girls and boys slouched against the walls and leaned on the railings. Some cried in the corners of the landings.

When the last boy exited, his face drained of all blood. Dormon walked from the dorm entrance. "All work detail is cancelled for the time. These dorms will remain unlocked so you may comfort one another for – for your loss." James stared at the man in disbelief. He must have a will like iron not to be weeping from spending more than a moment with those things. Dormon moved down the stairs to the courtyard below. The five glided out from the dorms, cringing guards followed reluctantly at their heels. The things flowed down the stairs and as they passed James, whispers in his head made him grip his ears to try to keep out the sound. *We've no eyes to see you by, but by and by we'll find you Bligh. Find you, Bligh. We'll find you, Bligh.* The whispers echoed in his head and he shook with fear. James watched as the things continued down, never rising or falling, out into the courtyard. *Run Rebecca,* James thought, *run hard.*

* * *

Dormon was certain the girl couldn't have gotten far. When he sent Postam out with guards and hounds, they had made for the lake reservoir. What they found had startled them. The girl must have gotten out, somehow, judging by the steel barred cover, and she must have been on the move. The guards had tracked all morning for her but the hounds had come across a scent that spooked them off the girl's trail. It seemed that she had that famed luck Arnorans were said to possess.

* * *

Rebecca pounded her fist against the bars of the cover. She was going numb from cold and lack of air. Her hands felt feebly at the edges of the opening, hunting for some way out. She searched desperately for a handle of some kind, nothing. She was beginning to see flecks of white and black float before her. She would be crying if she weren't surrounded with water.

She gripped the bars in increasingly unresponsive hands and planted her feet in the slimy sand at the opening. She pushed with all she had left but the bars refused to move. Slowly, slowly, her body gave up. She gripped the bars in loose fingers and her muscle slacked. The gray light from the surface taunted her, just out of reach. She was drowning. Her vision was nothing more than a thumbnail at arm's length in a field of gray. Spots flashed and flickered about and she became *calm*. Her arms loosed from the bars and she half floated, half stood, before them, *relax*. The thumbnail of vision grew to become bright white and warmth flowed into her. She felt at ease and knew everything would be well. She was dying but all would be well.

A voice whispered as if behind her head. She turned to see who was there. Again, just behind her head, the voice came again. *Rebecca don't give in,* it said. She wanted to ask why she should not but all it said was: *You have more to do than this; don't give in*. She felt the warmth flowing from her. *Calm, relax,* she thought. Something in her started sliding, shifting within her. *Calm, relax, calm, relax,* she thought. Whatever was moving began to flow, moving out from her, moving toward the steel bars. *Calm, relax, calm, relax, calm, relax.* Breathe!

The bars exploded outward; a rush of water pushed her from the tunnel entrance out into the gray light from the surface. She tried to fight for the air but there was nothing left. Her arm rose up, carried along with the canvas sack. She too rose slowly to the rippling surface above. She could see circular waves as the sack broke the surface of the water and she kicked with her last bit of life.

Air burst from her lungs like a raging torrent. Her chest heaved in glorious burning pain as the air rushed back in to fill it again. The cold leached back into her and her muscles clenched tight. Numbly she made her way, pulling the canvas sack to hold her head up, to the shore of the lake. She felt dirt below her feet and she pulled herself, coughing, onto the shore. She was alive.

When her breath returned, she crawled on hands and knees to the forest near the lake's edge. She needed to get dry and she needed to get hidden. Under the relative cover of the trees, she sat and pulled the canvas sack to her. She undid the lashing at the top and unfolded the material. She stood slowly and fought against her wet underclothes, peeling them from her shaking body. She pulled the woolen work pants on, they clung to her still wet legs, and the shirt as well. Falling to her backside, she pulled her coat around her and shook relentlessly. When her hands could hold still long enough, she slowly, painfully, buttoned her shirt and pants and pulled on her socks, then her boots. She wrung out her underclothes, as best she could, and stuffed them into a pocket of her leather satchel. She needed to get moving.

She looked back to where Valgerhold laid. A bright plume jetted from the Alchemy shop. *No small feats for you James Bligh,* she thought and moved into the forest.

She made perhaps six hundred yards before the fatigue overtook her. She struggled along the last few paces, falling to her face, rising, and then falling again. She had never felt so tired in her life, like breathing was an effort. She thought it was from the cold; she could still not feel her hands and feet. When the convulsions hit her stomach, she knew something was wrong. Her mind spun, the world felt like it was moving around her. She tried to puzzle it out but the pieces kept changing shape.

Dawn peeked at her eyelids. She realized she'd fallen asleep. She could not move more than her eyes. She could hear the sounds of morning birds beginning their day. The rain had let up but she could feel the dampness still on her clothes. She tried to remember where she was. *Forest, I'm in the forest and I need to get moving.*

"Why?"

I need to get away from someone.

"Who?"

I'm not sure, men, I think, blind men.

"How are you going to get away?"

I don't know but I need to go, now. Before they come; I know that.

"We understand; we will help."

As her eyes closed, she vaguely thought how strange a dream she was having. She had carried on a conversation with someone but she had never seen him; or was it them? She couldn't think well when she hadn't exercised. That's what she needed; she needed to move. Her thoughts faded back into those mixed ideas and images of dreams. When her eyes opened again, she saw it was darkening in the east.

Twilight, I'm in the forest and it is twilight. How? She thought.

"We helped," spoke a voice in her head.

She felt frightened at first, but her mind told her to be calm. She shouldn't move too quickly. If she moved quickly it might upset them.

Who are they?

"We are," spoke the voice in her head.

She tried to jump but her body failed to move. *What's wrong with me?*

"You have Reached too far, too soon," the voice answered. "Do not be afraid we will watch over you; rest now."

Rebecca's eyes closed and she had dreams of hounds baying. She knew the hounds were trying to find her and she wanted to hide from them, but she was only Rebecca, floating helpless in her weakened body. Snarling, snapping, whining, and the hounds vanished.

She dreamt of riding a horse, a shaggy horse. The horse smelled of soil and trees. It carried her on its back as she slept and laid with her when it was time to rest. The horse was warm and called out for its brothers and sisters as Rebecca slept. A deep mournful cry came from her dream horse, almost like that of a wolf, she thought absently.

* * *

The guards had returned empty handed at midday. Dormon was furious but there was nothing for him to do. The Blind Men waited for Dormon's best efforts to find the girl for them, and then they made to leave, seeing his failure.

"We have come far from our haunt. We hunted this land for weeks and you had the prey all this while. You should have taken the prey from the outset. We will go after the prey as we must. You will remain here and wait for our return. We have unfinished business with you." The Blind Man moved closer to Dormon and stroked his soul once more. Dormon fell to his knees at the touch and began to weep. The other four Blind Men watched; Dormon could tell they were hungry.

"We will find the prey and cull it. Our return will see us feed once more unless we are instructed otherwise by Mandagore Adarian."

Was this creature offering Dormon an option? He thought wildly. What would make Adarian give him a pardon from the Strynges?

"I will send out men to aid you," Dormon was surprised at the desperation in his voice. "My Commander will take a patrol and find the girl for you. They will hold her while you come."

"A fine offering but you have already proven incapable of tracking the prey," said the Blind Man.

"Then I will have them go farther west into the Wilderlands to hedge her off. If they cannot find her, surely they can prevent her traveling too far from you."

"*That will be sufficient for the time. If they fail at what should be your task, we will cull them and come for you also,*" the Blind Man said. The corners of its wide mouth twitched outward. Dormon thought he saw a hint of teeth.

"They will not fail, they must not," the last he said for himself.

The Blind Men poured from his office, in their strange way of moving, out to their black carriage. The driver sprang into the bench. His dark clothes and face still covered to the eyes marked him for what he was. He led the carriage from Valgerhold.

Dormon stood staring after the carriage. Those creatures had done more ruining his work here than the fire had. The children who had been examined would have nightmares for weeks to come and they would not be fit to work for days yet.

Dormon wiped sweat from his forehead and pulled his hand from caressing his chest; the Blind Man had reached into his body to fondle his soul through that spot. The passing of its hand was unfelt but the caress of the Blind Man upon his soul made Dormon want to sit down. *Edwin my life as well as your own are in your hands*, Dormon thought. *Where had the girl gone?*

Thirty-two: Voices

Rebecca opened her eyes.

Forest.

"Yes," spoke the voice.

Different though.

"Yes," spoke the voice.

Where are you?

"We are near," spoke the voice.

Will you not show yourself? I must thank you.

"You will frighten and we will have to react."

I will not move, I promise.

"A promise the Touched One must not break," spoke the voice.

Slowly, Rebecca pushed herself, up to lean against the fallen log where she lay. She was in deep oak forest now. The trees stood tall and thick, little underbrush filled the area. These woods were old. She could recall moving in her sleep but she didn't know how. *A shaggy horse carried me*, she thought.

"Not a horse," spoke the voice.

Stepping silently from the trees, a shaggy gray brown shape appeared. It carried a rabbit in its jaws and its eyes stared fixedly at Rebecca's, yellow-green meeting yellow-gold. Her heart began to race. *Oh, Father protect me*, she thought.

She had the distinct feel the large timber wolf in front of her began to laugh as it dropped its catch. It wagged its thick tail and relaxed visibly.

"We told you, you would frighten," spoke the voice.

Rebecca stared at the wolf before her in utter disbelief. She was not scared though, anymore; she felt safe with this animal.

"You carried me away from the forest near the lake, didn't you?" she asked the wolf, it cocked its head and looked confused. Rebecca stretched her arms and legs, she felt like she had slept for a month. The wolf tensed and a low growl rumbled from its throat. Slowly, Rebecca put her arms down and tried to talk again.

"You helped me back at the university," she said, speaking again to the wolf. It growled deeper and stepped forward, baring its teeth. Rebecca's heart thumped in her throat. *What am I going to do; I think he's going to hurt me,* she thought. The wolf sat down, wagging its bushy tail again, panting.

"Your sounds confused us, Touched One; we became wary. We apologize. We have brought food; you will need it." The voice sounded friendly enough but strange, as though many spoke through the one.

You carried me here, away from the university, away from the lake? She thought.

"We did. It has been a time since Touched Ones moved in our home. We saw you near the water; you could not move. We tried to wake you. You lay alive but unable to hunt. We pulled you away from the building on fire, nearer our den. You still could not rise and then the men came. They brought the loud ones, the ones that sniff when they should look. The loud ones were scared by our smells and went from you. We carried you on our backs to this place." The wolf looked on at Rebecca with unblinking eyes.

Then I must thank you, she thought.

"We are honored to help the Touched Ones,"

The wolf picked up the rabbit in its jaws and carried it to Rebecca, dropping it by her hand. She smiled at the wolf and asked it if it would mind if she tried to rise.

"Please do, we will have the others bring your skin sack,"

Another wolf appeared as if from nowhere, carrying Rebecca's satchel. She bowed her head to the wolf, it seemed appropriate, and it brought the sack to rest beside the rabbit. The two wolves stared at her now. She pushed herself slowly off the ground to sit on the log at her back. She took a deep breath and released it.

"You do well Touched One," she was unsure if one was speaking or both of them. "You Reached far for one so young, we saw. You Reached, and the water billowed like the clouds in a storm. You came to the surface of the water and you were cold. We were impressed at your strength to live."

I'm sorry but I don't know what you're talking about. I was drowning and something happened...

"You Reached, and the water billowed; we saw," the wolves loped into the trees and vanished.

Wait where are you going?

"We go to hunt. We will be near. We will follow you to the Other; the Other will help you." With that, they were gone.

Rebecca pulled her satchel to her and opened the flap. She pulled out the knife she had taken from the guard. *I have killed,* she thought. *I am a murderer.*

"What is this *murderer*?" She heard in her head. She looked around and found another wolf lying not far to her side.

Rebecca pulled the knife from the sheath and looked at the blade. She sheathed it and pulled a flint from a small pocket on the leather scabbard.

Someone who kills another, she thought to the wolf.

"Ah, we understand. A hunter."

Not quite, murder is not like hunting. You think about it beforehand and you plot how you will do it. It makes you evil.

"We do not see it this way," the wolf rose and walked over to sit at Rebecca's side. "We think about what we hunt before we hunt it. We do what we must to survive. This does not make us evil."

No, but you need to kill what you hunt to survive. I killed just to get away.

"Would you have survived without killing?" the wolf was looking into her eyes, she would say, with sympathy.

I'm not sure. Some men were after me and the one I killed held me for them. He was also trying to hurt me.

"Then this word *murderer* does not apply. You are a hunter, Touched One," the wolf set its muzzle on her knee. She stroked the great head of the wolf and felt a bit better. After a time, the wolf rose and walked into the woods, leaving Rebecca alone. She struggled to her feet, it was amazingly difficult to balance, and began gathering wood to make a fire.

She dressed the rabbit as Gene and Lester had shown them and spitted it to put over the fire. She had a warm blaze going when the wolves returned, their muzzles red, and full of energy. They silently loped into the little camp and gathered round Rebecca.

There were six that Rebecca could see, and they all had a similar shaggy coat of dense gray brown fur. The patterns varied but they were as much alike as not. They watched everything Rebecca did with complete interest.

"Why do you play with your food this way," one or all asked, it was a bit confusing.

We, I don't like to eat my meat raw.

"What is this shiny metal stick you use to tear at your food?"

A knife, we, I use it to cut, so I can take smaller bites.

"Why not just put your head in and tear off a piece to swallow?"

Because that is ill manners and besides it's too hot, I would burn my mouth.

She felt the wolves laughing and they began to lay down to rest. One sat farther from the others, watching the woods; others paired off, playing or licking one another. Rebecca ate amongst the wolves and when she had finished she leaned back against the log.

How is it that we can talk?

"None know, it just is, as we are."

I have never been able speak with any other animals.

"Because, you had not Reached then."

What is this Reaching?

"The Touched Ones Reach and we feel it. We can hear them and them us. You are a Touched One, you Reached and now we can hear you. It is, and we are."

Rebecca was puzzling again. The wolves reacted very strangely. They stood up, turned to Rebecca, and locked their eyes on her. She stopped all thought and relaxed.

What is wrong?

"You are on the verge, you attempt to Reach and we become wary."

I was just thinking.

"That may be but we felt your attempts to Reach, connect that which was not, link the chains where they had been only parts before. You were on the verge and we are wary because we are not yet accustomed to you."

I won't hurt you, I promise.

The wolves laughed again, returning to their activities. "The young do not always know that which will hurt and that which will not. Do not attempt to Reach until we have taken you to the Other."

"Yes, the Other will help you." That sounded the same but different, like she had spoken to one before and the rest had spoke in agreement.

Who is this Other?

"The Other will help you. He is not far by our paws but you will have to travel slowly. The Other will show you, he will guide you. We have known him for a time and he is admired. The men who are on your scent will not find you with the Other."

Men on my scent, the men are still after me?

"We will watch over you until the Other. Do not be afraid."

Rebecca tried to follow the wolves' advice but her mind kept trying to see shapes in shadows. Each time, a wolf would pad next to her and look up to her. She quickly learned how the wolves spoke to each other. It was body language more than anything. A lowered brow, showing of teeth, drop of the tail, raising the fur, each meant something different to the wolves. She couldn't begin to even wonder at how she was able to communicate, because as soon as her mind grazed the subject, a wolf would be at her leg staring upwards.

She followed the wolves for days through the forests. The trees gave cover from the light above so she walked along dappled grounds. The air was clean and just hinted at the warmth that would come with spring. She felt at ease with the wolves. They brought her rabbits and once a leg of a deer. She cooked over fires she started with the flint from the murdered – no hunted, guard – and ate surrounded by wolves she came to call friends. They seemed to know the route they led her by, so, she hadn't thought to look in her grandfather's journal for many days.

One evening her mind slipped at sleep, a wolf lay near her, lending warmth. Her mind wondered at where she was in the world and she remembered the journal. Her eyes came to life at the thought.

"What have you thought of Touched One?"

I just remembered something I have in my skin sack, satchel I mean.

She pulled out the leather-bound book and flipped to the maps her grandfather had traced along the yellowed pages. She found one that showed the border of Romara and the Wilderlands. They had been moving west, judging by the sun, and Rebecca gauged the distance from what she could remember. How far, one hundred, two hundred, miles in the past days?

Do you know maps?

"We know forests and plains, mountains and rivers."

Could you tell me about what lay near this place?

"Trees lay nearest, then the river that splits. From where we have come lay the wide undrinkable water, and to where we travel lay the rocks in the grasses that lead into the mountains."

Rebecca interpreted the words the wolves spoke to her and tried to determine her approximate location. Somewhere near the border of the Wilderlands she guessed. There was a bay to the east, undrinkable water. A river ran to the bay; it forked northwest of the bay. A space demarcated with stones and grass showed land leading into the Santeri Mountains. She looked to from where she had come. Valgerhold lay nearly two hundred and thirty miles to the east.

How have we traveled so far, so fast?

"You keep good pace with us Touched One. We hardly need to slow for you."

298

How far to this Other?

"Not far now, close by. We feel him and we know his workings."

Tomorrow then?

"Or the day after. Are you so anxious to be away from us?"

No it's not that, it's just that…

The laughter again, "We play Touched One, we understand your need."

When we reach the Other I will have him thank you properly. You have done much for me and I have done nothing for you.

"We ask nothing in return. You have been little encumbrance to us. We have continued to live and hunt and that is all there is for us. We ask of you nothing."

I thank you my friends.

Rebecca turned her attention to the journal. She wondered at the map that showed where she was, but moved on at the insistence of the wolves. She turned through the pages of the journal, coming to the section James and she had read most often.

There seem to be certain artifacts that need to be either found or created to pass through the Barrier. We were able to gather this… and with that the Tremen bade us farewell, our questions still unanswered.

"Tremen, you think on sad subjects Touched One."

You know the Tremen?

"We have memory of the Tremen. They are hunters like we but inventive like you. They sail the undrinkable waters and roam near the Lost Lands."

Sailors and explorers? My grandfather met them, I think.

"Yes, we recognize you, now. Your father's father walked our land at one time. Your eyes are the same but your face is of your mother and mother's kin."

Rebecca felt stabs of pain at her eyes. She felt the tears trying to come.

You knew my grandfather?

"We felt him and aided where we could, yes. You must not think on this now; we feel you on the verge, rest now Touched One."

She tried to clear her mind but it kept snapping back, fighting her. She instead enveloped herself in studying the lines in the journal.

There seem to be certain artifacts that need to be either found or created to pass through the Barrier. We were able to gather this… and with that the Tremen bade us farewell, our questions still unanswered.

What was that? She looked at the words again. Something had shimmered there, in the valley between the pages. A line of shimmering gold light, barely visible, reached out to her eyes. Something was there just out of sight.

"Rest now," she looked up and a wolf stared at her, inches from her face. "You are on the verge and we are wary."

Thirty-three:
Leap Without Looking

By midday, the forest echoed with the sound of running water. *The river that splits,* Rebecca thought. She followed the wolves out to the banks of the river, Gandis it was called on the map. She stared at the raging waters, spills of white swirled about and the roar filled the world. She looked north and saw where the split occurred. Two rivers from one, East and West Gandis moved roughly southeast and emptied into the bay, after much winding.

How will we cross this?

"We follow south to where the waters widen; we will wade through there,"

Is there not a bridge somewhere that we could use?

"North is a metal and wood span that reaches across this river valley. We will not follow you if that is your course. Men and machines use that path and we stay clear. South is much safer for us."

Rebecca turned north and squinted to see through the bright reflections from the water. She thought she saw it; a dark spider web of trellises forming a railroad bridge reached across the river. That would be the way her pursuers expected her to go, the easier way. She would not let them find her.

We go south then.

"Yes, Touched One, south."

She walked with the wolves, moving along the eastern half of the Gandis River, until the water calmed and slowed. The water was clear and ran more slowly for the width it had gained as they traveled south.

The river bed was smooth rounded stones that had been carried from the Santeri Mountains over the years. Rebecca judged the water to be about to her chest from what she could see.

"We will cross here."

The water looks like it will be deep for you.

"That does not bother us. We have crossed this way many times. You will be cold though. The water is from the mountain ice; it still holds much of its cold."

I will move quickly.

The wolves waded out into the slowly moving water. In quick order they crossed, moving swiftly, but still they were carried several yards downstream before they were on the opposite bank. Rebecca took off her boots and socks as two remaining wolves waited for her. She stripped to her underclothes, and felt self conscious of the wolves' stares. She tucked her clothes into the satchel and pulled all the straps tight to keep out any splashes. She edged into the stream; the water made her puff in gasps as she moved deeper. She made little wooing noises as the water reached her waist. She could feel the wolves laughing.

"You should have the fur like we, for as much time as you spend in cold waters."

Rebecca held the satchel over her head until the water got deeper in the middle. She floated on her back and kicked with her feet, trying to keep the satchel dry. She saw the other two wolves charge into the water in sprays of white. They quickly caught up and swam beside her. When she felt the slick stones beneath her feet she stood and followed the two out of the stream.

That was harder than I thought.

"You do well keeping that skin sack dry."

302

Thank you; I was a good swimmer back home. My father owned a mill near a river like this one, only not quite as cold.

"Come, we will rest and warm you before we cross the second."

Rebecca followed the wolves into the patch of sparse trees on this part of the land between the rivers. The sun felt warm on her skin so she continued on in her underclothes, hoping to dry them as she walked. The wolves chose out a small hill to rest on and gathered around her. She sat and pulled up her knees. Four wolves crowded around her, one to either side, one behind and one in front. She quickly felt quite warm again and the wolves thanked her for rubbing their backs and heads while they sat with her.

From the hill, she could see the second river. It still held much speed from the river's mainstream to the north. She could see small whitecaps in the middle, and eddies and whirls churned the waters in places. This crossing would not be as easy.

"No, not easy, we have lost brothers and sisters to these waters. We don't often cross here but to journey farther south will take too much time. We will cross here; the Touched One must be careful."

Rebecca agreed and they moved to the bank of the Western Gandis. Rebecca felt nervous seeing these waters close. They were deeper and the rocks more jagged. She wondered if she could cross without drenching the satchel. The first wolves moved in cautiously. She watched as they pumped their paws, moving downstream all the while. The wolves shook themselves as they exited the stream almost fifty yards farther down than they had entered.

"The waters are swift; be quick Touched One."

Rebecca waded into the edge of the river. She fought the current as she walked, struggling to keep to the rocks underfoot. When the water reached her knees, it was no longer possible. She crouched low and turned on her back, the satchel held aloft. She felt herself pushed down river and leaned her head back to see where she was going. She spotted the wolves on the far bank. They slid by her as she kicked to cross the river. She looked back and the two wolves that had waited moved in after her.

They flowed toward her paddling with all their strength. She felt her feet brush stones and she braced her feet against the next stones she touched. She was able to stand slowly and exit the river. She looked upstream; she was another thirty yards from where the first wolves had exited. She made her way to where they stood waiting; she could feel their tension as she approached.

What is wrong?

Instead of answering, they looked to the river. One of the wolves who had waited struggled against a whirl in the river. Its eyes were wide with fear and it fought against being pulled under. Rebecca's heart sunk. This wolf was about to die.

Before she could think she dropped her satchel and ran upstream along the bank. She dove into the river without a look. She stroked with arms and legs now, back across the river, moving down toward where the wolf was losing his fight. Rebecca aimed for where the whirl was and met the wolf in the twirling water. Instantly the waters were pulling them under. She had seen this before at home during storms. The rivers would rage and whirls would pull children under to drown. She remembered something her mother had told her once, she hoped it was correct.

Be calm, friend and take a deep breath, she thought at the wolf.

"We will, Touched One," came back in a panicked tone.

She grabbed hold of the wolf when he looked to have his breath held and plunged down into the whirl. The waters pulled the two under, the wolf kicked, trying to get to the surface, his eyes wide with horror.

Remain calm, friend, I will help you.

Nothing came from the wolf; he was in sheer terror.

The whirl pushed them to the riverbed and Rebecca felt rocks beneath her feet. The whirl's force lessened at the bottom and she was able to kick off for the surface at an angle once it released the two.

She broke the surface with the wolf hugged to her; he pawed at her shoulders, trying to get higher out of the water. She floated on her back and kicked for the bank. She felt strong jaws on her underclothes, pulling, and she realized the other wolves had come to pull them from the water. The wolf she had saved crawled out and shivered on the bank. He looked back at Rebecca as all the wolves gathered around her.

"Thank you, Touched One you saved us," it had the sound of all of their agreement.

You have nothing for which to thank me; it was what I could do to help for all you have done for me.

"You will have a place with us forever Touched One; we have never seen one of your kind save one of ours."

The wolf she saved from the currents walked to her with his tail between his legs and his head low. Rebecca sat on the stones of the bank and held out her hand, he licked her fingertips.

"We are sorry we panicked Touched One, we should have trusted you; we could have lost both of us."

No need to apologize friend; you did well for what was happening. I've never seen a wolf hold its breath before.

"We don't usually stay under for long."

The wolves' tension released and they all shook themselves dry. Rebecca gathered her satchel, after dressing, and followed after as the wolves made for a thinning wood that led off to rolling hills of grass and gray black boulders.

Thirty-four: Meeting the Stone Walkers

The party of wolves and Rebecca moved cautiously out from the sparse cover of the trees. The land became rolling hills of green and yellow grasses interspersed with stone outcroppings. This was an area of foothills before the range of the Santeri Mountains. The wolves told Rebecca they would soon enter the territory of the Stone Walkers. She questioned them as to who they were.

"The Stone Walkers are a touchy sort. They have a difficult life in the mountains and feel that any other not of their kind are weak. We feel otherwise of course."

Wolves? The Stone Walkers are another pack of wolves.

"Yes, but they are strange to us. If we were not escorting you to the Other, there would be disputes. Disputes with Stone Walkers are savage and we would have to flee for our own home."

The wolves pace ate up the ground leading into the mountain range ahead. The line of sharp jags and peaks of the Santeri reached skyward. The caps were topped in white snow and the mountains themselves made a dark mottled horizon stretching for as far as Rebecca could see north and south. The rolling foothills gave way to sharper inclines and rougher footing. The grasses dwindled, and were replaced with stretches of bare rock showing through the soil. The wolves slowed their pace and became tense.

"We must announce ourselves; if the Stone Walkers are near, they will respond and know we are here."

The wolves sat and leaned back their heads. One after another they began to cry out; the sound made Rebecca's skin prickle with its mournful tones. Again the wolves sung into the silence. Rebecca waited with the wolves, listening for a response. Rebecca strained to hear any noise. Crickets chirped and birds twittered to one another. The soft rumble from the river was only just audible. Then from some distance away, a lower more ominous response came from the mountains. The wolves pricked their ears to listen to the sounds. It seemed to surround them and Rebecca wondered if these Stone Walkers might not cause them some problems, despite what her friends believed.

The wolves moved forward into the mountains. They seemed on edge, swinging their heads from side to side looking for movement. They told Rebecca that they came this way to visit the Other, and the Stone Walkers would allow passage for such reasons, but the Stone Walkers often made the journey difficult. What exactly these difficulties might be they wouldn't say.

As the afternoon light began to wane toward twilight, the wolves led Rebecca through a narrow mountain pass. The wolves suddenly halted, sniffing the air.

"Be still Touched One, the Stone Walkers are near."

Rebecca felt her pulse quicken. She looked from side to side in the pass. The floor was crumbled rocks washed down the hills from rains over the years. The sides of the pass showed the weathering of time as well. Lichens and mosses clung to the rocks where they found it hospitable, adding gray greens to the blacks and dark grays of the rocks. The hair on the back of Rebecca's neck stood on end as a dark shape stepped soundlessly into the pass. More followed after, Rebecca counted thirteen in all. Their coats were just as dense as her friends' but where the wolves she traveled with were browns and grays, theirs were blacks and charcoals. The first to come into the pass stepped closer.

"Why have you brought one of the man kinds with you, Tree Dwellers?" the voice was harsher than she was used to.

"We escort this Touched One to the Other," her friends responded.

The Stone Walkers swiveled their heads to stare at Rebecca. Their stares were unwavering.

"We can feel it now; the young Touched One must not Reach while she travels our lands." That sounded like a command to Rebecca.

I promise I will not Reach while I travel your home, I thank you for passage.

She caught the feel of the Stone Walkers laughing; it too was a harsh sound.

"We warn you Tree Dwellers other man kinds walk our land. They seem to hunt but not prey as we know it. They pass up the goats and deer that venture into our mountains and send out runners to search the way you have come."

What do they look like?

"All man kinds look similar to our eyes, Touched One. They look like you only bigger and with shorter head fur. They have no female scents among them, and they carry the long metal sticks that throw fire and rocks at us."

Big men with guns, men were chasing after me from where we have come.

"Then perhaps these are your men."

I would not like them to find me.

"That is between you and them and these Tree Dwellers. We will do what we can to keep them from your trail but they try to hunt us when they see us."

Thank you, Stone Walkers.

"It is an honor to help the Touched Ones. Take care of this one, Tree Dwellers."

And with the last, the Stone Walkers vanished into the mountains. Rebecca began to worry. The Red Guard could have taken the train tracks from Valgerhold through the mountains days ago. For all she knew they could have brought the Red Fist Army into Romara to search for her. She just didn't know how badly the Blind Men and whoever had sent them wanted her.

"Be not afraid Touched One; we will see you safe to the Other."

She wished she could feel as confident as the wolves.

As night began to creep over the mountains, the wolves stopped to rest. They managed to find a brace of rabbits and they all ate them raw. Rebecca had to learn to eat her meat this way; for, there was not always time for a fire as they had traveled. Now though, beside the fact that she didn't think she could find enough wood here, she was afraid she might be spotted while she rested with a fire. The wolves gathered round her and nuzzled close as they drifted off to sleep.

Rebecca awoke with a start. That sound echoing through the mountains was the shot of a rifle; she was sure of it. The wolves were awake in an instant, looking as though they had not just roused from sleep. The moon still hung high in the sky; they had hours till dawn yet. The sound of the Stone Walkers cries filled the mountains.

"We must move quickly Touched One. The Stone Walkers give warning."

Rebecca gathered her satchel and trotted after the wolves. They led the way, sending out one or two ahead to scout the path. After about an hour running, Rebecca's lungs were burning. Her legs were tired from gripping the loose stones and finding footing in the ever rising path. She hoped they were nearly there because she was going to have to stop soon.

"No stopping Touched One, we scent man kinds near."

The news gave Rebecca renewed energy and she climbed and ran with the wolves, moving farther into the mountains. The energy she had gained from fear burnt off soon and she slowed. The wolves urged her onward. Soon, they stood at the peak of one of the lower mountains, looking into the valley below.

A makeshift camp had been set up and Rebecca could see men moving between the lean-tos and small tents. There were horse lines off to one side. The men wore rougher clothes, with no sign of who they belonged to, but Rebecca knew them for who they were. Red Guard. She could see a large bulky man with a shaved head and a beard, moving about, giving orders to the others in the camp. Postam had been sent to bring her back.

These men are those who would have hurt me back at the university.

"Then we will remain hidden from them. Come Touched One, something feels wrong in that camp."

Thirty-five: One Last Dash

Postam strode through the camp, feeling anxious. Anton had said he was to act as a net to catch Dulac but they had not seen sign of anything more than wolves and goats here. His men were taking their absence from the university as a holiday of sorts. They were often found lounging, sipping from hidden flasks or dicing in groups around the fire. Postam confiscated the spirits but allowed the dicing to continue. Whatever would allow the men to keep their minds from the one who had been sent with them, he would allow.

Postam had not believed what Ramon had said about the Blind Men when he first heard it. Any doubts he had vanished when the five arrived to cull Dulac. Postam shivered slightly as he looked into the mountains.

Now, he had one in his midst. In this very camp, one of the five had come to see that Postam was positioned correctly. As if he had not spent the first half of his life in the service of the Red Fist Army. The Blind Man's tent was no larger than any other and, for all Postam knew, it was empty save for the creature sitting in it. He had not seen the Blind Man take food or water since he had begun traveling with it. Moving through the woods on horses had proved difficult as well. The Blind Man rode his dark horse far back from the others so as not to send the other horses into a panic. The horse he rode seemed to have become accustomed to its rider, only just. The men were another story.

When the Blind Man had ridden out to the train leaving to cross the mountains, his men had nearly soiled themselves. They knew very well what this creature was and were not keen to be traveling with it. When the train had reached the last depot, the general store had been raided for as much liquor and whatever wards against evil as they had on hand. He had spotted one of his men riding with a garland of garlic around his neck. Foolish man. Folklore about the Blind Men journeyed toward the absurd, but the more Postam had traveled with it the more he thought that perhaps the stories didn't go far enough.

The light of day was dwindling and Postam, as he so often had, scanned the mountains for signs that someone approached. Nothing, as had been the case for days. Postam wondered exactly what use this Blind Man was if all it did was sit in its tent until dark crept over the mountains. Some of his men were recounting stories from their childhoods.

"I hear they can walk right through walls and grab your soul while you sleep."

"You know why it stays in that tent all day, because it would burst to flame if the sun touched its skin."

"Why you think it wears them smoked spectacles? I thought they won't suppose to have eyes?"

"It dresses a dandy that's for sure, I han't owned a set a clothes so fine ever in my life."

"You know how to kill one of 'em? I hear it takes a number of knives to do the job proper."

"Or one Palantean," the last sent the men into nervous laughter.

Postam turned. "Shut your mouths about the heretics. I won't have that title uttered in my hearing," he growled at the man who had spoken.

313

Suddenly the flap of the Blind Man's tent whipped open and the thing glided toward Postam in that strange way it had. It took a roundabout path, staying as far from the light of the fire as possible. This had become routine waiting for signs of Dulac.

Postam pulled his head from between his shoulders, trying to remember what the Blind Man had just spoken. Postam was not sure how Anton took the sound of their voices so well; he himself found it difficult not to slap his hands to his ears. Sliding his mind around what he could remember hearing before his ears tried to stop listening, Postam responded.

"No…no sign," he said, swallowing.

"Something comes, something not far from the current haunt."

The Blind Man, ignoring Postam's shudders, turned to look at the mountains.

"Have your men begin the hunt for the prey."

Postam hurried to follow the order, more to be away from the thing than to be dutiful. He assembled a group of his trackers and sent them scouting into the mountain range. Perhaps they would find Dulac and he could be back to Valgerhold in a few days, away from this nightmare come true.

Postam sent a group of six men armed with rifles into the mountain range. When Postam returned to look for the Blind Man, it had vanished into the night. No sound, no warning, it was just gone into the shadows of the deepening dark.

After a time, Postam heard a single shot. If those fools killed the girl before the Blind Man was satisfied, Postam would tear out their hearts before the Blind Man could tear out their souls. Shortly after the shot, Postam heard the deep haunting sounds of the mountain wolves they had spotted over the days. He figured his men were taking

314

pot shots at the animals. They hadn't managed to hit a single one since they had been here, the wolves seemed able to vanish as a gust of wind.

Postam paced the camp, issuing orders to men to secure the camp for the night. He set guards and had the horses put down for the night. He prayed that this excursion would end soon.

* * *

Rebecca headed southward through the passes and trails the wolves found through the mountains. The night had seemed to last on as they moved and Rebecca's vision had time to adjust to the light the moon lent. She still had to watch her footing in the steep areas, but the wolves and she seemed to be setting a quick pace.

The wolves headed more westerly now. They said they would arrive at the Other by day break at the pace they traveled. They told Rebecca they would be safe from her pursuers when they reached the marked grounds. It didn't make much sense to Rebecca but she trusted them and followed their lead.

Suddenly, she heard a whizzing sound by her ear and ducked to the side; the sound of the shot came after. She took shelter behind a large boulder and told the wolves to find cover as well. She poked her head over the boulder to see in the direction the shot had come. She spied three men, moving in the mountains toward where they were hidden.

"We are sorry we did not see your pursuers Touched One."

Don't worry about that now. Is there some way you could call out to the Stone Walkers, get them to distract the men while we make a dash for cover?

315

"We cannot convey such ideas over distances but we can call out for their assistance."

The wolves laid back their heads and howled into the night, a short cry followed by a longer. Some seconds later, Rebecca heard the response from the Stone Walkers, two quick cries in a row.

"The Stone Walkers come, Touched One."

The men bearing down on Rebecca hesitated at the sounds of the wolves so close. They stopped their advance and scanned the hills. Rebecca and the wolves took the chance and ran farther along. The men took another shot but the distance was too great and it whizzed off a rock well to the side of Rebecca.

The path from the mountains became less barren as the wolves led onward. Grasses sprouted from beneath rocks here and there and rich soil smell kicked up as Rebecca and the wolves ran.

The sounds of screams and two shots echoed from the rocks from where they had come. She heard snarling and snapping, and cries of pain, mainly of men. She hoped none of the Stone Walkers had been killed.

Rebecca could see trees ahead to the southwest. They were nearly there the wolves said. Rebecca chased after and she felt the relief of safety near to hand. The wolves ran into the forested land and Rebecca could feel their anxiety lessen; they too felt relieved. She slowed her pace as they did, to catch her breath.

"Halt, Touched One! Something moves."

Rebecca's heart pounded but she did as the wolves said. They arrayed around her, looking in all directions. Their ears pricked and their fur stood on end. She heard low rumbling growls from many of the wolves.

"A wrongness comes this way; we can feel it."

Can you tell where it is?

"It drifts between worlds, Touched One. We will not be able to hunt whatever it is. We must continue to the marked grounds; we will be safe there from men and this wrongness."

The wolves moved again, Rebecca placed at the center of the pack, wolves turned back to check the rear every few yards. Rebecca reached into her satchel and pulled the two knives she carried. She eyed every tree shadow like an enemy.

A black flash of smoky tendrils lashed against her and she spun, falling to the ground. The wolves were around her in an instant. She looked up to see a wolf give chase, snapping after the remains of the apparition; before it turned back to resume its guard on her.

"A Masked One, we must run Touched One. You will draw the Masked One to us but we will be safe in the marked grounds. Run, Touched One!"

Rebecca picked herself up and took hold of her knives. She ran, following the wolf in the lead. She felt her blood rush through her. *Masked Ones, they have to be Blind Men,* the wolves did not answer but she felt agreement from them.

"A bit farther, Touched One, we can feel the marked grounds now."

Rebecca was hurled sideways; she bounced off a nearby tree and fell bruised to the forest floor. She tried to get her breath back as the wolves gathered round. Their eyes told her they were frightened. They looked at her as though they would help if they could. She knew they would and she didn't grudge them any. She took a deep breath, gathering her wits.

"We can run Touched One we are nearly there."

I don't know if I can keep going my friends. I feel weak like I've had the energy of a day pulled from me.

"The touch of the Masked Ones, you must not let it have you Touched One."

What can I do?

"We don't know; we don't hunt Masked Ones."

The sorrow that came through with those last words made Rebecca want to cry. They were doing their best to get her to safety but they couldn't fight this. She gathered herself and tried to calm. She breathed a few times clearing her mind.

"You must not Reach Touched One. There is too much danger in it."

Tell me when you think the Masked One comes next.

"We will try."

She stood and walked more slowly, the wolves alert. She held a knife at the ready. She calmed herself, limping a bit from her attacks. She relaxed, trying to picture what she would do when the next attack came. She breathed slowly.

"Now, Touched One!"

Rebecca threw her lion pommel knife as hard as she could at the center of the black smoky shape hurtling toward her. The knife somehow stuck in the dark airy filaments and held in place. The mass of tendrils coalesced into the rough shape of a man. The shriek it emitted had Rebecca writhing on the ground and the wolves snarling and whining. She saw one wolf bolt for the man-shape's throat. The solidifying form whipped a materializing cane as the wolf got close and the wolf flew off wildly into the air. It yelped as it hit the ground and slowly worked its way to its paws again.

318

The shriek halted and the now fully-formed Blind Man stood before Rebecca and the other wolves. Rebecca, on her knees, held the second knife, staring on through watery eyes. The Blind Man attempted to pull the knife from its chest but it seemed incapable of getting a firm grip; its fingers passed through the hilt. Rebecca tried to calm herself and took aim with the second knife.

The Blind Man looked up in time to catch the spinning blade between its eyes. Its smoked spectacles shattered, the shards vanishing in dark wisps, and Rebecca could see now why these things were called Blind Men. Lids blinked over two gaping holes that seemed somehow to stare directly into her; the Blind Man walked toward her in its half gliding way. Rebecca could see the head was hollow inside the eyeholes, as though the skin somehow hung unsupported in the rough shape of a face. The two knives stuck from the creature's body, one in the heart the other between those malevolent empty blinking holes.

The wolves were at her sides, growling savagely at the Blind Man. It hesitated for an instant before it gripped the end of its cane in its other hand. It twisted the end and pulled a long vicious spike from the length of cane. It moved relentlessly forward.

"Run Touched One, you have pinned the Masked One here in this world. It will feel our jaws now."

The wolves circled the Blind Man like a wounded deer. They looked for the weaknesses the prey would show. Rebecca rose; the Blind Man's empty gaze tracked as though transfixed to her chest. A wolf leapt in and the Blind Man spun faster than Rebecca could imagine. The wolf yelped as the spike pinned it to the ground through the shoulder.

Rebecca screamed out; the wolves jumped onto the Blind Man's back and began tearing at its face. Shreds of black pulled away and vanished like smoke before they hit the ground. The Blind Man rose up and sent the wolves sprawling all around. The wolf it had stabbed lay trying to get up, to get away, but the Blind Man raised its spike above its head for a death blow. *Calm, relax, breathe,* and the world…grew…slow.

Everything moved as if the flow of time had dwindled to a trickle. The wolves spun from their attack to stare at Rebecca, their eyes wide with terror. The Blind Man was bringing its spike down; the injured wolf looked helplessly upward. Rebecca felt herself slip, like a sudden release. The air condensed in a tight sphere, moving away from Rebecca's outstretched right hand, bending the dim night light around its faint glowing, violet-blue edge. She saw the Blind Man turn its head, bits of its mockery of a face torn away leaving empty air. The wolves leapt in infinite slowness away from the hurtling sphere. She saw the injured wolf squeeze tight its eyes and try to get lower to the ground.

The sphere flashed away from Rebecca. The world rushed to catch up its time. The sphere took the Blind Man in the chest, exploding in a burst of bright, blue-white light. The Blind Man instantly evaporated from the center of its form outward in thin streams of black mist. The two knives dropped with a clatter to the forest floor and all was silent.

Rebecca panted in fear. The wolves gathered themselves from the ground and stared at her. They approached hesitantly.

"You should not have Reached, Touched One. You have not been guided you could have been lost."

I had to do something. Convulsions hit Rebecca's stomach like a punch. She doubled over and clutched her abdomen. *Something's wrong my friends.*

"We will take you to the Other; he is not far now."

Rebecca's mind began to swim, her pulse quickened, and she felt like her hand had been seared in frost. She drew ragged, rasping breaths and her eyes closed. She felt herself drawn up onto warm shaggy fur that smelled of soil and trees.

Thirty-six:
Meeting the Other

Rebecca opened her eyes. The light of the world overwhelmed her at first. She blinked several times before she could look around and begin her mind working. Her thoughts felt sluggish like the gearing in her brain had been greased with tar. She saw a wood slat ceiling. *A room*, she thought. *How had she gotten here?*

"We carried you on our backs," spoken into her mind rather than her ears. Rebecca looked around, trying to rise, but slumped back before she could move her head more than a few inches.

Where are you?

A padding of feet, the click of nails on the floorboards, and a large gray shape appeared at Rebecca's head. The wolf walked with a bit of a limp and it wore a kind of collar looped around its neck. A metallic disc hung from the collar, a glass face showed gears and springs of various materials, moving about inside, like an intricate mechanical watch. The device had no hands or dials to show what it was doing but its soft ticking and whirring made Rebecca feel warm for some reason.

Where am I?

"We brought you to the Other. Be not afraid, he will keep you safe."

Rebecca weakly reached a shaking hand out to touch the wolf's face, it nuzzled at her touch.

"You have saved us twice now, Touched One. We will help you in whatever way you ask of us if you ever come again to our home."

Are you leaving me?

"The Other has your care now. We will stay to see you rise but we are far from our home and we long for its familiar smells and sounds. We live for little more than waking each day and hunting and living our lives. We are not meant for adventures. We leave that to you." She smiled as she felt the wolf laughing softly.

"Rest now, Touched One. All will be well when next you rise."

Rebecca closed her eyes; the soft sound of ticking lulled her, she slipped off to sleep.

Rebecca opened her eyes and smelled food. She looked around and found a small bedside table set with a tray and a steaming iron kettle with a small ceramic bowl next to it. She pushed herself to her elbows, lying in the bed she found herself again. She looked up; making sure this was the same room she remembered. She struggled to a sitting position, letting the covers fall. She grabbed them back up around her chin when she realized she had been stripped. She looked wildly around the room.

The wolf wearing the strange device around its neck picked up its head from the floor where it laid. It looked at her with curiosity.

"What is wrong Touched One?"

Where are my clothes; who took them?

"The Other, we suspect, took them. He made noises that made us think he distrusted the smell of them."

A man stripped me naked? She was shocked and embarrassed. Her face heated and she felt more uncomfortable by the second. She heard a deep man's voice humming from below her, from beneath the floor boards. She looked around the room for anything with which she could dress herself.

The room was small and made from naturally finished woods. The warm light, filtering through the white drapery of the windows to either side of the bed, made the room feel homey. A wood door set with brass fixtures was set in the wall opposite the bed; it sat ajar. Other than the small table with the tray and kettle, there was little else in the way of furnishings. A woven rug where the wolf laid was the only adornment to the floor. A large wardrobe sat in the corner but she could tell the humming was approaching, climbing stairs by the sound of boots. She didn't trust her strength to carry her to the wardrobe to search it. Besides, how much more exposed would she feel if she collapsed halfway when this Other, whoever he was, came barging through the door?

The humming stopped just outside the door. The wolf pricked up its ears and its bushy tail began to sweep the floor behind it. The door creaked open enough for a man's head to peer inside. He seemed friendly enough by appearance. Copper-red hair, graying at the sides, framed a slightly plump-cheeked face with bright blue eyes. A beard of the same color grew from his face, grown longer and to a rough point at the chin. He appeared to be in his late middle years by the fine lines that showed around his eyes. He wore round glass spectacles and had a second and third pair dangling from leather cords around his neck. His eyes brightened, twinkling, when he saw her sitting in the bed. He pushed the rest of the way through the door, revealing a man who had not missed a meal in his life. He was short of tall perhaps a few inches taller than Rebecca herself. His smile seemed to say he knew something she did not.

"I see you have awoken. How do you feel my dear?" he asked, smiling broadly.

"Where are my clothes?" she said through gritted teeth, trying not to redden more.

"Oh, well, I had those burned; they smelled much the same as you do yourself at this point. Not that I can blame you, arriving in the company you did." He smiled at the wolf lying on the carpet. Rebecca took his comment as a personal affront to herself and her friends.

"We do not smell," she said in an outraged tone. She caught the distinctive odor of unwashed flesh when she pulled the covers tighter to her chin. "Well, they don't smell at least," she said half under her breath.

"They are what they are," he said, spreading his hands as to say there was no changing what was. "Just as you are what you are." The man walked into the room and sat at the foot of the bed. Rebecca scooted to the headboard and pulled her knees up to help guard her from the man. "Come now child, I have seen quite more than you can imagine in my time. Certainly I have seen older, and younger, finer and coarser than anything you hide. Let me examine you and see how you are coming along," he reached up and pushed Rebecca's hands down to reveal a leather cord around her neck.

She hadn't noticed in her anxiety at finding herself the way she had but she too wore a device around her neck. She looked down at the metallic case of the object. She saw it was etched in intricate designs, with patterns and swirls seeming to move around its body. The glass window revealed gears and cogs, springs and wheels all moving in their own fashion. She felt the object now more fully than she had. It felt like strength leaked into her from it. She was so fascinated by the discovery she hadn't noticed the man was leaning in

325

to inspect the workings as well, holding one of the dangling pairs of spectacles to look closer.

She jumped when she noticed how close his head was to her chest and yanked the covers to her chin. He gave her an amused glance and stood from the bed.

"You should eat what you can and drink the tea. When you have that down, you can wash yourself. Down the hall there is a washroom. There will be clothes waiting for you outside the door." He walked to the door and turned back to look at her. "Keep that," he pointed at the device around her neck, "in place until I can check it properly; without having you jump out of your skin."

Rebecca felt ashamed for being so suspicious of this man. So far, all evidence pointed to him having helped her without reason. The wolves seemed to trust him which gave the man more ground to stand upon. She spoke before he could close the door behind him.

"Wait," the door opened a hair and he looked back. "Thank you for helping me and my friends." She looked to the wolf on the ground.

"I would help the meanest of their kind they could bring limping in here, and I reckon he'd have a touch more trust in me than you." He said it with a smile which made Rebecca feel even worse.

"What is your name?" she asked. She tried to look relaxed while still hiding herself.

"Alaric von Magus," he bowed his head and closed the door behind him, resuming his humming.

Thirty-seven: ## The Way of It

Rebecca turned to the tray and pulled the ceramic cover from the plate. A feast awaited her from what she was used to eating. Meat of some kind in gravy, carrots and potatoes, warm bread with a jam jar waiting, peas and other vegetables. She figured the small bowl was to be used as a cup and she poured the tea from the kettle, it tasted of cloves, cinnamon, and other spices she couldn't name, and warmed her belly. When she looked at the tray a moment later, she found hardly a crumb remaining. She had never eaten so hastily in her memory. She drank the rest of the kettle of tea and made to rise from the bed. The wolf stood from the rug and came to watch.

"You do well Touched One. You felt near death when our brothers and sisters brought you to the Other. We could not help you ourselves for we needed help as well from the Masked One's wound. The Other helped us and assured us you would rise before the day was half spent. "We see he tells us true."

I feel like a fool thinking the worst of him. He must think me very childish indeed.

"We would not think so. The Other knows you have been through much. He is a kind soul. The Other will know you as we do; we are sure of it."

Thank you for your words my friend. How are you feeling? I was so scared for you back in the forest.

"We know, we were frightened as well. You should not have Reached, Touched One, even to save us. It was a very dangerous thing to do, untrained as you are, dangerous, but courageous as well. You must not let your courage get you injured; you are a special one Touched One."

I didn't really know what I was doing to tell it true. She looked at her right hand it was a bit red and sore. She flexed her fingers, loosening them. *I just wanted to stop the Masked One. I don't even know how I did it.*

"The Other will show you and it will be less dangerous. Come, you should do as the Other told you, then go to him. We will stay for a while yet."

Rebecca pulled the covers from the bed, wrapping them around her and walked, with the wolf at her side, from the room. She found herself in a wooden hall, a few other doors were spaced down it but the one at the end was opened. Light spilled onto the floor from inside, a towel hung from a hook, she could see through the opening. She padded across the wooden floor boards, the wolf's nails clicking as it followed. She stepped through and the wolf came along.

Inside, she found a small washroom or sorts. A mirror hung on the wallboards above a basin attached to them; copper pipes ran to and from it. She saw a wide round porcelain bowl with a flat bottom on the floor, a hole cut in its center with a grate fastened over. A set of copper tubes ran from the floor, through a set of valves, to a rounded metal housing with many holes directed down into the bowl. A loop of metal, supported around the bowl with rods attached to the floor, held a curtain that hung from hooks. She was completely baffled.

What do you suppose this thing is?

"The Other used it to wash us before he tended our wound and collared us with his device."

How does it work, do you think?

"The Other adjusted the position of those metal sticks and water rained from above, from that." The wolf finished, looking at the housing with the holes. The metal sticks Rebecca took to mean the valves. She stepped closer and turned one of the handle valves. Water poured from the housing overhead and grew hot. She turned the other valve and the water cooled. She dropped the bedcovers to the floor and stepped into the bowl, pulling the curtain around to keep in the water. She thought for a moment about removing the device around her neck but Alaric had said not to, so she left it. She found a cake of soap and washed herself clean. Brown water poured from her, circled the hole in the center, and disappeared. When she felt clean enough, she pushed the valves back and the water ceased. *What a marvelous contraption*, she thought as she dried herself with the towel hung on the hook.

She opened the door and found a folded set of clothes for her. She pulled on the shirt and pants, made for a boy it seemed in soft dark cotton, and walked from the washroom with the wolf. She continued to dry her hair as she came to stairs that led down. She padded barefoot down the steps and found the most comfortable room she had ever known.

Shelves lined the walls with books numbering in the hundreds if not thousands, squeezed into every available space. Several tall backed mismatched chairs of leather or velvet or wood sat around the room with more books piled at either side of them. The floor was covered in a woven rug with an intricate Beltari pattern. Small tables around the room held strange objects of metal and glass, wood and porcelain. They all ticked or whirred quietly, giving the room the sense of a living being. They seemed to call to her to examine them; to see for what they were meant. She hardly noticed Alaric reading near the fire in the river stone hearth, sitting in one of the chairs, his back to where she stood. A strange rifle hung over the mantel, with an elaborate firing mechanism. More wolves lay around him. They looked up when she stepped into the room. Her escort wolf went to Alaric and sat, staring at him. He snapped from his concentration and looked at the wolf by his leg.

"Yes, I think you can have that off now, if you insist," he said, leaning in to unlatch the collar from the wolf and setting the device on a stack of books to his side. "You seem to have lost the limp I see. You should be bringing down deer with no trouble."

He turned to look around the side of the chair at Rebecca. "Well, if you're quite comfortable now, I would like to check you also."

"I wanted to say I'm sorry I didn't trust you before. It's just that...I have seen a lot already. A friend of mine told me I should not just trust anyone just because I need help."

"Come, my dear, sit down here with your friends. They've been as jumpy as you waiting to see if you'd come out alright."

Rebecca walked over and sat on the floor in front of the fire, looking up to the man in the chair. He closed the book he had been looking through and leaned over to pull the device around Rebecca's neck closer; she lifted her chin, staring over his head, and bent closer in so he could see. He held up first one pair of spectacles, then the second, looking over the top of the pair he wore on his nose. He made considering noises and smiled once he was satisfied. "Looks good I'd say. You should be able to have that off also." He gently lifted the cord from around Rebecca's neck and laid the object on the pile of books with the other device. She felt a loss with its departure, like a bit of warmth pulled from her.

330

Rebecca felt a touch out of ease under the stare of the man. He seemed to be weighing her. She looked around the room so as not to have to meet his eyes. She found the book he had been reading; it was her grandfather's journal. She suppressed the urge to snatch the book from him, but she felt he had no right to be looking through it.

"I see you carried this safely enough," he said, patting the cover of the journal sitting on his knee. "Some of my brethren would have had this stored away in the Holding but it belonged with its rightful owners by my judgment. And look here, it's brought you safe to me," he said with a smile, leaning back into the chair. His stare had changed and Rebecca felt better about meeting his gaze. Whatever he had been weighing, he seemed to have found measured to his satisfaction. "Come now my dear, ask us a question; I'm sure you're full to the brim with them by this time."

She was bursting with questions but the first from her lips was, "What is that device I was wearing?"

Alaric smiled and picked it up from the books, tilted it back and forth as he stared at the object. "This is a stradeageaum, a technical name, it means strength device in some archaic tongue. What most would call it would be a Healer. It aids the body, lending strength to the host upon which it rests."

He handed her the object. She took it in her hands, one redder than the other. She turned it, looking into the glass face of the object. It was small enough to fit in the palm of her hand. A brass-colored case, etched in beautiful details, which housed hundreds of moving and working parts.

She let her mind wander through the object. She saw the gears and sprockets, ticking happily to their own time. Springs bounced back and forth or coiled upon themselves. Small gem bearings held the precise alignments of the parts. She saw hundreds of intricately worked pieces of various metals and materials silver, gold, steel, copper, and, suspended somehow within, a tiny pearl of quicksilver. She got lost among the turnings. She marveled at the complexity of the thing. She could follow all the workings but they made no sense. Some pieces moved without any connections to another. They seemed driven by some unseen force. She looked up at Alaric.

"How does this work? It makes no sense. I feel strength flowing from it but I don't see how that's possible."

"Try again, my dear. Look at the movements; follow their turnings," Alaric said, leaning against the arm of the chair and stroking his pointed beard. A grin grew on his face as he watched her.

Rebecca frowned at him but did as he said. She liked answers when she asked questions, not being led through pointless tasks. She resumed her study of the Healer. She followed the parts on their courses around the device. She leapt from part to part, seeing the links between the cogs and springs. Once more she lost the train of their movement. She was about to look up in frustration when something in the corner of her vision stopped her.

"There you see it," Alaric said in a breathy voice. "No, no, don't flick your eyes you'll lose it. It's a bit like trying to follow a spot in your vision. The more you chase it with your eyes the more it moves away."

She saw twinkling that led into the device. Golden sparks of light flitted into the brass case. She slowly followed the flow of light as it resolved further.

"Let them show themselves at their own pace, my dear," Alaric said, leaning in to watch close. He held up one of the pair of extra spectacles.

"What are they Alaric?" she asked, not looking from the Healer. She was nearly to the destination of the flow of light. Her eyes itched in a peculiar way and she made to rub them.

"No, no, my dear," Alaric warned in that hushed tone, like he was trying to sneak up on a startled rabbit. "Your eyes, they try to see in a way they have not become used to. That flow you are seeing, what do you feel when you try following it?"

Rebecca thought for a moment; she did feel something now she realized. Strength, strength moved along the lines of light into the Healer. She could see now why she couldn't follow the function of the parts; not all of them moved due to mechanical connections. Luminous golden struts held the pearl of quicksilver in place, formed from the flowing light. This gear, that spring, they were powered from the flow of energy streaming into the object.

"The Kilaray," she whispered in awe. She caught the barest nod from Alaric out of the corner of her eye. "They are so...beautiful. I had no idea they would be so..." She pulled her eyes reluctantly from the device and stared through teary eyes, partly from straining, partly from the feeling she had seeing the Kilaray. Alaric's bearded face held a warm grin.

"That's the way of it my dear," he said reverently. "That took you no time at all, amazing." He leaned back into the chair and took a deep breath. "I should have known you'd have caught on as quickly as that, with those eyes you have."

"Alaric are you..." she didn't know how to ask it right. She felt a bit foolish. "Are you a Philistari?"

He burst out with a laugh that startled her. He gripped his round belly and gasped as he rolled in the chair. "Me?" He managed before collapsing back into another fit of laughs. "Oh dear, if my brethren could hear that." He exploded again, eventually tapering down to little giggles. Rebecca was in shock. She thought this man was laughing at her; how was she supposed to know? "Oh my dear, my dear, you give me too much credit," he said after his fits subsided and he wiped tears from his eyes. "No, I am not Philistari," he held in a last laugh before going on. "I can't see them, you see, without these," he said, pulling on the leather cords attached to the spectacles, "and even then it's the barest hint at their flows and movements. No dear, I'm afraid there aren't any Philistari left to us, Father help us."

"Then how did you know about the Kilaray? How do have this Healer?" she asked trying to recover from her shock at the man's laughter.

"I, my dear," he said, rising regally from his chair, "am Alaric von Magus, once of the Grand Masters of the Garmonian Order of Mecharicals." He finished with a bit of a bow over his belly. She stared wide eyed at him. He sounded as if she should recognize the titles, the only things she had even heard before was, Garmonian, and Mecharical. He twisted his mouth and slumped back to his chair. "I knew you'd be ignorant of certain facts but I had no inkling I would be starting from scratch with you." He sounded a bit deflated. "Mecharicals, dear, are of the Third Order of the Touched, we can manipulate the Kilaray through our works, like the one you hold in your hand. We have learned to touch without seeing, as it were. We use, or should I say, used our skills in the aid of others, as did all the Orders. We teach from what we learn and discover knowledge through our work."

"So Mecharicals are like Kilaray…teachers?" she asked a little confused.

"That would be one way to put it. We aid the untouched with what we can. We teach them the use of our creations for their benefit. I could have shown you how to check that device without your ability to see the Kilaray. The little sphere of quicksilver, you see, it had become smooth and unperturbed. If you still had need of the healer it would have rippled and danced about."

"So anyone can use this without the ability to Touch the Kilaray."

"Correct, but we restrict the use of Healers to only those who vitally need them because the body can become accustomed to the device, we call it attuning. With the continued use of Healers the body loses its ability to heal itself. Just as with muscles, the systems that rebuild the body can become atrophied."

Rebecca handed him the Healer and he took it by its leather cord. Rebecca felt the loss of warmth again with the Healer's departure. She looked at her hands, the redness had gone from her right hand; she was amazed. She sat considering her hand. The wolves stared at her, she noticed, and a second question leapt at her. "Can you hear them also, the wolves I mean?"

"Aye, I can hear them; all with the Touch can hear the thoughts of certain animals. Not all, by any means and only if they wish you to hear them. They have the control of it not we. These Tree Dwellers here know me and often treat with me. The Stone Walkers come reluctantly but they too allow me to hear their words. We believe the how of it relates to their natures. Animals often feel the Kilaray; they know what the ripples in their movements mean. They can tell sometimes when a storm is forming, or a ground quake coming, or see things that we cannot. Our ability to Touch the Kilaray calls to them and they can hear our thoughts. Words are meaningless to them, but I like to hear my voice so I speak as I think to them."

Rebecca smiled at the wolves around her and stroked the nearest one's back. She was glad that they had chosen to speak to her; they had saved her life. She brought her thoughts back to her questions, something she had seen while traveling with the wolves. "Alaric I think I may have seen the Kilaray before and not known it. In my grandfather's journal there was a shimmering between two pages before I could look further the wolves stopped me. They said it was dangerous to…"

"To Reach, yes, it can be quite dangerous attempting to manipulate the Kilaray without training." He looked at the journal, through his multiple spectacles, turning it about. He seemed to be searching for something he hadn't seen before.

"How can Reaching be dangerous?" she asked hesitantly. He stopped his examination of the journal and looked over the top of his spectacles at her. His face became grim. He set the journal down on the ground and stood up.

"Come with me, this is better understood with a little demonstration," he said.

Rebecca stood and followed as Alaric led the way; the wolves remained behind. The cottage was smaller than Rebecca had first thought. The ground floor consisted mainly of the reading room. A short walk led to a kitchen with an iron stove and more valves set in the wall over a basin. A small woodblock table held more of the meal Rebecca had eaten. Alaric snatched a roll of bread and continued out the door set in the wall of the kitchen.

The house was made of dark brick, with climbing ivy doing its best to engulf the building. A slate tile roof, streaked in green and black moss, topped the building. A flag stone path led through the shrubbery and trees, to a larger building made of stacked stone with a copper-lined roof, green with weathering. The area around the two buildings was part of a clearing in the woods. Rebecca could see a gravel trail lined with stone walls leading out into the trees. All around the clearing stood wrought iron poles with orbs atop them. The orbs shone with a soft white light. There was no fire inside them to make them glow and she saw no other method for how they worked. She stopped and stared at them. The light they cast seemed to shine mainly on shadows, illuminating the darkness around them. Alaric turned from his destination when he noticed she wasn't following.

"Incandeogeaums," he said around a mouthful of the bread, "or Incandeos for short, light devices. Come, there is more to see." Rebecca tore herself away from staring at the globes and followed Alaric to the stone building.

Alaric tugged the large wooden doors open enough to walk through and led the way into what, Rebecca could only assume, was a workshop of some sort. Inside, the tables and benches were covered in parts and pieces. Half-built contraptions hung from the rafters above or sat on the clay tiled floor or lay on a stools or tables. The floor was made a maze with all the objects strewn about. Alaric picked his path as though he could have done so blindfolded. Rebecca had the urge to tiptoe to keep from running into the objects.

"Too much for one man alone, I'm afraid," Alaric said, turning in a small circle and gesturing to the objects. "Once this many devices and machines would have been the work of an hour or two with the numbers of Mechanicals in my Order. Now, I'm sorry to say, I may never get them all working again before my time is spent. Ah, but why linger over sore areas when there are more *important* things to worry us. Come, here is what I must show you."

Rebecca moved closer to where he stood in the shop. Light from large windows cast shafts on a wooden frame on three legs. Two vertical masts extended from the frame with two metal spheres at their tops; perhaps two inches separated the two spheres. One of the masts was hinged as to be able to move closer to the other. A crank handle was placed in the side of the frame and a glass disk between two woolen pads attached to it. Rebecca had no idea what she was supposed to be looking at.

"This works in a way like the clouds of a storm," he said, cranking the handle, making the glass disc spin between the wool pads. "The fixed sphere stores the energy from the movement of the crank. After a few turns there will be enough to show you a parallel principle to what you need to learn."

After about four or five turns, Alaric stopped and stared at her over his glasses. He took a deep breath and spoke in solemn tones. "Reaching is the first step to manipulation of the Kilaray. When one Reaches it is like the clouds of a storm roiling together. Energy, the energy of the movement, is stored in the clouds like energy is stored in this sphere," he said pointing; Rebecca noticed he didn't touch the sphere or go too close. "When enough energy is stored, the clouds need to regain balance with the surrounding environment." He walked to the side of the frame and took the hinged mast in his hand. "This sphere is like the surrounding environment." He slowly moved the sphere closer to the other. With a loud crack a jolt leapt from the fixed sphere to the other like a small lightning bolt. The air smelled strangely similar to a storm as well. "Balance must be restored," he said, stepping away from the frame. He moved to a table containing a smaller version of the frame with a few differences. He gestured her to come closer.

This frame had smaller spheres and the crank connected to an engraved bronze disc with no wool pads to carry the energy. His face was set in grim determination.

"You must learn to manipulate the Kilaray but this must always be remembered." He looked like he struggled against his better judgment. "The Kilaray can...destroy with the energy that moves along them. This frame is linked to pull power from the Kilaray in a fashion similar to Reaching. Stand back a touch when I tell you." He began to crank the handle; the disc turned slowly, the etched pattern on it revolved. After the first turn the pattern glowed with sparks of light. Golden like the sun, blue-violet like lightning, and green and fiery orange like fireworks, streams appeared as if from nowhere. They drew down onto the bronze disc. They flowed to one of the spheres, collecting and intensifying, in a multi-hued white haze. Alaric held one of his extra spectacles up and studied the sphere. "Step back now; it won't be but a second longer."

Rebecca did as he said, watching the glowing flow of Kilaray into and around the sphere. It seemed to be agitated, rippling and vibrating; Rebecca could hear a discordant hum from their movement. Alaric stood back from the frame. A tiny stream snaked from the second sphere, sinuous and smooth, nearly transparent. It moved closer and the haze of light around the first sphere reached for the thin line. As the two met, everything happened at once. The sphere fractured like an egg cracking, sending a piercing sound, like a high pitched gong, around the room. The metal shattered like glass and ripped toward the second sphere, carried along on the flow of Kilaray like the jolt from the first frame. The second sphere exploded as the shards of the first tore into it. A wave of pressure blasted out from the frame and back, raising clouds of dust from all around. The building rattled and the mechanisms hanging from the rafters swayed slightly. The flow of light equalized around the areas where the spheres had been and faded away. A fan of metal filings was all that remained of the two spheres.

Rebecca turned to Alaric with horror. If that is what happened when one Reached, she would be killed if she attempted it.

"I won't ever do it again," she said in a whisper.

"You will, and I will help you to do it. You must be readied for what you must do," he said, walking to a stool near a workbench to sit down. He seemed suddenly shaken. "A man by the name of Charles Broheim was supposed to bring you to me. Arriving as you did, I suppose something went awry. The wolves are close-mouthed about whatever went on in the forest, they don't believe in gossip, but they were shaken by whatever it was you did." He pulled a second stool up and gestured her to sit. Reluctantly, she walked to where he was and sat on the stool. "Tell me, what happened dear?" he said once she was seated.

Rebecca ran her fingers along the lines of her palm. She thought back to everything that had happened to bring her here. She struggled against the feel of tears. She talked, not looking from her hands; the palm she stroked, she realized, was the one from which she had sent the sphere hurtling toward the Blind Man.

"Broheim is dead," she said in a thick voice. "It's all my fault; I got him killed, and a friend of mine." She felt the tears trickle down her cheeks and drip into her palm. "I should have listened to both of them, if I had they would both be alive. I am so very foolish. I should have seen it coming but I didn't – I was so blind."

Alaric cleared his throat and sniffed. Rebecca peeked up at his face; he brushed at one of his eyes. "My dear, I believe you are neither blind nor foolish. Some things happen whatever we do to stop them and this, I am sure, was one. Charles was a friend, a good friend; he could look after himself. If he couldn't stop what happened, no one could have. From what I've read from him, he thought you quite a brave young woman. You must not blame yourself. The ones responsible for his and your friend's deaths are the ones to blame, not you."

"But if I had just listened and been more cautious, if I had just seen what I was doing would lead to... if I had just let them kill me..."

"Enough of that," he said, putting a hand on her shoulder and pulling her chin up to look into her face. "You would have done no one any good by dying. Your heart knows that too, or else you would

341

have given up before you made it here. You're letting your mind fall into a trap; self doubt leads to despair. You are too important for that."

"Why am I important?" she pleaded. "I don't even know what I'm doing here."

Alaric took her hands in his and looked into her eyes. "These hands will bring about a rekindling of a fire that has gone out of this world. You must be readied for your task in the resurgence of the Three Orders."

"I don't want to be readied for anything; I just want to get my friends out and be left alone. I thought maybe you could help me. I can't do anything without help, I'm just a little girl," she said.

He chuckled and patted her cheek. "You are very kind, my dear. I am too old and too fat to be of any help but in what I can teach you. Just a little girl, you say. Rebecca Dulac, daughter of Tomas and Sophia Dulac, two of the most gifted Mecharicals of their time. Why do you think Charles and the Brotherhood of the Three Knives were waiting for you? The world needs your help Rebecca. You are the only one that can fulfill what needs to be done."

Rebecca's head spun. "The *world*? I told you I couldn't even help my friends. And my parents weren't Mecharicals. They were ordinary people like everyone else." She knew she lied to herself. She and James had talked this through; she had come to the conclusion that something like what Alaric was telling her about her parents was true. Alaric looked at her askance as though he could tell she lied also.

"Your father was a Mecharical; he crafted pieces in his early years that never saw their equals. Your mother, by rights, was Philistari trained; she became a Mecharical because of your dad. Her father was none too pleased about that, but he came around eventually, especially

342

when he saw your brother and you. You wouldn't believe that stone-faced man would weep like a babe." Rebecca couldn't remember her mother's father; he was a soldier of sorts Rebecca had thought. "Your brother was very near being sent to the Palantean to be trained when the wars broke out. No dear, you are far from just a little girl. You are our last hope to see the Three Orders of the Touched reborn. You won't just help your friends if that can be done, you will help the world."

Rebecca felt very weak and very small all of a sudden. How was she supposed to do as Alaric said? She had so many questions, so many doubts, so many fears. He wanted impossibilities from her. She meant to tell him he had the wrong person but what she said was not what she expected.

"How am I supposed to help?" she said in a little voice. The words came not from her mind but from somewhere inside her; somewhere she didn't know had been there. It was that place that she felt move when she had Reached. She heard the words from her mouth and knew they were the right words to have said, the true words of the heart.

Alaric's face lighted with joy. "That's a girl," he said. "Come, let us have supper and we will talk near the fire."

Alaric made more food back in the little house. They sat and ate at the woodblock table and he gave the wolves each a helping of meat. After they had all eaten, Alaric made more of the spicy tea and Rebecca and the wolves sat on the floor in front of the fire while she and Alaric spoke.

Rebecca told him everything of what had happened. From the train out of Arnora, to her meeting Broheim, from the beating Postam had given her, to the disaster in the courtyard, Alaric listened intently and urged her to continue. She told of the journal and the script and Reaching for the first time in the woods. It was dark out before she had arrived at the part about the Blind Man's attack.

"A Blind Man you say," he said with a startled look. "Great ghosts, what did you do?"

"I tried to run but it kept coming at me. I couldn't see it all the time; it turned into wisps and vanished," she said, sipping her tea to wet her mouth.

"That's the way they move between the worlds. If you picture our world as a sheet and the world of the First Father as another, the space between is devoid of the Father's touch. Disorder reigns, there nothing exists completely, that is Discordia. That's from where they come.

"The Kilaray bridge the worlds, the Father cannot touch our world or the Kilaraic energy would destroy it as the spheres were destroyed, but the Links are a way to touch the world of the First

344

Father. Strynges and other creatures of Discordia can sense the Links between the worlds and are drawn to those who can touch them, they feed on our spirits. Strynges can press themselves against our world in the form we would know as Blind Men. They wrap the fabric of our plane around themselves as a mask. They are very hard to stop; so tell me what you did?" He sipped from his tea bowl.

"The wolves told me when it came again. I did the last thing I could – I threw a knife and it stuck into it. It still came so I threw the other. The wolves went to attack it. They said it was pinned?" She was more frightened of the Blind Men after what Alaric had told her, creatures of Discordia wanting to attack her.

"The Brotherhood would induct you on the spot if they heard what you've told me my dear," he said, shaking his head. "A pity you didn't have a third blade that would have finished the job. One to pin the flesh, two to pin the spirit, and the three to sever the link, three knives will end a Strynge. It would have killed you still with only two in it so tell me what drove it off and what, I assume, frightened our furry companions here."

Rebecca hesitated; she tried to remember what she had done. "The Blind Man was going to kill one of the wolves, it was hurt, and the Blind Man was going to stab him. I was frightened but somehow I calmed myself. The world slowed and something formed in the air near my hand." She looked into the palm of her right hand. "It shot out toward the Blind Man, hit it, and exploded. Then the Blind Man disappeared."

"My dear, you are very lucky you didn't tear yourself to bits," he said concerned. "Your hand was singed when the wolves brought you here, I figured you had tried to Reach but I hadn't known you had dispatched a Strynge."

"So I killed it?" she asked with hope.

"I dare say not. It will take time for it to press itself against this world again but you destroyed only its flesh. It will look more human when it reworks its mask, but it will remember you certainly."

Rebecca shivered. She didn't like the thought of that thing out there still, trying to get her. "Can it come to get me here?"

"No, not here, when we built this place, we marked the land to ward them off. Around the perimeter of the grounds you saw the Incandeos; they are part of a network of bars to their crossing here. They can't see in the full light, that's the reason for the smoked spectacles. Mind, the light devices are the last line of the network and they wouldn't make it that far. We Mecharicals were known to have a sense for mischief and we couldn't help but use that sense to devise some nasty traps for the likes of them."

"What about men? The Red Guard was after me before the Blind Man attacked," she said.

"Men wouldn't enter here either. There are Screeners to stop the untouched. Animals and the Touched would not notice their illusion, but it looks like the forest ends in a sheer cliff into the ocean. If they had the courage to forge ahead they would trigger another defense that would hold them long enough for me to deal with them. You are quite safe here, unfortunately you cannot stay here."

"Why not?" she asked.

Alaric took a deep breath and sat his tea down. He leaned forward from his chair and took up Rebecca's grandfather's journal. He flipped through the pages of the book and came to picture of the cliff with the trees growing from them, the Gates of Yuriah. He set the book on the floor in front of her and turned it for her to see.

"Touch the book my dear," he said. She did as he told her. The hidden script on the page seeped back into the parchment. "That effect is caused by the Kilaray Linking your family to that book. I can teach you to control it. When you have control you will be ready to go through that." He said pointing to the gates. "I don't know what you will find there, the Barrier has been sealed for as long as our histories can tell. We don't know how it was formed or why but we suspect that it holds the key to fulfilling the Reached Vision. You must go through and find what was lost; we hope that to be the Three Orders. You can't stay here because eventually, you must go there."

Rebecca stared at the page; the constellation above the rock cliffs named it for what it was, the two arching pillars partially covered by the trees. The Gates of Yuriah, her mother had told her it was the most important of the constellations. It must never be forgotten. Now she knew why.

"How do I go through; from what I've read no one can pass through alive?"

"Your father's father, Martan Dulac, was a part of the Homeland Expeditionary League that rediscovered the Barrier. That is his journal. The script that he wrote in is a handy little trick of Shintish work. The Pictsies don't like to be seen by many but a few of the Shintish Pictsies still hope for the day when they can be known again."

"Pictsies," she laughed, "are you making fun of me? Pictsies are pure fancy, childish tales about Shints and Shunts stealing and hiding people's belongings, only to sell them back to them."

"So wise of the world are you, my dear," Alaric said, looking quite amused himself. "There are things in this world that many would believe only fancy but I can assure you the Pictsies are not. They had something to do with the creation of the Barrier, they and the Tremen.

347

The most the Pictsies would tell Martan was that there would come a time when they would help to find what was lost. I sent messages to the Shints, the Shunts would never help, when Charles said you were coming; I haven't got a response as of yet."

"What about the Tremen?" she asked. "The wolves told me they were sailors and explorers."

"I'm afraid there is no hope there. They broke from us, we think, about the time when our ancestors first were able to touch the Kilaray. Something happened then, something horrible. A war of some kind ravaged the world. Men fought men using the Kilaray as weapons. The Tremen were caught up in the turmoil and were enslaved, used for their knowledge of the Kilaray. When the war ended the Touch was lost to men until Arnora was found. The Tremen have never forgotten the sins of our ancestors. They journey the seas and have little interest in human affairs. Their home in Tremore has not known humans since your grandfather's last visit. They have small colonies in the southern half of the Wilderlands, mainly ports for restocking their ships. The women are able to read the Kilaray in the air around us to navigate. The men can see the Kilaray on the land to hunt and track. I don't believe they will break their silence until we are all wiped from existence."

Rebecca remembered then about the journal. The section that was missing had mentioned the Tremen.

"Alaric I think part of the journal has been lost." She flipped to the section and showed him the pages. "I thought I saw something in the valley between the pages. I think it may have been the Kilaray."

He took the book and snatched up his multiple spectacles, switching from one to the other. He shook his head after a time and handed her back the journal. "I can't see it my dear. You give it a look and see if you can tell me what's there."

She took the journal and stared at the pages. She let her eyes wander up and down, back and forth, across the pages slowly. The wolves pricked up their ears and their eyes went from Rebecca to Alaric. He waved them off and they resumed watching Rebecca. She ignored everything but the two pages. Slowly she caught the first spark. She shot her eyes to the spot and it was gone.

"Slowly, dear, slowly," Alaric said, "you must work slower until you learn."

She started again. Gradually the sparks of light flickered along the dark valley between the pages. Rebecca's heart leapt. The light resolved into a two parallel lines extending the length of the page. They were so close Rebecca thought at first they were one line. But she could see now there was a hair fine space between them. Thin strands webbed over the space and, in the middle of the two lines, two small circles stood atop one another. She described what she saw to Alaric; he frowned and stroked his beard.

"I think that the pages have been sealed with Kilaray. I don't have the skill to get them back and I wouldn't know where to start to teach you the way of unraveling it yourself. I think I know who would be able to help but we will have to worry about that later. Come now, it is late and you must sleep. Tomorrow we begin your training."

Rebecca left Alaric in the reading room and walked up the stairs to the room she had woken that morning. She remembered the sheets were still in the washroom but upon smelling them she decided against reusing them. She checked the wardrobe and found an old leather coat and some blankets. She put on the leather coat, it was a bit too large for her, her hands just poked out of the sleeves, and what would have been mid thigh length on its owner fell to her knees. It felt comfortable though so she lay down and covered herself with the blankets. She brushed her eyes as she slipped off to sleep.

Her mind wandered in her sleep, trying to break through the web between the lines in the valley of the pages. The webbing held tight and she gave up the task. She dreamed about the two spheres of the second frame Alaric had shown her. Instead of the spheres, she stood in the place of the first. The Kilaray gathered around her, humming as they moved. She tried to stop them but she shattered to pieces and streaked toward the second sphere. *Tomorrow that might happen to me*, she thought in her dream.

Rebecca awoke in the early morning hours. Her eyes felt tired still, and she rubbed them to clear her vision. She rose from the twisted blankets on the bed still in the leather coat; she'd had more rough dreams. Mainly they consisted of either being caught by Blind Men or tearing herself to pieces. She trudged to the washroom and splashed her face with water from the basin set below the mirror attached to the wallboards. She stared into the mirror and was startled at what she saw.

Around the iris of either eye streams of gold and green sparks of light flitted about, moving into and around her eyes. She rubbed her eyes, trying to brush them away but they were still there when she looked again. Her heart pounded; *what was happening?*

"Alaric," she called out. "Alaric, come quickly." She heard the sounds of rustling sheets and the click of nails on the floorboards from down the short hall. A moment later Alaric stood in the washroom door, placing his spectacles on his nose and blinking to see.

"What's the matter dear?" he asked. The wolves padded up behind him staring around his legs.

"Can't you see them?" she said rubbing at her eyes. "They won't go away."

He walked into the washroom and took her wrists. "Don't dear, they are still working." He held up one of her lids and peered close, taking up another of his spectacles. "Ah, they seem to be excited to have you know them, my dear. The Kilaray will come easier to your sight when they are done. It's sort of like using a muscle you've never known before, it will strengthen in time. Don't worry; your eyes will not be harmed and none will be able to see them at work."

She looked into the mirror again; she felt uncertain. Alaric went from the washroom the wolves following after. Rebecca washed herself and went downstairs after redressing. She smelled food from the kitchen and went in to find Alaric making first meal. She sat and ate with him.

"I see you've found my old travel coat," he said smiling. "That coat has seen me safe through many miles. It belongs to you. I fear it would fit me less than you now." He patted his belly; Rebecca smiled.

When first meal was eaten, the wolves spoke to Rebecca.

"We will be leaving you now, Touched One. We are long from our home and we wish to return."

I wish you would stay with me. I have felt better having you close.

"We are not adventurers, Touched One. We know only our lives and the hunt. We have been honored to help you but we are what we are."

I understand; I will miss you. Please be safe on your way home.

"We will always be glad to have you in our home Touched One."

She hugged them all and said a few more parting words and they loped into the forest, vanishing into the trees. Alaric assured her they would be safe and escorted her to the large brick workshop to begin their day.

Alaric stood before the frame with the ruined spheres. He had her sit and watch as he fitted two new spheres, pulled from a drawer below the workbench, atop the masts. Then he turned to explain.

"What I showed you before was what happens when one Reaches. The Kilaraic energy builds; eventually the container can no longer hold the imbalance between the world around and itself. Like a dam holding against a flood, the power grows too great and the forces balance, destroying the container. But, if a Link is made from the container to a target, the power can flow along it and balance in a more controlled fashion," he finished. He turned to the frame and moved the spheres so they were touching. "This is the link," he said. He cranked the handle, the bronze disc rotated, and the sparks of light flowed along the etched pattern. The first sphere began to gather the flow of light and Alaric moved the spheres apart slowly. The glow around the two spheres stretched, thinning in the space between but it was an even, multicolored, whitish glow from one sphere to the next. He stopped cranking and the glow faded leaving the spheres unharmed.

"This frame is one way we Mecharicals are able to manipulate the Kilaray. You are able to do it without any aid. The danger lies in not knowing how to form the Links in your mind. You must have a target to transfer the Kilaray to or else they will attempt to balance themselves..." he grimaced, "um, unpredictably, I would say."

"Whenever I have Reached I've had ill effects afterwards. If that happens every time I won't be able to do much," she said worried.

"You must learn the technique first. To gain control of the Kilaray is quite a challenge but, once you learn, it will grow easier. Come outside into the open air; we will begin with the easier parts."

Alaric led her out a rear door of the workshop into a round garden. The gravel stone paths were raked neatly into patterns around large rocks and trees that seemed to have been grown to please the eye. The little garden was quite peaceful.

"This is a meditation garden. The Beltari used these for years before we knew them. They help to calm your mind so you can concentrate easier," he said, leading her to the center of the garden. "Now, the Three Orders developed with focuses in certain aspects of life. Mecharicals, the Third Order, focused on knowledge and the teaching of others. The Philistari, the First Order, worked to know the will of the First Father, and guide others."

"And the Second Order?" Rebecca asked. Alaric grinned with a knowing smile.

"The Palantean, would consider themselves...apart from the other orders, pride always was a weakness with the showier aspects of the Touched. The Palantean focused on the body, or should I say the protection of it. The word itself means 'those who guard'. They developed skills that forced the body to attune more quickly and powerfully to the Kilaray."

"The Philistari brought the other two Orders into being. The Palantean arose first to protect the first Philistari. They had their start in your country actually, soldiers found with the Touch trained by the

Philistari. They formed their own order and developed what I will teach you today."

"Alaric, I am a little frightened," she admitted reluctantly.

"That is good, it will keep you sharp. Now, to start, what is it you used to calm yourself before? Most of the Palantean I have known focused on some aspect that worked in time with the Kilaray, heartbeat, say, or breathing."

"Breathing," Rebecca said, "I try to control my breathing and I calm myself."

"Good, now there are several states you will pass through. Time is not fixed and will move in relation to the Kilaray's flow. The Palantean called this the Easing, the world slows around you. This state is precarious because you are out of phase with the world. The Kilaray will attempt to bring you back into balance. Hold against them. The next state is called the Stillness, the world will halt, the Kilaray will present themselves."

"I don't know if I'm ready for this," she said, biting her lower lip. "What if I go wrong?"

"I will be here, to bring you out, if it comes to that." He walked to the edge of the garden, picking a stone from the side. He set it atop a boulder in front of Rebecca. "When you reach the Stillness, find a Link that flows into this stone, once you have it in your mind let the Kilaray bring you back into balance, this is called the Quickening. It will allow you to pass the flow to your target."

Rebecca steeled herself. She breathed in and out, focusing on each breath. The world slowed, the light of the day intensified. The leaves moved on their branches as though the air had become denser. She felt something inside her slipping; she tried to hold it back. She was going to lose it; she thought about the exploding spheres and panicked.

The world snapped back to speed and Rebecca fell to her knees panting. Alaric was at her side holding a whirring glass globe. Etched into the glass were spirals and patterns. Within the globe a series of rings spun wildly; symbols on the rings glowed like the patterns of the bonze disc of the frame. The rings slowed and the illuminant patterns dimmed.

"Great ghosts, my dear that was close," Alaric said. "You almost let the Kilaray fill you. Tell me what happened?"

"Something…" she panted, "something inside me slipped away and I couldn't hold it back. Alaric I don't think I can do this."

"Yes you can dear, try again. This time more slowly, you try to work too fast. I will be ready this time in case you need me," he said, holding the globe up. "This will draw you back."

She nodded and stood up. She tried again, breathing more slowly. She worked her way back to calmness. The world began to slow. *Easing,* she thought. She felt a tug at her, she was ready this time. She found what attempted to move and held it in place. It felt close to her heart. The tug became a pull; she held tight. The world became more defined. The light bloomed to blinding brightness. She felt the world halt. The air stilled; her heartbeat and breath were all she could hear. The blinding brightness drew down and she could see forms in the air. Glowing strands of gossamer thin light moved around her; she was amazed at the sight. She thought she could hear words spoken to the place she held in herself.

She looked around slowly; everything seemed to have glowing wisps of light moving into and around it. The rocks, the trees, even the ground itself, all seemed to have thousands of fine tendrils of energy flowing into and through them. Some of the threads of light connected all she could see. She looked down at her chest, from where she could feel the pull, and saw a multitude of hair-thin strands tying her to all around her.

She picked out one particular strand, coppery green, and followed it into the stone atop the boulder. She felt the bonds that held the stone together move along the strand. She concentrated on the Link and let go her hold of the pull in herself. She felt something pass through her, moving out to the stone along the link. The world brightened again and in a flash time fell back into place. She dropped to her hands and knees again as the flow passed from her.

Alaric helped her to a sitting position. He talked to her but she couldn't hear his words. She felt that place near her heart like a newly found hand. It felt more defined, stronger. She looked at Alaric and noticed he was very watery. She blinked and he became clear.

"Are you alright my dear," he was saying. "Are you hurt anywhere, do you feel sick?"

"It's my soul," she said through numb lips.

Alaric laughed with relief. He took her from beneath the arms and helped her to her feet. "Walk dear, it helps to walk. Come let's see what you've done."

He half supported her to the boulder where the stone had been set. A neatly formed crystal, the color of glacial ice, sat where it had been. She looked at it in complete wonder.

"I felt the link holding the stone together. I didn't know what to do so I just let go and I felt something flow through…my soul. It is, isn't it?" she said picking up the crystal delicately; it felt warm in her hand.

"We think so. Every one of the Touched has the same feeling when they first learn some control," he said, sitting her down on the boulder. "You did well for a first go; more often the target is destroyed. Your mother, I heard, was left with a smoking crater her first attempt."

"Why did they never tell me Alaric? Why was this kept from me?" she asked.

Alaric sighed and sat on the boulder next to her. "Your parents were some of the few survivors of the Scouring. Some fled the Homelands, taking refuge in the Wilderlands, hiding in the towns and cities. Others went underground, like your parents. We covered up the past by destroying the Old Religion's archives after we salvaged what we could. The Holding stores what we managed to recover; there it waits for when it will be used again."

"Why did Adarian do it; why did he ruin everything?" she asked, looking into the crystal.

"That is a sad and complicated question," he said, sighing. "Mandagore was once a good man, one of the best of the Palantean. He was a rare find actually, Felsofese born. He grew strong, and confident in his own abilities. . .overconfident would be more accurate."

Alaric looked at her with hurt in his eyes. "He was betrayed. Mandagore trusted the untouched of his land of birth but they deceived him. People he had come to know and love were killed because of it. He sought vengeance for his lost friends by the laws of the land. The ones responsible for the murders were powerful and influential, aristocrats and politicians; Mandagore's friends had been rebels, freedom fighters. The results were not to Mandagore's liking; he took matters into his own hands.

He convinced several other young Palantean to join him. Slaughter would be a kind term for what they did.

The other Palantean were charged with bringing Mandagore to justice for his actions. He and the other outcasts went into hiding. When they reemerged again, they had a twisted sense of things. They believed it was the right of the Touched to rule the untouched. Mandagore felt that if this had been the way of things, his friends would never have been killed. They set about trying to seize power from the nations.

Eventually they were driven out of the Homelands at the cost of the Philistari. Mandagore never forgave those responsible for his exile. He paid them all back with pain and suffering."

"He blamed himself for what happened to his friends, didn't he?" she said, looking up from the crystal. Alaric nodded slowly.

"He had always known what to do, how to solve problems, what would come next. When he didn't see the betrayal coming, he saw it as a personal failure. He couldn't forgive himself for the deaths of his friends."

Rebecca sat considering the crystal, and Alaric's words. "What happened to him when he was exiled?"

"No one knows for sure; we do know that his guilt lead him to cruel savagery. It had an effect on his soul, twisting and deranging it. He lost his Touch and was driven to near madness even before he fled into the Broken Lands," Alaric said.

"You can lose the Touch?" she asked concerned.

"One's soul allows the Kilaray to flow through it to manipulate the links. If your soul is corrupted, ruined, the Kilaray cannot flow; you would be cut off. I doubt you'll have to worry about that my dear," he said, placing a firm hand on her shoulder, "but it is something to keep in mind. You must always try to fend off those feelings that would lead you to corruption. Vengeance, guilt, hatred, these will begin to leach into your soul if you cling to them."

"How can I stop myself from feeling hatred toward those who took everything from me? It's all I want, but to end every last one of them, Alaric," she said.

"Your feelings are natural, my dear, but you must let them pass. If you dwell in that place it will affect you in the same way as Mandagore."

"What can I do to stop the feelings?" she pleaded. "My heart aches every time I think about my friends, my mother and father, my brother."

"Remember what they meant to you. Remember their love, that is what matters, that is what you need. That Link lingers long after those you felt love for have passed. Don't forget what was done to them, but don't let that rule over what they were to you."

She nodded and let Alaric pull her to his side, putting his arm around her shoulder and resting her head against his chest. They sat for a time then Alaric began to hum in his deep voice. Rebecca recognized the tune as *Pretty Girl on My Arm*, a song about an older man wooing a younger woman; she punched Alaric in the ribs with a smile.

"Oh, I see your spirits are up, my dear," he said, rubbing his side with a grin. "Shall we continue with some more lessons then?"

Forty

The Skip Tracer

Wren waited at the dark wooden counter in *The Gilded Woman* tavern for his mark, sipping at a silvered glass of wine. The crowd was beginning to thicken as the sun edged down. This was a higher class tavern, which meant wine was served more frequently than ale, but being in the Wilderlands, there was always a chance for a brawl to break loose. If Wren were not working, he might be well into his cups by now, but some things could wait; he had a job to do tonight.

He enjoyed this part the most, the hunt. His quarry was already well in hand; she just hadn't realized it yet. Wren had his problems but when he was working few could match his skill at collaring Skips, breakers of New Dominion laws. He was focused purely on finding his mark; Wren had traced this one for days. When on the trail, he could take his mind off his dragging urge for the syringe in its leather case in his coat pocket, for a time at least.

He was dressed in a fine brown wool coat over an embroidered grey linen shirt. His boots he had polished that morning and his black woolen trousers had been pressed for him. He had shaved his cheeks, had his longish dark hair tied back in a satin black ribbon, and looked as respectable as he ever would. He rolled his shoulders to ensure his Stitcher's Rig was properly seated. If the tavern keeper, chattering away at him, knew he wore that, he probably wouldn't be acting as friendly. The vest-like harness had garnered its wearers – assassins, cutthroats, and other underhanded murders – the name Silvarish Tailors in bordering countries. The Stitcher's Rig held his needles, slim throwing knives, lined up the sides of the vest in sheaths attached to it, concealed beneath his coat.

He brushed his moustache straight with his fingers and stroked the line of a goatee beneath his lower lip. He needed to look the part of a Wilderland regent or barrister, someone of importance, someone with coin; his mark could smell gold like a dog could scent a trail. He hoped his look of importance would draw her to him.

The tavern keeper chatted to him about the necessity of having a good stock of Homeland vintage wines, marked of course for proper sale; he was a loyal citizen after all. Wren ignored him but gave the impression of interest. Wren despised loyalists, those who had obtained trader's marks, and decrees of working rights from the New Dominion. Strictly speaking, his work made him a loyalist but he had his standards. *Where was she?* He had Hodgens drop the name he was using among the hidden world of thieves and cutpurses that Skip Bureaus sometimes associated. He had assured Wren this mark would track him down. If Hodgens was wrong with his information Wren would not be pleased.

Wren searched the crowd coming in for a night's drinking and carousing. Men in quality cut coats and high top hats moved in through the swing doors of the tavern. They moved past the large stand mirror near the door where the doorman checked their reflections, rumors of Blind Men had been drifting through the Wilderlands lately. After they proved human, the doorman took their overcoats and hats. The tavern's house ladies began filtering through the men, batting eyes and hiding giggles behind hands. They could tell a fat coin purse at fifteen paces. Soon enough, the tables filled with the local chancellors, barristers, council leaders, and all the influence peddlers of the local industries who clung to them. Women, painted for the evening, sat on their laps, wine clutched in their free hands. Wren chuckled to himself; which form of whoring he found more honest he couldn't tell.

Just then the light clop of heeled shoes on the floor boards announced a woman in well cut silks and lace; she sidled up next to him, leaning on the counter. She smelled strongly of rosy perfume and wore too much rouge and powder for Wren's taste; a freelance courtesan by her look, her hair trussed up in a construction of tight curls and ribbons. She examined Wren from the corner of her dark painted eyes. This could be her. She fit the profile. Any normal man would be panting and drooling on himself for the chance to chat this woman up. That made Wren remember, he was supposed to be acting a normal man. He turned to the woman and fell into his role.

"Why, good madam, I don't believe I've seen a finer offering of Wilderlands beauty since I arrived here," Wren said, bowing as he took her hand, kissing her knuckles softly.

"How kind, sir," she said in a smoky voice. "Silvarish aren't you, by your accent of course."

The qualification made Wren realize she had seen his tattoos when he took her hand. The blackbird, imprinted on the web between his thumb and forefinger of his right hand, named his clan, Night Birds. The two peaks of the mountains Mraxis and Mraidan – the sun a red spiral over the point of Mraxis, the taller of the two – on the inside of his wrist indicated his township. They had been imprinted there when he was eight years old, a year before he was taken by the Red Fist Army and given another tattoo on the inside of his left forearm, a crudely scrawled blue snake, but that was not important now.

"Your ears tell you true, Madam," Wren said, straightening and doing his best to look besotted with the woman. "Tanis Forleroy, by name, Mraxian Silvarish by birth. Now, might you give my life meaning and purpose by granting me the honor of hearing your surely sonorous name?" He sipped his wine and hoped he wasn't spreading it on too thick.

"You Silvarish gentleman are a gilded tongued lot," she said with a smile. Her eyes darted to the ring he wore on his right forefinger and judged the expense of his wool coat. "Sandia Evelwick," she said. "Would you be so kind as to offer me a glass of wine, kind Sir Forleroy?" She stepped closer, looking up into his eyes and parting her bright red lips a bit. Oh, yes this was his mark; she knew how to enchant her prey.

"But...but of course," Wren said, darting his hand into his coat pockets, looking befuddled. He produced a coin purse and laid a gold strip, minted with the Traders Mark, atop the counter. The mark made Wren tug at the dark-blue silk scarf tied at his neck. The woman missed the motion as she watched the gold strip and weighed the contents of the coin purse with her eyes before Wren could put it back. "We'll have two bottles," said Wren to the fat balding tavern keeper. The expense he hoped would be justified in this woman's bounty. "Send the other up to my room if you would."

The woman smiled at Wren and took his arm in hers, brushing his hand lightly with her finger tips. "Are you here on business, Sir Forleroy?" she asked, doing her best to present Wren with the best vantages of her bosom. Wren had to hold back a smirk, if only this woman knew what business he was in...

"Aye, I have been tapped to be the prime solicitor of New Harn here," Wren lied, gesturing around. He flashed his best smile at the woman. "So far, I have thought to refuse. Now though, I may have to reconsider." The tavern keeper set the bottle of wine on the counter with another silvered glass and bowed his way away, taking the gold strip and biting it as he turned. Wren laughed to himself; that was the only *gold* he had in his purse at the moment.

Wren poured the woman a glass and offered it to her. She took it greedily and took large sips. Wren measured the woman for what to expect later. She was well built; she had a fine silhouette, hips and shoulders in good proportions. Her face had a displeasing look to it though, a weasel-like quality. She had the same eyes as a rodent as well, dark and unforgiving, shifting continuously. Wren supposed the men who had fallen for this woman's guises had got what they deserved but he was not interested in comeuppance. The bounty for this woman's collaring was what dominated Wren's mind. He gulped the rest of his wine and poured another glass. The woman smiled at him in a slightly condescending manner.

"Madam, if I could be so bold as to ask if you have not been reserved for the evening, I would gladly offer you my coin purse for as long as it will pay for your services," he said.

"Good Sir Forleroy you are too generous," she said, pressing her hand to his chest. "I would be pleased to accept your offer."

Wren smiled a broad, drunken looking grin. He offered her his arm and she took it, making sure to snatch the bottle of wine and glasses before Wren led her to the stairs at the back of the room. Men at tables and booths craned their heads to watch, eyeing Sandia Evelwick greedily, wishing they could take Wren's place for the evening. They wouldn't be so keen to replace him if they knew the way this woman worked. She dabbled in poisons.

In the upstairs hall, Wren led Sandia to his room. He unlocked the door and pushed it open for her; she walked through graciously. Wren entered and locked the door behind him. Turning, he couldn't help but grin with his usual mischievous smile. He hoped she took it for wine soaked enthusiasm. He stepped closer to her, shrugged off his coat and Stitcher's rig in one motion, folded them together to conceal the vest, and tossed them onto a chair near a small table by the door.

"Sir Forleroy, your room is so large it must have cost quite a sum," she said, the corners of her mouth showing teeth as she smiled.

"This," Wren said, shrugging, "I've known finer, but one does with what one can." He hoped he had the right amount of arrogance for the character he played. To tell it true the room was bigger than most he spent his time, by about three times. He usually slept in basements and cellars with thin mattresses on the floor boards or stone.

There was a knock at the door. Sandia stepped around Wren and pulled it open. She returned with the second bottle of wine after relocking the door. She walked to the table at the side of the door and set the two bottles and glasses down. She filled the glasses with wine, upending the first bottle into one. She searched her skirts for a blade to uncork the second. Wren took note of the glint off glass as she returned her hand to her skirts to replace the blade. Wren knew what she had done and chuckled lightly. He very shortly would be turning purple in the face and dying.

She strode to him and offered him a full glass of the wine. Wren smiled at her over the rim of the glass. She held her own to her lips and they both drank deeply. Wren felt the effects very soon. His lips tingled and his eyes blurred a bit. He hated dying, almost more than his need for the syringe pocket.

"I feel a bit odd of a sudden," said Wren, his voice cracking.

"Perhaps you should sit here on the bed," said Sandia, mock concern on her face. She escorted him to the bed and sat him down. "Take another drink Sir Forleroy. You sound parched."

Wren played her game. He finished the glass of wine and handed it to her. She stood and placed in on the bedside stand. She returned to him as he began to cough. His head was pounding. It felt like the blood in his body all pushed to get out of his eyes.

"I…I can't…" Wren croaked around a swelling throat.

"Can't breathe? Well that *is* the point now, isn't it Sir Forleroy," she said, harshness coating her voice. "You men are so easy sometimes. Now do be quick about it and die would you."

Wren keeled over on the bed; spasms wracked his torso and his limbs quivered. He felt the familiar pangs that came with death. His vision narrowed, his breathing slowed, he felt his blood halting, and then at the end, his last breath on his lips, he heard his Murmur.

Sandia Evelwick started searching Wren's corpse before he had even stopped shaking. She stuffed her hands into his trouser pockets and patted his body down, looking for concealed treasure or weapons. She popped his forefinger into her mouth, slid his ring free and into her pocket, and then loosened his linen collar to see if he hid a necklace. She paused at the curious brand hidden beneath the scarf. She started to pull the silk lower to get a better look…

Wren seized her wrist in his chilled fingers. "That will remain hidden," Wren said his voice a cracking whisper. The woman fell loose legged to the ground as Wren opened his eyes and sat up. "Sandia Evelwick, I collar you for a Skip for the murder of Tanis Forleroy."

It took a moment for the color to return to the woman's face and with it so too did her wits. She dashed her hand for the blade hidden in her skirts and made to slash at Wren's throat but he was too quick, his hands blurred at the edges. He grabbed her other wrist and in an instant had dragged her to her feet, had her arms pinioned behind her, and was fishing in his coat pocket for the thin copper and steel manacles hidden in his coin purse.

"You should be dead," she cried. "You drank enough to kill an ox. You should be dead."

"I don't usually do what I should," Wren said hoarsely. He searched her body roughly, looking for more weapons hidden in the folds of her dress. He felt a thick lump hidden on one leg. He lifted her skirts enough to pull it from beneath; she harrumphed her outrage. "Only returning the favor," he said into her ear. He looked at what he had found; a fat stack of coins and his ring could be felt through the purse's thin leather, as well as a glass vial, empty but with faint traces of liquid still clinging to the walls. "I'll be taking this for proving guilt and this," he tossed the purse up, catching it with a clink, "for expenses."

Wren made himself comfortable as he sat in the dimly lit shabby office of the local Skip Tracer's Bureau. Hodgens was filling in the proper documents for the transfer of the bounty at his rickety little desk. Piles of papers covered the desk and posters of Skips and other criminals plastered the walls.

Wren pushed aside a stack of papers with the heel of one of his boots, propped on Hodgens' desk, to look at the fat little man. He wore a worn tweed cap and smoked a thick cigar, his pudgy fingers pointed along the lines of the bounty transfer document.

"And, you say she *killed* you?" Hodgens said, looking up from the document.

Wren nodded lazily, toying idly with the leather syringe case in his pocket. Hodgens shook his head and returned to the parchment.

"Well, that qualifies as personal harm I would reckon," he said, puffing out a cloud of smoke. "That earns you an extra bonus. Woo, hoo, Wren I swear you are the best at finding the loopers. That woman cracked I tell you, she kept going on about a demon. 'He's a demon I say, a demon straight from Discordia'," Hodgens mocked in a high voice.

Wren shrugged his shoulders as he looked around Hodgens. There was a strange machine perched on a tabletop behind him. Wren noticed it started to clack and tap, steel and brass hammers swung wildly, spitting a long strip of parchment out one end.

"Ay, Hodge," Wren said, "what is that? I thought those things were supposed to be banned."

Hodgens turned, "Oh, well, you know how the law works, Wren, personal exceptions for friends of friends and so on. Anyway, it's a tap-writer. We have one in each of our Bureau chief's offices to get the latest Skip info. We'll see what's come in when I finish this up."

Wren stood and paced around the room, looking through the stacks of stained paper filling every surface. Lots of people were made criminal in the Wilderlands since the New Dominion had made deals with governors and town councils. Wren never went after the ordinary folk the New Dominion had turned outlaw. Touched folk, those with particular talents and gifts that were deemed heretical, were strictly off Wren's plate. He walked around to the tap-writer and watched as it spewed out words and images in little dots of dark ink.

"All seems in order here," said Hodgens at last.

Wren turned to him and took the sheet of parchment after Hodgens stamped it with his seal and the trader's mark. Wren tugged at his silk scarf again. "That is your copy of the bounty payout. Go to the counting house and give them that and they can either deposit it or pay out the lot to you, whichever you prefer. I'd suggest the deposit; we are in the Wilderlands after all," Hodgens pink cheeks grew pinker still as he laughed. "Now, let's see what I can find for you, if you're up to it."

Wren nodded and walked around the office, going over the walls of the tap-written images of the wanted. Young, old, men, women, even children looked back at Wren from reproductions of silver-transfer images. Wren read the charges from burglary, to murder, to document forging, and dealing in unmarked goods. Wren discarded those with crimes such as suspicion of heresy, possession of blasphemous objects, hiding suspected heretics, and speaking against the New Dominion.

"Bast! Wren you gotta see this one," Hodgens said, holding up the long strip of parchment. Wren walked over to see. "Now, I know how you are about these things, Wren, but just hear me out."

Wren looked at the dotted image of a girl still in the head of the tap-writer. It clicked away finishing up the border of the silver-transfer image. Hodgens ran a knife along the parchment to cut it loose from the roll.

"Let me read you the payout first before you get all superior on me," said Hodgens. "To the successful retainer of this wanted individual: alive the sum of four hundred thousand in gold strip will be paid. Dead, the sum of one hundred thousand in gold strip will be deposited in an account of their choosing."

Wren felt the pit of his stomach lurch. For either sum he could stop all the running around, getting himself stabbed, shot, and killed. Then his mind looked for the poison needle hidden in the pillow. Why would someone pay that much for, from what Wren had glimpsed briefly, a kid?

"What did she do?" Wren asked.

"Does it really matter, Wren? This has got to stop with you. You could be retired twice over if you would just put off these standards you have."

Wren grabbed the paper from Hodgens sweaty grip. He stared down at the girl in the image and felt his stomach heave once more. Staring up from the paper at him was a familiar face if a bit older than the last time he had seen it in a silver-transfer. The dark ink didn't do the girl justice but he could clearly tell her eyes were very pale, dark hair framed a frightened face. This image had probably been taken when the children of Arnora had been moved to the holding camps, before they were shipped to Romara. Her face was a girlish form of one Wren knew personally; she was defiantly Seb's sister, Rebecca.

Wren's heart pounded in his chest; he quickly read the charges: Murder of a Red Guard soldier, destruction of New Dominion property, incitation of a riot resulting in the death of a Red Guard soldier, escape from reeducation facilities, suspicion of possession of blasphemous materials, and suspicion of heretical attributes. *Definitely Seb's sister*, Wren thought after he read the charges. Wren's mind spun.

"Are you all right, Wren?" asked Hodgens.

Wren looked to the pudgy little man and thought quickly. "Hodge, you said every bureau chief has one of these tap-writers. So every bureau is getting one of these bounty sheets right now." Hodgens nodded, looking worried. "So every Skip Tracer in the

370

Wilderlands can look this kid up and go after the payout." Again, Hodgens nodded. "Fates favor me for once," Wren said to himself.

"Does this mean you'll take the job?" Hodgens asked, appearing more hopeful. "Because you know I get a tenth of the payout for turning you onto it."

Wren was torn. With the coin he got for turning the girl in he could buy a ship, a crew, and sail the seas like any Silvarish boy would have dreamed. He also had a debt to pay, and a promise to keep. Wren folded the parchment and stuffed it into his coat pocket. Hodgens eyes lighted with joy.

"I'll just need you to sign this Tracker form so we can make sure the payout is clean when you find this one and I'll need…"

"Look Hodge, remember what I asked before I took this last Skip?"

"Got it right here, Wren. You can use my washroom if you want to do it here." Hodgens leaned over to his desk and pulled several small glass vials from a drawer below. "I'll draw up the paperwork and you can go do what you need to do."

Wren took the glass vials and moved into the washroom to the back of the office. He sat on the porcelain flusher and took off his coat, after pulling a leather case from inside the coat pocket. He unlaced the case and rolled out the glass and metal syringe. He placed all but one of the glass vials into the slots to hold them in the leather and assembled the needle.

He stuck the point through the corked vial and pulled an amount from the container, replacing it in the last open slot in the case. He examined the color of the liquid in the syringe, very pale blue, low quality. He shook his head, pulled a leather lace from a pocket, and rolled up his left shirt sleeve.

Near a vein on his arm was tattooed a blue snake, faded over the years, but still distinguishable. Tears filled his eyes as he pulled the leather lace tight around his arm and stuck the needle's point into the vein. He pushed the plunger down and was immediately wrapped in warmth. It coursed through his arms and legs and his eyes could see more clearly. His heart pounded excitedly, his senses were on end. Wren threw back his head and twitched with the ecstasy of the chemicals flowing through his blood. He looked at the veins in his left arm and watched as the color shown through, staining the branching vessels a deep dark indigo.

He started to hear the whispers of his Murmur in his head. *Good Wren, good boy, you have missed me. So long away, but I knew you would return. You always do.* He felt a stroking along his soul as its grip tightened and released. Wren put the syringe back in its case, rolled it up, and replaced it in his coat pocket. He stood and, before turning to leave, looked to the mirror over the wash basin.

I wait for your final husking, Wren. You are mine, remember that. You need me more than I need you. The Murmur whispered seductively in his ear. Wren could see it there, a skull-like head, shimmering, smoky, transparent skin, waving as if currents in the air were blowing it away. Its voice whispered into his soul for it had no lower jaw to form real words. *We see one another again, Wren. You need me now, like before, like always.* It stroked his cheek with its skeletal fingers; its skin looked like thin white silk moving in a river, fading to nothing. Its malevolent eyes met Wren's in the mirror, hazy white met grayish blue-green. *You can't escape me with death you know. You have tried often but I always bring you back. When I have husked you clean your body will be mine, Wren.*

Wren strode from the washroom, unconcerned about anyone seeing his Murmur, the urge in him sated for now. Hodgens immediately pestered him about signing and sealing documents; Wren ignored him. He concentrated on what he had to do. What to do when he found Seb's sister? He had made that promise a long time ago and that payout was very enticing. What was more important now, coin or the Fates laws of a promise? *I'll have you in the end either way.* Wren felt the chill caress of that place near his heart he knew was his soul.

Forty-one: Knocked About

Rebecca knelt on the gravel of the meditation garden. Her body ached in more places than she knew she had. Her skin was slicked in sweat and caked in dust from the ground. Her panting breaths couldn't seem to get her burning lungs enough air. The loose cotton clothes Alaric had given her to wear, she had come to realize, were meant to allow free movement in lessons like the one she was currently working at. She pushed the long scarf holding back her hair into place on her head and got to her feet again.

The air was warm and the sky clear. The sun beat down at nearly midmorning upon the garden and, if she wasn't already overheated, Rebecca would have enjoyed the day thoroughly.

"Closer, my dear, you nearly got them all that time. Just missed that last by a hair." Alaric's voice ushered from behind a wooden wall from which he had been tossing Bashers, heavy balls with whirling arms that flew maniacally through the air driven as if by crazed spirits. They had walloped Rebecca for the past two hours and she had the bruises to show for it. The idea was to have her fend them off with a heavy wooden stick, which, because she was so exhausted, was nearly impossible for her to lift.

"Alaric, for Father's sake, I can barely lift this bloody, Father forsaken, stick anymore," she shouted back at him, trying to clear her vision. "Can I at least have five minutes rest? I need to catch my breath."

"No, my dear, and I might say you sound a bit testy." Alaric's head popped above the wooden barrier. The wall was marred and splintered where Rebecca had managed to send the Bashers back. "You had a rest an hour ago and, I say, you did worse afterwards."

"I'd like to see you swing at these things for two hours," she yelled back, brushing sweat from her eyes. She noticed a particular dark area on her sleeve when she wiped her mouth, her nose was bleeding. "That one got me in the face you know. I thought you said you had some control over these things."

Alaric giggled and ducked behind the wall. Rebecca would make him pay for that one. "Ready dear?" Alaric called behind the wall. "Here they come."

Rebecca saw the twirling arms around the ball's leather coated body moving fast at her as she readied the stick. She tried to calm her mind, that had been the whole point of this lesson - calm under pressure, but she wanted to blast down that wooden wall. She ducked as the Basher rushed at her. She swung wildly at it, trying to maim its arms, but a second flew too fast for her to see and took her from behind, hitting her in the back of her thighs. She felt pain course up through her legs and she fell flat onto the tiny gravel stones.

Rebecca heard the recall whistle blow and knew Alaric had called off the Bashers. He poked his head above the wall and the Bashers floated back to him like pleased pups. He set the Bashers down and walked to where Rebecca laid on the gravel. He knelt down with a grunt and checked to see if she was conscious.

"You weren't even trying that time," he said, offering her a jug of water. Rebecca pushed herself up and looked at him sidelong through narrowed eyes. She flopped over reluctantly onto her backside, wincing at the pain from her thighs. She took the jug in two shaking bruised hands and sucked down as much water as she could.

"You were doing better at the start, my dear," he said, sounding disappointed.

Rebecca stared at him in disbelief. "I wasn't at the point of falling over at the start, Alaric. I wasn't bruised over every inch of my body. I wasn't on the verge of strangling you either."

He shook with laughter as he dabbed at her face with a towel he carried. She pulled away. "Why are you pushing me so hard all of a sudden? We spent days trying to repeat what I first did to the point where I could do it with my eyes closed now. Now, you have me swinging sticks, running for hours, and trying to push boulders around with the Kilaray. I don't understand what you're trying to do."

"We started slow so now we are making up ground, my dear." He said, leaning closer and taking her face in his hands, forcing her to hold still while he dabbed at her nose. "If you would stop being so resistant, we could go faster."

"Resistant? You must be insane. Broheim told me you were a bit odd but he didn't say anything about being a madman," she yelled. "Alaric, I have been fighting as hard as I can to do what you're asking me, but you keep pushing harder before I'm ready. What is going on?"

He sighed heavily and stood up, offering her his hand. She took it and limped along as he led her into the workshop. She followed feeling apprehensive. When Alaric didn't answer a question immediately it was usually something important. He took her through the maze of machines to a corner where a steel and brass device sat with a spool of parchment at one end.

"This is a tap-writer. It's connected, using the Kilaray, to another with a contact of mine. He is my liaison with the Pictsies, a fellow by the name of Bertran Gabriel. He owns a book shop in Nor Harbor, south of here. The town is a bit of a haven for people who…well, who need hiding."

"The Shints want to help, but they won't risk their necks without some assurances that you can get through the Gates. My plan is to push you as hard as I can so you can demonstrate to their representatives that you can."

"What does it matter if it takes a little longer for me to be prepared?" she asked, brushing away a dribble of blood from her nose.

"Because he also sent me this," Alaric held up a piece of parchment Rebecca was quite disturbed to see. "This is a bounty sheet for you. The payout on it is more than most men would see in three lifetimes."

Rebecca took the sheet and read the charges; the last two left her hands shaking, *blasphemy and heresy*. She looked up from the bounty sheet. "This says they'll pay for me dead also," she said.

"Death bounties are rare; any Skip Tracer with an ounce of brains will know that it means you're to be considered dangerous," Alaric said, quite angry. "Dangerous, bast!" he looked at Rebecca. "Once it would have been considered an honor to have the least talented of the Touched sit at your dining room table. Now, we are hunted like rabid dogs."

Rebecca didn't know what to say. She had figured Alaric was just being hard on her. She realized now he was trying to get her ready to handle more than just the Gates.

"I don't have what it takes to teach you blade skills and it's difficult to carry rifles or pistols into most towns now or I'd give you mine, they've been banned to the commoners. The best I can do for you is to teach you to defend yourself with the Kilaray," he said, looking sad and scared.

Rebecca considered his words for a time. She had assumed she would simply walk up to the Gates with Alaric, do what needed to be done inside, and everything would sort itself out. She resolved to show Alaric that she would meet what was required of her. She looked at Alaric with a hint of a grin.

"Then we should get back to it; shouldn't we," she said, placing her hand on his shoulder. He smiled and smacked his thighs.

"I knew you had steel in you, my dear," he said, following Rebecca out into the meditation garden again. "This time I'll let you get ready before I send the Bashers."

"Don't lighten up on me now," she said, grabbing the heavy wooden stick from the gravel. "I'll never learn otherwise." She grinned now as she saw Alaric duck behind the wall.

She calmed her mind and saw the first of the Bashers hurtle over the wall at her. The Easing came on her and she held against the tug of the Kilaray; she had learned control over its release. The Basher slowed to a crawl, its whining mechanisms pitched down to a drone. She could see the arms spin like wind mills in stale air, its leather coating marked with a bright green stripe. She took aim with the stick and swung at her target.

The Basher flew off to lay battered on the ground, but she had no time to celebrate. The Quickening had brought her back to speed. She had practiced moving through the phases of Reaching and could now transfer from one to the other and back again. It was like having a rein on time.

The world slowed as she turned to see two more Bashers, aiming hard for her head and feet, blue and yellow markings indicating their increased skills. She jumped, moving faster in the Easing than the Bashers, and caught the blue one aimed for her head before landing. The world whipped back to speed in her excitement. The whine of the last Basher met her ears as it recovered from missing her feet. The world slowed once more and the whine sounded as if it came to her from underwater. She spun as it aimed for her stomach and took it from behind, to send it crashing into the wooden wall as she let time return to normal.

Behind you! she heard in her head.

She didn't have time to wonder at the words; she rounded instinctively to see one more Basher fly around the side of the wall. She hadn't seen any red striped before. She dropped to the ground and threw the stick end over end into its path. The Basher collided with the stick and went careening off course. The stick clattered to the ground, out of reach, as the Basher recovered and made for her face like a bullet. She could hear Alaric blowing the recall whistle but it was too late for that; its momentum would carry it onward into her.

Rebecca remained calm allowing the Easing to come, she went deeper and the world brightened to shimmering beauty. The Basher froze in mid flight, the Stillness. The Kilaray Links blossomed around her. She could see the hair-fine multicolored strands licking out from the Basher; they twisted out behind the arms like a corkscrew. She saw the connections she had with it and choose one. She reached out her arm and was surprised to see she could still move. She gripped the strand binding her to the Basher; it felt like the most taught line she had ever touched. She let the Kilaray move but she held tight to the link restraining the full torrent; the Quickening, the world flashed bright again.

She swung her hand holding the link and sent the Basher flying over her head as if tethered to a cord into the ground behind her. The whistle ceased as it dropped from Alaric's lips; he gaped at what she had just done.

"Haroo!" bellowed Alaric, jumping from behind the wall. "My dear, oh Great Ghosts." Alaric's feet crunched the gravel as he ran to her side.

Rebecca picked herself off the ground and turned to look at the ruined Basher behind her. The other three bumbled, whizzed, and whirred, waiting to be restarted. This one though was utterly still, silent, dead. Rebecca felt sad for some reason. She knew it wasn't alive but she hadn't meant to hurt it so badly.

Alaric hugged her and began ushering her into the house for a much deserved break.

"I didn't want to kill it," she said, looking over her shoulder at the inert Basher.

"That's what they are built for, dear." Alaric said, sensing her unease. "We can fix it, I swear, but you should rest after a show like that."

Forty-two:
Inner Workings

Alaric made mid meal and they took the food out into the garden to eat. Rebecca picked up the mashed red-marked Basher and examined it as she ate. She still felt sorry for wrecking it as badly as it appeared, but Alaric continued to reassure her that it hadn't felt anything and they could repair it.

"We designed these to be easily cleaned up. This is a time honored training method, my dear. Mecharicals for ages have had these in their shops, in constant repair. We would have the newest members of the Order do nothing but piece these back together when they first came to us." Alaric stuffed a large hunk of bread and cheese into his mouth and washed it down with tea.

"What do the red stripes mean?" Rebecca asked, rolling the crumpled ball over in her lap.

"Those, ah…well." Alaric had turned decidedly red and hid his face in his tea bowl.

Rebecca eyed him suspiciously. "You *are* a madman; aren't you?" she said, shaking her head. "The green are the easiest, then blue and yellow. Were you going to tell me there were more difficult ones or did you think it would be funny to see me laid out again?"

"I wouldn't have thrown it if I didn't think you could handle it, my dear. It's just…you were doing so well and I…I got a little overly enthusiastic. Now let me see that," he said, heaving the ball from Rebecca's lap. She munched on some apple slices while he fumbled the ball around. He switched his lenses continuously and pried the leather shell open to see inside.

"We'll have this back in the air in short order," he said, looking up. "I had hoped to bring you around to this eventually, but seeing as you have handily given me a teaching aid; I can show you how to get devices to work with the Links."

They finished eating and took the dishes into the kitchen then Alaric took her to the workshop. He cleared a table with a swipe of his arm, sending metal clanking and rolling all over the floor. Rebecca was amazed he could work in his sloppy shop. He thudded the Basher up on the workbench and pulled over a stool. He adjusted a lantern and pulled it closer to him. He gestured for Rebecca to come closer to see.

"Now, all Linked objects work by drawing energy from the Kilaray; that's what drives their actions. As you have seen there is a multitude of links that connect all objects together; the key is to find the ones that will do what you want and bind them correctly," Alaric said, peeling away the leather body of the Basher. Inside was a series of rings that moved independently in three axes. Centered in-between the rings was the main mechanism, a layered construction of gears and wheels that were now obviously thrown out of alignment.

"Try and see the links here, my dear," Alaric said, pointing at the main mechanism. He pulled down a leather strap with numerous glass lenses attached to it from a shelf. He stuck the strap on his head and moved lenses on little arms in front of his eyes. Rebecca laughed a little when she saw him in this contraption but she did as he asked. She gazed at the parts and more quickly the flitting sparks of light presented themselves to her. She could see how they tried to move through the Basher but were stopped in several places where the parts were misaligned.

"I can see where the links are broken," she said as Alaric searched around for tools. He pulled up several overly large mallets, a strange metal rod with several discs attached to it, and other bizarre implements.

"Not broken my dear just blocked. It would take something more serious to break the links than a crash into the dirt." He spun two of the discs attached to the rod; the point began to glow in a familiar way. *It is something to manipulate the links then*, she thought. "There are few things that can break the links. Severing the Kilaray Links can be devastating. It sends ripples out, tearing away more links in a chain reaction. There is a place where many links were severed sometime ago." Alaric looked up, his eyes magnified huge through the lenses. "Your grandfather Martan explored the region but could not get close enough to the center of destruction to see what happened there."

"Where was it?" she asked.

"The heart of the Broken Lands," he said, returning to the Basher. "He speculated that whatever caused the rent in the world at its center is the reason the land around it has been tormented as it has. Terrible things happen when the links are severed."

"Now, the goal here," Alaric said, turning his attention to the Basher, "is to simply realign the links that are blocked. The Kilaray will do the rest."

Rebecca watched as Alaric slid the glowing end of the metal rod into the Basher's mechanisms. She saw as the rod was drawn, like a magnet to steel, to one of the blocked connections.

"This next step is bit more energetic," he said, picking up one of the large mallets. "You might want to stand back a nudge there." He stood from his stool as Rebecca moved back. He braced himself and began pounding on the end of the metal rod, forcing the links back into position. They resisted his efforts and soon sweat had formed on his brow. He picked up a larger mallet. "Wants to play tough does it?" he said to no one in particular and hammered with full force on the end of the metal rod.

With a sound like a cork pulled from a bottle, the metal rod broke free from the Basher and sent it flying from the workbench. Rebecca jumped out of the way as the Basher hit a large device sitting on the ground, rebounded, and began to whine, its naked rings and gears spinning up to speed.

"Aha, there we go," Alaric said, wiping his forehead. "Just took a little persuading."

Rebecca watched the Basher begin to hover, its parts moving of their own accord, bending back into shape, and finally halting in perfect order. She could see the steady beat of the Kilaray moving the springs and gears of the Basher, an ever persistent source of energy.

"The parts, they moved by themselves?" she asked. She watched the Basher hovering contentedly above the ground.

"Of course, the metal bits are only secondary to the construct of links that make up these devices." Alaric indicated all around the shop. "Fixing these is a matter of finding the out-of-order links and putting them right. The Kilaray will mash the physical parts back into place as they want, form follows function."

As Rebecca looked she could see that the inner mechanism seemed changed now. The parts had moved into a different arrangement from where they had been before. The metal workings adjusted to suit the flow of Kilaray.

"The hard part comes when making these things from the start. You have to know what you're about before you begin. It's almost a matter of listening to the directions of the Kilaray than working from a plan," he said, taking off the leather strap with the lenses.

That got Rebecca thinking about what had happened when she had fended off this Basher.

"Alaric, do the Kilaray talk to you?" she asked, turning to him. The Basher floated over, nudging Rebecca's leg.

"Why do you ask?" He peered at her suspiciously.

"When I was batting at the other Bashers, I thought I had got them all. Then something warned me this one was coming. I think I heard something similar before, but I thought it was because I was dying underwater back at Valgerhold. Something spoke to me."

Alaric had become very quiet. He thought for a while and sat on his stool. After a time he spoke.

"Do you know why you can see the Kilaray outside of the Stillness?"

She shook her head.

"It's because they want you to see them. You have the Touch, as do I, or a Palantean would, but the Kilaray do not show themselves to me very well and not to a Palantean outside of the Stillness. It was a trait of the Philistari. They always had the Kilaray before them if they looked for them. It allowed them to do things that none of the other Orders could. If you listen, they can speak to you, guide you, tell you of what is to come."

Rebecca looked very skeptical. "You mean I can tell the future like some crystal ball reader." She laughed at the absurdity but Alaric remained quiet. She stopped laughing and felt a bit embarrassed but it was absurd, *wasn't it?*

"It is not an easy thing to read what is to come. The paths of our lives are not laid down as a book to be read; there are possibilities, chance, and choice. If you can learn the how of it, you can see ahead what might come. We call it a Reached Vision. The further ahead, the less accurate the vision will be, hazy and clouded by the possibilities of the happenings that lead to it."

"Then the Vision that said I would be needed could be wrong?" Rebecca felt slightly queasy.

"It could be. That is why we were not certain if it would be you, your brother, or some other child that we did not know about for that matter, that would be the child the Vision referred to."

"Then it could be someone else still," said Rebecca.

"Maybe but I doubt it for several reasons. First you have accepted the path before you. Second you show a strong connection with the Kilaray, this voice you speak of gives evidence of that. And lastly there is your grandfather's sword."

"What sword?" she asked confused.

Alaric took her around to a hidden staircase attached to the ceiling of the workshop. He pulled on a cord and the staircase descended. There was an attic above the rafters of the workshop that she hadn't noticed.

Walking up the steep steps, she entered what she could describe only as a shrine of some kind. Around the room stood pedestals with bits of battered armor. Shields hung on the walls with gaping holes in them. A tattered banner, a Blackbird emblazoned against a crosscut field of orange and green, hung on one wall. At the back wall, on wooden racks, hung swords of various designs, some curved gracefully, others straight and unyielding, and some tapered to elegant points.

She didn't realize she had stopped moving until she was nudged from behind. Alaric followed her up into the space; its low ceiling gave just enough height for them to stand.

"This is what we could salvage from the battle the New Dominion likes to refer to as Ronan's Folly. The Armor is beyond repair or it would be in the Holding. The swords, on the other hand, are still functioning very well." He led her back to the wall with the varying swords. They seemed to call, to sing to her, whispers in her mind, all with varied voices. One was set apart on a small stand on the floor; it sat on a patterned silk cloth of blue and gold. "These are Soul Blades," he said, reverent. "They were the weapons of the Palantean, each as individual as its owner. These here," he said, indicating the swords hung on the racks on the wall, "have lost their owners, their Mates. They would be able to attune to a new Mate with their previous owners death but alas, we have had no more Palantean."

"Why is this one separated from the others?" she asked, kneeling down to inspect the sword on the silk. It was beautiful, curved slightly, both edges sharpened to razor keenness, a narrow bronze guard covered in blossoms and blooms, a sinuous serpent wove in and around the blossoms to reinforce the guard. The hilt was dark black wood with shining silver wire worked into it in a lacey scroll. The blade had intricate etched symbols at its base, some looked almost like the Shintish writing in the journal, but others were clearly runes of some sort. The feeling Rebecca got from the sword was that it was feminine.

"That one is very special and I think you should take it when we leave. It cannot be yours; for, this is my third reason for believing that you must be the one to fulfill the Vision. This sword was Mated and still is to your grandfather."

Rebecca turned to Alaric standing above her with a sudden burning in her eyes. "My...my grandfather, Martan?"

Alaric shook his head. "Your mother's father, Ronan Arcand."

Rebecca felt her stomach had suddenly dropped to her feet. She had not known her mother's father; they had not talked to one another since after Rebecca was born. She thought back to her mother, crying at the news of Ronan's defeat at the pass, how her mother had been inconsolable; it made sense now, she had lost her father. She felt a pang of loss suddenly.

"You can't Mate to that sword because it is still attuned to Ronan." Alaric said, settling himself beside her. "You see, all of these swords were forged using methods to bind them with the Kilaray. In essence they are devices like those down below. The difference is that these swords have a life to themselves, a Soul of sorts."

Rebecca touched the hilt of Ronan's sword. It felt strange; she could almost feel it want to pull away from her fingers like some frightened animal. She touched the wood gently almost stroking it and the feeling settled.

"She, for some reason, has refused to give up her bond with Ronan," Alaric said.

"She?" Rebecca asked.

"The Souls of the blades have a female or male sense to them. They usually Mated best with Palantean of the opposite gender. The sword that we see is only the part that exists in our world. There is another half that exists in the world of the Kilaray. It is that half that makes these swords so extraordinary. These Blades in the hands of a trained Palantean are unstoppable...nearly."

"It couldn't stop Ronan from getting killed then," Rebecca said, dropping her eyes to the floor.

"Maybe. You see the Mating of the Soul Blade and the Palantean is one of the strongest links we know. The Soul Blade will know when the Palantean has died because his soul will have moved on. The link is released and the Blade can attune to another. We have never known the link to be mistaken. So, when we found that this Blade was still attuned to Ronan, we believed that he was still alive, but he never came back. We searched for him but we could not find him."

"Where could he have gone? Would he have run away?" She didn't like the idea of one of her family running from what was needed of them.

"If you think that of him, you surely did not know your grandfather. The man would have walked through a wall if it stood in the way of what he needed to do. No, I do not think he ran away, but I don't know where he could be. He is lost."

"Then that is why you think that I am the one for this Vision, because I'm of the blood of the lost."

Alaric nodded with a sad smile on his face.

"If I can't attune to this Blade, why do you think I should take it with me?" she asked.

"It just seems the right thing to do. I can't say why. If you feel you should leave it I would be proud to hold on to it."

Rebecca shook her head. She reached slowly for the hilt of the sword. It trembled beneath her finger tips. She let it settle before gripping the hilt.

Where is he? Where is my Mate? Who are you? Release me.

The words jumped into Rebecca's head so forcefully that she released the hilt and fell over backward away from the sword.

"What happened, my dear?" Alaric asked, looking concerned. He helped her so sit up.

"It...it spoke to me. It asked where Ronan was. I don't think it likes me," she said.

"Well, this could be a bit of a problem," he said, stroking his beard. "I figured at least you could use it as a normal sword when you go. Most bandits would flee if their prey were armed." He quirked an eye brow at her and a hint of a grin touched the corner of his mouth. "We could have you take one of these others," he said, pointing along the racks. "Or better still..." his face lighted with joy. He slapped his hands together startling her. "Oh yes, that will be perfect, a young woman for a Young Blade."

Rebecca looked at him, confusion clear on her face.

Alaric hurriedly found the scabbard for Ronan's sword. He sheathed the Blade and wrapped the silk around it, tying it with a bit of gold cording. He handed it to her; Rebecca took it reluctantly but the words did not come to her this time.

"Keep this with you. Perhaps with time, the Soul linked to it will come to trust you enough to allow you to talk with it," he said. "Now, come with me. This will be most exciting."

He led her down the steep stairs to the shop below and moved deep into the maze of machines and workbenches. Rebecca, the sword slung over her shoulder, picked her way through the mangled contraptions blocking the path. She found Alaric sorting through crates and cloth wrapped bits of metal.

"Where did I leave the poor thing? Half made for so long, I will have to apologize I'm sure. He certainly will be quite angry," Alaric muttered to himself. He threw bits of packing straw and old burlap behind him as he searched his shelves of odd possessions.

Rebecca chuckled to herself still in a haze of confusion. "Alaric, what are you looking for?"

He turned his head, still on all fours, strings of straw stuck in his red hair, to stare at her. "It's a sword of course. Well, almost. Look around for a length of steel about three feet or so. *You* won't be able to miss it when you see it; its links won't have been settled yet."

Rebecca set Ronan's sword on a cleared space on one workbench and joined the search. She sifted through Alaric's piles of disorderly clutter.

"You know," she said after a time, "you wouldn't have this problem if you cleaned this mess up."

"Mess," he sounded quite offended, "mess indeed. I know where every scrap of metal here belongs. It's all up here," he said, pointing to his skull through his ruffled hair, soot and dust smeared across his face. Rebecca shook her head and returned to the hunt.

She spotted it as soon as she turned back. Wrapped in an oiled cloth, something bright flitted through the wrapping. She slowly pulled the cloth out from beneath metal rings, gears, and springs, and blocks of wood. She could see the flow of light sparkling into what was hidden inside; the cloth could not block out the Kilaray.

"Alaric, I think I found it," she said, turning to him. He pulled his head from under a crowded table and scuttled over to her, still on hands and knees.

"Let me see, ah yes." He took it from her, unwrapped it, and cradled it like a baby.

The sword blade looked nearly complete; it was narrow, tapering ever so slightly to the point, and thin. The metal had turned dark in places from the air and in spots bits of rust marred the surface, despite the oiled cloth.

Alaric looked up with a grin. "He is not going to be happy with me."

Rebecca followed Alaric out of the clutter into a corner of the workshop that seemed dedicated to metal working. A large cold brick furnace sat at one side and hammers tongs and other metal tools lined one wall. This was by far the tidiest area of the whole shop, perhaps for the chance of fire otherwise.

"I will need your assistance in the last phase of the Blade's working, my dear," Alaric said, pulling on a thick leather apron. He had another set of lenses attached to a leather head strap hung from one of the rafters near an anvil. He pulled the strap down over his head and flipped lenses in front of his eyes. He turned some levers near the furnace and it roared to life, heat blasted from its opening. Alaric examined the Blade, turning it here and there, every few seconds folding a lens out of the way or moving another into place.

Rebecca let her eyes wander over the Blade as she took a seat on a stool, watching Alaric work. The Blade was quite handsome in her opinion. She let the Kilaray fill her vision. They moved around the length of steel with an energy she hadn't seen before. They didn't flow smoothly; there was disorder to their movements, cutting out in twists and points in areas. After Alaric had examined the Blade to his satisfaction he walked to the furnace and thrust it into the fire.

"I had to leave some of the tools required to forge Soul Blades behind when I left Garmon," he shouted over the roar of the furnace. "I can work the metal but the Kilaray I leave in your hands."

"What do you mean?" she shouted back. "I don't know what to do."

"You will. Just listen to the Soul; he will guide you. He knows better than you or me how to work himself into the steel."

Rebecca felt apprehensive. She watched as Alaric pulled the white hot steel Blade from the fire and brought it over to the anvil. He beckoned her to come closer.

"Now, as I begin to hammer, you align the Kilaray how the Soul tells you. I'm going to warn you now, he may be a little angry. Young

393

Blades do not know patience and he has been many years in the waiting."

Rebecca's eyes popped out of her head. She not only was being asked to do something she had never done before but she was going to have to deal with a potentially angry Soul.

"Ready then, here we go."

Alaric began to pound on the glowing steel. Rebecca tried to focus. She moved into the Easing. Alaric's hammer blows slowed to a crawl. She began to hear words coming from the Blade.

Important to you now, am I? Well, I am not a distraction to be picked up when you are bored, Alaric von Magus. Wait, who are you?

Rebecca was so shocked she slipped out of the Easing. She looked to Alaric.

"It knows your name," she said.

"Well he should I was the one who started his birthing, and it's best to refer to him as a kind of person. He won't take kindly being talked to like an animal."

Alaric returned the Blade to the heat for a moment. Rebecca readied herself.

"Set, my dear?" Rebecca nodded.

She slipped into the Easing and Alaric's hammering slowed.

Back again stranger? Where is Alaric? Why has he not finished my birthing?

"I am Rebecca," she said to the Blade. "Alaric couldn't finish you. He's sorry, but I am here and I can help."

A child? Alaric sends children to finish his work. Do you think you have the skill to bring me into your world girl? I think not. I have waited here for years while Alaric toys with his other constructions. I will not be crippled and made useless after my long wait by some child who wanders blindly into my world.

394

"Well, I'm all you've got right now," Rebecca said, angry at this Soul's attitude toward her. "If you would rather I go…"

Not so hasty, young one. Rebecca was it? Perhaps you can bring me along. We shall have to see; I suppose, if I have no other option?

Rebecca shook her head.

"Do you have a name?" she felt a bit odd talking to the metal. It was still white hot and Alaric's hammer was just now meeting the surface, sending a shower of slow motion sparks out from the blow.

You find this strange do you, talking to a Blade as you are?

"A little."

No inkling of procedures, I have no name yet. I will not know it until I am in your world as well as this one. Come, we are wasting time. You must begin by Reaching deeper. I will guide you from there.

Rebecca concentrated and felt the familiar tug at her soul. She slipped into the Stillness and the links flared before her eyes. Alaric's laced into the Blade as did her own. There was a third set from someone else but Rebecca could not see him.

We have time here but the process, once started, must be continued unto completion from this stage. If it is not, I will perish and I would rather not, if that could be avoided. It was from this third unseen person the words emanated.

"What are you?" she asked.

I am the Soul of this blade. I have been summoned and drawn to join the metalwork. Now, if your questions can wait; I would like to finally be birthed.

"Right, sorry," she said.

Then begin by feeling the links you can see in the steel itself. There are several that need to be pruned; others need to be strengthened, before it will be ready for me to join with it. I will tell you when you are nearing the final arrangement of each.

395

"But there are hundreds of them."

Then I suggest you get started.

Turning to the metal, Rebecca felt along the links tied to her and the steel. She found one that led to a kinked link.

"What do I do?" she asked.

You mean you have never done this before? Oh, Alaric you are a daring one aren't you? Let a trickle of the Kilaray's force flow along the link until you feel it is in correct balance.

She gently released her hold on the Kilaray flow. A torrent of force ripped through her soul. She thought she was going to lose control entirely.

Stop! Stop! The voice shouted in fear.

"I've got it," Rebecca said, frightened herself.

You must move slowly, especially without practice.

"Sorry, let me try again."

I have no choice now; do I? You have begun. There is no turning back, please be cautious.

Rebecca felt a wave of dread. This Soul depended on her now. She found another link; this one had looped several times on itself. She touched it and let her hold go, keeping tight rein on the flow.

Gently, gently, there that's perfect. The voice sounded much stronger now. *A few hundred more like that and we're done.*

Alaric remained frozen, the hammer still in contact with the steel of the Blade. Hours seemed to drift by as Rebecca worked each of the malformed links in the Blade. With each successful alignment the Soul's voice became more confident. Rebecca felt exhausted. She had never held the tug of the Kilaray so long and she didn't think she could last much longer.

You have almost finished my friend. The Blade is prepared and these last few links are the key to binding me to it. This one – the light pulsed bright gold along the thick link – *will bind my being to the Blade in this world. This one* – another thick link pulsed lightning blue – *will bind the Blade to me in your world. This last* – the thickest strand flashed a brilliant white – *must remain loose until I am Mated. They just need to be pruned and tied correctly. So if you will, let us be done.*

Rebecca found the golden link and sent a trickling flow of Kilaray along it. Its loose waving ends attached firmly to the Blade and tightened, forming a firm tie to the place from where the voice was speaking.

Good, I can feel this world fully now.

Rebecca reached for the blue link; it felt solid in her mind. She passed the flow of Kilaray onto it; it snapped out of her mind and formed a rigid strut between the steel and the Soul.

Ah, a body. This last will be most difficult. You must form one end and leave the other loose.

Rebecca nodded and concentrated on the last link. It whipped wildly now, like a kite in a windstorm. She reached and slipped, grabbed and missed. She held out her hand and physically held the link. She could feel the force flowing from her into the link immediately. She reined it back. One end jumped to the place where the voice had been speaking the other end moved in a controlled waving motion.

You have done it. I thank you Rebecca. Return now to your world and see what you have accomplished.

Rebecca let the Quickening take her from the Stillness. Alaric's hammer recoiled and jumped into the air. The world came back to normal; it seemed to move too quickly in contrast to the Stillness.

Rebecca slumped to her knees. She hadn't realized how much effort it would take to hold against the Kilaray for so long. Alaric dropped his hammer and went to his knees beside her.

"Are you alright; did you do it?"

"What does he look like?" she asked, fighting her way to stand. "Let me see him."

Relief washed over Alaric's face. "You did it then?"

Rebecca nodded and Alaric helped her up. They both looked on the Blade. The white hot color faded too quickly to be natural. A gleaming shine came on the thin, supple Blade; its edges honed to razor sharpness as she watched. Bright golden green runes etched themselves into the base of the Blade, cooling to black as they settled. The metal seemed to hum with excitement. Rebecca stared at the Blade with awe.

"What is his name? That's what the runes are; aren't they?" she whispered.

Alaric put his arm around her shoulder and nodded. "This one is called Astenos, it means balance or harmony, a strong name. Come, we must finish his construction."

Rebecca reached for the Blade, knowing he would be cool. She found he was lighter than he appeared. Alaric turned off the furnace and returned to the cluttered workshop. He brought Rebecca an assortment of wood blocks, and retrieved a silk-lined wooden box which contained several bronze guards and spools of various metal wires. Rebecca found the choosing was a matter of listening to what Astenos wanted.

Choosing out the materials the Blade called for, she and Alaric fitted the hilt together. The guard slid into place, a rough block of pale white holly following. The wood creaked as it was fitted into place, the guard hummed. The materials of the hilt began to flow like liquid into shape as Rebecca watched; the Kilaray pulled the materials into shape. Alaric placed the loose end of a spool of copper wire to the unsettled wood. The spool spun as the wire was pulled into the swirling grain of the hilt. When the Kilaray settled into the Blade and the motion about the hilt ceased, the sword was finally fitted with a beautifully honed hilt. An intricate bronze guard, meandering trees forming its open pattern, had worked itself from the metal. Thin copper wire was laid into the gleaming white wood of the long hilt in spirals. When the Blade was completed, it resonated in her hands; she could feel the last link she had formed snake its way into her, forming a tentative bond to her and the Blade.

"Now dear, this is what we call a Young Blade. He will be quite anxious to prove himself. You must let him attune to you gradually or you may be injured. Fortunately he knows you already. So, it should go a little easier, but you must be patient where he will want to be brash," Alaric said.

She was delighted with the Blade. She could feel his eagerness flow into her finger tips. The voice she had heard while Reaching came to her as if from the end of a long tunnel. She could barely hear it.

"He sounds like a whisper in my head," she said, straining to listen.

"His voice will strengthen in time as the attuning fully resolves and you have been Mated properly. He will be more clearly heard when you are using him for what he was created. Come, it is late and you need to rest."

Rebecca followed Alaric back to the house after retrieving Ronan's sword from the table where she had left it. The day had started to go pink; the sun had sunk into the trees. Rebecca was tired and still in pain from the Bashers earlier in the day. Alaric prepared her a plate for last meal and brought it to her while she sat in a chair in the reading room. She devoured the food. Astenos's working had taken as much out of her as two hours of swinging at the Bashers.

She bathed and changed clothes for sleep. She carried both swords into her room, laying them at the foot of her bed. She climbed beneath the covers and soon felt her eyes droop as she slipped off to sleep.

She found herself dreaming of a woman's crying. The woman desperately searched for someone, someone she had lost. She, though unseen to Rebecca, seemed to have a familiar sense to her like they had met some time long ago. She refused to listen to Rebecca's pleas to allow her to help.

A man entered the dream and watched as Rebecca tried to comfort the crying woman. He too remained out of Rebecca's vision but she had a feeling that he was familiar as well. He approached Rebecca from behind and laid an unseen hand on her shoulder.

Come, there is nothing you can do for her. She has lost her Mate. *The man's voice was in her head.*

"Astenos, is that you?" Rebecca asked, turning to look for him but finding only shadow. "Astenos, will you talk to her? She will not listen to me."

I cannot, not until she is willing to hear us both. It is against custom for the Soul to speak for his Mate to another. When we are attuned she will listen to us more willingly.

"I don't mind Astenos; please, she is so frightened and she might be able to help me find her Mate. He is my grandfather."

400

I am sorry Rebecca but she must wait. Sleep deep now; I will guard your mind from her. She may be dangerous.

"She isn't dangerous; she is just afraid and lonely."

That is what makes her a danger to us. She wants to be Mated again but cannot let go. If she attempts to attune to you it will kill us both. She is stronger than us now, we are still both young.

"What do you mean kill us?"

Sleep Rebecca, we will talk tomorrow.

Forty-four:
Sending a Message

Rebecca awoke the following morning with a deep sadness for the poor Soul she had met in her dream. She could remember the sobs of the Soul, the howling moans of a being deprived of its greatest joy. She looked at the silk wrapped sword, lying still at the foot of her bed. She stroked the sword through the silk in a reassuring way.

"I will help you find your Mate, I promise," she said to the sword.

She felt a surge of jealousy from nearby, not her own. She picked up Astenos, lying beside the other sword. His voice immediately burst into her head.

She is not yours to comfort Rebecca. You and I must attune. She must wait as I told you before; you will not attempt to talk to her.

The words she heard shocked Rebecca; the volume had increased and the anger in Astenos's voice was plain. "Do you feel no sympathy for your own kind? Are you so eager to join with me that you would allow another to suffer while you enjoy your new life? I do not think I would like to join with someone like that."

You have no choice now, child. I am yours and you are mine. The attuning has begun and cannot be stopped. I tell you again, do not attempt to talk with that other Soul.

"Just how do you expect to stop me? As far as I can tell you are just a length of sharp steel. You have no way to hold me back. I will help her."

402

Child, you do not understand of what you speak. Rebecca caught a hint of fear in the voice. *I can stop you and…and I will if you attempt to speak with that Soul again.*

Rebecca felt her body tense up; her muscles seized like they tried to pull away from her bones. Her body arched until only her head and heels touched the mattress. Her mind went wild, images and sounds began to flash across it like a storm. She began to shake and shudder in her bed. Her fingers were incapable of releasing Astenos from her grip. Fear, sadness, agony, all washed through her, leaving her in a state of panic. They all came unbidden from Astenos clutched in her fist. She thought she was going to die.

Then it all stopped. Her heart beat like it wanted to tear through her chest. She dropped Astenos as though he were a poison snake suddenly slithered into her hand. She scrambled away from him as far as she could. She clutched her legs up to her chest and rocked slowly in bed against the head board.

I…I told you…I would stop you. You see we are joined now. We are becoming two halves of a whole. Whatever I feel you will feel. I give you a taste of what will come if you attempt to speak with that Soul.

Rebecca felt embarrassed, humiliated, and angry. "I will never touch you again. I will never use you. You are cruel and hateful. I should have stopped birthing you when I had the chance to end you. I hate you."

She felt a wave of sadness and remorse wash through her, not her own. *You will use me I assure you. You are a foolish little girl who does not understand what she has stepped into. You will not speak with that Soul again.*

Rebecca sat for a time in her bed huddled against the head board until she heard Alaric rising for the day. He pushed open her door, poking his head in to see if she was awake. She met his eyes and anger pushed through her fear.

She scowled at him and spoke with her mouth hidden behind her knees.

"Why didn't you tell me he was such an awful Soul?" Tears leaked from her eyes.

Alaric pushed into the room and surveyed the scene. Astenos lay forgotten on the floor. Ronan's sword, still covered in the silk wrappings, lay on the bed; Rebecca cowered as far from the swords as possible. He swooped down next to her and Rebecca clung to him like a lifeline. She hugged him, crying into his shoulder.

"What happened, my dear? What happened?" he held her head and pulled her close.

"He hurt me. I told him I wanted to help the other Soul, and he hurt me. I couldn't stop him; I was so scared." Rebecca felt shame flow from Astenos lying on the floor. She turned to him and screamed.

"YOU SHOULD BE ASHAMED!"

"What did he tell you? What did he say?" Alaric asked, calming her a little.

"He said I couldn't speak to the other Soul again. I told him I would without him and he... he..."

Alaric looked on her with an extremely serious face. He looked at the sword considering it. He then picked up Ronan's sword, and stroked his beard, thinking.

"Rebecca, what did he tell you about speaking to the other Soul?"

"What does it matter? I just want to help her. She is so lonely without her Mate and I could help her if I could just speak with her."

NO! You must not.

"Shut up!" she wailed at Astenos.

"Did he tell you what would happen if you tried speaking with her again?"

"He told me he would stop me. I didn't believe he could and then he started hurting my mind."

"Rebecca, I do not believe he meant to scare you so much. What he says may well be true."

"What? You're taking his side but I ..."

"You don't know the customs of the Souls, my dear. We have never witnessed anything like what has happened here," he said, holding up Ronan's sword.

Rebecca, please. I am sorry.

"I'm not talking to you," she screamed at Astenos.

"But you must talk to him, Rebecca. He is a part of you now. What he said to you, what he did, might have been meant to protect you. Did he tell you what would happen if you spoke with her again?"

"In my dream, he said she could be dangerous, but Alaric she can't be; she is my grandfather's Mate. Surely he would not let her hurt me."

"He is not here to stop her Rebecca. Did he mention anything about what would happen if you tried speaking to her without him?"

"He said it was against custom and she might kill us both, attempting to Mate to me."

Alaric pulled air in through his teeth, looking at the silk wrapped sword. "I may have to take this away from you, my dear. Astenos, though reckless, knows more about this than we do. If she attempts to Mate to you it would tear both of your souls apart. You would be destroyed. I know you think he was being cruel to you but I think he

405

was frightened you may have continued without heeding his words. You must listen to him, my dear."

Rebecca was still angry at Astenos. She refused to touch him, but Alaric picked him up and placed him on the bed at the foot. He stood with Ronan's sword in his hand.

"I will put this back with the others. Perhaps, she will eventually move on. I am sorry I had a part in your pain this morning, my dear. This should be a time of joy, getting to know your new Mate, and I have tainted that. I will make you first meal you can come down when you are ready."

Stop him Rebecca.

"Alaric wait," she looked at Astenos lying on the bed. Alaric turned to her with an eyebrow raised in question.

I am sorry I did what I did. If it is any consolation, I felt the pain the same as you. I was trying to make you listen to my words, but you seemed set on going around me.

Do not let him take the other Soul. Keep her with us. When we are ready I will help you talk to her. It still will be dangerous but I will help you.

Rebecca was wary; she looked from Astenos to Alaric, waiting at the door. "He says to leave her here. He says he will help me talk to her when we are ready."

Alaric nodded and put the sword at the foot of her bed.

"Be careful dear." He turned and walked from the room.

Rebecca didn't feel like touching Astenos. She got from the bed and walked, limping, wide around the bed. She kept her eyes pinned to him set upon the sheets of the bed as she backed out of the room and closed the door. She walked into the washroom and scrubbed the tear streaks from her face and then hobbled down to the kitchen where Alaric stood preparing first meal.

She sat small on a stool at the wood block counter and watched him work. He gave her a bowl of tea before he continued chopping onions and beating together eggs. She sipped at the tea and listened to her thoughts.

She could feel Astenos in there, in her mind. He kept quiet and hidden, but she knew he was there. What was worse, she could feel pity for him. She understood that he had been frightened Rebecca would kill them both. Firstly, he was concerned for her before himself. She also knew he had not known exactly what he was doing to her at first; he had no experience yet. She wanted to be angry with him; she wanted to never see him again but she also understood that he truly feared what she had spoken of doing, of talking with Ronan's Blade.

"I suppose he may have been trying to guard me against myself," she said to Alaric's back. He had remained very quiet, unusual for him. "I don't know if I can trust him again, though."

I can promise you—

"I don't know if I will feel comfortable handling him again," she said over Astenos's words.

"If someone breaks your leg to stop you from walking blindly over a cliff, will you begrudge him when finally you see the edge and what would have happened if he hadn't acted?" asked Alaric as he poured the eggs into a pan over a flame.

Rebecca, please listen to me. I only meant to scare you a little. To stop you from doing yourself harm.

"You could have told me; you could have said something. You didn't have to hurt me," she muttered.

You seemed unwilling to listen. Your desire to help the other Soul, to find her lost Mate, your grandfather, had blinded you. Your words brought thoughts of our destruction to me from the customs of my world. I acted out of fear. Decisions made in a state of fear are rarely the right ones.

Rebecca listened to the words Astenos spoke; she heard the sadness, the remorse. She couldn't hold onto her anger. He probably had saved her life; she would have plunged forward in spite of Astenos.

She felt a trepid sense of hope from him. He said he could feel what she felt. He knew she was on a tipping point and was not about to sway her against him.

Alaric scraped a portion of eggs and onions onto her plate and laid thick toasted slices of bread beside them. His blue eyes twinkled behind his spectacles, seeming to know she had met some decision.

"What can you do to help me learn to use Astenos?" she asked, covering her reddening face with her tea bowl. A wave of relief swept from the Blade upstairs. Alaric smiled at her.

"There *is* steel in you, my dear," he said, fixing his own plate. "As I said before, I can't show you much. I was never a Bladesman myself, but I do have some volumes around here of stances and forms that should start you down the path."

Forty-five: One Last Task

Rebecca had spent over a week going over the books and diagrams Alaric had pertaining to the Bladesmen's art. She had done this with the lack of Astenos's presence. In spite of the link between them growing stronger all the time, she still felt fear when she touched his hilt. The memory of what he had done seemed to linger.

Alaric said nothing about her behavior, apparently feeling it best to allow her to come around in her own time. Rebecca could tell though that he was beginning to get anxious.

When she finally mustered the courage to try her hand at some of the forms she had studied, Astenos in her hand, she was completely unprepared.

Her fingers tingled in anticipation on the ninth day following Astenos's attack. She could feel his desire to make up for his actions seep from him in her hands. She stood in the meditation garden on a day threatening a storm. Alaric, standing in the open workshop doorway, watched her ready herself. He was finishing a scabbard for Astenos.

Rebecca reviewed, in her head, some of the forms she had seen in one of the novice diagrams. She stepped into the form, legs wide, arms loose, sword parallel to the ground. Instantly, the tingle in her fingers became a shudder up her spine, excitement coursed through her. She transferred her weight to her forward foot, raising the Blade above her head in both hands. An image of the next stage of the form flashed into her brain from Astenos; she moved as if she had been born to the task. She found herself halfway across the garden before she realized she had completed the stroke. Slowly the memory of the intervening forms she had moved through came to her. Some she hadn't even seen in the books Alaric had given her.

She looked up at Alaric, now standing much closer, he pulled a bit of leather cording taut with a cocked smile on his face. He nodded once and moved back into the workshop, leaving her alone with Astenos.

She thrilled at forming the next stance. She listened to the thoughts that came from Astenos; her fear melted as she continued. He seemed to guide her, if she let him, through maneuvers she wouldn't have believed she could do. The Blade spun in her hands faster than she could imagine, at times only a streaking blur. She was amazed that she hadn't managed to cut her own arm off. At this thought Astenos spoke to her; it was the strongest she had heard him, the most adamant.

Never! I will never draw your blood. You must never fear that I could allow myself to harm you.

At this Rebecca thought of his attack.

I would not have done you any lasting hurt. Soreness and bad thoughts are far from actual wounds. And I have apologized for my actions.

Rebecca didn't think of the attack again. The elation she felt working with Astenos drove the thought from her mind. When she had finally reached a point of exhaustion, she went to the workshop to find Alaric. She walked across the gravel path, sweat soaked to the skin, with a satisfying ache in her arms and legs. The storm that had been threatening finally broke as she covered the last few yards to the open door.

Large fat drops pelted the copper roof of the workshop as she moved into its dark interior, the grayish light from outside cast weakly through the windows. She could hear a metallic chatter from deep within the shop. She worked her way back to Alaric. He stood at the tap-writer, feeding a small bit of parchment into one end of the device. She approached and found the completed scabbard lying on the table beside the tapping machine.

She could just read the words Alaric had sent into the device around the clattering fingers of brass and steel: Prepare for our arrival. The child has been readied. The child comes.

Forty-six:
Watchers from the Gloom

They prepared for departure over the next couple of days. Alaric had grown almost obsessive about the devices in his workshop. Rebecca found this odd, being that since she had been with him she hadn't seen him so much as glance at the mass of cluttered machines. Rebecca commented on this as she helped him pull a swath of canvas over a particularly large contraption.

"These are extremely rare objects nowadays," he said in an affronted way. "If I have seemed negligent in my care of them over the past weeks, it does not mean that I shall remain so. I'd like very much to insure they are as reasonably protected as I can make them, if that is quite alright with you."

He has always seemed a bit negligent with us rare objects in my opinion, said Astenos into Rebecca's mind.

Rebecca smiled as she helped Alaric with the other pieces he wanted to cover. She had taken to carrying Astenos and Ronan's Blade around with her wherever she went. She had not yet learned the other Blade's name, and was not eager to broach the subject with Astenos; they had steadily grown closer.

When Alaric was satisfied with the securing of his devices, they set to prepare for their journey southward. Alaric explained that they would have to leave the protection of the marked grounds. Therefore, they would take certain artifacts that could aid in giving their journey relative safety.

Alaric retrieved his rifle from the mantel over the fireplace and set it with the other preparations piled in the reading room. Rebecca finished stuffing one of the bags with food. It seemed a lot to carry now that she saw it all packed and stacked in the room. One of the bags was dedicated to objects Alaric felt they might need, several Incandeos, the lighted globes from around the buildings, a Healer, "You never know when it will come in handy," Alaric said, a set of odd carved cubes that Alaric said were called Screeners, two wooden carvings that resembled lizards he called Salamanders, they felt oddly warm in her hands, and an assortment of other trinkets Alaric refused to leave behind.

"We'll need to disguise you as best we can for Black Bridge; it's a town not far from here. They don't have a Skip Tracer's Bureau there but it's best to be safe," Alaric said when all the straps on the bags and been tightened. "I run a small metal works in town. I told the townsfolk I was off to collect my nephew from Romara to come apprentice with me."

Rebecca cocked her head at this bit of information.

"*Nephew?*" she said, feeling a bit offended. "How am I going to pass for your nephew?"

"Well you haven't – ah, quite – urm. Well, should I say, you have a while to go yet before you – shall I say," his face grew red to match his hair and beard. "Not that you aren't quite a lovely young woman, it's just that." He stammered to a halt, eyeing her up and down. Rebecca knew what he was getting at. She knew she was underdeveloped for her age. Other girls she had known at Valgerhold, even Helen who was younger than her, seemed to have started on their way to a womanly shape. She felt a bit embarrassed but laughed at the desperate look Alaric was giving her, still floundering for words.

"Alright, alright, just stop looking at me like that," she said.

"Good, well then, there is a wardrobe upstairs in the spare room with some clothes that should fit you. We can hide your hair with one of my old hats around here, and that old coat of mine should do the trick for the rest of you," he said.

Rebecca found herself a short time later, standing in the reading room, dressed as Alaric's apprentice wearing a worn old leather cap, her hair tucked neatly into it. She wore the leather traveling coat Alaric had given her and fidgeted with the wool trousers she wore.

"I liked the other clothes better," she grumbled, "at least they didn't itch so much."

"Well, you look the part this way," said Alaric and handed her a hard leather case. "Here you can keep the Blades dry in this, and out of sight."

She pulled the top from the leather tube and slid Ronan's Blade inside, still wrapped in the silk to keep her hands from touching it. She knew it would feel better to carry Astenos but she placed him inside next to the other Blade and put the top back on the tube. She slung the leather case over her shoulder and retrieved her satchel, after checking that all her belongings were still inside. Alaric pulled on several of the bags they had packed, hefted his strange rifle and secured its strap on his shoulder.

"Well, looks like this is it," he said. "Ready, dear?"

Rebecca nodded, feeling her stomach lurch. They closed the door behind them and Rebecca took one last look around. The Incandeos on the iron stands still glowed with their shadow banishing light. A light rain fell from the slate-colored sky. Their breath was visible in the chill that had settled in that morning, adding to the feel of foreboding Rebecca had since she started preparing to leave.

"How long do you think it will take us to travel to Black Bridge?" she asked, feeling apprehensive.

Alaric nudged her forward, placing a reassuring hand on her shoulder. "I hope to be there before dark tomorrow but we shall see."

They marched into the thickly wooded forest that surrounded the clearing Rebecca had come to enjoy. This was the closest she had to a proper home in the last year and she was sorely missing it already.

After a while walking in the misty rain, Rebecca was glad for the coat and hat she wore. Her nose had begun to redden in the damp and she had a slight chill in her toes. Alaric trudged along merrily, humming in his deep voice. He had pulled on a travel cloak and a wide brimmed hat to keep the rain from him. Rebecca followed along under the weight of the bags, examining the area.

She saw strange blocks of stone placed here and there through the forest as she walked. When she asked about them, Alaric said they were part of the defenses of the grounds.

Finally, the forest began to open up a bit and she spied a series of metallic cubes set into the ground, stretching away to either side of the path they traveled. She recognized them for Screeners and turned to see the effect they produced. She was disappointed at seeing the trees they had come through.

"Come along a bit further," Alaric said, seeming to know what she was looking for. "You're going to have to look at it from the corner of your eyes or else you won't see it."

She moved out from the woods to where Alaric stood. She turned her head, slowly looking for something to change. The forest faded from view and was replaced with a most convincing vista of a sheer rock cliff, the ocean breaking against the jagged black rocks below. She thought she could smell the salt even and hear the roar of the pounding surf. The effect was quite disorienting with forest plainly in view before her and ocean cliff in her periphery.

"A little unsettling isn't it?" Alaric said, wiping the mist from his lenses with his thumbs. "If you couldn't see the links, you'd be completely convinced that what you saw was real. Come now, we should move along as far as we can today."

She pulled herself from the Screeners and followed Alaric to a dirt path leading south a ways from the forest. She had the urge to run when she realized she was no longer protected from those who had been chasing her, but Alaric set the pace.

The midday light was a diffused gray when they stopped to eat. The persistent misting rain had settled in to stay for the time, the result being their backsides were dampened as they ate mid meal, sitting upon a downed tree. Rebecca pulled her coat snug around her as she finished eating a heel of bread. She had an eerie feel in the back of her mind. She figured it was just her imagination but she could almost feel eyes on her. An itch began at the back of her mind, it came from Astenos. She could feel his eagerness to be of use, to protect her. She pushed the feeling down.

"Alaric," she asked, glancing to the forest paying close attention to the shadows, "is there anything in these woods that could, well…"

"Cause us trouble? I would assume so. But we should be more concerned about running into any of the Wilderlands patrols. They travel the trails here and there between Romara and the border towns, hunting for runaways and smugglers of contraband items. The New Dominion pays them for prisoners and bodies alike so they don't always investigate too deeply before they resort to drastic measures." He crammed a strip of dried meat into his mouth and wiped his hands. "Shall we get going then," he said, his voice muffled by the food filling it.

They walked for hours more after their meal. Rebecca's feet felt like they were three times larger than they should be. Her shoulders burned with the weight of the bags and she was sick of being wet. The sun had edged into the trees and in the growing gloom of night, Rebecca's feel of being watched grew stronger. She felt if she turned quick enough, she would see a silhouette on the trail behind them, waiting. Testing this thought, she spun around and saw an empty gravel trail leading off into the trees around a bend. The itch returned with new vigor; she could feel her hand's desire for Astenos's hilt. Alaric, seeming to sense her nerves, rummaged in his bag of objects and pulled out a sack with a spherical weight at its bottom.

"Here," Alaric said, handing the sack over to her. She pulled open the top and the Incandeo within rolled into her hand. She looked up for instruction, for it was not emitting any light at the moment. Its glass like surface was a hazy dull white color, clouded shapes moved within. "Give it a quick shake; that'll get it going."

Rebecca snapped her wrist and the dull clouds erupted in the whitish glow she had seen before. The shadows around her seemed to edge away, the blackness of the deep forest lessened. Feeling more confident, she resumed following Alaric toward Black Bridge, carrying the Incandeo huddled to her chest.

The watchers in the trees Rebecca had felt seemed, if anything, to be more interested in the two travelers though. Alaric began checking the mechanisms on his rifle as they walked now as though he too could feel the eyes on him. This did little to reassure her. Rebecca, seeing Alaric's unease, moved to pull Astenos from the leather case on her back.

"Do not move for that Blade, my dear," Alaric said from the side of his mouth, continuing to walk as though all was well. "If they know we know they are there, it might get a little tetchy."

"Who are *they*, Alaric?" Rebecca hissed back in a worried whisper.

"I am not certain but I think it best to let them reveal themselves when they—"

"Halt!" the voice came from behind them. They had heard no one approach. They did as they were commanded. Rebecca strained her eyes, looking around her, but she dare not turn to see who spoke. Astenos's thoughts buzzed in her head. She thought if only she could reach fast enough...

"We have been watching you for some time now. You carry certain items that interest us greatly," said the voice. Rebecca could tell the man who spoke was tall; it sounded as though the words came from feet above her head. She felt a rough hand snake around to grab the Incandeo from her. "Very interesting," said the voice above her. "Do you know what dangers this device could cause you, walking in these lands now? Though, I think, being what you are, you might not worry too much about such troubles."

"Stop trying to intimidate them Tagus," said a second voice from the trees, a woman's voice if Rebecca was not mistaken, but strange sounding. "Garin, Fayit, step into the light. Tagus let them relax and give them back their device."

"Yes Maien," said the voice above Rebecca.

She felt the Incandeo pushed into her hand. She took it and slowly turned to see who was behind her. She stepped back at once upon seeing him and ran into something massive behind her. She looked up to see a huge face staring down at her of the strangest creature she had ever seen.

"Tagus, you brute, you startled them," said the creature whose face she looked up to. It spoke with a womanly voice but different from the one she had heard before. Rebecca did her best not to grab for Astenos, but she felt like she had just lost control of her senses.

Standing before her were four very large, very strange, people. They carried bows and quivers, bristling with large arrows, hung at their sides. They wore mottled forest-colored clothing that blended smoothly with their surroundings. But the oddest thing about them was their size and shape. The shortest among them had to be almost seven feet tall. The man, who she assumed to be Tagus, was near on eight feet with a mane of black hair that looked more like fur than not.

In fact, they all had a distinctly animalistic quality to them, not quite bear or lion, but something of a cross between, with a touch of human thrown in for good measure. They appeared to be two men and two women, the men's manes grew into coarse beards on their cheeks and chins. Their eyes were what truly gave them their wildest look; she had seen eyes like this in her wolf friends, unblinking, measuring. They seemed to see through her.

Rebecca looked to Alaric for guidance but was disappointed to see him staring agog at their visitors.

"Close your mouth man, you look like a trout," said the second beastly man. He reached in an enormous paw-like hand and closed Alaric's mouth, with a click. This seemed to break Alaric's trance, for he began to bustle to remove his bags and with a broad grin, stuck out his hand to the man before him. The huge man cocked a sandy-colored eyebrow at Tagus and took Alaric's outstretched hand.

"Tremen! Great ghosts! Rebecca would you look...ha! My goodness but you are big aren't you?" Alaric seemed almost as surprised as Rebecca. She stood struck by the complete absurdity of what was happening.

She felt a mammoth hand on her shoulder. "We wish to speak with you, young one," said a rumble of a whisper in her ear. She looked sideways to find the huge woman, whom she had backed into, craning down to Rebecca's ear. Rebecca nodded her agreement, looking for Alaric to follow, but the two male Tremen were already into an in depth discussion with him about his rifle.

"You see it works with the Kilaray," Alaric said, holding out the strange weapon to the giant forms standing around and above him.

"Tagus and Garin will occupy your friend. Do not be frightened, we will not harm you. I am Fayit and this," the enormous woman said, gesturing to the impressive regal woman striding toward them, "is Maien. She is our Pride Mistress." Rebecca looked confused. "You would say our Commander, I think."

"Greetings, young one, what are you called by?" asked Maien.

"Rebecca," she said in whisper.

"And your Pride name, your people go by both I know," Maien asked.

"Um...Dulac, my name is Rebecca Dulac."

"Peace upon you Rebecca of Dulac," said Maien. She bowed her ginger-colored head and touched her huge paw of a hand to her chest. She stared at Rebecca with her unsettling sky blue eyes and after a moment spoke again. "We Tremen do not usually associate with your kind. Our paths parted long ago on uncertain terms. However, we have noticed you as we traveled back toward the sea. The men

420

thought you and your friend would cause us trouble. Fayit and I see, though, that you will cause us more than that."

Rebecca felt uneasy, judging by the huge paw-like hands and the arms they attached to, these people could end Rebecca and Alaric in a heartbeat. She looked over to Alaric who seemed to have forgotten that he was talking to two over large beast-like men; he was showing them more of his beloved devices.

"I don't mean you trouble," she said, trying to keep fear from her voice.

"You will though, whatever you do. You bring change on your back and with change come difficulties. Man kinds have always caused us much difficulty." Fayit nodded in agreement. "But we have seen what you bring. We have waited and have planned. All who have seen what the God Lights foretell know your pattern, young Rebecca."

"God Lights," Rebecca asked, "what pattern?"

"The Kilaray as you say, and your links to the world from which they come," said Fayit with a look of great joy in her face. "We see the God Lights and the patterns they form in the sky above. We see you in them or your pattern and what will come if you can find your way."

"We should not aid you, for we have been forbid interference since the last of your people treated with us. He persuaded some of our kind to divulge certain information which they should not have. Our people asked him to leave and made him vow never to speak of what he had learned."

"My grandfather, Martan Dulac, he visited your people. It's here in his journal." Rebecca lifted the flap on her satchel and pulled out the worn book. She flipped through the pages and found the place that mentioned Tremen. She held up the book for Maien to examine.

"He seems to have met Pictsies as well, your grandfather," said Maien, running her finger down the valley between the pages. "This looks to be sealed with one of their tricks. At least he protected his oath breaking well."

"He did not break his word," Rebecca said, surprised at the harshness of her own voice. "He didn't speak of it to anyone; he just…he just wrote it down."

Maien smiled, a series of sharp looking teeth visible behind her lion-like lips. Fayit snorted, "She has a point there, Maien, and a fierce streak I see."

Maien handed Rebecca back the journal and knelt down to look into her eyes. Rebecca still had to look up to her face. "I don't blame him for taking the knowledge, young Rebecca. You will need it. I doubt if you would receive this information from our people now even though your pattern would be clear to them. We have not fared well under this New Dominion that has taken hold of your lands. Its men intrude on our lands and steal what is ours. We are hunted when in your lands and killed or enslaved when caught. Many of our people would have us take up arms against the man kinds but those like us know you, Rebecca, can end our need for isolation."

"Rebecca, Rebecca, come you have to see this," Alaric called. Rebecca looked over at the three men. Tagus was shaking his head as Garin knelt and laughed, looking at the ground. Rebecca looked back at Maien, she smiled and stood, the two women and Rebecca walked over to see what had Alaric so excited.

"Well Garin, you great braggart, get on with it," said Tagus, looking amused. "We wouldn't want to keep our man kind companions in suspense."

Garin put his huge hands out before him and concentrated on the trail as if searching for something Rebecca could not see. His hands trembled for a moment and, before Rebecca's eyes, ghostly red gold shapes formed from the ground. They looked like her and, beside her, Alaric, a faintly less substantial image; on her back two shapes showed clearly, the Soul Blades. The images faded back along the trail, hundreds of images stretching back, diminishing the farther they went.

"This is how we tracked you. We can see these from those who touch the God Lights," said Garin. "This is how we knew we could approach you."

"You are hunted almost as much as we are," said Tagus grimly.

The images faded into the night and, as they did, Tagus froze rigid. His wide nose sniffed the air. Rebecca was reminded of the wolves going on alert. Astenos's thoughts hammered at her mind.

Now Rebecca, I am needed.

"Up! Garin, bows ready, Maien, Fayit take cover, hide the man kinds," growled Tagus. He pulled a large arrow from his quiver; Garin followed suit. They moved with animal-like grace into the forest around them. Then Rebecca caught the sound, hoof beats. Riders approached.

Maien and Fayit readied their bows but followed Tagus' command. Rebecca could tell that the men seemed to have taken charge with danger near. The two women herded Alaric and her into the dense forest.

"Alaric, how do I turn this thing down?" whispered Rebecca as she rolled the Incandeo around in her hands.

"Circle your hand above it," he said as he pulled his rifle to his shoulder, readying it.

Rebecca did as he said and slipped it back into the sack, stowing it in her satchel. She reached to pull the leather case around for Astenos, but Fayit put her huge hand on Rebecca's shoulder stopping her.

"Leave the Souls where they are, young Rebecca," she said in a growling whisper. "The men can handle whatever comes this way."

Rebecca waited, hiding behind a thick oak. She could hear the horse hooves pounding closer, they sounded like they were at a gallop. Suddenly the horses began to scream. She could hear men's shouts.

"Calm the damned horses."

"They caught scent of something."

"Quiet! What's that noise?"

A grumbling noise came from the sides of the trail ahead, like brick dragged over stone. The horses' screams echoed through the forest with renewed vigor. The men began to shout, panic lacing each unintelligible scream. Gun shots sounded through the depths of the trees. Then silence.

Rebecca looked over at Maien and Fayit. They had not slacked the tension on their bowstrings. They peered into the darkness with predatory awareness. Alaric, his rifle to his cheek, stared into the forest's gloom with as much interest.

Out of the blackness shapes loped. Tagus supported Garin who clutched his side. Maien and Fayit ran to them, sliding their bows away with practiced motions.

"What happened?" asked Fayit, looking at the dark stain spreading from Garin's side.

"There were twelve of them," said Tagus. "Now there are none. The last managed to get off a clean shot." Tagus set Garin down and Fayit began tending him.

"I tripped over one of the men," Garin said to Fayit with a laugh; blood began to slick his lips. "My own fault, don't tell Baro. If our brother finds out I got pecked by one of these man kinds, Fayit, he'll never let me…" Garin groaned as Fayit pulled up his tunic to see the wound. Alaric went to help her.

Tagus pulled Maien aside but Rebecca could still hear what he said.

"We can't move him Maien. There are more approaching, I checked. They bring one of the Masked with them." The words sent shivers up Rebecca's spine. Maien looked over at Rebecca with a concerned eye. "Maien we won't stand much chance one man down, a dozen or two more man kinds, and one of the Masked approaching."

"Hold him down, for Father's sake," Alaric roared. "He's thrashing like a mad man." Alaric held down Garin who was fought like a trapped animal; Fayit gripped his shoulders, trying to hold him still. Rebecca saw the watch-like Healer drop to the ground and knew what Alaric was trying to do.

She ran to help, dropping all her bags as she went to her knees. She grabbed the Healer and held it to Garin's side. Nothing happened.

"That won't help him," Tagus said, staring down at her. He had come to help restrain Garin. "When the death grip takes hold we fight to our end; it is our way. Your contraptions will not save him."

Rebecca looked to Fayit; her face was set in grim resolve. Maien walked to stand guard. Tagus knelt beside Garin and pulled a long savage looking knife from his belt. Rebecca understood at once what he meant to do. She had a sickening feeling; she had been in this place before, and she had been unable to stop what happened then.

"No!" she shouted, "You can't just kill him. He's still alive, he's got a chance."

Tagus shook his head and readied his knife above Garin's heart. "Go with peace, my friend," he said, raising the knife above his head.

Stop him! Astenos shouted into Rebecca's mind.

Rebecca acted at once; she leapt over Garin's chest, blocking Tagus' knife. A frightening roar filled the air and shook Rebecca's chest. She turned to look at Tagus, his face wrinkled with rage, baring sharp teeth. Garin whined, his feet scrabbling at the dirt. Alaric had bleached white, Fayit looked confused and angry, but Maien spoke.

"We must do this Rebecca; it is our way to ease a friend's passing if he has been mortally wounded."

"But he's not; he's just hurt bad, I can...I can save him." She was startled by her own words. "I...I think I can at least." Maien studied her for a moment; Tagus looked to her for orders.

"Tagus put away your blade, go scout for the coming men. Fayit and I will assist young Rebecca." Maien strode and knelt with graceful fluidity at Garin's side. Tagus disappeared into the trees, looking distraught. Rebecca felt her nerves now. She had started this; now, it was up to her to do something.

Garin's breath heaved in a labored way, each time his chest rising less and less. Rebecca calmed her mind. She slipped into the Easing. Astenos was at her side at once, giving her comfort. She slipped into the Stillness and found the links blooming from Garin binding him to the rest of the world. They seemed strange, alien, but she could see how they flowed all the same. Darkness leaked from his side; the links near the wound faded and were losing their vibrant colors.

You see the problem Rebecca, said Astenos, *now you can fix it.*

Rebecca acted slowly at first. She moved her hand out over the wound. She could feel pain, fear, death, seeping in near the darkening links. She could feel something within Garin's side, something metal, a bullet. She grabbed the links trailing from the bullet and eased them out of him. The bullet dangled from the links like a rock tied to a string. She set it aside and felt along the links that had been affected by the bullet. She sent flows of Kilaray down each damaged hair thin thread.

She fell over backwards panting as the Quickening brought her back to speed. Garin's roars of pain broke the night, Alaric, Fayit, and Maien toppled over as he sat bolt upright. He clutched his paw to his side as the skin began to knit back together with the flows of the damaged links restored. His howls of pain became silent and he stared at Rebecca with astonishment.

Tagus burst from the trees looking for a fight. He took a step and stopped at the sight of Garin sitting up, his side covered in blood but healed. He strode to Garin and knelt at his side. They exchanged a look and Tagus pulled Rebecca to himself. He bowed his head to hers; a deep rumbling purr came from his chest as he rubbed his mane of black hair against her head. Her leather cap tumbled to the ground. Garin did likewise when Tagus had released her. Tagus stood and pulled Maien to her feet. Fayit began the ritual with Rebecca as Tagus reported to Maien.

"They are minutes from here, Maien; we must get her out of here," Tagus said, nodding his large head at Rebecca. Maien nodded her agreement and turned to Rebecca and Alaric.

"You have done us a great honor and proved that we can trust at least some of your kind. We need to get you to safety. One of the Masked approaches. We can fight it but it may do us great harm. We would suggest you run with us. We can move faster than the men on horses through these trees even burdened with you, but the Masked one will catch us up."

427

"I believe I can give us a third option, Pride Mistress," said Alaric. Rebecca turned to him. He had a gleam in his eye. "I just ask you to get my dear friend to Black Bridge safely." Rebecca did not like the sound of this one bit.

"Alaric, you are coming with me. I need your help," she said. "I don't know where to go from Black Bridge and I won't know what to do."

"I have told you before Rebecca, I am too old and too fat to be of much help. Besides, I have every intention of rejoining you," he said, pulling off his bag full of devices. He fished out a metal and leather cuff and handed it to her. "This will let me know where to find you. You can't stop though Rebecca, not for me anyway. Keep moving on. South is the way you need to go. Get to Nor Harbor; find Bertran Gabriel, you must get to the Gates."

The Tremen were making their preparations seeming to know that Alaric's plan would involve a fight. Garin, Tagus, and Fayit stood in a circle, throwing hand gestures into the middle. Tagus threw a fist, looking triumphant, and the others looked crestfallen. Rebecca ignored them and tried again to get Alaric to come with her.

"Alaric," she felt her eyes burning, "I need you. You're my only friend now. If I lose you, I'm going to be alone again. I can't do this alone."

"You're not alone, my dear," he said, "Astenos is with you, and I will catch you up when I've dealt with this coming lot." Rebecca could tell he lied but she could see he would not be turned either. Tagus walked up to them.

"Mecharical, I will stay with you. I have won the toss. What is your plan?"

Alaric laid out his plan and after giving Rebecca the devices he felt she might need and keeping what he would need, they made to part. Maien, Fayit and Garin exchanged farewells with Tagus with rumbling purrs and head nuzzling. They did likewise with Alaric, leaving his spectacles askew on his nose but smiling. Rebecca hugged him and pecked him on the cheek.

"I expect you to come for me old man," she said, laughing through her tears. "If I have to track you down, you won't like me when I find you."

"I expect I would like you no matter how you find me," he said, pulling her close one more time. "Good luck, my dear."

"You too Alaric von Magus of the Garmonian Order of Mecharicals," she said. He swept in impressive bow over his stomach and began to hum in his deep voice as he set up the Screeners and shook one of the Incandeos into life.

Tagus bid her farewell and she set off with the three other Tremen. She could here Alaric's voice issuing from the trees, the glow of the Incandeo casting a white haze around their trunks.

Garin picked up Rebecca and sat her on his shoulders. Fayit and Maien took up the bags she had left. Rebecca gripped tight to the leather case containing the Soul Blades and clapped the leather cap back onto her head. The Tremen began to stalk through the forest faster than Rebecca had ever moved. The trees blurred to either side as the muscles in Garin's back writhed with his motions. Rebecca kept low, gripping hold of Garin's great bushy mane and leaning over him. She looked back now and then to see if she could spot the white glow of the Incandeo, and Alaric's trap.

A burst of fire behind her lit the trees and a spine-melting scream tore through the forest. A war roar rose up behind them and Rebecca felt the urge to make the Tremen go back. Blue-white flashes brightened the underside of the trees' canopies and men began to scream. Rebecca prayed Alaric's were not among them. The battle cries and explosions died away as the Tremen moved on at unbelievable speed.

It felt like hours before the Tremen stopped running and Rebecca was lifted off Garin's shoulders. Her back was sore from hunching down over Garin's huge head to avoid the low hanging branches. She focused on the pain in her muscles to avoid the pain she felt in her heart.

Alaric was back there, somewhere, and she had just left him. How many more people would be lost shielding her? How many more people would she leave behind while she made for safety? Surely she wasn't so important that anyone else should be sacrificed in her place. If she had just stayed back there, Alaric and Tagus would be where she was now. Two lives were certainly more valuable than hers.

Enough of such thoughts, Rebecca, Astenos's voice shook her from her brooding. She hadn't noticed her mind had strayed from her aches and pains. *Alaric did what he needed so that you can do what you need to do. Sacrifice is honorable but only when it is necessary, when there is some gain. Lives are not so petty that they should be squandered.*

She agreed of course, but she still had a hollow feeling in her stomach. Perhaps it would be best for her to travel on alone until she did what had to be done, or she was killed. She didn't know how far she could get but at least she could spare anyone else the danger she faced.

She finished stretching her back and joined the Tremen who were talking together as she approached.

"...should send one of us back. One of us could determine their fates," Garin said.

"Tagus stayed so that we could escape; what would we gain in possibly losing one more?" Fayit said back, her brows furrowed in concern. "Garin you've already been spared death once. Why tempt the Gods more with foolish notions of bravery."

"Foolish notions, Fayit what if Tagus has been captured? Would you see him in shackles; would you allow him to suffer that? I will go back. It will take me less time alone..."

"Enough!" Maien said with finality. "Garin you will stay with us. We promised the Mecharical we would see young Rebecca to Black Bridge and that is what we will do. Whatever comes of those we left behind is in the hands of others."

Garin turned his gaze on Rebecca, his mouth worked as though chewing on words he held back. Finally, he turned and stalked away to watch the way they had come. Fayit laid a huge hand on Rebecca's shoulder and turned to disappear into the surrounding trees. Maien squatted on her heels to look at Rebecca on more of an equal height; she was still heads taller than Rebecca.

"They were cub mates, Garin and Tagus," Maien said. "Tagus has always watched Garin's back. Don't worry yourself, Garin owes you his life and that will see that he follows your friend's promise."

"I wasn't worried," Rebecca said. "I...I think I should go back. You don't need to come I will be alright alone. If they are hurt I can help; I showed you I can."

"No. We all travel forward. If our friends succeeded in stopping those who came then they will join us as we travel. If they fell then your pursuers are still behind us. Either way it will be best to go forward," she said. "If our friends fell so that we could escape, we would dishonor them in returning to be captured or killed. Now you should rest while you can; we stay only as long as we need to regain our wind. Then we move on." She stood and disappeared silently into the dark trees, leaving Rebecca alone.

She was torn; she understood what Maien said but she still felt responsible. She wondered if she could slip away without the Tremen noticing. She didn't think it probable from what she had seen of their tracking.

Rebecca walked to where the bags the Tremen had carried were set and opened her satchel, pulling out the Incandeo. She snapped her wrist and white light lit the space around her. Trees loomed all around. It was amazing the Tremen could move so quickly through such dense forest.

She looked into the bag containing the devices Alaric had given her. She placed the metal and leather cuff Alaric had given her around her left wrist and it tightened itself to fit. These odd happenings grew less surprising to her now. She pulled out the wood carving of the lizard, the Salamander. She could feel warmth in her hands as she held the carving. She wondered if she would be able to figure out what half the objects were meant for without Alaric.

Clutching the carving to her chest she pulled her coat tight around her and used one of the softer bags to rest her head. She closed her eyes and slipped off to sleep, hoping to find better places in her dreams.

She could feel Astenos near, just out of sight behind her. The world was gray, as though a dense fog filled every crevice. Every direction she looked, the clouded fog persisted.

"What is this place?" she asked Astenos.

It is nowhere. It is everywhere.

"What do you mean?"

It is the place where what will come can be found. The possible futures lay all around us, each with equal possibility of happening, and each with equal possibility of never coming to be. They all exist at once here and so here is nowhere, and here is everywhere at once.

Rebecca looked around at the stark grayness. It felt so lifeless; she would try to wake...

Something sparked in the corner of her vision. She looked and it was gone.

"Did you see that?"

Yes.

"What was it?"

Your decision, it vanished when you chose to stay.

"You mean when I tried to wake up, that caused the flicker."

Yes.

Rebecca looked into the gloom, thinking. She would go back when she woke and find Alaric...

A clouded form billowed out of the depths of the fog. It moved toward her, growing clearer as it came.

She looked at herself as though from above. She lay amongst the trees where she slept now; her eyes opened and she gathered her bags. She set off into the trees. A flash of light wiped the image from her eyes. Now, she stood in the path where they had left Alaric and Tagus. She looked down on the scene again as if she were in the braches above.

The image of her looked around the trail; there were signs of fighting. She knelt down to pick up a broken rifle. Something formed behind her. She could tell the image of her didn't see what was happening. The black wisps of the apparition became a solid shape, a man shape. Her image self turned but it was too late, the Blind Man had her. It's hand swept into her chest. The white flash cleared the scene from her eyes.

The billowing receded and became uniform again. Her stomach felt frozen. She knew now what she had just seen. If she were to go back, she would be killed. She had just had a vision of her future.

Reached Visions are not so clear always. Only when the outcome is so final and so near are they as solid.

"I can't go back."

You can, it is your choice but you know what you would face.

"Then I go to Black Bridge."

The formless mass of gray came forward. The images were clouded and overlaid atop one another. The flashing white light was like a savage storm, clearing her vision before she could see what came. She saw faces, but they were burned away from sight before she could remember them. Places flickered through her mind, pausing here and there only long enough for her to know she was somewhere different from the last scene. Ahead of the storm of visions, like a lighthouse in a maelstrom, a spike of white stood, looming ever nearer. It called to her, beckoning. The flashes receded with the visions and one thing was clear, as the billowing gray came again, this choice held a much longer future than did the previous.

Feeling a deep sense of sorrow for Alaric and Tagus she slipped into deeper sleep. Astenos was there to watch her dreams. She could feel his back to her thoughts watching outward, guarding her mind.

The sun was still hours away when she was shaken awake. The Incandeo still cast its light around her and she was warmed through from the Salamander still in her fist. Garin's huge face filled her vision.

"It is time to move on," he said. He looked deeply distraught. She could tell he thought his friend dead.

"I am sorry," she said to him as she sat.

"You have nothing for which to be sorry. I was wrong about returning. Fayit was right in calling me foolish. I should accept what Tagus and the Mecharical did for us," he looked at the ground, unable to make eye contact.

Rebecca got to her feet and hugged him; she had to stretch to reach his neck even with him on knee before her. She felt his huge paw on her back and felt his rumbling purr from his chest. When she released him, he had a sad smile on his face.

Rebecca gathered the bags together and Maien and Fayit took them up. Garin lifted her onto his shoulders once more and they set off toward Black Bridge. They moved less quickly than before but the trees still blurred to the sides as they ran. The rain from the previous day had lifted but the moisture had produced a low lying fog that threatened to stagger the Tremen.

Dawn came and cast shafts of warm light through the trees overhead. Soon, the day's warmth burnt the fog away, except in deep hollows. The Tremen were able to move faster. An hour before midday, the Tremen stopped. They breathed heavily and their manes were laden with sweat.

"We near our destination," Maien told her. "We cannot venture into man kind towns in daylight; this New Dominion offers coin for our capture or bodies. You will have to journey the rest of the way alone."

Garin set Rebecca on the ground. She could see that they were on a steep hill leading down into a port. She could see the glimmer of the sea through the trees. She looked down into the town near the sea and could see a river running out into the port. A large bridge like a black web of steel and stone stretched out over the river from a wide main road. She could see wagons moving in and out from the port town. Ships were docked, their sails furled, and booms moved cargo to and from the piers. She looked to the Tremen.

"Where will you go?" she asked them.

"We travel on; we have an appointment further south. Intriguing news has met our ears and we go to investigate. If we could be assured of safe passage through the town, we would come with you," Fayit said. "Before the New Dominion, we would travel sometimes on your kind's ships, trading our skills for passage. Most man kind seafarers would trade us into the nearest government for our bounty now."

"I understand," Rebecca said. "I will go on alone then." She turned to Garin. "Thank you for carrying me." He bowed his head and put his hand over his heart. She gathered her bags from Maien and Fayit. "I don't know exactly what to say. You have kept your promise and I feel I owe you more than I can give."

"You will see us again, we think," Maien said. "Our fates are tied to yours now. Go with peace young Rebecca."

"Go with peace," she said to the three. She shouldered her bags and walked toward the main road. She stopped after a few steps and turned back; the Tremen had vanished into the trees. She was alone again.

Forty-eight:
Across the Black Bridge

The sun was high overhead by the time she reached the road leading into Black Bridge. The cobbles of the road were rutted from the wagons that had traveled along the road for decades. The bridge that gave the town its name loomed ahead of her. The moorings were made from dark cut stone. From either side of the bridge, two thick, black painted main cables arched up to the tower; it stood like a massive, dark stone trunk in the middle of the wide river. Support cables held the roadway above the river. The tallest of the ships' masts, traveling the river to the port, passed with tens of feet to spare.

There was a walkway on either side of the main road leading out over the bridge. A toll house stood collecting fares from the wagons entering and leaving the town. She could see a sign atop the house naming the town and another smaller underneath prohibiting firearms without special decree from the constabulary. A saying occurred to her as she read the small sign – *where arms are outlawed, the outlaws go armed.* Rebecca made her way to the walkway, pulling her cap down low to hide her face. She made note to keep her eyes open; she remembered the bounty sheet with her image on it.

The wind from the river below whipped at her as she walked across the bridge. She hoped she didn't stand out in the crowds of people traveling the walkways. The majority of the traffic was the wagons and carts creaking along the wood slats of the roadway. Horses' hooves clattered along like a continuous roll of thunder and the sounds of shouted directions from the drivers added to the general cacophony.

The far side of the bridge let out into an array of stone-paved streets. A brick building stood at the bridge landing; men in flattop, black-billed hats with the dark green wool coats of the constables milled about out front. Some were mounted on horseback others were afoot; they carried batons and pistols at their waists. Rebecca steered wide of them. She didn't know if she could trust officials of the town but she wasn't eager to try her luck.

Black Bridge lay on the main route from Romara, a hub for rail and sea travelers. There were other towns scattered along the railways but they were little more than train depots. This town seemed to have prospered from its location. She could see the signs of money flowing through the streets, women in fine cut dresses and men with their girths stretching the fabric of their well-tailored coats.

Once into the streets of the town Rebecca felt suddenly adrift. She had no idea of where to go next. She moved down one of the main roads toward the port. She read the signs outside of the shops as she passed along, hoping to catch sight of Alaric's metal works, the only landmark she could bring to mind. The buildings were crammed together with barely a narrow alleyway between; most were made from brick or stone but here and there wood slat storefronts faced out into the street.

The town seemed loud in her ears in contrast to the forest she had been used to for the past weeks. She thought she had forgotten the sounds of a town. Men boasted of their wares in shops, people haggled over prices, shouted arguments, all seemed to meld with the sound of the wagons in a way that made Rebecca nervous. Her stomach grumbled and she decided to take shelter in the nearest tavern.

She pushed the door open of the first pub she came to and stepped into its main room. The room was filled with several long tables with benches. A tall stand mirror stood at the door, an empty stool sat across from it. A brick hearth warmed the room. A few men sat together at one of the tables. They glanced over their shoulders as she came through the door, and then slowly turned back to their conversations. She approached the barkeeper standing behind the long counter opposite the fire. The barkeeper was a squat balding man with several days' growth on his chin. He eyed Rebecca as she approached.

"Little young to be out loose, aren't ya, son?" he said as he polished a pewter mug. "Perhaps you're running off then, are you?"

"I am looking for a meal, and some directions," she said. "I wonder if you would know where I can find a metal works owned by a man named Alaric von Magus?"

"Aye, it's down by the piers a ways, but ya can forget going there he left weeks ago for Romara to fetch his nephew," said the barkeeper. "I haven't heard he's back yet. Let me see what I can do for the meal then." He pushed his way through a swing door that wafted the smell of food from the kitchen as it swung back. After a few minutes he returned with a bowl of fish and potato stew and a loaf of bread. "Don't suppose you can be showing me some coin before I give you this then?"

Rebecca reached into her satchel and found a coin purse she had taken so long ago back at Landfall Station in Arnora. She pulled open the bag and pulled out a coin with a gold strip running through it, and the traders mark, a crude hand with a strange glyph on the palm, on its face. She placed it on the counter. The barkeeper slid it off and bit the edge.

"I won't be asking where you came by gold son, but a little advice; don't go flashing that purse too much. You'll likely find yourself stabbed in some alley." He dropped the coin into his till and fished out some copper and silver striped coins and slapped them on the bar top. "I say you look a might young for the stronger spirits, but this then..." he turned to one of the large wooden kegs behind the bar and filled a mug from one. "Now, what are you doing in Black Bridge son?"

Rebecca began eating and sipped at the mug – strong cider – the barkeeper had set on the bar. "I was heading toward Nor Harbor," she said. "Alaric von Magus was a friend of my father's. I meant to see him before continuing on." She thought the story sounded plausible. She just hoped this chatty man didn't start digging too deeply.

"And what are you heading to Nor Harbor for, then? Rough place, trying your hand at a seafarer's life?" By the look he gave her, he thought this idea a ridiculous one. "Or are you on the run after all," he said with a laugh. One of the men turned to look at Rebecca and the barkeeper at this. "They say that town swallows up those that don't want to be found. Ah well, if you're set on getting to Nor Harbor you can try and buy passage on one of the cargo ships. There's usually one or two heading that way. Just make sure you agree the passage before you go showing them sea captains any coin, son."

Rebecca finished eating the meal and left the mug half full; she could feel warmth in her cheeks that had nothing to do with the fire. One of the men at the table turned and shouted over his shoulder to the barkeeper.

"Oy, more wine over here you lazy sod."

The barkeeper's eyes looked murderous. "Filthy skip tracing scum," he mumbled under his breath. He turned to Rebecca. "They've been flooding the town for the last few days. Ships bring them in along with the rats. They're tracking some big payout coming out of Romara. They all think they're tougher than steel but most of them are like this lot, a drunken pack of weasels." He moved off behind the counter, filled a pewter pitcher, and took it over to the men sitting at the table near the fire.

Skip tracers. Rebecca felt the urge to run from the pub but that might get their attention. Instead she kept her back to them and waited for the barkeeper to return.

"Best keep away from anyone that looks like trouble, son. Most of this lot hasn't been in the game long, eager to try their hands at collaring a big catch their first go. Can't say as I blame them; someone's got to make some coin." He pulled out his watch and checked the time. "Say son, if you're interested in catching a ship out, you might want to get going before the tides go out."

She thanked the barkeeper and, with one last glance at the group of men drinking themselves into oblivion, she walked out into the street. She had a new feeling that eyes were on her back, paranoia. Every man she passed was trying to see under her cap, or reaching for a concealed pistol when he put his hand into a pocket. The green-backed constables moving among the crowd, looking here and there for trouble, did they spend more time examining her? She headed for the piers, moving quickly.

The streets sloped downward as she approached the port. She could smell fish and the sea on the breeze. The blue green waters shimmered in the afternoon sun. She walked, keeping her eyes down. She spotted Alaric's metal works shop; it was a small brick building with iron grilled windows. She fingered the leather and metal cuff at her wrist. She could see the sign announcing that he was away.

The piers bustled with activity. People were busy loading and unloading carts and wagons. Cranes lifted huge nets with crates or fish out of the holds of ships. Barges with thick fresh cut timber piled high waited to tie up further out in the port. Men with arms as wide as Rebecca's waist hefted sacks of grain. Ships were tied to the stone piers; their masts like a forest with canopies of ropes and furled sails. Gangplanks extended from the sides of the ships. At every gangplank a man stood with a heavy timber to prevent stowaways sneaking aboard. Rebecca moved into the crowd of people milling among the piers. She could hear men haggling passage for themselves or cargo with the ships' captains. She hadn't ever traveled by ship before and was at a loss as to how to get aboard. She approached one of the men standing guard at the closest ship, a gargantuan with scars on his face

"Get outta here ya filthy street rat," he barked at her before she could ask him anything. She moved on to the next and was likewise told to move along.

She approached a third vessel; it looked quick to her eye, which meant very little, but at least the guard had a smile for her.

"Run off have you, boy?" he said, leaning lazily on his heavy timber. "You have the look of someone off to see the world a bit. Just don't be trying to get on board Illandra's Heart without passage. I'd hate to have to end your journey before it gets started."

"I can pay for passage," she said. "But who is the captain?"

"Ah, earned a bit of coin did you? Or did you steal it?" His eyes twinkled at the thought. He smiled at her; he had several silver teeth showing. "Well, the captain's over that way." He pointed to a tall man with dark, graying hair in a well-cut dark-blue coat. "Name's Pell

Rhannon, best to call him Captain Rhannon though. He likes the sound, you see."

"Thank you," she said and made her way over to where the captain stood. He was talking to two shifty looking men that had a well used feel to them. Their eyes could not meet the captain's but kept twitching and darting between the Captain's chest and the ship.

"I won't be having no sneak thieves on me ship. Now, you two scuttle off before I have Davies limber up his swinging arm, you got it." His voice was airy like he was singing a song as he spoke. "Galloway said he saw you two fiddling with me merchandise below decks and I trust him a far sight more than the two of you, away with ya." He turned his back and caught Rebecca's eyes. She saw something register in his sea-colored eyes. He squinted at her then looked behind her, over her shoulder.

Suddenly, one of the men he had turned his back on had a dagger in his hand.

"Behind you!" she shouted.

The captain ducked sideways. The man with the dagger caught his sleeve, though, slashing it as he lost his balance. The captain moved in one motion, folding the dagger out of the man's hand and sticking it hilt deep into the man's thigh before rolling him hard into the ground. The man screamed and all heads turned to see what had happened, but it was already over. The second man ran off, covering his head with his hands as if expecting to be hit from behind. The man on the ground staggered to his feet and hobbled away into the crowd.

"You'll pay Rhannon," screamed the man as he vanished into the mass of milling people.

Everyone went back to what they had been doing as if nothing had happened. The captain walked over to Rebecca, pulling his coat sleeve to better examine the slash in it.

"Not a decent man in this Fates forsaken land; what's your name...boy?" It all came out in such a rush Rebecca had to think through what he had said. "Out with it, what are you deaf?"

"I...uh," she hadn't thought to ask what Alaric's alleged nephew was called. "Tomas, Tomas von Magus." The captain eyed her with skepticism, his eyes lingering on hers. "Well, I thank you for the warning...boy. Now move along." He looked over her shoulder again up the direction she had come. "I think a fair few people might just be looking to see what you be hauling in them sacks on your back." She turned to see what he had been looking at. She saw the men from the tavern making their way down to the piers. The captain made to walk past her but Rebecca caught his arm.

"Wait, I want to buy passage to Nor Harbor," she said. He looked at her hand clutching his sleeve with a dark raised eyebrow. She quickly released his arm. "Captain Rhannon, sir," she finished in a weak voice. She needed to make this quick.

"Nor Harbor, ay? Well, we be going to the south and the Fates might have me owing you something for what you did for me, but I don't give no handouts when it comes to me ship," he squinted, looking at her sidelong. "I expect to see something shiny before I let you up that plank."

"How much?" she asked desperately.

He scanned her from boot tips to leather cap and back, then at the men shouldering through the crowds along the piers. "Ten silver strip and you sleep on the deck with the crew." He began to move off.

"Five," she shouted after him, "and I want a cabin."

"Five! And a cabin you say," he spun about. "Well, you must certainly travel the seas often; you seem to think yourself a pirate. It's five gold strip for passage and the deck on me ship…boy, for anyone I don't owe." The way he kept saying 'boy' made her nervous, but she could see the men scanning the crowds around the ships, searching for someone.

"Two gold strips and a cabin then," she needed the cabin if she was going to stay hidden. "The smallest you've got is fine, Captain Rhannon."

He turned and she kept to his heels as he approached the plank leading up to the deck of his ship. He stopped, his foot on the plank, and looked at his guard leaning on his timber club. The guard looked pleasantly amused

"I don't suppose, Davies, you had a word with this young lad," he grumbled.

"Why, I just pointed you out to the boy, Captain," said the guard with a silvery grin.

"Three gold and you'll work my cabin, last offer, and Davies," he said to the guard under his breath, "we might be having company; keep an eye out won't you." Without looking back at Rebecca, he marched up the plank.

"You have the coin, son? *I can spot you a couple.*" Davies the guard finished in a whisper then looked toward the men moving closer to the ship.

Rebecca fished out three of the gold striped coins, a silver strip, and a copper from the purse hidden in her satchel. She tossed Davies the copper and walked up the plank after the captain.

She placed the three gold striped coins in his waiting palm. She held up the silver coin. "A silver strip for a word with you Captain."

446

"Words don't cost coin once you bought passage...boy. You got something to say, start to say it. Otherwise me cabin is going to need squaring away before we set out."

Rebecca put the last coin into her pocket and moved onto the ship. She heard Davies below talking to someone.

"You don't come aboard Illandra's Heart without passage and we're all booked up at the moment boys, so sorry." He sounded much gruffer than he had with her.

"We aren't looking for passage you sea gnat. We think we saw someone we is after," Rebecca heard from the pier below.

"Sea gnat? Well you can shove off then," she heard Davies say and then the clump of boots up the gangplank.

Captain Rhannon came to her and had her follow him into his cabin at the rear of the ship. Men were coiling lines onto the deck and setting the rigging. Davies pulled up the plank and joined the other deck hands in preparing the ship for departure.

Captain Rhannon walked her down a set of steps and into a cramped little room. Portholes along the back wall let in shafts of sun. The light-colored wood seemed to make the room glow with warmth. A little bed was set into the rear wall and small writing table was anchored to the floor at one side. Several rolls of parchment lay on the top of the table and a large map was tacked to the wall. The captain turned once she walked into the cabin; his face looked like a thunderhead.

"You either think you're very clever or you think me a fool...girl," he said in a quiet tone that sounded a shout for the anger in it. "You think tucking away your hair and wearing a boy's clothes will hide what you are? Whose empty headed idea was that, your own or did you have a crew devising this masterful disguise?" He plucked

447

off her cap, spilling her hair down to her shoulders. "Now who are you, *Tomas von Magus*, and who are you running from?"

Rebecca didn't know what to do. She stood in the middle of the cabin, staring at the captain, and feeling very exposed. "I…I stole some coin from my uncle and I ran away."

"Lies, care to try again? Or shall I have a guess? Did you see those three men that followed you down the pier? Looked very interested in you for some reason."

"My uncle was a governor in Romara," she said quickly, her cheeks reddening. She wanted to get out of this cabin.

"Tell me one more lie girl and I'll pitch you overboard when we get a mile out to sea," he growled. "There ain't no governors in Romara. Now let's have it out."

"I'm wanted by the New Dominion," she said under her breath.

"Skip Tracers, then, nothing I couldn't have guessed," he said, rubbing his stubbly chin. "Did you know that those two men I was pitching off this boat would have turned their own mothers in for a New Dominion bounty payout, girl? Most men would do anything to get into their good book. You're lucky you weren't snatched up, bundled up, and trundled up to the first New Dominion lackey they come across."

Rebecca felt a wave of embarrassment and anger. "Well, how long can I expect before you turn me over to a New Dominion lackey?" The smack across her face sent stars whirling in her head. She felt Astenos's rage and made to reach for the leather tube on her back. She was suddenly face down, her hands pinioned behind her back, on the bed, the captain's mouth inches from her ear.

"You listen, girl. I'll say this but once. I don't fetch for no New Dominion swine, you got it?" He released her and she pushed herself up onto his bed. "I took you on board me ship; I don't take no New Dominion handouts. I got me reasons, if being Silvarish isn't enough." He held up his right hand, a gray gull was tattooed onto the web between his thumb and forefinger. "Now, who are you and why are you trying to get to Nor Harbor?" He sat in the only chair in the room at the writing desk.

She rubbed her cheek where she knew a welt of his hand was forming. "My name is Rebecca Dulac and I am supposed to meet someone in Nor Harbor," she said scowling at him. "I was hoping to get there in one piece. If my coin isn't good enough for you, I can find another ship."

"I already took your coin girl, you aren't getting it back, and you'll keep this space clean while you travel with me."

"Can't you just let me take another cabin?" she asked. "I can pay."

"You'll be in here with me. The other cabins are taken with me trusted men. I go tossing them out of their bunks and I'll find me throat slit by morning," he said. "You can trust Davies, and Galloway. Stay away from the rest. You find yourself alone without meself or the other two nearby you get yourself someplace else."

"How long to Nor Harbor?" she asked.

"Half a month, maybe less, depending on the wind," he said. "Stow your bags, and leave that leather tube here when you come back out on deck." He stood and walked to the door leading up. "You got nothing to worry about until we make land...Dulac."

Forty-nine:
Illandra's Heart

Rebecca pulled her cap back on and stored her bags beneath the bed where several small compartments were built. She placed the leather tube holding Astenos and the other Soul Blade on the small bunk and turned to leave the cabin.

She could feel the ship moving as she mounted the steps to the deck. She found the captain stalking the deck, shouting orders to men who seemed to work twice as fast while he bellowed at them. She felt out of place; she had no idea what she was to do. So, she tucked herself out of the way and watched the piers drift off.

"Tomas, is it?" She heard in her ear. She turned to find Davies behind her. "Will Davies," he stuck out his hand. A small hawk marked his right hand; she shook it and he pulled her close to whisper in her ear. "You didn't fool me neither. I have an eye for the lasses. Don't worry; Pell's always a bit rough on the new folk." He released her hand and led her up a small flight of steps to a deck above the captain's cabin. Will was lean but well muscled; he moved with a grace and balance from time spent on rough seas. He had a similar way to speech as the captain as well as a similar look, if younger.

On the top deck, a large man stood at the wheel; his hair was white gold and his eyes were like flecks of the sky. He had a beard that came to a point at the chin, like Alaric's. He bowed his head to Rebecca as she approached but remained focused on his steering. The ship was being pulled out to sea; several small boats had lines running to the ship, and men with enormous arms pulled at oars that churned the port waters to foam.

Will placed his hands on Rebecca's shoulders, pushing her forward, as though presenting her to the man at the wheel as a prize. "Maxim Galloway, this is…what's your proper name then lass? We're all in on the story you know."

"Rebecca," she said to Will over her shoulder. "Rebecca Dulac."

"You don't say?" Will said, suddenly in front of her. "You wouldn't be related to that other Dulac then would you?"

"Will give it a rest for Father's sake," said Maxim. "Show the girl the ship and stay out of my way until we're at sea. Your mouth don't know when to stay shut." He twitched a grin at Rebecca, "Pleased to have you aboard."

"Great bear of a man don't know his history is all," said Will as he turned her to walk down to the main deck. "I'll show you the rest of Illandra's planks. She may look small and ugly in port but she's a right beauty at sea; I can tell you that."

The men on the ship were setting the sails as the captain lowered a small cloth bag to the headman of the towing crew. The smaller boats rowed back to the pier as Illandra's Heart picked up speed, heading into open water.

They passed the Captain as he made his way up to the main deck.

"Davies, you keep my new cabin boy occupied all day and I'll have you clean the barnacles off the side of Illandra's hull with your wagging tongue," he said stumping on. "I pay you to plot me courses not entertain the crew."

"Aye, Pell, I mean Captain Rhannon," Will said, making a flourished bow as he passed. "Wouldn't want the new hands to get lost though would we?"

451

He moved on down the deck. The masts of the ship stood high overhead; the sheets of the sails billowed in the late day sun. The ship rocked gently as it moved further away from Black Bridge, the buildings a mass of brick and stone at this distance. She could still see the silhouette of the tall black bridge tower against the hilled banks of the river, emptying into the port. Will led her to a set of stairs leading below deck. He showed her the other cabins and the cargo hold, talking away the whole while. He seemed unable to keep silent for more than a few seconds.

Finally, they reemerged from below decks and Will made way to the prow of the ship. Rebecca was thrilled at the speed at which they cut through the waves. She caught salty mists in her face when a particularly large wave crashed against the hull.

"You see her?" Will said, pointing to a carved figurehead of a beautiful black-haired woman. "She's Illandra. Do you know her story at all?" Rebecca shook her head; she had never heard the name before.

"Ah, I doubted you would, Arnoran by the sound of you. They never told no tales of naught but honor and valor up that way," he said with his silvery grin. "Her tale is one of love and tragedy, the best kind in my opinion." He proceeded to tell Illandra's story as the sun reached for the sea.

"She was a girl of the finest beauty. Her hair like ravens wings, her skin like copper in the sunlight. Her eyes could entrance a man for days; he'd die of thirst before breaking his gaze. And warm hearted she was atop it all. The Fates exceeded themselves when they shaped her.

"Now, there were two princes, Mraxis and Mraidan. They ruled together a land long forgotten to most. They were kind rulers and well respected among the people.

"Here lay the problem: Mraidan, the younger of the two, was forever overshadowed by his brother. Mraxis was always first among the two; Mraxis was said to be the better Bladesman, the finer dancer, the more handsome, and he held the most prominence in the rule of the land. As a result, Mraidan was forever in search of a way to out show his brother. Along comes Illandra.

"Mraidan was first to set eyes on her and he knew this beautiful woman would make him shine with her very presence. He asked for her hand in marriage. She asked for a day to think through his offer.

"The following morning, Mraxis was out to patrol the realm. He came upon a band of harriers assaulting a woman along the road. Mraxis dispatched the harriers and when the woman set her eyes on him she fell deeply in love with him."

Will placed both of his hands over his heart in a dramatic pose, his silvery grin shone in the golden sunlight. "Ah, the tragedy, when Mraidan returned to receive Illandra's answer, he found her in the arms of his brother. Mraidan lost his head, he bared steel and the two brothers fought a duel for Illandra's love.

"It's said the Fates themselves were witnessed above the duel, gazing down in horror and amazement. The two fought until near exhaustion; Illandra made to break them apart, for she did not want her love for Mraxis to drive him to kill his brother. She came between the two as each regained his second breath. They struck like savage beasts at one another their swords aimed for each other's hearts."

Will paused for effect. "She stood between the two brothers, pierced from either side through her beautiful chest. They say the two brothers' screams shook the ground around them for miles, the stone cracked beneath their feet, fire spat forth. Two mountains sprung from the spot where the brothers stood agonizing over what they had done."

Will held out his right wrist and pointed to the tattoo that lay there, two mountain peaks, a small red spiral for the sun over the smaller of the peaks. "The towns that built up around the peaks took the names of their fallen princes. We Mraidan still hold a grudge against our Mraxian neighbors."

"Davies, your lips flapping isn't getting us any closer to our destination," roared the captain from across the ship.

"Come along, Pell seems to be in a mood for a chat it would seem," said Will as they walked the planks toward the upper deck.

It was full dark, lanterns lighting the deck, before Will had set the course for them to follow southward. Rebecca watched as he used instruments, pulled from velvet-lined boxes, to scan the stars above, and check the heading on the large compass, suspended in fluid and mounted on a binnacle before the wheel. When the captain was satisfied, he left Will and Maxim to their tasks and escorted Rebecca to his cabin again.

"You'll be sleeping on a pallet on the floor," he grumbled to her, pulling out some spare blankets from one of the small cabinets built into the walls. "We wake early and work late on this ship. You are going to earn your meals like every other sailor." Captain Rhannon moved around to his desk and pulled out a small mirror from another hidden cabinet. He produced a metal basin and retrieved a pitcher of salt water; he proceeded to shave. "Well, what are you standing about for girl; the pallets are stored on deck in a chest near the main mast."

Rebecca turned and stomped out of the cabin. She was not some servant to be ordered around. *Work for my meals, will I? I paid the man and offered more.* She found the chest and unlatched the lid. She pulled one of the stuffed cloth pallets out and closed the chest. Entering the cabin, she threw down the pallet near the door, and turned to tell Captain Rhannon what she thought of his 'working for meals'. He held Ronan's Soul Blade, the blue silk lay on his bunk. His eyes traveled along the length of the sword with curiosity and admiration.

"What do you think you're doing?" Rebecca shouted. She stormed over to him, snatched up the silk and took the Soul Blade from him, careful not to touch it with her hands. "Do you root through all of your paying passengers' belongings or just those that save your life?"

"Save me life did you? You give yourself a bit more credit than you're due," said Captain Rhannon.

"That man would have stabbed you in the back!" she said outraged.

"Aye might be he would have, it's not like I haven't been stabbed before. Now, where did you come by that blade and its partner here," he said, rattling the leather tube.

Rebecca reached for the case with Astenos inside. Captain Rhannon held it out of reach. "Now, now, didn't your parents ever teach you no manners, girl? I asked you a question; answer it and you get this back."

Let's teach this man a lesson Rebecca. She heard Astenos in her head. *Perhaps he'll show you a bit of respect if we give him a closer shave than he's given himself.*

Rebecca smiled. "Find something amusing, girl?" said Captain Rhannon.

"The Blade you are holding is mine," she said. "The one you were looking at was my grandfather's. Now give me that case."

He handed her the tube. "What does a little girl be needing with a sword?" he asked.

"I use it to cut things," she said savagely, Captain Rhannon chuckled to himself. She could feel her cheeks redden.

"Girl, by the look of you, any man on this ship could pluck that sword out of your hand before you could pull it from its scabbard." He seated himself on his bunk and pulled off his boots, and coat. He threw them to Rebecca, "You can have them boots shiny by morning and I expect that slash mended. I just bought that, bloody coat." He lay down and rolled over, turning his back to her, he obviously had no fear of her, even armed with two swords.

Fifty: Warnings from a Dream

Rebecca was exhausted as she sat down on the pallet. She took off her cap and coat and laid them beside her. She felt miserable, tired, dirty, and lonely. She also didn't feel like sleeping. With nothing else to do, she decided to occupy herself with the captain's boots and coat.

She hunted around the cabin quietly; she could hear the captain's snores from his bunk. She found a small sewing kit and boot polish and brush. She seated herself and tended to the captain's boots; they were dusty from the piers but other than that in good order. She made quick work of them and set to mending the slash in the captain's coat sleeve.

Her eyes burned from the need for sleep; she kept drifting off as she passed the needle and thread through the wool of the coat. She pricked her fingers several times before she decided she had done as best she could. She set the coat aside, and lay back on the pallet. As tired as she was the thin pallet felt like a feather mattress. The gentle rocking and creaking of the planks lulled her to sleep. Astenos was, as she had become accustomed, somewhere close by in her mind as she began to dream.

Rebecca could hear a woman weeping quietly. She kept moaning something over and over.

I am sorry my love, I had no choice, you made me do it. I am so sorry.

Rebecca felt Astenos tense at the sound of the woman's voice. It sounded familiar to her and she decided to search for the woman. Astenos was close at her side.

Careful, Rebecca, she has awoken again. Astenos said.

"The other Soul, it's her again isn't it? Did the captain wake her? I swear I'll show him we can handle him," Rebecca said.

No, she slumbered for a time. Now, for some reason, she has awoken. The captain had nothing to do with it.

Rebecca journeyed through darkened halls inside her dream, Astenos warily following. The echoed moans, like laments for the dead, filled the stone corridors. The woman's sobs seemed to grow closer. Astenos stopped her.

We have grown closer over these weeks, Rebecca, though our mating has not yet resolved fully. I must teach you something if we are to approach the other Soul. It should not be taught yet but it must be.

Rebecca was anxious. She had forgiven Astenos for his attack on her the last time she had made to contact the other Soul Blade. She was not eager to have it happen again.

I believe I understand what has happened to this Soul's mate, and I am repulsed by it. You must understand that we Souls exist by strict customs. The highest of these 'The Soul shall cause no harm to his Mate' is instilled in us as we come into being.

"But that's only a rule. If I was to make a mistake and hurt myself, how could you stop it?" Rebecca asked.

You could not. I would feel our mutual Links grow close as my body approached yours. I would pull the Kilaray to me to adjust the flows of our links. I will not harm you physically. It is what we Souls are made to do. So when I tell you what I believe has occurred you must realize the full breadth of the action.

What I believe has happened to the other Soul's Mate is he somehow overcame the Soul's ability to keep from harming him.

"He hurt himself?"

I believe he killed himself. This is a taboo which has never occurred in memory. I do not know what would happen to the Mate but it appears to have driven the Soul insane.

Astenos's words disturbed Rebecca deeply. She did not like to think that any of her family would be driven to kill themselves. What had happened that would drive a man to do such a thing? She had never known Ronan but she had felt some kinship with him. Now, to learn he may have committed suicide seemed to taint that link.

I know how you are feeling, Rebecca. For me, this other Soul is as family. We Souls look upon one another as brothers and sisters. To have allowed herself to be used in such a way, it is sickening. I pity her but I am repulsed by her.

"Can you talk to her Astenos?"

Our link has grown stronger; I believe it will be safer for us to approach her.

They moved closer to the sobbing woman's voice. Turning down an ever-expanding maze of stone corridors, Rebecca and Astenos walked. A shape appeared, ghostly and incoherent, hiding at the end of one hall. Rebecca could not focus on her face; it seemed to slip in and out of clarity. She huddled on the ground in the darkness of Rebecca's dream; she continued to sob.

Rebecca could feel Astenos move closer to where the woman's form lay. Rebecca realized Astenos had become a more substantial shape from the last time she had seen him. He slipped in and out of focus like the woman, but he seemed to emanate a power that the woman seemed to lack. His appearance drifted, his face changing, but Rebecca could see hints of faces she had known. Her brother's, her father's, Broheim's, all men's faces she had known and loved. Rebecca saw Astenos crouch beside the woman; he seemed to talk to her, though Rebecca could not hear their words.

She says her name is lost to her. Astenos said. *It is forgotten; she longs for her mate, and for death.* Rebecca *moved closer to the two. Astenos held out a hand to stop her. Rebecca you must not approach! She says she can feel her Mate approaching; she believes you are him.*

Rebecca shivered. She had never dealt with madness before. She felt a sick sense in the pit of her stomach. "Can you tell her that I am not?"

I do not think she is capable of seeing reason. Rebecca, we should leave.

Suddenly, the woman was on her feet, running at Rebecca, her unsteady face contorted in rage and despair. Astenos's fear swept through Rebecca as he tried to restrain the other Soul. She was stronger than him, Rebecca could tell. She began to shriek at Rebecca.

You had no right Ronan, no right! I could not refuse you! Ronan stop, stop you must stop, NOOO!

Astenos toppled to the ground, holding the woman; she seemed to have collapsed. She rocked gently her legs pulled to her chest, weeping again. Rebecca was frozen where she stood. Astenos got to his feet, grabbed Rebecca's hand, and they hurriedly moved away. She knew now why Astenos had refused to let her contact the other Soul; if the woman had not stopped, Astenos would not have been able to keep her away from Rebecca.

I fear she has become too dangerous to be kept near, Rebecca. Astenos said when they could no longer hear the woman's sobs. *We are not strong enough yet if she comes again.*

"Astenos, what do you think happened to him, to Ronan? What would happen if he killed himself with her?"

I do not like to think on such things Rebecca. We Souls act at the edge of worlds. Our bodies and our souls are Linked as a three way bridge. We span the planes of the Father, the Kilaray, and your own world. That is why no mortal sword can best one of us. It is also why what has happened cannot be known.

"Why can it not be known?"

We Souls sever the Links of worlds. We reach a state where we can draw on the power of the Kilaray to divide the Links that tie your world to that of the Kilaray. They are controlled cuttings so as to prevent disaster but whatever we are used against is severed in your world as well as the Kilaray. He would be lost to your world, cast adrift between the planes of existence.

"Would it have to kill him? Could he still be alive?"

I do not know, Rebecca. As I said this has never been done before, I think it would be unlikely. I think you should dispose of the other Soul, Rebecca; drop her over the edge of the ship. We are in danger with her so near to us.

"I won't do it Astenos. I have to be able to help her somehow."

Why do you want to help her so much; she may be responsible for the death of your grandfather?

"I have a feeling she is important, Astenos. I don't know why, but I won't leave her behind."

*Then I will continue to guard your mind from her. You must take care, Rebecca. I will not be able to stop her if she wants to get to you. We will both be destroyed...*Astenos stopped abruptly; he tensed, and began to look around. *Rebecca you must awake! Danger approaches.*

Fifty-one:
Unwelcome Visitors

Rebecca opened her eyes and was filled with a sense of dread. The creaking of the ship met her ears, the captain's snoring, and, underneath it all, a sound below her in the hold of the ship, like water pouring. She got to her feet, pulled Astenos from the leather tube, and climbed the steps to the deck above.

Men slept in dark mounds on the deck of the ship. The sound of the sails rippling in the wind and the lapping of the water on the hull filled her ears. The moon was hidden and the sea was dark. She had an eerie feel creep along her arms and the back of her neck. Movement from the corner of her eye made her jump, a grey striped cat. It walked the rail of the ship, inspecting a line cast over the side. She moved, silent as she could, and looked over the rail. A small one black-sailed skiff was tied to the side of the ship; whoever had been in the boat was no longer there. She had time to hear the yowl of the cat and the sound of boots quickly approaching her from behind before she was fighting for her life.

Astenos was alive in her hand and her mind. A dozen or so men, six surrounding her, all carrying short swords or knives appeared on the deck around her. They slashed and stabbed at her with vicious fury. Someone shouted at the attackers.

"It's her! Get her, you fools."

Rebecca barely registered the voice. She moved through stances and movements faster than she had believed herself capable. Her streaking Soul Blade fending off the points and edges of six swords

462

like an ever moving shield. She realized she could hear other voices now, men waking at the uproar.

She moved into the Easing before she knew what she was doing. The six men around her slowed to a crawl, their faces clear in Rebecca's eyes. She recognized some of them, the men from the pub in Black Bridge. Anger overpowered her fear. She struck out at them.

She was vaguely aware that others come to her aid, men with clubs or hammers, crate hooks, and axes, or planks. She spun in fluid movements, working Astenos faster and faster; she felt a buzz in her mind and her finger tips from him, excitement. She slashed across the gut of one of the men; his shriek split the air. He groped at his stomach, where coils spilled out from his insides, his hands dark with blood. Rebecca felt sick even as she fought for her life.

The other five men edged back from her. They seemed wary now of getting too close. Captain Rhannon charged into the fight, barefoot, bellowing, and brandishing the other Soul Blade. Rebecca took advantage of the momentary chaos and ran another man through. He dropped to the deck with a gurgling groan.

Rebecca heard the sounds of men fighting behind her as she took on a third man. She didn't know why she had not taken the chance to run; she felt eager to fight. Her fear had evaporated like fog in sunlight. This was what she was meant for; she could feel a sense of rightness flow through her, but these were not her feelings. Astenos channeled his own feelings into her; the sense of purpose was his, she realized. This was what Alaric had meant about Astenos being a Young Blade; she felt reckless abandon as she charged after her opponent across the deck.

She traded strokes with the man, his short sword unable to match Astenos's superior skill. She felt the buzz in her hands increase;

something was happening to her. She could feel the flow of Kilaray pushing at her, Astenos called it on. His edges gleamed bright in the darkness of the night, too bright. She slashed at the man's sword; Astenos's edge seemed to catch fire in the night as he passed through the steel of the other sword, sending it to clatter on the deck broken, and into the flesh of the arm that had held it. She spun before the man could scream and when she finished the turn, the man's headless body lay twitching on the deck boards.

Rebecca turned and found several of the crew staring wide eyed at her. Captain Rhannon was gasping and seemed to have been slashed across one arm. She could feel her blood pounding in her head. She felt like vomiting as the adrenaline wore off. Will supported Maxim who had a large dark lump on his head. The quiet on the ship broke when one of the deck crew spoke.

"That be a girl, Captain," said a grizzled old sailor with patched pants.

"Ya think I'm a blind fool, Darris?" shouted Captain Rhannon. He had a strange look in his eyes as he watched Rebecca. "Will, what in Discordia happened? Where did these sea rats come from?"

"They jumped us Pell," Will panted. "They hit Maxim first, hit him with an oar."

Rebecca realized she stood a foot away from a body *she* had decapitated. She moved away without turning to look at it. She approached Captain Rhannon who still appraised her.

"I heard a noise below us," she said to the captain. "It sounded like it came from the hold."

The captain didn't take his eyes from her. "Darris, take Belwer and Stevens below. Search the hold." The three men moved off, picking up swords from the dead men lying strewn across the deck.

Finally, the captain turned to examine Maxim, his lump seeming to grow larger before Rebecca's eyes. The captain felt around on Maxim's skull, gently probing the wound.

"His skull's broke," said the captain. "Will, set him down; get some rags and a sharp knife. We're going to have to open this before it swells and kills him."

Rebecca knelt by Maxim's head as he lay unconscious on the slowly rocking deck. The men Captain Rhannon had sent below emerged holding a struggling man between them. He walked with a limp and had bandages wrapped around his leg. Rebecca recognized him for the man who had attempted to stab the captain on the piers. Understanding of what had happened dawned on her.

"Hold that worthless pig while I tend to Galloway, boys," said the captain. "If Galloway dies, we'll have us a right little party sending that dog off to join him." Rebecca knew the captain did not exaggerate. He would kill the man for his part in hurting Maxim.

Will returned looking frightened. His face was pale and his eyes shone wide in the low light. He handed the captain a knife. His hands shook as he held Maxim's head for the captain. One of the crew, Darris, brought a lantern over for the captain to work. Rebecca knew she could help Maxim, but doing so would reveal to anyone who saw what she was. She decided saving Maxim's life was worth the trouble.

"Stop, Captain!" she said before he stuck the point of the knife into Maxim's head. "I can help him."

"Girl, we haven't the time for you right now. This man is going to die if I don't ease the pressure growing in his head," the captain said.

"I know but I can help. Let me try," she pleaded. The captain's eyes searched her own. After a few seconds he nodded and moved the

465

hovering knife away. Rebecca breathed deeply. She laid her hands on either side of Maxim's swelling face. She Reached and slipped into the Easing, moving deeper as she had done with Garin. She saw the damaged links in Maxim's head and worked them into their proper place, sending flows of Kilaray through her Links into Maxim's. She knew what she did by instinct more than anything.

She passed through the Quickening back to the normal world. She saw Maxim's eyes flutter as the bits of bone in his head moved back into place, as though pushed from below. The swelling in his face lessened and Rebecca knew his skull was knitting itself together with the flows restored to normal. Maxim's bright eyes flicked open, staring into hers.

"You...you was in my head. I could feel you," he said. "Captain, I never felt nothing like it before. She...what are you lass?"

Rebecca looked at him worriedly and then to the captain. She could feel the eyes of the crew on her back.

"She's my cabin girl, one of the crew," said the captain. "Anyone else know anything different?" He asked the crew, looking around at them with savage threats plain on his face. "We are taking her to Nor Harbor and she is going to get there without a hair on her head harmed, or the Fates' curses be upon you." He stood up and helped Maxim to his feet. Will's face flicked from Maxim to Rebecca, as though he couldn't decide who the stranger was. The crew slowly acknowledged the captain's words, nodding and grunting their agreements.

Maxim thanked her as the crowd around her dispersed. Will seemed to have regained his senses, his silvery grin flashed in the lantern light and he laughed a nervous chuckle. The captain turned to deal with the prisoner his men held between them; Rebecca followed after him.

"Now, to flay our guest," the captain said as he approached the man. "Hallis, wasn't it? Well, we're going to see if you can swim your way back to shore with that knife wound in your leg, Hallis. First though, I want to hear what you're doing back on me boat."

The man tried to shrivel from the captain's glare. "We was after her," Hallis said, looking at Rebecca. "She's worth a fortune, you hear me Rhannon. Them others they was Skip Tracers; check them, see if I'm lying."

"Oh, I trust that they were at that," said the captain. "But you went for me hold Hallis. You tried stealing from me too."

Hallis looked around for help. He tried to appeal to his captors. He put on an oily grin. "We can be rich, boys. We turn that girl over to the New Dominion, we get the payout and we're rich men."

The two men smiled viciously at Hallis held between them.

"Hallis, you didn't hear the captain? She's his cabin girl. She's one of the crew," said one of them.

"You fools! You utter fools," Hallis shrieked. "You're throwing away a fortune. And you Rhannon, I know what you be carrying. I know."

"Boys, toss this trash off me boat," said the captain. The two men walked Hallis to the rail, he squirmed and struggled. They calmly laid hands on his back and pushed him over the rail. Rebecca heard the splash below and Hallis' screams dwindle as the ship sailed away.

Darris was at the captain's arm again. "Captain the dogs bored a hole in the side of Illandra's hull. We plugged it but we'll need to mend it when the hold has been dried out."

"They meant to kill us all," said the captain, distracted. He turned to look at Rebecca. "I want a word with you girl." He turned to Will and Maxim. "Cut that skiff loose and clean these bodies off me boat."

Will patted her on her shoulder as he passed. The captain led her back to his cabin. Inside, he walked to his bunk and sat looking extremely tired.

Rebecca could hear the crew above heaving bodies off the ship, and scrubbing the deck boards. The captain pulled a rag from one of the cabinets and tossed it to her.

"Best to clean a sword before the blood dries," he said to her. She looked down and saw the red stains over Astenos's blade. "Seems I was wrong about you girl. I doubt I could get that sword from your hands after what I saw."

Rebecca wiped off the blood and sheathed Astenos. The captain took the rag and cleaned Ronan's sword then handed it to her. She picked up the silk and wrapped the sword in it, the captain watched intently the whole while.

"Why would those men have gone to the trouble to follow you all the way out here, girl?" he asked her as she sat cross-legged on her pallet. "How much are you worth to them?"

"Four hundred thousand I think it was," she said frankly. "That was alive. Dead, I'm only worth a hundred thousand."

"A death warrant too?" he asked, running a hand through his graying hair. "I see, well you don't need to worry about the crew, now. Most of them are from Silvari, they hold the Fates' debts in high regard. You saved them from drowning at sea in the night; they'll see you safe to Nor Harbor. I reckon Hallis ran into that bunch of Skip Tracers after we set sail. They must have shown him your bounty sheet and they followed us."

Rebecca had come to a similar conclusion. Captain Rhannon heaved a heavy sigh. Rebecca knew he had more questions for her.

"What you did up there, I've heard of things like that before," he said. "It's why the New Dominion is after you? If they find out I have you aboard, every one of us on this ship is a dead man."

"If it comes to it, turn me over. I won't let anyone else die for me," she said.

"I told you girl, you'll make Nor Harbor without worry. I don't go looking for New Dominion encounters if I can avoid them. They would tear this boat apart if they knew one like you was aboard. I can tell you they would be mightily interested in what they found below," said the captain.

"What is it Captain? What did Hallis think you were carrying?" she asked.

The captain got to his feet and soaked a rag in saltwater, he dabbed at the slash on his arm, cleaning the wound. He spoke with his back to Rebecca.

"When I was a younger man, I fled from my home shores in a ship barely sea worthy. The Red Fist Army had taken Silvari and was sending all those who remained loyal to the old ways to prison camps, death camps would be a better term. Of the ships that fled, three in four was caught. I was Fate blessed." He turned and sat on his bunk, looking at the now pink rag.

"Will was but four or five when we found ourselves on a waterlogged rotten vessel in the middle of the Castean Ocean. We was going down, no land in sight, all hope lost. That's when our captain chanced sight of something in the distance. A vast ship, the likes of which I have never set eyes upon again, drifted toward us. We called

469

out to her crew but she had none that we could find. We lashed our sinking ship to her hull and boarded, hoping to make repairs."

"There was no crew, a ghost ship. She was adrift at sea. We explored her depths looking for salvageable goods. It had no sea faring goods that we was used to seeing. No sails or lines, we couldn't see how it moved. We delved further. That's when we found the stores."

"It had weapons and armor, swords, guns, cannons, of a make I have never seen. Strange devices scattered about, metal wheels and sprockets. They all lay unmoving as though waiting for whoever had left them to return."

A shiver went up Rebecca's back. This sounded like a larger form of Alaric's shop.

"We was afraid to touch anything. I'm not ashamed to say I was frightened by it all. We decided to leave after we had made repairs to our ship. That's when it happened.

"The captain spotted something. It rested on a pedestal under glass. We could tell it was old, older than the rest. It was covered in strange carvings and runes in several rows, of which, we could read only one, an old form. What was most disconcerting was the haze around it. A green mist of light clung to it. The captain reached out to touch the object...

"Next thing I know we was running for our ship. I held what we had took to me chest, the captain was dead. The vast ship had come alive before us. Lights shone down upon us as we ran from its hold and made for our rotting hulk."

"I was the oldest man on our ship, and so, I became her captain. I set sail with a child crew for the Wilderlands, the only land not yet affected by the Return. I still have it, the thing we stole from that ship."

"Can I see it?" Rebecca asked.

Fifty-two: A Tower of Light

Rebecca found herself standing knee deep in cold sea water. The captain had asked the crew to leave while he inspected the hold. The men that passed patted her shoulder or head as they left; some just with fingertips as though she were some talisman, or luck charm.

The captain fished a chain from around his neck. He approached what appeared to be a solid wooden wall. He put a hand to the wall, the chain dangling from between his fingers, and traced a pattern slowly along the wall. Rebecca heard a tiny click as the captain finished and a compartment popped open.

As soon as the compartment opened Rebecca could feel the objects within. The captain reached in and pulled a leather sack from inside. The compartment held shelves of small objects. Some were broken or covered in ages of filth but all, Rebecca could tell, were or had been linked to the Kilaray.

The captain turned, holding the leather bag in two hands. Rebecca could see the green mist the captain had mentioned. It was like a fog of light around the sack, permeating the leather material. The captain approached and pulled open the bag.

Inside she could see a dark metallic triangle; the captain removed the object in delicate hands. It was covered in lines and circles, etched deep into the metal surface, transecting one another. Rows and columns of tiny scripts covered every face of the triangle; she could see the Shintish sweeps and lines, the similar runic writing that was etched into the Soul Blades, others that looked like brutal hatches, and there, in a tiny row near the bottom, she could see an ancient form of Arnoran writing. The Arnoran hand was less refined and etched lightly onto the object as though not long ago added to it. The writing made her head spin, for she recognized the hand. She had seen it so often she hadn't realized how old fashioned it was.

For the crossing of worlds. A map? It was written in the same hand as her grandfather's journal. The last words "a map" were clearly a question. Rebecca was astounded by the artifact sitting not a foot from her. She could not help but reach out for the triangle. Her fingertips touched the surface.

Her vision was erased; the world streaked by her. The ship had vanished from her sight. The speed she traveled made her want to vomit, for she could feel her feet firmly on the unmoving floorboards of the ship. Abruptly the sensation halted.

She stared at a lush forest she had no words to describe. The trees she was used to were made for harsh winters; these looked like they had not seen fall in centuries if ever. Thick canopies of every shade of green stretched overhead, casting the forest floor in shadow. Rain poured down saturating everything. Wrist and arm-thick vines climbed moss-covered trees and flowers of every color grew wherever a surface could hold them. She could hear birds calling and animals of a kind she had never known. She looked around and saw, nearly swallowed in vegetation, stone structures.

They seemed to grow, as the trees and vines, from the sodden forest floor. Four carved forms stood twenty feet high, their faces eroded into vague rounded planes. Two, she could tell, were humans. The other two seemed out of scale, one too large, the second too small. She looked up and saw above her in the sky a familiar shape. Seven white stars, six, arching slightly, to either side of a central green at the foot of the columns – the Gates of Yuriah the constellation was called. Her vision blanked and she seemed to streak toward the constellation.

The green of the forest smeared before her. She closed her eyes to stop the feeling of travel without movement. When she opened her eyes again, her location was changed seemingly completely. A dark rock cliff faced her, stretching toward the sky above. She could see the Gates of Yuriah directly above her; she looked again at the cliff. Two trees grew from the rock face; sinuous white limbs reached for one another across a gap in the cliff. Their pale boughs and golden canopies partially obscured two white stone columns, arching slightly toward one another. She knew where she was now; this had been where her grandfather had stood, sketching on parchment that would eventually be bound into his travel journal. This was the actual Gates of Yuriah. Motion took her again.

She moved faster than either time before. Her eyes felt like they should be watering from the speed. Her head spun and she felt her stomach try to wretch. With great effort she peeled her eyes open to see what approached. A tower of light moved closer.

The suddenness of the stop made her step forward to balance herself. She stood at a gap looking toward the Tower of Light. The precipice she stood upon looked down on a lake at the foot of the tower. It appeared to be a round pit stretching off into the distance as though she stood on the top of a huge volcanic caldera. The Tower of Light reached skyward; it was the tallest structure she had ever laid eyes on.

From the center of the clear blue green lake, the shaft of the Tower rose what must have been a thousand feet skyward. She could not imagine what was casting so much light, and then she saw it. The

Kilaray wound around the Tower, a vast river moving upward, not light but Links. She could begin to see the structure held within the net of Links; pillars of stone supported level upon level, and, directly across from where she stood, an arched opening with the base of a bridge extended outward a third the distance to the edge of the cliff. She could not see how to get to the opening; she would have to be able to fly.

Without warning the vision ceased and she found the captain supporting her as she clung to the metallic triangle, the tendons in her hands standing out like cables. She pried her fingers from the triangle and the captain caught it.

"What happened to you, girl? I thought you were having a fit or a mind attack," said the captain.

Rebecca didn't know what to say so she just shook her head until her mind could puzzle out what had happened. She caught her breath and realized she could hear Astenos screaming at her.

Rebecca, answer me! Where have you been? Your mind felt distant but I could feel your Links near.

"I'm here," she said.

"Well of course ya are, girl. Did that trick you did to Galloway addle your brain? You haven't left me sight," the captain said. "Come, let us put this away, and get out of this water, and you can explain to me just what happened to you." The captain slid the metal triangle back into its bag and replaced it within the compartment, sealing it with the same pattern as before traced in reverse.

Fifty-three:
The Fate of the Holding

Rebecca felt the overwhelming need for sleep as she settled herself, still soaked to the knees on her pallet in the captain's cabin. She recounted what she had seen when she took hold of the triangle and he nodded, stroking his chin as he listened. Rebecca's eyes were drooping as she finished her journey with the Tower of Light. The captain seemed to take everything she said in stride, as though this was as to be expected. Finally he spoke.

"You've told me more than I'd like to know already, girl. You need sleep now. Don't worry about your chores in the morning. You've done enough for me this night to pay for your passage. It's hard enough finding a man that won't slit your throat in the dark, leave alone a man with as much skill at the tiller as Galloway. I'll have Will save your rations for you. I've heard what you did can wear on a man full grown, and you still be but a young lady."

Rebecca felt mildly annoyed by the backhanded compliments of the captain. She curled up on her pallet as gray light streamed into the portholes set in the walls of the captain's cabin.

Her dreams were unsettling as she slept. Her vision blurred and halted as it had when she held the triangle, only when she halted, a nameless man, his innards held in red slicked hands, faced her. His face shifted and she stood before James. She tried to apologize for killing him but she moved again.

Now she stopped in a forest clearing, Alaric ran from some unseen foe behind him. He limped on a leg dark with blood. He stumbled and fell as a dark form coalesced behind him. Rebecca screamed for him to turn but the Blind Man was on him already.

Astenos struggled into her mind. He grabbed her by her shoulders and pulled her from her nightmare into peaceful grayness.

Sleep my dearest Mate. Can you feel it? We are nearly joined completely. I will guard your mind from these thoughts of pain and fear.

When Rebecca opened her eyes, the yellow light that poured through the portholes made her eyes water. She rolled from her pallet and lashed Astenos to her back before she had realized what she was doing. She paused for a moment.

He had been the first thing she thought of. Not her soreness or the slight dull ache in her head from sleeping so late into the day. Not the fight from the previous night or the bad dreams. Her first thought had been to make sure he was near, close to hand, in case he was needed. She could remember his words to her. *We are nearly joined completely.* She could feel it now. It was like in her dreams, now in the waking world, like he was just behind her on guard for danger. She felt oddly comforted at his weight over her shoulder.

When she stepped, covering her eyes in the blinding light, from the cabin, hails of greeting met her from the men at work on the deck. She felt strange at being welcomed in this way. She had become accustomed to hiding and cringing away from the stares of men.

She could see crew scrubbing at dark stains, missed in the night, where a body had lain. These scrubbing men held smiles for her too. The captain seemed to know his crew well. They were glad to see her and she felt no fear as she strode onto the upper deck looking for the captain.

"Ah, the sun has come out at last," said Will as he saw her climb the steps. He leaned lazily against the rail of the deck. The captain and Maxim looked over to her. Maxim's bearded face broke into a warm grin, the captain nodded slightly. Will brought a wooden bowl to her with a cover overtop. "I was going to bring it to you in bed but Pell didn't trust me not to wake you with a kiss." Rebecca's eyes dropped to the deck and she felt her face heating. "I do adore the coy maids," he said, handing her the bowl.

"Will, you blathering idiot, leave the girl be," Maxim growled. "If you spent half your time minding your charts as you do chasing the lasses, we'd have sailed the extent of the world twice over."

Rebecca lifted the lid and found a fish stew, still warm, waiting for her. She devoured every drop and was disappointed to find the bottom of the bowl. When she had finished, she set the bowl aside and approached the captain and Maxim. They seemed concentrated on the navigation of the ship. Rebecca looked out over the bow. A wide landless expanse greeted her. The horizon was heavy with thick, dark clouds to the south; she could see the hazy mists from this distance that meant rain. The clouds lighted from within now and again.

"We be steering the ship around the worst of it," the captain said when he saw the concern her face. "We've seen worse than what's ahead by a long margin. No need to fret yourself. Will happened to plot us right into its path."

"You know Pell, that sounds like you don't appreciate my work," he said, pulling a hangnail from his finger.

"I value your skill Will, I'll give you that, it's your Fates-cursed tongue I don't appreciate," he growled back. "Why don't you two make yourselves useful and see if you can manage to plot us back onto course after we pass this storm."

"Gladly Pell — sorry, Captain Rhannon — I'll show our pirate slayer here my trade. Maybe I can find some real recognition of my artistry." Will put a hand to her back and led her down the stairs to the heavy rumble of Maxim's laugh.

"Why do you call him Pell if you know it annoys him?" Rebecca asked as Will led her toward the main mast. She felt a bit uncomfortable under the stares of the deck crew as she passed.

"Ah, he doesn't mind, at least from me or Maxim. We been with him the longest, you know." Will put a foot on the first rung of a rope ladder leading up the mast. "He saved us, took me from Silvari, got me safe to the Wilderlands, taught me to read charts, he's like my brother. Hope you don't mind the heights." Will climbed hand over hand up the moving ladder. Rebecca followed after; she recalled climbing a ladder in near darkness down a narrow steam vent.

At the top there was a perch built onto the mast. Will pulled out his instruments for charting the course and proceeded to show her how to use each in turn. She could see the ocean bending to either side of her sight from this vantage, the curve of the world. Will regaled her with tales of his adventures with the captain. Running from New Dominion galleons and avoiding the taxmen seemed to dominate the stories. She told him of her travels from Arnora and life at Valgerhold. He seemed to enjoy the part where she had tweaked the nose of Postam at the start.

And so her time aboard Illandra's Heart went for day after day. The crew took to her like a kid sister, telling stories and showing her how to do various tasks aboard the ship. She helped Darris, the patch-pants sailor, record soundings from the ocean floor. Maxim let her have her hand at the tiller wheel. The Silvarishmen of the crew seemed to love nothing more than to accost her with complements on her beauty, laughing with one another when she turned, blushing fiercely, from them to hide her face.

Stevens and Belwer, men she had met her first night on the ship, as it turned out were talented musicians. Belwer played a concertina in a rapid folk tune while Stevens, laughing and red-faced, kept pace on a fiddle. Will grabbed her hands and pulled her into the center of the circled crew, gathered round in the lantern light after last meal. The crew laughed and pounded out the beat on the deck boards as Will spun her to a dance she rushed to follow after. The captain chuckled with Maxim, smoking short-stemmed pipes and looking on.

The nights became warmer as they plotted southward. The days grew longer as High Month approached. Her birthday loomed not far ahead; she was almost fourteen now. She had been forced from her home a year ago, to find herself marched, with lost children, into the New Dominion's prison camps. She vowed to herself she would see them ended for all they had done to her and those like her. Every man on the crew recounted stories to her of the brutality they had found at the hands of the Red Fist Army, the Red Guard, or any other loyalist of the New Dominion, the captain included.

Every night since the first, she spent long hours telling the captain what she knew of the Kilaray. He had become a collector of Linked items after his encounter with the vessel at sea. He refused to tell her his stories though, of what he had seen to make him flee his country. She could only assume the worst.

She explained to the captain about Alaric and what he had told her of something he had called the Holding. She had come to the conclusion that is what the captain had found adrift at sea, a floating warehouse of Linked objects, weapons, and armor.

480

"Well, I'm sorry to tell you then that I know this Holding to be lost for good," he told her as he listened to her story. "That vessel, it sank. We watched as it drove itself down below the foaming sea, its ghostly lights shining on as it traveled deep. Finally, even those was lost to our eyes."

"But how did it sink, did you damage it at all?" she asked concerned at the captain's news. Alaric had said that the stores of the Holding waited until they would be needed again. If they were lost to the depths, how could anyone get to them?

"I told you we were scared at leaving our foot prints in the dust. If not for our captain we wouldn't have left a trace we'd been aboard. It seemed to me like it was trying to keep itself secret though. Like it was asleep until our captain woke it, and then it defended itself. A light took him in the chest. I don't know from where it came but his skin was charred to the bone when he fell over."

"A protection of some kind?" she asked. He shrugged.

"I can only say that we saw it go down deeper than a man could hold his air. It belongs to the fish and sea now."

"About the piece you took from the vessel, what would it take for you to let me have it when I leave?" she asked.

"I dare say it would take something more than gold strips could pay for," he said. "We paid for that trinket with a life, girl. You can see as I have become attached to it."

"What if I were to show you something that would prove that I might need it? What if I could show you that it was once in the possession of one of my family?" she asked, looking to the cupboards holding her bags.

"I say it would require some amazing proving even at that," he said, leaning forward from his bunk. She retrieved her satchel and

481

pulled her grandfather's journal out. She handed the book to him and let him thumb through the pages. He nodded and ran his hands over the writing. "This is interesting I must say. Your grandfather you say? He must have been on the Expeditionary League. Strange though he doesn't mention the triangle."

Rebecca had thought over this too. She had a feeling she knew where the triangle was mentioned but she could not show him because she could not see it either. She turned to the pages where the missing section was locked away. She pointed to the discrepancy in the text but the captain refused to see it her way.

"I see what you're showing me, but it's mighty convenient your proof is invisible. Girl, I tell you this, and know that I have grown fond of having you aboard; I would need to see some actual evidence before I parted with that piece. It is a reminder to me not to get tangled in things I don't understand. Letting you aboard went against that lesson; it seems so far to have let me off gently, but we'll begin to see New Dominion patrols soon and things may yet turn against me," he said.

Fifty-four: When to Keep Your Head Down

It seemed like the captain's words were like a beckoning call the following morning. The weather had turned dark, slate-colored skies stretched overhead and misting rain had Rebecca in the leather coat she had taken from Alaric. Her hair she had taken to tying back in a scarf and she had the leather cap pulled down over top to keep the rain from her face. The other men had pulled out various hats and scarves, and covered themselves in oilskin coats. The captain, his dark three corner hat pulled down low, was at the wheel with Maxim in a woolen cap and coat. Will had made a small shelter for himself and Rebecca at the rail of the upper deck from a tarpaulin stretched over the rail. They kept the brass and wood instruments as dry as they could while trying to take readings when the call rang out from a man in the crow's nest atop the mast.

"Ship's ahead!"

The call froze the crew at their posts; all heads looked out to catch sight of white sails on the horizon, the Red Fist billowing on a banner from its main mast. The already sullen crew turned to the upper deck. They now knew what it would mean if Rebecca were known to be aboard.

"Keep at your posts you curs!" shouted the captain. "It won't help things if we sink the ship on a sandbar before they reach us." The captain turned to Will and Maxim. "You two know what to do." They nodded, looking grim.

Will took her hand; Maxim followed after, clapping a hand over his eyes to shield them from the rain. The crew was silent as the three moved down the deck to the hatch leading into the hold. Rebecca felt anxious; Will's grin, which had shown even in the overcast day, was hidden behind a set mouth.

"Where are we going?" she asked when they were below deck, moving far back into the hold. Crates were stacked about held in place with nets and ropes, all bore the Trader's Mark on their outward facing sides.

"You've seen our legitimate cargo," said Will. "We keep our more lucrative goods in a secure location."

Rebecca turned to Maxim for answer. "He means the goods we smuggle to those what needs them," he said in a slow serious voice. "You should be safe in there with them until we get past any sniffing dogs of the New Dominion."

They came to the solid wall the captain had shown her that first night aboard. The hole that had been bored into the wall had been sealed with tar and wood. She turned to the two men beside her.

"I've seen that compartment; I can't fit inside," she said.

"Aye, Pell showed you his collection but we don't sell that." Will pounded on the wooden wall in several places. A narrow wooden door popped out and Will pulled it open. A thick, steel-braced panel blocked the opening. Maxim stepped forward and heaved his large shoulder against the panel. It pivoted upward, he held it aloft and Will herded her inside. The captain came down while she was still climbing through the door. He held Ronan's sword covered in the silk lining and her bags. He tossed them to her as she pulled her feet inside the already crowded space.

"Ya stay inside and don't make a sound till we let you out. No heroics, no sacrifices, it's how we get past the New Dominion," he said. He nodded to Maxim and he lowered the panel. She could hear the wooden door close as she huddled inside the space.

After what seemed like an interminable span she heard the clumping of boots above to one side of the ship, and then a sound of metal chunking onto the wood above. She heard more boots overhead, hard heeled boots that sounded like they were more used to marching than balancing on a rolling deck.

She was glad to have Astenos on her back even if she could not move to unsheathe him. She probed around inside her bags and found a sphere that fit into the palm of her hand. She snapped her wrist and white light filled the space. She looked around inside the secret hold in which she sat. Thin wooden boxes marked with faded green crosses indicated medicines, Beltari marked burlap sacks filled with some dark nuts or beans, and smaller wooden crates with the old Black Bridge trader's mark emblazoned on their sides, any of these would have the crew hanged for traitors. Something more caught her eye. A strange hatched writing she could not identify was branded onto one of the crates, below the strange writing was the word "Tremore" – Tremen goods.

Just then, Rebecca heard boots approaching slowly. They stopped now and again as though searching for something. She heard voices and looked to see if she could spot an eye hole. A small knot hole sat by her elbow, she shifted and positioned her eye near it. She waved her hand above the Incandeo to turn it down. The room went dark.

She could see several shadows cast against the hold walls. They were working their way back to where she was hidden. She listened to the voices on the other side of the wall.

"And you say you set sail from Black Bridge," a haughty voice said. It sounded strangely similar to the other Silvarishmen aboard.

"Aye, that be so," she heard the captain say in a grunt. All the song from his voice had gone.

"Captain Rhannon? Rhannon, Mraidian correct?" asked the voice.

"Aye," said the captain.

"And Illandra's Heart? Now, certainly you don't hold to the old stories now do you?"

"I see as that makes no difference to you." The captain sounded like he would like to tear this man's throat out.

They stepped closer to the rear of the hold and Rebecca saw the men in the lantern light. A snide man stood glaring at the captain like filth. He wore a red coat with brass buttons and a black bicorn hat with an enameled Red Fist pinned to its front. Rebecca could see pistols at his belt. The captain looked drab by comparison, but proud. The man thumbed his nose and Rebecca caught the sight of the tattoos on his right hand, the mountains and the sun over the taller peak, Mraxian. Branded into the flesh over the tattoos was a crude hand marked with a glyph on the palm. It looked to Rebecca like the Trader's Mark from the cargo.

"It's nearly High Month now, Captain Rhannon. You would show a beggar from Mraxis the hospitality of a friend this month; would you not? Well, I'll dirty my men's boots no longer on your...vessel." Rebecca heard other men's guffaws from the dark. "But, I would like to inspect the farthest reaches of your hold. I know

486

how some of our fellow countrymen sully our good reputations trying to smuggle unmarked goods; not that I'm accusing you of such."

"Be my guest, Mraxian," growled the captain.

Rebecca watched as her vision was blocked with wet red wool. She heard pounding on the wall in front of her face. Closer and closer to the narrow door the knocks moved. Finally, she knew she was found. The next knock would be on the opening. This red-coated man would hear the hollow sound from within and…

Thud, thud, thud came from the door. It sounded like the rest of the wall. Rebecca realized the second heavier panel made the space sound like it was a solid as the other areas.

"Well, good to find a decent merchant among our peoples still Captain," spoke the haughty voice again. Come men, his manifest checks out. Tell me Captain; you didn't by chance see a young girl while at port in Black Bridge?" Rebecca felt her eyes bulge as she strained to look through the hole.

"Aye, we saw plenty of young girls in Black Bridge. My navigator bedded a fair few I'd say," the captain said without any humor in his voice, but the red-coated man took it to be a joke, and laughed without any real heart in it.

"True, Captain Rhannon, true. You would be amazed how the girls seem to jump into my sheets when I speak with my native accent," he laughed at his own words. The captain was silent. Rebecca guessed, from his broad crooked nose and sniveling mouth, the man used his position as someone who could have a woman hanged, more than his charms, to get a woman into his bed.

When she heard Will's voice on the opposite side of the wall, she felt a great weight lift from the pit of her stomach. A wedge of light appeared and the heavy panel swung upward.

"We'll be into Nor Harbor at dawn," Will said as he stuck his head into the secret hold.

"That man, he was Silvarish?" she asked as she stepped into the hold.

"A traitor to his home," said the captain, holding a lantern near the crates. "He must have been caught by some holding to the old ways; he was branded."

"His wrist, I saw it. What was it Captain?" she asked as they strode from the hold.

"We called them Traitor's Marks. After the surrender, those that had turned on the Homeland Defense, what was found, got branded,"

"I hear the one who betrayed the First Born of Arnora got one too," said Will at her side. "Hardly fitting payment I'd say."

Rebecca agreed wholeheartedly. What was a burn to betrayal of your friends, betrayal of her brother? She would have seen the man dead that did it.

The day seemed to go too fast for Rebecca. Why did it always seem she had to leave her friends as they grew to know her? James and the others at Valgerhold, the wolves, Alaric, the Tremen, and now the crew of Illandra's Heart; she was perpetually on the run and it tired her more than anything else.

The crew all had advice for her as the day wore on. Nor Harbor, it seemed, was a bit of a den of thieves and cutthroats, villains and scum, refugees and the abandoned. It had been one of the first towns built when the Expeditionary League had returned with their reports. It had originally been built as an example of the Mecharical Age, using as many new devices as they could think of to fit out the streets and buildings. The men said the streets were lit with strange glowing orbs as were some of the buildings. The only reason any of it still existed when the New Dominion took control of the Wilderlands, was that it had, by that time, become overrun with outlaws.

It wasn't just visitors and merchants that were at risk in Nor Harbor, Red Guard and Red Fist soldiers had been found floating belly up in the port. Now, the New Dominion patrols were said to keep the residents of Nor Harbor in, as much as catch smugglers. Will suggested that she stay aboard and see the world with them which was greeted with many agreements from the rest of the crew.

"Ya don't want to get your pretty throat slashed in that Pit of Discordia," said grizzled old Darris.

"I have to find someone there," she insisted.

The following morning Rebecca woke to find the captain sitting in his bunk waiting for her to wake. He had remained closemouthed since the encounter with the New Dominion patrol.

"The men be right, girl. I could have you stay as one of the crew if you'd like," he said in a quiet tone not like any she had heard from him before. "Ya seem to be good luck to have aboard. We nearly never have such smooth sailing. And you're a right frightening sight with that sword you carry everywhere like some Palantean. Stay with us; you'll stay alive a lot longer than within the walls of that city."

She felt a longing to take his offer, but the thought of leaving her friends to rot while she saw the world made her feel ashamed.

"I told you Captain Rhannon, about Valgerhold, and my friends. There's a boy there who..." she felt her cheeks warming, "who I think I love. I wouldn't like to leave him to die at the hands of the men who have him."

The captain smiled, and pulled out a leather sack from behind his back. He handed her the triangular shaped parcel, she took it, and looked up into his face. There were tears on the rims of his eyes.

"I left behind me wife and daughter. I saw what those bastards that were coming were doing to our people and I ran," he paused and she saw him steel himself. "You bring fury down on them Rebecca Dulac, you bring the Blazes upon their souls. You fight for us like I saw you fight that first night, like a caged beast, and you send these evil men into the Pit of Discordia."

Nor Harbor was ringed with brown stone walls. She could see the stone piers from this distance. She stood on the deck at dawn. The day was still overcast but the rain had let up. The sea was a mirror of the sky, white caps splashed here and there and the grey-green water looked unwelcoming. She thought she could see why they had built the high walls.

All around she could see hills covered in dense forest. They felt forbidding; deep, dark stretches could be seen even at sea. Who knew what creatures lurked in forests like that. The city itself looked a jumbled collection of strangely square-shaped boulders. As Illandra's Heart moved into the wide horseshoe-shaped harbor, past vast harbor gates that reached to the top of the main mast, Rebecca could see the maze of streets.

It suddenly hit her that she would have to find her way through that labyrinth to one specific man. How many people lived in a city this size? Ten thousand, fifty, or more? Rebecca felt her heart drop. Astenos was there to bolster her spirits.

Fear not my mate. We will find your man and we will make him help us.

But Rebecca could not feel as enthusiastic. The captain bent his head to whisper in her ear as the ship coasted into the harbor.

"We'll be here till morning next. We have an appointment with some who shall remain unnamed. If you change your mind, you come running you hear, girl." He straightened and laid an encouraging hand on her shoulder.

Fifty-five:
Nor Harbor

Men in boats approached the side of the ship; they hoisted long thick poles up to the waiting crew of Illandra's Heart. The Captain handed down a cloth sack filled with the payment for the harbor master. The crew used the thick poles to guide the ship into her berth. The harbor was shallow; it was easy to tear out a keel on the rocks below, so the poles worked best to lever the ship into place.

The crew threw down lines to waiting shore men, and soon Illandra's Heart was docked. The men coiled lines and hoisted the sails, as booms moved into place to lift out the stores in the hold of the ship. Rebecca noted the glowing spheres atop tall iron posts dotting the piers. They didn't cast the same pure white light as Incandeos; it was a sickly yellow that made her feel even less like setting foot on the piers.

Eventually, the gangplank was lowered to the stone pier and there was nothing left for her but to walk down it or cower and wait to leave port.

Go, go, into the fight
The heart of Arnoran
Men will do right.
Back, back, they will fall then
To the Pit and the Blazes
We shall send them.

"Where did you hear that?" she thought to Astenos as she put her foot on the first cleat of the gangplank. The last time she had heard that sung her brother had bellowed it to his friends as they made to leave for the frontlines.

I can hear it still in your memory my Mate.

"Well, I'm not an Arnoran *man*."

Nor am I.

Rebecca smiled as she left the plank. She carried her bags tight to her, the reassuring weight of Astenos tucked next to Ronan's Blade over her shoulder in the leather tube. She had lashed all the openings with leather lacing as the crew had suggested. As she moved into the throng of people she thought it might be better to brandish Astenos and cut a path through, a thought that he heartily seconded.

The crew had given her advice on how to act when she thought someone threatened her. Most of which involved puffing out her chest and looking bigger, the first of which she shouldn't do and the second of which she couldn't. She was dwarfed by the men lumbering through the crowd. Women moved about in a fashion similar to cats avoiding being stepped on. She had no intention of darting in and around these thuggish men.

She decided on a more tactful approach. She began coughing heavily and frequently. A wide gap opened as men twice and three times her size skittered away from a potentially contagious child from abroad. She moved into a less populated side street off the piers and took stock of her possessions. She noticed the loosening of some of the laces and distinct finger smudges on her bags. She needed a place to hide her belongings or she would find herself worse off than she already was.

She looked for an inn to rent a room. The streets all sloped uphill from the pier. She found the backs of her thighs aching before she spotted a hopeful looking sign. It hung out front of a brown stone two-story building. The windows were arched and fitted with dense iron bars. The sign was what caught her eye, three daggers splayed out below the name, "The Three Knives." She ducked inside and was immediately stopped by a dirty, rough looking man at the door. He sat across from a large stand mirror that was cracked up the center.

"Stan' in fron' of the meer!" It took Rebecca a moment to understand what he had said. She stepped before the mirror and the man squinted sideways at her reflection. "Ee's na' a threat!" the man announced his accent was slurred with drink.

"Of course he's no threat you twice damned fool," said a man with a familiar accent. "You think them Strynges would take a mask of a scrawny little runt like that, you twit?"

Rebecca looked over at the man who had shouted. She could see his clan tattoo but could not tell what it was supposed to be. She stepped past the doorman into the dirty smoky room. There was only one patron; a dark haired man sat on a stool to the side of the barkeeper, his chin upon the counter. He had covered his ears with both palms at the first shouts of the barkeeper at the doorman.

"Was only doin wha ya paid for, Mannis. Can I 'ave a pin' now?" said the dirty doorman.

"Ah shove off ya twit," shouted Mannis the barkeeper.

Rebecca approached the bar cautiously. She had done her best to hide the fact she was a girl and it seemed to work for those who didn't look to close. She pitched her voice as low as it would go and spoke. "You have any rooms?"

"No, we're all booked up as you can see," barked Mannis. "What's a boy your age doing roaming these Fates-cursed streets?" The man with his hands over his ears stirred.

"Look, Mannis, I can take my coin elsewhere," he grumbled in a slurred voice. Rebecca looked over at him. He was Silvarish also, his right hand had a black bird on the web of his thumb and forefinger; she couldn't see the underside of his wrist. He had a sickly appearance, like a man with a fever. His cheeks showed days worth of stubble and he wore a mustache that came to points and a stripe of a goatee under his lip; a dark blue scarf was tied around his neck. He slowly sat upright and peeled open his slightly swollen eyes to stare at the barkeeper.

"You know you're not welcome in most of this town's pubs Wren. Now pay for another drink or I'll have that twit at the door show you the lovely streets of Nor Harbor. Can not you see I've got a customer?"

Wren looked to Rebecca; he struggle to focus on her face, and then his eyes bulged, showing bloodshot white all around. Rebecca had a dropping feel in her stomach, her fingers buzzed for Astenos.

"You alright there Wren, looks like you seen the walking dead," asked Mannis. "I don't want no corpses to dispose of. You know how the city watch looks on that sort of thing, even in this part of town."

Rebecca decided to find another inn, somewhere where the patrons didn't stare at her like they had just found their meal ticket. She apologized for wasting Mannis's time and moved for the door. She kept looking back at the man at the bar; he had turned to look dead ahead past the barkeeper; she could see his eyes lock with hers in the mirror behind the bar.

She trudged back out into the growing heat of the day. The streets were starting to steam from the rain soaked pavers. Rebecca would look out of place in her coat and hat if it continued to warm. She hurried around the corner of the narrow ally-like streets past grey, brown, and white stone faced buildings. All the lower floors had iron gratings, preventing intruders. Everywhere she looked the walls were coated in graffiti. The iron posts with the glowing spheres soon showed signs of the type of people who roamed the streets here. Empty sockets where the yellow globes had sat became more a rule than the exception.

Gangs of men caroused through the streets speaking loudly in drunken voices, whether still sobering from the previous night or getting drunk for the night to come she couldn't tell. As she worked her way through the winding streets that seemed to come in at every angle, she saw signs of a more dignified area. There appeared to be a city within this city.

The rough stone pavers widened in this area and the stone buildings were sheathed in colored plaster facings. Large windows stood open on second and third floors and shops appeared; their goods placed on wooden plank tables out front of their open doors. Her feet ached, unused to walking on such hard ground. She thought that maybe here she might be able to ask for directions.

She stepped into the nearest green grocer. A wary eyed fat man with his hair slicked back with oil watched her enter. He watched her every movement, apparently used to the usual fare of these streets.

He didn't say a word until she began sorting through some apples.

"You have coin I suppose? I mean to see it before you continue to paw my fruits."

"How much for these green ones?" she asked.

"A copper each." The price was outrageous; she had expected six for that price. She turned to walk out. "Stop! Alright a copper for three but I expect to see the coin first you mind."

She fished inside her pocket and pulled out one of the copper striped coins she had gotten from Black Bridge. The man dropped it into his till and came around to help her.

"I just got these in. No one in town has them yet. I worked a special deal with some friends in the town council to get first pick of the green goods." He sounded as though she should be impressed; so, she nodded with what she hoped was a passing expression. He seemed to find her look convincing and continued helping her with the selection. He watched her take the first bite with an expectant look. The tart snap hit her and made her eyes water; the fat man laughed at her face when she blinked to clear them. "They bite back don't they; great for pies. What else can I get you?"

"I was hoping to get some directions," she said as she munched on the tart apple.

"Well directions don't cost much; what are you looking for?" the man had become amiable since she had paid him.

"A book shop, run by a man named Bertran Gabriel," she said, looking over some more of the fruits on display. She had had far too few fruits in the past weeks.

The man tapped the tip of his bulbous nose with a thick finger. "Hmm, let me see, Bertram Gabriel." His eyes drifted to watch Rebecca and she noticed he had become silent. She looked at him.

"How much for these…uh what are these, exactly?" she pointed to the strange long yellow fruits bunched together at a wooden looking stem.

The man came to life again. "We're calling these bananas; I'd have to insist on a half copper for each, these *are* rare. They come from the Tremen lands to the south, very hard to acquire."

"I'll have one than, just to try it," she said.

He took her money and broke one of the fruits from the stem; he insisted that she eat it before him and tell him how she liked it, before he would give her directions. He showed her how to peel the bright skin away, revealing the soft mushy fruit. She hesitated before she bit into the thing. She smiled and gulped down the rest. He laughed and showed her out of the store. He pointed down the street and reeled off directions.

"The man's a real strange one though. I warn you, whatever it is you're looking for, find it quick. He gets very protective of his books," the man went back to his store and she left feeling a bit better about this town.

That was until she felt Astenos tingling at the back of her mind.

Someone is following you.

Fifty-six:
The Book Vendor

She turned to look over her shoulder, checking the leather case on her back. She could see no one. She quickly moved away from the green grocer's, standing in one place would not make it hard to spot her.

"Are you sure?" she asked Astenos. "I don't see anyone."

You should know I wouldn't be wrong about this. You must seek shelter or allow me out of this tube to protect you.

"No, not here." She eyed the men moving through the streets in this part of town. Dark flat-topped hats and faded green coats gave them away for the city watch. She could see the heavy batons, short swords lashed to their sides, a pistol in a leather holster; these men looked ready for a fight. They walked through the thickening crowds of the streets looking menacing. She made note of the directions the grocer had given her and darted up and down streets at a fast walk, hoping to lose her pursuer.

She stepped out into a wide boulevard with large shop windows on the street. This was the road where she would find the book shop. She clung to the walls, allowing women in fine cut dresses – the hems torn and dirty and showing signs of wear elsewhere – make moving cover for her. This must be the part of the city where the town council lived. Her father had often said that the last place to burn in a city would be the mayor's house, and the first repaired.

Men strolled along the streets in dark coats and top hats, giving her a spasm of fright; they looked like Blind Men at first glance. But

499

their rosy-colored cheeks and bulging girths gave them away for upper class men. She pushed her way through the crowd, keeping her head low, her bags tucked in behind her.

She passed a strange three-story dark building, its middle story painted in harlequins of dark violet and lavender. The round portico looked like a huge wine barrel on its side, a round door set back into the wall. The glowing globes mounted at either side caught her eye, true white light of Incandeos. She looked for a sign naming the building, the "Copper Keyhole." Perhaps they would have a room for her to rent. She hurried to the door and pulled at the etched copper knob. It didn't budge. A small slide opened in the thick iron-bound door; a set of dark eyes peered out.

"We open at dusk. Go away!" and the slide snapped shut.

Rebecca looked at where the eyes had appeared, feeling extremely confused. She moved on to find the book store and this Bertran Gabriel.

Your follower has disappeared, said Astenos as she moved down the wet streets.

"I lost him," she said relieved.

I do not think so. He was there and then he was gone. Rebecca, perhaps you should at least hide me beneath your coat.

She had the urge to follow his suggestion but decided against it. It would only make things worse if someone spotted him. She felt a sulkiness coming through their link.

"I'm sorry, but we can't risk it right now," she said, trying to console him.

Eventually, she found the door of the book shop she had been looking for, Bertran's Books. The sign was small and the windows were covered in thick dust as though the building was trying to hide.

She turned the handle of the wooden door and pushed through into a two-story open space to the sound of a tinkling bell.

The space was covered in wood – paneled walls, wood slat floors, and heavy wooden book shelves lined the walls and second floor. There was even a wooden candelabra dangling from the ceiling, small pink globes mounted on the carved wooden sockets. What was not wood was of luxurious materials: leathers, velvets, satins. Strange patterned rugs softened her footsteps. She approached a thick dark wood counter, its top covered in highly grained leather. Books were stacked atop; one was open as though whoever had been reading it had just stepped away.

The back wall behind the counter held shelves of glass jars, labels glued to their sides or hung from strings around their openings. Smells of herbs, spices, teas, and tobaccos filled her nose. Under all was the welcoming aroma of the books. Thousands and thousands filled the store, leather bound, or wood. Some looked like they weighed more than her. Ladders attached to slides ran along the shelves to reach the upper books and footstools were scattered about for the less lofty volumes. She turned from looking around at the store to find a man suddenly behind the counter.

She screamed at the abrupt appearance, and the man's eyes widened. He calmly returned to the open pages of the book lying on the counter.

"I suppose this is some new greeting of the younger people of this town? Fitting, the hordes of this city all seem to find that to be heard one must shout," the man said in low growling voice. Something felt wrong about him to Rebecca; it made the hairs on her neck rise.

"Are…are you Bertran Gabriel?" she asked.

His eye slowly climbed from the page he studied to look at Rebecca. His dark irises were pink rimmed, she had never seen anything like them; she looked away quickly. His pointed face slid into a mocking grin.

"Something disturb you girl child? You don't like my face perhaps? Well, I can assure you our feelings for it are mutual. Now, what do you want?" he said in that same slow growling voice. There was an emotionless tone to it.

Rebecca studied the man's appearance. His hair was bright blond streaked crossways with dark brown, like tigers she had seen at menageries that came to town every year when she was younger. His features were extremely pointed; his mouth and nose seemed out of proportion, almost muzzle-like. He had a blond beard growing from his cheeks, leaving his mouth and chin clean shaven. She watched his hands turn the pages and something seemed odd there too. His hands remained folded like a magician palming coins and balls.

"I'm looking for Bertran Gabriel, if you are he then I believe you can help me," she said, stepping closer to the counter. Again the man's pink-rimmed eye pivoted to look on her. It seemed to Rebecca as though his movements were almost marionette-like.

"I have no desire to help you girl child. Now, if you wish to buy or sell something I would appreciate you getting to the point." His languid attitude was starting to annoy her.

She undid the lashings on her satchel and flipped open the flap. She grabbed out the journal and laid it on the counter. Finally, something seemed to get the man's attention. His eyes clung to the cover like steel filings to loadstone.

"Where did you steal this, girl child?" his manner became defensive of the book before him. "I will have the name of the man you killed for it."

Rebecca was enraged. She pulled back the book. "I'll have you know that it is mine. Handed down from my father from his father," she did her best to seem threatening. "I killed no man for this book and you won't lay one finger on it until you answer my question – are you Bertran Gabriel?"

The man's expression of anger deflated into a pitiful sadness. "I know you must speak lies, girl child, but yes, yes I am Bertran Gabriel to the people of this city."

"Why do you say I lie about where I got this?" she asked, holding up the journal.

"Because the man I knew to have owned it is dead, as is his son and his son's son and daughter. The last must have perished with a friend; for, I have heard from neither in weeks," he said his eyes pinned to the cover of the book.

"Well, *I* am still alive," she said in a softer tone. "My name is Rebecca Dulac, Alaric von Magus was traveling with me until we ran into some trouble. I do not know if he is dead but I pray that he is not."

Bertran's eyes finally met her own and lingered there. His mouth twitched and then he harrumphed. "Oh, I see now. Yes, yes, you must excuse my behavior. The city folk here are always after something. Now, give me the book." The last was obviously an order. Rebecca hesitated and his expression flashed to anger. "I must see the book, girl child."

Her fingers buzzed with sensation from Astenos. Abruptly the man froze stiff.

"Who's there?" he said, looking behind Rebecca. "Who are you hiding?"

"I am hiding no man," she said. He eyed her warily; she was beginning to understand what the grocer had meant about this man.

"I must see the book, girl chi…, I am sorry, Mistress Dulac. I must ensure the uh…authenticity of the book and your words," his face became sly. She didn't know if she trusted this man, and Broheim's warnings echoed to her.

She reluctantly placed the journal back on the counter. He greedily pulled it toward him, sat with his strange hands and opened the cover like he caressed a lover.

"Ah, it is true," he panted. He turned the pages, running his finger along spaces where Rebecca knew script would appear if she touched the book. "I am believing your words now," the man said. "If Alaric's words prove as true; I shall help you contact the Pictsies." He whispered the last.

The sound of the door chime made Rebecca's head spin. A fat black clad man trudged into the shop.

"You! Strange little man do you have the books I requested?" he sneered at Bertran. "Or shall I hint to the city watch they might find interesting materials hidden among all this rotting parchment?"

Rebecca's heart pounded; Bertran closed the book and slid it across to her. "Get out, you devious boy child. I have no use for a third edition of this worthless dribble," he growled at Rebecca. His pink-rimmed eyes pleaded with her as he looked on. She understood he was helping her to leave without notice. "Perhaps someone at the Copper Keyhole will give you a copper strip for it, though I would doubt it." Rebecca slipped the book back into her satchel and darted,

504

head down, for the door. She could see the fat man turn up his nose as she passed through the open door.

She leaned against the closed door catching her breath. It was nearly midday, but the day's heat hadn't burned away the clouds. If anything, it seemed darker than when she had first set out. A brief shaft of light made her eye catch something small across the street in an ally. A flash of bright green, an apple core, whoever had eaten it had come past the same green grocer. She was still being followed.

Her heart resumed its hammering. She ducked down a side street looking for someplace to hide to get her senses back. She heard the sound of a group of men approach from the street she had just exited. They boasted loudly and laughed with too much bravado to be true.

"When we have that payout boys, I tell you what I'll do with my split. Whores, and plenty of them," this was met with cheers and wolf whistles from his companions.

"Then it's true; what they say, the girl is coming this way?" asked a second man.

"Aye, that's what I hear from all the Skip Tracers' bureaus, 'last seen in Black Bridge assumed to be traveling south'," said the first. "One hundred thousand sounds good to me." More boisterous laughs greeted that as the men moved on down the street.

Now will you let me out of this case? asked Astenos.

Fifty-seven:
Thrown Out With the Trash

Rebecca had a destination at least, the Copper Keyhole. She just needed to stay hidden until dusk. She kept to the narrow alleys, hoping to find someplace to lay low.

The stone sides of the buildings seemed like canyon walls as she moved down the streets and alleyways, away from where she had overheard the Skip Tracers. She could trust no one here. The City Watch would no doubt hand her to the New Dominion, any man could be a Skip Tracer, and if that barkeeper, Mannis, was paying to keep watch for the Blind Men, she had them to worry about too. What more could she expect to be against her?

The sound of an echoing peal of thunder seemed to answer her thoughts. She would have laughed if she didn't feel like crying. She moved on, hunting for somewhere to hide that would remain dry now.

She saw women in windows pulling in the lines of drying laundry strung across the alleys. They called down to her to hurry home before the rains came. She wished that she could heed their advice, but she had no home to which she could run.

The first fat drops splattered on the still damp cobbles of the alleys. She picked up her pace, as did the rain, taking turn after turn, trying to maintain her orientation. She could hear sounds from ahead over the soft hiss of the rain on the stones, a low mumbling of conversation. She came upon a group of people taking shelter from the rain beneath a covered area, near some rubbish bins. Their talk cut off as they heard her approach.

506

She ducked under the wood plank roof over the bins. Three older men were huddled together, two smoked short-stemmed pipes, the third sat against the stone wall resting his chin on his chest. They were dirty and smelled heavily of stale wine. The look they gave her was like that of stray dogs, not sure whether to expect a pat or a kick.

"Do you mind if I stay here until the storm passes?" she asked, brushing drops of water from her nose.

"Our hovel is yours," said the man against the wall. He wore a faded blue cloak that reminded her of something, but she couldn't say what. His companions made their goodbyes, with murmurs of what sounded like respect, and pulled swaths of oil cloth over their heads to walk through the rain.

Rebecca moved further into the little shelter, and crouched nervously across from the blue-cloaked man. His eyes were darkly shaded beneath heavy grey brows and there was a mark on his forehead.

"I apologize for my friends," he said, lifting his chin. Rebecca fell over onto her back side, his eyes were gone. Two gaping sockets stared out at her, the skull rims clearly defined. The mark on his forehead was a brand into the flesh, red and slick with the healing. It was a circle, a line descending from the bottom, and a half circle transecting the full one arching up toward his spotted wispy haired crown. "I apologize too, for my appearance," he said with a smile.

"No...no I'm sorry I didn't mean to..." she stumbled over her tongue.

"Ah, but what has been done cannot be undone, my child." His smile was reassuring if his gaze was unnerving. The way he said 'my child' brought recognition for Rebecca.

"You're a Cleric," she said. The robes should have been a deep blue, and the mark been displayed on a chain on his chest not branded into his flesh but she was sure of it.

"Once, my child, but now, alas, I am what I am." He spread his hands as though to display himself. "But you child, who are you? I hear the rolling hills of Arnora on your tongue."

"I uh…" She didn't think this man was in any position to cause her harm but she still felt caution was best. "I ran away from my uncle," she said at last.

"You need feel no obligation to tell me your secrets my child. We shall sit and tell one another lies while the rain passes." He straightened, bringing up his knees to rest his forearms upon.

"What happened to you?" she asked feeling abashed. "Who would do this?"

"This was punishment for holding to my convictions, my child," he brushed his hand down his face. "In the end, I am shamed to say, I think they proved that their convictions were the more potent." He laughed in a defeated way.

"What do you mean?" she edged closer, forcing herself to overcome her repulsion to this poor man.

"Adarian's Red Path, my child. We Clerics, when caught, were forced to yield to it, or were used as examples of the consequences. They told me, as they plucked out my eyes, that all my faith in the Touched was for nothing; that they would tear down what those gifts from the Father had brought us." He sighed. "You see they were correct now, my child, and I and my brethren were wrong. The Philistari are gone, as are the Palantean. The Mecharicals, if any remain, stay hidden, cowering, waiting for someone to bring back the light to this world. I fear they, as we all, will die in the dark in the end."

Rebecca felt the weight of the Cleric's words. The rain pounded on the planks overhead. She looked into her hands, searching for words to ease this man's burden.

"What if I told you, your faith wasn't wrong? What if you were right, and in the end the Touched would return?" she asked.

"I'd say you would be looking at your first apostle of the hopeless dream," he said, resting the back of his head against the wall, looking up blindly to the wooden plank roof.

Rebecca leaned over and laid a hand on the Cleric's scarred forehead. She Reached and found the seared links of the skin of his head. She passed the Kilaray through her to the dull damaged links. She slipped back to the world and the skin of the Cleric's forehead smoothed down; the color paled to leave a fine white emblem in the surrounding flesh. He looked at her with his blind sockets. As he felt his forehead, his chin trembled. Rebecca knew that had he eyes, tears would be spilling down his cheeks.

"Oh, Father above," he said in a thick voice, "forgive my doubt for you."

Fifty-eight:
Through the Copper Keyhole

Rebecca sat with the blind Cleric for a long time. The rain never let up but finally the light of the day began to diminish. She had to make her way back to the Copper Keyhole if she was to meet with Bertran. Before she left, she searched within her bags and found some of the gold striped coins. She pressed them into the Cleric's palm and told him what they were.

"Thank you, my child. You have given me back what I believed I had lost with my eyes. Faith can be broken as can a man's spirit but to mend either is harder than one could imagine. I have a need to walk amongst my wayward sheep," he told her. "I will do as I dedicated myself long ago; tell of the greatness of the Orders of the Touched and the First Father who grants them their power."

"Don't do anything that will bring you harm," she told him, worried at what his words might get him. "I must go; take care, Cleric." He held her hand to his forehead for a moment and then released it.

She pulled her coat tight and her cap down low and plunged out into the still pouring rain. One advantage of the storm was that the streets had cleared of all but the heartiest of the city dwellers. She made her way back to the boulevard she had left that afternoon, trudging through puddles and torrents in the streets. The windows were all closed now; flickering lantern light shone in most but here and there was the steadier glow, in pinks and yellows, from the orbs.

510

She passed several pubs, silhouetted card games on their windows and men standing in the front stoops to watch the rain. She heard raucous laughter and raging music from some of the doors as men or women would stumble out into the coming night, covering their heads with coats or shawls or oilskin sheets.

She found the odd shaped portico of the Copper Keyhole and hurried inside its barrel-like opening. She stamped her feet and shook her coat to get off the excess water. She tried the handle again; it refused to turn. Frustrated she pounded the door with her fist and the slide whipped open.

"What'd you want?" said the dark eyes that shone through the door slide.

"I want to come in out of the bloody rain," she shouted at the eyes. "You said you opened at dusk," she turned, gesturing to the fading light through the circular opening. "Well, it's dusk."

She heard a click and the slide snapped shut. She tried the handle and the etched knob turned easily in her fist. She heaved her shoulder against the heavy round door and a roar of noise collided with her ears.

Nearly every seat and stool was taken with men and women in their evening's best. She stepped into the room and her nose found exotic scents drifting in the air. The eyes at the door turned out to be attached to a wide dark skinned man. He closed the door when she had pulled her last boot through the opening and stopped her before she could move forward.

"You have to stand before the mirror first," the doorman said. Rebecca turned to find a gilded stand mirror at the raised step of the entrance. The doorman wore a belt full of knives lashed around his waist. She did as instructed and the doorman squinted at her reflection.

"She's clear!" he announced over the din of the room. Eyes whipped to see who had entered. Rebecca felt her stomach tense; the doorman had said *she's clear*. Another wide dark skinned man behind the bar waved to the doorman. "You're free to go," said the doorman at last.

"I thought you said you opened at dusk. What are all these people doing here already?" she tried to keep the annoyance from her voice.

"Most been here since last dusk," said the doorman, taking a seat at a stool near the door. "Others, they know how to ask in a friendlier way." He flicked a coin from one hand and caught it. Rebecca saw the shine of silver.

Shaking her head she walked into the inn's main room and was overwhelmed. The walls were painted in burgundy and violet diamonds; bright white Incandeos on wall sconces marched around the room. The dark painted floorboards were covered here and there in well worn Beltari patterned rugs. A fire crackled low in the large stone hearth at the side of the room. Square tables with many mismatched chairs filled the center of the room, and around the walls in alcoves, were velvet lined benches with small round tables. A dais across the wide room held several men playing instruments.

The music was similar to the Silvarish folk music the men on Illandra's Heart enjoyed, a fiddle player, a man on concertina, but with the addition of a handsome flutist. His lips cocked at her entrance and he bowed his head as he played to the upbeat tune. Rebecca felt her cheeks flush and she hurried to the barman to ask if Bertran had appeared.

512

As she approached she stopped dead, sitting on a stool at the bar and staring into the mirror, directly into her eyes, was the man from the Three Knives. He looked less shabby than he had before. He wore a brown wool coat and dark pants, both of which seemed like they could use some laundering; the blue scarf was still tied at his neck. His hair was loose and his cheeks still needed shaving, but some of the fevered look had left him.

"Wren, I let you in here as a favor. You go harassing my customers and I'll toss you out," the barman said when he saw Rebecca's face. "What can I get you lass? Don't go asking for anything too strong, I won't sell it to you." The barman's voice was friendly and deep. He reminded her of Gaston, the only other Beltari man she had ever talked to, back in Landfall station.

Rebecca frowned at the back of Wren's head and sat beside him at the bar. "I'll have some cider if you have any." She set a silver strip on the counter top and the Beltari barman slid it off, returning shortly with a mug and several copper strips. She took the mug and coins, sipping at the cider. She heard Wren chuckle softly and saw him shake his head. Rebecca ignored her urge to bolt for the door; she needed to talk to Bertran. Besides, she felt less threatened with the huge barman not two paces away from her. She turned to the smug-looking Silvarishman sitting to her left.

"I suppose you find yourself very clever," she said, filling the words with as much scorn as she could. She pitched her voice lower so he would lean closer. "It was you with the apple, was it not? It doesn't matter; so, do you mean to turn me in to four hundred or one hundred thousand in coin?"

He looked at her, a skewed grin on his mustached face, as he took up his cup of wine. "I haven't decided yet." He raised an eyebrow then turned to sip at his cup.

She turned to the barman and gestured him over. "Has Bertran Gabriel come here yet?" she asked him.

The barman shook his head. "He usually comes in a bit later; I'd be concerned if he didn't show in an hour or so. Don't worry lass, you're safe here."

She looked up at the Beltari barman. "What do you mean?" she asked, trying to stay calm.

He pointed to his eyes with his fore and middle fingers, "The Eyes, girl we know what they mean here. Safest place for you to be right now is on that stool."

Wren leaned over to her; his eyes had cleared somewhat since that morning. "I wouldn't bet on that myself," he whispered in her ear.

She turned on her stool to watch the men on the dais. They were quite good. Several people stood and pushed back some of the tables and chairs to clear a space to dance. Men and women made a circle and took turns jumping to the center in ones and twos to twirl about and stomp out the beat of the song. Rebecca soon forgot to be frightened, helped by the eager buzzing in her fingers and mind from Astenos. The flutist ventured over to the side of the dais closest to where Rebecca sat. He winked at her as he played and when the songs stopped he would stare openly. She smiled back and could feel her cheeks burning, helped along from the cider in her mug.

Wren, she noticed, watched the flutist with much more interest. He looked like a wolf about to attack. When he saw she was watching him, his expression shifted back to the smug haughtiness from before.

"Does that smile make other girls blush?" she asked. "It makes me want to slap it off your face." She heard a grunting laugh from the barman.

Wren smiled a grin that showed too many teeth. "Little sister, if we were elsewhere right now, I'd let you try. You should think about keeping yourself less noticeable, by the way. You look like you just ran off from the Homeland Defense."

"What would you know, *Skip Tracer*?" she hissed back, her eyes slits. "The man that owned this coat before me was a better man than you'll ever be."

"I have no doubt," he said, burying his smirking face in his goblet.

She saw the door creep open and a man in a hooded cloak came through. She could see the tiger streaked blond hair as Bertran pulled back the hood. She heard the doorman call out and the barman waved him in. Bertran caught her eyes and motioned for her to wait with a discreet hand gesture.

"Just what are you doing with that one I wonder?" whispered Wren.

"Didn't you figure it out when you were following me today?" she said back, feeling relieved that she could leave this man's company.

She watched as Bertran slipped into the farthest alcove from the door, near the steps leading to the upper floors, behind the dais.

"He usually takes our spiced Beltari coffee with whiskey," said the barman. "You go over and I'll send some food out when you're settled."

She stood from her stool and the room moved in way she was not used to; she caught herself on the stool. Wren looked at her with distinct concern on his face; it vanished the moment he noticed she had seen.

She leaned over to him. "Don't worry; I'm sure a bruise or two won't damage my payout," she whispered in his ear. She turned and walked across the room to where Bertran had sat. She felt strange; it wasn't like her to be so confrontational. Something about Wren had rubbed her the wrong way. She felt a doubling of dislike from Astenos. She told herself she would not drink anything other than water tonight. She could feel the Soul Blade's eagerness becoming belligerence.

She slid into the dim alcove where she had seen Bertran sit. She gasped and recoiled at what she found sitting in front of her. A too short man sat holding a porcelain pitcher, tipping out some strong smelling dark liquid into a teacup. Bertran was nowhere to be found. The small man's face was fox-like in appearance, with pink rimmed dark irises. Blond hair streaked in dark stripes tufted his head and was held back in a tail at his neck. His cheeks were bearded; his muzzle of a mouth and nose broke into a grin when he saw her reaction.

"I told you I disliked that face," spoke the growling voice of Bertran Gabriel from the jaws of this fox-like man. He lifted the teacup to his dark lips and sipped at the edge. Rebecca could see two thumbs on either side of his hands. Tufts of course blond hair spilled from his turned back coat sleeves, nearly covering his small strange hands. He wore a rust-colored velvet coat and a white shirt with lace at the collar and sticking out from beneath the coat sleeves. "You seem to be speechless; I trust my appearance has everything to do with that."

"Who...what are you?" she asked, relaxing a hair. The sounds of heeled shoes approached; there was a momentary blending of the man's face and a sound like a thick string plucked and the man she had met earlier sat before her. A woman approached in an apron, carrying a tray of bread and cheese with some exotic cured meats. She set the tray on the table and left the two to be. Rebecca watched as Bertran's face shrunk and distorted as though deflating and the little man sat before her yet again. He reached for the meats ignoring the bread and cheese and stuffed a strip into his mouth. He chewed, as all appearances would suggest, like a fox. His pointed dark fuzzed ears twitching happily.

The little man leaned across the table. "My name is Noe Avaka. I am a Shint Pictsie, and I am the one who showed your grandfather our tricks for hiding words."

Fifty-nine: Cracking the Seal

Rebecca watched the Pictsie expecting him to vanish and her to wake from a dream, but when he belched and took another sip of the dark liquored concoction she knew he meant to stay. She settled the weight from her bags on the velvet bench beside her and waited to hear more. When the fox-faced Pictsie stopped chewing and stared at her she lost her patience.

"Well?" she said exasperated.

"Well what, girl child? It is you that needs to do the talking," his growling voice said. "I'm the one that needs convincing; I can see you are persuaded as to what I am. What are you exactly; I do not yet know."

She understood he wanted some proof that she was who she said she was. She thought the journal would have to suffice. She pulled out the book and slid it across the table. She touched the cover, after checking to make sure no one could see, and turned open the book. Noe Avaka looked down at the pages, the parchment filling itself with script. The corners of his mouth turned up showing pointed teeth.

"Good, good, what else have you to show me?" he said, twitching his dark nose, and looking expectant.

"What else do you need to see?" she asked, frowning at the little man. "I am who I said I am."

"Then show me you can see the secret to this journal, the reason your grandfather sought me out in the first place," he said.

The missing pages, it had to be that. She flipped to the spot in the book and pointed to the valley where the pages should have been. "There," she said, "there is your secret."

"You are very irritable, girl child," he said, sipping at his teacup. "Why? Is it the drink or are you always this angry."

Rebecca calmed herself; she was angry. She was still thinking about Wren sitting across the room. The smarmy look when he saw her. The man was going to see how hard she would go down. Astenos's spirits lifted.

"I'm sorry; I ran into someone I disliked," she said. Noe Avaka bowed his head. She took a deep breath and let the Kilaray show themselves. The flitting strands of light jumped into her vision. She could see them moving along the valley of the pages in seemingly one line. "There are two parallel lines spaced so close they seem as one," she said in a flat voice, her eyes locked to the pages. "At their mid point is a shape like two circles stacked atop one another." She looked up from the page into Noe Avaka's face. "Do I need to show you more?" He shook his head.

"Now, down to business; Martan Dulac, your grandfather, cost me a sizable fortune for what I showed him. I will expect repayment of his debt to me, with interest I might add," said Noe Avaka, looking shrewd.

"I thought it was the Shunts who were supposed to be the thieves," she said absently. The Pictsie became very still.

"You insult me? I agree to help you, for reasonable recompense, and you compare me to those thieving weasels," he shook his head. "I should have learned from my dealings with man kinds; everything should be done according to your ways, no matter what peoples came before you." His face smeared and the twang sounded, Bertran

519

Gabriel appeared once more. "I leave you to unlock that seal, girl child."

Rebecca berated herself for a fool. "Stop, Noe! Wait, I was rude and should not have said what I did."

He stopped and looked first to the book and then to Rebecca. "I will expect payment for the work that I do. Shunts take what they have no right to; we Shints work for our fortunes. I keep a room on the second floor, come we will need privacy."

Rebecca followed the bright coated man to the stairs leading to the upper stories. The flutist on the dais winked at her as she passed – he really was quite handsome. There was a small hall to her right that led off to a rounded door; it would open out onto the alley at the side of the Copper Keyhole. A steep stair led to the floor above opposite the hall. She climbed after Noe Avaka.

The upper floor was less showy than the main room below. The walls here were fading slightly, lit with dim gas lanterns, and the window at the end of the hall was dusty. A staircase behind her would take her up to the third floor, but Noe Avaka moved down the narrow hallway, past several doors.

He slid a key into the latch of one and opened the door; yellow light bloomed from the room, making a wedge shaped pool in the hall. Rebecca slipped into the little room and closed the door behind her.

Noe Avaka had taken on his Pictsie appearance once again and waited for her in the middle of the room.

"Come, I will need some space to complete the pulling through," he reached out his two thumbed hands. Rebecca handed the journal to him and he set it delicately on the floor. Rebecca looked around the room. She judged that she was at the back of the inn; the shuttered window would look out on a common alley with the other buildings around the Copper Keyhole. The bed looked soft and there was a small writing desk set beneath the window. The lights were, as Rebecca could see, some of the stolen street orbs. Another of the strangely patterned rugs from Bertran's Books covered the floor.

Noe Avaka loosened his coat and collar and flexed his odd hands. He had opened the book to the missing pages. He laced his fingers and cracked his knuckles, turning at last to Rebecca with an outstretched hand.

"I take your word as one of the Touched to bond you, Rebecca Dulac." His tone had a formality that gave the words a feeling of a contract. She took his odd gnarled hand in hers and shook. "Then we begin."

Rebecca thought she had heard something from the hall, but as she listened the sound ceased. She turned her attention to what Noe Avaka was doing. He reached toward the valley of the pages like he meant to put his hands through the book. Rebecca could see the Kilaray brighten. Somehow he managed to touch the lines and he began to pry them apart. She watched as he strained against the unmoving set of minute lines, then they spread apart.

The spreading lines revealed a woven net of shining strands, all attached and knotted about the tiny circles; they remained where they had been, at the center of the valley. Noe Avaka wiped his furry brow with his long blond hairy forearm. He turned his eyes on the tiny circular shapes. Rebecca looked over her shoulder; she thought she had heard the sound again somewhere down the hall. Astenos became wary.

Rebecca knelt to watch Noe Avaka work. Gripping the little circles in either hand, he twisted the shapes around, back again, clockwise, and anti-clockwise. He repeated this several times. His hands slowed now.

"Ah, there you are," he said in a satisfied way. He spun the shapes around twice over and then began rotating them in a pattern that made little sense to Rebecca. She saw the lines and woven net flash, and Noe Avaka pulled away the little shapes; they faded into the background of the room. He began unraveling the netting holding the lines and that too was pulled away to vanish. Finally the two lines remained. Noe Avaka stuck his hand wrist deep into the valley, between the glowing lines, and gripped a hold on something.

He began tugging. He reached in his other hand and pulled with all his strength. Rebecca watched, open mouthed, as his hands pulled forth several pages from seemingly nowhere. They kept sliding out from between the valley and finally the lines on either side of Noe Avaka's hands faded into nothing.

Noe Avaka's head dropped and he breathed heavy. Rebecca went to his side. He turned to look at her.

"I expect payment, girl child," and he laughed.

Rebecca flinched as the door burst open, sending wood splinters from the jamb skittering across the rug. Rebecca found she had fallen over onto her side from the crouch she had been in. Noe Avaka looked as startled as she felt, his eyes wide, the blond hair on his head stuck up. Two men had kicked their way into the room and trained pistols on Noe Avaka and Rebecca.

"What is that thing?" said the handsome flutist from the dais, his pistol targeting Rebecca's heart, and looking at Noe Avaka.

"Dunno," said the fiddle player. "We'll just kill them both and sort it out in the end."

"Right," said the flutist.

He raised his pistol and took careful aim. She had been so foolish to think the man handsome. James was handsome; this man was pretty in a way not becoming a man. Rebecca squeezed her eyes shut, filling her mind with thoughts of James for the end of her life.

Her heart stopped as two pistol shots fired. The "tchunk" sound of the bullets hitting wood met her ringing ears. She felt no pain. As she reopened her eyes, she saw a haughty looking Silvarish man in a brown coat, standing over two dead musicians. He knelt to pull two narrow, hand-long knives from their backs. He pulled aside his coat, after wiping the knives and stuck them into a concealed leather holster lined with similar knives. He stood up and offered her his hand.

She looked to Noe Avaka who was lying on his back, propped on his hairy elbows, his feet out in front of him. He had one strange hand to his chest and breathed heavier rapid gasps.

"Are you alright?" she asked him. He looked over at her with wide shocked eyes.

"I...I believe I saw my history before me," he said in a soft growl.

"We have to get moving, little sister," said Wren, offering his hand again.

"Why should I trust you?" she asked, staring at the two dead men. "You're going to just do the same as they were."

Noe Avaka looked up at Wren as he got to his feet, and then back to Rebecca.

"This must be the man you did not like, if you do not trust him now," he said to her. Wren looked at Noe Avaka with an amused look. His face was all seriousness when he turned back at her though.

"If you wish to keep drawing breath, you'll take my hand, little sister," he said. The smugness had vanished. She looked at his outstretched right hand, the mountain Mraxis was pointing to a red spiral for the sun on his upturned wrist. "Take my hand, little sister," Wren said each word slowly and with force. Rebecca reached up and caught his hand. He pulled her to her feet.

"You'll have to leave the bags behind," Wren said, poking his head out the door and looking down the hall. Rebecca was shaking her head when he returned to look at her.

"I can't leave them; they're too important," she said.

"More important than your life?" Wren asked, pulling off his brown coat, and rolling it into a ball. His white shirt showed stains and many holes. He thrust the balled up coat into Rebecca's arms. "I can keep you safe, but we're going to have to travel light, and were going to be moving fast," he said. "The bags stay, or we wait here for the rest of the dozen or so Skip Tracers down there to come see what is taking these two." He finished, pointing at the two dead men. He turned to Noe Avaka's bed and sat down.

"I may be able to assist here, girl child," said Noe Avaka. The twang sound and Bertran Gabriel stood before her. "I will be able to carry your bags to wherever our destination may be."

"Good, give your luggage to the fox and let's get moving, little sister," Wren said as he rolled up his left sleeve, Rebecca caught sight of something blue. He leaned out and took the ball of coat from Rebecca. He fumbled around inside the ball and pulled out a small leather case.

Rebecca handed over her bags to Noe Avaka, she felt nervous giving him everything she had. She bent and tucked the journal into her satchel and handed that over as well.

"How do I know you will meet me where we go?" she asked as he pulled on the bags. Wren assembled what looked to be a syringe.

"You insult me again, girl child. We have a contract; it is I that worry for your end to be paid. Now, where am I going?" he said.

Rebecca pulled the leather tube over her shoulder for something to do while she thought. Wren pulled a leather lace around his arm, Rebecca watched curiously.

"What are you doing?" she asked.

"Never you mind, little sister," he said through gritted teeth, holding one end of the lace taut. She could see a blue serpent tattooed on his left inside forearm now.

Noe Avaka looked at the man warily also. But his eyes flashed back to Rebecca.

She looked at him. It came to her. They couldn't have left yet; it couldn't be dawn for at least a couple of hours.

"Illandra's Heart!" Rebecca announced. Wren tensed and looked at her through confused brows. She turned to Noe Avaka. "Go to the piers find a ship with a dark haired woman as the figurehead. Ask for Captain Pell Rhannon. Tell him I sent you and that I'm taking up his offer." Noe Avaka nodded and walked with her to the door.

He leaned over to her. "I see why you do not trust this man, girl child. Be wary of him; what he does is unnatural." Noe Avaka slipped from the door and down the steps at the end of the hall. She could hear chairs push back as he reached the bottom step.

"It's not them. Godge get up there and find out what's taking those two so long," she heard from the quiet common room below.

Rebecca turned back to Wren; he had just pulled the spent syringe from his vein. He began to shudder violently; an indigo hue coursed through the veins of his arm to his wrist and up under his rolled sleeve. She watched at a loss for what to do. His convulsions ceased and his eyes snapped open, there were tears.

He brushed them away and hurriedly put the case back into the ball of his coat. He pushed it at Rebecca.

"Keep that safe," he said in a flat emotionless voice. "I'm going to need it when we get where we're going. What's in the case?" he asked, looking at the tube on Rebecca's back.

"Never you mind, Skip Tracer," she said back.

His lips twitched into a smile. Rebecca could hear boots sliding down the hall.

"Here we go," Wren said. Rebecca would have said his face looked serene if not for the tears he had wiped away.

Wren grabbed Rebecca and pulled her to the wall near the door. They waited for the boots to come closer. A nose edged around the jamb. Wren grabbed the man from around the door frame and threw him, head over feet, to crash into the shuttered window. He hit the desk below and slid to the floor in a heap. The way the man's neck sat crooked told Rebecca his spine was broken.

Everything happened quickly after that. They were at the top of the stairs, looking down. Wren's hand flashed and a streak of steel flew. Rebecca saw a man, his legs twitching in death, with one narrow knife hilt protruding from between his eyes. Wren half pulled, half carried her down the stairs and knelt to retrieve his knife.

"Stay close. I stop, you stop, I run, you run. You see it's me, don't fight, otherwise run like the Blazes are on your heels. Got it?" he peeked around the edge of the stairway into the room. "Now, let's go!" he shouted and threw her out in front of himself.

Men shouted; she was suddenly enveloped in Wren's body. She heard pistol shots and the sound of steel hitting wood and then she was running down the hall toward the side exit, Wren right behind her. She was amazed he had not been killed. He pushed her through the door as she turned the latch and then threw her to the ground as a volley of gun fire rang out from the head of the alley. She felt something crunch beneath her.

His arms worked faster than she could believe. Shining streaks of steel flew from his hands, and wherever his hand pointed a man fell dead or gasping. Rebecca looked up from where she lay and saw five dead men ahead of them. Wren retrieved his knives without a sign of remorse.

Rebecca was relieved to find the rain had let up; at least they had one thing behind them. She crouched behind a rain barrel at the side entrance. Wren blocked the door, propping a loose plank under the latch. A hammering sound came from within the Copper Keyhole against the door. She tied Wren's brown coat over her shoulders like a cloak.

"Where did they come from?" she asked. She could not see how Wren had not been shot, but he showed no sign of pain.

"You walked into a hornet's nest, little sister. Every Skip Tracer or man with a pistol and a copy of your bounty sheet descended on this city two days ago." He pulled her to her feet and began dragging her down the alley. "Some halfwit in Black Bridge with a knife wound told tail of a girl dressed as a boy on a ship bound for Nor Harbor."

Rebecca felt sick. She should have had the captain gut Hallis instead of throwing him overboard. They came to a main street; Wren stopped and pushed flat against one wall. He edged to the corner and swiveled his head around to see.

"A City Watch patrol, stick close and stay low," he said, rolling out into the open street, Rebecca's hand caught in his. "Gentleman,

I'd like to claim my payout!" The four green backed watchmen turned to Wren, their guards slacked only a little and Wren released her hand. He moved in a blur; *no man could move that fast*, she thought. He threw himself at the startled watchmen faster than they could pull their pistols. He took the first and rolled him through the air into two others. He punched the fourth in the jaw in a way that snapped his head up and he fell like a sack of rocks. The other two he left struggling against their fallen companion, and they bolted down the street again.

Rebecca could see dark stains on Wren's shirt as he dragged her behind him. He seemed to have been injured after all, but it didn't seem to slow him down.

"Faster, come on, little sister, faster," was his only comments to her.

Shouts from alleys to either side gave Wren in instant to react. He wrapped around her from behind, covering her like a shroud, as a volley of gunfire let loose all around them. She could feel chips of the pavers spray against her legs and impacts through Wren's chest against her back, and then Wren was gone like mist. She looked around for a body but there was none to be found. Men mobbed in on her.

"Run, little sister," Wren shouted. He was moving through the crowd of men, stabbing and slashing with his knives. Rebecca reacted at once; she dug in her boots and dashed down the increasing slope of the street. More men appeared from side streets and opened fire. Wren appeared from nowhere shielding her as she ran. His hands whipped from holster to the air and men fell screaming. He vanished once more. She pulled the leather case over her shoulder and pulled off the cap.

Here Rebecca, I am here, shouted Astenos as her hand met his familiar grip.

She pushed the cap back onto the tube and ran full speed down winding streets. She turned whenever she heard shouts from men and soon ran down wider streets than she remembered, open streets. A call from behind her, and she spun ready to fight, it was Wren. He limped slightly; all his knives were gone. He caught her free hand and pulled her onward.

His hair was matted to his forehead and bloody streaks showed on his shirt. His limp, if anything, lessened as they moved, though. They came to an intersection. A mob of men brandishing an assortment of weapons moved toward them.

Wren looked to the alleys. "Up!" he shouted. He pulled her toward a low wooden roof. Rebecca pulled open the tube once more and stored Astenos inside; she needed her hands free. Wren lifted her and she pulled up to the roof top. He was behind her in a flash. They climbed to a second higher roof and a third and then they were above the streets. Chips of stone shattered as men shot wildly after them.

"Keep going," Wren said.

They ran, jumping the narrow alleys as they leapt from roof to roof. The mob of men chased after them, looking skyward for their quarry, sprays of gunfire, and shattered glass sounded as they leapt the gaps. Wren tossed her when the spans were too great and she rolled out onto open terraces. The streets became quiet as they moved toward the now visible harbor below. They came to a gap they could not jump and worked their way down to the ground again.

The street they took came to a wide circular intersection. Wren halted her. Astenos buzzed at her. She reached up and retrieved him now she was on the ground. Wren looked back at her.

"Give me that other one," he said, looking at the case. Rebecca hesitated then turned for him to take it. He pulled off the sheath and the silk and Rebecca put them into the tube. She felt the extra warmth of Wren's coat around her now.

"Why have we stopped?" she asked in a whisper.

"I can feel...others around us," he said, looking up to the roof tops. "Whatever happens, little sister, keep running."

They edged out into the circular intersection. Wren's head swiveled, trying to look all around at once. The streets ahead came in from three different angles. Rebecca felt exposed in this wide space. Wren pushed her to the ground as a dark blade streaked where her head had been a moment before. Wren twisted around a dark clad figure that had appeared from nowhere.

The two fought like snakes, the dark clad figure using two short knives, and Wren wheeling Ronan's Blade like he was born to it. Rebecca got to her feet and started to run to help him.

"Run, little sister!" Wren shouted from inside the twirling fight. Rebecca turned to run. She headed for the straightest route to the harbor.

A dark mist descended from the night, pouring a man shape onto the ground. The Blind Man placed its tall hat onto its dark haired head, and pushed the smoked spectacles over its hollow eyes. Rebecca saw the scar between those repulsive gaping lids, as though a knife had plunged deep into its mask-like face. It's charade of a visage looked more human than the last time she had seen it.

"We come forth; the culling shall begin," it said in its spine-shattering rasp, like life ripped from the world. It took a step, sliding more than walking, and another mass of black vapor poured from above in the second street, a third; all three paths to the harbor were blocked.

531

It took Rebecca a moment to realize Astenos screamed in her head. She had dropped to her knees with the first word from the Strynge's travesty of a mouth.

Rise Rebecca, we must fight. Get up; the Masked approach.

With great effort, she pulled herself to her feet and brought up Astenos's point in her two hands. The three Blind Men recoiled, covering their faces as though from the sun, and Rebecca realized there *was* light. A stream of Kilaraic energy passed through her into Astenos. The edges of the Blade shone like star fire in the night, a warm green gold color. Wren was beside her, panting.

"Go, little sister, run now," Wren pushed her to get her moving. "They've brought Husked Men."

Rebecca dashed forward. The Blind Men evaporated into the night, screeching at their loss, before she reached them. Astenos resumed his normal metallic shine, the glow faded like steel cooling. Rebecca ran with Wren driving her on. His head never remained in one place, continually scanning the street as they went. Rebecca could see the sails on Illandra's Heart unfurling.

"We're almost there," she gasped. She smiled at Wren, relieved; he smirked back. A dark triangular point burst through Wren's rib cage. Rebecca turned to see a dark-clad pale man, his knife pushed to the hilt into Wren's back, his face pressed close behind Wren's ear as though to whisper in it. Wren staggered and fell forward; the dark-clad man turned his dead white eyes on Rebecca. Her hands moved under Astenos's instruction; she couldn't have done so herself. The stroke was clean and fast; the dark figure took one step and his head fell away, his legs melting beneath him.

She turned to Wren. Gasping, blood streamed from his mouth.

"Keep…keep run…running, little sister," he stammered through slicked lips. She had led another man to his death. The weight of it was too much. She sheathed Astenos, carefully did the same for Ronan's Blade, and put them in the leather tube on her back.

She knelt beside Wren, still gasping through his punctured lung, and pulled his arm over her neck. She struggled as fast as she could with the man stumbling along with his dying strength. She fell more than once but finally she heard the crew of Illandra's Heart rushing up to her. They took the man from her and hurried her up the plank. She heard what sounded like blacksmiths hammering. She collapsed on the deck near Wren.

"Captain, this man's as good as dead," Will said. "The blade is in his lung, I don't know how he's not dead already."

Rebecca looked at Wren, his eyes were rolling toward her, his hand waving feebly for her to come closer. She crawled over to him. He pawed at the brown coat tied over Rebecca's shoulders, and she understood.

She reached into the pockets and found the leather case inside; she pulled it out. Her hands were wet with some blue liquid. She opened the flap and found the glass vials within shattered. She looked at Wren with utter loss on her face.

"I'm sorry," she said, "oh, I'm so sorry, they must have broken when we were running." The look on his face at the sight of the blue liquid dripping from her hands was worse than the four inches of steel poking through his chest.

"Ah, he's only a Mraxian anyway," said Darris, the grizzled old sailor. He held Wren's right wrist up for the crew to see. Rebecca didn't recollect crossing the space but she could feel men pulling her from Darris. He was covered in bright welts over his face and her hand ached now.

"It's High Month," the captain said at last. "If we treated that Red Fist traitor with respect we can surely show this man some for saving our girl here." He crouched looking at the shattered glass from the case, his face looked grim. "Will, take this man into the hold, pull out the blade and lash him to the walls. Tight mind." The men around the captain looked confused. "Am I still the Captain of this boat or do I need to find me a new crew, you Fates Cursed dogs!" Men rushed to comply.

Rebecca followed Wren with her eyes while she sat on the deck. The captain's face filled her vision.

"The men say I was a fool letting our luck charm walk away. I'm beginning to believe them. We could use some of it now for sure."

The captain pulled her to her feet. Will returned shortly, looking pale and frightened.

"We did like you said, Pell," he said in a shaky voice. "He...he died Pell, sure as I'm standing here and then he came back. I...I think he's a demon."

"No Will, he's no demon, just some poor twice damned fool," said the captain, sounding sad. "Now, to tend to other matters. Girl, our luck went under the moment you disappeared from sight. The City Watch claps a steel tie down on us till morning, our appointment runs late, some strange man comes running out of the night screaming that you sent him, and now you drag a near-dead Mraxian onboard."

"Noe Avaka, he's here?" she asked in bewilderment and relief.

"Said his name was something like that," said Will. "We didn't think he'd be dumb enough to rob you and then come here calling out your name; so, we locked him in one of the cabins until we could sort it out."

"We got more trouble coming, Captain," bellowed Maxim from the upper deck.

They all looked; the streets leading down to the harbor were filling with a mob of people. They could see the green-backed City Watch in that herd of people. The shouts and cries could be heard from the decks.

"First thing's first," said the Captain, leaning over the side rail. "How's that chain coming boys?"

"It's no good," said Stevens. "It's hardened steel, Captain."

"Pell, even if we get the chain loose the harbor gates are still locked," said Will.

"I know that, Will!" said the captain.

Sense slowly came back to Rebecca. Trapped and no way to go; she was back at Valgerhold all over again, at the bottom of a well fighting against a locked grate. She looked over the rail at the men hammering uselessly at the steel chain bolted to a solid granite pylon, and then out to the large slotted wooden harbor gates, barring their way. Rebecca thought back to everything she had learned and done before and since Alaric, rolling the leather and metal cuff around her wrist. Suddenly, a plan formed. She would not let these men die for the trouble she had brought down on them.

"Captain Rhannon, get those men up here and get ready to sail." He looked at her and barked a laugh.

"You bringing the fury, girl?" he said hopefully.

"I'm bringing the Blazes," she said and readied herself for what she had to do. The men below gathered up everything they had been using on the chain and ran up the gangplank. Rebecca heard heavy pounding on the deck boards behind her and turned to find a great hulking shape standing over her. She was pulled upward, as the crew screamed in outrage, but Garin's huge sandy-colored mane nuzzled gently against Rebecca's head, her cap falling to the deck.

"What are you doing here?" she gasped, when his purring had ceased.

"We had to complete our task and then we came to meet your Captain Rhannon. He is to be the man kind's envoy," he said. He looked up to the nearing mob of men. "Perhaps, Captain, we should be off?" The captain's face flashed from astonishment to anger in a heartbeat.

"I'm trying to help him to do just that," Rebecca said before the captain could explode. "See if you can help the crew to get this ship moving." He nodded and Rebecca saw Maien and Fayit emerge from below decks. The three took up the large poles and began pushing Illandra's Heart toward the harbor gates.

Rebecca focused on the chain and let the pull of the Kilaray build. She Reached and threw out her hand when she felt she would burst from the energy against her soul. A sphere of bright blue-violet light condensed from the air and streaked into the thick chain growing taut as the ship moved. The link the sphere hit exploded in a spray of white hot metal, sizzling as the bits hit the water, and the first part of her plan was done. She ran to the bow of the ship, startled crewmen throwing themselves to the rails to get out of her path.

She could see the five heavy locks of the harbor gate growing nearer. She let her mind drift over the group of locks; she Reached and the metal of the locks fell away like sand. One last task and they would be away.

She turned her mind to the water below them. She focused on the point where the two gates met and Reached out once more. A swelling bulge of sea water blasted forth sending the harbor doors wide.

Rebecca heard low thuds from the harbor. She turned to see puffs of smoke from the piers. Huge plumes of water sprayed up to either side of Illandra's Heart.

"Cannons!" shouted the captain from the upper deck and he issued orders to an already harried crew.

The men pulled lines as fast as she had ever seen them work. The sails caught the wind and the ship picked up speed. More thuds and plumes and ocean spray coated the deck. Men ducked their heads and braced for the next volley as the cannons were set for the next round.

Rebecca ran, weak-kneed, to the stern. She mounted the steps to the upper deck, bracing herself against the rear rail. She tried to focus her mind on what she could do to stop the immanent cannon fire. A shield of some kind, she needed something to keep the shots from the decks. She saw the flashes of light from the piers, the puffs of smoke; she needed to do something or they would be hit.

"Incoming!" screamed the captain and pulled at her wrist to get her down.

Suddenly, a wall of water shot up behind the ship. The stern dropped as the water rose, climbing upwards from the sea. Fish swam twenty feet above the harbor within the column of water, and then two billowing streaks tore into the wall as the cannon balls impacted it. Rebecca dropped to her knees, the column crashed back into the harbor, and its wave carried them out beyond the cannon range. Rebecca heard fading shouts of men as she dropped into deep darkness.

Sixty-two: The Monster under the Floorboards

Rebecca heard screams in the darkness of her mind. Astenos sat beside her in her dreams, his shifting face filled with concern. She felt strange even here in her mind. Exhaustion didn't begin to define her feeling.

You must rest my Mate, said Astenos when her eyes met his. *You did well, now sleep deep.*

The screams echoed on in her mind. She thought of Ronan's Blade, was it the Soul screaming? Was it herself? She didn't care at the moment. She slept on, her mind too tired to pull forth dreams. Eventually, even the sound of the screams faded.

She awoke in a small bunk. She put her hand to her throbbing head. The creaking of the ship sounded like her mind grinding in her ears. She was weak and starving, but she could feel strength, not her own, pouring into her. She looked down, the brass case of the Healer laid against her chest. She sat up and steadied herself on her feet. She reached out without looking and took up Astenos, belting him over her shoulder. She staggered up the steps of the captain's cabin past a pallet on the floor.

She squeezed her eyes shut as she stepped into the light. As her eyes adjusted, she saw the crew looking on her with what appeared to be a mix of fear and reverence. Their utter silence said more for their feelings than their faces. She slowly climbed the steps to the upper deck, looking for the captain.

539

Fayit stood towering over Will, pointing to the bright sky; Will's face was painted with puzzlement. Maxim was at the wheel as ever; the captain beside him. Rebecca approached the captain. He looked up, concern across his face.

"Should you be out of bed?" he asked her. "The Pictsie told us you would sleep for days yet."

"I'm alright," she lied. "How is Wren?" she asked.

"You gave us a scare back there, girl," the captain said, ignoring her question. "You're good to your word though, those were the Blazes if I ever seen them."

Will's silvery grin flashed at her and then faltered. He turned back to look at Fayit, seeming startled to find her there. Maxim's eyes flicked between the compass and Rebecca, trying to avoid her notice.

"Captain, how is Wren?" she asked again.

He sighed and came around the binnacle to walk with her down the steps to the main deck. He stopped and turned to look at her.

"That man you brought aboard, we're going to have to put him down, girl," he said flatly.

"No, I won't let you," she said outraged. "He saved my life in that city."

"He'd appreciate death now, girl," said the captain, placing a heavy hand on her shoulder. "He's like a rabid dog; you can't do nothing for it but put them out of their misery."

"What do you mean misery? Where is he?" she said angry and frightened.

"He's still tied up below. He broke Darris' hand two days ago, when he tore one of the ropes free from the wall," said the captain. "Girl, remember what I told you…about…why I fled." He pointed to the deck boards, and the hold below. "That is what they did,

Rebecca." A shiver went up her spine. The captain took her elbow and led her into his cabin. He sat at his desk and she on his bunk. He took a moment, obviously fighting against what he felt.

"I was a soldier in the Homeland Defense," he began. "The Palantean scratched us together to defend Silvari. We were quickly trained and poorly armed, but we found our fire to fight from the Palantean that had been sent to lead us." The captain had a faraway look on his face. "The Red Fist had pushed into Silvari's northern borders. They seemed an unstoppable horde. We did our best, striking at them from cover and slowing their advance. Somehow we started gaining ground and then we came upon the camps."

He looked up at Rebecca with a horrible expression. "Children, our children, Silvarish boys and girls half starved and all with blue serpents tattooed on their arms. They begged and screamed for what they called the Blue. We didn't know what they were talking about. Eventually, we found out."

"The Red Fist had concocted some...scourge. A blue liquid spiked into the veins, it did something to the kids. They yearned for more, when we couldn't give it to them, they went mad; we restrained them. Slowly, they're screams faded and we thought they had weathered the storm. We were wrong."

"Spasms took them after the screams stopped; they shook so violently we thought their spines would snap. Grown men wept for them. In the end they seemed to calm. That's when the horror of the Blue came upon them. Their eyes glazed over like the dead and they attacked us. Something from Discordia had taken their bodies and moved them like puppets. We lost men to children of ten and eleven years old. They used knives or sticks or their bare hands to tear at armored soldiers. Whatever we tried they couldn't be stopped. Girl,

541

we were trying to kill them as hard as we could. We put them down finally, had to remove their heads to do it, and I wasn't the first to flee from the sight."

Rebecca felt sick. She stared at the captain, feeling his horror.

"That is why we must put him down, because, in the end, whatever it is that has a hold of him will take him," he said. "He will turn on you and kill us all. He is and will be a Husked Man."

Rebecca stood in the hold of the ship, looking on the ruin of a man. He was tied hands and feet to the floor. His shirt was stained with blood and sweat and the floorboards showed deep gouges below his boot where he had scrabbled to free himself. His wrists were red and raw, and his face was contorted in a silent scream.

"His voice went out, just today," said the captain, standing at Rebecca's side holding a lantern. "The crew wanted to slit his throat, but I thought you should see him first. I'm surprised really; he should have been taken years ago, judging by his age."

Rebecca approached slowly; the captain caught her shoulder to stop her.

"Careful, girl," he said.

Rebecca knelt at Wren's side. His hands thumped the floor trying to pull loose. She brushed the sweat soaked strands of hair from his forehead. His scarf was still tied around his neck, but askew. Rebecca could see a strange scar on his neck. She put her finger to the scarf to pull it down to see.

Wren's eyes snapped open fixed onto Rebecca's face, his arm tore loose from the rope and locked around Rebecca's wrist like a clamp. The captain seized Wren's wrist, struggling to pull his hand from Rebecca, but Wren relaxed and struggled no further. He still held

Rebecca tight. The captain stopped his fight when Rebecca motioned that she was alright.

Wren mouthed something through dry cracked lips, his head shaking in refusal. Rebecca leaned in close to hear his hoarse words.

"I'm sorry my dearest friend. I couldn't resist them Captain Dulac. Seb, you have to forgive me, please. Please Sebastian," he hissed, and his eyes closed shut again, his hand falling limp.

Rebecca had gone cold, her mind quivering in confusion. She turned to the captain, with fury driving her determination.

"This man will live," she said to the captain.

"Rebecca, you must see, he will..."

"I don't care! You said yourself you're surprised he hasn't been taken; well, he'll just have to last a little longer!" she shouted.

"Listen, girl..."

"This man knew my brother, Captain!" she screamed in his face. "He lives!"

Sixty-three: Horrible Things

Over the following days, Rebecca became obsessed with Wren's survival. The words he had spoken while staring into her face haunted her. What had he to be sorry for; why did he need her brother's forgiveness? She tried the Healer on him but had given it up when she saw the Kilaray rushing into it faster and faster with no effect. It had been as if something was siphoning the flow of energy away. She dare not attempt healing him herself.

Rebecca moved a pallet into the hold to be near him should he wake, but after she began refusing to come up for meals, the captain intervened. He had dragged her bodily out of the hold and tied her to the main mast until she agreed to resume sleeping in his cabin. She snuck out after the captain began to snore and sat watching Wren the same night.

The captain turned to the Tremen for assistance. Garin carried her into the cabin the three shared; Maxim had given it to them to share with Will. They took turns standing watch to make sure she slept. She had looked on this as a betrayal of trust and refused to talk to them for two days.

Noe Avaka finally settled it. He agreed, for additional payment, to watch Wren and come to Rebecca if anything changed. She settled reluctantly for the compromise, and so, she found herself on the upper deck, watching the seas as they traveled southward.

Fayit and Maien took turns directing Will in his navigation of the ship. They pointed to the skies, speaking of the patterns in the air and stars. Will followed their instructions as best he could.

Garin sat beside Rebecca, the ship's grey striped cat nestled in his lap, he seemed as out of place as she felt. Finally, she gave up on her silence with the Tremen. In a voice cracked with lack of use she turned to the huge beast-like man.

"Do...do you know where we are going?" she asked. He looked at her as if the days of silence had not occurred.

"The women hunt for the location of the gathering," he said plainly.

"What gathering?" she asked.

"The God Lights show signs for the need of a gathering. We travel to where its location will be," he said. God Lights were what the Tremen called the Kilaray, Rebecca knew.

"Why don't they know where the location will be?"

"The God Lights have not settled yet. Do not worry, Rebecca of Dulac, the women know of what they do," he put one of his huge paw-hands on her shoulder.

That night Rebecca slept in the captain's cabin. She sat awake long into the night, thinking about Wren. Eventually, her lack of sleep took her. Astenos was as ever vigilant in her dreams.

Rebecca awoke the following morning with a strange sense that something wrong was in the room with her. She was instantly alert, her hand flying to Astenos's hilt. She sat up to find Wren sitting at the captain's desk, shaving his cheeks in a salt water basin. She saw his eyes flick to hers in the mirror, and the haughty grin came to his mouth.

He was shirtless; Rebecca could see healed scars across his back and arms. The place where the dark-clad man's knife – the Husked Man's knife – had plunged into his back looked as healed as the others. He had strange runic symbols adorning his flesh from his waist to his neck. Something seemed odd about those symbols, the feeling she had looking at them was that they were broken, all but one. The last seemed to hold some power to her. Three interlocking triangles surrounded with minute script were tattooed onto his back and chest, over the place Rebecca felt the pull of the Kilaray in her, over the location of his soul.

She stood and froze rigid, staring at Wren's reflection in the small mirror. A form hovered over his shoulder in the reflection. Its skull-like head lacked a lower jaw; its skeletal hands stroked Wren's head like a loved pet. Its whole form had the consistency of smoke and flowed like the thinnest silk in rushing water. Wren's smile never faltered when he spoke.

"You can see it too then, little sister," his voice was rough and cracked. "That doesn't surprise me."

"What is it?" she said aghast at the thing in the mirror. It looked at her with malevolent dead white eyes, and pulled close to Wren's ear as though to whisper in it.

"We called them Murmurs," he said, cleaning his razor in the basin and drying his face with a rag. He stood and pulled a clean shirt from the captain's bunk. "It has its advantages," he brushed a hand over the scar where the knife had been. "It'd take more than that to put me down; the Murmurs take care of their vessels. The captain took some convincing before he untied me, though. He has the big beasties just outside the door to make sure I didn't kill you."

"The captain told me...told me about the Blue," she said cautiously.

Wren's face looked grim as he nodded. "He spoke to me about that," he said.

"Well," she said, looking at him as he buttoned his shirt.

"Well, what?" he said with a laugh.

"You said you could feel others, other Husked Men," she said. "That's what you are; isn't it? You're like that one that stabbed you; you're one of them."

His eyes narrowed, as he looked at her.

"Not yet," he said, and he walked out onto the deck.

Rebecca ran out after him. Garin and Fayit were at her side when she came up the stairs.

"I'm not done with you, Skip Tracer," she shouted at Wren's back. Men on the deck turned to see what was happening.

He turned so quickly Rebecca thought he was going to attack. Garin began to rumble in his chest and Fayit's face was concerned.

"Done with me!" he said, laughing at her. "Little sister, you don't get to tell me when you're done with me. I saved your life in the streets of that town, remember?"

"And she saved yours, and all our lives from that mob in Nor Harbor, Mraxian," growled the captain, stumping down the steps from the upper deck. Wren looked over at the captain, anger flashing across his face. "She saved you again; for, when I saw what you are, I wanted to cut your head off. Right now, she's the only reason you're still standing on me deck."

Wren turned and walked toward the bow without a word. Rebecca stared after him.

"The Pictsie says he should be safe for the time, something to do with seals," said the captain, indicating his own chest where Wren's tattoos were. "It's why he hasn't been taken yet by the...the Murmur he called it."

Rebecca looked at the captain. "You said 'taken yet'," she said.

"Like I said before, there's no stopping it. The Pictsie agreed; eventually that thing that has him will Husk him out."

Rebecca found herself staring out to the waves ahead of Illandra's Heart. She stood silent beside Wren. He leaned against the rail watching the grey sea in the morning sun. He still had the blue scarf tied at his neck, the tails whipping in the wind behind him.

"What's with the scarf?" she asked.

He looked over at her, anger still on his face, but it melted as he looked into her eyes.

"It's a reminder," he said.

"Of what?" she asked.

"You ask too many questions, little sister," he said, looking back out to sea.

"Why do you keep calling me that? You know my name, Skip Tracer," she said emphasizing the title.

He shook his head, a wry grin jumping to his mouth, and refused to speak. So Rebecca went on, she tried to be less aggressive.

"Why is it that you didn't turn me in to the New Dominion, Skip Tracer?"

"Do you know what twice damned means, little sister?" he said instead of answering. "When the Red Fist took me prisoner I was younger than you. They had us kill before they began spiking us with the Blue. Our first victims were other Silvarishmen." He turned to

548

look her in the eyes. "They liked to pick our relatives for our first kills. They found my mother, put her against a wall, put a rifle in my hands, a pistol to my head. It was kill or die." He stopped; his face never even flinched. "Here I stand. Slaying your kin damns you in the Fates' eyes and the First Father's. I know where I go when my Murmur takes me."

Rebecca forced herself not to cry. The man was trying to make her turn away from him, but she wanted answers.

"What did you do to my brother?" she tried not to let anger fill her words.

He looked shocked and then his face hardened and his eyes became ice, his mouth in his usual smirk. "Something horrible," he said.

Astenos was at his throat before she had time to think. Tears welled in her eyes. The haughty smile stayed on Wren's mouth, but his eyes showed sad relief.

"Do it, little sister," he said in calm clear words. "Yours is the only hand I would find peace in taking my head."

Heavy pounding down the deck announced Garin's approach. He grabbed Wren like he meant to tear his arms off.

"What did he do to you, young Rebecca?" Garin said in a near roar.

"He finally gave me a straight answer," she said, sliding Astenos back into his scabbard. "Garin, would you take this man from my sight?"

Sixty-four:
Beneath the Scarf

Illandra's Heart sailed southward. Rebecca had slipped into a deep despondency. The crew stepped light around her as she sat staring silently out to sea. She sought the solitude of the crow's nest, finding the height and the silence a relief on her mind. So it was she that spotted the strange sail on the horizon.

The Tremen had been searching the skies, night and day, for a pattern to emerge that would point them to the gathering. The captain had begun to declare his impatience with their methods. Will had given up trying to understand the women and simply functioned as a go between for them and Maxim. Noe Avaka seemed the only one interested in talking to Wren, and so they remained holed up below decks. Rebecca refused to suffer Wren's presence.

She had climbed the mast to be alone as she had for the past four days. She carried her grandfather's journal aloft. She had forgotten it entirely in her distraction over Wren. She had begun to read what was on the new pages when Astenos tweaked her mind. She looked up, the late day sun showing a red ball in the western sky, and there it was. A sail, lit orange against the setting sun, floated on the arcing horizon. Rebecca thought she was seeing things at first but when the sail persisted she called out.

At twilight the ships met, the human-sized Illandra's Heart and the Tremen-scaled Benon Hurna. The ship was enormous, constructed from some strange pale wood Rebecca had never laid eyes on. It was carved and shaped like a piece of weathered rock, or some enormous bone. It had odd rigging too. Massive kites cast out in front of the ship, pulling it in even the lightest of winds.

When the ships were anchored and lashed together Rebecca waited with the captain and the gathered crew. From the decks, Rebecca could see that the vast majority of the Tremen ship's crew were women, their cheeks and chins lacked the beards of the men. Maien went to exchange formalities with the Benon Hurna's Pride Mistress. She returned looking concerned.

"The other Pride Mistress refuses to meet with the man kind's envoy," she said to Captain Rhannon. "She will allow only Rebecca aboard. They can see her pattern in the skies and know that is why the gathering was needed. They do not, however, see the reason I have brought other man kinds."

Maien sounded defeated. Rebecca was confused.

"Why won't they have others aboard?" she asked Maien.

"We have suffered losses at the hands of your kind," she said. "Our people hold a great dislike of the results of our dealings with man kinds. You must come, Rebecca of Dulac, the other Pride Mistress waits."

"She doesn't leave the ship without me," Wren said, walking toward the group around Rebecca and Maien. Rebecca's anger flared at the sight of the man.

"What are you doing here?" she asked.

"You didn't take my head when you had your chance, little sister, and my debt and promise was not made to you," he said, his customary smile on his face.

Garin rumbled deep in his chest; Wren seemed to take no notice. Noe Avaka stood in his natural form looking like he'd rather be anywhere but where he was.

551

"No man kind but Rebecca will board the Benon Hurna without the permission of her Pride Mistress," Maien said into the growing tension.

"Then no human boards the ship," Wren said, looking up into Maien's crisp blue eyes. "Including her," he pointed to Rebecca. "I have her safe keeping and will not allow her out of my protection."

"How dare you, you pompous, swaggering, evil man," Rebecca roared at him. "I trust them more than I will ever trust you."

Wren looked like he suppressed a laugh. Garin stepped in between her and Wren and things became riotous. Wren moved like the wind. He plunged forward, grabbing Garin's wrist and rolling backwards. He threw Stevens, who came to help, into Maxim and Will, knocking them to the deck boards. Rebecca moved to pull Astenos from his scabbard but Wren was on her in an instant, slamming Astenos back into the sheath. He grabbed her and pulled her behind him, restraining her hands in the process. He stood as a shield between the crew, the Tremen, and her.

"There was a promise before the Fates made. She goes nowhere I cannot go," Wren shouted at the stunned crew. Garin had regained his feet and stormed through the crowd roaring in anger. He went for the savage looking knife at his belt.

Wren pointed the jagged blade at Garin, who looked bewildered at his empty sheath. "I think not beastie," Wren said, an amused smirk on his face. "Now, you," he pointed the blade at Maien; Garin snarled in outrage. "Get back to that ship and renegotiate our boarding."

Maien put a huge paw-like hand to Garin's shoulder to calm him. When she spoke, the peace in her voice made Rebecca respect her nerve.

"You will never board that ship, Cursed One. We do not treat with creatures of Discordia or their hosts." Her voice was cool yet powerful.

Wren flinched at the words as though slapped, and he released Rebecca's hands. Something caught Rebecca's eye; Wren looked, for the first time she had noticed, unsure and defeated. He lowered Garin's knife and tossed it to clatter at the huge Tremen's feet. He turned to look at Rebecca; his grayish blue-green eyes searched her yellow-green ones. He reached out a hand to touch her face and she flinched away. He nodded with a sad grimace on his face and walked silently through the crew; they parted to let him pass toward the bow.

Noe Avaka's growling voice spoke with caution. "Perhaps an arrangement can be made," Rebecca looked at the little fox-like man; he was jittery as though about to take flight. "Pride Mistress Maien would it go against customs to meet aboard this ship?" he asked.

Maien followed Wren with her eyes as she spoke.

"I may be able to convince the other Pride Mistress," she turned to Rebecca. "You must take rein on that one, young Rebecca. If he insists on having your Guard Keeping you will be held to account for his actions according to our customs, just as I am held to account for Garin's."

Rebecca felt renewed heat growing in her cheeks. She didn't want Wren near her and now she would be held responsible for what he did. She moved to speak but Maien was already moving across to the Benon Hurna. Captain Rhannon approached Rebecca as the crew dispersed.

"I won't tell you, you were wrong to let him live, girl," he said with sympathy. "Maybe you should talk to him. It's hard to find a decent man in this world let alone one who will fight with that much fire."

Rebecca looked into the captain's sea-colored eyes and he grinned. He put a hand on her shoulder and moved off to check on Will and Maxim.

Rebecca looked to the bow; Wren watched the moon rise over the dark sea. She strode down the deck to give him a tongue lashing. As she neared he spoke without turning back.

"He did this himself," Wren said, putting his hand to his chest. Rebecca stopped dead to listen. She could see him rubbing the area where the symbol was tattooed over his chest. "It was your face that did it." He turned and that infuriating smile was back. "I thought he had come back to haunt me in that hold."

"What did you do to my brother?" She heard the words leave her mouth before she knew she had thought them.

"He found me when he and the First Born moved into Silvari. Your brother stopped his men from killing me when they saw what I was. I had been two days without the Blue. He looked at me with those startling eyes and then over my shoulder. I knew he saw it somehow, my Murmur. He had me tied up and sat with me until the ache left me. He made me an offer when my mind was clear enough."

Rebecca was entrapped she felt her anger leave her. Astenos, his eagerness to defend her ever present, listened engrossed.

"He summoned one of the Beltari men that had joined him at that point and together they set to work. I struggled to resist the Murmur's pull on my soul. They feed on our souls, you see, as the last step to make a bridge to take our bodies. Seb devised a temporary seal, an anchor to hold my soul to this world." Wren put his hand to his chest. "He told me that I would be able to live for a time, able to resist the urge for the Blue that the Murmur brings. But I could never use it again or it would speed me toward my end."

"Why, did you do it then?" Rebecca asked. "Why did you keep taking it?"

"It wasn't my choice. I was captured on a mission for your brother. The men that took me spiked me and the urge was back," he said. "Before I left on my doomed mission, your brother brought me to his tent andgave me the other end of his bargain."

Rebecca's hands were cold; she stepped closer.

"You will fail, Wren Tobias my friend, against your burden," he said, quoting her brothers words. It was as though she could hear them in her head. "I do not blame you. You must find her in her time of need and guard her as only you can. You, without fear of death, shall be her shield against it. Find my sister, Wren, after this night is through and what will be done has been done. She must fulfill what I now know I was not meant to do." Tears welled in both of their eyes. "I promised him, Rebecca Dulac. I promised your brother I would guard your life. Don't take that from me, I beg you. Don't make me an oath breaker as well as a traitor." He pulled away the blue scarf around his neck and there, branded into the flesh, was a crude hand, a glyph on the palm, the Traitor's Mark, Adarian's mark.

Sixty-five: The Gathering

Rebecca had to get away. She turned without a word, and ran down the deck. Men turned to watch her pass but she took no notice. She bounded into the captain's cabin and slammed the door behind her.

Her head thundered with emotions. She could not put her mind on one thought without others jumping in to join them. Wren was the one who had done it. He was the one who had betrayed her brother to the Red Fist. He was the reason she and all the others had been forced out of Arnora. He was the reason her brother was dead. Astenos raged with her anger and her hand ached for his hilt to fill it. She should take his head if that's what he wanted. She should end his miserable existence.

Yes, it must be a miserable existence; mustn't it? A thought bubbled through her roiling mind. No, she had no pity for the traitor. *Are you so sure? He did save your life and you his.* No, no, she had not known before; if she had, she would have left him to die on the streets of Nor Harbor. *Would you have?* Yes, yes I would have left him for the Strynges or the other Husked Men or anyone who would do it for her. *Are you so cowardly now that you won't do it yourself? Look him in the eyes as you do it, take his head and end his half life.*

Rebecca collapsed on the floor where she stood and sobbed. She could not do it. However much she now loathed Wren, she wouldn't be able to do that final task, not now, not in cold blood. How could her brother have done this to her? The man had betrayed him, had betrayed them all, why him?

Perhaps we will need him. That thought came through from Astenos. Rebecca paused in her grief.

"What do you mean *need him*?" she thought to him.

I hear your thoughts my dearest Mate. I feel your torment but your mind is reaching to save this man. You want to get rid of him as I wanted to rid you of the other Soul.

"It's not the same Astenos," she wailed at him. "He as good as killed my brother."

And the other Soul may have as good as killed your grandfather.

Rebecca did not know why Astenos had suddenly shifted his feelings toward Wren but she thought over his words to her. She heard shouted voices from above decks but she ignored them. She needed to think. She found her satchel and pulled it open. She searched through its contents for the small triangular compass her brother had given her. The one last thing she had left of him.

She found it and looked at its face. She could use some direction now if she ever had needed any. She watched the needle spin as she held it in her palm. The engraved patterns on the face of the compass looked oddly familiar. Lines and transecting circular patterns etched deep into the bronze face. The needle of the compass acted odd now too; it refused to settle in on north, but instead spun erratically. She wiped her eyes and focused on the shifting needle. A loud thud from above broke her concentration and she put the compass back to investigate what was happening.

Men were scattered across the deck, running to and fro. She found Noe Avaka as he ran for the lower deck.

"What's happening?" she asked in confusion.

"A sail on the horizon," he said in his growling voice. "I will not be pleased if I am unable to collect my full payment for my services to you." He darted off to seek the lower decks.

Rebecca watched the chaos of the ship's crew for a moment and then went to find the captain. He stood on the upper deck, holding Will's spy glass, looking northward. She approached him and he lowered the glass.

"It's Tremen," he announced. "It'll be here within an hour by me guess."

The confusion on the deck lessened but the tension was still palpable. Maien had not returned from the Benon Hurna. Men stared off at the pale sweeping lines of the approaching ship; their faces held anxiety, they didn't like waiting, these men. They were used to movement at sea.

Garin and Fayit watched the approaching ship with distinct apprehension. She joined them and it was Fayit that spoke.

"You know you will have to go with them, Garin," she said, never taking her eyes from the sail. A banner was becoming visible now, a golden tree on a deep green field. "They will need you if we read the pattern correctly."

Garin's mane of sandy fur ruffled. "I cannot leave, Fayit; I have a debt to young Rebecca."

"Your duty is first to me and your people," said Maien. Rebecca spun to see her striding up the steps to the upper deck. She locked eyes on Rebecca. "The other Pride Mistress refused my offer to meet aboard this ship." The captain threw up his hands and stalked over to Maxim leaning at the useless wheel. Maien stared after him. "She says you must come now if the gathering is to meet."

Rebecca looked down the length of the ship; Wren stood hidden in shadows at the bow, his back to the ship. *Sebastian sent him for you*, she thought.

"We wait for the other ship," Rebecca said. "If this gathering has been called because of me then it will have to be held under my terms. If the Pride Mistress aboard the Benon Hurna refuses to have Captain Rhannon and…" she paused for the strength she needed for her next words, "…and my Guard Keeper, then perhaps this coming ship will suffer we humans." Maien looked shocked for a moment then turned to Fayit.

"You were right about that fierce streak, I fear," she looked amused. "So be it. I will inform the Pride Mistress and return to wait here with you."

The second ship to approach was twice again as big as Illandra's Heart. The crew of this second ship, Rebecca could see, seemed mainly comprised of men. Their manes and beards in colors ranging from gold to ginger to brown. When the ship finally settled on the opposite side of Illandra's Heart, Garin was the one to board it.

She had talked to Garin and given him her requests, which is why she had tracked down Noe Avaka. The little man could seem to vanish if you didn't keep your eye on him, even in his bright rust-colored coat. He was meticulously examining some of the Linked objects Rebecca had carried with her in the captain's cabin. He froze as she opened the door and then relaxed when he saw it was her.

"You startle me, girl child," he said in his growling voice. "I see I have not made an arrangement with a pauper," he said, holding up a metallic cube she knew to be a Screener.

"Noe, we have never discussed exactly what my debt to you would be," she said, settling in beside him on the captain's bunk. "I don't have anything of value besides what I carry with me. But I can tell you I will see that you are repaid whatever you say is fair."

He looked at her inquisitively. "You are too humble, girl child. You carry with you a fortune that would make some of my people's wealthiest envious. Do not fear; I will wait for your debt to be filled."

"What exactly are you going to want as payment, Noe?" she felt a bit confused.

"Mistress Dulac you are playing the fool. Certainly you would not enter into a bargain without knowing the terms," he coughed a chuckle that died away with the look on Rebecca's face. "Well, I see then. Very well, we Shint Pictsies accept only one thing for payments from man kinds." He held up the Screener.

"Noe, I don't know if I can let you have these quite yet."

"No, no, girl child, I don't want to take what belongs to you. I want what you *have*." He put a finger to his head. "Your knowledge of the Kilaray, this is what I require. Your defense of this vessel has begun to settle your debt for what I have done for you. That was quite an impressive display of Link work. I would almost feel at ease in offering you more of my services from what I saw, almost."

"Well, I could use some actually," she said, seizing on the man's words. Noe Avaka became very still, his eyes measured Rebecca.

"What do you request of me?" he asked in a shrewd voice.

Rebecca went to Wren while they waited for Garin's return answer. She approached and waited for Wren to turn and speak. He kept his back to her. She noticed he had retied the blue scarf around his throat. She felt acid in her throat. She railed herself for what she was doing.

"When Garin returns I hope to board this second ship," she said, keeping the heat in her voice for strength. "Captain Rhannon and Maien will have two companions..." Wren cocked his head to listen, "...and I and two of my own will join them. Noe Avaka has agreed to be my second I...I will need you to be my first." Wren's head nodded in a jerky way and his hand went to his eyes.

"Thank you," he said in a thick voice. Rebecca walked away from him to await Garin's return. She would trust her brother's choice; he had always watched out for her. She just prayed for the strength to forgive Wren; she thought she would learn to breathe water first.

When Garin crossed the plank, he was alive with excitement. He spoke to Maien first.

"The Pride Mistress of Saied Freej has agreed to young Rebecca's terms," his face broke into a broad grin. "She has also agreed to allow the Cursed..." Garin halted as Wren approached; his face wore a more solemn expression. "...Wren of Tobias to board as young Rebecca's Guard Keeper. There is more Maien..." he moved close and spoke in a low rumbling whisper. Maien's face flashed in what Rebecca could only describe as relief and then she regained her composure.

"I must inform the Benon Hurna's Pride Mistress," Maien said, smiling at the end. "She will not be pleased with *his* attendance." She said to Garin, and he nodded in agreement.

Arrangements set, the procession of those to attend the gathering readied to board the Saied Freej. Six women from the Benon Hurna strode aboard Illandra's Heart, three men, the Pride Mistress' Guard Keepers Rebecca learned, stalked after them in forest-colored clothing. The women were bedecked in flowing robes of greens, blues, and grays, colors of the sea. Their manes were trimmed and groomed

561

and an exotic spicy smell drifted along after them. They eyed the human crew of Illandra's Heart with contempt but their greatest interest seemed to be in Rebecca. Their eyes widened at the sight of her and quickly resumed their animalistic measuring quality. When their eyes passed over Noe Avaka standing to her side, they laughed, but as they spotted Wren they became visibly disturbed. Their fur, which had been so well groomed, ruffled, and low rumbled growls came from their chests, loudest from the men's. Wren simply smiled and checked for dirt under his nails.

"Do you have to be so arrogant?" Rebecca growled at him under her breath as the Tremen passed. Noe Avaka actually looked amused.

"You took me on, little sister," he said, all the haughty sureness returned to his voice. "I won't start trouble for you, but I'll end it if they do."

Captain Rhannon went first, after the Tremen, carrying a crate Rebecca had seen before in the secret compartment in the hold. Will and Maxim followed him. Will turned to Rebecca and flashed his silver-toothed grin and then shook his head in disbelief. Rebecca walked up the plank that had bridged the two vessels, Wren a step behind her, followed by Noe Avaka, who had insisted he bring the satchel containing the Linked objects and her grandfather's journal.

The Saied Freej was enormous by human standards, built for people on average half again as big as a man. Rebecca had recollections of being younger trying to reach for cabinets made for adults. Tremen stood by to watch the procession of humans board their ship; their faces were hard to read but she would have said they looked on guard. A large Tremen man with a mane of dark brown greeted them as they boarded. He took the crate from the captain, handing it to another who carried it further onto the ship, and spoke.

"My name is Harnik. I am Saied Freej's Pride Mistress's Guard Keeper. I welcome the man kind's envoy and would have you follow me to the gathering room," he said.

They followed Harnik across the deck to a pair of massive, pale, caved doors. He opened them and warm light spilled out on the darkened deck boards. The six Tremen women from the Benon Hurna strode inside as though this were their ship, followed by their Guard Keepers. Captain Rhannon was far more graceful, bowing his head to Harnik as he passed through the arched opening. Will and Maxim followed his lead. Rebecca thanked the large Tremen as she passed and she heard Noe Avaka growl something similar; Wren's silence sounded loud in her ears.

The room had a low ceiling, low for the sixteen huge Tremen that stood awaiting their entrance. The room was slightly arched and seemed to have a feel of a cave or den of sorts. Ornately crafted lanterns hung from the ceiling and cast the room in a golden light. The banner Rebecca had seen trailing above the ship was hung from the walls at either side of a great empty throne.

Harnik spoke when Maien, Fayit, and Garin were inside and the door was closed.

"The gathering called for by the God Lights may begin. I present the Pride Mistress of the Benon Hurna, Sanjeen and her first and second, the man kind's envoy Captain Pell of Rhannon and his first and second, The Touched envoy Rebecca of Dulac and her first and second, and the Rogue Nation Pride Mistress Maien and her first and second."

Rebecca listened to the titles with great interest. *What was the Rogue Nation and since when was she the Touched envoy*, she though. She stared around the room at the faces of the gathered Tremen and her breath caught. Standing closest to the empty throne was a familiar face set in a black mane.

"Tagus!" she screamed and ran to hug the huge Tremen. She ignored the bursts of outraged growls and roars. He caught her and pulled her to him, nuzzling his huge black mane against her head. This was met with as much indignation as her outburst. "I thought you had been killed. Are you alright? Is Alaric with you?"

He smiled down at her and spoke in his deep booming voice. "I am well Rebecca. Your Mecharical friend fought well but we were separated during the battle. I would not fear for that one though, he is harder than he appears."

"What is this, Tagus?" growled Sanjeen the Benon Hurna's Pride Mistress. "Why have *you* come to this gathering? Why do you bond with this man kind girl?"

"I have birth right and duty to attend this gathering, Sanjeen," he looked to the throne and then back. "As for my bonding with this girl; she saved my friend from the death grip." His next words were for Rebecca alone. "You must return to your first and second Rebecca."

Rebecca could not hold back the smile as she returned to stand with Wren and Noe Avaka. She had feared for Alaric and Tagus, her hopes returned that he had somehow made it safely away as Tagus had. Wren leaned close to her, as she toyed with the cuff on her wrist, and whispered into her ear.

"You seem to have made friends in odd places," he said indicating Tagus.

An elegant Tremen woman stepped into the center of the gathering room. Her mane was nearly as dark as Tagus' and she wore a flowing deep blue gown with jagged gold embroidered patterns. She spoke in a breathy voice and Rebecca knew she was a Pride Mistress.

"I am Aleren, Pride Mistress of the Saied Freej, King Ship of the Tremen peoples. I welcome you to this most significant of gatherings." She paused to look at the others encircling the room. "I am pleased to see so many of our brothers and sisters here, as well as other branches of the Tree," she looked to the humans and Noe Avaka.

These words seemed to have meaning for the Tremen; for, they all bowed their heads a moment. Rebecca and Captain Rhannon followed their lead and waited for Aleren to resume her speech, but it was Sanjeen that spoke into the silence.

"You bring dishonor on the King Ship, Aleren," she growled with contempt. "The feet of man kinds and Pictsies have not sullied our decks in centuries, but that is nothing to allowing this…" she pointed at Wren with rage clear on her increasingly animal like face, "this cursed thing to walk freely into our sanctum."

"If you have something you'd like to say to me beastie," said Wren, "I'll have it out here and now."

Rebecca was horror-struck and the Tremen growled their rage. Tagus stepped into the center beside Aleren. A roar that shook the lanterns hanging from the ceiling tore from his mouth.

"Silence!"

The hiss of the flames dancing on their wicks was the only sound that could be heard.

"You, Sanjeen, have dishonored this gathering with your outbursts for the last time. You, who know our ways, will hold to the

565

customs of our people or *you* will be asked to leave this ship. Wren of Tobias is Rebecca's Guard Keeper. He will be afforded our courtesy as we would show her. She would also be well-warned that her Guard Keeper's actions will be held to her account," Tagus finished looking into her eyes and she understood his warning. He stepped back to allow Aleren to resume. She continued in a stately manner Rebecca respected.

"We can see in the God Lights the need for this gathering. This pattern has not been seen in many centuries. Not since the Tree was split and our races parted ways has such a need been observed by our eyes." She looked to the humans and Noe Avaka standing farthest from the throne. "Your ignorance of our ways will be forgiven for we have held our seclusion closer than our former bonds to you. This has been our error."

The Tremen from the Benon Hurna and several others standing around the room bristled at this; they obviously felt otherwise. Aleren raised her huge paw-hand to settle the others.

"Tagus has convinced us of this error. The Rogue King's words have made us see reason in light of the pattern of the God Lights," she said.

Rebecca looked to Tagus. *Rogue King*, what was this about? She turned and found Garin's eyes and his face said for her to wait. Aleren still spoke.

"Rebecca of Dulac, would you step forward?" she asked. The other Tremen pricked their ears at her name.

Rebecca looked around nervously before stepping into the center of the ring of gathered Tremen. She felt suddenly small, not just in comparison to the massive forms of the Tremen but because she didn't know what these people would ask of her.

566

A murmur of voices went around the room. She could hear snippets of what they said.

"So bright her pattern."

"Yes, yes I can see it."

"Dulac? But he was the thief was he not?"

"The eyes Sanjeen, can you see the eyes?"

She felt like she was being prodded and poked from their stares and gaping. She had a great desire to be out from under their scrutiny. Tagus's presence was reassuring though. He nodded to her and spoke, turning her and placing his huge paws on her shoulders.

"You see now what Maien and I saw when we first tracked her pattern. She is the one who can bring us out of our dark times. You see the companions she brings with her, the man kind who brought us back what was stolen from us," he indicated Captain Rhannon. "A Shintish Pictsie, one of our lost little brothers, and yes one of those who would be our enemy but one who has managed control of his demon."

Rebecca's heart stopped, expecting another retort from Wren but she could see from his grimaced face it would not come. Rebecca felt relief wash over her.

The Tremen however looked to struggle with Tagus' words and it was Sanjeen's voice that spoke for them.

"How can we be sure, Tagus? What if we are mistaken; she could bring ruin on our heads as well as salvation." Rebecca was glad to hear the moderation in her voice now.

"What are we to do, Sanjeen; wait until our people are shackled to the last cub?" said Tagus. "Should we delay while the New Dominion steals our lands and kills those who stand in their way? We

567

are diminishing, Sanjeen. We all know it. This girl may offer us a chance to change that."

The Tremen looked thoughtful, even Sanjeen. Captain Rhannon cleared his throat and spoke for the first time.

"I be but a sailor and smuggler but I've seen what this girl can do, and I doubt that the legends of the Philistari could match what I did see with me own eyes." He looked at her with pride on his face. "She has been naught but a blessing from the Fates since I met her. I owe her my life several times over as do most of me crew."

Rebecca was touched by his words. Her cheeks felt warm and her nervousness lessened. Garin stepped forward and spoke next.

"I attest to her skill as well. She brought me back from the embrace of the God Lights. If you refuse to see her pattern for what it is then you are all blind," he directed his words at Sanjeen.

"What would you have us do Tagus? Are we to break custom like the last time we had dealings with humans?" Sanjeen asked, glaring at Maien. The other Tremen nodded at her words.

Rebecca felt the mood in the room turning against Tagus. Whispered acknowledgements of Sanjeen's words raced along the line of Tremen. She understood little of what was happening but she could only benefit with the Tremen behind her.

Speak Rebecca; they will listen to your words, said Astenos

"I do not ask you to betray your secrets," she said into the growing din. Silence crashed on her ears as they listened. "I don't know if I am who you think I am—"

"You see the girl admits—"

"Silence, Sanjeen," roared Aleren. "Please, continue Rebecca of Dulac." Again the Tremen's ears pricked.

"Um…I don't know if I am who you think I am, but I could use your help. I never wanted any of this. I wanted to live my life with my family but the New Dominion stole that from me. I have been lost ever since, trying to find some peace, but I will never know it with the New Dominion extending Adarian's rule further and further.

They hold my closest friends in a prison. They hunt me like a rabid animal. I want peace but this is all those like the New Dominion understand." She pulled Astenos from his scabbard, holding him above her head; she could feel the pull of the Kilaray at her soul. His edges gleamed too bright in the lantern light; the Tremen gasped. "I don't know how far I can get alone, but I need to get to the Gates of Yuriah." More gasps and growls of outrage. "I only hope to find something to end the New Dominion." She sheathed Astenos and waited.

"This girl speaks the double talk of man kinds. Dulac, the name of the last human we treated with. She is the descendent of thieves and liars. She says she doesn't want us to betray our secrets, and then asks us to allow her what we vowed to protect?" Sanjeen's words were full of contempt.

"What *we* vowed to protect!" Noe Avaka said his voice full of indignation. He looked shocked that he had spoken but quickly regained his composure. "*We* vowed to protect the Barrier Port, Pride Mistress, the Pictsies not the Tremen. It was placed in your lands but we sealed it away. Only one of the man kinds can open it, I believe that to be Mistress Dulac. I have already aided her and will continue to do so without the Tremen if needs be."

Rebecca was quite shocked but gratified at Noe Avaka's words.

"You will never find the Barrier Port, *hider,*" hissed Sanjeen at Noe Avaka. "You may have sealed the Port, but its location is known only to us."

"Not anymore," Rebecca said. Sanjeen's eyes popped and the snarl on her face made Rebecca step back into Tagus. Wren launched himself between Rebecca and Sanjeen; empty handed, the cold look he had on his face held the massive woman at bay. Rebecca needed to cool the fires she had started and began to recite what she had seen while holding the metallic triangle Captain Rhannon had given her.

"In a dense forest that seems to have never weathered a winter the Gates of Yuriah are hidden, below the constellation of the same name." Sanjeen took a step back at Rebecca's words. "They stand like two arching pillars in a cliff face; two trees twined together partially block their view." She felt Tagus's huge paw on her shoulder again.

"Do you know Rebecca? Have you seen what is within?" he asked in an astonished voice.

Rebecca nodded and looked around the room, catching all the eyes around her in a defiant glare. "A Tower of Light," she announced, they gasped. "It reaches skyward, taller than anything I have ever seen. It stands in the center of a huge…uh," she couldn't think of how to describe the pit; she had no words for its breadth.

"A huge crater that stretches a mile across," said Tagus. "The ground heaved and the winds that followed the Tower's impact flattened trees for as far as the eye could see. How have you seen this place Rebecca?"

"She has not!" bellowed Sanjeen. "Dulac, Tagus, Dulac, the girl has been filled with the stolen knowledge of our people. She has never seen the Tower, she couldn't have."

Her words fell on the silence that had gripped the room. Noe Avaka held a triangular shaped covered object above his head; a green mist leaked through the leather covering. The Tremen were transfixed on the object in the Pictsie's strange hands.

Tagus took the object from Noe Avaka and pulled the triangular shape out. His eyes flicked from its engraved surfaces to Rebecca then to Sanjeen. She stood, panting through her gaped mouth. She seemed to have lost some of her fight.

Maien spoke for the first time. She seemed conspicuously reserved in the presence of the other Tremen. She wore forest-colored tunic and cloak, lacking the grandeur of the other Pride Mistresses but Rebecca thought she looked just as regal as Aleren, despite her attire.

"When she first crossed our path," Maien began, talking more to Aleren than the others, "she carried a book. Her grandfather had included what he learned from the Rogue Nations, from me." Snarls and growls met these words. "He had sought to hide the information until it would be needed. There was a Pictsie seal within the book, hiding the pages from our world. That seal has been opened." She looked to Noe Avaka. "Rebecca is guided by the God Lights like no other I have known, Aleren. They bring to her those that she needs to help her. How can we deny the God Light's pattern? Our own signs have been hardest for us to see but it is there." She turned now, addressing the others. "A Tremen pattern must be added to Rebecca's or the doom you fear will be all but a certainty."

"She is the herald of change, Sanjeen," Maien said imploringly. "This gathering says as much. Man kinds, Pictsies, others," she bowed her head to Wren, "and for the first time in three decades I am allowed in the sanctum of the King Ship. I do not ask forgiveness for what I betrayed of our people. I only ask that you see that the outcome I foresaw has come at last, Sanjeen, my sister."

Rebecca was astonished at Maien's words. She had never said anything about knowing her grandfather, and she had been cast out for what she had told him.

Sanjeen refused to answer Maien's words and instead spoke to Tagus.

"Despite my sister's words, you can see for yourself this man kind child is a thief. She comes aboard a ship of thieves, bearing stolen artifacts of our people, and in possession of our stolen knowledge."

Tagus' look of astonishment flashed to anger.

"I do not believe your words, Sanjeen. Your anger at your blood kin has blinded you. Captain Pell of Rhannon has returned to us what was stolen. Rebecca has seen through the Barrier Port using this," he hefted the triangle, "which was given to the man kinds to prove when the herald had come. Her grandfather's crimes shall not have any bearing on her. He sought only to prepare the herald of his people, a task for which we should have undertaken ourselves."

Sanjeen looked to the others surrounding her for support; they refused to meet her eyes. Her belligerence shriveled a little without their backing and she was silent. Aleren moved to the center of the room once more. Order seemed to descend on the Tremen with her retaking of the gathering. Tagus resumed his place by the throne, Sanjeen melted back into the others that had come from the Benon Hurna, and Maien resumed her post beside Garin and Fayit. Noe Avaka took Wren's arm; he reluctantly left Rebecca's side to stand near the door. Rebecca felt Aleren's paws on her shoulders as she went to follow and knew she was to stay.

"We have had heated words in this room. Change brings fear, fear brings inaction, and that we cannot afford. Maien's words have been too long from these walls; we have forgotten her skill at reading the pattern in her absence. What is clear to us all is the need for a Tremen to go forth from this place with Rebecca of Dulac." Sanjeen shifted uneasily. "What is the question is the number of Tremen and from which nations."

The Tremen all seemed to shift now. They clearly had doubt even now. Rebecca felt her cheeks heating under their watchful glares. She doubted herself as well.

"Sanjeen, would you volunteer any of your Pride to follow Rebecca to the Barrier Port?" asked Aleren. Sanjeen scoffed and refused to answer. "Nageel?" Aleren asked of another woman standing at Sanjeen's side. "Ornea?" again silence. She turned to Tagus with pleading in her face.

"I will follow Rebecca of Dulac!" said a gruff voice from near the door. Rebecca spun to see Garin, his eyes locked on hers. "I owe young Rebecca my life and volunteer myself." Rebecca's heart swelled for her friend.

"You know that is impossible my friend," Tagus said in a sad voice. "Your duty is to Maien and she will be needed for the Choosing."

Rebecca felt her stomach drop. Garin looked defeated but Fayit placed a reassuring paw on his back. "I will take my brother's debt as my own." She came to stand beside Rebecca and Aleren. "I have seen this young one's pattern as you all have but I refuse to ignore it as you do. I shall leave here with Rebecca." Maien's eyes were filmed in tears as she looked on Fayit with a prideful smile. Fayit nodded to her.

Aleren waited for others to speak but it was unnecessary; no one else moved. They all looked ashamed in Rebecca's opinion. Aleren spoke once more; her voice sounded sad.

"Then the number of Tremen shall be one, and of the nation which all of Tremore has turned their backs on. It is done." A bell sounded low from somewhere in the ship and the Tremen bowed their heads. "Rebecca of Dulac you have our blessing to pass into our lands to seek out the Barrier Port, known to you as the Gates of Yuriah."

"Thank you," Rebecca said to Aleren. "I thank you for your help, as much as you have seen fit to give." The Tremen around the room looked more shame-faced.

Sixty-six:
Pages from the Past

The Tremen from the Benon Hurna made their way from the gathering room. They seemed eager to put the events of the evening behind them. Maien stood silently as they passed. Sanjeen stopped and for a moment Rebecca thought that words would pass between them. Sanjeen shook her head and marched quickly through the carved pale doors. Some of the tension that had weighed on the room seemed to have left with her. Harnik sealed the doors when Sanjeen was gone.

The ten Tremen that had traveled to the gathering aboard the Saied Freej remained after the others left, as did Captain Rhannon. Will and Maxim looked anxious to leave; they had remained close-mouthed the whole time, seeming to not truly trust their eyes. The remaining Tremen moved closer and began talking quietly. Harnik removed the object that had been inside the crate Captain Rhannon had carried aboard. Rebecca craned her head around to see what appeared to be a massive crown.

"We best be off, I suppose," said Will hopefully.

"Rebecca, you must stay a little longer. Some of what has passed here must be explained if you are to travel our lands," said Aleren. Will's shoulders hunched.

Tagus handed the wrapped triangle back to Noe Avaka as he spoke.

"What you have seen was a sign that we have awaited for centuries." The other Tremen that remained watched Rebecca now. "I cannot tell you what you will find within the Barrier Rebecca, for its secrets are meant for those who finally breach it. We were meant to keep secret the Barrier Port from any who sought to find it. We constructed the Traveler you used to see the Tower. It was made to be used by man kinds who could touch the God Lights but only one with a particular pattern, your pattern, would see the Tower."

"But all anyone would have to do is find the constellation of the Gates to find this Barrier Port," Rebecca said. Tagus shook his head.

"The star markings move with the Barrier Port. The Pictsie could better explain it than I."

"The Port is in drift," growled Noe Avaka. "Our skills work between the planes of worlds. We cast the Port loose after it was sealed. The exact location will remain unknown until it is finally opened."

"How can Fayit show me to this Port then?" Rebecca asked. There was silence. "You mean you don't know? Noe?" She turned to look at the Pictsie. He shook his head.

"The Port can only be found and opened by the one meant to breach the Barrier," said Maien. "Your grandfather was told this when I spoke to him of the Barrier Port."

Rebecca remembered the pages Noe Avaka had pulled from the seal. She pulled open the satchel Noe had carried and pulled out the book. She quickly found the lost pages and began to read where it had left off.

There seem to be certain artifacts that need to be either found or created to pass through the Barrier. We were able to gather this description of something the Tremen Pride Mistress called a Traveler. A sketch of the Triangular object covered one of the missing pages, followed by her grandfather's understanding of it. *I believe it is some kind of a map showing the location only to the rightful entrant. These people are truly mysterious; they seem unwilling or* unable to tell me what they sealed within the Barrier. I am not sure but I think they are hiding something from us. I will continue my inquiries.

Several days seemed to have passed by the dates of the next entry into the journal. *Continuing my exploration of Tremore, I stumbled across a book written in Shintish. It describes the need of a World Strider. I wonder if it has anything to do with this Barrier Port. The Tremen Pride Mistress I spoke to seems to have become more reluctant to speak with me. I must tread more carefully if I am to discover anything more about the Barrier and its contents.*

A few more days' time passed in the journal and the writing that followed seemed hurried, frantic. *The legends are true. Oh, Father above, guide me. Maien, the Pride Mistress has told me something truly amazing. This Barrier Port she has referred to; it is the Gates of Yuriah. How can this be? Some trouble seems to have erupted around Maien's help. Hostilities toward me and the other members of the Expeditionary League are becoming violent. I believe I have broken some taboo in speaking about the Barrier Port. I will remain as long as I can. Maien seems frightened of the repercussions of what she has told me. She has promised me though that she must show me one more thing before I leave. She has planned a meeting in a temple later this evening.*

The following entry seemed subdued to Rebecca. *We are found. Maien has been seized; her Pride and followers are to be exiled. I pray forgiveness for what my actions have caused. They call me thief. We are to leave the Tremen lands forever. I fear I have failed in my goal to treat with the Tremen. What's more I may have destroyed any chance for further advances with their people. They are to send Maien's Pride to the Wilderlands. Their nation has been cut off from their home. My pride and eagerness has cost my friend much. The League and I will sail from Tremore at dawn.*

The following day's date topped the page; a letter was attached midway down in another hand. *We are a miserable lot. The Tremen emissaries we have built relations with seem to scorn us. I am a fool. A messenger*

has given me a letter from Maien; the wax has been broken already. They
obviously have read what she has written to me.

Martan of Dulac, I wish these words could be delivered to you in person, but some things can never be. My words will no doubt be inspected by the other Pride Mistresses, if not the King himself. What I have told you has been the truth. You have seen how we Pride Mistresses read the God Lights; you understand that the Creator tells us what may come. What I have done, I have done because I believe you are connected to the pattern that will bond our people together once more.

Your histories are incomplete. Seek the Pictsies; they may be of assistance. I have instructed this messenger to deliver the Traveler to you. Even my strongest opponents know that it should have been sent to your people long ago. Keep it safe.

The messenger gave me a sealed stone container. They say it will open when
we leave Tremore's shores and with that the Tremen bade us farewell, our questions
still unanswered.

Several pages seemed to have been cut and placed between older pages. Their dates were later and the yellowing of the parchment less. Rebecca turned through them. They were mostly drawings of mechanical workings, parts of a watch or clock. She had to look twice before she believed her eyes. Two very familiar objects were drawn into the added pages. One a large pocket watch, had belonged to her father, the second a triangular compass belonged to her brother. She looked up from the pages and she knew she had everything she needed to find the Gates already. She had had them since she had left Arnora.

"Noe, what is the World Strider?" she asked.

He quirked a smile before he spoke. "I dare say that is you, girl child."

"What have you found, Rebecca?" asked Maien. "I see Martan kept my letter."

"He did everything for me," Rebecca said, feeling sadness for never having known her grandfather. His words had accompanied her for her whole journey, had brought her some comfort even in the most desperate places. "I believe I have everything that will lead me to the Gates. I will need help in understanding how to make it work." She turned to Captain Rhannon. "I will also need someone to take me where I need to start."

"Well, I carried you this far, girl. Did you think I'd leave you in the middle of the sea once we done what we come here to do?" he smiled.

Rebecca turned to Maien and Tagus. "What will you do now? I could use your help if I could have it."

"We must attend the Choosing," said Maien and she looked to Tagus. "Our King has vanished. Our crown was stolen but your Captain Rhannon has returned it to us."

"I am sorry my grandfather caused your exile," she said, feeling embarrassed.

"It was my own choice to aid Martan. You have nothing for which to be sorry. You have proven to those who were here I was not as wrong as they believed; even if they refuse to admit it now. You may have influenced their thinking as well." She turned to Wren when she spoke next.

"Wren of Tobias, if you are to act as Rebecca's Guard Keeper you must be bound to your duty. I will perform the linking ceremony if you are both set in your decisions. It must be agreed upon by both

579

Guard Keeper and Charge." She looked at Rebecca and Wren. Wren nodded his agreement without hesitation; his usual grin was nowhere to be seen. Rebecca waited with an unsettled feeling; Maien's words had a feel of finality, of something that could not be undone. A nudging at her mind from Astenos, her ever present guardian, made her nod her head in agreement.

Maien raised her paws level with her head as she spoke. Her words reverberated inside Rebecca's head. "Wren of Tobias you are charged with the protection of Rebecca of Dulac." An aura of red-gold light formed around Maien's finger tips. She laid one paw upon Wren's head and another upon Rebecca's. Maien closed her eyes and Rebecca felt warmth spread from beneath her paw. It raced along her spine and into every fiber of her body. "Rebecca of Dulac your life and safety are now bound to Wren of Tobias. Guard Keeper, you will be able to find your Charge wherever she may be. Keep safe our hope Wren of Tobias." Rebecca turned to look at Wren; his face held a seriousness she had not seen there before. He nodded to Maien and thanked her.

"Maien, we must depart if we are to reach Tremor by the second sunrise of the Choosing," Aleren said. "To our guests, we bid peace upon you." The remaining Tremen bowed their heads and murmured, "Peace upon you."

Rebecca hugged Maien, Garin, and Tagus, receiving their bonding purrs in return. Her Tremen friends did likewise with Fayit. Captain Rhannon thanked the Tremen for the honor they had shown him and passed through the massive carved doors. Noe Avaka bowed to the Tremen, his strange hands outstretched before him and recited words in a language Rebecca did not understand. *Tor a Sporsa so a Arada propea garder onas multo.*

"What did you say to them?" she asked as they emerged into growing dawn on the deck of the Saied Freej.

"In your words I said, 'May the Seeds of the Tree grow together once more,'" he said, wearing an amused grin. "It has been long since I was called little brother," he laughed, "longer still since I was called *hider*. Change follows close at your heels, girl child."

Sixty-seven:
One Last Link

Rebecca had a sad feeling departing from the Saied Freej. She felt comfortable with the Tremen there. Now, she was to be set out into an unknown land to find the Gates, which she was not sure yet how to do.

Fayit was taken aside as she followed after Rebecca; Maien, Garin, and Tagus spoke words with her. Garin unbelted his savage blade and handed it to her before they parted and she took it gratefully. Maien pressed something into Fayit's palm. She looked at the object, nodded and slipped it into a pouch at her belt.

The Benon Hurna had already parted and grew smaller in the increasing gray light of dawn. The Tremen unloaded supplies onto Illandra's Heart for the journey and the crew was busy storing them below decks. Wren had a reserved manner as he walked the plank back to Illandra's Heart.

When there was no point in lingering any longer, the anchors were hoisted and the sails set for the journey. Rebecca was exhausted. The whole of the night had been dedicated to the gathering. Fayit followed Will, Maxim, and the captain to the upper deck to lay in a course for the Tremen lands to the southwest. Noe Avaka took his leave and went to sleep below decks in the cabin the Tremen had vacated. Rebecca found Wren standing at the bow watching the Saied Freej depart.

"Aren't you going to sleep?" she asked him. He shook his head.

"Murmurs are loudest in sleep. It's when we are most open to their words," he said, never taking his eyes from the shrinking pale lines of the Saied Freej.

"Do you know how long you have?" she asked carefully.

"Long enough to see you through what you need to do, I think," he said calmly. He turned and looked her in the eyes. "You will do it for me; won't you? Before it takes me completely; you'll take my head."

She looked into his face. She had many feelings for this man, hate and loathing not least among them. Now, all she felt was pity; something she hadn't thought she would ever feel for him. Not after what he had done. "Yes, I will give you that if it comes to it," she said plainly. Rebecca could see the boy her brother had found with the relief that washed over his face.

"You need sleep, little sister," he said smirking. "I can feel it." He tapped his chest where his soul lay anchored to a tattoo her brother had given him. She knew what he meant, she could feel a vague sense that someone watched her from behind. It had come with Maien's bonding.

"I'll see you later, Wren," she said and went to find the captain's cabin.

The sun was already past its apex when Rebecca rose. The captain lay snoring on the pallet. She had fallen asleep in his bunk and he had not wakened her to take the pallet. She belted Astenos over her shoulder and crept out of the cabin.

Wren sat leaning against the wall near the cabin door. He had a covered bowl near him which he handed to her as she stepped into the

583

light. She removed the cover and saw a stew of fish and vegetables. She sat beside him and ate the bowl clean.

Noe Avaka staggered into the light not long after. He covered his eyes from the glare and walked to join them.

"I don't suppose you have saved a meal for me, Cursed One," he growled at Wren. Wren laughed and pointed to the kettle across the deck.

"I can't feel you in the back of my head, Pictsie," Wren said. Noe Avaka scurried off to the kettle and scooped a bowl of the stew. He picked out the bits of fish and popped them into his mouth. "I like him," Wren said, watching the Pictsie sort through his stew. "He doesn't mince words. Most around here think I'm contagious, those that don't seem to think I'm invisible. What I wouldn't give to knock a few skulls about. Nothing makes a man acknowledge your presence like a fist in his gut." Darris who had been passing stopped to look at the two of them sitting against the wall. His hand was still wrapped in bandages and splints from what Wren had done to him - she really should tend to his hand, she thought. He seemed to realize he had paused and hurried away.

"Not everything can be settled with fists and weapons," said Fayit. She had appeared silently from the upper deck.

Wren laughed silently and looked away from the Tremen. "No, but they can settle most things well enough."

"You sound like the men of my people. Garin was impressed with your skill, Wren of Tobias. He wouldn't admit it but you took him unaware," said Fayit.

"That was just to get your attention. If I had meant any harm it would have been done," said Wren. The cabin door banged opened and the captain stumped up the stairs to the deck.

"The uplanders of Mraxia liked to flaunt their wealth in the preparations of their children," the captain spoke to the air. "They wasted their coin on frivolities." Wren had a wry grin on his mouth; he seemed to have heard much the same before. "Dancing, music, and fancy words will do for you little on the seas. The blade now, that comes in hand and Mraxians were ever boastful of their skill with a sword," he said to Fayit.

"No boast, Mraidian," Wren said as he put his head back against the wall, "just the way of it. We had practice swords thrust into our hands when we learned to stand, between *dancing* lessons," he smiled. "My time with the Red Fist, while unwanted, did sharpen some skills."

"Might be you should try your hand against someone who could show you a thing or two about the Bladesman's art," said the captain, looking to Rebecca with a sly expression on his face. Wren looked at him with incredulity clear on his face.

"I wouldn't want to bruise you Mraidian, it being High Month still." Wren said smirking.

"Well, that holds between us, but I wasn't talking about meself," said the captain. He held out a hand to Rebecca and lifted her to her feet. "What about our girl here then?"

The crew gathered around to watch. The captain had found some practice swords – carved narrow wooden staves in reality – and Rebecca and Wren stood facing one another on a clear portion of the deck. Rebecca, her hair tied back in a scarf, held the wooden stick in her hands. She recalled her practice with Alaric, swinging at the Bashers; she touched the cuff at her wrist with a smile. She was determined to bring some humility to her smirking Guard Keeper. Astenos spoke encouragements into her mind as Wren tested the weight of his practice sword. The crew heckled Wren, he being the only Mraxian aboard. He seemed to smile broader with each desultory comment.

"Rules be this," bellowed the captain, stepping into the center of the gathered men. "First to three hits wins, no strikes to the head. I don't need any more cracked skulls aboard me ship. Touch blades and begin."

"Don't worry little sister. I'll go easy at first," said Wren.

"You will try," Rebecca said, a smile crawling across her face.

Rebecca touched blades with Wren and was immediately barraged with lightening quick strikes. If this was going easy, Rebecca would believe Wren's boasts. He moved like a viper, a strike at the body – blocked at the last second, and a second to the feet – avoided only by chance. Again and again he came at her, until she found herself at the edge of the onlookers. He swung at her shoulder and she dodged sideways, rolling to her feet.

She had only a moment to recover before he attacked again. Rebecca needed an edge. She Reached and slipped into the Easing. She watched as Wren moved; he seemed quick even here, but at least she could defend herself better. Astenos drove her hands now. Even separated as they were, she could allow him to direct her movements. She began pushing back against Wren's attacks.

The Quickening, she was back to speed. Wren's eyes were widened in shock. She had landed a blow against his forearm; he shook out the pain. The crew roared with laughter and jeers. His eyes narrowed and a twisted grin slid onto his mustached face.

"You're cheating, little sister," he panted.

"No rules Mraxian," shouted the captain from the sidelines. "That's one to our luck charm!" The crowd yelled with joy.

They took their places once more. This time Rebecca was prepared for Wren. He dashed forward and she spun to catch him as he passed. Somehow he avoided the blow and had caught her blade with his own, spinning it nearly out of her hands. She moved into the Easing once more; she would move more quickly than Wren here, but something was different. Wren moved just as fast as he had before, just as fast as she. Rebecca was shocked; she fought to maintain the Easing as she fended off Wren's strikes.

He caught her foot with his blade and pulled her off her feet, driving his blade down at her chest as she fell. Rebecca whipped back to speed with the Quickening. Wren's blade hovered an inch from her chest. The crowd began to taunt Wren once more; some of the men had money on this fight.

"One to the Mraxian," said the captain. Wren pulled her to her feet.

They took their places once more. Rebecca slipped into the Easing; she felt Astenos at her back, on point. Wren was there waiting. They struck at one another in the Easing. The crowd around, their faces painted with awe, moved as if in cold honey.

To the captain and the others, Rebecca and Wren were as two smearing shapes, their blades barely visible as they swung at one another. The crowd had become silent as they watched. The only sound was the splash of the sea, the wind rippling the sails, and the echoing clack of wood on wood. The fight paused; the two duelers panting, their clothes showing rings of sweat now. The captain couldn't call the point.

"It...it was her point," said Wren, breathing hard. No catcalls broke the silence this time.

587

They held their places for half an instant and the flashing blurs resumed. Moments seemed to pass as the streaked shapes of the duelers danced around one another. None of the crew had ever seen anything like this. None had waded through a mob of men turned beasts, trying to tear each other's hearts out. None had seen those streaking motions rip through that mob, leaving swaths of men on their backs staring blind to the sky through death filmed eyes, but the captain had. Palantean moved like this, they and the children that had been spiked with the Blue. The motion ceased once more. Rebecca rubbed at her thigh.

"His point," she gasped. Her hair flew loose behind her, the scarf holding it back in disarray.

Rebecca had become obsessed with defeating Wren. She slipped once more into the Easing and found him there. Astenos's weariness was nothing to her own. Wren was slowing as she was; the strikes came further and further apart. She Reached deeper and the world stalled, the sails above still in mid ripple, the waves to the sides of the ship frozen like ice. The crew seemed to bloom with multicolored strands that reached out all around. She could see the Links of the world tying everything together. Everything before her eyes showed the streaming lines of Kilaray, except Wren. He stood stationary for once, his face a portrait of grim determination. And then she saw something that froze her stomach.

Above Wren's shoulder, the phantom form of his Murmur clung to him. It, unlike the rest of world around her, still flowed as though it was caught in a windstorm. Its dead eyes snapped from Wren to her, and its voice entered her mind.

"He is nearly mine; you will not have him." The sound was the voice of despair.

She could see a tendril of black snaking into Wren from the Murmur. Wren's own Links were tangled in the tendril; they did not tie him, as did the other men's Links around her, to the world. There was one hair-thin thread laced around the symbol on his chest and back, the anchor her brother had formed. The Murmur's macabre hands worked at that lacing as it looked back to him, trying to untie it from the seal. She could see the waving loose ends of other Links that it had untied from other symbols on his body that was why they had seemed broken to her; they no longer held their ties to Wren. There was a second thinner thread Rebecca could see; one that tied her to Wren. It had a strange feel to it and Rebecca knew at once it was the bond Maien had formed between them, the Link of the Guard Keeper to his Charge. Rebecca slipped out of the Stillness and moved with effortless speed toward Wren.

Their blades crashed into one another, splintering as they met, coming back to speed. The broken staves clattered to the deck. Wren smiled until he saw the look on Rebecca's face.

"A draw!" cried Noe Avaka. "Marvelously done, girl child."

"You saw it; didn't you?" Wren panted under his breath. Rebecca nodded. "How much remains of the anchor?"

"One thread," she said feeling sick.

"My last Link to this world," he said with an amused look. Rebecca wondered how he could see humor in such things.

"There is one more Link, Wren," she said as crewmen began conspicuously passing coins between one another - most were passed to Noe Avaka. Wren looked to her with confused hope on his face. "Your Link to me still holds."

Sixty-eight:
Seeking Answers

The days grew hotter as High Month waned and they plotted further south. Fayit had taken to Will as a fellow navigator. He had never traveled this far south, few men had. There were no ports for human ships to find harbor. They had passed into the Tremen territories two days ago. Fayit found Will's methods of charting courses amusing, while Will simply watched, trying to see what Fayit followed in the skies.

Rebecca, Wren, and Noe Avaka spent most of their time together. Wren seemed to know as much as he had boasted about fighting, armed or with hands and feet. He taught her techniques for handling people larger than she – which would be just about everyone except Noe Avaka. They spent their days tossing one another around the deck or sparring with wooden staves. Wren started to correct what he called, "the wild slashing of an untrained stripling," showing her how to handle a blade unaided by Astenos. Astenos took offense and Rebecca had to steel herself from showing Wren how an "untrained stripling" could still break his arm.

On one of these occasions something occurred to Rebecca, something she had begun noticing about the way the crew looked at her. She only noticed in contrast to the way in which Wren eyed her. The crew had a look she could not quite define, almost of longing, she had not sensed before from them. It was a comment from Wren that sparked the understanding in Rebecca's mind.

It had been an especially hot day, the sun brought tears to the eyes if glanced for too long. Not the smallest puff of cloud wisped over head to break the heat and the humidity had increased. Wren had removed his shirt, his strange tattoos catching worried glances from the crew as they went about their tasks. Rebecca, following his example, removed her own, working only in a dark undershirt and loose cotton pants she had taken from Alaric's home. The crew began to linger a little longer in their passing and Wren eyed them like a guard dog.

"What's wrong with you?" she asked as she caught her breath from blade work.

He broke his glare from one of the men who had been watching as he carried a coil of rope toward the bow. "Sea dogs, too long away from a woman," he said in an under tone.

"What are you talking about?" she asked confused. Wren's look of disbelief lasted only a second before his grin climbed back to his mouth.

"Little sister, have you not seen the looks on these salt crusted sea urchins' faces?" he chuckled to himself. "I'd say you're the only *human* woman within two hundred miles of this ship. That sort of thing begins to grate on a man's...brain." His smile became increasingly mischievous as he watched her. She felt the stares of the men around her now and her face felt warmer than it should. She had noticed her clothes feeling a bit snug in recent weeks but she hadn't thought twice about it.

Pulling her shirt back on she turned to Wren feeling embarrassed and angry. "What's wrong with you then, Skip Tracer?" she hadn't used the term in days. "You're a man, if a vile and smug one." He laughed softly but there was a sad look on his face.

591

"One of the first things that goes when you're on the Blue, little sister, is the desire for much beyond that next spike. I might not feel what these fellows around here do, but that doesn't make me a complete blind fool." It felt odd being complemented by a man for her appearance, especially this man. She decided to take out her growing embarrassment by beating some of the mirth from him.

Later, after she had sent Wren away rubbing his bruised thighs and arms, she went to find Noe Avaka. He and Rebecca sat together in the cabin he had taken as his own, determining the use of the compass and watch she had carried out of Arnora. She allowed her mind to wander while the Pictsie explained the markings on the Traveler. He translated the lines of foreign text to her; all seemed variations on the same phrase, "For the crossing of worlds." The etched lines and circles had something to do with holding the alignment of the planes of worlds. The markings on the compass seemed to correspond to the Traveler's at times but when she would look again they would have changed their orientation.

Rebecca noticed how the compass's needle spun wildly except when she focused on holding the image of the Gates in her mind, the cliff face with the arched pillars. The etched pattern on the compass face would settle at these times and then she could feel the tug of the Kilaray. The feeling was magnified in the presence of the Traveler. She still didn't understand how the watch would help. It kept the beat of time with its steady tick, tick, tick and its glowing face had come in handy in Valgerhold for a portable light, but it still seemed nothing more than an interesting aspect to a normal timepiece.

Noe Avaka was of no help where the watch was concerned. He insisted that time was linked to the planes of this world alone; the other worlds were timeless, existing everywhere at once. He simply repeated, "The World Strider will know when time is true," whenever she asked how the watch worked with the Traveler.

Whenever the three were together though, the talk eventually turned to Wren and his seals. The three would sit together on the deck of the ship in the dark and discuss how his seals were made. He had been uncomfortable about talking at first, saying that Sebastian had tried time and again to break the hold the Murmur had on Wren's links. He had not been able to tie Wren's links to the other seals for long; the Murmur was always able to unbind them, all but his last, the one holding Wren's soul in place. Noe Avaka was the one to have turned the talk toward Astenos.

"An interesting aspect about the Palantean weapon the girl child carries; creatures of Discordia flee before them, if they can. Few man kind objects can harm them, for most weapons do not work in but this plane of worlds," he said as he gnawed on a dried bit of beef from last meal.

"Murmurs don't flee before anything," Wren said. Rebecca agreed; the Husk Man she had killed had not even flinched when it came for her after stabbing Wren.

"Strange that," said Noe Avaka. "Perhaps they fight because they are tied to the flesh of their hosts. Strynges will slip back into Discordia unless they have been pinned." Rebecca remembered her experience with that particular aspect of Strynge behavior.

"Look, I'm telling you there is no way to separate the Murmur from the host. Once it tangles itself in your Links it pulls more and more of your soul away until it can take you," said Wren exasperated. "The surest way to cut a man's soul from a Murmur is to take his head before it Husks him out."

So sure of himself, this Wren, my Mate. We could cut the most entrenched of the demons from this world when our Mating is complete, whispered Astenos in an offhand way. It made Rebecca's mind sizzle though.

"Wren, did my brother have a Blade like mine with him when you knew him?" she asked hesitantly.

He shook his head. "He was a good Bladesman, best I've seen, but he got his steel from the same place as the rest of us, from the men we killed."

This thought hit Rebecca hard. She knew her brother had to have killed men, but to have it said so plainly was different, it was more real. She had something more in common with her brother now, though; they were both killers.

"Soul Blades cut like steel in this world," she said after a moment. "They also can cut in the world of the Kilaray. They can cut Links, Wren."

Noe Avaka shook his head with a worried look on his face. "Severing Links is a dangerous thing, girl child. Cutting the ties to the world of the Tree Father can do damage like no other. The Broken Lands, girl child, is what comes of severing links."

"No, not always, Noe – Ronan Arcand did it," she said and for the first time she had spoken what she knew from Astenos to others. "He...he severed his own Links."

Noe looked horrified. "Why, would a man do such to himself? He would be lost with no way of returning to this world."

"I'm not sure, but he did and nothing happened to anything but himself," she said. "Wren, we can cut the Murmur's ties to you."

He looked frightened. "No, I...I won't let you, not...not yet." His head cocked to the side as if listening to something. "I won't be able to keep you safe without it." His words became hollow. "It brings me back, little sister… I'm why he can't die." His words sounded strange on that last, a note that made her skin prickle. Rebecca knew it was the Murmur, somehow; it was speaking to him, through him, protecting itself.

"Alright, Wren, I can't do it now," she said, trying to pacify the Murmur. Wren's smirk came back to his face.

Rebecca reached out in her sleep later that evening. She needed to talk to Astenos. She found him waiting for her in her mind. His form was becoming more solid all the time; she knew their link had nearly resolved completely.

"Can it be done, Astenos?" she asked when she found him. She paced back and forth in the place she found him, a warmer feeling version of Valgerhold's courtyard, the trees in their surrounds pink with blossoms. She had become determined since hearing the Murmur speak through Wren.

It might be possible.

"What do you mean *might*? You said we *could cut the most entrenched of the demons from this world*, Astenos."

Astenos seemed sheepish. *I sometimes speak higher of us than I should, Rebecca.*

She looked at his shifting face in disbelief. "You sounded sure, Astenos. I can tell when you're bragging."

Some things, Rebecca, I know from where I come into being; the customs for instance. Other things I can only speculate upon. It might be possible to separate the demon from Wren's soul but we might kill him in the process.

"Well, we are going to find out Astenos, one way or another," she said.

Not long ago you wanted to kill this man, Rebecca.

She fell silent. Why did she want to help Wren? She still held what he had done against him. She thought of those symbols adorning Wren's skin; her brother had a hand in those marks. Perhaps it was that Wren was one more thing she had left of her brother. One last person who had known him, had talked with him, laughed with him.

"I don't want to see him taken, Astenos. Too many have died already around me. I will save any I can from being lost."

I see; then I will assist you, my Mate. It will not be long yet before we are complete.

Sixty-nine:
Fannith Cove

Fog enveloped Illandra's Heart. Rebecca wore the loosest lightest clothing she had. The crew mopped at their heads as they entered into the dense cloud, not just for the heat. Fog this thick could hide a mountain, let alone a rock outcrop, that could tear the keel out of a ship like it was made of parchment.

Fayit stood close by Maxim, the captain to the other side. She directed his steering as though the day were not obscured in an impenetrable mist. Fayit had said they would reach a Tremen outpost this day. From there they would set out on foot.

This was by far the strangest birthday Rebecca had known. Standing on the upper deck of the ship, staring blindly into nothingness, waiting with growing anticipation for a jolt which would mean the ship had hit rock, and listening to a woman whisper directions to Maxim, his knuckles white on the wheel. Even Wren, ever assured of himself, looked uneasy, leaning against the rail to Rebecca's side.

"What's the matter Mraxian," said the captain, never looking from dead ahead of the ship, "think the Fates be against us?"

"It's been long since the Fates have been with me, Mraidian," said Wren. "I just hoped to reach land without taking a swim."

"On that we can agree, Mraxian," the captain grumbled. He chewed at the stem of his short pipe.

Suddenly a pale gold beam of light flashed through the fog and a haunting, bellowing sound echoed out from an invisible shore. The mist broke in places, clinging to the cooler water. They had sailed into a cove; steep forested hills reached up from the rocky shoreline, their tops hidden in misty clouds. A tall lighthouse sat at the mouth of the cove, directing the beam of light out to sea; a long curved horn mounted atop the sweeping cylindrical building.

Growing out from the shore was a village of a sort Rebecca had no comparison to. The buildings blended smoothly with their surroundings, white and grey to match the bark of the trees growing up in the middle of the cleared path-like streets. The roofs were arched and covered in a type of deep green thatch. The walls reminded Rebecca of the Tremen ships, like weathered driftwood or shells, the remains of something once alive.

Piers stretched out from the shore and several Tremen ships were moored at the docks. Fayit guided Illandra's Heart into one of the berths. Huge Tremen in forest-colored clothes paused to watch the human vessel moving into their port. The crew moved about the ship, forcing themselves to stop staring at the shore long enough to prepare the ship for docking.

"Captain Rhannon, you and your crew will not find trouble here," said Fayit. "With the blessing of the gathering, we will be shown quarter. I will see that you are supplied for your return to sea, but you will not be allowed away from the docks."

Rebecca turned to the captain; she had not thought about this since leaving the gathering. She would be leaving the captain and the crew behind. She felt a sense of loss as the ship came to rest at the pier.

Rebecca forced herself to gather her possessions as the crew worked above, readying the ship for when it would depart. Illandra's Heart was one more home she was leaving; more friends that would be left behind. This time though she would not be alone. The thought brightened her spirits a bit.

On the deck the crew had all gathered to see her off. Will and Maxim, the captain, Stevens, Belwer, and Darris and all the others stood shoulder to shoulder smiling at her.

"We carried you as far as we can take you, girl," said the captain. "We hopes this accounts us even with the Fates this time,"

"We're gonna miss you, lass," said Maxim in his deep friendly voice.

"You're one of the few girls I've not stolen a kiss from," said Will, flashing his silver toothed grin and placing his hands over his heart. "Ah, the tragedy." Rebecca went intensely red.

She saw Darris shuffling his feet and looking at the deck boards; he held his broken wrist at his waist. She went to the grizzled old sailor and put her hands on the bandaged hand. A moment later he smiled through his whiskers and pulled off the splint.

"I thank you, dear, I do," he looked to Wren and his face hardened. "You watch this girl's back Mraxian or you'll have us after you like the Blazes."

Wren bowed with a flourish. "By your command, so do I obey."

Fayit and Noe Avaka stood waiting for Rebecca and Wren at the gang plank. Rechecking that she had not forgotten anything, Rebecca trudged down the plank with a heavy heart.

Fayit led the four up the piers to a tall Tremen man with a dark mane. He had a line of a scar running though the fur on his face. He eyed the group with a measuring glare.

"Jergan of the Fannith Cove Tremen," he said in a hoarse voice. "Why have you brought this vessel into our lands woman?"

Fayit rummaged in her pouch and pulled out a small ring, Rebecca would be able to fit it over her whole hand; it bore the tree symbol from the Saied Freej. She showed it to Jergan and his eyes widened.

"I had heard rumors from the women that the pattern had changed," he said in a breathy voice. "What do you require?"

"Supply the man kind's vessel and see them out to sea once more. For us, I will see to what we need," said Fayit. "Does Lelin still call Fannith Cove home?" Jergan nodded.

"She has become Head Council to the Pride Mistress; you should find her near the Council House. Peace upon you."

Jergan put his hand to his heart before moving past the group, directing other huge Tremen to Illandra's Heart. Rebecca took one last look at the ship before she followed after Fayit.

"I'm going to need a metal works," Wren said to Fayit. She nodded.

"Our smiths can make whatever you need," she said as they walked into the village.

"A meal would not go amiss either," growled Noe Avaka.

The heat of this place was worse for the dampness of the air. Rebecca felt like she breathed through a sponge. Wren's face shone with sweat; Rebecca could feel trickles down her back. Noe Avaka had loosened his shirt and fanned himself with his strange hands. The heat didn't seem to faze Fayit though. She marched along the paths of the village with ease.

Rebecca could see Tremen moving about the village, carting supplies to and from the piers. There were several round buildings she would not have been able to identify if not for the Tremen working in the open air outside of them; seamstresses, fletchers, smiths, all the various crafts of a human village except operated and scaled for the huge people of the town. Everywhere she looked the Tremen who spotted the group would stop what they were doing and stare. Children, cubs Fayit called them, roamed the streets, marked by their smaller size, the youngest would be just shorter than Rebecca; they lacked the great manes of the older Tremen.

A woman with a white-gold-colored mane greeted them as they wound through the canopied paths. She wore a gown of deep green with jagged silver embroidery around the loose arms and hem. She had that way of carrying herself that gave Rebecca the impression of regality.

"Fayit," said the woman, "your feet have been long from our soil."

"Change brings that which we never expected, Lelin. It's good to see you again."

The woman smiled. "How is Garin? Does his humor still hold?"

"He misses you, Lelin. Perhaps you will see one another again some day." Lelin nodded thoughtfully. "I bring the herald, Lelin. Will you assist us in gathering what we need?"

The woman looked around Fayit to Rebecca. Her pale eyes widened and her mouth twitched into a surprised smile.

"Oh, I see," she said. "Yes, Fayit, come, come, you will rest while we gather what you require." She led them to a round building with gray hardened mud walls.

The structure's curved sides were perforated with windows; above each, the wall jutted outward to cover them from the rains. The building was raised above the ground on a platform of pale wood. Walking through the curved archway leading into the building, Rebecca had the same feel of a den or cave from the Saied Freej. The only flat surface was the floor and that was covered with stuffed fabric cushions. The building consisted of one giant room divided here and there with thin fiber screens. In the center there was a stone plinth where a packed clay hearth and chimney had been constructed. The smoke was directed up through the peak of the ceiling.

"Rest here in the Council House," said Lelin. "I will see to your lodging and that you are fed." Noe Avaka perked up at this.

The Tremen at first seemed reluctant to help but soon the villagers offered up whatever assistance they could lend to – as they insisted on referring to Rebecca – the herald. Seamstresses measured the group, even Wren, though reluctantly, and promised to have clothes more suiting to the environment ready for their departure. Wren made arrangements with the smiths of the village to forge what he needed.

They were ushered into a sort of Tremen inn. It varied slightly from the Council House in that it was not quite as large and had places where meals would be taken, and sectioned-off areas Rebecca assumed were rooms, though they had no doors. They spent that evening eating the Tremen meal they prepared. It consisted of a kind of wild boar, a variety of fruits, and dense dark bread. They bathed and were shown where they would sleep. It seemed too late for the brightness of the sky, the Tremen lived closer to the equator.

Rebecca pulled the three items she knew she would need to find the Gates of Yuriah from her satchel and laid them out on the cushion upon which she sat. She felt her tired eyes drifting off as she studied the patterns of the Traveler. She focused her mind on the Gates. She could see the cliff face, two white trees growing to partially obscure the arched stone pillars, but nothing came of it. She tried locking in the etched designs on the compass's face to no avail. And through it all she felt a steady rhythm she had not felt before; something brought her eyes around to the watch. Tick, tick, tick, the hands marched around the face of the watch as they always had. The dull green glow seemed to pulse with the steady progression of the thin metal arms.

Coming no further with the objects, she finally gave up. As Rebecca lay down to sleep, the haunting call of the lighthouse horn sounded, ushering out Illandra's Heart. A feel of great loss washed over her. She longed for the gentle rock of the ship at sea.

The following morning, Rebecca was awoken from a troubled sleep. She had visions of desperate times, war, pain, loss. The worst part was that it had come to her in that place she knew that Reached Visions emanated. She shivered; she had the feel of being surrounded.

Then, as sleep left her and the sense of feeling someone close by remained, she sat up. There was a strange sense in her body now she realized; it had been that which had woken her. It felt as though every nerve in her body were on edge. She was worried at first, but then a great sense of joy flowed through her from Astenos.

I can feel your world through you, my Mate, he said.

Rebecca knew what had happened almost by instinct. She could feel everyone in the inn's sectioned room, not through herself but from Astenos. It was as though she had opened some never before used eye for the first time, a newly discovered sense. The feeling faded slightly but she could still feel the dull sense of connection with her surroundings.

We are joined, Rebecca. Finally we are whole.

Seventy:
For the Crossing of Worlds

"Something funny?" asked Wren as they collected the knives and narrow sword he had had made.

Rebecca realized she had a smile from ear to ear. She had been experimenting with her new connection. Astenos's joy at the sensation was almost worth the effort it took Rebecca to use it.

"No, it's just..." but her mind trailed off in feeling around her through the village. Tremen eyed her as she walked along the paths, Wren at her side. She could feel their presence before she saw them. She reached out toward Wren and recoiled. It was like running her mind over ice, ice so cold it burnt flesh. She removed the look of terror from her face and followed after him with a strengthened determination to cut the Murmur from him.

The Tremen seamstresses had been true to their word. When Rebecca and Wren returned to the inn they each found a neatly folded set of Tremen clothes outside their rooms. The cloth was soft and yielding yet felt extremely tough. The colors ranged from deep greens to grays and browns, in patterns that would blend neatly with the forest around them. Wren fastened his Stitcher's rig over his tunic and belted on his new narrow sword. He seemed more comfortable being properly armed, his swagger became more pronounced, more threatening.

The day's mist had rolled in again. The mountains around the cove protected it from the worst of the raining season but the mist was unavoidable. One thing was certain as they prepared to set out; they were going to get wet.

When they found Fayit, she had a pack on her back as well as her bow and quiver of arrows at her hip. Noe Avaka, his new cloak dyed a deep orange to fit his tastes, wore a bundled bag on his back. He alone was unarmed. Instead he leaned on a thin pale wooden staff that reached the top of his head.

"We Shints have never taken up arms," he said, looking offended that Rebecca would ask such a thing. "Discretion is far more effective than brute force." The term *hider* began to make some sense now to Rebecca.

The four, their supplies on their backs, prepared to leave Fannith Cove. Fayit would lead the group into the steep forested mountains but it would be up to Rebecca to point the way once they were deeper into the forest. Noe Avaka reassured her that, "The World Strider will know the path." This did little for Rebecca other than thoroughly knot her stomach.

As they walked the path-like streets, Tremen came out of shops or stopped along the roads to watch. The procession – two humans, one marred with a parasite from Discordia, a Shint Pictsie, and a member of an outcast nation – walked from Fannith Cove, making for a most solemn parade. The looks the villagers cast them varied from awe to fear to plaintive concern. Lelin escorted them to where the village became wilderness and spoke a few short words.

"Tread carefully, Fayit," she said. "The Masked have been seen stalking this land of late." Her eyes flashed to Rebecca for the briefest instant. "Man kind's touch of the God Lights has been soft for far too long. Like a candle to a moth, she will draw them on, Fayit. Take care, my dear friend. Peace upon you, upon you all."

"Thank you Lelin, and Peace upon you and Fannith Cove," said Fayit, touching paw to heart. The three others spoke similar words and thanked Lelin for her aid.

They marched from the path-like streets into the surrounding trees. Shortly, Rebecca found herself in the densest, wettest forest she had ever known. The ground beneath their feet was sodden and their feet sank deep into the mulch of the forest floor. Vines climbed the trees and moss grew thick everywhere. The sun, grayed by the mist, beat weakly through such canopy cover; the whole of the forest was cast in a weak green light. Fayit offered to carry Noe Avaka after a few hours of walking through the pathless forest. He kept vanishing beneath ferns and wide leaves that grew near the ground. He accepted gratefully and clung to the Tremen's sandy mane.

Rebecca could hear whispers in her mind in addition to the exotic bird and animal calls. Creatures lurking in the undergrowth knew they were passing through their home. None of these animals seemed to want to speak to her as the wolves had. She followed Fayit, Wren brought up the rear, and she listened to the unintelligible words of the unseen beasts of this forest.

When it became too dark to travel further they made camp. Rebecca retrieved the salamander from her satchel. She had finally figured out how the carving was used. She set the lizard-shaped object beneath a pile of wet tinder gathered from the forest and after a moment, fire burst into the logs sending up a plume of steam and sparks as the wood instantly caught flame. As they ate, Rebecca focused on the compass, trying to decipher the location of the Gates.

When morning came, Rebecca gathered the salamander from the ashes of the fire; it didn't look the least bit singed. She slung Ronan's Blade over her shoulder, still cased in the leather tube, next to

Astenos, worn openly now. Wren checked his knives for rust and sheathed them, covering himself in a deep brown cloak. Fayit stood waiting with her bow and quiver for Noe Avaka to finish packing his bag. In repacking her satchel, placing the salamander within, she brushed against the triangular Traveler inside.

A flash pierced through her mind. Further into this forest, stone statues, their faces eroded, stood sentinel over the place they needed to go. Not the Gates themselves that is not where the Traveler would take them. She had been picturing the wrong place in her mind. The vision vanished; she stood in the camp again. The others watched her, Fayit measuring, Wren concerned, and Noe Avaka with a look of interested knowing.

She lifted the flap of the satchel and took out the Traveler. The compass in her hand spun wildly back and forth, its design changing with the needle's direction. She focused her mind on the image of the statues, gripped hold of the Traveler, and the compass began to pull at her hand. She could feel herself slipping away from where she was now, moving deeper into the forest. Suddenly the sensation ceased.

Wren pulled her out of her trance. He had wrenched the Traveler from her hands.

"What are you doing?" he yelled. "You were fading."

"For the crossing of worlds," she said absently. "It's not just a map is it Noe?" She looked at the fox-like man. His pink-rimmed eyes sparkled.

"You had to see it yourself, girl child," he growled. "The World Strider cannot be shown the path."

"I understand. Everyone come close," she took the compass in her hand as Fayit and Noe Avaka moved in.

"What are you doing, little sister?" Wren said, picking up the Traveler.

"I'm not quite sure myself," she said. She closed her eyes and could feel the three others around her through Astenos. She held the compass and felt its needle spinning here and there within its case, its patterned face exactly matching the Traveler's etched lines and circles now. She felt something else, a steady tick, tick, tick; the watch kept time in their world. She saw the statues in her mind and reached out to the Traveler, touching it with her finger tips and mind.

The green mist expanded from the triangular faces of the Traveler, growing in intensity as it engulfed the four. Rebecca saw the blinding white light through her closed lids. She held the image of the weathered statues in her mind, the raining forest, the abandoned structures growing from the forest around them, and she felt the ground drop from beneath her feet. Her stomach lurched and she felt a strange wind blow at her from everywhere at once. Tick, tick, tick, became a humming metallic rattle, time had sped forward. Someone was screaming, babbling incoherently. The words slowly came to her ears, enveloped in the white light that washed the world away.

I feel him near, my Mate. I killed him. Bring me death, oblivion, nothingness. Forgive me Ronan, you made me do it. I hate you, I love you. Ronan, oh Father, bring me my Mate. The words were screamed in a hysterical rant and Rebecca understood where the Traveler had taken them.

I am here, Rebecca. I will hold against her. Astenos bellowed desperately. *Move quickly, take your friends through; take them back to your world.*

Rebecca opened her eyes, still holding the image of the statues in her mind, and she saw Astenos's shifting form. He struggled against a woman, her arms flailing to reach Rebecca. Wren stood blocking her,

608

his back turned and his narrow sword in his hand. Fayit was roaring something Rebecca struggled to hear through the streaming wind.

"Back, Rebecca, take us back; we must return to our world," she yelled.

"We can't, not yet," she screamed over the rush in her ears. "I understand now. The time isn't true yet." She pulled out the watch from inside the satchel. The face glowed brighter than she had ever seen. Its hands spun around and around, the ticking a high pitched whine, too fast for their world. She Reached and the ticking slowed as she moved into the Easing.

Astenos battled the other Soul; she tried clambering over him to get to Rebecca. He fought with a strength she knew he had gained from their joining. The other Soul broke free from Astenos and moved with infinite slowness toward Rebecca as the Stillness came over her. The beat of time from the watch met her ears. The shifting faces of the Souls were frozen, mid form, and her breath caught. Her mother's face stared on her with a look of mad rage. Astenos was suspended in mid flight for the other Soul, her father's face awash in fear. The tick, tick, tick of the watch drew her from her petrifaction. The compass needle held its position as she looked at it. *Time to go*, she thought, as she touched the Traveler once more. Closing her eyes and focusing again on the statues.

The ground slammed into Rebecca's feet and she toppled to the wet soil. A cloud of illuminate white-green vapor billowed out from where they stood, dispersing as it moved away. The wind had ceased and Rebecca could feel rain pouring from the dense canopy overhead.

"What, where?" Wren staggered to his feet, looking for a fight. "What did you do?"

Fayit and Noe Avaka looked around as they gained their feet. Above them, through a break in the clouds, seven points of light were visible. Three white stars arched together to either side of a seventh green star centered between. Statues grew from the forest and for the first time Rebecca recognized what they were. Two humans, a taller Tremen, and a Pictsie stood over them, awaiting their arrival.

"This was where we sealed the Port," Noe Avaka said. "Tremen, do you see? The watchers still stand," Noe Avaka bounced with excitement.

"I see little brother," said Fayit in a calm voice. "Rebecca, are you well? I must say I am glad to feel the soil beneath my feet again."

"Who, what were those people?" Wren said, sheathing his narrow sword. "Where did they come from?"

"The man was Astenos," Rebecca said, brushing the mud from her knees. "I still don't know the woman's name. They are the Souls bound to the Blades I carry."

"How, I thought they existed in another... plane, or world," he asked, attempting to bring back his confident manner but failing.

"They do, we passed through their world to get here," Rebecca said, staring at the compass.

"When we cast the Port adrift, it was into that world it was sent," said Noe Avaka. "We could have left from any location, the Kilaray world touches everywhere, every time, at once, and still arrived here, but the World Strider had to locate it. Only the World Strider would be able to bring us back here."

"Well, where are these Gates?" asked Wren, finally managing to retrieve his haughty attitude.

"They are that way," said Rebecca, pointing to where the compass needle now settled. She packed the Traveler, no longer emitting the green mist, back into her satchel along with the watch and the group set out into the vine covered forest.

Everywhere were signs a civilization once existed here: the foundation of a wall, covered in moss and crumbling, the foot of a statue, the body would have stood twenty feet if it could be found. The forest here had been quick to reclaim what had been taken from it. Vines lashed around huge cut stone blocks, pulling them from where they had been placed. Trees several feet across grew up from the center of where once had stood a building.

"What happened here?" asked Rebecca, as they walked past a row of what had once been pillars. "Where did everybody go?"

"The man kinds, Tremen, and Pictsies who built these structures abandoned their homes when the Port was sealed," said Fayit. She seemed reserved, as though she were in a sacred place. "The people who lived here sacrificed their homes to keep the Darklings from this place, to save what was kept inside the Barrier."

"Who were the Darklings?" asked Wren. "I've never heard of them."

"The Darklings were man kinds, mainly," growled Noe Avaka. "They bent their Link-working abilities to evil ends."

"They could touch the Links?" asked Rebecca. "I thought the Philistari used their skills to help."

"Not Philistari, girl child, this was long before your kind would touch the Links again, before the Tree split." Noe Avaka looked sad. "Our kinds, yours, the Tremen, and mine, lived alongside one another, the Great Tree of the Father Touched. Great things came of those times, much fortune, much knowledge, but the creatures of Discordia were drawn to us, your kind most of all." His pink eyes flashed toward

Wren. "There was one such creature that pressed itself on our plane. We knew it only by its turning of our most ambitious friends to seek power with their skills."

"What was it?" Rebecca asked.

"We called it Wanderer," said Fayit, her fur ruffled. "It twisted those it corrupted, damaging them beyond their ability to touch the links. It offered them their skills back if they would join with it."

"To what end?" asked Wren.

"Opening this plane to Discordia," said Noe Avaka. "The Darklings were willing to destroy what the Tree Father had created to touch the Links again. Our people were ravaged in the war that sprung up. Creatures poured forth to aid the Darklings, Strynges not the worst among them. One of your kinds had a Reached Vision on the eve of our most dire struggle. Yuriah Penterius saw we would win, but at the loss of many man kinds. He saw too that your people would be unable to touch the Links for many centuries afterwards."

"He had the Barrier built," said Rebecca. Noe Avaka nodded.

"We built it together; Pictsie seals prevented the man kinds of the Darkling forces from entering. The Tremen guarded its location, and when we sealed the port the people who lived here went to join the final struggle," said Noe Avaka.

"But what were you trying to protect, was it the Tower of Light?" asked Rebecca. They had walked for some time and the forest was changing. The sounds of the animals had faded as they walked, now the silence gave the trees an eerie foreboding feel.

"Not just the Tower," said Noe Avaka. He stared up at what had suddenly loomed from the forest. The trees stopped short of the massive stone wall before them. For fifty feet before the cliff the ground became hard black stone. As far to their right and left as they could see, the cliff face stretched. The clouds broke again, revealing the seven starred constellation named for the pillars of stone below them. "The Tower came long before, we built *this*," he gestured to the massive stone wall facing them, "to protect those we sealed inside."

It felt strange, after so long beneath the tree cover, to come suddenly out into the open. The group walked toward the cliff; its dark stone face stretched skyward. The height was hard to judge. It seemed to meet the clouds hundreds of feet above them. The stone beneath their feet looked as though it had melted, flowing toward the great wall to become part of it. Two white shapes clung to the cliff face; Rebecca knew before they reached them they were two white trees.

She could not see how it was possible; the wall of rock seemed of one piece, solid. Yet, the trees roots sprouted from the black stone, supporting their sinuous forms as they reached toward one another. Their boughs were sheathed in golden leaves making Rebecca think of the ring in Fayit's belt pouch.

The cliff seemed to be completely impenetrable until they approached the two trees. There was a gap below them fifty feet across. At either side the black stone changed and two arched columns of a smooth white material, somewhere between glass and rock, grew upwards two hundred feet.

"How…" Rebecca had to wet her mouth before she could continue. "How do we open it?" Fayit and Noe Avaka, so different in appearance, had the same look of unknowing; it would have been comical if not for their situation. "You must be able to tell me how to open the Gates; your people made them."

"We created the Barrier, and sealed it, kept it safe. Yuriah Penterius created the lock; it is to you we look for how the Gate shall be opened," said Noe Avaka.

Rebecca had that feel in her stomach of when too much was expected of her. They had come this far, but they would go no further – not unless she could open something that had not been known in centuries. She quelled the panic that began to form in her and calmed her mind. Slowly, slower than it had taken in a long time, the flitting motes of light appeared before her eyes.

Chains of golden Links stretched across the gap in the rock cliff. They were so thick, so tightly netted together, that they seemed as solid as the rock around them. The columns supported the strands of Kilaray Links, and they flowed through them. Rebecca approached one of the glassy pillars. Patterns formed within the depths of the material, not visible to any eye but those who could see the Links. Hesitantly, she touched the glassy pillar; the surface felt warm. She looked upward; the Kilaray Link barrier blocked the entire height of the pillars.

"What do you see, Rebecca?" asked Fayit.

"I see a problem," Rebecca said, walking back to them. "I don't know how we can get through. There is a web of Links barring the opening from ground to the top of those columns."

"Can't we just walk through?" asked Wren, looking into the opening. "It seems wide open. I can almost see the trees on the other side."

"You might not see it but, if you cross beyond those pillars without unlocking it, your soul would be pulled from your body," said Noe Avaka. "The power that flows from the Tree Father is vast."

615

Rebecca studied the opening once more as Noe Avaka spoke. Her eyes wandered from the opening, to the pillars, to the golden topped trees. A twinkling in the limbs caught her eye. Why were the trees here? They only partially hid the stone pillars, and their presence would only draw the attention of anyone who found this place. The wind rustled the leaves and the twinkling caught her eye again.

"The trees," she said, tracing their sinuous lines arching out from the wall toward one another. "The lock is in the trees. It is the trees." She knew she was right before the words left her lips. The golden leaves tangled together in the forms of the trees, the stone pillars were a decoy. The Gates were the trees. Rebecca watched as the golden lines of the Kilaray twined up the white bark of the trees, flowing from either side of the cliff face and meeting in the middle twenty feet above the ground.

"I have to get up there," she said, removing her possessions and pulling the two Soul Blades over her shoulder. She ran to the base of one of the trees.

"Wait, little sister, are you crazed? You can't go up there you'll break your neck," Wren said, chasing after her.

"I have to, now give me a lift," she said. He stood without moving. "Wren, I can't reach it myself." He breathed deep and lifted her to the closet root. She pulled up and climbed the pale bark of the tree. Higher and higher she climbed; the branches became thinner yet remained as solid as the trunk of the tree. She was into the golden canopy of the tree, moving closer to where the two met. She could see the sparkling light of the Kilaray traveling along the limbs toward the middle.

"Be careful, Rebecca," Fayit called up to her. She seemed small from this height and then Rebecca caught sight of something else.

From above, she could see two glowing patterns at the base of each tree and she knew she could not open the Gates alone.

"Fayit, Noe, I need you," she said. Wren jumped and caught the roots and began to pull himself up. "No, Wren, I need them." The patterns she could see were made differently from the one which the Barrier had been constructed. The pattern beneath the tree she had climbed had been made using Tremen hands; the opposite tree's pattern was different from either of the others, Pictsie forged.

"What do you need, Rebecca?" called Fayit. She approached the base of the tree and the pattern ignited in a red-gold light. Fayit gasped and the flow of Kilaray along the tree Rebecca was on halted and then reversed direction, feeding into the glowing pattern. The tree's limbs hummed beneath Rebecca's hands and knees.

"Noe, go to the opposite tree," Rebecca called down. Understanding flashed across his face and he hurried to take his place. The Pictsie pattern bloomed like blue-green fire as his feet touched the spot. Rebecca watched as the flow reversed in the opposite tree. The leaves of the second tree vibrated on their branches, and resonate tones filled Rebecca's ears.

She climbed the last limbs to the center of the two trees. Perched between the two she searched around for something, anything, that would tell her what to do. There was nothing.

"I don't see anything," she called down in desperation. "What do I…?"

She went rigid as the flow of Kilaray filled her. It felt like an ocean current forcing its way through her chest. The golden strands of light between the two arched pillars pulled away from the ground as the bonds passed through Rebecca and into the two trees. Noe Avaka and Fayit howled with the force of the flows around them. Rebecca's

617

hands were clamped to the branches to either side of her; she could feel the Kilaraic energy rolling through her harder and faster than she ever had. She would be scoured away with the power. She felt her soul pulling loose from her body. One more second and she would be dead, one more heartbeat and that would be her last.

She was dead, she had to be. The flow had ceased. She must have died, but then what was that sound. Someone called her name, and she felt hands now, lifting her. Her head felt heavy as the hands hoisted her onto someone's back.

"Rebecca, Rebecca," she knew that voice but whose was it? "Come on, little sister, open your eyes, come on." She cracked her eyes and immediately wished she hadn't. The light made her brain hurt. She felt herself moving, and was set on the cold ground.

"Is she alive?" asked another voice, a growling voice.

"She draws air," a voice higher above her.

Rebecca tried her eyes again, more slowly. She saw three faces over her, all painted with concern. She swallowed and tried to move. Her hands felt like they had been dipped in frozen fire.

"There you are," said Wren, a smile fighting with the worry on his brow. "You did it, little sister."

Rebecca turned her head and saw she was on the ground, laid before the gap. The two pillars still stood but the Linked net was gone. The two white trees no longer touched; their forms had bent away from one another. It was done; the Gates were open.

Seventy-two: Strangers in the Forest

It took Rebecca almost half an hour before she could sit up straight. Noe Avaka went on about what she had done.

"A conduit, girl child, you funneled the energy from the Gate through yourself. Remarkable you weren't killed really." He paced back and forth and ran his strange hands through his tiger striped hair. He stopped suddenly and looked at her shrewdly. "I lent you myself for that bit of Link work, girl child. I won't add that to your account but don't expect me to deduct any of your debt either."

"Noe, I don't care if you double my debt; just let me rest. My mind feels like it's been forced through a knot hole." Rebecca said as she laid her head back on her satchel. "I need something to eat."

"Quite right," said Noe Avaka. "A bit of tea and some meat and you'll be on your feet in no time."

Fayit stood silently, watching through the open Gates. Wren stood from Rebecca's side, as Noe prepared food, and joined her.

"What are we going to find in there?" he asked her; his hand unconsciously squeezed the hilt of his sword.

"It has been a long time," she said to him. "I know as much as you about what to expect." Rebecca watched the two; they were more alike than she would have thought. Fayit's hand was gripped to the savage blade Garin had given her.

They decided to make camp in the forest they had come through. "We know what dangers to watch for here," Fayit had said. Rebecca slept deep that night.

In the morning, they rose and broke camp; soon, they stood before the Gates once more. No one seemed to want to take the first step into the unknown. Rebecca broke their hold, gripping Astenos's hilt firmly, she stepped toward the gap. She heard the foot falls that told her the others were behind her. Soon Wren had taken up the lead, his narrow sword unsheathed and ready.

The stone of the walls arched together overhead, giving the feel of a cavernous long hall. The slick walls reflected the light from both sides of the Gates, so though the walls were black they could see well enough. Slowly the wall's texture changed; it became lighter in color, almost the color of sandstone. The arched opening at the far side grew larger as they approached. The gap in the forest on this side seemed less defined. Eventually they emerged again into the open.

Rebecca turned to see the Barrier from this side and her breath caught. This side of the barrier looked like an enormous city wall. Layer upon layer of columned walkways stretched off into the distance. The Barrier wall looked less natural and more hand crafted.

"What do you make of this?" asked Wren, crouching down to something on the ground. Rebecca broke her gaze from the wall to see what he had found. A print, wider than Rebecca was tall, pressed deep into the soil. It had the marks of four, three-foot long, claws where the toes had touched. "I'd say we should keep an eye out for whatever left this." They all agreed.

They moved into the forest on this side of the Barrier; the difference was not apparent at first. It took Rebecca a while to realize the sounds of the animals had changed, a subtle difference in the calls, as though they spoke with a different accent. They walked for hours with no direction. The compass, having passed through the barrier, now appeared to function as any normal compass, pointing north.

They made camp for mid meal and ate quickly, they didn't want to remain stationary for too long.

The apprehension Rebecca had felt upon crossing the Barrier had left her, frustration replaced it. They had no idea what they were looking for; they had not spotted a path, or even a game trail. They were about to stop when a strange call tore through the sky above them. The forest became silent instantly, not a cricket could be heard. The call was a throaty bellowing cry; whatever it was it sounded large. Rebecca looked around; the others eyes were white all around. They progressed more cautiously from that point on. An hour passed since they had heard the call when Astenos tingled in her mind.

She stopped for a moment and felt it again. "Something comes," she said as the others stopped to look at her. Fayit reached down and hoisted Noe Avaka up onto her shoulders. Wren pulled his cloak over his shoulder to gain access to his knives. She could feel it coming closer.

A cracking of trees crashed toward them. The lower plants rocked as whatever was coming approached quickly. Suddenly, a man burst through the underbrush before them at a run. His eyes were wide with fear but he was smiling.

"Velto!" he cried as he bolted past them.

"What in the Blazes was that?" asked Wren, sheathing his sword.

"I believe he said, 'Run!'" said Noe Avaka.

"Run?" asked Wren, but before he could ask more, a second person burst through the trees. She stopped; her face bright with excitement. She grabbed Wren's arm pulling at him, and shouting in a panting voice.

"Velto! Velto!" she yelled.

"What are you talking..." he began but a thundering roar cut him short.

"Orae es a cronus a velto!" she bellowed, pushing Wren forward and reaching out for Rebecca's hand.

"She said, 'Now is the time to run!'" Noe Avaka said as they quickly followed after the man who had passed them.

The trees behind them began to part as they ran; not just the smaller ones but trunks a foot across too. Foot falls shook the ground beneath them and they dashed deeper into the forest. The woman ran flat out through the trees, her legs flashing in the broken light from the canopy overhead. Rebecca's lungs started to burn. Whatever chased them was catching up.

A clearing opened up in front of them with a river running through it. They would have to wade through to cross. Suddenly, the creature that chased them broke through the forest and Rebecca could see it for the first time.

A mammoth beast on four legs, standing as tall as some of the trees. It spotted them and bellowed from a mouth that could have swallowed Fayit whole. Its back was covered in what appeared to be small trees and plants and a coating of moss, perfect camouflage. Its mouth dripped froth and its eyes were caked in a yellow slime. It rocked its head back and forth, brandishing two huge red horns that grew from its snout. Its red-striped throat rumbled as it pawed the ground, digging deep furrows with massive claws, about to charge.

A dark shadow passed overhead, covering most of the clearing. Rebecca looked up and caught sight of bright tail feathers. A throaty cry above broke the tension. The huge beast halted and looked skyward. It slowly backed into the trees and vanished more quickly than Rebecca could believe for such a massive creature.

"What...was...that?" panted Wren, holding a stitch in his side.

"I...I...don't know," said Rebecca, catching her breath. She looked around to find the man that had passed them staring at them. "Noe, could you thank them, please." The man held a javelin with a foot long metal spike at its end. He was bare-chested and wore little over the rest of him. His face was painted in bright blue and red patterns, the sides of his head were shaved in jagged shapes, and the rest of his hair stood in a blue-painted crest atop his scalp.

"Ah, yes," said Noe Avaka, climbing down from Fayit's shoulders. He approached the man tentatively and spoke. "Uh, let's see, multo gatzi, imo amicus." The man's eyes widened and he laughed.

"Cev, proximo; em oporto ecce," he called over his shoulder. The woman who had grabbed them came closer and gaped at Noe Avaka.

She was equally as exposed as the man. She had a thin strip of fabric bound around her chest and wore loose fabric coverings over her hips that left her legs bare. Her skin was the color of copper in the sun and her hair was like a raven's wings. Her dark eyes studied the group, lingering on Noe Avaka and Fayit, but dispensing a good amount of disbelief for Rebecca and Wren.

"Ens, visago," she said in a husky voice, looking at Wren, and motioning around her mouth with a smile, "Ets simi es ona gonga." She laughed as did the man. Wren looked dumbstruck.

"Illandra," he said in a whisper. Rebecca looked to the woman and she saw what he was talking about. If the woman's head had not had jagged patterns trimmed to her scalp, and had her face not been painted in green and yellow shapes, she could have been the living version of the figurehead from Illandra's Heart. "What did she say?" Wren asked quickly.

Noe hid his mouth behind a strange hand. "She said, 'His face, it's like a goat'."

Rebecca barked a laugh before she could stop herself. Wren's face crumpled into a mischievous smirk.

He stepped forward and pointed at the woman. "Look here, you savage…" but whatever else he had to say was lost when the woman grabbed his hand and rolled him over her to the ground. Rebecca threw her hands up to stop the man from running Wren through with his javelin.

"Noe, tell them we don't mean any harm." Noe translated quickly. "Tell them we came through from the Gates and we could use some help." The two quickly shifted their glares to Noe when he translated the last. The woman spoke to Rebecca, stepping closer and looking down at her; she stood a head and a half taller than Rebecca.

"She wants to know if you are speaking true," said Noe Avaka.

Rebecca nodded and the woman whipped her head around to the man.

"Nico, nos oporto egi a pardra," she said. "Nico, we must take them to father," translated Noe Avaka.

The group followed, in a tight knot, the two people they had met. They chattered away in their tongue obviously in an argument. Rebecca listened to Noe Avaka's translation. The man, Nico, wanted to return to hunt the beast that they had run from; an anset Noe Avaka said they called it. The woman, Cev, seemed to think it best to take them to their father; he seemed someone of importance from what Noe Avaka gathered. Fayit eventually was able to catch on to the words, it was in a dialect she was familiar with, and she too related what the two said.

"I believe that animal was sick," Fayit said. "Nico wants to stop it before it causes any harm to their people."

"Well, he can do it later," grumbled Wren. "I don't trust these people, little sister. They're backwards savages." He eyed the woman with anger plain on his face. "Just look how they're dressed." He seemed unable to take his eye from the woman's strong legs. Rebecca smiled to herself; he didn't like the fact that she had gotten the better of him, but his eyes seemed to like following her outline. She thought maybe some of the effects of the Blue were finally wearing off of him.

"They warned us," said Fayit. "They did not have to stop for us."

Wren shook his head, but his eyes lingered on Cev's form. Suddenly, the two stopped ahead of them. Their argument had become louder; their arms flailed wildly as they shouted at one another. Fayit and Noe stared at one another and translated what they said.

"Apparently, Nico, thinks if they return without proof of stopping the anset, their father will be most displeased," said Noe Avaka.

"Cev thinks he will be more displeased if they get us killed tracking down the creature. She says Nico is being an over proud…"she paused and looked to Noe for help. "What is 'aozzi'?" she asked.

Noe looked delighted. "It refers to a type of burro I believe," he said. "This man kind woman is quite amusing."

"Yeah, quite amusing," said Wren, looking annoyed. "What's happening? Where is he going?"

Nico had stopped his arguing, turned, and started walking back toward the group. He passed them without a glance and stalked into the trees, hefting his javelin. Cev looked concerned and then approached Noe Avaka; she spoke quick words.

"She says that she may have gone too far with her brother," said Noe Avaka his head turned slightly to speak to the rest of the group. "Nico, she says, is desperate to prove himself worthy to their father and may get himself killed in the process. She seems to be asking us if we would join her in bringing back her brother."

"No," said Wren hurriedly.

"Yes," said Rebecca, right on top of him.

Cev looked between the two of them as though trying to decide who was in charge. She settled on Rebecca and Wren folded his arms looking disgusted with the woman.

"She says she will be glad to take us to her father, but she can't leave her brother to hunt the anset alone," said Fayit.

"Tell her we will help her," said Rebecca. Fayit quickly related Rebecca's words and the woman's face broke in a warm smile. She grabbed Rebecca's hand in hers and shook it. She turned to Wren and her eyes narrowed. His infuriating smile seemed dipped in animosity. Cev looked to Wren and spoke quickly.

"Decoro em egeno ima a suspensum emo amicus des ona arada por em?" she said, smiling with a vicious grin. "Would you like me to hang your friend from a tree for you?" Noe Avaka said happily. Wren leered at Cev and spared some for Noe Avaka.

"Tell her I'm watching her," Wren growled.

"She says 'I noticed'; and she thinks you should not gape so openly at women or you'll end up with flies in your mouth," said Noe Avaka as he turned to follow Cev. He began chattering away to her.

Rebecca felt sorry for Wren; he looked so helpless staring after Cev in open incredulity. She patted his arm before she turned and followed after Noe Avaka and Fayit.

They caught Nico halfway back to the clearing they had last seen the anset. He refused to listen to his sister and forged across the river. They had no choice but to follow. He paused to find the tracks, and stalked through the forest, his javelin ready. It became clear that they were not going to be able to turn Nico in his pursuit. Grumbling, Wren pulled his sword.

"If we can't stop the fools," he said, marching after Cev, "we might as well join them."

Fayit followed Wren's lead and readied her large bow. Rebecca looked to Noe Avaka; he seemed on the edge of flight.

"Come along," she said, unsheathing Astenos. "Maybe you'll learn something to make it worth your time." Reluctantly he nodded and followed at her heels.

They moved through the forest as quietly as they could, best to have every advantage they could on the creature. After about an hour, a rutting noise echoed through the trees. Nico crouched down, edging forward slowly. As they emerged from a copse of head-high plants, Nico held up his hand for them to halt, and then gestured for them to move closer slowly.

The creature stood in a valley below them. It pawed at the base of a tree with its clawed feet, ducking its massive head now and again into the hole it created. It kept shaking its head to clear the yellow scum from its eyes and froth dripped from its munching jaws. Every few minutes spasms would wrack the great beast and it would moan a deep sorrowful sound that vibrated the ground beneath them.

"Cev says the Anset has the shaking sickness," whispered Noe Avaka. "It gets into the creatures' brains and drives them mad. These animals are usually docile but this one has been raiding the villages nearby, destroying and killing whatever gets in its path."

Rebecca watched the great beast and felt pity for it. It seemed confused now and then, looking around in fear. The plants that grew from its back seemed ill as well, now that she could see it better. The leaves were wilting and brown and the moss showed bare patches of pale flesh beneath in spots.

"Nico says, their father sent them to bring it peace," said Fayit. "These creatures seem to be held in high regard with these people. He keeps saying this is a dishonorable way for the anset to live. I believe we should help them," she said, turning to Rebecca; she stroked the savage blade again. Rebecca agreed; she could see the anset was in pain and fear.

"What do we do?" she asked.

"Cev has already wounded the creature," said Noe Avaka. Rebecca looked and could see a trickle of blood from a hole in the anset's front leg; the javelin stuck deep into the flesh seemed like a twig. "They usually divert the creature's attention while someone gets beneath it to run it through the heart. She says it will be difficult with only one javelin among them."

Rebecca looked to Fayit's bow; her arrows would do little against such a massive animal. It would be up to her, Wren, or Nico to get below the beast. Noe Avaka translated Rebecca's words and they agreed. The six moved slowly into their positions. Fayit, Noe Avaka, and Cev would drive the beast toward the others. They were to work their way beneath the anset.

Rebecca hid behind a tree, looking across to where Wren stood. He shook his head and muttered to himself, but his face was set in that almost passive look he had in Nor Harbor when he had saved her. She had no fear for him but the others could be killed with one swipe of those huge clawed feet. The forest around them seemed to hold its breath to see what played out.

Fayit stepped out from behind a tree and called to the anset. It spun about and locked on to her. It started to stagger forward when Cev jumped from cover and started shouting at the animal's side. The ground churned beneath its weight as it rounded on the new threat. It took a step back and Fayit fired a bow shot at its flank. The animal bellowed and turned back to Fayit. Noe Avaka popped out of nowhere and began shaking his staff and shouting. The animal, faced with three fronts, started to turn. Fayit fired another arrow to convince the beast.

It turned and lumbered toward where Rebecca, Wren, and Nico were hidden. It was nearly past Nico when he ran from where he stood to chase along its side. Rebecca and Wren followed suit. The three chased along the flanks of the animal, trying to time their sprints for its soft, pale, red-striped underbelly. The stink from the creature made Rebecca scrunch her nose. It smelled a mix of decaying vegetation, sweat, and rotting meat.

Nico darted beneath the animal and made to force his javelin upward, but somehow the animal sensed he was there and swatted at him. He dodged sideways just missing a fatal strike. He tumbled on the ground and was on his feet again in a flash. The anset changed course, veering toward Rebecca and Wren. They followed it, trying to move toward the clear space between its galloping legs.

Wren seemed to see a hole and made for it. He ran along beneath the creature's heaving ribcage a foot above his head. He reared back his narrow sword and plunged it upward. The roar of pain shook Rebecca's teeth and the anset stumbled, knocking Wren from below it. He seemed to have missed his target; the creature regained its footing and lumbered on, spilling a trail of blood from where Wren's sword was still stuck. Rebecca turned her head to see Wren. He staggered to his feet; Cev stopped to check him before returning to the chase.

Rebecca's legs burned from her all-out sprint through the uneven forest. She could see Nico intermittently between the animal's striding legs. His jaw was clenched in determination. Rebecca could see he was nearly in place for a second attempt when Astenos spoke into her mind.

He won't make it, Rebecca. The shock of the words threw her footing off and she nearly fell.

"What?" she thought to him. "What are you talking about?"

The beast is about to change direction. Tell this Nico to stop or he'll be trampled.

"I don't know how, Astenos."

Desino orae!

"Nico, desino orae!" Rebecca screamed at the top of her lungs. Nico turned to look at her in confusion. "Desino! Desino!" she screamed. He fell back just as the anset turned toward him, stepping where he had been about to jump. She didn't have time to be relieved because now the anset knew it was being followed. It dodged wildly back and forth. Rebecca was alone to bring the animal down.

Up, Rebecca, go up. Astenos roared in her head.

She jumped and caught hold of the anset's back leg. Its skin was thick and tough, forming huge wrinkles in the flesh which she used to climb its thundering legs. She was nearly shaken loose as she reached its hind quarters. She kept low on the anset's rolling back, clinging to its wrinkled skin as it shook to get her off. She progressed into the plants growing from the creatures back. The smell of decay increased. The plants were coated in a thick oozing muck. She worked her way toward the anset's head. Abruptly, the anset stopped. Rebecca had to grip tight to a four inch wide tree trunk to keep from being thrown off.

She regained her senses and dashed forward, bringing Astenos up above her head. She dropped to her knees, squeezing her eyes shut, at the base of the anset's skull and plunged her Blade deep into the flesh. A spray of hot blood splashed across her cheeks and mouth. She had to hold onto Astenos, as the anset's legs gave way, their connection to the creature's rotting brain severed.

Rebecca let out the breath she didn't realize she had been holding and panted with exhaustion. She fell back onto her elbows. Her heart felt like it would burst through her ribs. She wiped her face on her sleeve. She opened her eyes and looked at an expanse of open sky.

The Anset had stopped short of a vertical drop that appeared from the forest. Rebecca sat up and walked the length of the anset's head. Gripping the red-colored horns growing from the animal's snout, she leaned out over the drop and her breath caught. A hundred-foot plunge to the treetops below faced her.

She looked out over the vista from atop the animal's head – trees as far as her eye could see. She squinted at the blue sky around her and she spotted something that, for the second time, made her breath stop. A shape moved up there. It looked huge but it was hard to judge from below. Its wings were black, silhouetted against the sun, as it circled overhead. It twitched its wings and soared off behind her, vanishing above the treetops around her.

"Rebecca," called Fayit, finally catching up. Rebecca turned to see the path cleared through the dense forest. Wren ran beside Nico, Cev and Noe Avaka, a little behind. "Are you well?" she panted, looking concerned and excited. Rebecca nodded that she was and pulled Astenos from the Anset's neck. Fayit lowered her down and she wiped the blood from Astenos with some leaves.

"Nico seems to think you know their tongue," said Noe Avaka when he arrived. "He says you told him to stop just before the creature turned."

Rebecca thought for a moment; *is that what she had said?* "It wasn't me. It was Astenos," she said. They all looked at her. "He told me what to say."

"Well, he saved Nico's life," said Wren. "That thing would have crushed him if he hadn't stopped." Cev watched the group speaking and after a few seconds scrunched her brow in concentration, speaking in an unpracticed way.

"Th-than-thank you," she smiled at Rebecca. The looks shifted from Rebecca to Cev. Her smile broadened and she laughed.

Seventy-four:
The Icari

They had trouble retrieving Wren's sword. The anset had fallen on it, pushing it deep into its chest. By the time they had pulled the blade from the creature's body, Rebecca, Cev, Nico, and Wren were blood soaked, and covered in gore. The anset, Nico said, was not safe to eat, not when it had the shaking sickness. So, the carcass was left for the forest to consume. Nico cut the huge horns from the animal's snout for proof of their success and they walked to a nearby stream to wash themselves.

Cev and Nico dove into the deep dark water without hesitation, their painted faces and hair coming up clean. Wren and Rebecca stood at the edge and looked to one another. After the anset, they wondered what might be lurking below the surface. Nico and Cev assured them it was safe and Rebecca and Wren followed after them. Cev and Nico whispered to one another as they watched Wren and Rebecca swimming. Cev's eyes kept wandering over Wren's bare chest, stopping to examine the tattoos and the brand on his neck.

It was too late to set off for Nico and Cev's village so they made camp near the stream. Nico and Cev marveled at the salamander when Rebecca pulled it from her satchel and showed them how it worked. They gathered round the fire, Rebecca's and Wren's clothes draped over rocks near the flames to dry, and shared last meal together. Fayit and Noe Avaka worked as interpreters between the humans. Cev remarked on Wren's tattoos and the brand on his neck.

"She wonders what that hand around the Tree means," said Fayit as she sipped at a cup of tea.

"Tree?" asked Wren. "What tree?" He hastily rewrapped the still damp blue scarf around his throat.

"She says she can understand some of the other markings but the Tree should not be surrounded with other symbols," Fayit looked at him like she agreed with what Cev said. "And it shouldn't be hidden like you do." That, Rebecca could tell, was Fayit's opinion. Rebecca felt the tension rise around the campfire. Wren's surprised face flashed to his haughty smirk in an instant and Rebecca could tell his venom was about to come out.

"Well, you can tell it to the men who held me down and seared it into my neck, beastie." He looked like he wanted to hit Fayit; she in turn rumbled deep in her chest as she showed her teeth.

"Stop!" Rebecca said. "Wren, calm yourself." He looked at her and his eyes tightened slightly. Cev leered at Wren now.

This man should be beaten until he learns to act more civil. Astenos spoke into her mind as Cev spoke. She looked to Noe Avaka and shook her head slightly to stop him from translating.

"What did she say?" roared Wren.

"Nothing, Wren, sit back down." He was looming over the fire staring at Cev with heat in his eyes. He heeded her words and sat beside her, turning slightly away from the group. "He didn't choose the symbol," she said, "and...and it should not have been done to him." Wren's head snapped around to stare at her in disbelief. "He didn't earn what that symbol implies." Noe Avaka translated her words and Cev nodded. She asked a question.

"She wants to know what it means," said Fayit. She looked to Rebecca then to Wren.

"Tell her," he said. "All of you know; why shouldn't they?" He laughed to himself.

Noe Avaka explained and Nico and Cev looked to one another; they looked startled, then angry. "They say this man Mandagore Adarian should not have defiled the Tree with his hand," Noe Avaka said.

Cev stood and walked to face Wren, she squatted in front of him her face set in a grimace. She took a twig from the ground and began drawing on the dirt in front of him. She spoke and Fayit translated what she said.

"The Father above," said Fayit as Cev drew a triangle in the soil, "first sent forth the Listeners." Cev drew a curved line tipped with an arrow at its end, extending from the base of the triangle; she pointed to Fayit. Fayit inclined her head slightly. "Then the Father sent forth the Teachers," Cev drew a second line, curving away from the first in the soil from the base of the triangle. She pointed to Noe Avaka. "Lastly, the father sent forth the Children." She drew a third straight line between the two; this one she tipped with a small circle. She gestured around to Rebecca, and Nico, herself, and lastly pointed at Wren. Cev dropped the twig and looked into Wren's eyes. The symbol she had drawn was the glyph inside the palm of the hand of the Traitor's Mark on Wren's neck. "She says she was wrong; you are right to keep such a symbol of pride covered." Cev stood staring down at Wren, his face was awash in astonishment.

The rest of the meal passed in relative silence. Rebecca felt her stomach unknot slowly as the conversation returned and the topics shifted to lighter fare. Cev joined Rebecca and chatted away to her, Fayit translating for Rebecca and Astenos volunteering more of his knowledge of the language. Soon Rebecca was teaching Cev more

Arnoran words. Nico had moved around to sit beside Wren; Noe Avaka joined them to help. Wren seemed to take to Nico after a while and Rebecca felt easier.

Rebecca envied the ease with which Cev seemed to pick up the language. She still chattered away in her own tongue but she slipped more and more of the words Rebecca had taught her into that chatter. As the night wore on Rebecca began to drift a little and so thought she had slipped off to sleep when she heard Cev speak.

"Es…tiss man, Wren, you…um," her eyebrows knotted as she looked at the fire and Rebecca sat up to listen. "Is this man, Wren, yours…loved one?" She turned to look at Rebecca with a smile. Fayit chuckled to Rebecca's side. Rebecca's head whipped to look at the Tremen woman. The men across the fire stared at the women; Wren looked like he had just been punched in the gut.

"Uh, no, he's…my, my, uh, friend. My Guard Keeper," Rebecca stammered. Cev looked to Fayit for the translation.

"En es ere amicus, alto ere Palantea," said Fayit. The last word Rebecca recognized. "One who guards." Cev smiled and nodded her understanding.

Cev leaned in and whispered into Rebecca's ear; Astenos chuckled in her head as he translated.

He would be handsome if he would shave that fur from his lips, Rebecca laughed out loud and looked at Wren. His eyes narrowed as though he had heard and understood what Cev had said.

In the morning, Rebecca woke stiff from sleeping on the forest floor. Cev lay next to her; they had fallen asleep whispering to one another. The woman was maybe three or four years older than

637

Rebecca. It felt odd having another woman of an age with her to talk with, even though Rebecca understood half of the words she said.

Rebecca looked across the fire and saw Wren sitting where he had the previous night. She knew he didn't sleep often times, and when he did, he muttered in his sleep and thrashed about. He broke his eyes away from where Cev laid soundly asleep and met Rebecca's. He pinched his eyes as though trying to clear them, but Rebecca could tell it was a diversion.

Wren was older than Cev by about as many years as she was older than Rebecca. He had mentioned something about a lack of women grating on a man's mind once, and Rebecca thought she understood. Wren's insistence on calling her 'little sister' seemed to have convinced him that she was just that to him. She felt a similar bond to the man now.

After so much time spent together they had grown closer, though she still held a deep enmity for what he had done. But the defense she had given for him last night diluted that enmity somewhat. She thought she might even believe what she had said. She could not see Wren betraying her; the only thing that seemed to frighten him was that she would be harmed. Perhaps her brother had felt the same for him. The thought felt odd in her mind though; Wren had told her that Sebastian had known Wren would lose against his Murmur. That brought her mind around to what else she had not known about her brother.

He had known; she was sure of it. Maybe he had learned of Reached Visions. But if that was true, why had he sent Wren out in the first place? It was as though he had used Wren to betray himself, like the traitor was in fact Sebastian. That made her feel sick in her stomach but it was Wren that stopped her mind's wanderings down that path.

"The Fates, they have a sense of humor," Wren said quietly to her.

She stood and covered Cev with the cloak she had used for a blanket. She walked across the camp to where Wren sat. His eyes had returned to Cev's sleeping form.

"What are you talking about?" she asked as she sat beside him. He sighed in an odd way and looked at her with a wry grin.

"Illandra reborn lies across from me," he said to her. "Me a son of Mraxis, and what would the Fates have for me but to have us despise one another, cruel humor. Perhaps they know me too well." Rebecca smiled and slumped her head against his shoulder. He froze rigid as steel for a moment; she could feel his breath catch. He relaxed slowly, as though he had felt a friendly touch for the first time in his life, uncertain of what it was. Her heart went out to her friend.

"I don't think you despise one another," she said softly. "You're like two strange cats thrown together for the first time. Your fur is still ruffled."

He laughed softly. "Little sister, we're more like a leopard and a pit viper," he said, turning to look down at her head. Nico began to rouse from sleep and Cev shifted beneath Rebecca's cloak. Fayit marched into the camp with Noe Avaka. Rebecca looked up into Wren's face with an impish grin.

"She thinks you're handsome," she said and stood, leaving him looking bewildered. His head whipped from Rebecca to Cev. To confound him further, Cev stretched her arms as she sat up, looked across the dead fire to Wren, and scowled at him.

The camp was cleared after first meal and Nico and Cev each took one of the massive red horns. Cev walked next to Rebecca; Fayit strode along beside them. She seemed to find female company more pleasant, even though they weren't Tremen. This left Wren, Nico, and Noe Avaka to travel together.

Rebecca could hear Wren laugh every now and then, pitched for the women to hear. Cev would smile viciously at this and whisper something into Rebecca's ear. Usually it was something funny about Wren, his appearance, the way he smelled, but always something about him. Rebecca began to find this downright childish after a time.

"You know, if you are so intent on talking about him," she whispered, "why don't you just talk *to* him?" Fayit filled in the words Cev didn't catch.

"You do not know the man, Rebecca," she said haltingly. "It is best to, um..." she made a gesture like pulling a rope, muttered something, and Fayit gave her the word. "Yes, draw the man on. That way they are so pleased when you let them near." She smiled as though this made absolute sense.

"Then you do want him near you?" she asked a little confused.

"Him? No, no, no, never him." Something about the way her eyes jumped to Wren made Rebecca doubt the woman's conviction.

Rebecca followed along and the more she talked to Cev the more she liked her. Wren's futile attempts at getting Cev's attention had ceased and when Rebecca turned to see them, the three men were talking heatedly about something. Nico was smiling and urging Wren to go forward, Noe Avaka was shaking his head desperately. Finally, Wren picked up his pace, a fiendish expression on his face. Rebecca had a strong feeling this was going to be bad.

Wren fell in beside Cev and she looked coolly ahead. Wren looked back to Nico who smiled fiercely, holding back a laugh. Noe Avaka looked ready to bolt into the trees.

"Nico says you dance well in the binding rings," he said to the air. Fayit hesitantly translated what Wren had said. "He says…" he looked back to Nico; he urged Wren to continue, "…that you are always prickly before your father forces you to join the other women." Cev stopped walking after Fayit reluctantly translated the words at Cev's urging. "I told him," his eyes narrowed, "that the men should be the ones to fear the Father binding you to them." Nico snorted with laughter and Rebecca looked confused. Fayit rolled her eyes and sighed finally telling Cev what he had said. Cev's cheeks darkened and her head whipped around to her brother; he stopped his mirth short at the dark gaze she cast him.

She looked back to Wren; the fire in her eyes should have singed his moustaches. "You, you…" she looked to Rebecca for help, Fayit answered instead.

"Are a cruel man, Wren Tobias. You should not speak of what you do not understand." Wren's smile broadened. Rebecca thought a pit viper would have been a kind comparison. Cev snatched up the anset horn and stalked away, Fayit following after.

"What is wrong with you?" Rebecca groaned. "What was that about anyway?"

Noe Avaka explained as he caught up. "The binding rings are a traditional marriage ceremony. The women dance, allowing the music to lead them to the man that the Father has sent for them." Rebecca looked cold fury at Wren as understanding bloomed. "Cev has danced in the rings for several years, since she was old enough to wed." Noe Avaka looked reluctant to finish. "She always leaves the rings last, alone. Her father assures her that the Tree Father is waiting for the man that will suit his only daughter."

"I agree with Nico," said Wren, "there aren't men made to handle that woman." His smile faltered only a little as he said it. If Rebecca had believed he meant what he said she would have stabbed him with one of his knives. As it was she settled on punching him in the short ribs; he doubled over with a grunt.

"You are an utter fool," she hissed at him. She stormed away after Cev and Fayit.

After several hours of walking through the forest, Rebecca heard the sounds of people ahead. A soft hum of conversation drifted through the trees, the smell of cooking and fires permeated the forest smells of rain and leaves. Cev's face brightened as she picked up her pace.

She had been more reserved since Wren had insulted her, walking for stretches of minutes without saying a word, staring contemplatively at the ground. Rebecca had tried to apologize for Wren but Cev would turn her head away as though the smell of the words Rebecca spoke was distasteful.

The forest path widened and became a packed dirt trail. After a short distance, set stone replaced dirt. Rebecca caught sight of the first building and stopped short, causing Cev to turn to see what had happened. She beamed at the look on Rebecca's face.

Like living stone, the building grew from the ground. The base was like a tree trunk, tapering and branching as the building's height increased. Soft glowing orbs, suspended in webs of woven fibers, hung from steel posts around the building, leading out along the stone streets; the posts twined like iron vines, no two the same. The openings in the building were nearly hidden, windows and doors worked in seamlessly with the walls around them, almost like knot holes. Bright patterns were painted onto the surfaces, symbols above the doors named what it was, a sort of school Cev said.

A woman herding a flock of children called out to Cev; she turned and lifted the anset horn over her head. The children, wearing similar buff-colored fabric wrappings as Cev and Nico, cheered and the woman's wrinkled face split with joy. She wore considerably more clothing, a cloak, pinned with a silver broach, over her shoulder dyed a deep violet color, a tunic and open skirt of soft white material, and she wore large brightly colored feathers; they were woven into her white hair and splayed out onto her curved back. Then the woman caught sight of Fayit and Rebecca, and the look of joy evaporated. Her dark eyes widened in fear, and she clutched the children tight to her. They for the most part seemed interested in the newcomers, their faces wide with curiosity.

"Come, I will take you to father," Cev said, looking concerned.

The hum of voices they had heard came from the men and women bustling about the village. The words may have been different but the sounds could have been from Arinelle, in Arnora; the noises of towns were the same everywhere. Men leading goats, or driving mules pulling carts laden with goods, lined the stone streets. Women carrying babies in bundles on their backs, or leading older children by the hand, wove through the throng of people toward the school they had passed. Men and women of an age with Cev and Nico gathered in groups gossiping and laughing, their clothing baring tanned skin. Craftsmen pounded steel, carved wood, or chipped stone, their apprentices watching closely to see the way of the skill. Rebecca began

643

to notice a hush that they left behind them as they passed along the streets.

The sound of activity was quenched as the six moved through the village. It was like a wake of concerned anxiety trailed them. Men and women stopped what they were doing to watch them pass, most with looks like the old woman they had first seen. Slowly, by ones and twos, men put down their hammers, or saws, or chisels, women handed their children to their aged mothers, or dragged them along behind, young men and women stopped their conversations, and fell in behind the group. Soon they had a chain of men and women following them in complete silence. The people looked like they had been transplanted from every corner of the world. Every combination of skin and hair dotted the tail of people. Rebecca caught worried whispers from them when she would turn.

Cev led them through the meandering village past more of the extraordinary buildings. They came to a great round plaza. The stone work in the plaza was laid out in three interwoven rings; Rebecca could see where generations of people had worn the rings into shallow bowls. At the head of the plaza, a series of the strange buildings grew close by one another, their branches connecting the trunks to form one structure. Cev led them toward a wide opening at the foot of one of the trunks. Huge men in thick leather armor stood guard, a long pike in hand and a short horn bow and quiver of arrows at their sides. They clapped fists to hearts when they spotted Cev approaching. Rebecca and Fayit received a less welcoming reception.

"Desino!" the guards shouted in unison, snapping up their pikes and pointing them at Rebecca and Fayit. Wren appeared, as if from the air before Rebecca, his narrow sword in one hand, a knife in the other. The guards didn't take to this well and started to move on Wren. The crowd made noises of astonishment.

"Palantean Desino!" shouted Cev and Nico at once. The guards stopped without hesitation, snapping back into their standing positions, but eyeing Wren warily.

"Wren, put away your weapons, for Father's sake," Rebecca said urgently. He complied and the guards' knuckles loosened slightly on their pikes. The crowd resumed its solemn silence.

Cev spoke heated words to the two men as they looked directly ahead, their faces like stone. The group proceeded into the building, Rebecca turned to see Nico speak to the two men in a friendlier manner. The two guards returned to their posts and Rebecca could see the grins on their faces.

Cev led the group into a sort of chamber. The stone walls seemed even more like a hollowed tree from within. The windows around the building cast the room in spots of light like the forest canopy. All around the chamber were painted, patterned images of snakes and birds, lions and deer, even an anset and a massive winged creature Rebecca could not identify, all in stylized forms. The center of the room showed a mosaic of tiles of deep greens and blues, laid out in the symbol of the Tree Cev had drawn.

She led them to a man sitting cross-legged on a cushion on the floor. He was gray at the temples and his face was like leather, but Rebecca could see the resemblance between Nico and him. He wore an indigo cloak, pinned with a gold version of the winged creature Rebecca could not identify. His chest was bare, showing well honed muscles. He wore a loose white breechcloth, held with a thick leather belt. His cheeks were as smooth as Nico's, and his hair was long and held braids with more of the bright large feathers interwoven. His eyes were closed as if in meditation but he spoke in a strong deep voice when Cev stopped before him. Fayit whispered to Rebecca what he said.

"You come before me daughter," he said. "You have returned with more than that with which you left."

"The anset died well, father," she said in a voice filled with respect.

"But, neither you nor my son ended the great animal's suffering," he said.

Nico stepped forward and spoke, sounding irritated. "What was set before us has been done, father. What does it matter how the goal was achieved?"

The man's eyes flicked open, and stared yellow-green fire at his son. "It matters Nicolias because it was your goal to achieve. Not this girl's," he pointed at Rebecca. Fayit looked at the man and then at Rebecca as she finished. He seemed unsurprised to find two new people, a Tremen, and a Pictsie standing before him.

"Father, this is Rebecca," said Cev. The man stood and walked over to stare down at Rebecca; their eyes could have been a reflection in a pond. "Rebecca, this is my father, Talic," she said in words Rebecca had taught her. "He is the Chief Elder of the Icari."

"You have done what my son was sent to do," he said and Rebecca felt nervous. "You risked yourself to help my blood." He looked to Nico; his eyes sparkled with a mix of anger and relief. He placed his strong hands on Rebecca's shoulders and his face split in a smile like Cev's. He released her and walked to Nico; Nico stood looking to the floor in embarrassment. "You should not be so disheartened, my son. Your bravery and courage have brought peace to the great anset. I am pleased to see you well." He put his hands on

Nico's shoulders and shook him a bit. Nico looked up with a grimace. "Do you remember what I told you when I set this task before you?"

Nico nodded and spoke. "Yes, father. The path to any goal may have many obstacles and many opportunities."

Talic finally seemed to acknowledge the rest of the people standing before him. "My son, you have earned your place among men." Nico's face looked ecstatic, but a little confused.

"But I did not slay the anset, father," he said abashed.

"You have done far more than bring peace on that poor creature, my son. You have brought the ones who will lead us out of our isolation. You have found the World Strider," he said staring into Rebecca's eyes.

Talic sent Nico to the other Elders, bearing a knife with a bone hilt carved into a bird's head he pulled from his belt. Nico all but ran to comply. Cev remained with the group. Talic examined each of the newcomer's faces. His eyes seemed to measure them, judge them. Rebecca felt uneasy under that gaze. Noe Avaka remained unruffled; he looked on Talic like a lost treasure. Fayit seemed to measure the man gaze for gaze.

Wren shifted a little but his self confident air remained. Talic's eyes twitched when he looked into Wren's face. Then like lightning Talic seized Wren, locking his arms around Wren's throat and pinioning Wren's arms behind him. Talic's face was contorted in rage.

"Cevara," he called with cold fury to his daughter. "Retrieve the guards. This man is a spy for the Darklings." Rebecca's heart pounded as she hurried to Wren's side. Talic's grip was like a vise; Wren could not wriggle free.

"Stop," Rebecca shouted as Cev ran from the chamber looking back in fear and concern. "He's not a spy for the Darklings," Talic looked her in the face and it was difficult to keep her eyes on the man.

"He has a Taker bound to him, child. It will tell its kind where we are," Talic growled and Wren's face bleached white. Wren's eyes snapped to Rebecca's, pleading.

Guards raced into the chamber carrying pikes, and javelins, and putting arrows to bows, all of the points trained on Wren's heart. Cev stepped to Rebecca's side. Her face was painted in concern as she looked from Rebecca to Wren and back. Talic released Wren and stepped away.

"Guards, bind this man eyes, hands, and feet and feed him to the halicarras," said Talic. The guards moved to take Wren and his hands whipped to his knives. Rebecca reacted in an instant.

Astenos's blade filled the room with star fire light, like a molten strip of gold green sun. The guards halted at once and Talic pulled Cev behind him. A space opened up around Wren and Rebecca. Wren's hands held two narrow blades; he looked like a viper about to strike.

"This man is not to be harmed!" Rebecca said. The guards' faces never broke from their target. She heard her words echoing in the chamber's silence. She knew she had spoken in these people's tongue, the words flowing easily from Astenos.

"Palantean Desino!" called Talic after a tense moment. The men lifted their points, and slacked the pull of the bows but remained encircling the chamber. "Child, you do not know what you are doing. That man is not to be trusted; he is bound to a Taker." Fayit and Noe Avaka had frozen in place unable to speak.

"I know," said Rebecca, lowering Astenos, the light fading. The guards eased a hair. "He is in control though, and I have taken him as

648

my Guard Keeper." Talic looked worried at this and he seemed to look between the two quickly, his head flashed to look at Fayit.

"Why have you joined these two, Listener?" he asked roughly.

Fayit shook her head, "It was not I; my Pride Mistress bound them. She believed he could be trusted well enough."

"Um…Yes, and I quite agree," said Noe Avaka, stepping forward hesitantly. "He has been tied to this world, his soul sealed to an anchor." Cev's eyes looked to Wren's chest; she looked horrified. Talic considered what they told him.

Soon, other men and women entered the chamber. They were as equally graying as Talic, their cloaks and clothes of a similar type. They jabbered quickly to determine what was happening. The chamber was filled with gasps of astonishment as they spotted Rebecca, Fayit, and Noe Avaka, and then hisses of revulsion when Talic explained Wren. An argument broke out between the older men and women. Nico returned; the sides of his head had been shaved of their shapes, a green cloak pinned over his shoulder with a silver anset. He bore a tasseled javelin. He took up a position next to his father. Cev shifted to stand beside Rebecca; she took Rebecca's hand and squeezed it.

The majority of the men and women agreed with Talic's first inclination to feed Wren to the halicarras, whatever they were. But some of the older wizened members examined Wren and Rebecca; they too seemed to examine the Link binding Wren as her Guard Keeper.

The argument ceased and Talic turned to face Wren; Rebecca felt nervous. "You will be watched for now. At any sign that your Taker is gaining control, you will be put down." Wren looked relieved. He replaced his knives in his Stitcher's rig. "You will be disarmed as well." This Wren did not take well to. Rebecca had to stop him from saying anything. "Guards will be sent to the Barrier Port." He spoke to Rebecca now. "With your crossing, World Strider, the Barrier will be able to be crossed anywhere along its length. Your Guard Keeper may have brought ruin on what should be a time of great joy."

The guards waited for Rebecca to take Wren's knives and sword; it felt like removing a snake's fangs. Wren's sense of security removed, his eyes flashed around, never in one place for more than an instant. Rebecca handed the weapons to Talic, he in turn handed them to one of the guards. Cev's look of revulsion for Wren seemed to be permanently adhered to her face.

Seventy-five: A Glimpse of the Horizon

All but two of the guards left the chamber. The last two clung to Wren like his shadow. Rebecca sheathed Astenos and waited for Talic and the other Elder Council members to speak. Talic looked on the newcomers with heavy thoughts clear on his face.

"Father, this man Wren," said Nico after a moment, "I believe he can be trusted."

"So new to the place of men and yet already you speak as if a seasoned member of the Council," said a bent-backed old man in a deep gold cloak. "Talic your son seeks to take your place as the most forward speaker among us." Nico looked annoyed and abashed at once. Talic looked from the gold cloaked man to his son.

"Why do you speak for this man, my son?" Talic asked.

Nico recovered quickly, "He aided us in the anset hunt. He drew first blood. I would not believe it of him to betray us to the Darklings." Talic looked appraisingly at his son and nodded.

"My son will take up the watch of the World Strider's Guard Keeper until we reach a decision," he said. "Guards you may leave us." The guards hesitated. "Go!" roared Talic. The two guards spun on the spot and marched from the chamber. The Elder Council members shifted their feet, looking uncomfortable with Wren left relatively unguarded. "We must deliberate," said Talic to Rebecca and the others. "Cevara, Nicolias, show our guests our village. We will meet again at dusk, before the evening's festivities. Nicolias," Talic said with emphasis, "know that you will be held to account for your watch on this man." He finished pointing to Wren. Nico nodded looking grave.

Cev and Nico escorted the group from the chamber. The crowd that had gathered to see them in remained outside of the Council chambers. Cev seemed angry at seeing the mass of people awaiting their exit.

"What are all of you doing?" she shouted. "Go about your tasks; do you have nothing better to do than await the Council's words?" The crowd looked shocked but slowly they began to disperse with angry mutters. Cev turned to Rebecca with rage clear on her face.

"How could you allow this," she said, pointing to Wren, "to be bound to you, to even allow it near you?"

Rebecca was stunned; Wren looked like a dog with his tail between his legs. Rebecca backed him instantly. "What I do is my choice," she growled. "I trust Wren with my life." Wren gathered some of his confidence at this. Rebecca drew on Astenos for the words to continue; she spoke to Cev in her own tongue. "You seem to be as fickle as the wind in a storm. A short time ago you could not keep your eyes from my friend; now, you seem to want to skin him." Cev looked like she had been slapped. Her eyes narrowed as though she were about to attack.

"Stop this!" said Nico. "Cev, you will do as father instructed, as I will do as I was instructed. Come we will show you our home," he said, turning to the others.

Rebecca clung to Wren's side; Noe Avaka and Fayit a little way apart as Cev and Nico walked them through the village. Cev kept her eyes forward, her back as rigid as the iron posts that lit the streets. This left Nico to do the talking. He pointed out places of interest, where the council made their announcements, the binding rings, the trying grounds, apparently a place for warriors to test themselves against one another. Rebecca looked in amazement as Nico showed how the ansets were used.

She spotted the great heaving shapes in a cleared space. Their massive rolling backs sported an array of vegetation. Groups of men goaded them gently with heavy wood poles as they pulled huge slabs of stone into place. Once in place the men rubbed the ansets under their throats, making the creatures groan; the ground vibrated with their content. This apparently was how the beginnings of the structures were started. Cev seemed to loosen with the pride that came from the next location.

"...and these are the halicarras we keep," said Nico, halting before a railed-off pen. "The green one is Cev's, mine is the spotted gray one." Rebecca closed her mouth when she realized she gaped like a fish. Turning, she felt less foolish. Fayit stared wide-eyed, Noe Avaka trembled slightly. Wren seemed to be startled out of his reserve.

Before them, several great beasts sat basking in the sun. They had heads like hawks or falcons, sharp beaks in shades of black to yellow. Their sharp eyes locked onto the group, judging whether they were prey. Nico put his hand on Rebecca's shoulder nudging her forward.

"Do you want to see them closer?" he asked with a grin. "They will not harm you."

Rebecca warily allowed herself to be led forward; Wren followed close. Nico showed the group to the halicarra he had identified as his, it was slightly smaller than a horse; Cev separated from the group to see to her own. She scratched the beast roughly behind its skull; its feathers ruffled as it let out a squawk of pleasure. The animals had huge wings; folded under them a two-clawed fingered appendage

653

protruded from where a hand would be on a man, used as a foreleg. Its hind legs were veined and muscled beneath the short hair that covered them. Tails with splays of feathers swished flies from the creatures. The colorful feathers varied greatly, from brown to gray, red to green and they had protrusions on their skulls like the first buds of antlers.

"These are halicarras," said Nico. He grabbed his beast's head and scratched its jowls. It opened its beak and snapped playfully at his hand. Its eyes though, made Rebecca nervous; they never changed as they blinked, always they looked like a predator's.

"What is wrong outsider?" said Cev viciously as she turned from her halicarra. "Are you afraid the halicarra will see your friend's Taker and attack?"

Rebecca narrowed her eyes. Nico's and Wren's expressions were mirror images; they looked guarded like they expected to have to tame two wild beasts.

"Nico," Rebecca asked. "What do you keep these creatures for?"

"We use them to hunt healthy ansets," Nico said cautiously. "We ride them."

Rebecca stepped close to Nico's halicarra, allowing it to sniff her hand. She stroked the creature's beak and rubbed gingerly at the base of its skull. Cev smiled and walked away for a moment. She returned shortly with two harnesses, handing one to her brother.

"If you are so brave, outsider," she said, dropping the harness over her halicarra's neck, "perhaps you will not mind taking a flight."

Wren made to stop the escalating feud but Rebecca and Cev spun, glaring at him with identical expressions of challenge. He raised his hands as though to surrender and turned to Nico; he, looking at Wren's face, shrugged and began lashing the harness to his halicarra.

"Girl child, perhaps this is not the best of ideas," said Noe Avaka cautiously.

"I agree with the Pictsie, Rebecca," said Fayit. "You do not know these animals."

Rebecca looked fury at the two. "If she can do it, so too can I," she said, following Cev's lead and hopping onto the halicarra's shoulders.

The animals stood and shook feeling into their rested muscles. They strained at the harnesses strapped around their beaks, making harassed hissing sounds. The halicarras' feathers ruffled as they strutted out from the posts they had been tied to. Cev looked to Rebecca with displeasure and heeled her green halicarra's shoulders.

The beast took off like a shot; it ran in a lumbering gait, stirring up the ground of the pen as its huge wings beat strongly at the air. It rose with Cev on its shoulders, its strong wings pulling it into the sky with each stroke. Rebecca bit back her anxiety and kicked at the spotted gray animal's shoulders and she felt the muscles heave beneath her.

Wind tore at her face immediately as the animal gained speed and then Rebecca's stomach left her. The animal stretched out its neck and beat its wings, drawing them both into the open sky. Slowly Rebecca stopped herself screaming and regained her senses. She looked down and saw the grayish-colored space of the village fading away into the green of the forest that surrounded it. Astenos thrilled at the energy flowing through her and she slowly began to enjoy the flight.

She spotted Cev on her green halicarra not too far ahead of her. She pulled at the harness and leaned, trying to get the animal she rode to move toward the other. It refused to budge from its course. Panic seeped into Rebecca, if she could not steer the animal she would be up to its whims.

"Right, you fool, right," she screamed over the rushing wind. Her eyes watered from the onslaught of air. She saw Cev, a small shape on the horizon, turn to look back. From this distance Rebecca could still see the concern in the woman's face. Perhaps, she thought, she had gone a touch too far in her support of Wren. This was very nearly suicide.

"Oh, Father, how do I turn this thing," she thought to Astenos. The creature, as if by command, veered toward where Cev flew. Rebecca understood at once. It was like the wolves, only not. She could hear the animal's thoughts but they were wildly different, instinct and intuition, more than anything else.

"Higher," she thought and the halicarra beat its wings with renewed vigor. The trees dwindled below her to a variegated green expanse. She drove the halicarra toward Cev's and the animals' wingtips edged closer. They flew like geese, one ahead, one behind, riding the draft of the leader. Cev turned to look at Rebecca and the anger had vanished; the woman's streaming black hair whipped behind her as she screamed out to Rebecca.

"I am happy to see you," she said in Arnoran. "I am sorry for my words to you."

"Me as well," Rebecca shouted in the rush of air in Cev's tongue. "How about we go back?" Cev smiled and nodded. Her halicarra twitched its wings and spun about dropping in altitude. The sight spurred Rebecca's thoughts; these were the creatures she had seen soaring above her in the forest. She marveled at the animal below her for a moment and spun the halicarra to follow after Cev's.

A gleam on the horizon caught her eye mid turn. A speck of white just barely visible, it was hard to judge the distance; the air hazed the vista and the speck vanished like a mirage. Rebecca knew she had not imagined it though. She thought it looked to be a spire of some sort, a tower.

The halicarras returned to their pen like pigeons to their cotes. Cev landed first, kicking up a plume of dust, as her green halicarra beat its wings against the momentum of its flight. It landed at a gallop and Rebecca knew what to expect as she held tight to the reins of the beast beneath her. She lunged forward as the animal reared back to slow itself. Landing with a bone-jarring impact, the halicarra squawked its pleasure and its breath came in blasts through its beak-like nose. It cantered to where the others waited; Rebecca watched its strange forelegs kicking at the dirt as they extended from its wings.

Wren was at her side at once to lift her down from the halicarra's neck, his haughty grin returned to his face.

"You proved yourself, little sister," he said, looking amused and relieved.

Cev pounced from the neck of her halicarra and rubbed its side, and then she strode next to Rebecca, clapping a hand around her shoulder. Wren looked baffled; Cev spoke and Fayit translated.

"Do not speak to the new rider, Darkling. She must have a drink of bast fruit juice to commemorate her first flight." Cev's displeasure with Rebecca seemed to have vanished somewhere in the skies. She looked on Wren in a way Rebecca took to mean that she had accepted him as well.

"Bast fruit?" asked Wren. He laughed.

"What is funny?" asked Nico in Arnoran.

Rebecca giggled too before she answered. "Bast means something bad in our tongue," she said.

Nico's grin made them cringe. "Then our languages have something in common," he said.

Rebecca found herself staring at a blown glass jar of brown congealed liquid. Cev had called for the substance as she ushered the group into a tavern of sorts. Men laughed and cheered as Cev and Nico explained what had happened. Fayit and Noe Avaka looked relieved not to have to translate angry words. The jar was slammed down on a lacquered counter and Rebecca eyed it warily as she sat on a stool.

"A first drink for a first flight," announced Nico. He slapped Rebecca on the back and the men and women gathered in the tavern chuckled and cheered with laughter. Cev pulled a large cork from the jar and the dark skinned man behind the counter slapped six narrow glasses on the bar top. Cev looked to Fayit and Noe Avaka as she spoke.

"Do you want to join in the toast, Listener, Teacher?" She smiled in a devilish way. Fayit and Noe Avaka shook their heads.

"I think you man kinds can take this drink alone," said Noe Avaka. Fayit nodded her agreement.

Two glasses were removed from the counter and the barman poured the brown slop into those that remained. Men around the tavern laughed and jeered the people about to drink the ooze that had come from the jar.

Cev pulled Wren by his scarf to join them and Nico, Rebecca, Cev, and Wren each took up a glass of the thick jellied juice. Rebecca tipped back the glass with the rest of the group and the people in the tavern cheered.

"Bast!" they all shouted in unison as they slammed the empty glasses on the counter top. It felt like liquid fire dripping down Rebecca's throat, her stomach like a crucible to catch the fire. She breathed in heavy pants and felt sweat come to her forehead and cheeks.

"Alright, Darkling?" Cev said, looking to Wren panting next to her. "Whether I like you or not you're Icari now." She smiled and reached out a hand to Rebecca. Rebecca took it still blowing out the burning feel in her mouth.

Seventy-six:
A Night to Remember

Wren sat easier with Rebecca at his side. It was an odd feeling listening to her two new friends; Rebecca listened to the Icari as Fayit, Noe Avaka, and Astenos translated their words. Cev and Nico related stories over several more glasses of the jellied juice; most contained a near fatal incident with the halicarras. Cev and Nico displayed the scars from each at the finish of the story. Fayit and Noe Avaka had difficulty translating, gasping for breath as the group laughed together, tears streaming from their eyes. Rebecca leaned against Wren and he put an arm around her shoulder as they listened to Nico tell a tale about a second or third flight Cev had taken.

"…so, so the harness, the harness slipped around, my fault," Nico said, gasping for breath. "I had been angry; she had made light of me, saying I could not throw a javelin to knee height of a juvenile anset to save my life. I thought to teach her a lesson. I loosened the girth strap and slapped her halicarra into flight." Nico's voice slurred slightly. Cev wiped at her eyes as she listened. "So, Cev is supposed to be practicing hard turns, the harness slips and she is dangling from the halicarra's neck like a bauble, screaming her head off." They all roared with laughter. "She turned back to the pen at once, hanging on for her life. She touches down and the halicarra drags her through a pile of dung. She dismounts, bleeding from her head, covered in the stinking slop, steps up to me…"

"…and I stuck a wad of the heap right in his face," screamed Cev. They all bellowed with joy. Rebecca's stomach cramped from the laughter. Cev leaned over the table, at which they all sat, and pulled back her hair to show a pale line of a scar, long healed, along her scalp. Rebecca pulled air through her teeth as she looked. Cev moved for Wren to see.

"Oh, very nice," said Wren as he rubbed a finger along the scar through her dark hair. Cev looked up laughing, realizing who had spoken; she bit her lower lip to keep the laughter small. Wren smiled in a way Rebecca had not seen before; it was affectionate. She put a hand to his stomach as Cev sat back down, still guffawing.

A young boy burst through the door of the tavern and his eyes were white all around. He hurried to Nico's side.

"Nicolias, sir," the boy panted, "the council has reached a decision regarding the Darkling. You must come at once."

The laughter died in an instant. Nico and Cev looked to Rebecca and Wren with deep concern. The group rose from the table and Rebecca squeezed Wren's hand as they left the tavern.

Cev and Nico spoke in whispers at the head of the group. Even Astenos could not pick up what was said. A deep sonorous bell toned somewhere ahead as the group came into the plaza where the Council chamber sat. The day had reached dusk, the light fading as the sun reached for the forested horizon. The soft glow of the orbs suspended from the posts increased with the lack of light, brightening the dark spaces that had been trying to form.

Cev fell back beside Rebecca and put her hand to the scruff of Rebecca's neck. She pinched it fondly and smiled.

"Do not worry for your friend, Rebecca," she said in sporadic Arnoran. "All will be as the Tree Father wills." She looked to Wren and grimaced in a meaningful way.

The six gathered at the head of the opening of the Council chamber. The people of the village gathered behind and around them. The women wore dresses and ribbons around their necks; the men wore finer garb as well. Rebecca thought this strange for the occasion. They cast the group in looks of awe and worry. The members of the Elder Council exited, one by one, from the dark opening of the Council chambers. Talic was last to step into the growing dimness.

A hush washed over the gathering; the members of the Elder Council looked to one another. One last tone from the bell and Talic spoke.

"You come before us for the ceremonies of this evening; most have heard rumors of one of the matters of which we have decided," he announced, his voice carried in the plaza more than it should have. "The members of the Elder Council have debated and reached an agreement. Firstly, we have a new man among our ranks." Talic looked to his son, full of pride. Two young girls brought forth the red anset horns and Talic took them, holding them for the crowd to see. They cheered and several men shook Nico in congratulations.

The crowd grew silent as the other members of the Council raised their hands. "Secondly, and most importantly, we have newcomers to our world. Their arrival signals the time of release from our long isolation." The crowd cheered again; Talic and the members of the Council waited in deep concern for the cheers to cease. "The World Strider has unlocked the Port back to our home. But she has brought a...Darkling...in her wake." Rebecca heard the strain with which he spoke the last. The crowd's enthusiasm quieted. They looked to the six people standing at the head of them.

"We discussed his arrival and Viewed what may come. We have judged him..." Talic looked to the group and measured each, "trustworthy, for now." The crowd let out a held cheer, the likes of which Rebecca had never heard. Talic raised his hands for quiet. "We must look to our borders. With the coming of the World Strider the Barrier has been breached. Our...Darkling...friend is but a taste of what may come; be vigilant!" Talic raised his hands and the Council Members followed his lead; a stream of light flew forth from their fingers forming a glowing haze above the gathering in gold, white, and blue. "Now, let the ceremony begin!" cried Talic his voice echoed through the plaza.

Men blew on tubes of wood casting the plaza in a reverberant hum. Drums beat out a tribal rhythm. Rebecca caught Cev's eye and she smiled, grabbing Rebecca's hand and dragging her away from the crowd toward a house not far from the plaza.

* * *

Wren's heart dropped from where it had been pounding in his throat. He had not had so much fear in nearly half his life. He watched as Cev drew his Charge away from him. He could still see, vaguely, what she saw; feel what she felt, in the back of his mind. Ever since the Tremen Pride Mistress had bound the two together he knew what Rebecca was thinking. He could feel her pull at him, like she had a line tied to his very being. He could tell, for instance, she was moving into the main room within the house, and that she was happier than she had been in a long time, she felt safe. Wren couldn't decide how he felt.

Right now he felt strange, stranger than he should. The Blue was one thing, taking all thought and desire, but this was something entirely different. Wren watched as the beautiful copper skinned woman drew his Charge up to a warm room within the marvelous house. He could almost see her through Rebecca's mind, like the vision of a memory in his head. Cev had her back to Rebecca and was removing the cloth bindings around her chest...

Nico grabbed him by the hand and shook it vigorously, breaking his concentration. "Congratulations, Darkling," Noe Avaka translated. He felt his heart drop with the term. Darkling. Is that what he was? He had always thought of his Murmur as a malicious being intent on stealing the meat from which he was made. But to discover it could report to other creatures of Discordia made him feel sick, dirty. He grimaced at Nico, facing him with a mild drunken smile. The jellied ooze they had imbibed had numbed Wren's face a bit.

It was feeling anything that felt strangest to Wren. Pain, fear, anger, all but humor came to him as though through a screen, another result of the Murmur. But he felt something for the woman who had taken his Charge, something he had not felt in his entire life. Eight when he had gained the tattoos of his land, nine when he had been forced into the camps, gaining more markings that would steal his life from him; he had never experienced this emotion. Desire. A deep desire, like a man dying from thirst first spotting a pond, he wanted the woman. Cevara. A good name, a strong name.

He looked to Nico drawing him into the crowd of strangers. He should open his veins now. Death would surely be easier than seeing the copper skinned woman watch in horror as his Murmur took his body. But that would leave his Charge unguarded. Why? Why had Seb done this to him? Wren thought he actually...loved the girl. She was young and spirited like he liked to think he would have been if not for the Red Fist. When she touched him like she had recently, like a friend, like a brother, he had almost felt...human again.

But you are not; you are mine, Wren. Never will you be free. His Murmur brought him back to what he was. Tainted. Cursed. He should seek out the halicarras and feed himself to them. *I will not let you,* spoke the Murmur.

Wiping a regretful tear from his cheek, he hoped passed for a tear of laughter, he allowed himself to be drawn into a dance. The men of the crowd allowed women to pass through to the rings in the center of the plaza. Young toddlers to old grandmothers, they began to dance. The younger girls had yellow ribbons wrapped around their throats the older wore deep blue. Women of marrying age wore white tied loosely around their necks.

The women were beautiful, like exotic gems of infinite diversity. He danced the twirling motions of these people, people he had inaccurately thought were savages. They were a good people, better than he would ever know. He smiled as he changed hands from woman to woman. Dark, smiling, creased eyes changed to pale open eyed golden-haired youngsters. Girls of nine or ten, women of fifty or seventy he danced with them all. He spotted Nico again, his cloak of green fabric loose at the clasp; the man chatted with a woman thrice his age but his sister reflected through the wrinkles, obviously his mother. Nico hugged the woman and bounded back into the fray of dancers.

Wren's vision blurred a bit and he looked to where he knew his Charge had reemerged. Rebecca stood in a deep green dress of soft fabric, tiny beaded straps laced over her bare shoulders and a narrow golden ribbon wound around her thin neck. He had tried to tell her once that she had a pleasing figure, but that had ended poorly. He seemed to stumble over his words when truly telling women they were beautiful; he could lie to them well enough but the truth bungled his words. Rebecca's dark auburn hair fell in waves, setting her face perfectly. Her stunning eyes, so like Seb's, reflected the moonlight. As he gazed at the girl, she locked eyes with him and grinned. She seemed awkward, coltish, and coy, unable to see that she was becoming a beautiful woman. Her hair was adorned with feathers, like all the women around him, but smaller. Men seemed to gaze at her like the youngsters; they knew she was not of age.

"Cursed One," called the fox-faced Pictsie. Wren turned to see him; his strange face was lit with joy. "You man kinds do know how to celebrate." Wren knuckled his forehead and grinned. He could see men hesitantly approaching the Tremen beastie, trying to get her to dance. He smiled broader; *that would teach her to be so judging of the man kinds,* he thought. Wren worked his way across the rings of dancing women in time to see his infatuation emerge.

She stood like a warrior in front of the dark opening. She wore a similar dress as Rebecca's but white; her figure made Wren's heart pound harder. An aged woman stepped into the light behind her and Cev turned to hug her. *Grandmother,* Wren thought. Rebecca turned and did likewise and the three edged into the crowd of growing revelers. Wren nudged and pushed his way to his Charge. Her face broke in a grin when she saw him near.

"What do you think?" she asked shyly, spreading her skirts and twirling.

"Absolutely gorgeous," he said, grinning his best. She squinted her eyes and half heartedly punched him in the ribs. He bent and hugged her and she looked abashed.

"What was that for?" she asked.

"Nothing, little sister, nothing at all," he said contentedly.

Cev moved into the crowd, pecking men and women on the cheeks and hugging passersby. She edged toward her father and she wrapped her copper arms around him tightly. Oh Fates, what he would give for her to do the same to him? Wren turned and pushed Rebecca into the crowd of moving dancers; she disappeared with a laugh. He edged his way across the crowd back to where Noe Avaka sat.

A yellow skinned man lit a pipe for the Pictsie as he approached. Wren fell in beside the two.

"This plant they burn, Cursed One," said Noe Avaka, "it is quite relaxing. I would say much more that that goop you four drank earlier." Wren smiled and took a puff of the long pipe the man had lit when offered. His mind spun with the fumes.

The music was nearly as intoxicating as the smoke. Deep hollow hums from the pipes and a carrying rhythm from the drums made Wren forget he was an outsider here. Noe Avaka elbowed him after a time and spoke shouted growling words.

"This is the Binding Ceremony!" he called, directing Wren's attention to the center ring. "The Bindings will be temporary for a period, and then they decide if they will become permanently wed."

Wren noticed the men gathered on the outskirts of the three interwoven rings set into the plaza stonework. Men within years of his age gathered in clumps around the center ring. He could see Rebecca dancing in the ring nearest him, she was slicked with sweat and laughing her heart out with girls of her age and younger, the ones not yet of age to be wed. Older women moved slower in spirals in the farthest ring, looking longingly to the center ring; their time had long past. Men of all ages filtered through these two rings, dancing toddlers and wrinkled grandmothers about. The middle circle was where the women danced like they had been taken by the Fates, spinning and jumping to the music. This ring remained for the women alone; men stood hopeful all around it. Wren could understand that they believed the Father drove them to the men gathered round the rings.

Now and again a woman would spin wildly out from the ring, to be caught in the outstretched arms of a man on the outskirts. Wren laughed and cheered with each catch. The women would open their eyes and look to the man that had caught them. They would move off together and begin to chatter to one another. Wren watched as members of the Elder council, in pairs, joined each couple, forming rings with the smiling couples. A golden haze formed around the couples. The Elder Council members congratulated them as the haze dwindled. Noe Avaka nudged Wren again.

"What is it, Pictsie?" Wren asked pleased.

"This man tells me they have a milder punch of that bast fruit juice on the far side of the rings. Would you mind gathering us some?" asked Noe Avaka. His pink eyes wide with cheer.

"Not at all, fox-man. Be back in a moment," Wren said, pushing to his feet.

He edged forward into the crowd. The drums pounded out their steady beat like a heart wild with exhilaration. He spun the younger girls about as he passed through their ring; they giggled and gathered when he had let them go. Into the oldster's ring, he bowed respectfully and kissed hands or a cheek here and there, more giggles. He exited the rings and gathered three cups of the punch. He sipped at his glass and gagged slightly. It was barely more palatable than the goop from the jar.

He laughed as he passed through the throng of women. How he did like the press of female flesh. He slipped through the younger girls, sweating and falling around in exhaustion; he caught Rebecca for a turn. She laughed and hugged him tight.

"Isn't this great?" she screamed.

"The best, little sister." She pushed him out of the youngsters ring and he found Noe Avaka once more. Fayit sat smiling next to the Pictsie. The man with the pipe had vanished.

"Perfect timing, Cursed One," laughed Noe Avaka. "My Tremen friend and I are parched and she is willing to sample your man kind beverage."

Wren handed a cup to Fayit, bowing over it; she smiled at him for once. He slapped a cup into Noe Avaka's hand, ruffled the Pictsie's tiger striped hair, and sat beside him. The three downed their glasses.

"Bast!" they cursed in unison. They looked to one another with smirks.

"More?" asked Wren. They nodded quickly and he set out for the far side of the plaza again. The women were ready for him this time; he found it most difficult slipping through the ring of young girls. Rebecca seemed to drive them on. Girls of five or six grabbed his hands and pulled him into raucous spinning dances. He had not laughed so hard in...in ever, now that he thought about it. He bowed his apologies to the youngsters and fell into the groping grasps of the aged mothers and grandmothers. He barely escaped with his shirt this time. He filled his cups and made to return but he looked to see the place where the Tremen and Pictsie had sat vacated.

He drained the three cups, feeling instantly the spinning haze of fermentation, and started to edge once more into the twirling women.

He spotted Cev in the marriageable women's ring; she spun about like a top in the center ring, her skirts spinning out around her, her black hair streaming behind her. She truly was beautiful. The numbers around her had dwindled. He had been a fool to insult her; he hoped she found herself in the arms of a good man, a better man than he. Shaking his thoughts straight, he pushed into the oldsters. He leaped about with pinches to more than his cheeks and entered the youngsters' ring.

Rebecca and her gang were waiting this time; they piled on him and threw him around like a sack. She was laughing and had that impish grin she got; her cheeks were red with excitement. She released her grip on his hands and he spun about; the music came to a sudden halt as he felt something run into him full force.

Gasps ripped through the crowd. The silence broke Wren's surprise like a knife severing a taught line. He looked down at his chest and saw Cev, her eyes just now opening. She looked amazed and horrorstruck at once. Wren slowly understood what had happened.

The center ring was devoid of all but himself and Cev. She stood pressed to him breathing heavily, her eyes locked like dark pools on his grayish blue-green. She shuddered slightly and looked to the head of the plaza.

Talic stood like a statue, his face like stone, glaring at the scene before him. Wren could feel the noose tightening around his neck already. Talic's only daughter had been driven by the Father into the arms of a Darkling.

"I'm sorry," Wren said hastily.

Cev looked at him with concern that melted away as she gazed up to him. Wren thought it odd that she could scream with her mouth set so contentedly. Cev looked away toward the sound Wren had heard and he realized it had not been her.

Women and men screamed as dark shapes slithered through the people gathered on the edge of the plaza. Wren could feel the pull of his Murmur now and realized what was happening.

"I need my weapons," he said to Cev. Her eyes were wide with fear and anger. She nodded and grabbed his hand, pulling him away from the rings.

Seventy-seven:
New Links

Rebecca watched Wren and Cev standing pressed to one another in the center ring. She laughed to herself. She couldn't think of a better way of getting the two together. The girls around her looked shocked and smiled broadly at the last two people in the binding ring. Astenos pulled her away from the sight.

Trouble Rebecca, he spoke into her mind. *Come for me. I must protect you.*

Rebecca heard the screams from the edge of the gathered people and turned to watch the dark clad men appearing as if from nowhere. Husked Men, she knew by the way they moved. Like serpents on legs they laced through the throng, striking out with their dark knives.

"Velto!" she shouted at the girls around her, in their tongue. "Velto! Velto, orea!" *Run! Run, now!* She ran from the ring of girls still held in confusion and bolted for the door where she had been dressed for the celebration. Astenos waited with her other possessions.

Where had they come from? She thought desperately as she belted Astenos around her waist over her dress. She pulled him from the scabbard and dashed back into the mass of people. It was chaos in the plaza as she stepped into the dimness. Men ran clutching women and children, shielding them from the Husked Men that dropped from roofs or appeared from dark shadows. Already Rebecca could see the motionless heaps of the dead in the plaza. She hurriedly looked for her friends.

Fayit drew long thick arrows from her quiver in practiced repetition. The points struck the blurred black shapes and they fell to the ground with each impact. But they were not down for good. Soon, the black-clad men stood and reentered the fray, sporting set arrows from their sides or chests. The Murmurs that had possession of those bodies kept them from death.

Noe Avaka sprinted through the running feet of the crowd, his tiny form distinguishable for the deep orange cloak billowing behind him. A young girl was in front of him, screaming in terror; Noe Avaka was leading her away. A midnight hued figure chased them with intent. Suddenly an orange cloaked Strynge stood where Noe Avaka had been running. The Husked Man looked on it in confusion. Rebecca heard a twang like a plucked string just before Noe Avaka reappeared and whipped his thin staff around him. The knees of the Husked Man he struck bent the wrong way and it collapsed. Noe Avaka grabbed the little girl's hand and scurried for cover.

Where was Wren? Rebecca hunted through the milling frightened crowd. She spotted heavy leather armored guards moving into the fight now. The Husked Men descended on them like flies on a rotting carcass. Their short dark knives flashed in the hovering light of the plaza. Men bellowed as the blades separated limbs from bodies or slashed through the thick cuirasses to spill entrails onto the stone pavers.

Rebecca grimaced and raced into thick of the battle. Astenos gleamed in the night as she allowed him to take control. She spun and twirled him around her, blocking the dark points of knives and slashing at pale death-like faces. They were difficult to strike, seeming to slip away just before she made contact. Three dark shapes

673

surrounded her and she knew she had bitten off more than she could chew.

Two lines of streaking silver took two of the Husked Men between the eyes. They fell to the ground convulsing.

"Take their heads, little sister!" yelled Wren as he sprinted for her. He wore his Stitcher's rig and his narrow sword was in his hand. Cev ran along behind him bearing a javelin, a quiver of arrows and a horn bow at her side. Rebecca acted at once. She slashed at the thrashing forms on the ground severing the Husked Men's heads. She turned about in time to catch the last before it could move. Dark bluish-black blood poured from their necks.

Wren and Cev flew to her side, Wren insured she was alright and the three quickly looked for targets. Like the arrows from Fayit's bow the three leapt on the attackers. Wren spun wildly, mirroring his opponent's motions. Cev twirled her javelin around her, slashing with its point and cracking bones with its haft. Rebecca could feel the flow of the Kilaray as Astenos sparked into life, his blade growing bright in the dim light of the plaza. The commotion slowed as she let him take over. She could see the Husked Men's faces now.

They were devoid of fear, blanked of all expression. Blue veins laced up their necks and cheeks toward their dead white staring eyes. Female faces looked out from some of the dark cowls. Rebecca felt a shudder of regret with each stroke as she sliced at their necks.

Nico rushed to join them, Talic, a dark blade protruding from his shoulder, at his son's side. Rebecca could not tell how long they fought, it felt like hours. They fought back the attack and slowly the sounds of destruction and death ceased. Rebecca let the flow of Kilaray pass and the plaza dimmed as she wiped the dark blood from Astenos. Talic stood panting, his son at his side for support. Wren and

Cev were near one another, Cev's pure white dress and scarf spattered with blue-black sprays. Talic turned to Wren like an overlooked enemy.

"You brought this!" he bellowed, pointing his javelin at Wren's throat.

"No!" Rebecca shouted in time with Cev's denial. Cev stepped between her father's steel point and Wren.

"Father he did not call them," Cev insisted. Talic looked stricken; his eyes flashed from Cev to Wren.

"Cevara, he is one of them," Talic cried. "You must see that. How else would they know to find us here?"

"It was you," said Rebecca as understanding dawned on her. "Like moths to a flame we draw them on, those who touch the Links." She looked to Fayit as the huge Tremen approached, Noe Avaka at her side. "It was yours and the Elder Council's Link work that pointed us out." Rebecca turned to face the intimidating man. "Talic, there will be Blind Men next, Strynges. The Tremen said they had seen them in the forests near the Barrier."

"Since the Barrier Port was locked in place," said Noe Avaka thoughtfully, "*any* who are near it can pass through its opening." Rebecca nodded and Talic looked concerned.

"We must prepare then," said Talic and he slumped forward, Nico caught him. Rebecca was at his side in an instant.

The Husked Man's blade was inches from Talic's heart but Rebecca could see the darkening Links of the Chief Elder spreading from the wound, poisoned blades. She slipped into the Easing and gripped tight to where the blade was sunk.

She heard whispers from all around her. She turned to see what made the sound. Ghostly forms clung to the bodies of the dead

Husked Men around the Plaza, like malevolent vapors. Wren's turned to stare at its compatriots. Rebecca glared at them as they finally succumbed to the wind that seemed to pull at their smoky forms, fading into the dark and Discordia. She returned to Talic. She passed a flow of Kilaray through the damaged links and pulled the blade from the Chief Elder's shoulder.

Time whipped back and Talic pulled air through his teeth as the flesh of his shoulder knit back together. He grabbed Rebecca's hand, his enveloping hers, and squeezed it tight.

"Thank you, World Strider," he said in a thick voice. He stood with a worried look from Nico and Cev and turned to Wren. Wren's eyes were wide, his face pale. Talic stepped close to him, and gripped hold of Wren's hand.

"By the Tree Father's rules you have been bound to my daughter, for the time of trial," he said reluctantly. Wren shook his head in weak refusal, looking worried, trying in stutters to apologize. Talic's face darkened. "You will not dishonor her by refusing Darkling. You will not deny the will of the Tree Father; you will be bound for the time specified."

"Do you accept the will of the Tree Father, my daughter?" Talic asked, taking one of Cev's shaking hands. She bit her lower lip and looked to Wren. He still shook his head, silently mouthing, "No, No, No," over and over again. Cev reluctantly took Wren's left hand and laced her fingers with his. She looked her father in the face, stood straight, and breathed deeply.

"I accept the Tree Father's will," she said. Talic looked disturbed.

"World Strider, will you stand for your friend?" asked Talic. Rebecca didn't know what was happening but she stepped to Wren and Talic.

"Yes, I will stand for Wren," she said a little confused. Wren looked to her like she was pushing him off a cliff.

The four stood together in a ring, linking hands. Wren's fingers were like ice and she could feel them trembling. Talic's were like warm hard leather, stone steady. Rebecca felt something move through her. Somehow Talic pulled on the Kilaray through her. She felt the world slow and she watched in amazement as a thin thread snaked out of Wren's chest. It was weak and duller than the finger-thick cord extending from Cev. Talic interwove them in an intricate knot. Wren had one more Link now; a new one Talic had somehow pulled from the seal on his soul. The pull of Kilaray ebbed and when the world returned to normal, she could see a dim aura of golden light around Cev and Wren.

Cev looked scared and shivered; Wren turned to her, shocked. Rebecca understood now what had just happened. The two had just been joined. Talic released Rebecca's hand and took his daughter's shoulders to stare into her face.

"I am sorry to be the one to bind you to your man, my daughter," Talic said regretfully. "He fights well but he has not long left to himself. I fear, even if you accept him, you will be a young widow." He glared at Wren and called to Nico to follow him. Nico appeared frightened as he watched his sister, still holding Wren's hand. He hurried to catch his father.

Cev released Wren's hand and turned about to follow after her brother and father. Wren watched her go, looking like he had lost something. He turned to Rebecca and knelt down; his face was set in determination.

"I want you to do it, little sister." He looked like he struggled; his eyes looked to Astenos. "When you can do it, cut this *thing* away from me, or take my head." His eyes flicked to Cev, walking away from them.

Rebecca joined the people moving through the plaza, attending to the wounded. Wren went to help the Icari plan for what would come. She heard Noe Avaka translate his words to the Elder Council for him as they walked. They looked doubtfully at him but as Wren spoke and explained the tactics of the Husked Men their doubt faded.

Fayit helped carry the dead, gently comforting women crying over lost husbands or children clutching tight to a motionless parent. Rebecca felt sick. She turned her attention to what she could do to keep from seeing the dead. She had a hand in each one of those deaths.

She had opened the Gates and allowed the enemy to enter. Tears filled her eyes as she healed wounds. Men, women, and children, all were equal targets in the eyes of the Husked Men that had attacked. She knew more would come and she felt anger boiling for herself.

"Thank you, World Strider," said a man as she healed over a patch of skin where his arm now ended in a stump. He felt the healed stump regretfully. "By the will of the Tree Father I will live to fight another day; even if on that day I use a different hand than I did this night."

She marveled at the man's courage, but she felt rage at the First Father too. How could this horror be his will? How could he allow something like this to have happened? She stepped lightly around the body of a girl, the yellow ribbon tied at her neck soaking up the red from the slash beneath it. She hated those responsible for this disaster.

She hated herself for not being able to stop it, and she hated the First Father for allowing it.

"You have heavy thoughts on your face, Rebecca," said Fayit as Rebecca stared at the young girl lying on the stones of the plaza. Rebecca felt a heavy paw on her shoulder. "Some things that happen in this world are hard to bare, but bare them we must. Mourn for the dead, but do not let their deaths weigh down your soul." Rebecca looked away from the girl's lifeless figure and cried into the huge Tremen's stomach.

"It's my fault, Fayit. Death follows me everywhere like a shadow," she sobbed wracking gasps into Fayit's tunic.

"Your hand did not slay these people, Rebecca," she said softly. "You bring the dead peace in ending their killers. It is the best we can do for them. Live for those that were lost Rebecca, because they cannot do it for themselves now." Rebecca looked up into Fayit's wide face. Her eyes were wet, dampening the fur of her face. She brushed a huge paw through Rebecca's tangled hair.

Rebecca bit her lower lip and held back her tears. Ending their killers would bring the dead peace. She could feel the rightness of the thought. She would do for the dead what she could, her best to stop those that had killed them from killing others. It wasn't vengeance; that, Alaric had told her, led to a damaged soul. This would be justice.

"We will bring the dead their peace, Fayit," Rebecca could hear the strength return to her voice. Fayit nodded and looked proud.

"You are a fierce one, my friend," she brushed the tears still trickling from Rebecca's cheek. "Now go, do what you can for those that live."

Rebecca still felt sick as she tended to the wounded Icari, but the hollow sense she had felt had left her. When the last gashes and severe injuries had been seen to, she went to find the others. She passed the line of bodies, grimacing as she watched their loved ones weeping over them. The smaller forms hurt the worst. She had danced with some of those girls and boys not three hours ago, now they would never dance again. Noe Avaka sat trembling not far from the opening to the Council Chambers. He seemed to be weeping, leaning on his staff. Rebecca went to him; he looked up as she approached.

"I am sorry, girl child. I wish I could have been of more assistance," he growled through his tears. "B-but my people we have never fought our enemies. W-we hide from them. I spoke of discretion, but it is really just...cowardice." Rebecca sat beside the tiny fox-like man and put her arm around him. He shook like a leaf in a thunderstorm as he wept.

"I saw you Noe," Rebecca said, rubbing his tiny back through his deep orange cloak. "You didn't look like a coward when you saved that girl."

He smiled hesitantly. "You, you saw that then...well, well, yes. I suppose I did at that, didn't I." He sniffled, twitching his dark nose, and wiped his eyes with his strange hands. When he looked back at Rebecca, he lowered his voice and leaned in close, the tremulousness of his shoulders was gone. "Do, do you suppose I should count that as a service to the child. She is young, I understand and no contract was agreed upon, but still..." It felt strange for the smile that came to Rebecca's face.

"I think you should let this one pass without payment, Noe," she said, standing from the Pictsie's side. He nodded his agreement and Rebecca turned to enter the Council chamber.

The Chamber was under heavier guard. Two rows of armored guards stood with their pikes ready for another attack. When they saw it was Rebecca, they snapped to attention slanting their pikes to allow her to enter. Rebecca had healed several of these men's wounds. As she walked into the interior of the Council Chamber, she heard heated words echo through the space.

"This should not be our fight, Talic," said a man, his voice shook with anger. "The girl may be the World Strider as you believe but this attack comes on her back."

"What would you have us do Janero; we knew this day would come. The Barrier cannot be resealed," said Talic. Rebecca could see him now in the chamber. Wren stood silent to the side of the chamber. The Council had sent out men on halicarras to search the surrounding areas and fast fliers had been sent to warn the other villages scattered throughout the forests, as he had advised. Cev sat cross legged beside him, looking plaintive. Nico stood beside his father but he too was silent. "Even if it could be resealed, would you have us hide in here forever?"

"Perhaps," spat Janero. He spotted Rebecca approaching and his eyes narrowed. "Ah, here is our *World Strider* now. Let us hear what she would have us do, Talic. She has already done so much for us." That hurt Rebecca deeper than she would have believed.

"Show some honor, Janero," shouted Talic. "She can understand our words." Janero's eyes widened a little in embarrassment but his indignation was greater. He folded his arms and inclined his head. He reminded Rebecca of Sanjeen from the gathering. He was balding and pale skinned. He lacked the eyes that many on the Council had, the yellow-green color that was a sign of the ability to touch the Links. His cloak of pale gold was clasped with a boar. The other members looked

682

thoughtful, considering. "We thank you World Strider for healing our people's wounds. I personally benefit from your arrival. In more ways than one," he said the last in a low voice, his eyes flashing to where Wren stood next to his daughter.

"I must apologize," said Rebecca to the Council as she stood before them. "I should have realized what would come from my actions."

"There is no need for apology," said a grandmotherly woman in a deep blue cloak; her dark skin was wrinkled and her hair was whiter than its once black color had been. Janero sniffed his belief to the contrary. "What was done was done by our ancient enemies. We were sheltered here to protect what the outside world lost. Some of us had come to believe that shelter would remain for other generations; that they would not have to face what would come when it was lifted." Her eyes narrowed at Janero. Rebecca liked this woman. "We have known we would have Darklings to contend with when you finally arrived. That doesn't ease the pain of what has happened this night. I am heartened to see that you too feel the pain of our people."

"I-I do at that Council Member," she stuttered, holding back the tears that wanted to flow. "I know little of your history, and little enough of what I have come here to do. All that I do know is that I must go...to a tower of light." She felt her stomach flutter as she saw the council tense at this last. Janero shook his head in refusal.

"What do you know of the *Torret so Incandeo*, child?" asked a tall yellow skinned man. He had the eyes. He rubbed at a whisker-free chin considering her.

"Does it matter, Sanir?" grunted Janero. "She cannot go. It is forbidden to approach the Tower."

683

"Enough, Janero, let her speak," said Talic. His voice did not raise but Janero shrunk back as though Talic had roared at him.

"I have seen it..." Rebecca started.

"Nonsense!" shouted Janero unable to contain himself. Talic glared at him and he resumed his shrunk shouldered look of indignation.

"I saw it when I used the Traveler that brought my friends and me to the Gates of Yuriah, the Barrier Port," she said.

"What did you see of the Tower, child?" asked the grandmotherly woman.

"It stands in a, uh, crater," she remembered. "It stretches for a mile across or more." The Council members became far more interested than they had been, and they already had looked ready to pounce on her. "At the base of the tower is a lake and the tower stands at its center. Light, Kilaray light spirals around the spire, reaching toward the sky."

"Do you know why the Tower cannot be approached, child?" asked Sanir the yellow skinned man. "What guards the Tower?"

Rebecca shook her head. "No sir, the Traveler only showed me the Tower," she said, feeling foolish suddenly. Janero looked victorious as he sneered at the Council.

"My son and daughter have told me you have ridden the halicarras," Talic said into the growing silence. Rebecca thought this an odd statement, completely off target. "Cevara tells me you did quite well; most are injured in their first flights." Talic's eyes hit on Janero like a whip crack and the man's victorious face shattered. "Some never fly again after their first attempt. We have bred our halicarras from their natural cousins to the north. I believe you have wolves and dogs on the outside as we do?" Rebecca nodded. "Our halicarras are to what guards the Tower, as dogs are to wolves. Falicarna, their pack leader, is deadly, at best."

Rebecca felt her stomach leap. Dogs had lost their predator's eyes, the eyes the wolves had. Rebecca could remember seeing how the halicarras had looked at her, like a hawk eyeing a wounded rabbit. What would these other creatures be like? Rebecca already knew, now that she thought about it. They would be vicious enough to have made approaching the Tower forbidden. She had to swallow and steel herself before she could continue.

"I understand," said Rebecca. Janero leered at her in an unfriendly smirk. Fayit entered the chamber, Noe Avaka, looking more confident, at her side. "I, we must still go." Janero's eyes bulged. Talic nodded as he turned to the Council. Their faces were painted in worry and consideration.

"I do not believe this should be allowed, Talic," said Sanir. "It is too dangerous."

"I reluctantly agree," said a stooped back man in a violet cloak.

"I say let her go get herself torn to pieces," hissed Janero. "Good riddance. We will block the port and wait out the Darklings."

"Shunta," spat Wren from Cev's side. "Coward," Rebecca heard through Astenos. Cev's eyes were wide in shock but her smile was full of pride. "I walk with this girl for my debt to her." Cev hesitantly translated his words for the Council to hear. "I have no fear of death, for what I am prevents that. But they," Wren pointed at Fayit and Noe Avaka, "have no such oath to keep them and no such protection to guard them. They follow her because…because they believe in her." Noe Avaka nodded; Fayit stood taller, looking proud. There was a moment of silence in which Janero looked to be boiling over.

"Father, I will follow the man the Tree Father has chosen for me," said Cev, standing at Wren's side. "I will follow the World Strider to the Tower." Cev took Wren's hand and squeezed. Talic looked proud and frightened at her words.

"I acknowledge your bravery my daughter..." started Talic.

"I will follow her as well, father," said Nico; he smiled at his sister and Wren. "I think I like my potential brother's words. I can hear the truth in them."

"Madness!" roared Janero. "Talic, you cannot allow your blood line to perish in a foolhardy stunt."

Talic watched his son, measuring him. "Are they the fools, Janero, or are we?" He looked to the grandmotherly woman. "Vania, what say you?" The woman looked at Rebecca, grimacing in fear. She nodded. "I say they will go as well." Talic turned to Rebecca and walked to her, standing over her. "You must take care, World Strider. We have known of your arrival for many centuries but what would occur afterward," he shook his head.

"We must prepare for our reentry into the world that has been lost to us," he said, announcing to the Council. "Despite our dissenting members, we cannot remain, nor are we, hidden from our enemies any longer." The Council nodded, Janero was forced to concur. "Then we will see it done." The Council members began to disperse. Talic remained.

"Cevara, you have not finalized your decision yet I trust," Talic said to Cev. She shook her head. "Then you will show the World Strider to our home for the evening, you will spend your first bound day under honor guard. Dark... Wren Tobias, you will be welcomed into our home as the Tree Father guides, Nicolias will guard your honor. Listener, Teacher, you will stay with us?" Noe Avaka nodded with Fayit. "Then we should all rest, for the day brings great change."

Seventy-nine:
The Honor Guard

Rebecca and the others walked across the plaza toward the home where she had been dressed for the ceremony of the evening. It seemed two lifetimes ago. Cev walked at her side to the house; Rebecca had believed it a wondrous place to live when she had first seen it. Nico had his arm slung over Wren's shoulder and sputtered out broken Arnoran as they walked, telling tales about Cev. Wren looked like he was going to be sick.

"...she punched him, right in the nose. The man went flat out. All he had said was that he thought her face attractive," Nico shook his head. "I think I am supposed to be telling you things that will make you glad of the Tree Father's decision. To tell it true, she is more vicious than a halicarra with a chipped beak." He grabbed Wren by the back of the neck shaking him lightly. "What is wrong man, you look queasy."

Rebecca couldn't help but smile a little. She turned to Cev and tried to say something good about Wren.

"He...uh," she looked back at Wren and he caught her eye, "he has nice eyes." Cev laughed.

"Yes but he still looks like a goat with that fur on his face," she said for Wren to hear.

They entered the house and Cev and Nico's mother and grandmother awaited them, Aleya and Hendra. The two women looked relieved to find them all safe. They had set a meal for the group and they ate hungrily. Rebecca sat at Cev's side, Nico at Wren's. Rebecca gathered they were to act as honor guards for the newly bound couple until Cev decided if she would keep Wren or if the bond would be broken. Rebecca hoped it wouldn't *have* to be. Cev, no matter how she disparaged him, kept flashing her eyes to Wren. Wren, for his part, stared in open-eyed astonishment, now and again shaking his head to clear it.

"You fought well, Wren," said Aleya at the head of the table. "Perhaps that is why the Tree Father chose you for my daughter. She *is* strong willed and could use a strong hand." Cev's cheeks flushed bright red and her eyes locked to the short table at which they were gathered. Wren choked on the fruit wine he had sipped.

"Mother!" Cev growled. Aleya laughed in a musical way. Rebecca and Nico looked to one another with matching grins.

"I thank you, madam," said Wren, recovering slightly, "but I...I wish I could be a better man for your very fine daughter. I only hope the Fates and the Father will see it in their power to let it be so, though I would not deserve it." Noe Avaka translated for him, looking sadly at Wren as he finished. Wren now stared at the table. Rebecca's vision blurred as tears tried to form.

"A humble man at heart, a strong man to the world, and a brave man in the fight," said Hendra, beside her granddaughter. "The Tree Father would do well to keep a man like this."

"All will be as the Tree Father wills," said Talic, stepping into the room where they ate. "It is good to see you here wife." Aleya stood and walked to her husband; she put a gentle hand to his face and kissed him deeply before all the eyes in the room. Rebecca felt like she was intruding; she averted her eyes but she saw Cev and Wren look on the scene with similar faces of longing. Their eyes met as Talic and

689

Aleya broke apart. Cev frowned slightly, biting her lower lip; Wren compressed his lips and ran a hand through his longish dark hair.

"Come, we shall all find sleep, for the morning waits for none," said Aleya, smiling to the group.

Rebecca followed Cev to the room she had at the top of the house. It was small and round with a low padded platform for sleeping. Trophies of horns and feathers adorned the sloping walls. Warm golden light came from a small orb set into a lantern. They washed the evening's dirt and blood from themselves and Cev lent her some of the strange buff-colored bindings to sleep in. Rebecca was glad there were no men in the room; she felt far too exposed. Cev sat cross-legged on the platform in front of Rebecca looking very tired.

"You must tell me, Rebecca," she sounded worried. "Is Wren a good man, beneath the skin, here?" she put her hands to her chest where her heart was. "What is left of him is it good?"

Rebecca didn't hesitate. "He is one of the best men I have ever known." Cev looked relieved and Rebecca lifted her worry from her. She had another burden now. She had to save Wren for more than her own connection to him, because she could not break Cev's heart.

Eighty: Wide Open Skies

A strange voice woke Rebecca. The sun had not risen in the small rounded windows; it was still dark out. Cev was curled next to her, looking peaceful. She listened for the sound wondering how it had not awoken Cev.

What has you up so early, my Mate, asked Astenos. *Your friends still sleep and you could use some more yourself.*

"Did you hear that call?" she thought to him. She felt a prickle through their link; he was concerned that she had heard something he had not. "Maybe it was a dream."

I would have heard it there too, Rebecca. He seemed to hunt around her, using their connection to check for danger he had missed. *What was it? What did you hear?*

"I thought it was you at first, but it felt too...far away to have been." She too felt concerned now.

I will keep watch. Rebecca, be ready but you should rest.

She lay back next to Cev and closed her eyes thinking about the call she had heard. She thought it had said, "I know you," but it was odd. She knew the words were not directed at her. She snuggled closer to Cev, feeling the warmth of her soft breathing on her cheek; it was that that made her realize she had gone cold. As she closed her eyes she had the feel of being watched.

Cev woke her from a tangled dream she had been having, something about a dark skinned man and an older man with dark hair but that was all she could recall. Rebecca felt her eyes had been packed in cotton as she stretched. She stumbled from the room following blindly after Cev and the smell of cooking from below.

"You have a fine figure young woman," said Aleya as Rebecca stepped into the room. "I wondered why you had covered it in so many wrappings." Rebecca looked up, snapping from her sleep haze in an instant. Wren and Nico sat at the table, Cev folding her legs to sit across from them.

Rebecca stood in the rounded opening of the room in the skin revealing bindings Cev had lent her. She had not thought to change. She felt her whole body flush as she saw Wren hold back a smile. Nico watched her passively. Aleya smiled warmly thinking her words would be met well.

Rebecca's eyes bulged and she heard herself make a squeak; Cev looked up to see what was wrong. She looked from Rebecca to Wren; suddenly, Cev's leg twitched and Wren yelled, rubbing at his shin. Cev beckoned Rebecca to sit down, glaring at Wren. Rebecca took small steps, trying to hide her bare stomach and legs with equal desperation with her hands; she refused to run from the room.

"Thank you," Rebecca responded at last to Aleya, forcing the words out.

Wren's grin slowly slid onto his face as they ate first meal. The heat never left her face. He leaned over when Aleya stood to greet her husband.

"I tried telling you *that* last night, you know," he whispered. He grunted softer this time and rubbed again at his leg. Cev smiled at him; her eyes dared him to say another word; Rebecca laughed.

The meal was finished and they all dressed for the day. Rebecca politely refused the Icari clothing Cev offered her changing back into those the Tremen had made her. Aleya hugged each of the group before they left. Fayit bowed a bit for her to reach. Aleya in turn bent for Noe Avaka. She looked Wren seriously in the face, whispered something in his ear as she hugged him and kissed him on the cheek afterward. She held Nico tightly, looking at the freshly shaved sides of his head with pride. Cev smiled at her mother's embrace. Rebecca she came to last. She put a hand over her mouth, holding back tears, and Rebecca heard her whisper, "So young for such a burden," before she wrapped her arms tightly around Rebecca. Aleya kissed her husband before he led the group out into the day.

The plaza was filled with people moving with purpose. Rebecca noted the number of men bearing weapons. They formed up in ranks and looked like a formidable force. Bowmen, and pike men, men with long knives just short of being swords; all gathered to the calls of their rank leaders.

"We received runners in the night," said Talic. He looked exhausted. "Riders from our northern most villages, they were hit in the night. The Darklings seemed to have been expecting your crossing, World Strider, and there were men with them." Rebecca felt her stomach lurch.

"I am sor…" she began.

"No need," he cut her off. "Wren's advice lessened the damage they inflicted," Talic said. He looked over to Wren walking beside his daughter. Rebecca felt relieved but Wren looked like he had gotten a reprieve on the gallows. "You know of what you speak, Wren Tobias."

Talic led the group through the winding village streets. Everywhere they went men and women looked harried. They moved about with wide eyes expecting to be pounced upon.

"I would have you take a caravan of juvenile ansets but time is short," Talic said as he led the group to the pens where the halicarras were kept. "Under the circumstances these will be the fastest way to the Tower.

"They have been prepared for you departure, World Strider." He directed their view to the six beasts standing in the pen, stretching their necks and twitching with pent up energy. Rebecca looked around to the others. All but Cev and Nico looked like they were going to be sick. "The animals we have chosen for the three who have not flown before are our most docile." Rebecca thought if those snapping beaks looked docile, she was a rabbit. "Their natural instinct is to follow the flock leader. Wren will not need to be able to hear their thoughts. I'm afraid their natural instinct is also to eat small creatures," he said, looking to Noe Avaka. There was the sound of a plucked string and the man Rebecca had known as Bertran Gabriel stood before them. Talic nodded.

"Falicarna will know when you have entered his territory." Talic removed a bundle of fabric and unwound it. It contained six blue feathers; they were longer than Rebecca's forearm and hand. The halicarras in the pen squawked, their feathers ruffling, and pulled at the men holding their reins. They looked frightened. Talic quickly rebound the bundle, handing it to Nico. "You should land near the cliffs before you catch site of Dandaria Falls, release your mounts, and then each of you take one of those. I will not tell you they will aid in your approach but perhaps..." He shrugged in a way Rebecca took to mean as the Tree Father wills. Her stomach did a back flip.

Rebecca was relieved to see she was not the only one who looked to be second guessing what they were doing. Talic walked them into the pen to the animals. Rebecca's had a crest of yellow-orange feathers, making points to the side of its skull with its small protuberances of tiny horns. She tentatively let its dark beak nuzzle her hand. Her satchel and other supplies had been slung over the animals hind legs like saddle bags, careful not to interfere with its wing movement. Fayit's looked gargantuan; it was almost as tall as she with a spotted brown head and shoulders. Wren shied close to his dark mount; its feathers were slashed with black and brown; he jumped as it pecked at his face. Noe Avaka's was the smallest of the group and by far the brightest, in red, orange, and green.

Talic and Nico grasped forearms, and Talic nodded quickly. He did likewise with Fayit and Noe Avaka. He rubbed Cev's shoulders and hugged her. With Wren he hesitated, and then grabbed his forearm. Again, Rebecca was last for goodbye. He took her right hand in both of his, knelt, and bowed his forehead to her knuckles. Rebecca looked nervously to the others. He stood and wrapped his arms around her. She liked this much better.

"Be fast, be safe, and the Tree Father be with you. Good flying," he said to the group. He pivoted on the spot and walked from the pen. Men met him as he walked and he issued them orders.

Rebecca heard caws and turned to find Nico and Cev mounted, stroking their halicarras jowls. There was nothing left but to mount hers. She pulled up onto the harness and stroked affectionately at the yellow crested halicarra. Noe Avaka still needed a boost; Fayit sat gingerly. Wren took a deep breath before pulling up on the dark halicarra; it snapped at his boot.

"Oy, I thought these were supposed to be friendly," shouted Wren in outrage.

"Father said docile, not friendly," said Cev smiling at him. "See how docile he is, he did not take off your foot."

The men standing at the sides of the halicarras ran to clear the path. Cev, followed by Nico, kicked lightly at their mounts and they ascended into the air. Fayit followed their lead; Rebecca could hear Noe Avaka gulp as he kicked at his brightly feathered animal.

"Alright, Guard Keeper?" Rebecca shouted over to Wren. He looked at her like she was mad. "I'll follow you up." He nodded and his head jerked as his halicarra took off like a bullet from a muzzle. Rebecca had a feeling Talic may not have gone out of his way to find *all* of them docile animals. She smiled as she watched Wren cling to the reins, rising after the formation moving into the sky.

"Ready," she thought to the halicarra. It shivered along its spine, swishing its tail feathers. She looked up to the clear blue sky. "Then let's go!"

Eighty-one: Windswept

The wind whipped at Rebecca's face as she moved into formation behind Wren's dark halicarra. She could hear his shouted nervous laughter. She leaned forward on her halicarra and thought for it to fly faster. Her hair streamed behind her and all sound was washed away in a deafening roar. She moved up wing tip to wing tip with Wren. His mount seemed to be trying to twitch the burden from its neck.

"We'll just see about that, you vengeful beast," she heard as she slowed up beside him. He looked over at her with anger clear on his face. "I accidentally pulled one of its feathers loose," he shouted over to her. "It's its own Fates-cursed fault."

Rebecca loved this; it was the freest feeling she had in her life. She passed along the thought to the halicarra. Rebecca got from it a sense she should hold tight. Suddenly, the animal rose higher above the formation, she could see the five other faces follow her upward as she soared over them. Tight now, she needed to hold tight now. The animal folded its wings and dove for the tree canopy below. She passed the others in a multicolored blur. She felt her stomach in her throat and she could not help but laugh.

"Who is that that carries you?" said a voice she could not identify. It was not spoken to her; she had just overheard it. Her halicarra's feathers ruffled and she felt it shiver between her knees. It pulled up from its dive and raced to rejoin the other halicarras. They too seemed to twitch in the sky.

Rebecca, what was that? Astenos asked worried.

"I don't know, Astenos," she said, looking around. "I think it was the same as last night. Keep watch alright."

Always! He responded. She could feel him stretch out as far as he could.

They flew over more villages distinguishable for the grayness of the stones. She saw other halicarras moving in the air above these villages, going off on patrols or to run messages. Rebecca found this absolutely amazing. She knew every rider out there could touch the Links in some way for they would not be able to fly the animals otherwise. She understood now why these people had been shut away from the rest of the world. For some reason they had maintained their affinity for the Kilaray while those on the outside dwindled.

She saw moving stands of trees here and there in the forest below, ansets walking through the dense greenery. She could see why they had developed the vegetation covering on their backs. When they sensed the halicarras overhead, the ansets held still and they blended into the canopy below. Rebecca could not tell which trees had been ambling forward and which had remained stationary.

Rebecca closed her eyes after a few hours in the sky. The wind had frozen them and removed every drop of moisture. Her face felt numb from the constant flow of air. When she reopened them, she latched onto the spark of white on the horizon. It was clearer this time. A shimmering haze blended it away from the ground so that it seemed to float in mid air. A spire stood out there. It was impossible to tell how far it was, even knowing how large the tower had been in her vision. Then, as it had appeared, it vanished over the horizon.

The sun was high overhead when Cev startled her from a doze she had dropped into.

"It is your turn, Rebecca. Nico and I have taken the lead; our mounts must rest in the rear. Just head north and think of the Tower. The halicarras all know where it is," she shouted through the wind. "Here have these," Cev held tight to her green halicarra, wrapping her feet into the harness straps and the animal rolled over top of Rebecca. Cev dangled above Rebecca, reaching out a leather strap to her. Rebecca quit her gaping and took the offered item. Cev rolled back to Rebecca's opposite side.

The object reminded Rebecca of Alaric, a leather band with tabs to adjust it and two crystal lenses to cover her eyes. She fingered the cuff on her wrist then pulled on the padded goggles, looking over to Cev.

"I advise drinking some water, and keep your mouth closed," she shouted, smiling. She ran her tongue over her teeth where Rebecca could see several dark spots. "Flies seem to aim for the face."

Rebecca took a swig of water from the canteen at her side and nudged her halicarra forward. She flew up the center of the "V" to where Nico was now. He looked back to her and nodded. He waved his hand around in a circle over his head and his grey spotted halicarra dropped below the others, falling to the rear.

"To the Tower," she thought to the halicarra and she felt it shiver again, but it flew on.

The wind at the lead was worse than the rear. Her halicarra beat its wings harder, having to fight through the gusts that came at them. The others behind her fell into her slipstream and she knew why they had to take turns. She felt the strain the animal was under.

She pulled the hood of her cloak up over her ears and pulled it snug around her. Abruptly, her halicarra snapped its mouth and an explosion of feathers and blood flew back into her face. She could feel the animal lunge its head as it swallowed what it had caught mid flight. She looked back - ducking her head low to her chest to keep from throwing off the flight - to Cev, flying behind Wren, a wake of fluttering feathers streamed from her hood and cloak. She saw the woman laughing as she shrugged as though to say, 'what do you expect.' Rebecca turned back and rubbed her halicarra's skull. She followed her mount's lead and rummaged in the pack below her knee for some of the food that had been loaded for the flight. She munched on some dried meat, keeping her head low to keep out the bugs.

The sun had passed its zenith and was on its way toward the trees to her left. Rebecca was exhausted. She could feel the heat of the halicarra below her from the strain of its time in the front. It beat its wings intermittently, trying to glide a ways before having to beat twice to keep the lead.

"Rebecca," shouted Cev as she moved up the center. Rebecca turned to look at her. Cev shot a signal for her to fall back. Rebecca nodded her understanding.

"Alright, back we go," she thought to her halicarra, waving her hand as she had seen Nico do before she had taken the lead. She felt relief from the animal. It angled its wings a little and Rebecca was thrown forward as it slowed and dropped. It quickly caught up behind Wren again. Rebecca pulled off the goggles and could see clearly again. The crystal lenses were smattered with yellow goop from insect strikes. She didn't want to guess how many she had swallowed. She wiped the lenses clean, splashing them with water and rubbing them on her cloak. She replaced them over her eyes after she rubbed the sore places where they had sat. She thought her halicarra had made another dive before she realized that it was her eyes that had caused her stomach to leap.

A series of waterfalls danced over hard black cliffs, jutting from the forest below. The sight was breathtaking. Deep pools sparkled through the gaps in the trees and cloudy mists blurred where the falls terminated. She could just see on the horizon a greater fall gushing from a vast expanse of rock. Cev led the formation down lower to the forest. The air seemed to become water logged as they dashed above the river roaring to compete with the rush of the wind in her ears.

Cev led the group to a clearing near the river. She made a large circle above her head then pointed down. Rebecca knew she meant for them to land. One by one the halicarras spiraled from the formation toward the clearing. Rebecca watched the green of the clearing tear away in dark brown streaks as the others landed. She led her halicarra in and felt another wash of relief from the animal.

Eighty-two: Callings in the Night

She braced as the ground swept up to meet her and felt the jarring impact. She felt warm now without the onslaught of the wind. Her halicarra trotted up to the others. All the animals puffed, their strong chest muscles heaving in and out. Rebecca hopped from the animal's harness to ease its burden and immediately wished she had waited a moment.

She found herself collapsed in a heap; her legs were dead from clenching to the halicarra's neck. The yellow crested halicarra came to her and nuzzled her cheek. Wren, Noe Avaka, and Fayit learned from her mistake and lowered themselves gently to the ground.

"We will go on foot from here," said Nico as he removed the packs from his halicarra. "We will travel until dark, and then make camp. It will not be safe to walk the cliff forests at night for more reasons than the drops."

"What about these?" asked Wren; he reluctantly scrubbed at the dark halicarra's neck he had ridden. It seemed to have warmed to him a hair but he had to yank his hand back as it snapped its dark beak at his fingers.

"We will let them hunt. They can be called back when we need them again," said Cev, rubbing her forehead to her green's upper beak.

Fayit helped remove Noe Avaka's packs and Cev, Nico and Rebecca went to each animal in turn, sending them off to hunt. They leapt into the air, staying close to the tree tops. Noe Avaka waddled up to Rebecca and she heard the twang as he shriveled back to his normal form.

"Quite…quite amazing creatures," he said in a huffing growl. "My backside won't stop aching for a month, but still quite amazing."

Nico came around to each of them in turn as they headed into the forests that surrounded the clearing. He held out the large blue feathers from the cloth bundle. Rebecca lashed hers to Astenos's scabbard, then helped tie Noe Avaka's to his staff; it stretched a third the length of the pole. Nico told them where they had come from and the reaction of the halicarras began to make sense.

"Until about a decade ago, those aspiring to the Elder Council had to make a pilgrimage to the base of the steps of the crater of the *Torret so Incandeo*. They had to retrieve and return with a feather of the pack leader of the valicarras, the creatures that guard the tower. This proved not only their bravery but their worthiness. It calls upon the days when our people first came to this land, when first we gathered the young of the valicarras to breed our halicarras," said Nico as they passed into the forest. The silence that followed them was eerie. The animals in the trees could sense the feathers and vanished.

"What happened ten years ago that changed that?" asked Wren, looking around them warily. Nico shrugged.

"The last member to join was Janero," said Nico. "Of eight men and women that set out, he was the only one to return bearing the smallest stub of a feather. He told of the new pack leader, Falicarna, he called it."

"Bringer of Death," said Fayit, tightening her paw on her bow. Nico nodded.

"Most believe Janero left the others to save himself," said Cev.

"I could see that," said Wren, smirking.

"Well then he was wiser than we," said Nico, looking serious. "There is a reason no one has made to join the council since Janero; no one who goes for the feathers returns. These," he said hefting his javelin bound with a blue feather, "my father managed to gather from the last pack leader when he joined the Council."

"No man had ever returned with six," said Cev, looking proud. "It is why the council defers to him."

"Why is this Falicarna so vicious?" asked Noe Avaka. His pink-rimmed eyes searched the dark spaces around them as the sun was setting.

"Janero spoke of something strange happening to the Tower," said Nico. "He said the valicarras that soared around its peak called out to something inside. Then the Tower shook, rumbling the ground around the crater base, and the Kilaray light around it intensified. The valicarras became more protective of the Tower and the surrounding area."

"Unfortunately for Janero and his group they happened to be making for the roost of the pack leader at the time," said Cev, looking grim.

Rebecca shuddered to think about what such a creature would do to a man. She felt Astenos strain to feel for anything around her.

They dared to travel only a little farther in the growing gloom of the forest. Rebecca snapped the Incandeo she carried into life and the group made camp. They feared to make a fire; they were attempting to avoid notice for as long as they could. Rebecca draped her cloak over the white glowing orb to dull its light. The group huddled together around the pool of light. Fayit took the first watch, saying she could not sleep with her nerves on edge as they were. Rebecca took her place next to Cev, Nico beside Wren, and Noe Avaka bridging the four of them.

Rebecca could tell she was not the only one to have difficulty finding sleep, as tired as they all were. Noe Avaka grumbled softly, switching from side to side. She could hear the soft click of Cev's eyelids blinking as she watched the darkness around them. Watching Fayit's constant scan around the group, she finally allowed herself to drift off.

Long, white columned corridors swept away from her. Astenos was at her side. The ceiling seemed to fade away into white nothingness above her. It was impossible to tell where it stopped, or *if* it stopped. She could hear a soft whimper from ahead of her, and a strange voice speaking to the sound.

"Astenos, where are we?" she whispered. The voice ceased, but the whimpering continued. She had heard that sound before.

Careful Rebecca, I feel something stalking us. Astenos whispered back. Rebecca's spine tingled.

She walked forward cautiously, leaning to see around the curved corridor. A soft sob and Rebecca placed the sound. The other Soul was here with them. She seemed to have woken once more. There was something different though, but Rebecca could not say what it was.

She walked slowly forward and the corridor gave way to a round inner room. The pattern on the tiled floors narrowed here becoming spiraled mazes on the floor of the room. Rebecca noticed something else strange about this place.

"What is casting this light, Astenos?" she asked quietly.

I do not know, Rebecca. Careful, up ahead, can you see her?

Rebecca could, the woman's diminished energy was pale in the light of the room. She knelt at the room's center, reaching out to something Rebecca could not identify. She stepped into the room onto the tiled maze floor. The woman turned and locked her shifting face on Rebecca. Astenos grabbed Rebecca's upper arm as the woman stood.

"Who are you?"

Rebecca's eyes popped open. She was sweating; Astenos hunted around for the source of the voice. She could see the gleaming points of light still, like the reflection of cats' eyes in the night. She sat up. Fayit turned to look to her.

"The sound woke you?" she whispered.

"What sound?" she asked confused.

Fayit pointed to the north and Rebecca could just faintly hear the echoing of a haunting call.

"I believe we are known," Fayit said. "I will try to sleep if you will take watch." Rebecca nodded, there was no way she was going to be able to go back to sleep.

Fayit took her place and Rebecca eventually heard the huge breaths of the woman slow. Rebecca sat watching out from the camp. Wren twitched in his sleep, moaning slightly. He was coated in sweat. She would help him when she could, but now she needed to get to the Tower.

"Come!"

I have found it Rebecca. Whatever it is; it is not human, but not a Darkling either. Astenos said feeling nervous. *It knows we are here, Rebecca. We should wake the others.*

Rebecca wondered to herself for a moment. "Is it nearing us, Astenos?" she asked him.

Yes, Rebecca, we should leave this place.

"Tell me before it gets too near for us to escape, or if it stops," she said, thinking, trying to remain calm.

What? Rebecca we need to leave now; it moves quickly.

"Please, Astenos," she said.

Very well, but we will not have long to wait one way or another.

Rebecca kept tightening and releasing her grip on Astenos's hilt. She tried to fit the puzzle pieces of what she was doing here in her mind. There were too many to remember. Her friends in Valgerhold, her brother, both her grandfathers, Ronan's Soul Blade, the Gates, now the Tower, everything seemed to fit, almost. But they fell apart as she let the pieces go. She should wake her friends and go back to the village. The Tower had nothing to do with why she was here, she was sure of it now. This was some wild goose chase; it was the Icari she had come here for. She could get them to help her set her friends free. Then what? Where would they go from there? What would hold the Icari to her after they went beyond the Barrier? What would give them any reason to help free her friends in the first place? She liked to think Cev and Nico would come to her aid but she wasn't sure. She was lost again. What was she doing?

It has stopped, Rebecca. Astenos said, shaking her from her thoughts. *How did you know it would stop?*

"I had a feeling. I think I know what it is, Astenos," she stood quietly, careful not to wake the others. "Do you trust me, Astenos?"

Do you even have to ask, my beloved Mate?

"For this, yes, I had to ask." She tightened Astenos around her waist, picked up the tube containing the other Soul Blade and crept silently into the forest toward where whatever had called to her waited.

Eighty-three: Eyes in the Dark

Rebecca shivered not just from the cold and damp of the night. Astenos remained on guard. She could feel him stretching his limits to feel for everything, anything.

It feels wrong, Rebecca, he said shaken. *I can feel nothing around us except the trees and soil. Nothing stirs for hundreds of yards around us. No bird, no insect, nothing.*

"I can feel it too, Astenos," she said, sensing the emptiness around her. The trees seemed to watch her progress through the dark forest. Astenos guided her as well as watched. He could feel the source of the voice ahead. It was alone and it waited was all he could tell her.

She began to hesitate with each step forward. The darkness grew and the silence pounded on her ears. The moon cast everything in a blue gray tint through the canopy above.

Rebecca stopped dead in her tracks. She felt something ahead of her now. Astenos buzzed for her to take him.

"Touch that Soul, and you will die before you can twitch."

The nearness of the sound made her fall over on her backside. Two green circles of light appeared, hovering within a dark silhouette. They floated closer and Rebecca could see something like a head, but it was too big to be a head, and it had something, two large shapes jutting up from above the spots of light, like horns. Eye shine that is what she saw, it was the reflection of the moonlight off the inside of some creature's eyes. They were huge eyes.

"May I allow him to shine so I can see you," she asked as she had to the wolves, in her mind. She could feel the creature considering her, its head cocked quickly.

"I like politeness. You may draw your weapon, child, but keep his point to the ground or you will lose your arm."

She slowly pulled Astenos and switched her hand position so as to keep him pointed to the soil. He grabbed at the Kilaray as soon as he had cleared the scabbard. The green-gold glow blinded her for a moment and she shielded her eyes. The trees lighted from below. What stood beneath them, bigger than the largest horse she had ever laid eyes on, was what she knew instantly to be Falicarna, Bringer of Death.

"Human names have no meaning to us, child. But I do like that one." She could feel his amusement.

It looked like the halicarras in a way but in another it didn't. The huge slightly spiraled antlers that grew from its skull would have come to Rebecca's chin if she stood at their base. The dark blue crest set behind the antlers fanned as it stepped closer to her. Its eyes were a yellow green color and this startled her most of all.

"You wonder if I can see the God Lights." He lowered his head and stared his huge eyes into hers. "What do you believe?"

"I would say yes," she said to him.

"Wise you are for such a young soul. You must watch this one close, Astenos." Rebecca looked to her Soul Blade then back to Falicarna. She had a sense that he was amused again. *"We are the guardians of the Tower, child. The Tower sent by the Creator. We can see all his creations, all that he touches. That is why I have called you here."*

710

"You can see Ronan's Soul Blade," she said, the understanding dawning. "It was you I heard in my sleep. She is always near me and…and I overheard you talking to her."

Falicarna nodded his great antlered head, closing his eyes thoughtfully. *"She is stricken, nearly lost. Hers and Astenos's kind are good beings. But they can be used for twisted purposes as the one who hunts you has done with the Soul he carries."*

"Mandagore Adarian?" She realized suddenly how close Falicarna was to her. "Can you help me to stop him? Will you help me?" Falicarna looked sad.

"We are bound to protect the Tower, child. We cannot leave it while its purpose is unfulfilled."

"What? What purpose? I need help Falicarna, as much as I can gain. I want to help my friends; I want to bring the dead their peace," she realized she was crying. "Please I am begging you; what do I do?" He stepped so close she could smell the wild air on him. He gently wiped a tear from her cheek with his black beak.

"You nearly have what you need to gain what was lost. You need only my permission to enter the Tower. I must ask why you carry a bond to one tied to a Darkling?"

"Wren? He is my friend, my brother sent him to help me," she said, scrubbing the tears from her eyes, feeling foolish. "I want to help him too. He has been joined to another of my friends in the binding rings. I want to cut the Murmur from him but I dare not, not yet."

"Why do you fear to act?"

"I don't want to lose him,"

"Life is full of loss, child; if you fear to take action because you may lose something, you will shrivel away in despair. This is

711

not your way; I see it in you already. Fear not, you will know when the time to act is upon you."

"Then do you allow me to enter the Tower?" she asked hopefully.

"Do not question me on that. I will tell you when and if I decide. Now, I see a Link has been drawn from you to a young man. He is far from you at this time, to the northeast. What can you tell me of this bond?"

"What? What bond?" Falicarna lowered his head and moved in closer to her she sensed from him that he felt she was hiding something. "I…I don't…" but she did. "James," she gasped. She felt it now; she couldn't believe she hadn't felt it before. "I…think,"

"The way of it does not come with thinking, child. Think first, and after, not during the Link work. Let the Creator guide you through that."

"I love him," Falicarna moved back a hair, turning his head to examine her better.

"Good, remember that bond. It is one of the strongest, most flexible, and hardest to find. Once found it is difficult to hold and easily lost. This last question is the most important; answer it true. I will know if you lie to me."

Rebecca could feel the sweat on her palms.

"Why do you seek to end this man Mandagore Adarian?"

She thought for a moment. She hated the man even though she had never met him.

"A strong emotion is that one, hate – powerful and deadly to those that hold it in their souls. But this is not the true reason or you would not have made it here. Hate can carry one only so far."

712

She decided she wanted justice, but it was still vengeance to her in her heart. He had killed her whole family, imprisoned her friends, and destroyed countless lives.

"Vengeance comes from hate, child. Justice is truer to where your heart lies. Vengeance drives Mandagore Adarian, vengeance for the loss of those he loved. Revenge is a self-feeding fire. There is always someone else to blame."

"I want to stop him, though. I don't want him to hurt anyone else," she said desperately. "I just want the killing to end."

"There it is, child; that is what you truly feel. You are kind; hold to that kindness in the times to come; it will be as hard to hold as love. You have killed and you are good at it, as am I, but never have you enjoyed it. Always you sought to end the killing as fast as possible, justice not revenge. That is what makes you different from Mandagore Adarian, Rebecca Dulac, never have you thrilled as you watched the life leave a man.

You may return to your friends. You have my permission to enter the Tower of Light. There you will be tested once more. Be strong; for, what you do will be difficult."

Eighty-four:
Torret so Incandeo

Rebecca stepped into the dim glow of the camp. The others were awake, their faces wide with terror. Wren turned to her, looking furious.

"Where did you go? I felt you leave and I woke but then you vanished; it was like something enveloped our link in smoke," he yelled and Cev looked on him worriedly. "What were you thinking, little sister; do you know what's out there?"

"Yes, I do, Wren," she said calmly, sitting down near the covered Incandeo. "And we don't need to fear it anymore." She pulled the cloak from the globe, lighting all of their confused faces in white. She pulled her legs close and wrapped her arms around her ankles

"Where did you go, girl child?" asked Noe Avaka delicately.

"We have been allowed to enter the Tower." Rebecca was still shaken from her meeting with Falicarna. *How had he seemed to know what was in her heart,* she thought.

Wren knelt by her now, looking like he was afraid she was going mad. "Little sister, Rebecca, what did you see?" he asked very quietly, brushing a stray hair from her face.

She looked up and tears dripped unbidden from her eyes. "I think it was…I don't know but maybe he was…Do you believe in the Father, Wren, or the Fates, the Tree Father, the creator, whoever it is you talk to when there is no one else to listen?" She looked around at the worried faces of her friends. "I mean really believe, do you think he exists out there somewhere, watching over us, listening?"

Cev knelt by her side and wrapped her arms around her. Rebecca shook as she clutched her legs to her chest. "I do believe, Rebecca. Tell us, what did you see out there?"

She felt a wave of joy and fear, feelings too big for her soul to hold in, as she sobbed and laughed at once. "I think maybe…he is His messenger, Falicarna. His name isn't right though," she said, laughing through her tears. "He isn't the Bringer of Death."

"Why do you say that, Rebecca?" asked Fayit softly from above her.

Rebecca felt that place in her middle where she felt the Kilaray; it felt warmer. "I met him out there." The others looked frightened for her. "He brought me hope."

* * *

They didn't bother to set a watch for the rest of the evening. Rebecca lay huddled in Cev's arms until she slipped off to sleep. Wren watched feeling desperately scared. He could see what she had seen in vague glimpses, mainly two glowing spots of light. Wren went to the two women whose bonds he carried.

"I think she's asleep," whispered Cev. "Bring me her cloak, please." Wren gathered the Tremen cloak. They covered Rebecca and laid her down to sleep. Noe Avaka came to relieve their guard of her. Cev took Wren's hand and she led him to where Nico and Fayit whispered together.

"What do you think?" asked Wren quietly. "Do…do you believe her?"

"I think whatever happened out there scared her to her core," Fayit said.

715

"It sounds…too true to what the Elders say," said Nico, shaking his head slowly. "The ones like my father who actually met the pack leader. They said it was as though it could read your soul like a book. I believe her Wren. We should trust her."

Wren nodded; he felt a stab of pain at his soul and knew his Murmur was getting close to breaking his anchor. He forced his face to show nothing. He focused on the warmth of Cev's hand in his, her forearm wrapped around his. The soft squeezes she gave his palm now and again to make him remember hers was still there. The pain receded.

"Then we go forward," said Cev. "We can always go back; can't we?"

Wren smiled at her. "Sure," he lied. "If things get tetchy we turn back." He knew this was his last day left to himself. His Murmur's excitement was palpable. Soon he would be what he had always been fated to become. The worst part was that when the Murmur took his soul, used it to move into his body, there would be nothing left of the dim coal he had found hidden inside him. That strange spark he hadn't thought capable of existing inside him. The love he felt for two women. One like a sister, the other…well not quite a lover.

"What are you grinning at?" asked Cev as they returned to where Rebecca and Noe Avaka were.

"Nothing, my dear, nothing at all."

* * *

Rebecca awoke warm, huddled between Cev and Wren. If not for the change of sleeping arrangements, Rebecca would have thought last night a dream, except for the feeling in her heart.

The solemn silence as they ate first meal gave more reality to what had happened. She could see the look of concern on each of their faces as they watched her. They finished eating and washed in a nearby tributary of the main river that fed the falls. Then they broke camp and hiked toward the Tower of Light.

One thing seemed brighter from the evening's activities, Wren and Cev were much friendlier this morning. Perhaps tending to a near-hysterical girl would do that to people. The thought brought a smile to Rebecca's face. She would see the two married if anything else like last night happened to her again.

Hours they hiked through steep cliff covered terrain. The talk had resumed among the group. They seemed to trust to one part of Rebecca's tale; they had been allowed passage to the Tower. Nico said that they would have been set upon this close to the Tower otherwise.

Before midday, they reached Dandaria Falls. The cliffs they edged along stopped short and a gorge opened up before them. Plummeting down into the gorge, the falls turned to cloud before they reached the pool below. Rainbows shone in full circles in the mists below. The thunderous roar of the ice blue water that gushed from the river shook small pebbles beneath their feet. Rebecca could not tell where the water source was but she could see a storm on the horizon, no, not a storm. She looked up in astonishment and realized why the horizon had become so dark.

Behind the falls a flat topped mountain rose toward the sky. Rebecca had seen it from its top and there it was a mile across. How wide was the crater at its base five, ten, fifteen miles? She realized it was larger than that as she turned to look down from where they had traveled. The ground seemed to rise and fall in ripples back as far as she could see. It was like the stone and soil had become water and froze at the instant a drop fell on its liquid surface. Now she knew where the water that fed the river originated. The lake within the crater; it had to be. The water squeezed through cracks and pores of the rock, forming rivulets that built to a deluge. She could see the sun shine on the dampened surface of the sides in places.

She broke her feet away from where they seemed to have rooted and caught up to the others. They worked their way around the lip of the gorge and found a trail marked long ago with cut stone sculptures. Rebecca shuddered slightly as she looked at the stylized figures of the valicarras.

Eventually they found themselves at the base of the crater. Overhead shapes wheeled in the sky. Rebecca could tell from the ground, from the points extending from their skulls, they were valicarras. The crater wall was stepped where erosion or sheer weight of rock cleaved the mountain. Cliffs and walls snaked up the sides making a giant's staircase. But for people, Fayit the tallest among them, each step was like climbing a hill. Here and there the stone had been carved into actual stairs, making the climb somewhat easier. Always there was the threat of the rocks giving way.

Rebecca was worried for Wren. He looked pale and too sweaty; he too would rub at the symbol on his chest when he thought no one was looking. She had been told she would know when the time was right, it was not now. She climbed onward. Three hours, and the top of the crater was in sight. The stone leveled out a little here and they hurried up to see what their efforts had gained them. The vision in the Traveler could not prepare her for the sight.

She could see clouds down there, floating above the lake. The crater's interior wall would be impossible to descend. Its bowl-like face was nearly vertical and it had been blasted smooth as glass from the impact. Words came to her mind that had nothing to do with the description of a piece of architecture as she looked on the gleaming spire that rose from the center of the lake.

Love, beauty, hope, joy, salvation these were the words that filled her mind. Like purest white snow, the columns of the Tower marched around and around its slowly tapered form. Higher and higher the structure reached until it was impossibly high and impossibly narrow. Rebecca could see the light; she looked to her friends and knew that they saw it too. Somehow even Wren seemed to watch it.

From the base to the tip, from the tip to the base, streamers of light flowed. The fountains of light seemed boundless. Rebecca felt her cheeks, too cool as a breath of wind rolled along the top of the crater; she felt them and found them wet. She was here finally, after so much heartache, she looked upon the *Torret so Incandeo*, the Tower of Light.

Eighty-five:
This Far Together and No Further

"How...er, erm, how do we uh..." Wren trailed off, his face full of awe. Rebecca knew what he meant to say. How would they get into the Tower?

From where they stood they could see the vast arched opening directly across from them. The only problem was the half-mile of open air separating them from it. A bridge cantilevered out from the side of the tower, stopping a third the way to the crater lip. She remembered thinking she would have to be able to fly to reach it. And, as though the thought summoned them, six of the wheeling shapes broke from their patrol of the Tower's top.

"Look out, here they come," Wren shouted, reaching for his narrow sword. Rebecca seized his hand before he pulled an inch of steel from the scabbard.

"No weapons, Wren, you have to trust me." His face was wide with fear; fear for her not himself she knew. His lips compressed and he slammed the sword back. Cev stepped close behind him and took hold of his hand. He turned back to her and a significant look passed between the two. Wren nodded.

Shadows passed over them as the six valicarras descended. Rebecca saw how much larger Falicarna, at their lead, was than the others. They touched down, flapping their wide wings to land lightly upon the crater lip. The six animals, their heads and feathers twitching with the urge to attack, walked closer to the group waiting for them. Falicarna halted his fellow valicarras and approached Rebecca.

"Your friends seem nervous child." Amusement was in his voice. Rebecca turned to look at her friends. Wren gripped the sides of his head staring at Falicarna in disbelief. Cev and Nico looked reverent. Fayit smiled and Noe Avaka shuddered.

"I can hear him, little sister," said Wren. "He's in my head." Falicarna tilted his head at Wren.

"I see why you like this man, child. He is valiant at heart. I hope you can help him as you desire." Rebecca knew these words were for her alone. *"You seem ill equipped for you journey to the Tower."* Falicarna spoke to the group again. He looked to his wings and front appendages, and then looked down over the lip to the lake below. *"A long way to fall I think."*

Cev and Nico smiled, Wren looked like he was going to be sick and shook his head slightly.

"Oh, Fates not again, my legs are still sore from the last time," he said in a groan.

"We could leave you behind, Darkling." Wren stepped forward, looking like he meant to punch Falicarna in the beak. Rebecca was shocked but she got that amused feel from Falicarna. *"Very valiant, child,"* he whispered to her again.

"I trust my young friend told you I had granted you permission to enter the Tower?" The group nodded. *"Then, if you will step lively to my brothers and sisters behind me. I will carry you myself child."* Falicarna lowered his huge head to the ground and Rebecca took hold of his antlers without hesitation. He raised his head and she slid down his blue plumed neck to his gray-and-white shoulders.

721

"Fear not, Teacher, we would not harm you even if you were not a guest of my young friend." Noe Avaka jerkily took hold of the valicarra that had lowered its head for him.

"These creatures are qui…quite a bit larger than the last animal I rode, girl child," growled Noe Avaka, clinging to his valicarra's neck.

"All in place? Then hold tight!"

The valicarras leapt from the crater lip swooping down into its interior. Rebecca could hear the shouts of surprise from her friends behind her. She hugged Falicarna around his neck, pressing her face into his indigo feathers.

"Thank you for this, Falicarna," she thought to him.

"You do not have me to thank child. You gained entry on your own."

The valicarras beat their powerful wings and they gained altitude, heading for the cantilevered bridge jutting from the side of the Tower. Falicarna and the other valicarras set down without the jolts Rebecca was used to from the halicarras. Rebecca and her friends slid to the white stone-like surface of the bridge.

Rebecca stood for a moment before Falicarna. He lowered his head to look her in the eyes.

"Remember what was said, child. I can be of no more assistance to you once inside the Tower." He looked to Wren, Rebecca followed Falicarna's stare. Wren looked shocked but nodded his head after a moment when Falicarna finished what he had to say. *"Watch your friends inside child. There are pitfalls meant to keep what is at the heart of the Tower safe. Tricks of the mind and soul await you."* Rebecca had the sense that if he could smile Falicarna would be grinning from ear to ear. *"We await your return, child. I believe your term is 'good luck'."* And with that, the

722

valicarras leapt from the edge of the bridge, flapping to catch the drafts that would allow them to soar around the Tower's peak.

Rebecca turned to Wren and he looked determined. She dare not ask what Falicarna had told him, it felt wrong to pry. The six moved toward the arched opening waiting for them. Rebecca realized why the tower seemed so strangely pure white. Surely this spire had stood for centuries but Rebecca could spot not a single mote of dust anywhere on its surface. As they neared the entrance, they passed through the cascading, coruscating wall of Kilaray light. It felt warm and when they exited, all of them had wide smiles that stayed with them. That was until they entered the opening of the Tower.

The light of the day vanished as they walked further inside the vast port. The walls were like polished glass inside the Tower. Light seemed to permeate the air around them. Rebecca had a sense she had seen this before. The opening let out on a curving corridor; it stretched away to either side of them. Rebecca looked up and she knew what she would find. The ceiling vanished in whiteness; it was quite disorienting. There had to be some limit to the height of the corridor, but the way the all encompassing light vanquished shadows, it was impossible to tell.

"Where is the light coming from?" asked Wren as he stared around the space. No one could answer.

The group huddled close as they set off. Rebecca led them to the right. It seemed the direction she had headed in her dream.

They traveled around the space for an hour, causing Rebecca to worry. They had to have circled the entire circumference of the Tower by now. Where was the room she had seen? For that matter, where was the entrance they had come through?

723

"I believe, Rebecca, we are back to where we set out," said Fayit. Rebecca was unnerved to hear the fear in the Tremen's voice. "I cannot see where we entered though."

"What are we looking for, Rebecca?" asked Cev, staring around the space open mouthed. "I see no other corridors."

"There was a room," said Rebecca. "I know there was." She looked around desperately. "It was right that way," she said, pointing and something changed. The tiles on the floor flowed in patterns in the direction Rebecca pointed.

Oh, Father I can feel him, gasped Ronan's Soul Blade in Rebecca's head.

I am here, Rebecca, I have her! Astenos roared in her head. She could feel him struggle against the other soul.

"Is something wrong, Rebecca?" asked Nico. "I say this place is unsettling but you look terrified."

"It's nothing. Come, we must hurry." They moved toward where the tiles had changed. They walked for what seemed like too long but the room never appeared.

"This is getting ridiculous," said Wren after a time. "It's like we are right where we started again." He pulled one of his knives and set it on the ground. He looked up to the group. They understood he was leaving a marker.

They set out again toward where the room should be. Wren watched the rear; his knife dwindled away around the bend in the corridor. "Well, we've moved at least," he said, turning back to the group." They walked on and finally they spotted something up ahead. They picked up their pace and then slid to a halt. Ahead of them the corridor looked the same, the changed pattern directing them to where the room should be, but sitting in the middle of the floor was Wren's knife.

Rebecca sensed the group held their panic at bay. Cev gripped Wren's wrist, and he rubbed the mark on his chest looking ill. Noe Avaka began to pace back and forth. Fayit caressed the hilt of the savage knife at her belt. Rebecca needed to do something or they were going to start to crack.

"In the dream I had, the pattern on the floor weaved back and forth like it is that way," she pointed and began to walk, talking as she did. She heard the scrape as Wren picked his knife off the floor. "I walked for a short time and then the pattern…" she concentrated on the floor, "…began…to change." Slowly the tiles weaving back and forth split off and the corridor seemed to change once more.

The curving inner wall stopped short and the outside wall continued around, forming a round room. The ceiling stretched far above them in the vanishing light. The tiles on the floor spiraled out in patterns and mazes within the room. At the center a shape sat. It was indistinguishable as Rebecca looked on it. It seemed to be blurred and out of focus though all around it, the tile mazes, were crystal clear. Rebecca's skin prickled. She could feel Astenos struggle with the other Soul harder now.

"What is that?" Wren said, pointing but not at the object at the center of the room. There was a banner lying on the floor not too far from the opening. Wren stepped to it and knelt down, the rest of the group came to form an arc behind him. Rebecca had seen it before, green and orange slashed diagonally, a black bird like the one tattooed on Wren's right hand at its center. "It's a Silvarish Night Bird banner. What is this doing here?" he reached out to touch the fabric.

"Perhaps you should not do that," growled Noe Avaka cautiously.

Wren turned to look at him. His fingers brushed the green side of the banner.

Flash! The room was gone. They stood in a field looking on a battalion of lightly armored men. Their coloring and the way they held themselves told the group the men were Silvarish. A man on a snorting black stallion rode into view carrying the banner. With his mask closed Rebecca couldn't see his face but she could feel his eyes. He reached to his waist and pulled a narrow sword from its scabbard. She knew at once before the blue-violet light shone from the Blade this man was Palantean.

"We march for the gap!" he roared and the sound of the men around them erupted in a deafening bellow.

Flash! The room returned. Wren was on his backside and elbows; he had fallen over from his crouch.

"What was that!" he shouted the sound of his voice echoed around the room, dissipating too quickly.

"Tricks of the mind and soul, Falicarna told me," whispered Rebecca. Her words should not have echoed for as long as they did. The tiles around the room began to revolve, groaning as the small stones grated against one another. The figure at the center of the room looked slightly clearer. Within the mazes of newly patterned tile work laid a blue and gold scarf, singed and torn in places.

"I think you should wait here for me," she said to her friends. "I don't want any of you to be hurt."

"You can leave that right there, little sister," said Wren, getting to his feet.

"I agree with Wren, Rebecca," said Fayit, laying a paw on her shoulder. "We should not separate."

"We said we would follow the World Strider," said Nico.

"...and follow you we shall," finished Noe Avaka.

Rebecca felt concern for them, but relieved that they wanted to stay with her. She nodded reluctantly and the group stepped to the next item. The ground behind them rumbled. When they had gathered around the scarf, the rumbling increased to a roar.

The tiles and the stone behind them fell away, splitting and cracking like a parched lake bed. The crumbling stonework tumbled upward toward the light obscured ceiling and vanished, leaving a bottomless darkness behind them. Rebecca looked around at her friends.

"Well it seems this room has decided our way, little sister," said Wren.

"Shall we see what comes of this, then?" asked Noe Avaka, reaching out for the blue and gold scarf.

Flash! They were at the top of a fortress wall looking out over a green rolling landscape. Rebecca knew these fields from her father's description of them. This was the Bastion of the Palantean, in Arnora. A slim young man stepped into view, looking out at those peaceful fields. The blue and gold scarf whipped in the winds at his throat. Rebecca's heart leapt; she thought at first it was her brother but he had never been that tall.

Another boy appeared before them; he was younger and looked quite content. A similar scarf whipped out behind him, chasing his streaming blonde curls.

"I love this view," said the golden haired boy. "Don't you Ronan?"

Rebecca could feel the tears in her eyes she knew the older boy. It was her grandfather, Ronan Arcand. He turned to the youth and clapped him on the shoulder.

"I told you Mandagore, it's Master Arcand, here," Ronan said, looking on the boy fondly. Rebecca felt like she was going to be sick. She knew this boy could not be anyone else, Mandagore Adarian. "If the Captain or Commanders heard you, you wouldn't be able to sit for a week."

The boy smiled mischievously. "It's not like I haven't been whipped before, *Ronan*." Ronan ruffled the boy's hair and gave him a shove to move him along.

Flash! The room came back, looking more sterile in contrast to the last scene. Wren's eyes were wide as he stared at Rebecca. She could tell what he was thinking.

"Who was that man, Rebecca?" asked Cev confused. "He had your face."

"It..." but she couldn't get anymore out.

"That was her grandfather," said Noe Avaka. "A very honorable man he was."

The group moved away from the scarf as the tiles began turning once more. They made sure they cleared the space as a helmet appeared, and the ground behind them gave way, crumbling upward. The helmet looked like leather fitted with bronze fixtures. It was weathered and sat on a small pile of red sandy soil. The group gathered around the helmet and Cev bent to touch its surface.

Nothing. She looked up at the group. "I do not understand," she said.

"This far you come together..." Noe Avaka said, looking at the tile floor; he seemed to be tracing some tiny script set into the patterned tiles. He followed it with his finger. "...and no further. Alone you must go." He looked up.

Rebecca shook her head. She turned looking for something, anything. "I won't. I won't leave them behind," she shouted at the room. The tiles below her friends' feet moved; they did not seem to feel them but the mazes and patterns shifted. Circles formed around the five sets of feet and moved them toward the round edge where the tiles ended in a deep dark drop. Cev dropped the helmet in her surprise. It rolled to Rebecca's feet and came to rest, as her friends were dragged toward their deaths by the accursed Tower.

Eighty-six:
Abel's Tale

"Stop!" she shouted in panic. "Please stop! I'll do it, just don't kill my friends."

The circles of tile containing her friends halted and then the gap between her and them broke away. Rebecca cried out as she watched her friends brace for the fall upward; it did not come. They stood suspended on five islands of tile over black of immeasurable deepness.

She fell to her knees and wept.

"We are alright, Rebecca," shouted Cev. "You must continue."

"Go, little sister, but be careful!" Wren yelled to her. "We'll be here when you get back."

Rebecca crawled to the helmet and, taking one last look at her friends, she took hold of it.

Flash! Rebecca saw the snowy mountains of a land she had never set eyes upon. Pink blossomed trees stood all around her in a stone paved garden. Snowflakes fell slowly to the meditation garden's paths, making a hushing sound. A small red bridge spanned a babbling stream ahead of her. She heard someone approach over the crunching gravel.

"You have done well, Abel." She turned to look; a man stared at her as he spoke. He was Beltari she could tell from his smooth dark skin. She stood, putting her hand on her knee for support and froze. Her hand was the color of oiled mahogany. She pushed to her feet and saw the man from too high up. "Your finding the Dulac man's journal has brought his family comfort. An Arnoran man comes to request you join them in their Bastion, one of the Palantean."

She heard words come from her mouth. "Who is it?" Abel said with a grin.

"He said his name is Ronan…"

"Arcand, the man is relentless," said Abel. "Take me to him. I feel if I don't agree to go he will bind me like a lamb and drag me there."

"Then, you mean to go?" asked the Beltari man.

"Yes, I believe I do," said Abel.

Flash! Rebecca was back in Arnora. Atop the very wall she had seen her grandfather as a young man. She saw through this man Abel's eyes, she knew it.

"Are you sick for your home already, Abel?" asked a gruff voice behind her. She turned and Abel answered.

"Ronan! By the Father, it's good to see you," said Abel in his deep strong voice. He took Ronan's outstretched arm and pulled the other man into an embrace.

"Hello, Abel," said an older man that was Mandagore Adarian. His face was strained a bit now like he had seen too much that hurt his soul.

"Young Mandagore," said Abel, embracing the golden haired man. "I am sorry about your friends in Felsof, I heard."

Mandagore compressed his lips and nodded. "The courts will bring them justice, I pray. I am leading some of my command to see if we cannot influence the court's decision."

"What do your friends call themselves again my young friend, *Adarianites*, was it not?" Mandagore nodded, looking somewhat proud and embarrassed. "Have faith my friend, the Father will see all goes as it should," said Abel, turning to Ronan.

"What have you dragged me here for this time, Ronan?" asked Abel. Mandagore slipped away as the two turned to walk the fortress wall. He seemed angry to Rebecca. A group of young men and women appeared at the end of the wall to meet him and they vanished together.

"My daughter, she has given birth," said Ronan, looking grim.

"Congratulations, man!" said Abel, slapping Ronan on his back.

"The father is Tomas Dulac," said Ronan, looking significantly toward Abel. Abel smiled.

"Sophia took to the boy when I returned that journal; do you remember?" asked Abel still smiling. Ronan nodded looking upset.

He has the eyes Abel, but he is…" Ronan sneered, "Mecharical."

"Ronan, you Palantean hold to much stock in your division of powers. Every new life brings chance for great things. It is time to rejoice my friend."

"I want you to do a Reading of the child, Abel," said Ronan, stopping. "My wife refuses. She thinks I am being a fool. You are the best I know with Readings."

Abel became serious. "You don't lend any credence to these theories about the dimming your people see in their Visions. It is a difficult task at best, Ronan…"

"I have a feeling about this child, Abel," Ronan looked frightened. "Please."

"Alright, Ronan, alright," said Abel. "Let's just stop to get them a gift first. You would never think of such things, I know, but I'm sure it would mean something to Sophia."

Flash! Flash! For the briefest instant she thought she could hear her friends call out to her, "What do you see Rebecca? Rebecca!" Flash! Flash!

Flash! Rebecca caught her breath. She was in her home in Arnora, in the main room. A squalling baby boy was clutched in Abel's strong dark hands. Rebecca's mother watched half in fear, half in hope. Ronan held her father from behind, pinning his arms behind him. Tomas struggled to free himself.

"I can't say for sure, Ronan. I'm sorry it may be the child the Philistari have been predicting, but the Reading is muddled," said Abel. Ronan released her father and he rushed to Abel, grabbing her brother from his dark hands. He spun and shouted at Ronan.

"You, bastard! Get out of my house," her father roared. She had never heard him so angry.

"Calm yourself, Tomas, please," said Ronan gently.

"No father, he is right. You have become obsessed with the Philistari's Visions," said Rebecca's mother. "You are not welcome in this house, Ronan Arcand. Leave."

Ronan looked like his heart was being ripped from him. "Sophia, would you deny me sight of my grandson?"

"Yes," roared Tomas. "Get out of here before I have you removed."

Ronan hesitated a moment then turned and walked from the room. Sophia stepped to Abel.

"Sophia, I'm sorry, he told me you both had agreed to this," Abel said desperately.

"We know, Abel. You should go, please," her mother's face filled her vision and Rebecca wept along with Abel.

Flash! Abel's dark hands held another bundle this time. Yellow-green eyes stared up into his face, her face. Rebecca looked upon herself, bundled in a soft white blanket. Abel looked up and Rebecca's heart felt like it would burst once more. They were in a workshop of some kind.

"What do you see, Abel?" asked a thinner, bespectacled, red-haired Alaric von Magus. "Is it her? Is it the child the Philistari saw?"

She heard a soft weeping from beside her. Abel turned and saw Ronan with his hand pressed over his eyes. Sophia had a hood pulled up over her dark hair holding her father's shoulders. Behind them, watching from the darkened window, a young man with a dark moustache stood watch. Rebecca knew at once, with a stab of sorrow, he was Broheim. He wore a Stitcher's rig bristling with knives. This must have been after the Brotherhood of the Three Knives had formed, after the Exile and the last of the Philistari.

"I thought you should at least see your granddaughter, Ronan," Sophia said, patting her father's arm. "Her name is Rebecca."

"Do you want to know, Ronan?" asked Abel.

"I don't care anymore." Ronan said thickly. "You were right, Sophia, I was obsessed."

Sophia looked to Abel; the question Ronan would not ask clear on her face. Rebecca saw the scene bob up and down, through Abel's eyes. Sophia bit her hand and tears came to her eyes.

Flash! Rebecca longed for the relative serenity of the last scene. Winds tore at the red sandy soil beneath them. Men were falling fast all around her.

"Abel, we have to push them back," screamed Ronan, his blue crested helmet blocking out all but his eyes which burned with fury. "We are betrayed!"

Abel had known this day was coming. Ronan pulled that amazing sword from its scabbard, filling the gap in its lightening blue glow. He tore into the Red Fist soldiers as they poured over the crest of the gap. The red horizon beyond the stone walls of the gap over the Broken Lands billowed and roiled like the Blazes of Discordia. Men fell before they knew they were dead to Ronan's Soul Blade.

Abel felt the pull of Kilaray; his vision blurred away from where he was.

Flash! Flash! A young girl screamed for her friends who moved away from her on stone discs. The scene shuttered. The girl crawled to a helmet lying beside her, his helmet. Flash! Flash!

"Come on Abel you're hurt," bellowed Ronan, grabbing Abel by his golden cloak and pulling him down from the peak of the gap. Abel could see the swath of death Ronan had laid bare with his Blade. He could hear the roar of thousands of the Exiled regrouping just over the peak. Mandagore was out there somewhere. *How could it have come to this*, he thought desperately.

"We won't make it out, Ronan," Abel said. He could feel the bullet burning in his thigh. "Not both of us."

"What are you saying? Come on, we'll fall back and take those Felsofese cowards together. Bast! Why did I trust them? I should have listened to you," Ronan dragged Abel behind a rock outcropping.

Flash! Flash! The young girl had the eyes as she gazed out in horror from scenes she didn't want to see. A form stood before her, it looked to Abel like a man on his knees. Flash! Flash!

"Oh Father, Abel," shouted Ronan.

It hurt to breathe. Abel looked at his chest and saw the dark spot spreading from the bullet wound. "Stay with me my friend, I'll get you a Healer, and you'll be alright."

"Ronan she's coming for you," said Abel laboriously. "Leave me, my friend."

"What are you talking about, Abel? You're in shock, hang on. Here, Elora, guard Abel," Ronan said, handing Abel his Soul Blade. She sparked into life in Abel's hand. Abel could hear her voice dimly in his head. Ronan rummaged in a dead medicine man's bag. He rifled out the contents. Abel turned and saw the horde of the Red Fist Army, pouring like enraged ants from a hill over the crest in the gap.

Flash! Flash! The young girl stood, tears running from her eyes; she had to be the child he had seen so long ago. Rebecca, Sophia said they had named her. She held her own Soul Blade now. Astenos, *where had that name come from?* Somehow he knew it was right. Understanding dawned in Rebecca's face as she neared the form of the kneeling man before her. Abel could see the blue crest on the kneeling man's helmet. She opened the leather tube on her back and pulled out a blue and gold silk bag. She pulled the cord loose and hesitated.

"Help me, Astenos. I know what I have to do," she said, bracing herself. She reached into the bag and pulled out Ronan's Soul Blade. Elora, sparked into life in the girl's hand. Rebecca looked like she fought with a bolt of lightning. Flash! Flash!

Ronan was on his knees over Abel. The horde was almost on them. Abel could hear the Felsofese coming up from the opposite side. A Night Bird banner drifted by them, and Ronan's scarf pulled loose from his neck. Abel knew the time was now. He lifted his helmet from his head.

"Abel what are…?" Ronan said as Abel shoved Elora hilt deep, screaming in madness, into Ronan's chest. He looked into Abel's eyes and understanding shone through. "It was her. It's Rebecca." Abel nodded.

"I'll miss you my friend." The red sky dimmed as a wave of light washed over him. Ronan's body slipped away. Abel could feel a slight ache in his head where the bullet had entered; he could feel Elora tumble from his fingers. Then, Abel felt nothing.

Eighty-seven:
The Strongest Link

Rebecca could feel the red sandy soil under her knees. The Red Fist Army was coming, they were going to be on them soon. The Felsofese were approaching from the opposite side. Ronan knelt over her as she lay dying.

No! She was in the Tower of Light and she knelt on a flowing tile floor before a man on his knees.

Hold to me, Rebecca, hold to me, pleaded Astenos. *We are one, hold to me.*

Ronan, you are mine. Where are you, I can feel you? ranted Elora in Rebecca's mind.

She felt Elora spark to life as Ronan hunted through a medicine man's bag for a Healer. She could see a girl in her mind, holding Elora, kneeling before a man on his knees. She understood now, what she had to do.

No! The girl was her. She was losing herself to the dead man, Abel. Ronan's Soul Blade roared in Rebecca's head.

Block her out Rebecca, cried Astenos. *Please hold her out.*

Let me in, Ronan. Why do you keep me away? screamed Elora.

Rebecca crawled to the man on his knees and felt the soil sticking to her damp hands. Where was she? She looked up and saw the strange light of the room; she looked down and saw a patch of red ground. She could hear her friends calling to her; she could hear the Red Fist Army roaring. She was in the Tower of Light and she was in the battle strewn gap.

738

Hold to me, my love, said Astenos weakly, desperately. She felt his Links slipping away from her. She could feel her own being pulled apart, torn into two different worlds. *Hold to me, Rebecca.* He begged weaker than when they had first been Linked.

"Astenos, Astenos, I can hear you, stay with me," she cried.

Elora raged stronger in her mind, she was trying to tear Astenos's Link with Rebecca away, trying to bind herself to it. Rebecca knew what she had to do. Abel was showing her in her head. She crawled weakly to where Ronan's body, drifting between worlds, knelt somehow in the Tower of Light. She lifted Elora with her last failing strength.

Rebecca found Astenos's Links to her; it was like grabbing lines in a windstorm. She held tight to the closest one, she felt his love for her flowing along that Link, thinner than spider silk, stronger than the thickest steel. She felt it slip and she focused her entire mind and soul on holding tight to that Link.

She lifted Elora...

Abel lifted Elora...

...and he...

...and she...

...plunged Elora hilt deep into Ronan's chest.

Rebecca's mind whirled about, Astenos held out the storm that was Elora. Her screams left Rebecca's mind and calm swept over her, infinite calm. She was being pulled away. Astenos was at her side she could feel his embrace of her soul; he held tight until the pull ceased. The relief and the love that washed through her from him gave her strength to take a breath. Her heart began to beat. Blood began to flow through her veins.

She had fallen over backwards with the power that had washed out from what she had done, like all the waves in all the oceans crashing at once upon her. She had died she knew it. Astenos had caught her and brought her back.

"Thank you my love," she said to him. She heard the words repeated from outside of her head.

"Thank you my love," a gruff voice said.

Rebecca pushed to her elbows. Ronan Arcand knelt, steaming from every inch, with his own Soul Blade pushed hilt deep into his chest. He looked up and locked eyes on Rebecca, and then toppled over onto his side. The shock of what she had just seen made it hard for her to think.

"Rebecca, oh Fates, are you alright?" Wren said, falling to his knees and sliding up to her. "I couldn't get to you, I'm sorry. Are you alright? What's wrong?"

"Rebecca, this man is injured," said Nico at Ronan's side. Nico looked over to her and his eyes were wide. "I believe this is the man we saw before. Rebecca, I think this is your grandfather."

Rebecca pushed to her hands and knees and crawled to where Ronan had collapsed. He was on his side, unable to lay on his back for the two and a half feet of steel protruding behind him. His labored breathing looked painful. Without a thought Rebecca slipped into the Easing, then down deeper into the Stillness where she could do her Link work.

Rebecca now knew the Tower must be a physical bridge to the Kilaray world. All time existed here at once and it was here that Ronan had waited until she could find what had been lost to her world.

How the Soul Blade had managed it, Rebecca had no idea. Every vital organ had been missed; the chest piercing stab was little more than a flesh wound. What Elora had not been able to do was keep from cutting Ronan's Links to the world. The one last tie she had clung to had been her love for him; it had kept him from drifting away completely, like a kite in a storm she had anchored him to herself. It had saved him and it had driven her mad. Rebecca pulled her from Ronan's chest and sent flows of Kilaray along the damaged links in his ribs and muscle and skin. She slipped back through the Quickening and watched in relief as Ronan's wounds knit together, their Links restored; all of his Links restored.

Nico helped Ronan to his feet; Wren helped Rebecca to hers. They stood like some skewed reflection, looking at one another. For the first time in fourteen years Ronan Arcand looked on his granddaughter. He touched his thumb and forefinger knuckles to the bridge of his nose in Arnoran salute and the face shield of his helmet collapsed on itself, revealing his face. Tears ran freely from his eyes.

"Hello," Rebecca said weakly and smiled.

Ronan stepped, Nico aiding him, to Rebecca. He hesitated for a moment and then wrapped her in his strong arms, holding her head against his chest, where so recently a Blade had extended. Rebecca's strength broke and she wept with joy and relief.

"You came, Rebecca, you came and you saved me," Ronan said through his tears.

They stood for a time clutched to one another until they both had gained enough of their strength to let go. Ronan held her at arm's length, examining her like a glorious treasure.

"You have Sophia's face," he said, looking overjoyed. "Where is your mother; is she with you? I want to see her." He looked around for the first time, spotting Rebecca's friends, expecting his daughter to appear. He turned back to Rebecca and the look on her face made

Ronan's fall, the understanding was immediate and terrible. "Tomas?" he asked reluctantly. "Your father, is he here?" Rebecca looked to the floor. "Oh Father, child, I'm sorry." He wrapped her up again and this time the tears were for their mutual grieving.

"How did you find me?" he said after they had recovered.

"My...my friends, Ronan," she said, wiping her eyes to clear them and trying a smile on her face. "My friends helped me."

Ronan saw the others now for the first time. His face split in wonder as he looked on Fayit and Noe Avaka. He cocked his head slightly at Cev and Nico.

"You!" he bellowed as his eyes met Wren's. "You're one of them!" Elora was in his hand and his weakness seemed a thing of the past. Rebecca launched between Wren and Ronan as his Soul Blade streamed for Wren's neck.

"No!" Rebecca shouted. She had Astenos in her hand, catching Elora an inch from the blue scarf tied around Wren's throat. "He is my friend too, Ronan."

Ronan looked at her like some tainted thing and shook his head. "He is a Husked Man, Rebecca. They don't have friends. All he has is a grave waiting for him to fill it."

"Well it will have to wait," Rebecca said. "He helped me, saved me, more than once. Sebastian sent him to help me."

Ronan faltered and his sword point lowered. Rebecca thought it safe to stand down a bit. Ronan looked up with a little excitement on his face.

"Your brother, surely that one must be here," he said carefully. Rebecca shook her head. "Oh, Father!" Ronan fell to his knees, Elora clattering on the stone tiled floor, and he clapped his hands to his face to hold out the world. "Oh, Father, no, no, no."

"Little sister," Wren said, eyeing Ronan sideways as he whispered. "We...we should probably get out of here. When you...did...whatever you did, this whole place rang like a bell, the floor reappeared - I don't think it really ever was gone, and the Tower shuddered."

Rebecca could hear it now, like some giant bell still reverberating with a massive strike from the claxon. The floor beneath her feet vibrated still. She turned to her grieving grandfather and went to his side.

"Ronan," she whispered, "Ronan, we have to leave. We have to get out of here."

He looked up and his crisp blue eyes were red all around.

"You're all I have left; aren't you, dear one?" he said at last. Rebecca nodded.

"Come on Ronan, we have to leave," she whispered, taking his arm over her shoulder, Nico taking the other. "Come, Grandfather."

Eighty-eight:
On the Edge of Worlds

The group ran from the intact room within the Tower. The corridor was much less troublesome on the way out, but the distance seemed to have increased. The Tower shook several times. One such knocked the seven people off their feet, sending them sprawling on the tiled floor.

"Come on!" roared Wren, grabbing Ronan's arm from Rebecca. "Old man, I won't let you get this girl killed." Ronan looked like he wanted to commit murder but he allowed Wren to help take his weight.

They ran for the spot of light they saw up ahead, not the strange light of the Tower, but the normal light of day. They could see the arched opening as they ran. The corridor began to shift. The interior wall pushed out toward the exterior, narrowing the corridor along which they ran.

"I think this place wants us out," said Noe Avaka, panting. Fayit took him onto her shoulders and the group doubled their pace. They were almost there, almost. The wall was closing in; they were going to be crushed.

Seven people burst into the light of the day as the interior wall thudded the opening closed. The cantilevered bridge shook violently. The group staggered back and forth with its waving motion. Rebecca looked back over her shoulder; the Kilaray light intensified, sparking wildly out from the Tower. She looked over the edge of the wide bridge and saw the lake below rippling wildly with the Tower's vibrations. Rebecca's vision blurred with the motion, the bones in her head rattling.

"Falicarna we need you!" she forced out with all her strength.

"We come!"

She looked up and saw seven wheeling shapes break from the hundreds that now flew around the Tower's top. Her breath caught; a blinding light like seven suns shot skyward from the Tower. *Oh, father! What is happening?* she thought.

The valicarras lighted on the edge of the bridge, waiting for their running passengers.

"I had faith in you child," said Falicarna as Rebecca caught his antler, pulling herself up. The valicarras plunged from the bridge and Rebecca's vision cleared. She watched as the spire behind them, from the now steaming lake below, to the blinding tip seemed to ignite. The Kilaray light around the spire pulsed in waves outward further and further. The valicarras rode through the waves. They landed on the lip of the crater and the group dismounted in time to watch the Tower do what it was meant to do.

Stillness swept over the land. All wind stopped. The flow of the river, pouring from the crater's walls, froze in mid rush. The very air seemed to sizzle with the pent up energy. Rebecca saw the Tower beginning to implode, brighten before she heard or felt it. Like a wave, the air pushed out away from the expanding light at the middle of the Tower. The pressure wave was overtaken by the light, so the Kilaray blast hit them before the wind.

Had they not dropped to the ground when they saw what was happening, they would have been blasted off the crater's lip. The force tore at Rebecca's hair; she could feel the skin of her face rippling in the rush of wind and Kilaray light. Her ears gave up trying to

745

comprehend the sound. So it was pure silence as the Tower collapsed in on itself from top and base toward the blinding light at its heart. Rebecca's eyes were next to surrender to what was occurring. Everything washed away to white, heatless light. She could not tell how long it lasted; it could have been years, and it could have been an instant.

The last feeling she had before the force of the blast relented was in her soul and through Astenos. She felt the warmth there that had started with Falicarna's words to her. Astenos laughed and cried with joy.

Can you feel it my love, he roared through their link, *the power of it, the love.*

She could, it was like the hand of the Father washing over them.

At last, the sounds of the world returned, slowly like cotton wads pulled from her ears. The light faded too. She turned to see an ever expanding wave front sweep out in all directions from the crater, from where the Tower had once been. Streamers of light trailed the front and she knew at once, from their infinite diversity of colors, that light had been the Kilaray the outside world had lost the power to touch. It would return to that world now. That is what the Tower had been meant for. Like some enormous storehouse of the lost Touch, it was now released, riding back on the crest of that wave.

She sat up and looked around for her friends. They all wept with tears of joy. Falicarna looked on the empty crater with what she knew was amazement. Rebecca blinked to clear her vision and stood shakily.

"Is everybody alright?" she asked, hearing her own voice as if from down a long hall.

"What?" asked Wren; he rubbed at his chest. "Fates, what did you say? If feels like my head is wrapped in a wool blanket. Are you alright, little sister?" He pushed up and Rebecca saw Cev beneath him; he had covered her with his body to protect her. Rebecca smiled. He pulled Cev to her feet. Nico helped Fayit to rise. Noe Avaka sat covering his ears, his head sunken into his shoulders and his eyes wide.

Rebecca felt a wave of relief wash over her as she looked on her friends. Fayit walked to where Ronan lay staring at the sky. She pulled him to his feet and Wren went to help her. Suddenly a buzzing in Rebecca's mind made her blink. Falicarna turned and looked to Rebecca his head cocked to the side, he whipped his head to Wren. Wren looked up, his eyes white all around. The sudden dawning of what was happening was a hair too late.

She felt herself grabbed around her upper arms and pulled down the crater sides toward the forest. She moved too fast; the world slipped in and out. Thundering wind raged in her ears as the two Husked Men that had grabbed her dragged her along with them.

She saw the forest for a flash and then the terrible wind raged and the colors dimmed to grays and blacks. The sun, a black disc in the sky, cast no light here; the Father could not touch this place. She knew the washed out world she was dragged though by the feeling of despair in her soul; it was on the edge of Discordia that Husked Men traveled.

* * *

Wren felt them too late, his Murmur held out its connection with the others until it could not help but pass the pull of them to Wren. It had betrayed him; or had he betrayed it. No matter it all came to the same thing; the Husked Men had her. He could feel her fear as she was pulled away. That way, he could point to her. He could feel her tied to him.

Ronan looked to Wren with rage in his eyes.

"You did this," he roared. Wren shook his head in desperate denial.

"No, I didn't," he said. He felt a stab at his soul and knew his Murmur yearned to join its kind, carrying Rebecca to whoever had sent them. "I didn't; but I know where she is."

Fayit looked to Wren in understanding. "After her, Wren, you must catch her."

Ronan looked confused and then his face hardened. "After her boy, the Father curse you if you lose her. Do you hear me? The Father curse you."

Cev looked at him with fear as Nico took Ronan from Wren. She took up his hands.

"Save her Wren," she had tears in her eyes. "I believe you can." She wrapped her arms around his neck and kissed him on the lips.

"Run you cursed dog!" roared Ronan. "Run like the Blazes are on your heels."

Wren began to trot away, pulling his knives from his Stitcher's rig. He picked up the pace and felt for where Rebecca traveled. The words Falicarna had spoken echoed in his head: *Your time is near; you must not lose the child.* He bounded down the side of the crater; he slipped in and out of the world, allowing his Murmur to pull him to the edge of the world, where time went slack. They were that way, up ahead. She called to him like a magnet to a compass. Wren ran now, jumping and sliding down the crater that had taken them hours to climb in minutes.

He was in the forest; they were heading north. The trees' colors dimmed and faded as he slipped in and out, leaping yards at a time as he passed through the worlds. Men appeared, his hands flashed and the knives seemed to freeze as they left his grip. He knew they would find their marks before they left his hand; those men had guns.

He was gaining ground now. More men ran across his trail as he slipped after Rebecca and her captors. He stayed his hand, leaping over their running heads. He could see from this between-world view the javelins they threw and horn bows they fired at the men with guns to his side. There must be some kind of battle going on around them. Not his concern.

Faster, faster, faster he had to catch them. He had never moved so fast in his half- life. He could see more Husked Men, chasing after Rebecca, not to help her he knew. He pulled his narrow sword. The first didn't have time to flinch for their knives before their heads came away from their shoulders. He could see the shocked dead eyes of their Murmurs extending from where the heads had been. Their stolen bodies dropped beneath them.

The others now knew they were being chased. Wren flung out his hand and moved in motions taught long ago in his home. The knife took the Husked Man that had stopped between the eyes, putting it down for a moment. His sword hand feinted and the second Husked Man missed with his blade, catching Wren's thigh as Wren hit his mark in the throat, sending up a slow speed shower of blue-black blood.

He was off, he closed his mind to the pain inching up his leg; his Murmur would tend to it as he moved. The Blue helped with the pain of the Murmur's healing but heal it, it would. Wren felt a bullet rip through his left shoulder but continued on. He could see her now no

749

more than a bright light in the gloom of the world through which he traveled. He tore past a Strynge. It was culling some poor soul it had caught. Not his concern, he couldn't save them all, but he would save his Charge. It would be the last thing he did in this life. He could feel the strands of his anchor fraying as his Murmur scrabbled at the weakening seal.

There, there she was. He whipped his hand to his Stitcher's rig and it flashed with the speed he gained here. The Husked Man on her left tumbled in a rolling heap as it lost its grasp. Another moved to take its place. He could hear her screaming for him now; he could see her yellow-green eyes, blazing with fear and fury.

"Wren, Wren, help me," she screamed. "I can't Reach, I can't, not here."

He could hear the panic in her voice. He knew what she meant even though he didn't understand the Kilaray; he knew they did not touch this netherworld. She could not touch the Kilaray Links, not here.

"I'm coming, little sister; hold on!" he bellowed as the Husked Men increased their frantic flight. He drew on some strength he hadn't known he had and kept pace. They were faster than him here, or they should have been.

He sheathed his sword and whipped his hands to his vest and out, sending two streaking silver lengths of steel toward his two targets. They crumpled in two rolling heaps out of this world and back to the normal one. Wren caught Rebecca before she could be blown away into the winds that tore at this place. He wrapped her up in his arms, tumbling out of the grayness and into the vibrant living world.

* * *

750

Rebecca tumbled out of the edge of Discordia into pandemonium. Wren had his arms wrapped around her and they rolled over and over with the velocity of their exit from that place. She realized he screamed in pain when they finally rolled apart. She crawled to him as men roared and the ring of gunfire broke the forest sounds. Icari raced by them, throwing javelins and firing arrows at the invaders that moved through their forests. She focused her mind on Wren and dragged him behind a cropping of moss covered stone.

His feet scrabbled at the dirt under his boots and his hand tore open his shirt over the symbol on his chest. Rebecca could see the life of the symbol flickering feebly

"Now, little sister, it has to be now!" he screamed, his eyes wide with terror. "Take my head; let me leave this world as a man." He screamed and his eyes flashed over dead white and back to their grayish blue-green.

Rebecca began to cry. "No Wren, not now. I don't know how to do it yet; I can't do it."

Wren grabbed her hand and put it to Astenos's hilt. "You promised me, little sister." His eyes pleaded. "Pleaaaa," he screamed and began to shudder, Rebecca could hear the hollow voice of his Murmur at the end of that scream. Rebecca pulled Astenos from his scabbard and he sparked to life. Rebecca pulled Wren to his knees, panting. He lowered his head to make the cut easier for her.

"Now, now, now, little…little, sister," he gasped.

Rebecca wiped her eyes and the anger that filled her was terrible. *Not now, Wren*, she thought. She began to swing the Blade down at his bowed head, she screamed with the pain of it.

A foot, six inches, one, *I am here my love, my Mate.*

751

Rebecca's friends caught up eventually. The sounds of the battle had long since gone quiet. Ronan walked under his own strength as he and the others pulled up short around Rebecca. Wren's body lay against her as she leaned on the moss covered rocks, Astenos still clutched in her hand, her other arm around Wren's chest.

Cev covered her mouth as tears spilled from her dark eyes. Nico put his arm around his sister's shoulder as she wept.

"How do you feel, once Cursed One?" asked Noe Avaka.

"Alive," Wren said through a hoarse scream torn throat. Cev was at his knee at once, kissing his hands, his face, and his lips.

Ronan looked amazed. "What did you do, child?" he asked in a whisper.

"She cut it from me," said Wren, his voice cracking on the last word. "I have it back; I can feel myself, my soul again." Cev pulled Wren to herself and Rebecca stood.

"We need to get back to the village, Rebecca," said Nico. "We have gathered the halicarras but we need one more."

"No, that will not be necessary," said a voice in all of their heads as a dark shadow passed above them. "I will carry the child."

Eighty-nine:
The Flight of the Icari

The group landed at dusk in the pen for the halicarras in Cev's and Nico's village. It seemed that the Icari had come out victorious in the battle. Though their weapons were vastly less powerful than the soldiers of the Red Guard that had come with the Strynges and Husked Men, the people of this world could touch the Kilaray Links.

The halicarras in the pen shivered and pulled as Rebecca lighted down on her massive mount. Falicarna had flown the entire journey at the lead of the formation. Ronan took her yellow crested halicarra, and seemed to take to the flight as she had. Word spread quickly of their return. Members of the Elder Council began to gather around the pen as Rebecca and her friends landed. The looks on their faces were one and all identical, utter disbelief, as they looked on the group and what they had brought with them. They gazed on Falicarna like they must be hallucinating. Talic, as Rebecca knew he would, was the only one who seemed capable of speech.

"World Strider, it is good to see you safely back. My heart warms with the sight of my blood with you," he took her hand and bowed over it. "You bring two...guests with you I see."

Janero ran to the pens, holding up his yellow cloak, his knobby knees flashing in the dim light. Rebecca could tell from the way the man ran he meant trouble. "Talic, Talic, we must seize this child. She has destroyed the Tower. She is..." Whatever else he thought of Rebecca was lost in an incoherent scream as Falicarna let out a shriek aimed at him. Janero's eyes looked like they meant to leave his skull as he turned and ran from the pens with his hands over his head, his yellow cloak flapping in the wind.

Talic turned to Rebecca. He knelt and examined what she clutched in her fist, a gift from Falicarna, seven arm-length indigo blue feathers. He smiled at her, his face wrinkling like thick leather.

"Where do we go from here, World Strider?" he asked for all the Icari behind him to hear.

Rebecca knew the answer to this question with the tug she felt from the northeast. She knew how to get there too, because the feathers that bound her to these people had not been Falicarna's only gift.

It took some time to gather the numbers of soldiers Rebecca had asked for. She had no idea what to expect, but judging by the lengths to which her enemies had gone to get her, she thought to be prepared for the worst. Nearly two hundred men had volunteered for what Rebecca had told them she meant to do. She marveled at their willingness to help her.

Men were not all she would take with her. Falicarna had told her what the limit to the gift he had given her was. One use, the farther the distance the fewer the numbers it could carry. She thought she must be pushing the bounds of those limits as the men squeezed in around her. Men on a dozen multihued halicarras, fit for battle, gathered round her, waiting. Several others sat rider-free waiting for Cev, Nico, and amazingly Wren to mount up. The dark halicarra he had flown nuzzled at his shoulder, he had to duck before it nipped his ear.

Wren had gained more than his soul when Rebecca had cut the Murmur from him. She knew, like others would have on the outside,

Wren had gained some affinity with the Kilaray, enough to ride the dark halicarra at least, with the Tower's release of energy.

"Is everyone ready?" she asked nervously.

"As ready as they're going to get I think, little sister," said Wren, looking at peace with Cev's arm around his waist.

"Let us begin, dear one," said Ronan, pulling on his blue crested helmet; its face shield slid into place as it settled.

Rebecca held up the glowing white triangle and set her mind on the place she meant for it to take them. Whoever had sent the Tower seemed to have known what would be necessary after its purpose was fulfilled. Rebecca didn't need to be able to read the runic script to know what was etched deep into its metallic faces, 'For the crossing of worlds.' The white glow stretched out, enveloping the mass of men and halicarras around her. They felt the ground beneath their feet drop and the world was blown away in a wind that came from all directions.

We are here, my mate, said Astenos.

We will show you the way, said Elora.

* * *

James knew something was happening. Valgerhold had become like a military outpost in the months since Rebecca had slipped Dormon's grasp. Since then, Dormon had acted increasingly unhinged. He walked the halls in disarray, his eyes wide and muttering to himself. James had caught a snippet on one occasion, "Can't be culled, anything but that, anything."

Postam had returned weeks ago, his once bald head covered in dirty matted hair. His beard was longer and he had a general disorder to him. The biggest difference was that his face looked like it had been mauled by some wild animal, perhaps wolves. He took weeks to recover his usual menacing manner, but it was nothing to what it had been.

James laughed to himself as he waited for Jason Ganty to pick the lock to the dormitory door. The children here seemed to have been forgotten for the most part, except by the Romaran teachers. James had seen a number of them smiling as they walked their groups to the shops to do their daily work. They could tell something was happening too. This night felt different though to James.

"Hurry you, blasted slinking dog," hissed James.

"I almost have it, Bligh. Your insults aren't going to speed it along," said Ganty.

"James, what's the rush?" asked Gregor.

"I can feel something strange. I don't know why; we just need to get to the courtyard above, quickly," said James dreamily.

The door clicked and Ganty made a satisfied sound. The girls waited for them on the landing of the dormitory level. Elizabeth stood with a smirking grin between her dark curtains of hair, holding up the set of lock picks James had made for her. Helen stood behind her, looking pleased.

"We have to go," said James to the children on the landing.

"It's her isn't it?" said Sam, stepping forward, her blonde curls dancing with her excitement. "It's Rebecca I know it."

James compressed his lips. He would not say it, but he had the same feeling. Something had called to him for the past few nights. He had found himself more than once in a dazed state, standing next to a cooled piece of iron, looking to the southwest. Angus Freen, the forge leader, would come by and place his leather-hard hands on James's shoulder to wake him. He never said a word about it though; he seemed to know what James felt.

"Mind on your work, lad," was all he would say.

Last night, that call had woken him from his sleep. He had dreamed of flying, and raining forests and…strange antlered bird-like creatures. He shook his head as Helen took his hand to get him moving. He and she had tried to fill the space Rebecca had left when she had escaped. It hadn't been enough.

If the treatment had continued like before Rebecca had left, the Arnoran children here would have broken. With Dormon and Postam's attention on other matters, the Romarans had turned Valgerhold into what it had once been, a school. They could not escape, Dormon's attention had not lapsed that much, but they no longer made weapons. The food had become almost normal too.

They filed onto the catwalk in the library now. He was really drifting tonight. He didn't remember descending the stone staircases or waiting for the door to be picked. He had a dire need to be outside, to look up at the sky. He felt the cooling winds of the Romaran night as he stepped onto the open courtyard atop the library. Soft murmurs of questions floated from the other's mouths. He turned to look. They were all here, every boy and girl that had known Rebecca. He could see the members of the Second Born in an arc around him. Arthur held that sewing kit Rebecca had returned him; Elizabeth clasped the brush, Mac was tumbling his glass lens in his growing hands. Michael had his arm around his sister as she clutched to the wire-wrapped mirror that had belonged to their mother. Gene, his brother at his side, held the fox-carved folding knife. James realized he was rubbing his wrist and looked down. She had given him that back too, his father's watch.

757

A silence swept over the group and James could feel it; something was happening. He looked to the southwest; he knew she was that way. The midnight violet sky was speckled with stars, not a cloud marred the clear view of the night. What was that? he thought. There on the horizon, like a spike of light reaching to the heavens. The hair on James's arms stood on end.

"Can you feel that?"

"What is it?"

"I feel...warm."

Whispers came from behind him. They could feel it too. The spike vanished and the world seemed to hold its breath. The soft wind that had ruffled his dark blond hair stilled. The cries of hundreds of wolves broke the night's silence, sweeping out from the school through the forests now plumed in greens. It was coming, something great, something powerful. The horizon brightened, dawn approached. *Wait, it was too early for dawn*, thought James, *and the sun didn't rise in the southwest*. It was her; he knew it at once.

A line of bright, blinding light lit the horizon sweeping toward them. He didn't hear a single gasp of fear. James could see the wisps of variegated light trailing the blinding line, arcing across the night sky. It lit a swath of forest beneath it as it came ever closer. It was almost upon Valgerhold.

The light was glorious, filling them all with a feeling of love and hope. James spun to watch it pass like a wave front washing out across the sea. The streamers of light in its wake seemed...brighter now.

"Do you see it?"

"Oh, Father, can you feel it?"

The world breathed out; a blast of wind trailed the light and the trees swayed with its passing. It howled around the two dormitory towers and blew the children's hair back away from the glistening faces. James felt his cheeks too cool for the night and touched them. He found them damp.

When it was clear whatever had happened had alerted the guards, James knew it was time to return.

"Back inside, we have to get in. It won't be long now ..." he stopped his mouth still open. *Where had that come from?* He thought. "Hurry Rebecca," he whispered.

His prediction came true several hours later. Before dawn, the first shouts of the guards tore through the courtyard. James rushed to the stained glass window of the owl holding the lantern. Something had just flown overhead. It was enormous. He pressed his face to the glass to see through the gray dawn. A spot was just there, out over the trees. It was joined with one, two, no four others. The five spots grew larger; *were those wings?*

"Everybody down," James screamed as the five flying creatures bloomed in size, flying at the window with blinding speed. The glass shattered and a tube of wood rolled to James' feet.

He quickly pulled the parchment within out, unrolled it, and read:
James,

Get them down. Keep them safe. We are coming. No heroics!
Love, Rebecca.

"Aye, Captain," he whispered with a grin. "Everyone up, Ganty, get that door unlocked. Gregor round the younger kids up. We're being rescued."

Ninety: **A New Day**

The white triangle had deposited them in a clearing in the forest near Valgerhold. Rebecca could see the abandoned pots and jars of the camp where she and her friends had prepared deer they had caught. Rebecca, Wren, Cev, Nico, and Ronan had flown to the school to deliver Rebecca's message. They gathered now, readying for the battle to come.

The flight had two purposes, first to warn her friends, second to see what they were to face. Ronan, Noe Avaka, and Talic were hunkered down around the Incandeo's white light. Ronan sketched out a plan, Noe Avaka translated for him. Fayit put a huge paw on her shoulder as she looked on the small lights of Valgerhold.

"All will be as it will be, Rebecca; worry cannot change that," she said kindly.

"I know, Fayit, but I'm still scared," she whispered. Fayit patted her shoulder and returned to the waiting Icari. They smiled as she approached; they saw the Tremen as a sign of good luck.

Nico stepped to her side next. He bore a leather helmet, a plume of orange and gold feathers ran along its crest.

"This was Cev's when she was younger," he said. "She wants you to wear it into battle." He handed her the helmet. She had reluctantly agreed to wear traditional Icari garb for battle. The buff-colored bindings left her arms, legs, and stomach bare, but fortunately a rider's battle gear also came with leather armor to cover some of her exposed flesh. She wore a deep blue cloak pinned with a stylized valicarra, a sign of her place among the Icari. Rebecca proudly took the helmet and looked to Cev. Her face broke into a wild excited grin.

"I believe we are prepared, child," said Falicarna into her head.

Rebecca felt her stomach leap. She pulled back her hair, tied it with a scarf, and pulled the leather helmet over her head. She walked to Falicarna and stood by his side. He had allowed her to harness him so she could ride more securely. A rider's gear also included a set of woven straps that latched to the harness on the mounts so they could fire bows from the air.

Ronan stood; pride showed through the mask his face had become with the approach of battle.

"They'll be expecting the ground assault here and here," Ronan pointed to the map he had drawn in the soil. You and the other flyers will attack from behind at their flanks. Sweep wide and stay low until you're around. The sun will be coming up soon, keep it to your backs and it will hide you from their fire," he said, in an assuring way. "Talic and I will lead the ground forces. I know you've seen death, Rebecca, but battle can be overwhelming, keep your senses."

She pulled up and pulled the goggles down over her eyes. Cev and Nico mounted up behind her. Talic handed Rebecca a bone bow and a quiver of arrows. She latched the straps looped around her bare thighs to the harness around Falicarna.

"Good flying, World Strider," said Talic, putting a warm hand to her calf.

Falicarna leapt into the sky; the others on the halicarras followed after. Wren clung to the dark halicarra at the tail of Rebecca's group. He tested the bow he had at his side. Her breath caught as she watched the rainbow of halicarras lift from the clearing, groups of 'V' formations climbing skyward behind her.

Anton Dormon sat watching as a group of birds lifted into the dawn sky. What he wouldn't give to fly away with them. That light and wind that had rushed overhead had set his men on edge. Edwin Postam stood in his office looking ragged and half crazed. The howling that had come with the light had set him looking to the walls for attack. What had Anton shivering, were the three man-shaped things that stood in his office.

"You say she's here," he said, hating the fear that shook his voice.

"*We are not wrong about this, human,*" rasped the Strynge with the scar between its eyes.

"Edwin ready the men," said Dormon. "It looks like you are going to get your revenge on the girl at last, my friend."

Edwin Postam looked mad as he smiled. He turned and rushed from the office, leaving Anton alone with the three Blind Men. They had appeared from the shadows not two hours ago. He had thought their threat to cull him was about to be carried out. Surprisingly, they sought help. They had tracked the girl into the legendary Barrier to the southwest; the direction from which that light had come. They too seemed unable to apprehend the girl. They had slid from the dark shadows of his walls, pouring into his office like a menacing fog.

He was glad now he had followed his instinct and gathered troops from the Red Fist Army. Something about the girl had set off an alarm in his head, the alarm had told him to be careful. The Red Fist troops were heavily armed and disciplined; they would repel any attack the girl could have mustered in her absence. Once put down, he would hand the girl to the Strynges and this ordeal would be done with once and for all. He would escape this with his soul intact.

Anton heard shouts from the gates at the front of Valgerhold. It had begun; the fool girl was attacking from the front. This would be over soon, thank the Father.

* * *

James gathered the children in the library farthest away from the windows; he could hear the younger children whimpering. The shouts and gunfire filtered through the walls. It sounded like a battle raged out there. He prayed to the Father like he had not done in a long time.

"Please, First Father, watch over, my friends, and Rebecca. See her safe to me, I beg of you," he whispered, covering Sam and Mac with his arms.

* * *

Rebecca let Astenos work through her; he guided her shots as she wheeled about in the growing light of the day. Falicarna lined her up for a strafing run; he read her thoughts, leaving her to focus on firing the bow. She saw the death rain of arrows falling among the blocks of men. They wore armor, unlike the Red Guard. These men seemed better trained too – Red Fist Army, Ronan had identified them.

Astenos made her lean back as a whizzing gunshot flew past her leather-covered ear cowl. Falicarna tumbled over, dodging between the volleys of fire; she hung from the straps lashed around her thighs straining with the blood that rushed to her head. She aimed above her toward the ground and men below and fired down on them. She saw men fall to her shots before she was right side up again. She could feel the pull of Kilaray at her and she let Astenos guide her.

The air condensed beneath Falicarna and she watched as ripples from the impact of the retaliation fire pounded against her shield.

"Well done, child," laughed Falicarna in her head.

Ronan was down there. She could see the blue streaks of his Soul Blade tear long lines through the Red Fist's ranks. The Icari were at his rear, firing bows, and stabbing and slashing with their javelins. She saw a streak of silver and looked back to see Wren pull up from a dive toward the mass of men below.

"Please, Father, let this end soon," she prayed.

* * *

Edwin Postam had taken an arrow, a bloody arrow, in the arm. He watched in horror as the savages, from the Father knew where, tore into his ranks. Their screaming calls were more terrifying than their vicious fighting. He took aim with his rifle on a leather-faced man with a blue cloak bearing down on him. He fired and saw the shot's impact but nothing happened. It was as though the ball had vaporized as it flew at the man. Edwin Postam saw his death come on the head of a foot-long spike of steel. He cursed the girl's face as the javelin pushed into his chest.

* * *

Anton Dormon's hands were shaking, *shaking*; he could not believe it. *What were those things in the sky?* Men rode the backs of beasts from Discordia. No not Discordia, he knew that much. The Strynges at his back, *they*, he knew, were from Discordia. He fingered the Arnoran revolving pistol at his hip.

The battle rages were dying down now. He should have demanded more men, all the men. He should have demanded Adarian himself for the Father's sake. This was like the old times again. He had seen the miraculous acts of the savage looking men and women down there. Bullets, that should have hit, missed. Bayonets twitched aside at the worst possible time. He saw, as impossible as it had to be, the incandescent streaks that were the sign of a Palantean down there. *What had he unleashed? No, not him.* This was Adarian's doing as sure as he was about to be culled. He felt the looming things behind slide to him.

The men on the animals were landing in the courtyard now. The one on the large blue creature with the antlers caught his eye. She pulled off the gold and orange plumed helmet and looked directly into his eyes through the glass of his office window.

"We told you we would be back, human," said the Blind Man just over his shoulder. *"We hunger for a soul to get back to our haunt, and yours will have to do."*

He felt the first enticing caresses from the three things behind him. He reacted in the only way he had left to him. He had a sad feeling that he would have been going to a better place had he helped the girl below him. He drew the revolver as lightning fast as he could as the Blind Man grasped hold of his soul.

* * *

Rebecca heard the shot from Dormon's office and saw a dark spray against his window. She knew it was over. Wren, Cev, and Nico cleared the courtyard of the Red Guard that remained, rounding up those that surrendered. The trees in their surrounds bloomed with pink blossoms as she ran to the door leading to the dorms. She could feel him nearby.

She Reached and the doors, from the courtyard to the library, burst open. A stream of children ran from the floors above. She felt tears run down her cheeks as they circled around her cheering. She froze and clapped her hands over her mouth.

Stepping just now into the light of the new day, his hair longer than she remembered, a scattering of growth on his cheeks, was the most handsome man she had laid eyes on. He paused as their eyes met. The Arnoran children around them went silent; they opened a path between the two. James stood rigid.

"Arnorans!" he bellowed in a voice deeper than she had heard from him. "Our Captain returns!" He snapped a salute and all around children followed suit.

Rebecca felt Wren at her back, Cev clutched to his side. Ronan just now marched into the open doors to the courtyard; Talic had his arm over her grandfather's shoulders in a victorious embrace. Fayit walked surrounded by a band of cheering Icari. Noe Avaka was carried into the courtyard on two men's shoulders, looking immensely surprised. She felt a familiar hand in her back as Wren pushed her to get her moving.

This is your man, my love? asked Astenos in her head. Her feet carried her to him, gaining speed as she moved.

"Yes," she whispered in her head as James caught her up, pulling her to his mouth. "This is my man," she said as his soft lips pressed down on hers.

When James put her down, Sam spoke.

"What do we do now, Rebecca?" she asked, joy in her voice.

Rebecca turned, wrapping an arm about James's waist and spoke to the gathered children, Icari, and Romarans that were filling the courtyard.

"Now, now we free your brothers and sisters, sons and daughters, friends and countrymen. Then we go home."

A cheer rattled the stone walls. The children and others were as one in hopeful jubilation.

Ninety-one:
Janonin's Fate

Mandagore shook with the Wanderer's fury. He lay curled on the marble floor of his palace. He had tried to stop the breaching of the Barrier. He had used the Wanderer's own creations to search her out. How could this thing blame him? He clutched his scarred hands to the sides of his golden haired head and screamed.

The worst part, worse than the pain, was the red and black cloaked men and women around him, watching in sheer terror. This was to be a demonstration to those who followed Mandagore that he was only a man. The Adarianites looked like they were going to vomit. The searing pain, jabbing into his brain and soul, relented and he quivered on the floor with the ecstasy of its cessation.

The hooded figure stepped so Mandagore could see its waxy bloodless toes poking from its deep red robes.

"You will not fail me again Mandagore," the lights of the room became bright again as it paused. "I have given you your power; *I am* your power. You will proceed with my design. Set your *men* to destroy the girl. You will travel to the heart of the Broken Lands where my creatures wait to be set on this plane once more." The dimness that had persisted while it spoke vanished. The room seemed to gain life that Mandagore had not noticed it lacked while the Wanderer was there. It had slipped away with its last word, vanishing to wherever it lurked.

Shanone came to his side at once; Mandagore pushed the woman away. He pushed to his knees, and quickly to his feet. He would not kneel, even to the Wanderer. He refused to wipe at the tears that had come to his eyes.

He turned to Shanone, looking like death flew on his heels. "Gather your forces. They will be coming," his voice was just above a whisper. "Shanone, do not fail me." She nodded looking frightened.

"Never Mandagore," she said breathlessly.

Mandagore gathered his Soul Blade from where he had dropped her. Janonin no longer spoke to him; she had long since gone silent. He didn't need her words to do what he had done with his Blade; she was bound by her customs. She could no more break them than Mandagore could refuse to reenter the Broken Lands. She would protect him, praying every time it was necessary that she would fail. And he would kill with her. He had a new name on his ranks of those he hated and would see dead. Janonin would do her work as she had hundreds of times when it came to it. Mandagore would bring her to life, blazing her red-gold glory on the girl's face, as he cut her down.

An Excerpt from the Next *Children of the Links* Novel

"It's hunting us whatever we will do or not. No matter how hard we run from it, nor how desperately we deny it, it's making of us what it will. Destiny, fate, it has come for us. Can you accept what I see bearing down on you, Lucian, what I see bearing down on me?"

Sebastian turned from Lucian in his tent. The lantern cast him in a warm orange light; his skin glistened with sweat. Sebastian stood stripped to the waist for the heat even at this late hour. Lucian could see the many scars that marred his body; they all had scars now. Sebastian was a handful of years younger than Lucian but one would never have known it from the look on his face, turned just enough for Lucian to see the pain that had hardened it. Sebastian stared at the silver transfer he kept with him always, the one of his sister. He turned and looked up from the small image to stare into Lucian's eyes; his yellow-green irises were hard to hold for long.

"What have you seen my friend?" asked Lucian, feeling his body go cold; his hands felt made of lead.

"I have sent out Wren with his Night Birds." Sebastian ran a finger over the image without seeming to notice.

"I know Sebastian, but you have not answered my question." Lucian felt his stomach tense. It had to be a Reached Vision. He had called his Hammer – his core of young commanders – together so quickly that the ripples of rumor had already washed across the camp. Lucian had heard everything from Sebastian having keeled over dead to Adarian having marched into camp to surrender. Lucian had watched as Sebastian's Hammer exited, heavy thoughts on their faces. Liana had tears on her cheeks, and she was known as one of the hardest amongst them. It wasn't like Sebastian to hesitate, and for that Lucian knew his words brought ill news.

"Tell me Lucian, what do you know of the Ru'han monasteries?" Sebastian's back was still to him as he spoke.

"A fair amount, as much as any man can say to know. The monks are said to have been scattered throughout the Broken Lands. Kept to themselves mostly; I reckon they're long dead now. What does this have to do with tonight Sebastian?"

"They followed the Red Path, true?"

"Aye, rumor says they started it."

He nodded as if Lucian's words had answered some great question for him.

"When this night is through and what has been done is done, I need you to secret yourself within our enemies." Sebastian tucked the picture into the pocket of his deep blue coat lying over a stool. He stood and stepped within a pace of Lucian staring up into his eyes. "I need you to be loyal, trusted, a perfect Red Fist soldier."

So, that explained the stolen uniforms; Lucian felt sick. How long would he need to play this masquerade? He plucked at the embroidered fist on the front of the deep brown coat, folded over his arm. He looked up to argue the point with Sebastian.

Sebastian put a firm hand on Lucian's shoulder; his peculiar gaze froze the words in Lucian's mind. "I know how hard this is for you my friend but…" Sebastian looked down and shuddered, "…but she is going to need you." He looked up again and tears filmed his eyes, but a warm smile was there too. "You know how hard a promise can

be to keep. I know I won't be able to keep the one I made to her."
There was no question of whom he spoke, his sister, Rebecca.

Lucian nodded regretfully. "I will do as you ask. Just…just tell
me there is a purpose to it, Sebastian. Tell me we will see the end of
the Red Fist."

"Not today my friend and I fear this night will grow far darker
before you see the light of a new day." Sebastian turned and walked to
his pallet on the floor of his tent. He picked up his black shirt – black
so as not to show his men and enemies if he had been wounded – and
pulled it over his head, lacing up the front. He retrieved his sword
leaning against the stool and pulled on his coat, touching thoughtfully
where the silver transfer was tucked. To Lucian he looked like a man
on his way to the gallows. Lucian remained standing in the tent waiting
for more. Sebastian stepped as if to go around him without further
word but stopped when he was shoulder to shoulder with Lucian. He
never turned his head from looking out to the camp as he spoke.

"I know now I was not meant for what Rebecca must do,"
Lucian did not know what he was talking about. "Hearts of lions,
Lucian. That is what this world will need. Make sure yours is amongst
them when the time comes…for I know now mine will not be."

Lucian Gaston sat up from his dream. He wiped at his sweating
brow and swung his legs over the edge of his bed in the inn. He
gripped the sides of his shaved head, resting his elbows on his knees.

The dream refused to leave his thoughts, ever since Landfall
station. Ever since, like a waking dream, he spotted that familiar face
across a sea of children. Lucian chuckled to himself remembering that
day. The girl had spirit to match her brother's.

He stood and peered out the dusty, cracked window pane. Only a few glowing squares of light could be seen dotting the small village, maybe he wasn't the only one having trouble finding sleep this night.

Lucian walked to the small battered wardrobe and pulled out the dark gray coat within. He sneered at the red fist on the left breast and threw it over his shoulder as he sat to pull on his boots. If he couldn't find sleep he might as well make use of the time he had.

Stepping from his room he found two Red Guard men sitting on stools to either side of his door, asleep. Their long rifles leaned against the wall. He hated these men, they like most in the Red Guard, had joined after the Red Fist swept the Homelands. They saw profit, a chance to find an easy meal, or, like the man that had led to his meeting Sebastian's sister, easy looting. He walked past the dozing guards and down the small open hall that looked over the main room below. He spotted two dark-skinned Beltari men at a table playing high card below. He walked down the stairs and to their table. They had goblets of wine at their elbows but each looked barely touched as Lucian stepped up to the two.

"Captain," spoke one of the men as Lucian stopped before them. A bleary-eyed bar mistress strode to him bearing a steaming tin mug of coffee – or what they were passing off as coffee here. Lucian noted the yellowed eye she tried to hide while proffering the cup. He took it graciously from the woman; the village folk knew they had no need to fear the three Beltari men in Red Guard uniforms. After Lucian had sent two of the other men under his command, if you could call them men, to the village healer for attempting to force themselves on the daughter of a mason here, word had spread.

"Thanks to you, good woman," Lucian whispered taking the mug in two hands. The plump woman made a small curtsy and murmured how he was no trouble at all.

"Up early, Captain," said the other man, giving his cards a disgusted look. "Or up late?" These two knew why he had brought them to this isle in the middle of nowhere. Sebastian's last words to him echoed through his memory.

"It amounts to the same thing, Travere. How would you two feel about an early morning stroll?" Lucian pulled his coat around him as the men put their cards down and stood from the table.

"Say, the halls of the brig, Captain?" said Dandolan; he was clearly going to win the hand. They each buckled on their Beltari swords, extremely long hilted weapons with blades that increased in width toward their points. "Maybe have a look at the sea afterwards?"

Lucian nodded with grim satisfaction; his men knew what they were about. The three made their way to the door of the inn. Lucian addressed the bar mistress as she approached to see them off.

"In the morning, answer their questions. Don't give them reason to question you too deep. I would advise not staying here after we're gone. I can't vouch for who will replace me but I reckon he won't be as peaceable." Lucian tipped the woman's chin up and gently thumbed beneath her bruised eye. He handed the woman a small purse of coins and thanked her for her hospitality. He hoped no harm came to her.

Pressing out into the not-night-not-yet-dawn dark, Lucian approached the horses the two men had prepared, dark horses. Lucian climbed into the saddle of one and set off for the high stone walls of the prison not far from the village. The air was already damp with humidity; it would be nearly unbearably hot when the sun rose. Hopefully he would have his quarry and be ship-bound by then.

His last conversation with Sebastian ran through his head as Lucian walked his horse forward over the cobbled streets, the horses' hooves ringing off the plastered building walls. Dandolan and Travere's heads barely swiveled but he knew they kept watch all around. He had finally tracked down what Sebastian had meant for him to find all those years ago. Sebastian had seen the only way Lucian could have found what he had would be if he were trusted in the ranks of the New Dominon.

The looming towers were dark – they were always dark – as Lucian and his two countrymen approached the iron-grated entrance of Branengat Prison. A stark edifice of stone faced them; windows, mere cracks between the huge stones, dotted the wall here and there. Lucian's eyes were drawn unconsciously toward the tower tops. A fat prison guard stepped out of a small gatehouse and took up a lantern held on a hook just outside the door. He waddled up to the three horsed men.

"Captain Gaston? What can I do for you this early morning?" He scratched at his scraggly beard and wiped his forehead with a gray-coated sleeve, pushing his flattop hat askew.

"We're here to question one of the prisoners," Lucian said, dismounting and casually tying his horse to the rail near the gatehouse. His men followed suit. The guard looked puzzled, his mouth working in a wet lipped 'O'.

"Well, I'll call some of my men to see you to…" the guard began moving toward the gatehouse door.

"We will see ourselves to the man I wish to question." Lucian cut the fat guard off. Dandolan moved forward to the gatehouse door, blocking the guard's entrance, and retrieved the ring of keys from the man's belt.

"In that case Captain, I'll need to ask who you mean to question. For the records you know." The fat guard looked worriedly from Dandolan to Lucian.

"Of course. We mean to see Kai'den Jita Danto," Lucian said calmly.

The fat guard's eyes widened and even in the orange light of the lantern Lucian could see he had gone sheet white. "We ...we have no... no prisoner by that name, Sir. I really must insist on calling some of my men to see..." So intent he was on Lucian, the fat guard didn't notice Travere slip behind him. The slim blade slitting the man's wobbling throat silenced any more objections. They had begun and would not stop now until dead or on their way to Romara.

"Put him in his place in the gatehouse." Lucian said to Dandolan. "Make it look like he's sleeping." Lucian moved with Travere toward a port door near the gate. Dandolan caught up quickly, jangling as he trotted up to unlock the door.

"You're sure he's in here, Captain?" whispered Travere. "It's been years since the Exile's return; he could be dead."

Lucian shook his head slightly as they moved into the dim hall of the prison. The two guards barely had time to acknowledge him before Dandolan and Travere were at their throats making quick work of their grim tasks.

"He's not dead." *He can't be.* Lucian wouldn't believe Sebastian could be wrong.

They moved stealthily down the halls. The prison cells here were for people who were meant to be forgotten political enemies of the old Felsofese nobility, rebels who stood against the New Dominion, and people like Kai'den Danto, people who the enemy could use. Lucian approached the iron-barred gate that let into the dark confines

776

of the halls of cells. A wide-shouldered guard sat on the opposite side of the bars; he stood as the three came into the lantern light.

"Where is your escort…oh? Captain, I didn't realize it was you. That fat slob Parry at the gatehouse should have sent word." The guard walked to the gate and unlocked the iron-barred door, swinging it open with an echoing screech. "Let me light you a lantern and I'll take you to who you mean to see."

"That won't be necessary," said Lucian, taking the lantern from the guard. "I know my way."

"I understand, Sir, but procedure…" the wide guard looked incredulous, hand drifting to the steel baton at his belt. Lucian stared into the man's face; a quick gesture and Dandolan had snapped his neck before more than a last gasp exited his lips.

"Bring his body," Lucian said, pulling the keys from the dead man's limp hand.

The three moved into the bleak interior of the prison cells. They moved in a circle of lantern light past row after row of darkened square rooms. Thick wooden doors with heavy locks hid men and women, or corpses for all one could tell. The smells of decay and human waste mixed with the mildew of the stone walls, making for an unpleasant miasma of despair. Soft whimpers and screeching cries were all that could manage escape from the sealed cells, where men and women were slowly driven mad from isolation. Dandolan and Travere's faces showed the burden of being in such a place; sickened sneers hardened their faces. They moved on climbing a spiral stone staircase at the end of one of the corridors.

The New Dominion, and Adarian himself, wanted this prisoner kept in the most inescapable cell possible; they wanted him where he could still be milked for knowledge but where none would know he existed. Branengat Prison itself sat on a stone outcrop in the gulf of Beltarus. The small village housed the prison guards, the minor industries needed to maintain its functions, and the families of those who worked here. It was a six mile swim to shore for anyone who managed to escape the confines of their cell, an improbable feat by itself. If the currents didn't pull them under, the mammoth sharks that patrolled the waters for seals would see to them. Lucian hoped that Travere's man could be trusted when they arrived at the sea.

Climbing to the highest floor of the eastern tower of the prison, Lucian and his men found a round room. Four heavy steel doors with multiple locks faced them. Rust crept in at the hinges from the damp salt air filtering in through the small grated windows at the top of the room.

"Which one is he in?" asked Dandolan as he stepped into the room.

"That one there," Lucian said pointing to a door that looked like it hadn't been used in many years. The hinges were rusted solid, but there was a faint hint of scrapes in the dust at the foot of the door where a hatch could be lifted for feedings.

The three moved to the door and Travere knelt to look through the opening.

"There's definitely someone in there," he said, standing and waving a hand before his nose. "Smells like he could stand his chamber pot being emptied."

Dandolan searched through the ring of keys for one that matched the lock as Travere set the dead guard on the stone floor and began stripping him.

"It's none of these, Captain," Dandolan said, turning from the door. Lucian moved forward with the keys he had taken and tested them. Finally with a shuddering click the first lock's clasp gave way. Working quickly, Lucian removed the remaining two locks. The cell door groaned as he pulled at the handle. It swung open reluctantly and ground against the stone floor just wide enough for them to slip inside.

The stench was nearly overwhelming as Lucian looked on the emaciated man kneeling on the stone floor of the cell. The lines of his skull were clear beneath the pale yellow skin of his face. His gray-white hair was overgrown, his beard falling to his chest. If not for the steady rise and fall of his slat-ribbed chest Lucian would have thought the man dead. He sat upon his feet as if in meditation. His robes, once deep ochre, were brown with dirt and sweat. Lucian began to move when the man spoke.

"Why have you disturbed my concentration?" His voice was a hoarse airy whisper from lack of use. The shock of the question halted Lucian mid-stride.

"Kai'den Danto?" Lucian asked.

"It is impolite to answer a question with a question, young man," the shriveled old man said, as though Lucian were a schoolboy disciplined by the headmaster. Well, if this man was who he was said to be that comparison was not far off.

"I apologize, Kai'den. We have come to set you free," Lucian spoke, moving to help the man to his feet. He froze as the man opened one steel gray eye to stare at him from the floor.

"You cannot set me free, for freedom only comes at the end of my Path. We are all set here of accords beyond ourselves. So, unless you mean to cut my Path short, I ask again, why have you disturbed me?" The man's eye closed as Lucian stood up straight, looking down on him.

"Captain, just grab him and let's go," hissed Travere. "We haven't got much time."

Lucian whipped his head around to stare at Travere with a look like murder. Men like Danto took their beliefs as serious as life and death; to him, his Path had led him to this place and he meant to stay until it led him elsewhere. Lucian knew he would not go willingly unless Lucian gave him good reason. And this plan would only work if Danto cooperated.

Lucian knelt and looked into the skeletal man's face. "We have come because I was set to find you." The man's steel eyes opened slowly to stare into Lucian's. "An old friend saw that I should find you and bring your skills to aid in the defeat of the New Dominion."

"You are Beltari I see. Your people cast mine out long ago for our beliefs, to drift the Broken Lands. Others came and sought to learn our ways only to corrupt them and make war on their enemies. Now, from your own lips, you seek to do the same. I ask you this, why should I leave this cell, Beltari?"

Lucian was at a loss. He felt Dandolan and Travere's impatience beating at his back. Lucian looked up at the stone ceiling, he could see to the east the sky was creeping toward gray. Time was not on their side. Suddenly the western sky grew bright. The kneeling man looked up, noticing the strange light.

"What is that?" asked Dandolan.

The brightness grew steadily. Lucian focused his attention on the small windows atop the cell. Suddenly, a line of bright white light washed across the windows, like a wave in the sky moving out from the west. The little man on the stone floor rose gracefully from his knees and stared up to the windows until the light vanished behind the stone walls of his cell. Lucian began to hear horns and bells ring out in the night as it passed. The little man turned on the spot and stared down at Lucian.

"Dawn seems to break in the west, but a fool could mistake this for an omen. I am convinced Beltari. Let us leave this place." The man offered Lucian his hand and when he took it Lucian was surprised at the strength he felt. "Tell me Beltari what do you know of us Ru'han Monks?"

Lucian supported Danto's minimal weight as they made their way down the spiral stairs of the tower. The horns and bells continued to sound as the four shambled down the dark stairs. Travere had sealed the murdered guard back in Danto's cell, having dressed the small man in the guard's uniform; it hung on him like a child in his parent's clothing. Lucian was grateful for the dimness of the corridors.

Guards began pouring into the halls as the four made it to the ground floor. It seemed they had found the dead man at his post in the gate house. Lucian handed Danto to Dandolan as a group of wide-eyed guards rushed up to him. Lucian cut them off before they could begin.

"We were attacked. It was an escape attempt. Up that way," Lucian pointed toward the stairs at their back. "Our escort was injured. We'll take him out."

"Aye Captain," said the man in the lead. "Did you see what they looked like? Who were they after?"

"They were in our own uniforms. I'm not sure who they sought but they have but one way out and it's down these stairs. See that they are captured." Lucian ordered and ushered Travere and Dandolan, carrying Danto, down the corridor. Lucian could hear the men forming up ready to storm the upper cells as they moved into the darkened halls.

Danto began to walk under his own power as the four moved toward the lower depths of Branengat. The stench of the halls lessened as they hurried down stairwells and dark passages that had long ago fallen into disuse. The Felsofese aristocracy had many a man vanish in their time, and the New Dominion that took their place made use of their tools when Adarian came to power.

Creeping down a seemingly dead end hall, Lucian held up the lantern and pulled a roll of parchment from his boot. He had found the document in his search for where Danto had been sealed away. He found the cobblestone with the wavy lines indicated on the parchment and began pacing in the prescribed order. Two left, one forward, three to the northwest and finally he took one step back. Suddenly a sound of rasping stone on stone echoed from behind the sealed end of the hall and small hatch appeared in the stone work. Dandolan heaved a shoulder against the stones and the hatch pushed open.

Lucian heard the approach of running boots and knew his lie to the guards had been discovered.

"Quick they can't have gotten far!" sounded from around the corner.

The four poured through the opening and found a passage more cave than hall awaiting them. Dandolan pushed the door closed behind them and they heard the stones' counterbalancing thud as it sealed itself.

A draft blew at their faces as the four men made their way down stairs carved from the stone foundations. The walls became slick with moisture and the tunnel filled with the smell of salt-sea air. Slowly the lantern light was joined with a gray light from the end of the tunnel.

They stepped onto a makeshift quay carved at the base of the rocky island. Huge boulders churning the sea to foam concealed the cave entrance for the most part. A sailor would be crazed to attempt to explore the cave mouth. The sea rushed in and out at the little pier and the roar of the sea reverberated in the interior of the cavern.

Hurriedly Lucian found the bundles he had prepared when he devised this plan. The four men stripped off their uniforms and pulled on seafarer's garb. As they were rolling their uniforms into the sacks a hollow thudding sound came over the roar of the waves. Lucian turned to see a man in a small boat pushing his way into the cave mouth. The sides of his boat had been padded with thick wool-stuffed leather sacks and he levered the boat to the pier with heavy wooden poles.

"Hurry along," said the old sailor as he reached the four. His eyes looked ready to fall out of his head; they darted from the rocks at his back, to the four men, to the heavy Beltari blades. He looked as though he was second guessing his decision to aid them.

Lucian helped Danto into the rocking boat then lowered himself down. Travere and Dandolan handed him the bundled uniforms and then they too climbed in. The small boat sat low in the water as the now five men made for the cave mouth.

"I'll be taking my pay, Travere," said the jittery old sailor. He looked like he wanted the words back as soon as Travere raised his eyebrows to the man.

"Give it over, Travere," said Lucian as he took up one of the heavy poles and began pushing at the boulders. Travere pulled a hefty sack from within one of the bundles and tossed it to the old sailor.

As they cleared the boulders, Travere and Dandolan took up the oars and pulled them out toward a small fishing vessel drifting half a mile off the coast of the rocky prison island. Lucian could see the beams of light from the prison walls searching the island and the sea. He smiled as he watched the prison growing smaller.

"What makes you stare so at that place, Beltari?" asked Danto. He studied Lucian with a master's eye, a Kai'den's eye, weighing him, searching for weaknesses, and determining his prospects as a student.

"Branengat makes for an appropriate place to leave a dismal life behind," said Lucian. He reached into one of the bundles in the bottom of the boat and felt the familiar hilt. He had refused to wear the traditional weapon of his home over his uniform. For all those years he had played the loyal soldier all the while hoping to find some way to end his commanders' rein. It would have been too painful to wear his honored weapon over the lie that was the Red Guard uniform. He slung the blade over his shoulder and closed his eyes, taking a deep breath, feeling the weight of the weapon on his back. He opened his eyes and met Danto's steely gaze. "It seems my time at the masquerade is at its end."

About the Author

Adam Dyer was born in 1981 in Washington, D.C. The middle son of three boys, he often found himself drawn into the pursuits of his brothers. The diverse interests of his siblings allowed him the opportunity to dabble in a wide field of subjects and hobbies. A consummate tinkerer and lifelong artist, he bounced from majoring in mechanical engineering to eventually graduate with a Bachelor of Fine Arts. His constant love of stories and reading led him finally to direct his energy toward writing. *The Tower of Light* is his first novel. He lives in Atlanta, Georgia where he studies and teaches the martial arts.